Main

Song of the
Golden Scorpion

Other works by Alma Luz Villanueva:

Short Fiction

Weeping Woman: La Llorona and Other Stories

Novels

The Ultraviolet Sky
Naked Ladies
Luna's California Poppies

Poetry

Mother, May I?
Blood Root
Planet
Vida
Desire
Soft Chaos

Song of the Golden Scorpion

A novel by

Alma Luz Villanueva

WingsPress

San Antonio, Texas
2013

Song of the Golden Scorpion © 2013
by Wings Press for Alma Luz Villanueva

Cover painting, "El Cisne" © 2004 by Liliana Wilson.
Variations from the original created by the artist for this cover.

First Edition

Print Edition ISBN: 978-1-60940-346-1

Ebooks:
ePub ISBN: 978-1-60940-347-8
Kindle ISBN: 978-1-60940-348-5
Library PDF ISBN: 978-1-60940-349-2

Wings Press
627 E. Guenther
San Antonio, Texas 78210
On-line catalogue and ordering:
www.wingspress.com
All Wings Press titles are distributed to the trade by
Independent Publishers Group • www.ipgbook.com

Library of Congress Cataloging-in-Publication Data:

Villanueva, Alma, 1944-
  Song of the golden scorpion : a novel / by Alma Luz Villanueva. -- First edition.
     pages cm
  ISBN 978-1-60940-346-1 (pbk. : alk. paper) -- ISBN 978-1-60940-347-8 (epub)
-- ISBN 978-1-60940-348-5 (mobipocket ebook) -- ISBN 978-1-60940-349-2
(pdf ebook)
  1. Mexican American women--Fiction. 2. Women physicians--Fiction. 3. Older
women--Fiction. 4. Young men--Fiction. 5. May-December romances--Fiction. 6.
Mexico--Fiction. I. Title.
  PS3572.I354S66 2013
  813'.54--dc23
                              2013026560

*To my son, Jules Villanueva-Castano, the goodness
of his heart and Spirit, that always inspires me.*

*To the ancient, alive, lovers, El Popocatepetl y La Iztaccihuatl,
whose images I saw in Mexican restaurants, markets, pan dulce
bakeries, in the Mission District, San Francisco, growing up.*

*A el corazon de (mi Mamacita's) Mexico lindo y querido,
where I now live.
A el corazon de Madre Tierra, Mother Earth,
where we ALL live.*

*To the next 1,000 years—one people, one planet,
into the Sixth Sun, QUE VIVA*

PART I

Gamble everything for love,
if you're a true human being.

—Rumi

Someone was knocking just as she began to undress, "Shit," Xochiquetzal muttered (friends called her Xochitzalita, and it wasn't that hard to say once you got used to it, 'Shweetzalita'). There was no eye-hole-peep to look through, "Fuck," she breathed out. Her skin was salty, dry yet luxurious from la mar, and her hair was still wet, coiled on top of her head. Her dreaming, relaxed, exhausted from swimming in la mar head. She didn't want to deal with a maid. She wanted to stay in this state of ocean dreaming; but the knock became louder.

"Quien es, who is it?" she hissed. Who the fuck is it, almost escaped her thirsty lips. She made a mental note to pour a full glass of bottled water; then the hottest shower, a nap, a dream. Later dinner. A slow walk on the sand to watch the full moon rise; one day after, waning. But still pregnant, full of clear erotic light. Her skin itched with salt, the Mexican sun.

Xochiquetzal thought of the handsome, very young, Mexican doctor she'd escaped, Like an idiota, she couldn't help thinking. Brilliant, hermoso, but too damned young for me. Her body clenched involuntarily, with the memory of his confident eyes gazing into hers as they spoke of past lives, Kubler-Ross, his work in the ER—and when she told him it was her birthday, that she was old enough to be his mother, he said, "Maybe I'm your gift." Those beautiful, clear, wise, young/old eyes staring into her. Into her. When he went to get drinks, she ran. She escaped.

There was laughter on the other side of the door—"Who the fregado is it?" she raised her voice.

"Es yo, tu amigo."

El cabron, he followed me here, her mind flashed awake, he followed me here. Then, her body flashed awake.

"Go away!"

"No." She heard the smile in his voice.

"I'll call security!" She felt her thirsty lips wanting to curl into a smile. She forbade it.

"I'll show them my medical credentials and tell them you're my patient," he said with his charming, way too charming, accent (he made English sound inviting, warm). "Here in Mexico they'll believe me, el doctor." Then he laughed again, that sense of confidence he exuded. That magnet. She loved his accent when he spoke English, though he spoke mainly Spanish from their conversation on the beach, switching back and forth. Spanglish. Right now it was English for her pocha benefit; he wanted her to understand every word.

"Sinverguenza," the word escaped her mouth, making her smile (one without any shame, nada, zero, zilch...shameless).

"Si, es yo, Javier." More laughter. She put her face to the coolness of the door (the AC was on at seventy degrees), and she thought she heard him breathing.

"What do you want?"

"Tu sabes, you know."

"You're old enough to be mi hijo..."

"Qué rica," he laughed, the 'r' rolling in 'rica,' conveying pleasure to her ears. Senses. "I am not your son, let me show you, Xochitzalita," he nearly sang to her.

His voice penetrated her in a stream of clear, erotic, full moon light, or the muy caliente Mexican sun; her body flushed with sudden longing. I'll probably regret this, she warned herself as she opened the door to find him standing there in his still wet trunks, bare chested, slim like a boy, flared shoulders of a man, and smiling with that unwavering confidence. A doctor, a god, she thought briefly—is there a fucking difference? She wanted to laugh, but firmly refused to.

"I was about to take a shower, Javier, before your rude knock..." Xochiquetzal realized she was smiling, in spite of her inner command to be irritated, to stay in charge. He stared directly into her eyes—large, dark pools of wonder that have witnessed birth, life, death in the ER. His eyes held no age, only wonder, terror, endless curiosity. He was a small boy of six; he was the eighty-eight-year-old man whose life he'd saved the day before. The infusion of energy that had made him pack a few things, drive directly to Vallarta, swim in la mar at 4 a.m., cradled by the clear, streaming light of the sensual warm waves. Always a woman's body, her secret salt on his tongue.

"This is my fifty-eighth birthday," Xochiquetzal almost whispered.

"What magic potion do you take, *mamacita*, you look in your forties, and you know what they say about older woman, younger man," Javier paused, smiling como un sinverguenza, shamelessly, into her eyes. "You know I'm your gift, Xochitzalita."

"It must be the yoga," she laughed weakly. "My son's close to your age, he's thirty, you're thirty-four, as I remember."

"*Qué rica,* let's wash this salt off." Now he spoke Spanish, that beautiful Spanish that entered hidden childhood sections of her brain: trust.

Xochiquetzal turned on the hot water, the way she liked it, almost unbearable. "What do they say about older women, younger men?" Her body flushed open like the ripest, red rose, so suddenly, she almost fell to her knees (red, fleshy petals floated so slowly). She was embarrassed. She was surprised. She was trembling.

"Are you trying to cook me?" he laughed deep in his throat. "Let me show you what they say." Javier gently took the pins out of her coiled, wet hair, and it fell past her firm shoulders, damp with curls. She held her kimono closed, but her hair was past her small, still girlish breasts, and the tips of the curls on her back reached the deep purple lotus blossom tattoo at the sacrum, the very small of her back (where the kundalini serpents slept). No man, except for the tattoo guy, had ever seen it. She felt ridiculously like a virgin—five years of celibacy—and the yellow/red tongues of fire leaping from the center of the lotus, etched on her flesh, danced.

"Mamacita," he laughed with joy, "your hair is so beautiful!"

He laughs like a boy, like my son laughs, still laughs, the boy still alive in the man. Xochiquetzal held her breath as the flames danced higher (as the serpents began to stir).

Javier took her hand and led her into the shower. "Make it cooler, por favor." Then, he did it himself. He took off his trunks. He was perfectly brown. Beautiful. Erect.

I can't talk or I'll weep, I'll start crying and scare the shit out of him, she thought, staying silent, gazing directly back into his eyes. And he saw the same thing—pools of wonder that have witnessed birth, life, death. No age, only wonder, terror, endless curiosity.

Xochiquetzal let her kimono fall to the tiles, and she walked the one step into his boyish arms. Their strength surprised her as they enclosed her forcefully, gently. As they began to kiss—his thirsty lips on her thirsty lips—it was such a gift, just this long, sweet, deep in her mouth, kiss. She began to weep, but it didn't matter, as the water encircled them, their joyful, melting bodies.

"This is what they mean, Xochitzalita, this is what they mean." Javier lifted her body slightly from the tiled floor, and she surrendered to his hands, his arms, his chest, his lips, his tongue that sent jolts of lightning to her tongue. *This is the deepest play*, she heard—did he say it, did she say it, it didn't matter.

He lowered her to the cool tile floor, the warm water caressing them. "Fuck me," she wept, "fuck me."

"Don't you want an orgasm first, I know my anatomy," Javier smiled gently, provocatively.

"No, no, fuck me."

"This is what they mean." His soft, commanding mouth found her breasts, left and right, caressing each nipple with his tongue until she reached the edge of orgasm (With my breasts, she wondered, weeping). She wanted to touch, to hold, to stroke his lovely brown penis, but he wouldn't let her. Then he tasted her secret, salty/sweet place, smiling to himself—the engorged, erect clitoris. This woman has orgasms, he noted with pleasure, and she has pubic hair like a woman, not shaved like a girl, yes... And he heard her, "Please please please fuck me now please Javier please..."

He held himself up on his hands over her, lowering himself so his erect serpent stroked her belly. "Please please please..." she chanted, lifting herself up to meet him.

"Am I your son?" He stared into her eyes, waiting for an answer.

Xochiquetzal stopped undulating, moving, chanting, her eyes flashing anger, and his serpent stroked her again, slowly. "No," she wept, "no."

"No what, tell me."

"You're not my son, cabron..." As he entered her it felt like a membrane gave way, a boundary she'd created to protect herself against the world—and she heard it again, *This is the deepest play*. As he entered her to the tip of her tender womb (now pulsing with a life of its own... birth, life, death, birth), she remembered his eyes from a dream. And then she forgot as the dance of the living filled her, convulsing her with ripples of orgasms like birth from her womb. This is the balance of labor, giving birth, multiple orgasms, she thought suddenly, seeing her womb filled with her unspilled monthly blood.

As he began to convulse within her, filling her with so much joy, his orgasm, joy, her rational self wanted to shout, "Do you have AIDS, herpes, I forgot to ask..." Then she remembered he was a doctor, didn't he pledge to do no harm, him and his beautiful uncircumcised serpent. She let it go, she just let it go—At least I won't get pregnant, the thought flashed across her mind almost making her laugh out loud. And these womb orgasms, is this new or what. Now she was smiling.

"What's so funny, I see your smile," Javier smiled into her eyes.

"I forgot to ask if you have any sexually transmitted diseases, you know like AIDS, herpes," she murmured.

"Ayy Xochitzalita, soy un doctor, no te preocupes, don't worry, te quiero otra vez, I want you again, this is what they mean by older woman, younger man, Xochitzalita, after this I'm going to give you an orgasm directly upon your sweet, engorged clitoris..."

"Ohmygoddess it sounds like a fucking prescription," she murmured, giggling like a teenager.

"Pues it is, it is," he laughed with her, picking her up in his strong, boyish, man arms, turning her around to face the cool tile, the waterfall of lukewarm water that enveloped them, steam rising from their bodies. "Qué hermosa tattoo, un lotus muy caliente," Javier laughed softly, lowering himself to his knees. "I'm licking your lotus, your fire, Xochitzalita.." And he did until he nearly drove her loca.

This is the deepest play.

She clutched the cool tiles as he entered her from behind so deeply, so suddenly, so perfectly, she wanted to scream at the top of her lungs like a wild animal, a tiger, a lion, no, a female jaguar. The sheer pleasure, the sheerest of pleasures—This is why we live, this moment, this moment, now, her silent scream. She photographed this moment in her mind, the tiny blue butterflies floating in the tile at her fingertips.

"I'm so glad I found you, Xochitzalita, I'm so glad I found you," and he meant it, in that moment, every atom of his body, his mind, his soul, meant it. Javier remembered her eyes from a dream, and then he denied it.

"I feel like screaming, I want to let you know, but I'll rouse the dead." She tried to laugh but instead she began to weep again, with joy, this moment, this is why we live, now, this joy.

"Rouse the dead, let me hear it, I'm your gift, you're my gift, que los chingan," and he thrust deeper, if that were possible.

Deep, inhuman, or truly human, the first human sounds escaped her mouth, and he joined her in that song.

"Quiero ver tu cara, tu cara hermosa...I want to see your face, your beautiful face," Javier sang to her, turning her around to face him.

"I'm not perfect, I'm not twenty-five, I don't think I was ever perfect but now I'm fifty-eight." Xochiquetzal couldn't bear to meet his perfect eyes, not a wrinkle. She looked down at his lovely serpent and missed it, him, inside of her, that sweet dance of the living.

"Look at me, hermosa, look at me." Javier waited until she met his eyes, and it made him want her more because she was weeping. He entered her blindly as though he'd die, that moment, if he couldn't feel the tender tip of her womb. He entered her fevered, pulsing, pushing, pulling birth canal, and he saw the fine lines of living in her face, and a rush of tenderness filled him.

"I've held the still born, Xochitzalita, I've seen death in the faces of teenagers, the very young, and what I see in you is life, perfect life, give birth to me, Xochitzalita," Javier wept openly, sobbing in that hoarse masculine way, clutching her to him, kissing her eyes, her cheeks, filling her open mouth with his tongue.

And they gave birth to each other—his moans, her moans, his tears, her tears, his death, her death, his life, her life, that moment of birth.

This is the deepest play.

They fell asleep in each other's still wet arms, the AC blowing its cool wind across their naked, damp bodies. Just birthed. He was thirty-four. She was fifty-eight. Just birthed. Timeless. His mouth sought her flesh, her trusting neck, as he dreamed, as she dreamed. They dreamt of miracles which they would forget the moment they opened their eyes. Yet the miracle would remain. Alive. Just birthed.

This is the deepest play.

Xochiquetzal woke up first. It was almost dark but she could see Javier's face. "Diosa, eres tan hermoso, Goddess, you're so beautiful," she whispered. She carefully disengaged herself from his strong, sweet limbs. "I'm so fucking hungry," she murmured, wondering if she should wake him, but he looked like a trusting boy sleeping (reminding her of her son, Justin). She didn't have the heart to wake him. His eyelids trembled as he dreamt. She wanted to enter his dreams.

"Who is this boy/man who's a doctor?" Xochiquetzal asked the violet twilight. And then she remembered El Nino Doctorcito, the little boy doll saint, in her favorite church in San Miguel de Allende. Surrounded by his toys, a stethoscope around his neck, a small black doctor bag in his right hand (with the tiny, sensual angel milagro, miracle, pinned to it). The healer. She thought of the candle she'd lit before her journey, placing it in front of El Nino Doctorcito. As she'd stared at him, the little boy doll saint, for a moment she saw his tiny, pink lips smiling. And now, she remembered what she'd whispered to him as her candle burned in front of him, with all the other lit candles, and the photos of the healed at his doll feet wrapped in black cloth shoes.

"Heal me, Nino Doctorcito, heal my hidden, almost fifty-eight-year-old, beat-up, bitter, wounded, untrusting heart that I may love again, heal me."

This is the deepest play.

As she dressed in the bathroom, putting on the last of her make-up, she decided to leave him a note telling him to meet her at dinner.

"A donde vas...Where are you going, Xochitzalita?" Javier's voice was husky with sleep and satisfaction, making her womb contract involuntarily.

"El Nino Doctorcito," she murmured, smiling. "I'm starving so I was going to leave you a note to meet me..."

"Oh no you don't, you can't leave this room without your physician, mujer," he laughed languidly.

"Okay then, quick, get up, where are your clothes anyway?"

"In my truck, and how are you able to walk around after what we just did, I'm still in paradise, Xochitzalita, ayyy... Come here, dame un besito, no mas uno... give me a kiss, just one."

She laughed, "I'm not falling for that trick, Javier, so I'm going to the far end dining place, where we met at the end of the resort's beach." Just met, she reminded herself, her body still glowing.. "Meet me there when you get dressed."

"How can you walk, I can barely lift my head, estas Amazon. See you there, Xochitzalita, but you're mine after we replenish our bodies." His voice was soft, satisfied.

"It's a deal, see you there."

"Un beso, mamacita, no mas una."

"I don't trust you, estas malo," she laughed.

"Es la verdad, Xochitzalita."

This is the deepest play.

She made a delicious salad with every vegetable in the buffet and ordered a vino tinto, waiting for him to join her. Did I make him up, this Nino Doctorcito, this beautiful man who tells me he's my birth day gift, younger man, older woman, maybe I did make him up. Except her humming body kept singing its new song, yes this was a new song.

This is the deepest play.

She'd never had multiple orgasms like this—from her breasts, from her nipples, from her no longer bleeding womb (there was a new depth, song). He hasn't gotten to my clitoris yet, she realized, sipping her vino tinto, el prescripcion. This made her smile like an idiota, but she didn't care. Maybe I made el doctorcito up...

"Did you miss me?" Javier was in jeans, a soccer t-shirt, sandals, and his boy eyes were fastened on her, laughing.

"Do you really work in Emergency?"

"Do you have something that needs fixing, Xochitzalita?"

She blushed in the darkness as he sat down opposite her. They both turned simultaneously to face la mar, her undulating waves making love to the sand in the darkness. From the northern tip of Alaska to the southern tip of Brazil, each endless wave making love to the willing, thirsty land mass.

"I think you already did that, doctorcito," she said loud enough, only for his ears.

"Como no," he laughed, "and there's more to come, mamacita, let's eat, I need fuel for the healing."

She put the salad between them, laughing with him. Ayyy Diosa, he's read my mind, the healing, and I'm healing him, something in him, el niño doctorcito. "Why do you call me mamacita, I used to call mi abuela, my grandmother, mamacita..."

"I certainly don't mean it in the way you meant con tu abuelita. Aqui en México, there's mama, and then there's *mamacita*." He smiled into her eyes so intimately she became instantly wet, ready for him. Now.

What is he doing to me? she asked herself, enjoying every single moment. Something's burning up in me, something's melting away, something's becoming so soft, soft, soft...

"What are you doing to me, Xochitzalita?" he murmured, taking her hands in his. People turned to stare for a moment, then looked away, smiling at their palpable intimacy.

Yes oh yes this is the deepest play.

She watched him load two plates full of chicken mole, tortillas, sliced fruit and more, handing her one when he returned. "Clean your plate, pochita," Javier teased as he ate with obvious joy. She was aware of people stealing looks at them from time to time, curious.

"Are you embarrassed because I'm twenty-four years older, tell me the truth, Javier." Xochiquetzal faced la mar as she asked. She couldn't bear to look at him, yet she had to know. The truth.

"Look at me, Xochitzalita, look at me right now." The softness of his voice held an edge of command. She heard the steel in his voice, and it soothed her. The man rose to meet her. Equal.

She met his eyes. He x-rayed her soul. Where have I seen those eyes? she asked herself, I've seen them before.

Javier stood up so suddenly, she almost knocked her wine glass over in surprise. "I've missed this," he murmured, kneeling next to her. He kissed her deeply, sucking her breath away, his soft, full lips, his hands firmly around her back, holding her to him, refusing her efforts to pull away.

So she surrendered. To his sweet, caliente, unrelenting kiss. His unyielding, tender hands on her back, holding her to him. In public. And she didn't care that people were staring.

Slowly he pulled away, keeping his eyes on her, still kneeling. "Does that answer your question, mi locita?" He smiled shamelessly into her eyes, her ripening womb, as soft applause reached their ears, and people went back to their dinners.

"Mamacita," she laughed, tears filling her eyes. "You're the first man, in my life, to meet my gaze," she whispered.

"Quieres mas vino?" a waiter asked, smiling down at them. He filled their glasses to the brim.

"As I was telling you on the beach when we met, when I forced you to talk to me," Javier smiled mischievously, making her wet, making her want him this moment, now, again, now. "I feel I've known you before, another life. I wasn't just saying that as a, tu sabes, a pick-up line. Something about your eyes, Xochitzalita."

She thought of the flash of dream she was trying to remember— I'll find it in my dream journals, almost as old as him, she reminded herself. "I think I've dreamt you, so I know the feeling, yes something about your eyes, tu hermoso, tan malo ojos...your beautiful, very wicked eyes." Xochiquetzal looked directly into them (Most men turn away, most men...), and saw they held the candle's flame right in their dark centers. "And don't you dare leap up and kiss me again," she laughed.

"I'll try not to, Xochitzalita," Javier smiled threateningly.

Three young, handsome waiters appeared with a large piece of chocolate cake with one candle burning. Am I in fregado paradise? she wondered. Am I on the same fregado planet, Earth? And where do they find all this eye candy ayyy... They began to sing, "Happy birthday to you..." in their lovely Spanglish, and Javier joined them, laughing at her surprise. "Blow it out, señorita, blow it out, make a wish, esta momento," the waiters urged her.

Xochiquetzal was momentarily frozen to the spot, each young, handsome face laughing, urging her to blow out the candle—and Javier's face was the most handsome of all, his. The knowledge it held. The play. She looked into his young/ancient eyes and blew out the single flame. In that flame, she knew him centuries ago; if only she could remember the dream. You will, she told herself, in your dream journals, maybe in the last one, yes.

"Qué bien, feliz cumpleanos, happy birthday," the waiters said in unison (in their beautiful, sexy Spanglish voices), as one took the dinner plates away, the second poured them coffee with a full shot of kahlua, and the third sliced the cake in half, serving them both. Javier gave the third waiter some pesos, "Por todos, gracias."

"How do you know I love kahlua in my coffee? How do you know I love chocolate cake? And how did you tell them to do this wonderful thing..." she began to weep, with joy/sorrow/joy.

"I know pues todo, everything, Xochitzalita, and if you start crying I'm going to have to kiss you again." He threatened to stand, placing his palms on the table to push himself up. Smiling.

"Don't you dare, Javier, no more applause from my fellow diners..."

Instead, he stood up, leaned over to reach her lips with his, licking her slowly, softly, making her wet, making her want him. Now.

"Vaya el cuarto!...Go to your room!" someone yelled to much laughter, and then another, louder round of applause. Then someone gave a grito (a loud, Mexican cry of joy and sorrow that sends shivers up a human's spine), and Javier gave one in return to more laughter. "Cuarto cuarto cuarto cuarto," they sang in unsion.

This is the deepest play.

Finally, as they stood up to leave—after another coffee and kahlua, some creamy flan, two more vino tintos for Javier—a round of gritos pierced the air. A man shouted, "El regalo de cumpleanos para la señorita...The birthday gift for the young woman!" to loud laughter. (Young woman, Xochiquetzal smiled...maybe I do look in my forties, Javier in his mid-late thirties, young woman, she kept smiling.) "Regalo regalo regalo regalo..." voices echoed with play. Before Javier could join in with his grito, come-back, Xochiquetzal ran away, down the steps toward la mar. Loud male whoops followed her, laughter.

"How do they know he's my gift?" she began to laugh.

"Correle, hombre, se fue...Run, man, she's gone!" Everyone laughing, echoing, "Correle, correle, correle, correle..." Then she heard a piercing grito—"Javier, I bet, oh my Goddess," Xochiquetzal couldn't help giggling like a señorita. "Senorita," she sighed, walking into the warm, erotic, moon-filled waves. They reached her ankles, her knees, finally her blissful fifty-eight-year-old thighs, as she pulled the already short bandeau-style, black with fuchsia, beach dress, higher (made in Bali, her favorite place on Earth). The wet warmth of la mar soothed her; cooler than the day but still warm, and a sudden night breeze licked her flesh, lovely.

Suddenly she wanted to give a grito to la mar, to the night sky, the stars raining down their ancient light, the erotic, full moon that bathed her, everyone, in her translucent, glowing, pregnant path.

Javier grabbed her from behind so forcefully she cried out. He put his lips on her neck, kissing her hard, then softly like small butterflies landing one by one. "Don't run away from me, Xochitzalita, you know I'll always find you." His voice was soft, firm, playful. She felt his swelling, his man's warmth. His gift, el regalo.

"But I want to run away..."

"Porque, mi Xochitzalita, tan mala..."

"So you can find me, Javier."

He slowly turned her around to face him, grinding himself into her, her mouth finding his, his tongue finding hers. "I'll always find you, Xochitzalita," he murmured, and then a large, moon-filled wave covered them. Laughing, spitting la mar, she opened her mouth wide and gave a grito to the Mexican night.

"Mamacita, que pasa?" Javier laughed, picking her up in his strong, boyish arms. El doctorcito. The healer.

Yes oh yes this is the deepest play, el regalo.

A bottle of chilled champagne waited in a sweating, metal bucket, surrounded by sliced mangoes, papayas, pineapples. And a plate of chocolate truffles, hand-made in the hotel kitchen. Someone had turned on the lamp that Xochiquetzal's deep purple, fringed, traveling shawl was wrapped around. It glowed its soft, purple light that made her feel at home anywhere she traveled in the world.

"How did you get them to do this, how?" she laughed with delight.

"I'm an upper class Mexican doctor at home in his own country," he smiled so confidently. That unwavering confidence that wouldn't let her ignore him as she tried to on the beach, at first. She was taken aback by his response, for a moment—her innate aversion to any class system (the 'all men are created equal' theory she'd heard all her life in the USA, but rarely saw in daily living, politics, the news). Here was this man, this thirty-four-year-old Mexican doctor, simply saying the truth... upper class and at home in his own country.

"I guess you know, from your travels to my country, el otro lado (the other side), that I have a hard time with any class system."

"Xochitzalita, in Mexico you are automatically upper class." Javier popped the cork smoothly. "But I know estas una pochita del otro lado, you can't help it," he laughed.

"A Yaqui Indian pochita," she shot back.

"Ayy, estas una India tambien, que bien, you're my pochita Yaqui." He gave an intimate version of his more public grito, pouring her a glass of champagne. "Dame la boca...Give me your mouth," Javier commanded, kissing her. "El regalo," he murmured into her open mouth.

"And how do all those Mexicans know you, regalo regalo regalo?" Her voice was jagged, her breath catching on his soft lips, his words, "El regalo."

Another intimate grito; it went right up her spine, the kundalini, from her lotus on fire. This guy makes me wet, want him, with a grito, his soft mouth, tongue, the words, el regalo—I'm road kill, she sighed inwardly. Foreboding and delight in equal measure, and she knew... You can't pick your gift, your gift picks you, el regalo.

"We're all Mexicans at home in our own country, Xochitzalita, this is how we play, it was in our honor, this new love." Javier paused, looking into her eyes. "In this moment, right now, I'm so happy, I love you," he said in English. He waited, then said, "Tell me you love me, Xochitzalita."

She was shocked, she wasn't ready to say those words...I love you.

"Tell me you love me, Xochitzalita." His gaze was unwavering. He waited. And what she saw at the center of his dark pools of endless curiosity, wonder: faith. The kind she'd had at thirty-four; to believe. In the impossible.

"In this moment, this very moment, right now, I love you," she whispered, tears filling her fifty-eight-year-old eyes of new wonder.

"Ayy Xochitzalita, besa me, un besito, un regalo," he laughed softly. "Did you see those pobrecito, confused gringos, yet I think they enjoyed it, the Natives enacting some strange ritual, now for el prescripcion..."

"I want more champagne, some mangoes, those truffles, por favor," she giggled.

"You want champagne more than *this*?" He softly, so slowly, grazed his wet tongue over the inside of her lips. "A woman's labia, her lips, so similar, let me lick tu mango, mi amor," he smiled playfully, intimately.

"You'd better stop that..."

"Qué...What?"

"Your words make me want you, what in el fregado are you doing to me, el regalo, gritos, mangoes y mas..."

"Primero el prescripcion, then el regalo, and yes I can make you want me with my words, just with my words, Xochitzalita, y mi lengua...my tongue." Javier gently lowered her black bandeau top with the fuchsia flowers, and slowly kissed her breasts, each one, butterflies landing, covering her, making her wild. New.

This is the deepest play, el regalo, the gift.

She lit the large, cinnamon scented candle she'd bought in the hotel shop with two, huge bottles of water, chocolate bars, cartons of juice, for in-room-emergencies. They didn't offer room service as the resort was all-inclusive, but they had the store. How did he get them to deliver the champagne feast? she wondered, with fresh pleasure, as she watched him sleep. "Hermoso hombre sonando en mi cama... beautiful man dreaming in my bed," she whispered. How does he know how to make love to my clitoris, like an old lover, an experienced lover, an upper class Mexican doctor at home in his own country, yes... Xochiquetzal smiled at the peace in his open, dreaming face.

She'd begged him to stop, she wasn't capable of one more orgasm, she'd fly apart, she'd cease to exist as flesh and blood, she'd become random pleasure bliss molecules merging with sea air moon light star light his breath, he'd breathe her in... Is this how it is when you leave your body, when you die, does everyone simply breathe you in? she wondered, deeply wondered, as her body pulsed with its own strange and private joy, separate from her persistent rational self, yet claiming her for its own. The body, spirit, soul. One blissful human being. That moment. That very moment. As she gazed at his open, dreaming face—his lips wet, parted, as though he wanted to tell her his dreams.

They dreamt in separate bodies, separate dreams, but they dreamt suspended in the same sky, the same timeless sky, where their souls simply knew each other. Timeless. They laughed as shooting stars pierced their dreaming bodies, as they remembered their endless preparation for death, for birth, always death, birth. Endless curiosity. Endless wonder. They dreamt. Side by side. His leg wrapped around her hip. Her arm flung over his chest, his heart. That pulsed. With life. Her heart. That pulsed. With life. El regalo, the gift. Endless wonder. They laughed. Suspended in the same timeless sky. Where their souls simply knew. Each other. Timeless.

Was this the deepest play?   *Yes.*

Xochiquetzal... *I speak to a beautiful man with no words, only a stream of light flows from my mouth and he understands. He opens his mouth, a stream of light, and I understand. Joy.*

Javier... *I fly across the impossible ocean to meet my love, I can't reach her, her long blonde hair hides her from me. I return to my own country. To dark haired women. Or I will. Die. Again. To the light. I see the light. A wise woman. Give birth to me, I've held so much death.*

She woke up to him inside her, so gently, from behind, stroking her gently, his arms, his hands, holding her to him as though she might try to escape, but she had no desire to escape. No Desire. To escape. They made love without words, only sounds of joy, ecstasy, searing pain/pleasure, as though in a dream.

"Let's go to town, I don't think I can bear to face our fan club," Xochiquetzal laughed from somewhere so deep inside her body, her still pulsing womb—a place she'd forgotten to remember, until now.

Javier frowned with disapproval, and for a moment she thought he was serious until he smiled at her. The smile of the boy in the man, beautiful. As he watched sunlight fill the room, her eyes, he felt happy like a boy on a summer morning with a day of play in his wide open hands. "I have to warn you, my truck is a disaster, I clean it out once a month maybe. My car I save for formal occasions, my truck es para jugar...for play."

El Nino Doctorcito and his toy cars and trucks, of course, she smiled at him. "I don't care if we go by burro, I just want to go to a strange place for desayuno... breakfast, walk around like tourists..."

"My truck is a burro," he laughed softly. "And you can be the pochita tourist, I'll be your Mexican guide," he murmured, kissing her, making her wet in spite of herself.

"No, I mean it, no, you'll have to roll me around in a fucking wheel chair, Javier, I'm not kidding, no, no, I mean it..."

They walked to the end of the resort's beach where his burro waited, and she laughed when she saw his teenage burro full of dents, scratches. Proof of many joyful, and probably muy loco, adventures. When he opened the door for her, a machete fell to the ground, as well as beer, juice and water containers. She leapt backwards, laughing. "What in el fregado is a *machete* doing in your burro, Javier, ayyy Diosa y Dios tambien!"

"I told you it was a disaster," he smiled happily. "Every Mexican travels with one, just like the gabachos travel with their pistolas. At least ours is hand to hand combat, mi pochita Yaqui."

"Woman hacked to death in Vallarta by insane physician!" Xochiquetzal stood, watching him pick up all the cans and bottles, placing them in a large plastic bag in the back of his burro. He slid the large machete under her seat, smoothly.

"Here, it's your weapon in case your lips drive me absolutely insane," Javier said in a serious tone, his eyes conveying concern for her safety. There didn't seem to be any shocks in his burro, which made her laugh out loud with irrational joy. And he laughed with her.

"I have one more day, Xochitzalita, then I'm expected back in the Emergency."

"Only tomorrow?"

"I'll come to see you in San Miguel at the end of the month, te juro...I promise... if I can stand it to the end of the month that is. You'd better get the machete to protect yourself, I think I'm going insane right now."

She gazed at his face, his mouth, as he said this, and her joy didn't leave her. Then she kissed him, meeting his tongue with her own, quickly. "Maybe you need your machete, doctorcito, maybe I'm going insane," Xochiquetzal laughed. Like she used to laugh so long ago.

Javier found the perfect place. Not fancy, wonderful home-cooked food, and facing la mar. The coffee wasn't strong but it was hot and tasty with sprinkled cinnamon.

"Do you miss your fan club?" he teased.

"We were going to have to do el tango next," she smiled at the clear mirror of la mar, "but seriously, that's never happened to me, that public display of I don't know what." She was glad she'd chosen to wear the deep-green, bandeau beach dress, with tiny white sea shells sewn into the fabric, and bare-shouldered, the heat.

"Pobrecita pochita Yaqui ayy," Javier laughed deep in his throat, in his groin, his still celebrating groin, and suddenly leaped to his feet. He looked like a college student in his black t-shirt with charging red bull (from the bull run in Spain), well-worn jeans; only his expensive leather sandals gave him away.

"Not here, Javier, por favor not here," Xochiquetzal collapsed into giggles.

"Pochita Yaqui, I'm going to kiss you in every public place in Vallarta!" And he pulled her to her feet, still laughing, and kissed her so deeply her legs felt like water. Like la mar, that constant rolling, that constant light-filled dance. Of sex. Her legs felt absurd holding her up, when she only wanted to lie down. Dance. Water. Dance. Sex. With. Him. El doctorcito. Javier.

And of course, the sound of a male grito reached their ears, making them laugh, stop kissing. His legs felt absurd holding him up—dance, water, dance, water, with her. La pochita. Xochitzalita.

Their chorizo omelettes with home made green tamales arrived, served by the woman who made them. Her long, grey hair was braided, coiled at the top of her head. She exuded gentleness and strength at the same time, in equal measure.

Mi Mamacita, Xochiquetzal realized, tears filling her eyes. Gentleness, strength. Her presence.

"You both look like you need your strength, comida fuerte," she said in Spanish, smiling, placing the large plates on the table. Fresh, warm, corn tortillas in a basket covered with a rainbow cloth. She remembered such mornings, needing comida fuerte, after a long night of love. "Estas cansados...You look tired..." she laughed, "then, you must eat."

Although it made her blush, somewhere below her neck (her breasts, her nipples, her waist, her wet ripe vulva), it also felt like a blessing. From Mamacita. The grandmother.

"Ay Mama, yes we need la comida," Javier smiled at her like a charming son, "gracias por los tamales perfecto, y un cerveza tambien, una Victoria, Mama."

"Una Victoria para me tambien, Mama, gracias," Xochiquetzal smiled at her as one stray tear slid beneath her sunglasses.

"Porque llores, no llores...Why are you crying, don't cry." Mamacita placed her feathery hand on Xochiquetzal's shoulder.

"Because I'm happy, Mama."

"Qué bien, que bien, your love is new, que bien," she smiled to herself as she walked away. Her memories of love. When they were new.

"She reminded me of mi Mamacita, that mixture of gentleness and strength, and of course she made the most delicious tamales. Sweet and spicy ones."

"I know, Xochitzalita, I know, but if you don't stop crying I'm going to have to make love to you right here on the sand, and then you'll really hear some gritos, and you'll become a Vallarta legend...."

"Callate, shut up and kiss me."

And he did, leaning over the table, feeling her inner lips, mouth, with his soft, hungry tongue.

"Give her a break, hombre, a woman has to eat," Mama teased as she placed their Victorias down. The Victorias, icy cold, felt like frozen joy in the hot Mexican sun.

They ate in silence. Their hunger surprised them, and Javier ordered more tamales, tortillas, Victorias. After her second Victoria, his fourth, the sun began to sing a new song in her sensory-filled mind/body/mind/body, and it was entirely in Spanish.

"At this moment, I'm so happy, Xochitzalita, I love you." He waited, fastening his eyes on her.

She sighed with exaggerated impatience, smiling. "Okay, okay, at this moment, this very moment, I love you, mas loco Javier."

"Qué bien, pochita hermosa."

And then she saw his eyes follow something in fascination. Flirting. She turned around in time to see a lovely woman, in her twenties, giving her best smile to him.

"Es nada, Xochitzalita, the women play like that in Mexico."

"I see." She paused, considering his words. "I suppose that's what we're doing really, playing." She sighed with hurt and relief—the truth.

I'm twenty-four years older, about her age, get real old girl.

"No, pochita loca, it's you I choose to be with now, this moment."

"I get it, we're playing right now, this moment, and it's okay. I imagine you get a lot of that, and why shouldn't you? Well, I suppose I get my share..."

"Do you smile back?" A tinge of jealousy edged his voice.

"When I feel like it," she laughed. This is how it should be—light, play.

"Ah, la feminista pochita."

"We're just getting to know each other, Javier, so I get that you'll flirt with women, just don't do it when you're *with me*. The same goes for me, and yeah la feminista pochita." She met his steady gaze with her own steady gaze—equals.

"I want you, right here on the sand," he said softly.

"You like the chase, the conquest," she smiled, "el conquistador."

"To your little Yaqui."

"The Yaquis, Javier, were undefeated, didn't you know that?"

"Ay pochita tan mala." He leaned over the table and lightly licked her lips. No kiss. Just this teasing memory. "Do you remember?" His voice. His tone. So intimate. Her womb clenched.

"What, cabron?"

"El prescripcion, esta noche, tonight, again, Xochitzalita." His tongue found hers, so very softly.

This is the deepest play.

"Do you want me, this moment, pochita?"

"I hate to feed your big, fat ego, Javier, but the truth is, I can't even believe it, yes." Her womb clenched again in ripples. Of pleasure.

"This is what they mean by older woman, younger man." He smiled with the knowledge of her womb, her orgasms, her tender birth canal.

She threw a piece of tortilla at him. "You won't be happy until you're wheeling me around in a fucking wheel chair," she laughed softly.

"Only if I can fuck you in the fucking wheel chair, Xochitzalita." Her strength provoked him, drew him to her—and he remembered his old love in Spain, her long blonde hair. Her strength.

Something changed in his eyes. Something switched to sorrow. "What are you thinking?" she asked.

"Of an old love. She was strong like you, una feminista. We'll talk later, let's have this day for just us."

"I agree, very wise, let's take our time telling each other our sad stories, and let's be brief if we can help it. Life is so short, let's be happy, right now, this moment." Yet she made a mental note to ask later, to find out about his old love that brought such sorrow to his almost always laughing, endlessly curious dark eyes.

"Yes, very wise, we'll talk later, but today is for us, Xochitzalita," he smiled with a mixture of sadness/play. "And now, let's walk to the next Victoria."

"You're not leaving a tip?"

"These little stands don't expect one." His tone became defensive, authoritative. His country.

"If someone cooks and serves me food, I tip them." Xochiquetzal reached into her purse and pulled out forty pesos.

"That's too much, pochita."

"It's not enough, she was wonderful." She placed the pesos on the table.

"Estas una pochita, Xochitzalita." Javier tried to disguise the trace of anger that rose in his throat. His authority questioned. Didn't he command people in the ER, didn't she know that...he was an upper class Mexican doctor at home in his own country.

"You called her *mama*, Javier, remember?" She heard the anger.

Just like Clara, that strength. He laughed, taking her by the waist, claiming her for his own, this moment. Now. They walked away.

"Gracias," the grandmother called, taking the forty pesos into her work-worn hand. Many people made forty pesos daily, she knew. "Gracias a la pochita," she murmured.

Xochiquetzal wore her straw sun hat from Taos, keeping a shadow over her face, the relentless Mexican sun. She briefly wondered if he noticed her face wrinkles in direct sunlight—Stop, she told herself, stop. "I wish I'd brought my camera now, damn, look at all these great images." She swept her hand in a wide arc to include the street, the stalls piled with color, the people minding their own business. No fans here. Of course he hadn't tried to kiss her in the street. Yet. No gritos. And she realized she missed it; his public kiss, his shamelessness, sinverguenza.

Cut it out, she told herself, or you're sure as shit road kill, twenty-four years younger and an eye for las mujeres, and them for him. Get real, old chickie, it's a normal thing, he's a young man, a doctor-god, a

Mexican at home in his own fucking country, get real.

"You could take photos of me," Javier teased, "and someone could take our photo, me kissing you all over Vallarta, gathering our new fan club, los gritos, Xochitzalita."

He keeps reading my fregado mind, she thought. "Look, this stand has throw aways, that'll be just fun." She bought one and immediately took his photo.

"Wait, wait." Javier placed a wide, black, glittering with gold, sombrero on his head, no smile, the deadly stare of Zapata, all will (but no horse).

"Perfect, just perfect," she laughed with delight. "Such a handsome jefe, but where's tu caballo...your horse, Javier?"

He instantly rounded up a very handsome young guy to take their photo together. He flashed her a lovely smile of hola, and Javier waited to see her response. She flashed hola right back, glancing at Javier playfully. Keeping the sombrero on, he swept her into his arms, in the middle of the busy market place. "Ayy pochita," he murmured, kissing her deeply (tongue to tongue, soul to soul), knocking her Taos sun hat off. In the full glare of the 1 p.m. Mexican sun, to the sound of scattered gritos.

That's it, his soul knows my soul, the thought came like lightning—and then a question: What does it mean?

"Otro foto, amigo." Javier's voice took on the tone of command.

"This time no kiss, let me breathe." Her body felt so fluid as though she had no control of the molecules that held her together, him together, this bright day together. Only la mar knew the secret of dissolution, and then creation. Only la mar knew how to play with the molecules of humans, the world. First destruction, then creation. That chaos. That soft, soft chaos.

Was this the deepest play? Yes

Javier wanted to force her for a moment, and then he remembered Clara, her strength. Instead, he took her by the waist, spreading his physician's hands to claim her right breast, tenderly.

Later Xochiquetzal would call this photo, Doctor Zapata y La Feminista. Neither of them had smiled, looking straight into the camera. And that photo captured what they truly were—equals. Only her mouth was slightly upturned, trying to match the staged moment of seriousness. Play.

Equals at play.

How does his soul know mine, and how does mine know his? she thought as the hermoso young man took their photo again.

"Buy the sombrero," she urged Javier, "it makes you look like Dr. Zapata."

"I could make love to you with it on," he smiled tan malo, "okay, I'll do it." As he wore the show-stopping, black with glittering gold, sombrero down the street, she began to realize what an exhibitionist he was. Flamboyant came to mind, making her laugh out loud.

"Do I look funny to you, Xochitzalita?" he stopped to gaze at her.

"No, no," she laughed, "I was just fully realizing what an exhibitionist you are, pero estas muy hermoso y loco tambien...but you're very handsome and crazy as well." This time she kissed him, drawing him to her.

"Ayy mamacita!" some guy yelled, laughter.

"I like that you kiss me, Xochitzalita, more, mamacita, more," Javier laughed.

They left the stalls of piled, colorful, glittery, hand-made, hand-painted things for sale, and began to walk on the main street parallel to la mar. A few people were begging, their hands out, watching them pass by.

"If you give them pesos they'll never work, come on, time for my next Victoria." But she slipped out of his arm that held her and walked over to a young Indian woman with a toddler in her arms. The toddler was very quiet, for a two year old, until he began to cough a deep, rasping sound from the center of his small chest. Xochiquetzal reached for some pesos as the young mother told her she needed money for medicine, her child's cough. Javier knelt down to see him, and the woman drew back, afraid.

"Soy un doctor, señora." His voice was gentle. The woman simply offered her son to him, beginning to weep quietly. "We need to get your child to a hospital now," he told her in Spanish. Javier stood and whispered in English to Xochiquetzal, "This child is dying, help her up, I'm getting a taxi."

Javier went directly to the nurse's station, with a look she hadn't seen yet—full command and anger. He briefly spoke to the nurse, and then she disappeared for a few minutes, bringing a doctor who seemed irritated.

Xochiquetzal sat with the woman, her arm around her, and she watched her baby, trying not to cry. She thought of her own son at two, the sheer health he exuded, and she simply couldn't believe this baby was dying, could simply die on the street in his mother's arms. He continued to cough that awful, deep rasping from such a small, frail body. She touched Javier's glittering sombrero with her fingertips, while keeping an eye on the baby, and then back to him with the doctor on duty. They appeared to be arguing; she couldn't hear what they were saying until, "I'll give you 3,000 pesos, my cell number, the hospital where I work, you must admit this child now." (In Spanish.) Javier raised his voice, staring the other doctor down with those eyes. Those piercing, Zapata eyes. The doctor relented—she'd have to stay, be her child's nurse as they were under-staffed, an over-flow of patients.

Javier walked over to them, glancing at Xochiquetzal with sheer disgust at the situation. Anger. He knelt down next to the mother, explaining the situation to her. "Si doctor, gracias, gracias," was all she said. He placed his hand on the baby's small, listless head, so hot, his eyes registering a moment of despair.

"I'm going to get her settled in, make sure they start the medications."

"Take your time, Javier." She gave him a look of, what she hoped was, encouragement. And more encouragement to the mother, as he helped her to her feet. "Qué te vaya bien, señora, tu niño...May it go well, señora, your son."

"She turned to face Xochiquetzal. "Qué Dios te guarda, señora, gracias, gracias...May God take care of you, señora, thank you."

Javier led her past the swinging doors to where some hope might be. Just before she entered, she turned to give Xochiquetzal the most brilliant smile, and she realized how young this mother was. So young, still lovely. And Indian. The lowest rung on the Mexican class system's ladder.

Javier finally emerged looking thirty-four, forty-four, fifty-four, sixty-four, seventy-four... She stood up to meet him, touching his somber face with her open hand. No words, just touch.

"They started his medications. If he lives through the night he might live. I gave them my cell number, Xochitzalita, let's go."

She picked up Zapata's sombrero, holding it by it's wide brim. "Is it because she's Indian..."

"She's Indian, she's poor, she's uneducated, she's powerless, let's get the fredgado out of here." His voice was strained with anger, and she heard it, tears.

"Zapata was an Indian and this is why he fought a century ago, the same fucking fight," she said softly. "Right now, this moment, I love you, Javier." She x-rayed his soul with her eyes, and kissed him in the silence of the hospital. A kiss of friendship. Solace. Her soft lips. His soft lips. Touch.

"Esta momento, te amo como no sabes, Xochitzalita...In this moment, I love you like you don't know." His voice broke. Tears fell slowly. Rain, rain, he was grateful or he'd explode, he knew; but then he made them stop, falling.

They stopped at a small restaurant, open air, by la mar. Only locals ate here, so people stared as Xochiquetzal entered, but Javier's cutting glance made them go back to eating, talking. Also, she was still carrying his sombrero, and she could hear their thoughts, Why is that pocha carrying un hombre's sombrero y mas joven...and younger. Of course, she knew she looked at least ten years older than him— "Mamacita," she murmured. She was beginning to realize the full command of his stare, his Zapata eyes. Even without the sombrero he looked like Zapata, without his caballo/horse, she smiled to herself. But that confidence that commanded my attention on the beach, followed me to my fucking room, ay Diosa, Dr. Javier Zapata.

Walking from the hospital to find this little restaurant, Xochiquetzal had tripped on the uneven sidewalk—Like Bali, she thought, with potholes to fit an adult body. She'd fallen onto her right knee, catching herself with the palms of her hands, springing right back up to her feet.

He'd tried to help her but she was too fast, she was already walking, laughing at herself, telling him about the potholes in Bali (and of course, India, she'd fled India, the crush of poverty).

"Look, your palm is bleeding, why don't you let me help you, Xochitzalita?" Women at least pretend they're helpless once in a while, that illusion of el hombre es jefe, the man in charge, his mind took notes.

"If I'd waited for you to help me, Javier, I would've fallen flat on my face, suffering more damage than a bleeding palm. I travel by myself, and I like to travel by myself, it's by choice. I can take care of myself, como no." She pressed a tissue to her bleeding right palm's raw ache.

"Como un hombre fuerte," he muttered. "Like a strong man."

"Como una mujer fuerte." His words slapped her. "I choose to be with you here, this moment, is that enough for you, Javier?"

Leaving the young mother, the dying child, he was in a sullen mood, so she let it go to sadness. And her sadness of this reality. Life unedited. Mexico. Beauty, joy, sensuality, poverty and death, unedited. Not on the scale of India; plus she couldn't simply flee Mexico. Her grandmother, great (great great...) grandmother's country. And her grandfather's (great great...), as well.

Is this my country? Xochiquetzal asked herself in the sad silence of their walk; and when Javier had taken her hand she'd wanted to say yes, but she knew it wasn't true. She remembered Virginia Woolf's words: As a woman, I have no country. As a woman, I want no country. As a woman, the whole world is my country. And the image of the small, sweet, vulnerable, oxygen-blue Earth spinning in the darkness of endless, eternal space (the mind of the Goddess, God, Mystery, Creator), filled her mind, comforted her. And, yes, the warmth of Javier's young, male, knowledgeable, healer's hand also comforted her.

He took out his cell to check for messages, nada—Should've I stayed? he asked himself for the fiftieth time, but he knew if he'd stayed the care would've been the same, the same medications. But I could've overseen the care, he countered, and then the reality. El Jefe, el doctor in charge didn't want me there—I would've ended up punching el chingado.

"Any messages?"

"Not a fucking one," he smiled sadly. "I'm starting to talk like you now, Xochitzalita. I was thinking I should've stayed, but they wouldn't let me, I'm not authorized to practice at that hospital, que fucking triste. And that jefe doctor, I probably would've had to knock him out, who knows, me in jail, fregado." Javier sighed on the out-breath, and then told the waiter he wanted una cerveza, a Victoria (sold only in Mexico) with a shot of tequila con limon y sal...with lemon and salt.

"I'll take some of that, sounds good." The older waiter raised an eyebrow of disapproval—a man's drinking order—then shrugged as in whatever.

Javier leaned over the small space between them, kissing her softly, sadly. "I'm sorry you have to put up with my country's deeply imbedded fucking macho pinche mierda, Xochitzalita."

"It's not your fault."

"Didn't I just want you to fall flat on tu hermosa cara...your lovely face...so I could take fregado care of you? No, brava that you caught yourself, that only your palm bleeds." He inspected her injury and kissed the bloody scrape, tenderly, in each spot. Then he moistened a napkin and carefully cleaned the injury of visible and invisible dirt, germs.

"Do you have any antibiotic ointment in your room?" His Zapata eyes x-rayed her womb, and he wasn't even wearing the sombrero. Javier picked up the glittery sombrero and placed it on her head, laughing into her eyes. "Let's give los machos something to look at, la feminista."

"Yes, Dr. Zapata, in my first aid kit," she laughed softly, kissing him back with fresh passion. A deep kiss, her tongue licking his inner lips, searching for his sweet tongue. No one here did a grito, made any comments, laughed. They discreetly looked away at the pocha wearing Zapata's sombrero, kissing the young

upper-class Mexican.

"Ayy mamacita, dame mas...give me more," Javier murmured, licking her inner lips slowly with his tongue, sending shivers to her willing womb, his swelling serpent, her now released serpents from the kundalini where the lotus on fire once held them, coiled, sleeping.

"Es tan hermosa en mi sombrero, Xochitzalita."

"It suits you more, but I must admit I feel muy macha wearing it," she laughed. He was on his second tequila con limon y sal. She continued to sip hers—The burning tequila, the cool beer, salt to lemon, just like life, his sweet lips the balance, she thought, as their food arrived.

"I want you to wear it tonight when I give you el prescripcion, por favor," Javier laughed intimately just for her. "Look behind you, look," he gestured with eyes bright with pleasure.

The most beautiful, mixed-race, mestiza, chocolate-skinned, blonde girl of about six was standing in the back of a truck gazing out at the sea. She looked like she was gazing at the length of her life; such wise six year old eyes. All she wore were white cotton panties on this hot night. Twilight. Her tiny breast buds unselfconscious, and her hair caught the sparkle of all available light. What would happen to her in this Mexican town? Xochiquetzal wondered, and Javier already knew.

"She looks like my old love, Clara, must've looked like as a girl," he almost whispered.

"Where is Clara, what happened, if you don't mind my asking."

"She's in Spain, married, with a beautiful child of her own." Javier finished the tequila, then the Victoria, and ordered more as warm, fresh tortillas de maize were placed on the table in a covered basket. "She wouldn't come to Mexico to be my wife, so she found a very rich man in her own country is what happened, Xochitzalita, she loves someone else now, a man of wealth, that's what happened." His eyes were wounded; the same look when he understood the baby was dying.

"I'm so sorry, Javier"—tears filled her eyes for his pain—"do you still love her, I think you do, you still do."

He looked into her eyes for a long while before he answered. "I'll always love her, and she'll probably always visit me this way." He indicated where the beautiful girl-child had been, now gone. "But right now, this moment, Xochitzalita, I love you, your green-gold eyes, your thick dark hair, your still bleeding palm where you caught yourself." Javier smiled a smile that encompassed all sorrow, all joy—and then he gave a grito. Not a loud one, but loud enough for la mar to hear.

Xochiquetzal remembered, as the first clusters of bright, burning stars appeared, how each true gift in her life had come with blood. Every time the omen was—blood. The list seemed endless as she thought about it—her son's birth (the bloody placenta, cord, his tiny beautiful, bloody body that emerged from her own bleeding body), the blisters on her feet bleeding as she traveled alone for the first time, her menstrual blood coming unexpectedly the first day, the first class she ever taught, how the chemicals in the darkroom cracked her hands, bleeding, until she learned how to avoid contact, her grandmother's last words, dark blood on her lips, her blessing, her own mother's labor 58 years ago, blood, as she entered the light—yes, the list was endless. And now, this thirty-four-year-old man, she fifty-eight, the blood as gift. When he'd kissed her palm, he'd tasted her blood—she didn't know this.

"On the beach you said you were my gift, remember?"

"Como no, your birth day gift, and I still haven't given you a regalo."

"Yes you have, Javier."

"Not *that* regalo, a proper one, but I will, you'll see, Xochitzalita."
He laughed a little too loudly and the waiter returned with his order
of tequila y Victoria, bringing one for her as well, la macha, la pocha.
As he placed their drinks down, he suddenly felt like giving a grito, as
he often did in his youth for no good reason; but firmly told himself
not to and sighed. He liked this strange couple—he an upper class
Mexican, she an upper class pocha—the fire between them.

Xochiquetzal was reluctant to stop at Senor Frogs, more drinks;
he'd had five Victorias with tequila shots. "I'll drive back to the hotel,
so how about one drink and we head back, walk on the beach, a regalo
in the shower…"

"Now you're tempting me." Javier checked his messages one more
time. "A fucking message from el jefe doctor at my hospital, later." I
wonder how many people are waiting for care in Emergency…I wonder
if the lines are long and I'm not there. He fingered the sombrero for a
moment, then placed it on his head.

Senor Frogs was touristy, women with exposed navels, bright
thongs between las nalgas…their butts, peeking over their low rise
jeans. The ones who sat alone scanned Javier and licked their glossy
lips. Xochiquetzal watched it as a kind of social experiment, refusing
to feel one atom of jealousy. She watched his relaxed, slightly drunk
face register pleasure; his love of female worship. And she realized, he
expects female worship, that's what he's used to, that's why he followed
me to my room, I didn't give it to him, el doctor de Emergencia. She
saw the male arrogance on his face as each woman beamed their
availability. Worship.

"Hey look, I'll take a taxi back, I'm not into this scene."
Xochiquetzal turned to leave and Javier grabbed her arm, holding on
to her.

"Do I have to fucking find you again, pochita loca, if you go I go,
vamos juntos…we go together. This is, what do you call it," he paused,
bringing her into his arms, "eye candy, es todo, that's all."

"You're used to female worship, aren't you, you're used to getting
your way, Dr. Javier Oscar Gomez Villatoro." She tried resisting the
pull of his arms, his gravity, but his intimate smile, just for her, was like
the sun.

"That's Javier Zapata to you, mi feminista. One more drink, a
margarita this time, and you drive el borracho to the hotel, okay?" He

said it, Oh kay. He wanted her to sit on his lap, but it felt too much like being in a old time cliche Mexican movie. The ones she'd seen with her grandmother. La puta on the guy's lap in the bar. She'd have to wear deep red lipstick and a blouse off her shoulders.

I'm too old for this shit, she thought, or maybe I'm weirdly too young, I've never been properly socialized as a woman. The one time I wore a thong, it felt like a chingado melvin, as my son, Justin, and his friends, used to joke around with each other, making each other's shorts go up their butts. I threw them in the trash and went commando for the rest of the day. I remember going panty-less as a little girl, the cool wind on my exposed self. That's what I felt like thong-less (that tight piece of material gathering dingleberries), when I took it off, free like a girl.

The women had gone back to the business of being hot, single women (in their exposed thongs, riding the curve of their hips), hanging out at Senor Frogs in Vallarta, when he'd grabbed her arm and wouldn't let go. They'd sit on his lap, each one; and they'd give him whatever he wanted. That night.

"You're used to being worshiped, aren't you? Especially after you drop the info about being a doctor, they must really lose their thongs. Is that why you followed me, because I wouldn't worship..."

"Callate...Shut up," Javier covered her mouth with his. "I followed you because I haven't seen anyone so fucking real and alive in a long chingado time," he murmured into her mouth. "I would've broken down your door if you hadn't opened it, Xochitzalita, you make me desperate, entiendes...understand, mi amor feminista?"

"Mi amor?"

"That's right, I'm claiming you and you don't even have to worship me, in fact I'd be immensely disappointed. If you ever worship me we're through, is that a deal?" He kissed her eyes, one by one, laughing. Then landed on her mouth, inhaling her words of protest.

"Estas bien loco, doctor," she finally managed to say. "Stop kissing me, stop."

"And if I stop you'll take a taxi and run away, though you can never ever run away," he laughed, still wearing the Zapata sombrero.

"I give up, especially when you're wearing that sombrero."

"In that case, I'll wear it everywhere we go." His young man's smile was dazzling in his semi-drunk state, and the black with gold glitter sombrero made him strangely irresistible. She could see his dark stallion. She could feel the energy he held between his young man's thighs. She could see the dark, sultry command at the center of his eyes. She held her breath for a moment, worship.

They took a taxi to his truck, and when he opened the passenger door the machete fell out again. He picked it up, making wide slashing motions. "This is my scalpel, Xochitzalita, my friend and my foe." His voice was sad again as he thought, in a blur of faces, of all the people who had died no matter what he'd done trying to save them.

"Throw your scalpel in the back and get in, Dr. Zapata, and take off that sombrero," she laughed. "You know, most women where I come from wouldn't get in a truck with a machete, ayy Diosa!" The giant margarita she'd finished at Senor Frogs (and she suspected an extra shot in their drinks, the bartender liked them), made her consciously focus on things. His machete (his scalpel). His hard to maneuver gear shift. The way back to the hotel.

"Your word is my command, Xochitzalita, when you're with me even La Muerte…Death swims in la mar, I saw her at 4 a.m. swimming next to me, what a beautiful laugh she has." In that moment, Xochiquetzal saw the boy, the innocent naked boy, in Javier's eyes. The one who believed in magic.

"Too many tequilas for you."

"Not enough, never enough, mi amor." He closed his boy eyes and slept.

Xochiquetzal guided Javier to the room, his eyes barely open like a sleep walker, smiling at the dream behind his eyes.

"I should leave you here in the hallway," she teased him. She was sweating little rivers after walking up the stairs, leading him slowly. Salty sweat drops burned her eyes, and she took note that Javier was sweating, but only a fine sheen like mist. Like a real Mexican, she thought, I'm such a fregada pocha.

"I'd have to break down your door, Xochitzalita, and then I'd have to have you arrested as your personal physician, a danger to yourself." He laughed at his own joke.

"Soy borracho, I'm drunk, gracias gracias…" he murmured as she undressed him, pulling the sheet over his lovely, bare, brown shoulders. The room was just right with the air conditioner. "El regalo en la manana, mi amor." Javier passed out, smiling.

After she moisturized her face, the quick version, and brushed her teeth, she stepped into a fast, cool shower, and, still damp, lay next to him over the sheet just to feel the slight chill in the air conditioned room. Outside, in mid-October, it was so hot you began to sweat in four seconds (the pochas/gringos anyway); so either an air conditioned room or leap into la mar. Or drink cool Victorias con tequila y sal, or a frozen pina colada—she wished there was room service.

Quickly, automatically, instinctively, Xochiquetzal scanned the white walls for scorpions; since moving to her house in San Miguel she'd killed around twenty-four of the hideous, little monsters with stingers slightly raised. So far, no scorpions in this hotel room, but she couldn't relax. Once, she'd almost stepped on one; plus, to her shock, they didn't even fight back, scamper away; they simply waited to die. They're so horrible, pre-historic, pre-landmass, no, pre-human, yes, that's it...they don't even know we exist, so they don't fear us. A cockroach runs away, fights back, wants to live; but a scorpion just waits to die. Why do I hate them, why are they so repulsive to me? "I'm becoming the fucking Scorpion Hunter," she exhaled, with one last scan. She opened the sliding door a crack, and there it was: *la mar.*

The lamp, with her traveling purple shawl, spread its circle of softness, an edge of violet, around their bodies. Xochiquetzal could hear la mar calling her, over and over, like a mother, like a lover; her song of return. And she remembered the boy, el doctorcito, with magic in his eyes, who swam with Death at 4 a.m., and heard her beautiful laughter. She thought of the baby in the hospital, his young mother, sleeping next to him, holding him in her sad, strong arms.

Slowly, Xochiquetzal uncovered Javier to see his nakedness in the violet light. He moaned with pleasure and flung his left arm out as though to grasp something, someone, and she wanted to enter his dream, to join him there. She cradled his sleeping serpent in her hand, feeling its sweet weight, his Quetzalcoatl twin brothers, and then slid down his legs to his stubborn, boney feet (imagining his long journey to this moment, his first steps as a baby). And she saw a tiny black mark next to his left nipple, so she bent closer: a tiny crescent moon. She licked the tiny crescent moon, his left nipple, his right nipple, and they hardened as he moaned softly, his serpent slightly stirring. Her open palm, the wounded one, swept across his flared chest as he breathed evenly, and in that moment (within the violet light), she sensed his joy, his sorrow. His freedom.

Javier was absolutely beautiful. A new, unexpected thing. He was whole the way the young are whole. Without any effort. The beautiful young. Yet she could also see tiny lines of worry on his smooth forehead, and she remembered The Look at the hospital as he argued with the other doctor.

"Mi amor, mi doctorcito," Xochiquetzal whispered, "I'm trying not to worship you." She entered the sheets, pulled the top one over them, kissed his slightly open lips gently. Like a mother. Like a lover. She wrapped herself around his dreaming body, his delicious body.

Entirely like a lover.

Her desire for him pounced on her—a ferocious, starving jaguar—opening her wide. And as the jaguar's paws, mouth, teeth found her, she breathed in Javier's sweaty, young man's sea-salt scent. She smiled as the jaguar consumed her. Wasn't this what she'd always wanted, secretly. To disappear. In desire. In dreams.

"Xochitzalita, despierta, wake up, tengo café." He repeated this until her eyes finally opened.

"Oh my Goddess, don't look at me, I'm hideous!" she tried to laugh.

"You just have some mokos in tus hermosa ojos, no big deal."

"You have an excellent imagination, and do I smell coffee ayy," she sighed. "Were you up at dawn or what?"

"First I stared at you for a long time, your chi chis de niña, your long legs, your hair wrapped around your face, and I didn't recognize you," Javier laughed softly. It was true, he hadn't recognized her as she slept; caught in the web of her dreaming, she was far away. So he dipped his fingers into her vagina, gently, sniffed them, licked them. Then, he recognized her and claimed her again. Like a wild animal. She has a son my age, Javier reminded himself, but she's not my mother, no she's a beautiful, so alive, feminista y loca mujer, and I want her. He tried to read her memories on her skin like a physician; a small stretch mark from pregnancy, her son; and an uncensored jolt of jealousy pierced him. He tamed it with tenderness, stroking the small, brown stretch mark, the slightly rounded belly. He licked the stretch mark, but nothing woke her up. He kissed her soft nipples, licking them so tenderly until they became hard. She moaned, clutching herself closed.

"I was molesting you in your sleep," Javier laughed.

"That's okay, I molested you last night when you passed out. What did you do to me?"

"What did you do to me, cabrona?" He tried to kiss her, but she bolted to the bathroom to pee and brush her furry teeth.

When she returned wrapped in her black Japanese kimono with a golden dragon on the back, Javier whistled. "La Empress, desayuno is served."

"How did you get them to put this on a tray, it's all-inclusive, don't tell me, you're an upper class Mexican jefe-doctor at home in his own country," Xochiquetzal laughed, reaching for a pastry. There was bread, ham, cheese, papaya, watermelon, mango, a plate of pastries, a large pot of coffee with cream in a small, clay pitcher, and packets of sugar wrapped in a napkin. "And where did you hide all this stuff, I didn't even see it."

"You learn quickly, grasshopper." Javier poured the coffee. It smelled so rich, a drug for the fully awake.

"Grasshopper?" she laughed. "Grasshopper, I'll give you a grasshopper." She wanted to tackle him, spread him out on the bed, her willing victim, sacrifice, regalo, gift, and devour him. "After the coffee, ayy gracias."

"Mi amor, dime, mi amor...My love, tell me, my love," Javier urged her. The boy, the man, who swam with Death looked at her so evenly. She had no choice.

"Qué me chingas," she laughed, trying to hide her desire, as her womb clenched. "Mi amor, Dr. Zapata, hey where's tu sombrero?"

"That's for after el desayuno." He smiled brazenly, then sipped his coffee.

Xochiquetzal picked up something wrapped in a velvet red cloth, bound in thick, black thread. "What's this?"

"Un regalo, open it."

A pair of blood-red, garnet stones set in an exquisite, silver seashell spiral design, earrings, fell to her open palm. The wounded one. "They're the color of blood, so beautiful, Javier, they're so beautiful." Tears filled her eyes, just joy.

"I told the woman on the beach what you were like."

"She must've thought you were locito," she smiled, tears starting to fall, just joy.

"No, she understood me perfectly, now put them on for me,

Xochitzalita." Javier poured more coffee as he gazed at her. "Perfecto," he smiled, handing her the hot cup. "Tomorrow morning, early, I have to drive back, to work all night in el fregado Emergencio."

"Won't you be tired after the drive, can't you sleep first?" She sipped the rich, hot coffee as her brain clicked to full spectrum, awake. She tried, briefly, to remember her first cup of coffee in the morning at thirty-four, his age, when her son, Justin, was six. She hadn't had the heart to tell Javier his name, both with a J.

"I see you've never been a new resident," he laughed. I've spoken to doctors in the USA and they're treated like puta royalty compared to los Mexicanos, much better pay tambien." Javier checked his cell for messages, his face becoming dark, stern, sad...el doctorcito. "Still no message about Juanito, so I'll call them after."

"After what?" He looks nothing like my son, Justin's taller, hazel eyes, more self-contained, both handsome. Javier is not my son.

"El prescripcion, but first let's eat," he smiled, sensuality opening his hermoso face. After the eclipse. The thought of another death. Another loss.

Javier peeled the ripe mango carefully and, as the juice filled his hands, he caressed her small niña breasts, her rib cage, her belly, her inner thighs. "Lie still, let me do this, mi amor." His voice a blend of doctor, play, command, sensuality.

"I'm getting so sticky, you like playing doctor, don't you, being in fucking control..." she giggled with an edge of embarrassment as the juice was spread all over her. Then he began to lick the sweet mango juice from her nipples, and unexpected swords of pleasure pierced her from the inside out. She moaned. He placed slices of mango all over her body, laughing like a boy as he did so (El Nino Doctorcito playing with his sacred toys, flashed across her mind).

"Was I dead before this?" the words escaped her. "What are you doing?" Xochiquetzal almost yelled, feeling something wet between her thighs.

Javier loomed over her with a slice of mango between his teeth; then holding the slice in his right hand, he said, "I'm trying to eat your mango, señora, callate...be quiet."

"You are totally deranged..."

"And you love it, callate, mi sabrosa...delicious, Xochitzalita." He went back to his sensual surgery, and she began to writhe with unbearable pleasure. "Don't move, do you hear me, amor, don't move."

Death smiled as the slice of wet mango slid so perfectly into her birth canal, as he licked her mango, as he sucked her sweet juices, as her body lost all control, as he swallowed the wet mango. Whole.

Yes oh yes this was the deepest play oh yes

The kundalini snakes became one beautiful, blue like water, snake, as it stretched from her lotus on fire, exploding with white light to her crown chakra, and beyond to the stars. Her snake had danced this way before, but it had been years since the journey to the stars. Older woman, younger man, the blue like water snake dancing.

Where is she taking me, Javier suddenly thought at the moment of his orgasm, her orgasm, his orgasm, Where is she taking me to... He saw a white, pulsing with light, orchid blooming behind his closed eyes. He saw the golden center flush with purple streaks. He flew toward the pulsing light of the orchid, into the golden center.

Yes

"You have an advantage, don't you?" Xochiquetzal tightened her legs around him, face to face, to feel her clitoris send its orgasmic surrender, victory, like la mar, wave upon wave, her floating grateful body. Her fifty-eight year old body. His thirty-four year old body. There was no time, no years, only surrender, only victory, only la mar. She was sticky with mango juice (her juice, his juice), and she wanted to shower. But she had no desire to move away from his scent, the curve of his neck.

"Are you speaking of my knowledge of anatomy, my expertise, mi sabrosita...my delicious one?" Javier smiled, eyes closed. "This is what they mean by older woman, younger man." His voice trailed off. And then, he remembered the boy, Juanito, the way his eyes tried to make him stay at the hospital. He could be my two year old son, Javier thought, Clara's daughter is two; and he saw the child as beautiful as Clara's in Vallarta. It made him sad/happy all at once, to see her beauty.

Javier sat up and dialed the hospital, and instantly his voice became authoritative as he asked about Juan Gonzalez, that he was a doctor inquiring, that he had to know his status *now*. He stopped speaking and glanced over at Xochiquetzal, "They're checking," and back to the nurse on the other end. His shoulders slumped forward. His head dropped as he spoke a clipped, 'Gracias," and hung up.

"Juanito swam with Death this morning at 5:20am, Xochitzalita, he's being reborn it seems." Javier looked directly into her eyes, expecting her to look away, but she didn't. His magical boy eyes brimmed with death, sadness, wonder, endless curiosity.

Xochiquetzal met his gaze with a mother's knowledge of loss, death of a child, endless curiosity. She took Javier into her arms, cradling his head, his body. "Yes, you're right, he's being reborn as we speak, yes he is, little Juanito."

Javier straightened up to look directly into her eyes, holding on to her hands (and she realized no man had ever looked so clearly, fearlessly, into her eyes). "He could've lived if his mother had the pesos to pay, the knowledge to insist on medical care, early in the illness, if she wasn't an Indian." His voice held an edge of steel. His dark Zapata eyes glowered with sadness. "I need a couple of shots of tequila or a tequila sunset, whatever they call it, it's almost sunset, Xochitzalita, let's get the fuck out of here."

They walked slowly down the beach with their tequila sunsets— the bartender laughed, "Tequila sun-set, como no," pouring a triple shot for Javier.

"What am I going to do for six more days after you leave tomorrow, I can't believe you have to go." Xochiquetzal focused on the intense sunset colors that married sky, sea, earth. She reminded herself that she barely knew him; their third day together. But it didn't help. Her body already missed him, the thought of his absence. And she remembered…This is what you do when you start to love someone, you begin to memorize them, I can't, he's thirty-four, I can't memorize him. She looked at his somber profile, and she couldn't remember his eyes, exactly, the way they held the light in their dark centers.

"I'll come to San Miguel for at least four days at the end of the month, te juro, I promise, Xochitzalita, go swimming, sailing, go dancing," his hand tightened around her shoulder, "just don't have too much fun." Javier stopped walking, holding her by both shoulders, staring into her eyes. He x-rayed her soul. She x-rayed his soul (and she memorized the light, the fire, exactly, in spite of the voice of logic that said, You won't survive this).

The sky flared with a deeper violet, sudden beauty, as the sun extinguished itself on the horizon. Where Juanito swam with death, life, birth.

"You gave birth to me, Xochitzalita mi amor." Javier's voice was clear, calm. He remembered the light-filled orchid, the pulsing yellow center, orgasm.

"And you gave birth to me, la verdad. Your first words to me were, 'I've lived many lives before this one,' and I thought, I've never heard this line before," Xochiquetzal laughed softly.

"I think it was the fifth or sixth thing I said to you, after I asked if you'd read Brian Weiss' books about past life regression, and after I told you I'd driven to the coast after saving an eighty-eight year old man's life the night before." Javier smiled sadly, finishing his drink. "I was a man waiting to be born, Xochitzalita, and I love saying tu nombre, your name. Remember at first, when you told me your name, I said, 'What kind of name is that?' But now I love it, I love saying it. Tell me again what it means, Xochitzalita."

"I'm glad you chased me down, that you found me, that you were a sinverguenza cabron," she laughed. "I renamed myself when I went to university, after a Mayan myth/history section...Xochiquetzal is the Goddess of love and beauty, may as well aim high and I was so young," she smiled.

"I'll always find you, Xochiquetzal," he returned her smile, "like this, so I can look into your wise woman's eyes. What do you see in mine, tell me the truth, la verdad."

She smiled, she wept, just joy. "I see a man who swims with Death at 4 a.m., who hears her laughter, who knows there is no death, only endless wonder. I see your boy eyes, your wisdom."

They swayed into each other's arms and, kissed so deeply, they heard Death laughing her beautiful laugh in the waves. Her laugh of endless wonder. Birth.

Is this? The deepest? Play?

"Let's swim, let's swim with Juanito, come on!" Javier took off his t-shirt and began to lower his jeans.

"I only have on panties, no bra, I can't..."

"No one's here, only Juanito, come on, swim with me," he spoke in Spanish facing la mar. "I'm waiting, Xochiquetzal, I'm waiting, and so is Juanito." Javier turned, looking at her with a mix of command, and she saw it: loneliness.

She stripped off her dress in one movement, piling her things next to his. She ran toward him, toward la mar y Juanito. Toward death, life, birth. They swam in the dark, silky water side by side. They rose and fell with each wave, weeping, laughing. And then they heard it, Juanito's sweet laughter.

The deepest play, yes.

"Why won't you let me take you into my mouth, I want to..."

"Tell me you love me, no in this moment mierda, shit." Javier's voice was sad, sweet. "No, no, don't, next time in San Miguel I'll give myself to you, your slave de sexo y amor, sabrosita...delicious one," he said, so seriously (a smile in the center of his dark eyes).

"But why not, Javier, must you be the one in control...I want to make you lose all of your fregado, chingado physician control, doctorcito." Her voice softened as his eyes took her in, unwavering.

"I want you again, I want to be inside of you, mi amor, next time, we have years, como no..." he smiled.

"The Mayan Goddess, Xochiquetzal's brother was Quetzalcoatl, did you know that..." She leaped to change the subject, years. But his words echoed, "We have years," and she silently answered, I cannot, must not, memorize you, I couldn't stand it if I did, when you must leave me, la vieja, the old woman.

"Ay que pendejo...what a dummy...no," he laughed softly. "Does that make me your little brother, Xochitzalita, does that make me Quetzalcoatl...tell me you love me, no this moment right now, tell me you love me, Xochiquetzal..." Javier felt his body merge with her body, his skin with her skin, his blood with her blood, his maleness with her femaleness, now.

"Tell me, tell me..." he wept with joy, just joy.

"Te amo, I love you, te amo," she wept with joy, just joy.

He felt his sperm explode into millions of stars, father to the cosmos, hijo del sol, hijo de las estrellas...son of the sun, son of the stars...hijo de la mujer, son of the woman, padre de luz...father of light, white light filled his head, his pulsing body. "Quiero servir te, mi amor...I want to serve you, my love." Just joy.

Is this? The deepest? Play? Yes

Just joy.

She woke up at pre-dawn reaching for him, expecting her legs to still be wrapped around his sabroso body, expecting his scent to fill her senses, expecting to see his boy eyes, el doctorcito. Of wonder. The space was empty, cold, forlorn. She ran to the bathroom. Gone. Every trace of him. Gone. She heard his voice, "Qué rica," the rolling 'rrrr' (like a purring gato), his soft laughter, lips, hands. Gone. It's only been three days, why do I feel this way, surely I am fucking road kill, she thought, lying next to where he'd been just an hour before. She sniffed his pillow, there it was. His scent. She burst into tears, briefly, saying out loud, "I will not be road kill," which made her laugh.

Then she saw a piece of paper on the tile, picked it up: Soy tu regalo, y tu eres mio. Te amo, no esta momento, te amo. Dr. Zapata con el mango en la boca, tu cuerpo sabrosita...I am your gift, and you are mine. I love you, no this moment, I love you. Dr. Zapata with a mango in my mouth, your delicious body.

"Pathetic but true, road kill, el regalo, and how does he enter my mind," Xochiquetzal muttered, making herself leave the bed (that place of dried mango, his, her, juice). She wanted to fling herself back down on the bed and weep, sob; Road kill, she reminded herself, get up and move, you are too old for this shit. She thought of the maid trying to figure out all that stickiness, and for a moment she was tempted to wash the sheet in the small bathroom sink. "Oh fuck it, she's seen worse I'm sure." And the recent memory of ripe mango slices on her body, in her body, made her shiver, smile—no shower. She dressed, some fuchsia lip gloss, thin lines of green pencil on her eyelids; and she knew his scent, his saliva, his sperm, his DNA, were with her. Sticky. Proof of all that. Joy. Just joy.

She remembered his black with glittering gold Zapata sombrero, and ran to the closet: gone. She wanted to sob again—And ruin my eye liner, she sighed. It was so silent in the room in the pre-dawn almost light, and she suddenly wanted to see the sun rise, rise, rise, bring la mar, each wave, to life. To life, la vida.

A small, very tiny, voice that seemed to come from her womb, more of a whisper, an inaudible whisper: *luz luz proof memory just joy padre de luz joy memory proof luz*

Is this   the deepest   sacred play?

It was barely light as Xochiquetzal walked to breakfast, the restaurant at the end of the complex (where they'd gathered their fan club). A cooling breeze still lingered. Workers sweeping, raking leaves, watering the wide lawns, greeted her as she passed, "Buenos dias," smiling intimately (this had confused, unnerved her when she first came to San Miguel). She returned their morning greeting with a smile she didn't dare smile in her own country: intimacy. She saw Javier in one young man's sensual smile, and she returned it. Mexican men are in their bodies, she thought, I love it, am I learning this, was I dead before?

She piled her plate with mangoes, next to her just cooked omelette with everything in it, green hot salsa on top. She always tipped the omelette woman, and in response she would say a brief prayer of gracias por los veinte pesos. To invoke further tips that day, then thanking her directly, "Gracias, señora." "De nada, que sabroso omelette, gracias." There was always extra ham, mushrooms, tomatoes at the center, with fresh hot corn tortillas in a covered basket. To invoke a blessing, a mutual blessing, gracias.

This was the understanding Xochiquetzal had with El Nino Doctorcito in her favorite church in San Miguel. She imagined her lit candle burned out, replaced with a freshly burning one; and she realized she was in a country of people who breathed their gracias in prayers, listened to their dreams, lit candles on altars, as her grandmother, Clara, had done. This tendency of her spirit wasn't strange here, it was daily life. It wasn't 'magical realism'(she hated that literary gringo term, as though the reality of millions was simply a fairy tale, a 'myth'); no, it was just reality, the human spirit. Unedited. The human spectrum. Poverty, Juanito, his Indian mother...to que rica. La vida. Unedited.

Suddenly she wanted to be grabbed from behind, to be lifted to her feet, to be kissed sinverguenza...shamelessly, in public. She yearned to hear a loud ass grito in her own pocha honor; in Javier's upper class Mexican at home in his own country honor. When she told him her son's name, "Justin, with a J like you," he laughed, saying, "Qué rica," softly in her ear. "But I'm not your son, soy tu amador...I'm your lover."

"Surely I am road kill beep beep y que rica," Xochiquetzal murmured, rolling the 'r' smoothly as she'd done in her childhood (to Mamacita's final approval).

With her third cup of coffee, she opened the book she brought for the trip, her solitary, monk-like, Zen-like trip. The one she thought she'd read entirely through by now: The Book of Secrets by Deepak Chopra. When Xochiquetzal first saw the book's title in the book store, she'd passed it by smirking; but then it hauled her back, shouting, Buy this fucking book, pendeja, dummy! She opened randomly to this: "Ecstasy changes everything. The body is no longer heavy and slow;

the mind stops experiencing its background music of sadness and fear. There is a dropping away of personality, replaced by the sweetness of nectar (mango juice, she smiled). This sweetness can linger a long time in the heart—some people say it can be tasted like honey in the mouth—but when it leaves, you know beyond doubt that you have lost the now. *The secret of ecstasy is that you have to throw it away once you've found it.*"

Warm, salty tears reached her mouth; the taste of honey, the taste of salt. The taste of gratitude. And loss. "I let you go," she whispered, "I let you go."

A line of pelicans flew by so gracefully, Xochiquetzal forgot to breathe (pleasure, ecstasy). La mar was filling herself up with the rising sun, and Juanito's sweet laughter mingled with each clear, dawn wave. The secret of ecstasy is that you have to throw it away once you've found it, the silence of the pelican's wings echoed.

She finished the perfect omelette, put the book in her bolsa, exchanged smiles with La Senora de Los Omelettes. And she walked to the end of the resort, onto the sand, to the chair she was lying on when she first saw him, floating in la mar like an otter. In fact, she'd thought he was an otter until she saw a beer bottle, to the otter's lips, glinting in the sun. Then, he defied evolution, and emerged from la mar, to lay down in the lounger next to her, smiling, eyes closed; yet she felt his eyes on her. Through those long lashes, she noted, ignoring him.

Xochiquetzal placed her bolsa on the chair (taking only her canvas travel purse), the thick hotel beach towel over it, spread out over its length. She claimed the lounger for the day, and then she tried to throw away the ecstasy of their three days (Maybe I'm your gift...) as she walked toward the small town of Bucerias, further up the ever-changing-colors-dawn-beach.

A lone jogger passed her, "Buenos dias," he greeted her, gone.

"Buenos dias." And the ecstasy returned, remained in her womb, her tender dark womb. Their mysterious child who would become itself in spite of his/her parents. Xochiquetzal felt her/him floating in her alive, pulsing, so new, womb. And she no longer felt alone, but pregnant with a secret. Their mysterious child would become itself. In time.

Then she played with it, with throwing away her ecstasy, as she walked away, from the place they'd met, to Bucerias, and it kept returning now now now. She took her digital camera out of its pouch and began to record the ecstasy of that moment: the horizon merging with sea, no up or down, her feet crunching painfully through hard piles of stone, crushed shells to soft sand again, the warming tide, the hungry dog in the distance whose stare made her body remember fear, the market place in Bucerias brimming with hand-made treasures as well as junk. Xochiquetzal felt fully human—equally strong, equally weak, equally wise, equally stupid, equally alive, equally dead, fertile, potent, barren, ecstatic, despairing, full, empty now now now. Now.

I didn't tell him I'm a photographer, a former professor of photography, a photo journalist sometimes, all my travels, adventures, my sporadic aspiring poetry, she thought, smiling. That throw away camera with precious images, can't wait to see Dr. Zapata wearing his sombrero, La Feminista with her Taos sun hat, standing side by side, smiling, unsmiling, in between public displays of affection, gritos. Those delicious, embarrassing kisses...I wonder if the hermoso young guy got a kiss in action. Xochiquetzal laughed out loud, and turned to face the Mexican sun, growing warmer each second. I have a lot to tell him, next time I guess.

She let the Balinese sarong fall to the sand, her Taos hat on top of that, and underneath her travel purse with her camera in its pouch. Ecstasy greeted her, engulfed her, cradled her, as she floated, swam, she gave a sudden grito like a lunatic. A silver-splashed dolphin spun in the air, joy, in the distance, and she laughed her childhood laughter, wonder, and then it let her go now   now   now...

Now.

Floating on her back, face to the now hot Mexican sun, she thought of him driving to his town, his hospital, at least eight hours away. Xochiquetzal wondered if he was bored on the long drive, was he calling one of his chicas (which she knew he had, at least three or four...); she wondered if he was laughing with her right now, this moment, now now now, as they made the day and time to meet; she wondered if he'd tell her all about la vieja...the old woman... pocha feminista he'd met in Vallarta y una Yaqui tambien jajajaja; she wondered if they'd laugh at la vieja's stupidity, her seduction, the spectacle she'd made of herself, gracias a el suave Dr. Zapata, his mango tongue, mouth, hands...she wondered if he'd tell her about that too, the helplessness, surrender, joy, ecstasy of her orgasms, older woman, younger man; she wondered if he'd mimic her orgasmic singing, la vieja tan pendeja. She could hear their laughter, so she dove deeply into a wave, its rush of silence.

Yes, Xochiquetzal felt exposed, naked to the bone's juicy marrow, under the young Mexican sun, fully human. La vida. Unedited. She wept with this feeling, this truth—strong/weak, wise/stupid, fertile/potent/barren, and her salty tears disappeared into the collected tears of the world, the Earth. La mar. It held her up, all those tears, billions of years held her up as she floated and wept, exposed and naked to the young Mexican sun. Fully human, unedited. Just sorrow.

She placed her hands over her womb, trying to measure her loss—sweet and salty—and she thought of their mysterious child lodged ecstatically in her dark, empty womb. She thought of Juanito swimming with his death into re-birth, and then she thought of Javier swimming in la mar at 4 a.m., hearing Death's laughter, the eighty-eight year old man's life he'd saved bringing him to la mar, Vallarta, to swim like an otter with a beer to his lips, not allowing her to ignore him. Javier.

Is this the deepest sacred play joy sorrow

Javier picked up his cell so many times during the drive like a habit, a space to fill, the unexpected silence after esta mujer, Xochitzalita. He suddenly wanted Teresa to meet him tomorrow at the usual time after he'd slept a few hours, after the ER, she was sweet, sabrosita. Or Juana, or—but his hand kept disobeying him as he put his cell down, not hitting the speed dial, each name, Las Sabrositas, Las Chicas.

He hit the steering wheel with impatience, boredom with the long drive, the silence; and then he did something unexpected. He simply looked out the window at the human chaos; people on the side of the road waiting for a bus, families grouped together, teens standing aloof and alone, other teens leaning into their parents laughing, an old man with his old burro carrying rainbow sprays of fresh flowers, firewood, making their way to the center of town, the next town, and he making his way to his town, his sick and wounded people, maybe a child as young as Juanito, or even younger.

"Maybe I can save one life tonight, maybe just one, maybe more," Javier murmured in Spanish as he watched the human chaos whiz by his window. The crushing poverty of his people, and the laughter of his people, moved him beyond words. It always did, since a young boy, when he looked. Unedited. He thought of Xochitzalita's wise eyes and how they held him; and he realized he couldn't superimpose her face over Teresa's, one becoming the other, interchangeable, convenient, diverting. One face becoming the other face; one body becoming the other body, her moans becoming anyone's moans, her laughter, her words, interchangeable, convenient, diverting. It had been the same with Clara; she was only herself, uniquely herself, Clara.

Javier picked up his cell, wanting to talk to Xochitzalita, but he knew she wouldn't be in her room. But he tried anyway, and after the desk clerk connected him to her room it just rang and rang endlessly. Her scent came to him; mango, the orchid scent of her womb. That's what he'd decided, that orchid scent, but he didn't tell her, that her womb was an orchid. A lush purple one. With a golden center. Where he was born again.

And as when he was cradled on her thighs, her endless skin, her inner wetness on his tongue, he tasted her. He inhaled her lush, purple orchid as he drove. Javier put his head out the window and did an ear-splitting grito—a joyful, sorrowful grito—and people laughed and waved as he sped by.

Javier thought of Clara's scent, trying to make it come to him, across la mar, Madrid, that scent of over-powering jasmine on a full moon night. Layers of jasmine, virginal, seductive jasmine. He waited, alert, waiting, willing it to come, but it didn't arrive. He picked up his cell to speed dial Juana, almost touching the button, seeing Clara's face bleed into Juana's.

And then, the subtle scent of an orchid came to him, and he gave another grito just for himself, softer, intimate. Full of longing. "No eres mio, Clara, no eres mi amor…You aren't mine, Clara, you aren't my love." A brief scent of jasmine, and she was gone.

Xochiquetzal settled herself in the lounger she'd claimed earlier; nothing had been disturbed. Mexican families were on the other side of the hotel boundary, sitting under umbrellas, eating delicious, home-made food, their children leaping in the waves. The upper class Mexican families (and the mostly gringo population) sat with her on the hotel side—same beach, same sand, la mar. She thought of Javier, the upper class Mexican doctor at home in his own country, and smiled (the Energy Child's left foot twitched).

She looked at the deep green/blue/purple opal stones, the bracelet on her right arm; it reflected every color of the sun. She couldn't resist them, or the opal earrings set in pure, white silver. As she'd held them to her ears, the guy selling them in his stall said, "Just stick them in, you know how, señora, to stick it in," smiling into her eyes. "You've got to be kidding, give me a fucking break." He apologized, still smiling. She bought the gorgeous opals and left, hearing his "Mamacita" tossed at her back.

The image of Javier taking out the lovely, garnet, sea shell earrings he'd given her, and gently putting them back in, on the sand, holding her face in his hands, came to her. "Don't take them out until I see you again, Xochitzalita, promise me." She hadn't taken them out, she realized, and it suddenly seemed very stupid.

Well, that's it, Xochiquetzal thought, that's what I am here, Mamacita, hot mama, hoochie mama, hot tamale Mamacita, that's me. I'll probably never hear from Dr. Zapata again, he has his story of the year, la pendeja vieja pocha feminista Yaqui India. "Ayyy Diosa, what a chingada pendeja I am," she moaned to the hissing waves, "road kill, that's me."

She closed her eyes and saw her car packed with what she'd called the essence of her loca life, those last days in Taos. She'd given away her just-broken-in black leather couch, all the front room furniture, dining room table, chairs, bed, year old mattress, warm blankets, good sheets, two beautiful comforters—in other words, everything. She only sold the washer/dryer because someone actually offered to buy them. She'd had no desire to sell, only the desire to give things away (like the ecstacy, but she didn't know that yet).

"Are you sure you want to give away all this stuff, it looks like good stuff?" the young, Indian looking guy asked, in heavily accented English. He swept the room with his eyes, longingly.

"I'm going to Mexico, can't take it with me."

"Sounds like dyin'," the other Indian guy said, but his accent was different. "Hey, I'm from Canada, here on a treaty that says I can cross as long as the rivers flow, the sun shines, you know *that unbroken treaty,*" he cracked himself up.

"I just came from Guatemala, no treaties," he smiled at the other guy. "Can you understand my English?"

"You can talk to me in Spanish."

"Naw," the Canadian Indian interrupted, "the dude's got to learn

English, blend in, como no."

"I came with my family, we have very little furniture, can I have this couch, señora?" the Guatemalan asked with his soft eyes.

"My bed's harder than the treaty," the Canadian laughed.

"Take whatever you want or need, and take the rest to the second hand. I want good karma if I ever return," Xochiquetzal laughed with him. "Can't take it with you, that's the damn truth, whether you're dying or going to Mexico."

"Why you going to Mexico?" the Canadian asked. "Seems like you got it all here."

"To be reborn," the words popped out.

"Si, yo se que dices, señora...I know what you mean," the Guatemalan smiled shyly.

"English, dude, English, or you're going to be reborn in Guatemala," the Canadian guffawed. "Yeah, I got you and there sure ain't no treaties for that. You're on a vision quest, am I right? You some kinda Indian?"

"I'm a Yaqui, my grandmother was from Sonora, the undefeated ones," Xochiquetzal smiled.

"Yo lo conocen, señora, los Yaquis...I know them, the Yaquis," the Guatemalan looked into her eyes. "Son muy fuerte gente, los Yaquis... Very strong people."

"Dude, you're going to be joining the Mayas in Guat if you don't stop talkin' that Espanol, por favor, dude, por favor," the Canadian laughed with exasperation. "So you're going to join your gente, your people, now he's got me talkin' el Espanol, dude, I give up. Take some of them magic shrooms, I would, send me a dream, okay?"

"Send me un sueno tambien, señora, por favor, okay, send me a dreeem," the Guatemalan smiled broadly. "Mi nombre es Manuel... My name is Manuel, so you can find me, señora."

"My name's Hector, Hector The Protector, send me a good one, a real vision quest kinda dream, promise?" he smiled into her eyes.

"Absolutely, I promise to send you both the best vision quest dream I can get hold of," Xochiquetzal laughed instead of crying. How do they simply understand me, get me, she wondered. I could draw a diagram for most, let's face it, white folks, and all I'd get is the she-must-be-insane look. And that's why Mamacita always told me to never, ever, tell 'other people' about our dreams, how we shared our dreams every morning. How she taught me to dream, mi Mamacita, tan clara...so clear...her name, Clara. She watched them begin to load her former life, the things she'd gathered for over thirty years, into the truck, and as Manuel handled her beautiful black leather couch with tenderness (now his couch), knowing his large family would sit on it, eat on it, sleep on it, it became a thing of use, not a possession. "All I need is the fucking essence of my life," she murmured. This is a taste, just a taste, of what it will be like to leave my body, my old amiga body.

After they left she sat with her favorite large pillow on the wall behind her, four smaller ones on the thick, warm rug. Taos was cold in the winter and this rug had comforted her. Their parting, joyous laughter as they packed all the furniture into the large truck; their repeated "Thank you, gracias, señora." And finally, "Safe journey and watch those Mexicans, and those undefeated Yaquis too," laughter, and they were gone.

Sunset. Slight chill. She started a small fire in the fireplace. The wood left over from the winter. Soft snow on the dry ground. Ice. Sky wider than her dreams had held her for four years. Taos. The Pueblos.

Early morning dances in winter, freshly fallen snow glittering on peaks at 7,000 feet. Tesque Pueblo by Santa Fe. The group of men singers, handsome in their ribbon shirts, entering the central plaza, the drummers leading the way. The bare-chested buffalo dancers, deer dancers with fox tails swinging to the drums. The women bare-armed, sashed at the waist, star headdresses that never toppled, tied to their chins with leather. The spectators bundled in warm boots, jackets; the elders in beautiful, woven, wool blankets. In spring the women and girls dancers would go barefoot, and the men and boy dancers would keep their soft leather shoes on. The women were closer to the Earth Mother, so their feet were bare.

Further south of Santa Fe, she'd gone to San Felipe Pueblo in spring on a hot day. The sky and earth came together in heat, after the swirling snow. That bone cold beauty. Her two years of celibacy; her last lover a beautiful Balinese on the coast, Sanur (his private, thatched hut by his small hotel, the ocean all night). Xochiquetzal sat in the shade with the Pueblo women, while the white people melted in the dry, hot sun. She knew this was bold, maybe even questionable, but she couldn't bring herself to sit with the white spectators. I'm a Yaqui from my grandmother, from Sonora, Mexico, she told herself as she sat down.

A very old grandmother, wrapped in a light, fringed, blue shawl with a pattern of yellow butterflies, turned her head to stare at her: "Do you have children?" Her voice was absolutely direct, no cushion of friendliness.

"I have a twenty-seven year old son." Her voice sounded like a child, but it was all she could manage. There was a pause as the women glanced at each other, waiting for the grandmother to speak.

"Soon you'll be a grandmother," she smiled, brief as lighting.

Then, all the women descended on a feast laid directly on the earth. Xochiquetzal sat watching them, with longing, but not daring to be that bold. She sat very still.

The grandmother turned again. "Aren't you hungry? What's your name anyway?"

"Xochiquetzal, is my name." She wanted to ask hers, but didn't dare. Still that child's voice came out.

"Well, that's a mouthful, say it again."

"Xochiquetzal, it's a Mayan Goddess," she said very quickly.

"I like that, a Mayan Goddess. You can call me Grandma, come on let's eat."

Xochiquetzal commanded herself not to start sobbing with joy, to be that ridiculous. Her own grandmother dead, reborn many years ago; and her mother reborn, no father (only a story or two...he returned to France when she was still in the womb). She was used to being an orphan, and now here was Grandma inviting her to join them. In the feast laid directly on the dry, warm earth.

The older women pretended to steal each other's food, much laughter; the younger women piled food on their paper plates. "The young women need their strength for *the love*," another grandmother laughed. Xochiquetzal took a serving somewhere in the middle, she hoped; not too much, not too little. She didn't want to draw attention to herself either way. Too much, too little.

Back to the shade, her plastic chair, and she started to nibble the delicious chicken taco on thick fry bread, sipping the can of still chilled Pepsi. She watched the maybe twelve-year old boys standing guard at what looked like a sanctuary. There were elders—men and women—sitting inside, and they were being served their feast with cans of chilled soda. The boys stood guard with rifles held across their chest, their eyes staring straight ahead. Vigilant. Fiercely. When a priest tried to enter, they blocked his way with rifles extended, in a row, like a gate—eyes fierce, no words. Xochiquetzal was spellbound as though watching something forbidden; the priest was turned away. He exchanged some words with an elder, a man, whose face remained impassive. The priest nodded in a gentle gesture, staying in front of the row of boys cradling their rifles in their slender boy-arms. Only his angry feet betrayed him as he walked away, kicking dust into the air, each step.

He must be hot in that black dress, Xochiquetzal noted, his red face perspiring. The four boys relaxed, vigilant, with their rifles now across their thin chests. And her heart sang these words, *They are undefeated*, as Mamacita used to say, "The Yaquis are undefeated." She heard Mamacita do a grito, the ones she used to do when she danced, hiking the hem of her dress up over her layered stockings, to rancheras on the radio. Xochiquetzal would join her in this undefeated dance when she felt her grandmother's spirit soar; her still thick, long, grey hair falling to her waist. During the day, she wore her beautiful hair in a tight, coiled bun, always with her going-out, old lady dark hats.

Xochiquetzal had seen, felt, an entire people, a Pueblo of people, who were undefeated. She was unaware of her tears; she was only aware of the boys holding their rifles across their thin, boy-chests, the women laughing and joking with each other, glancing her way occasionally, curious. And the sound of Mamacita's defiant grito, in her memory's ear, as she danced with her granddaughter, secretly. As she brought the hem of her long dress over her knees, the layered stockings, joy.

A new group of dancers entered the plaza, circling with beautiful rattles in their hands—painted with sacred images, some with feathers swinging. The constant heart beat of the drums led them, with the full, deep voices of the men singers that sounded at times like they were crying; then joy would spring up again. Strength. Power. Prayer. As the dancers passed the sanctuary, the boys with their rifles, they shook their rattles fiercely in that direction, pausing slightly, moving on, each row of dancers.

She began to notice black and white striped men with stiff yellow hair sticking straight up (punk-like, making her smile), zig-zag lightning bolts on their chests, animal pelts down their backs; and they were the only ones going in the opposite direction, weaving in among the dancers. They joked, taunted, teased the dancers, pausing to flirt with the beautiful, young and older women.

"Heyokas, sacred clowns," Xochiquetzal murmured with delight. One of them spotted her among the women; his eyes just stopped. She held her breath. The heyokas began smashing watermelons open directly onto the ground, and women ran out to collect the ripe, red pieces for their families. She sat absolutely still.

The one that spotted her approached, dancing as he walked, with a wicked smile, ear to ear. He laughed as he took a huge bite from the center of the piece in his left hand, juice dripping down his bare, striped chest, over his yellow lightning bolt which pointed skyward (not to the earth).

Oh man, here it comes, Xochiquetzal braced herself for anything, heyokas—yet she couldn't help it, she laughed out loud. His yellow, spiky, punky hair reminded her of Justin when he switched to a neon blue Mohawk at sixteen. I guess I've always been surrounded by heyokas, him and his friends, my students—neon blue, yellow, red, pink, purple and rainbow spiky, punky teen hair. Justin's high school track team, and his death defying surfer friends, the wild heyoka crew. She smiled, in spite of herself. The gathering silence, tension. Grandma and the women watched with sideways glances, and no one spoke or laughed.

His smile widened to expose his teeth, almost threateningly, with no shame that he was dripping with watermelon flesh, juice, seeds clinging to his chest. He liked that she laughed in spite of her caution, fear, obvious dread. Suddenly his face became stern, forbidding: "What tribe are you?" His voice held no kindness; the lightning bolt going skyward. A couple of awkward seconds; he took another huge bite.

"I'm Yaqui, my people are from Sonora, Mexico," the words flowed out with no help from her. They came from her grandmother, Clara, her voice. "Our people are undefeated." She tried to smile, but her facial muscles wouldn't obey.

He wiped his mouth, his chest, like a child would. He took one more good look at her, head to toe, even leaning in a bit for a close up. Xochiquetzal could smell the so ripe watermelon. He threw his head back, laughing wildly, then he yelled, "Welcome, sister!" and danced forward to give her a huge, red, ripe slice from his supply tucked in front of him.

"Thank you," she said in her own voice, but he was already back in the circle of dancers. He turned once, lifted his watermelon, laughed, and began weaving his way in the opposite direction. Tears filled her eyes as she took a good-sized bite from the cool center, juice running down her chin, neck.

The woman next to her handed her a wad of paper towels, poked her in the ribs with her elbow. "I think that guy liked you, but then he's such a flirt," she laughed. "My daughter's out there dancing so I hope those guys don't kidnap her." She laughed again like a young girl.

"How old is your daughter?" Xochiquetzal smiled in gratitude, her facial muscles finally unfrozen. The paper towels, to be included, her laughter.

"Look, there she is," the woman pointed, "the one with the parrot feathers fan. Kinda cute, ain't she?" An understatement, she was striking with her thick, straight, black hair to her waist. "She's eighteen going on forty, wants to go to college and I know she will too."

"My son's twenty-seven and he's in college right now. Your daughter's beautiful. She should go to college, absolutely."

"We should get our kids together, make some grand babies," she laughed, poking Xochiquetzal in the ribs again. "After college, haya!"

The drummers and singers paused, and in that pause loud yelling like gritos, rising laughter, announced something new. Men carrying what looked like large wash tubs came running into the plaza and placed one in front of the women, then ran away. A spiky yellow-haired heyoka, not the same one (his lightning bolt pointed sideways), came dancing up to the wash tub, facing the women, smiling with deranged joy. She looked at the women next to her for a clue, and what she saw was attention mixed with their own joy. Laughing that wild laugh, the heyoka began taking fresh ears of corn from the tub, passing out handfuls to the women. Each woman accepted hers wordlessly, slightly bowing her head. The first, tender, sacred, spring corn. He laughed as he gave Xochiquetzal a beautiful ear of yellow corn, just one, and she bowed her head in gratitude. She bit into it, as the other women were doing. Sweet.

"We're Corn Mothers now, you know, gotta eat every kernel," the woman next to her laughed, handing her more paper towels.

"I'm saving mine to cook later, I'm a Corn Grandma," the grandmother in the butterfly shawl said loudly, but she took one, sly bite.

Xochiquetzal finished every sweet, newborn kernel, and she wanted more. La mar came into focus. The Pueblo faded to an almost still ocean. Pelicans glided by in a graceful, wide-winged line, hungry, searching for movement in the glittering, lake-still sea. What do they see, she wondered, trying to imagine the pelican's vision of flashing, silver fish, and it brought her fully to the present. La mar. The memory of red, so-ripe watermelons mingled with the recent memory of el prescripcion: mango slices covering her body, mango juice drying on her body, sticky. Sweet. The butterfly kisses of Javier's soft mouth, tongue, over the stickiness as he ate every slice. As he devoured her sweetness.

She ran out to la mar, diving into the warm, welcoming wetness. Salt stung her eyes. Every inch of her, every cell, felt alive in the ancient, sacred Madre Mar. Ocean. "I miss you, Dr. Zapata, I miss your eyes of wonder." The Energy Child's left hand opened, a tiny flower. "I miss you, Mother, I miss you, Mamacita, I always will." Xochiquetzal gave a grito of just joy, laughing, and she remembered once again how sorrow, loss, sorrow, transformed into joy (the flashing, silver fish in the darkness).

She swam following the coast line, floating face up to the Mexican sun, swam some more. She gave a grito to the sun. A dolphin leapt in the distance. "I miss you Justin, your heyoka ways, but I'll see you soon, hijo, and I bet you're surfing right now hundreds of miles north in la Madre Mar, I love you, Justin." She swam following the coast line, floating, swimming back to her lounger where she'd met Javier, until she was exhausted and happy in her human skin. Her fifty-eight year old woman's body.

Then she went to get a cold pina colada, and she knew it would be extra strong as she laid her ten peso tip on the counter.

The phone kept ringing, finally waking her up. She fumbled for her Timex glow watch: 2:10am. Then Justin flashed across her mind, an emergency.

"Justin?" Xochiquetzal was still half dreaming so her panic was disguised in that huskiness.

"Y quien es Justin?"

She struggled to place the voice, who would ask her this question. Then his eyes came to her, staring at her boldly across the miles. In her half dream. "Javier, do you realize it's 2 a.m.?"

"Quien es Justin, Xochitzalita?" His voice was sad, angry, tired.

"He's my son, you idiot, remember, Justin."

"Ay, soy pendejo...I'm an idiot...and I'm tired too. I'm on a break after almost non-stop emergencies, save some, lose some, but there is no death, tell me there is no death, Xochitzalita."

"There is no death," she murmured. His voice clenched her womb, and the Energy Child's right hand opened, a tiny flower.

"I know I'm a selfish cabron to be calling you at this hour, but I had to hear your voice, Xochitzalita, to know you remember me, that you haven't forgotten me."

She laughed softly, refusing to emerge from the half dream. She was awake but she was dreaming—his eyes his eyes his eyes. "They felt sorry for me tonight at dinner, our fan club, Javier, they asked where you were as though our marriage had ended and I'd never see you again."

"Te quiero, Xochitzalita, cabroncita."

"You don't know me well enough to love me, Javier, not yet." His eyes x-rayed her soul in this waking dream, and she almost remembered the other dream years ago.

"I love you anyway so callate, shut up, tell me you love me, Xochitzalita, or I won't hang up."

She heard the play in his voice (and the exhausted loneliness), saw the wonder in his eyes, his eyes. "In this moment, right now, te quiero, Dr. Zapata," she laughed into the waking dream, his eyes.

"You're still cheating with that 'this moment, right now' mierda, but I'll take it for now, do you hear me, La Feminista?"

"I hear you, Dr. Zapata, and I also see tus ojos...your eyes."

"Do you feel my mouth on your mouth, my mouth on your niña nipples, on your sabrosita mango, my tongue, do you remember, Xochitzalita?"

"I remember your mouth, your face, your eyes, stop."

"Never."

"Ever?"

"Not ever."

"You're in my dream right now, I miss you, Zapata, I miss tu sombrero."

"Porque me llamas Zapata...Why do you call me Zapata?" Javier smiled. He heard the longing, desire, in her voice.

"Tus ojos tus ojos tus ojos, tu sombrero y tu caballo." She saw him on the dark horse in her mind's eye, very ancient, very young. In the waking dream.

"I'm being beeped, I'll call you tomorrow at midnight, is that okay?"

"Just let it ring till I answer, but the next night I'm going to Vallarta..."

"Why are you going to Vallarta?"

"To dance of course."

"La Feminista," Javier groaned. "Only to dance, promise me, cabrona."

"I'm a one guy at a time kind of feminista, you promise me, you and your chicas, I know you've got them on your fucking speed dial," she laughed softly in the dream.

"Te juro, mi pochita...I promise."

"Liar."

"I promise. Tell me again, Xochitzalita."

"What Javier con los ojos hermoso...with the beautiful eyes."

"That there is no death, mi feminista sabrosita." His voice held equal measures of pleasure, pain.

"No hay muerte, no mas la vida, Dr. Zapata...There is no death, there's only life....y te quiero en esta momento...and I love you in this moment."

This is.   Deepest play.

Xochiquetzal...*I wake up in my dream. Nothing but sky. Nothing but sea. I feel the emptiness of dying, the fullness of living. I see an eagle gliding over the waves, hungry, searching for a sea snake. I feel the sea snake's longing to be eaten, rising to the surface. "How beautiful they are," I say out loud. I don't recognize this voice. I don't recognize this dream. The same voice tells me, "They dream a different dream here, now you must dream this dream." "I'm afraid to love," I say in my own voice. The eagle flies with the writhing snake in its powerful, irresistible talons.*

She wrote the words down in her dream journal—They dream a different dream here, now you must dream this dream. Her journals of over thirty years, almost as old as Javier, and as old as Justin, she reminded herself. She'd also glued photos to them for visual echoes, and she smiled at this memory. She'd add photos later, of Zapata, La Feminista, el machete on top of the empty bottles, cans, the beauty that had followed them all day (all waiting in the cheap, throw away camera). And then, she remembered she had no photos of Juanito, his young mother. Tears filled her eyes. *They dream a different dream here, now you must dream this dream.*

Xochiquetzal wondered how many people Javier saved last night, simply helped, and how many he couldn't save. "There is no death," she whispered, running out to the soft, warm waves. The rising Mexican sun gently kissed her. She tried to feel Juanito's spirit in the vastness of the merged sea/sky horizon (like the dream, the eagle, the snake, she remembered); but he was gone. The eagle had carried him, in his powerful, irresistible talons, back to birth. Life.

She dove deeply, eyes open with salt, and a long, bright-green snake swam by, undulating, almost touching her. She rose to the surface and laughed, giving a grito to the sun that would soon burn her with its kiss. "I'm afraid to love," she echoed her own voice. In the dream. This dream. Here. This side of the border.

Her morning pina colada was still cold, creamy, delicious. She spread herself out to dry on the lounger, in the warm shade—the same lounger where he'd found her. The last loungers at the end of the resort's stretch of beach, where the non-guest Mexicans came to enjoy their own beach, la mar.

His fearless smile, words. She trying to scare him away, "It's my birthday and I'm fifty-eight years old." "Maybe I'm your gift, que rica."

"I'm afraid to love, especially someone twenty-four years younger than me ayy Diosa," Xochiquetzal laughed softly as she closed her eyes. She saw herself walking on her favorite sunrise, sunset mesa in Taos, the summer before she left with the essence of her loca life packed so tightly in her Toyota not even a toothpick would fit anywhere, finally. And she tried at the last moment—a small box of favorite things, some favorite books. Not one more toothpick.

It was late August, the monsoon afternoon rain had been earlier, and the air was so fresh with moisture, the ground still dark, the sky billowing with impossibly thick white clouds, hovering over the joyous earth. Dancing. Sky/Earth. She walked to the very end of the mesa as the sun began to set in a sea of forever changing waves of colors; and she thought of her son, Justin, who was now gone after a month of laughter, tears, joking, fighting (their new boundaries of mother/woman, son/man). The scent of the damp, dark, maternal, ancient Taos earth made her miss him even more.

Xochiquetzal stood at the edge of the mesa; her favorite place at sunset, sunrise, where she rarely saw another human being. Only the blackest, rainbow-winged ravens. Only the largest red-tailed hawks hunting, and the fiercest, spiraling golden eagles rising out of sight on invisible currents of wind straight to the sun. Only the silence created by those wings...lifting, falling, lifting, flying.

Lightning began to flash in the distance. She tracked it with her eyes. Low rumbles of thunder joined the lightning, those ancient allies of Sky/Earth. She felt the thunder ripple throughout her body, head to foot, and the white lighting strikes moved closer. The hairs on her body stood on end as though waiting for a lover to touch her for the first time. An expectancy. Her body felt it, head to foot, rippling. She tried to see the Thunder Dragon in the approaching darkness; she tried to imagine its long, powerful body lashing its lightning tail; but what she saw was even more beautiful. More mysterious.

She saw the dark, lacy curtain of female rain (the brief rains were male), and she could hear the kiva prayers, the young men deer dancers with their two wooden sticks in their hands, hunched forward, creating four legs in all; their deer antlers pointing skyward, soft feathers fluttering as they danced. Always praying for fertile, female rain. The brief male rain. For the marriage of Sky/Earth, corn, squash, beans, watermelon. Even if she ran, she wouldn't make it to her casita, so she watched the dark, lacy curtain of female rain approach. Sudden slivers of white light pierced the dark lace, rearranging the molecules of fertility into a thunderous dance. Fertile fingers of dark female rain caressed the earth as Xochiquetzal waited to be drenched.

An expectancy.

Just before the dark, alive, shifting, lace curtain reached her, a perfect zig-zag, shimmering, white-light lighting bolt pierced the earth directly in front of her, making her laugh. It looked like a cartoon lightning bolt, it was so perfect; and for that second, one split second, it glowed just for her.

There was a tiny, white-light lightning bolt embedded in the lotus tattoo at the small of her back, the sacrum, hidden in the rising orange, red flames. Where Javier had licked her. The first man to see it, the purple lotus. The first man to touch it. But only she knew where the tiny white-light lightning bolt glowed. Just for her. Sky/Earth. Her body. His body. He was the first man to see the lotus, touch it, lick it until he drove her muy loca wild. After five years of celibacy. No wonder.

The female rain had enfolded her, completely. She closed her eyes, raising her face to the full, fertile, mysterious, dark body of female rain, weeping. "I want to love, I no longer can have children, Mother Rain, make me pregnant with love."

Xochiquetzal had forgotten she'd said these words, so her eyes flew open, fully expecting to see the Taos mesa, the female rain all around her. "Javier," she murmured to la mar, the bright-green, undulating snake. The tiny, white lightning bolt hidden in the orange, red flames of her lotus glowed and itched. Her body. His body.

Sky/Earth.

She was still damp from her final swim, but decided to check her email at the hotel's internet room. Emails from a couple of friends, an old student now friend, an e-card from Justin. When she opened it, a mermaid appeared in all her glory to the tune of "Dock of the Bay," the title of the e-card: ESTOY CELOSO...I'M JEALOUS, making her laugh. Then she saw a jumbled email address with 'Javier' woven into it—a Mexican Yahoo translated to her USA Yahoo. Even our emails are in Spanglish, she thought, smiling at the jumble, and clicked it open.

EL TIGRE

Soy el tigre.
Te acecho entre las hojas
anchas como lingotes
de mineral mojado.

El rio blanco crece
bajo la niebla. Llegas.

Desnuda te sumberges.
Espero.

Entonces en un salto
de fuego, sangre, dientes,
de un zarpazo derribo
tu pecho, tus caderas.

Bebo tu sangre, rompo
tus miembros uno a uno.

Y me quedo velando
por anos en la selva
tus huesos, tu ceniza,
immovil, lejos
del odio y de la colera,
desarmado en tu muerte,
cruzado por las lianas,
immovil en la lluvia,
centinela implacable
de mi amor asesino....

THE TIGER

I am the tiger.
I lie in wait for you among the leaves
broad as ingots
of wet mineral.

The white river grows
beneath the fog. You come.

Naked you submerge.
I wait.

Then in a leap
of fire, blood, teeth,
with a claw slash I tear away
your bosom, your hips.

I drink your blood, I break
your limbs one by one.

And I remain watching
for years in the forest
over your bones, your ashes,

motionless, far
from hatred and anger,
disarmed in your death,
crossed by lianas,
motionless in the rain,
relentless sentinel
of my murderous love.

Querida, El Maestro Pablo Neruda, poeta de amor y tigres...poet of love and tigers...ayy Xochitzalita, this is how I feel, mi amor asesino, but I promise not to tear you limb from limb, yet it is how I FEEL right now, this moment (I'm cheating like you jajaja). Soy El Tigre and I want only tu sangre en mi boca...your blood in my mouth...and I did taste tu sangre when I licked your wound in Vallarta, and it made me very very hungry por tu sabrosita sangre, tu sangre en mi boca, mi cabroncita, feminista pochita Yaqui, tu sangre, only your blood in my mouth. Are you still wearing the blood red earrings I placed in your ears by la mar, after we swam with Juanito—when I see you in San Miguel, I want to lick them, one by one, como El Tigre, tu boca, tu sabrosita mango, desnuda...nakedly. Te quiero, El Tigre.

She answered:

Querido Tigre, Yes the earrings are where your fingers left them—today I saw a beautiful, bright-green snake in la mar swimming with me, and I wasn't afraid, not one bit, usually I'd be a little bit afraid, cautious, okay terrified, but not today, it was so beautiful and I felt you sent it to me. (The snake, el regalo jaja...I love jaja for haha, our Spanglish.) I wish you could've seen it, today that is, you've probably seen them before, your coastal visits. I have to admit, I'm glad you taste my blood in your mouth because I also taste yours—and that you secretly tasted my blood in Vallarta, I don't know why but I like it, that you know what my blood tastes like. Next I must taste yours, Dr. Zapata, como la Mujer Tigre ayy Diosa. Something's shifted in me, I can't tell you in an email or long distance, so will tell you (maybe) when you visit, when I see tus ojos hermoso...your beautiful eyes. I miss you, cabron Dr. Zapata, I miss your eyes, yet I only have to close my eyes to see you staring at me with the fierceness of El Tigre. I just closed my eyes for a moment to see you—Are you afraid to love, la verdad...the truth, I need to know your own secret Tigre truth. Gracias por Neruda's wondrous poem, gracias por El Tigre, mi sangre en tu boca, Javier. And know this, La Tigress wants to devour you, right now, this moment, te quiero xoxo

Midnight—After the fifth ring, "Javier?"

"No, es El Tigre," he growled deeply, laughing softly.

Xochitquetzal smiled, still in the dream. "You haven't met La Tigress yet, she wants to eat you up."

"I'm willing."

"What an easy victim you are, yummy..."

"And I'm not afraid to love, you, Xochitzalita."

She burst into tears, still within the dream.

"Porque llores...Why are you crying?"

"Because I'm old and bitter and you're not, you're the young, fearless tigre, Javier," she sobbed.

"Xochitzalita, there is no death, there is no age, there's only our timeless souls, I always know you, amor..."

"You do?" she tried to laugh.

"Always."

"Okay, I'm La Tigress so you better watch out cause I'm kind of starving..."

"Eat me up, mi amor, I'm willing," he laughed softly into her ear, "eat me all up."

She blew her nose away from the receiver, returned. "You'll be sorry, yummy young man meal."

"Eat me up, Xochitzalita, with your tigress teeth." The left ear of the Energy Child bloomed opened, the tiniest seashell, listening.

Xochiquetzal...*The sky, the sea, life, death, Juanito's sweet baby laughter washes over my feet, and a large, dark eagle swoops directly in front of me, staring at me for that second, those fearless eagle eyes of a hungry soul, an ancient soul, a soul that's flown to the sun and back, a soul that remembers each star, grasps the bright-green snake in its powerful* *irresistible talons, as the beautiful sea snake remembers flight. "How beautiful they are together, flying," I say in my own voice, "I love their hunger," and Juanito's sweet baby laughter reaches my open fifty-eight year old hands, each wave washing over my open hands, his laughter, fearlessness. "Am I afraid to love, Madre Mar, Juanito?" I remember female rain.*

After Javier sewed up the deep gash of the young man's wound—a teenager racing around on his big wheel motorcycle, flying over a cement tope, speed bump—he suddenly wanted to speed dial the Numero Una Hermosa on his cell. He shut his eyes and visualized her lovely twenty-two year old face, unblemished, her large, perfect, erect breasts, her dark nipples that filled his mouth. He got hard thinking of her, that youthful perfection; his finger poised over her button. She would come as usual tomorrow at 4 pm, then they'd go out to eat after incredible, mindless sex. That's what he always wanted after his ER shift—incredible, mind-blowing, mindless (no thinking, no talking) sex. And he kept her believing they might get married someday, have eight children, just as he did the other hermosas on his speed dial (four chicas in all).

He almost pressed the button down just to hear the ring begin, and then he thought of their best conversations: her latest shopping spree, the latest telenovela episodes, her desire to quit university and have her babies young, what their combined DNA would produce. She was a dyed blondie with dark, sensual eyes like Shakira; they'd have lovely, dark-eyed daughters who could dye their hair blonde eventually, and handsome dark-eyed sons.

"What kind of life do you think you lived before?" he once asked her after the great sex.

"Javier, that's a sin in the eyes of God." She'd gone on to talk excitedly about the current infidelity on her favorite show. "Would you have a lover outside of our marriage?"

"That would be a sin in the eyes of God," he'd answered in a voice dripping with sarcasm, but she didn't hear it. He remembered how bored he'd become if he stayed next to her for one more moment; how he'd leap up to shower to escape her voice.

He thought of asking her to tell him, "There is no death." He thought of putting slices of mango all over her body. He thought of sending her Neruda's poem, El Tigre. He'd never given her an orgasm with his mouth; she'd always serviced him, taking his penis into her mouth, dutifully, until he ejaculated all over her. "Are you happy, mi amor?" she'd ask and he'd never answer, never giving her that. He'd close his eyes in what looked like bliss, but he was really trying to shut her out until he found the strength to run to the shower. Escape.

Javier thought of Xochiquetzal, and her deep woman's orchid scent filled him, her eyes laughing into his, her voice calling him "Dr. Zapata," her niña breasts he could almost devour. "Como El Tigre," he murmured softly, remembering the taste of her warm, salty/sweet blood. His whole body felt like an erection, and he wanted to hear her voice, "There is no death, Dr. Zapata." He wanted to taste her sabrosita mango until her deep moans, the endless rippling of her body, drove him crazy; until he entered the rippling, the endless rippling of her ocean, her golden center orchid, and she took him somewhere he'd never been. Peace.

Xochiquetzal watched the Mexican sun bring rainbows to the waves, white light to each pelican wing as they flew in graceful groups, skimming each curving rainbow. She thought of the truth of her words last night, "I'm old and bitter, you're the young, fearless tigre, Javier." She breathed in the sun, as in the Buddhist practice of tonglen: breathing in pain, breathing out joy. "Hermoso, my fearless tigre," she breathed, sighed. He's going on thirty-five, I'm going on sixty in two years, get real, why did he find me, why did I open the fregado door, why did I allow him to bring me so much fucking joy, why is my empty womb so fucking full, why does he say "I'll always find you," why do I believe him, why am I old/young/bitter/sweet, why do I miss him, his body, his mouth, his eyes his eyes his eyes, his face, his strong, sweet hands, his perfect twin feet, his fearless laughter, his fearless tears, why?

She slowly let the immense, undulating rainbow engulf her. She floated on her back, found her erect, engorged clitoris and made love to herself, to the wide pelican's wing, to the rising Mexican sun, to the ecstatic rainbow mar that held laughter/tears/life/death/age/youth/tigers/poets/pain/pleasure/fear/love/sorrow/

ecstasy/cruelty/kindness, endless life, equally, yes equally, exploding into shimmering shards of rainbow waves, la mar, wholeness.

Forty more minutes to her first pina colada, 10am when the bar opened; she put her watch back in her beach bolsa. She wrapped herself in the soft, silky lace of her orgasm, but now her fleshy orchid clenched itself with longing. To be filled. To be filled. To be filled with. Him, el doctorcito.

She closed her eyes and saw the final box she'd forgotten to pack in her Toyota. The box filled with her favorite books, beautiful things, sacred things. It was the night before take off to El Paso, the border, and it was nearly midnight. The waxing full moon was setting on the far mesa, her favorite mesa where the lighting bolt had found her standing, and the casita was entirely empty except for the sleeping bag, one pillow, her morning travel clothes piled neatly next to it. Only moonlight filled the casita now, and no matter how hard she tried she couldn't find any room for her beloved books, fourteen in all. She could place them on the seat next to her, but then there'd be no room for maps, snacks, the four day navigation from Taos to San Miguel. From the map, she planned to drive for four days, stopping to sleep in El Paso, Chihuahua, Gomez Palacio, Aguascaliente to San Miguel.

"I'm homeless," Xochiquetzal whispered, "I'm fifty-six with not even a fucking couch or a bed, homeless," and she began to weep in the empty, full moon casita. "What have I fucking done? Hector and Manuel were right, I had it all." She wrapped the sacred things she couldn't live without in plastic, squeezing them into an impossible space. "The essence of my fucking life," and she began to giggle. "This time I've really lost it," she said to a wandering cloud, "even Justin thinks I'm a kook," and she laughed until she cried again, so alive in the full moon's light, in her fifty-sixth year. Homeless.

At the El Paso border she couldn't find the international crossing into the heart of Mexico. *The heart of Mexico!* She followed directions to a busy morning bridge where hundreds of Mexicans crossed over to their day jobs of hotel maids, gardeners, housekeepers, cab drivers, child care workers, construction workers, field workers; all the jobs that couldn't be filled, cheaply, by los gringos. She wondered which ones wouldn't return that night, keep going to San Diego, Los Angeles, San Francisco, Seattle, Iowa, Chicago... As she made a U-turn, a woman in her twenties caught her eyes, held them, smiled with joy, complicity— We both cross the border today, they seemed to say, Qué te vaya bien. Xochiquetzal thought of her grandmother crossing the storm-swollen river as a young woman (her mother holding her baby brother, both drowned). "Qué te vaya bien," she whispered, smiling. Then tears filled her eyes, fell, as her Mamacita's spirit filled her heart to bursting. In the final days of packing the car with the essence de la vida, Mamacita's spirit wings ached in her chest with tenderness, with pain. The journey home, Mexico. She was taking Clara's spirit home eighty-six years later.

Short bursts of a cop car siren, flashing lights; she pulled over. A young, Mexican cop strode to her open window. "You're not in Mexico, you're in El Paso, Texas, ma'am."

"I'm lost, I can't find the international crossing into Mexico (she almost said heart), the interior. I'm trying to get to Chihuahua by nightfall, I'm lost," Xochiquetzal repeated.

He saw how packed her car was, to the hilt, "You evading the law?" he smiled. "Where you going to?"

"San Miguel de Allende," she smiled back cautiously.

"I have family in Guanajuato, it's so beautiful there, I go back at least once a year." He gave her directions, watching her write them down carefully, and as she turned on the motor, he said, "Qué te vaya bien en el corazón de México!"

"Gracias," she laughed. *El Corazon,* the words echoed, his joyful smile, he knew. The heart. Then she heard a grito. She turned to look and he was laughing, waving.

Xochiquetzal carefully followed the directions she'd written down, the warmth of his voice in her ears (the first grito, she now realized on her lounger in Vallarta). At the stop light a thin, hungry looking teenager stepped in front of the waiting cars, filled his mouth with something, lit a match to his open mouth. Fire. A line of fire. The essence of his life, breath. Every driver rolled down their window, cash in their hands. The teen approached, face smeared with smoke and dirt, and she handed him five dollars. "Gracias," he murmured. "De nada," she answered. De nada, it's nothing, it's only the essence of your life, your body's breath. She thought of Justin, the breath in his body safe from fire, from hunger. "De nada," she whispered to a flowering, spring tree whose blossoms kept falling in a white circle.

Xochiquetzal sipped the cool, sweet pina colada, still wet and sleek from riding the waves. She wondered if Javier was sleeping after his night shift or getting a fuck in with one of his chicas; she knew he had his chicas. A Mexican doctor at home in his own country, por favor. She let it go, there was nothing she could do, nada, nothing.

Tonight she'd go to Vallarta, a night club, maybe dance. She sighed with longing. She didn't want to dance; she only wanted to be held. By him. The Mexican doctor at home in his own country, her son's age. "Dr. Fucking Zapata," she muttered, closing her eyes, seeing his eyes laughing into hers. "Eat me up, Xochitzalita."

She saw herself driving the essence of her life over the USA/Mexican border, the huge, green with white lettering sign that made her laugh out loud: REVISION. She didn't know that 'revision' meant 'inspection' in Spanish; instead, she imagined two heyokas, with their striped bodies, running out to place the sign just for her viewing pleasure, inspiration, as she crossed. REVISION. As in to see things freshly, for the very first time (in English). And Xochiquetzal crossed into the rainbow.

She drove into the desert thinking of the older man in the wheelchair in El Paso, trying to wheel himself up a curb. She was about to stop and help, when he stepped out of the wheelchair to push it up the curb. She drove on laughing—revision. She thought of the hundreds of murdered women in Juarez (she'd just sped through), her long drive alone (blown tires, radiator, engine), and the wide expanse of shimmering, dry desert made her silent, dry-mouthed, terrified. Alone. Life unedited. Revision.

After an hour or so of straight desert driving, Xochiquetzal saw a Green Angel truck and the guy waved at her, making spit return to her mouth. Her eyes were beginning to burn from the Mexican sun's potent glare in spite of her full strength, polarized sunglasses. She took a sip of water, willing it to go directly to her eyes. As she finished a wide turn at the top of a long hill—nothing but naked desert below, the sun's tongue on fire—an old man, dressed entirely in white, with a battered, straw hat, walked into view, face to the sky, his eyes challenging the sun's light. Smiling. Ecstasy. Revision.

He climbed it in this heat, she thought, and here I am sweating in my car. "Ayyy Diosa," she muttered. And smiling with either enlightenment or insanity... "What's my excuse," Xochiquetzal laughed a little too loudly. At the bottom of the hill she accelerated to seventy then eighty miles per hour, making the vision of a shower in Chihuahua, dinner, a glass of cold chardonay, a bit closer. From the far right she saw something dark approaching, spinning wildly, throwing dust and sand in its path. Then another one, two more. Little tornadoes, she thought, continuing at eighty, the wind from the vents teasing her face (she blasted the AC occasionally, but feared to use it non-stop, over-heating the engine in the dry, desert heat). Then she felt it; the entire car lifted from the ground, and for a moment it felt like flying, weightless.

Deep in her mind...the wise voice, she'd always called it, as her grandmother called it...deep in her body, she heard, *We are your wind allies, slow down, we'll protect you, slow down.* Trembling with terror and wonder, she slowed to sixty, and four little tornadoes whirled madly to the right side of her car for miles, through the wide expanse of emptiness (only spirits lived here). Occasionally, one would leave to dance alone, only to return. To guide her journey. Revision.

A small town loomed into view, and Xochiquetzal was greeted by a young man in a wheelchair sitting by his tope (cement speed bump, rather than stop lights, signs), a basket in his hand. She slowed and placed twenty pesos in it. "Gracias," he smiled, seductively handsome. "De nada," she smiled back. She looked in her rear view mirror fully expecting the young man to leap from the wheelchair as the older man in El Paso did; but he remained sitting, his basket extended like a blessing.

After the silence of the desert, the ecstasy of the old man, her whirling ally tornadoes, the sounds of a small town alive with people, music, eyes following her every move (la pocha, mas gringa, loca sin hombre, esposo), the sensory overload threatened to drown her. So she swam to fresh tacos, cerveza, agua mas agua, smiles of curiosity, distrust, welcome. And the sounds of her childhood tongue, Spanish, cradled her in comfort.

Xochiquetzal opened her eyes to the glittering mar... "Revision," she murmured, smiling. She crossed into the rainbow.

First she'd check her email before a nap, her disco night in Vallarta—Disco, are you insane? she asked herself again. Just take the nap, have an early dinner, you can always change your mind. Javier's message glowed on the screen:

> Xochitzalita, querida, did I tell you your secret scent is an orchid's scent, a fully blossomed deep purple wild orchid with a golden glowing center hidden in el corazón of the rainforest. And I am el tigre celoso, jealous of your distant

fertile orchid scent. Not fertile because of children (to me any way), but fertile because of the spring you carry (for me, el tigre), how can I wait for the end of the month?

El Maestro Pablo Neruda...

Ay todo de tu piel vuelve a mi boca,
vuelve a mi corazón, vuelve a mi cuerpo,
y vuelvo a ser contigo
la tierra que tu eres:
cres en mi profunda primavera:
vuelvo a saber en ti como germino.

Ah from your skin everything comes back to my mouth,
comes back to my heart, comes back to my body,
and with you I become again
the earth that you are:
you are deep spring in me:
in you I know again how I am born.

(When I read El Maestro's poetry from my student days, I feel old yet brand new.)
Did I give birth to you as well, Xochitzalita, I think I did. I'll think of you dancing tonight, enjoy los cumpleanos but don't forget you were born in me and I in you. And so people have been born and people have died in mis manos, my hands since I've seen you, mi amor, but now I know no hay muerte, no mas la vida siempre jamas, ...but now I know there is no death, there's only life forever and ever...mil besos para tu profunda (sabrosita) primavera...a thousand kisses for your profound (delicious) spring, tu orquidea, orchid.
El Tigre

She replied:

Tigre de mi corazón,
I'll be fearless like you and tell you that my orchid self misses you shamelessly, and I want to devour you limb from

limb, your sweet curved banana NOW, this minute, now. If someone else reads this how they'll laugh at all of these cliches, but I can't help myself. I think something potent has been born in me, a gift from you, so as I approach 60, yes 60 (don't forget this truth), I'm becoming potent/ fertile, fertile/potent. I need to find a dark room, the womb where I create my photos... I didn't tell you I'm a photographer, I was a professor of photography at the university and sometimes journalist (also a very bad, sporadic, sometimes inspired poeta). I think my images, my *vision*, revision (as in a new way of seeing), will be different in Mexico, knowing you, mi Tigre... I dreamt these words, "A different dream is being dreamt here"... la vida unedited con gritos tambien jajaja... Only this life, this moment, te quiero, La Orchid

PS—Neruda's poetry, his words, potent/fertile, gracias.

The phone kept ringing until Xochiquetzal picked it up, glancing at her watch, 9:30am. "What?" was all she could say.

"Qué what, buenos dias, disco girl!" Javier laughed wickedly into her ear.

"Ayyyy soy muerta, I got in at 4 a.m. or so, the long ass cab ride back ayyyy."

"Are you hung-over, mi amor?"

"I hear glee in your voice, no I'm not, just sleepy."

"Did you dance the ancient disco dance?"

"Okay, now you're being mean, it was the dance of my so-called youth, Dr. Cabron (he laughed). I ended up dancing a line dance with some muy wild Japanese women, and they were really good dancers. It was all too hilarious, the ancient dance de los discos, and we got free drinks too," she giggled, keeping her eyes closed.

"Cabrona, when I come to San Miguel we'll go dancing."

"What's your favorite dances?"

"Salsa y hip hop."

"Ayy Diosa," she laughed, wedging the phone, his voice, to her ear. "I can just see you doing the salsa hip hop."

"No te haces loca y mala, Xochitzalita."...Don't get crazy and bad. He tried to sound stern, serious, but it was no use.

After lunch and lots of coffee, she filled her water bottle with papaya-mango juice, and found her usual favorite lounger at the end of the resort's boundary. She gazed at the waves softly breaking, full of light, on the newborn sand, wishing she could see him floating like an otter. Then he'd follow her to the room, and they'd begin again. She thought of the charming Guanajuato cop she danced with last night, her last dances, how he assumed he'd join her, or she at his hotel. How she pretended to go to el bano, toilet, and escaped to a taxi, back to the safety of her room. What if the cop followed me and wouldn't go away, she asked herself. I'd call the front desk for back up, he's not Javier, those eyes, the dream I can't remember, yet.

As Xochiquetzal sat in the back of the taxi at 4 a.m., hurtling back to the hotel in Bucerias, she had to admit, smiling to herself, slightly altered by the three margaritas on the rocks; I had a fucking blast doing that line dance with those Japanese chicas. What great dancers they were, those smiles of pure joy, and the free margaritas that came to our table.

Gazing out to the tempting, wet waves, the words came to her: *As a woman, the whole world is my country.* In her own country she'd been called spic, wetback, greaser, dirty Indian, by the white kids growing up; and guera (light-skinned), gringa, by the Mexican ladies in the neighborhood. Here in Mexico, she was a pocha, chicana, guera, gringa; one or all of them put together. She who'd stopped eating table grapes for over ten years, and not allowing Justin to eat them either; signing petitions, joining the picket lines at Safeway, people hissing as they entered the supermarket, "Why don't you go back to your own country, why don't you go back to Mexico." Cesar Chavez, Dolores Huerta, The Farmworkers, these were her people, as her grandmother, Clara, was her flesh and her blood. As her grandfather, Luis, the sixteenth child of eighteen, of a farm worker's family in Texas. He started working in the fields at six, the story was told; her flesh, her blood. Xochiquetzal had crossed into the Mexican rainbow.

"I'm at home in the world, the rainbow world, I'm at home between earth and sky," she murmured. "My DNA belongs to this earth, my soul to the fregado cosmos." She smiled at her bad poem and, closing her eyes, she remembered the small hotel she'd stayed at in Gomez Palacio, mid-way to San Miguel. It was recommended in her AAA travel book, but she couldn't find it on the small, crowded streets, cars honking if she paused too long, sweat dripping so fast and the sun glaring right behind her exhausted eyes. She stepped out of her car, leaving the motor running, hand brake tight, the cars behind her sounding their horns, men shouting; she raised her left hand, silence, and ran to the taxi in front of her. He guided her to the entrance, smiling as she paid him twenty pesos. A kind man, seeing her exhausted face, ran to help with her luggage, carrying it into the coolness of the lobby.

The cool lobby with fans churning wind over her sweat-salty body (she was a wetback, but coming from the opposite direction), oh the whipping fans churning the cool wind. The small pool with stone frogs spitting water from their open mouths, surrounded by lush, tropical plants. I've landed in Bali, she thought, and it soothed her, as a sweet young (so handsome, Aztec looking) waiter brought her a chilled bottle of water, ice in a glass, and a perfect margarita on the rocks. Bali, Mexico, Europe, Asia…As a woman, I want no country. The whole world is my country, yes oh yes. Xochiquetzal crossed into the rainbow.

At the final border crossing into el corazón de México, the border guard swept his eyes around her over-loaded Toyota, and back to her visa. She waited for the signal to begin a full inspection (revision), wondering if she could fit everything back in. She willed herself to be neutral, a human arrow being shot into the heart. Of Mexico.

"With a name like Xochiquetzal Colette Aguila, andale, y que te vaya bien!" he laughed, waving her through. A miracle. The tornado allies, a miracle. The old man smiling directly into the sun, a miracle. All the way down, past Aguacalientes, getting closer to San Miguel de Allende, these small human, inhuman, miracles.

She remembered the Canadian Indian, Hector's words, in Taos, "You know, that unbroken treaty," (laughing) speaking of how he'd entered the USA. Maybe I'm taking advantage of that unbroken treaty between us humans and the world, the Earth, before maps, borders, when all we did was migrate, the thought streaked across her mind like a comet into a vast darkness. A brief streak of light from an ancient, human memory—Maybe that's what Hector really meant, she realized, driving into Leon, looking for a sign to San Miguel de Allende. After the toll roads, that were fairly straight forward, Leon was a big city with a maze of streets.

"That unbroken treaty, yeah," she laughed out loud, and continued to drive down what looked like a highway, searching for a sign with her destination, nada, nothing. Xochiquetzal drove at least forty miles until it fully dawned on her, in the melting noon day sun...I'm fucking lost, I'm really lost, where the fregado am I anyway... She found a taxi with its hood open, a guy working on the motor. A handsome, café mocha colored guy with the greenest (green!) of eyes, and a smile to stop any woman's heart. Are most Mexican men this handsome, she wondered, thinking of the young man in the wheelchair at his tope, the Aztec looking waiter ayyy...I've been to Mexico before, come on, she told herself, must be the handsome, scenic route.

She told him she was lost, looking for the highway to San Miguel de Allende, sweating her usual buckets. He looked at her sharply, as though assessing her, and laughed, "You're at least forty miles from your turn off, I'll take you there." In Spanish, then that smile. Victor handed her an icy soda, and told her to go sit in the shade, under that tree, smiling that pure sun smile. "Quieres agua...Do you want water?" he asked, laughing at her sweating, exhausted, lost pocha self.

"Tengo agua en mi auto, gracias." She returned his smile with an effort to be slightly in charge, not dying from heat exhaustion, and a longing she'd refused to acknowledge for these past years appeared in living color. His greenest of eyes. I'm on fire, Xochiquetzal thought, waiting in the shade, sipping the Diosa-given, icy cold soda; after these four years of celibacy and mourning, my cells are starting to fire up. Well, let them, good. "Let them fire up," she sighed, thankful for the canopy of filtering leaves over her not so tired, recovering head.

She watched his muscled, young man's arms deal with the motor, and thought, Oh my Goddess, I'm becoming the lecherous older woman watching young men's glistening muscles ripple, fuck. Then she wanted to howl with laughter, but she knew it was nerves and road exhaustion; the fourth straight day of driving in the glaring Mexican sun, clouds gathering, slight sprinkle, and the Mexican sun would conquer the blue sky again. Plus, Victor would probably leap into his taxi and speed away from la loca, and who would blame him, la pocha loca ayyy. This thought sobered her, but she giggled her heart out where la loca lived, somewhere hidden in her celibate, no more monthly blood, dark, so tender, alive womb. And one by one, her cells came to life, burning, burning, burning, alive.

Victor drove like a maniac to the San Miguel de Allende highway entrance, another toll booth to pay a few pesos to. And to her, and probably his, surprise she kept up. As Xochiquetzal paid him for guiding her, for getting her found, he quickly kissed her on the cheek. "Bien viaje y que amor te encontrarse...Safe journey and may love find you," he smiled right into her eyes. Mama mia, I believe my celibacy days are over, but he's too young, his thirties, and I will not be the older, lecherous woman drooling on young men's rippling muscles, ayy Diosa.

Xochiquetzal opened her eyes, feeling the sweaty-salt clinging to her dry skin. "La mar la mar la mar," she whispered. And what did I do, I'm involved with someone twenty-four years younger than me, and watching a lot more than his rippling muscles. That slice of mango dangling between his teeth, my kundalini snakes having a fregado field day, every cell alive. She laughed out loud as she dove into the silky movement of the wave that had journeyed from Africa to reach her, this silky moment, now.

She ordered a Tequila Sunset, as the bartender called it, the last drink she'd had with Javier, when she'd pulled off her dress to swim with him, with Juanito. She sipped, extra strong, and it was sunset. Tomorrow she'd go sailing, so she had to be up at 6 a.m. sharp. As Xochiquetzal gazed at the shades of lilac, violet, shimmering in the womb of la mar, the setting sun licking her once more until dawn found him young, virile, newly born, her lover... She thought of her April arrival in San Miguel. Purple trees, the purple jacaranda trees of spring; purple trees laughing, purple trees weeping. Purple clouds flowering everywhere, visible from her roof. That view of wide sky, clouds gathering.

And the pure, white dove that came to visit for three sunsets, sitting next to her, no fear of her. How she knew the spirit of Mamacita, Clara, visited her in the pure, white dove; the part of her Xochiquetzal had carried for forty years like a cherished burden. Now she would carry only her clear light: Clara. Her name, Clara...clear light...the pure, white, fearless dove. Never moving those three twilights as she wept goodbye to the cherished burden (of Clara's soul). Mamacita was finally home, her home, México lindo y querido; and she remembered Mamacita's voice singing in the morning. "México lindo y querido, si muero lejos de ti que digan que estoy dormida, y que me traigan aqui, México lindo y querido...Beautiful, beloved Mexico, if I die far away from you, tell them that I'm dreaming, and bring me home, beautiful and beloved Mexico."

Mamacita had taught her *dreaming, ensueño,* from the time she could speak; and the dream had brought her granddaughter home... México lindo y querido. Her mother, Florinda, had protested this dream training, "It did me no good, Mama, and she has to live in the real world, no dreaming." So Clara had taught her secretly, a finger over her lips...Say nothing, our secret.

And because of this training, Xochiquetzal dreamt/felt the fearful, violent dreams of the country of her birth, the color codes of each day: green, blue, orange, the dreaded, ridiculous red. She dreamt bombs falling on families, mortally wounded children dying in front of their mothers, the shock and awe of her country (the so-called president she called The Emperor Idiot). She tried to make sense of his outrageous stupidity, his shock and awe show making millions of Muslims the enemy world wide by bombing Iraq (and not tracking down bin Laden). She'd tell herself, He's doing his weird part, the birth pains into the Sixth World December 21, 2012, the end/beginning of the Mayan Calendar (the unfolding of the human spirit), and only one thousand years of evolution to go (her dreams kept telling her). But in Taos she kept dreaming the dream of her country; the dreaded, ridiculous color codes, daily.

When she'd gone to Bali her dreams shifted; she felt lifted up by an island of dreamers. Were they one thousand years ahead, she wondered. Her dreams were crystal clear in full, iridescent color: joy/sorrow in focus. In San Miguel she didn't feel lifted up by an island of dreamers, but her dreams began to join a different dream that was being dreamt. In Mexico. Unedited. No headlines. No color codes. Fear in the body, not in the soul. A different dream, unedited.

Xochiquetzal remembered her fear of someone breaking the glass in the roof top door and entering. A thief, a rapist. Her second week of arrival, hanging up laundry on the roof, April winds strewing purple petals, thick mountain dust making her sneeze; it slammed the door shut. No key, locked out, dinner on the stove. House swept, windows washed, she felt in control, humming with it, control. Will. She looked down to her bedroom patio, too far. She could scream AYUDA... HELP, too much pride. She picked up the brick that had wedged the door open, and smashed the thick glass on the fourth, determined hit. The April wind sang through the opening, México lindo y querido, and after the third twilight, the pure, white, fearless dove never returned.

It took a full week for the glass guys to arrive, and she had to take a taxi to their shop to convince them to come; the job was too small. Xochiquetzal slept for a week with her Swiss Army knife open on the night stand, with the roof door an open invitation to all thieves and rapists. Maybe I can open my intruder a bottle of fregado vino, she laughed at herself finally. No one entered, stole, raped. Fear in the body, not in the soul, let it go, let it go, fear.

Xochiquetzal crossed into the rainbow.

The first star appeared, Venus, or the more ancient name, Quetzalcoatl, burning himself into the dark flesh of sky. The star doesn't *will* itself to appear, it simply appears. I didn't *will* Justin's eyes, mouth, hands, feet, tiny penis, his baby brain, in my womb; they appeared, his life within me. Whenever I start to think I'm in control, here in Mexico, over this border, this dreaming border, I get my ass kicked, she thought smiling, this truth. Javier following me to my room, me opening the door, it was like a dream, no control, no will. Yes, a different dream is being dreamt here, but I'm twenty-four years older than him, it can't last, maybe a year, I cannot memorize him or I will suffer die suffer when we finally and inevitably part (will will will).

"Why did I open the fucking door?" Xochiquetzal murmured (no will no will)... and the Energy Child's right ear bloomed opened, the tiniest seashell, listening for Javier's voice, laughter, tears, his grito of joy, sorrow.

Is this the deepest sacred play joy sorrow

5:30 a.m., she opened her eyes, he didn't call as she'd asked (as he'd promised). She gave herself permission to close her eyes for fifteen more minutes. I miss his voice, damn it, I do, fregado. Maybe he'll never call me again, I'll never see him again, Dr. Gomez and his fregada chicas. And me, la vieja pendeja mamacita. "Ayyy que rica," she moaned.

She was glad she ate breakfast, the soft salt morning air made her hungry again as she stood at the rail of the speeding boat watching dolphins leap into sunlight, over and over; their sleek, perfect bodies, *joy*, making her senselessly happy. Just because. They leap. Just joy.

Then the all male crew began their entertainment—a skinny, wiry, yet attractive, guy, with a big mouth, obviously their leader, began. "Someone asked me if we have any sharks here in Mexico, and I told him we only have friendly Mexican sharks here. The Great White Sharks only eats white people, so that's where they live en el norte, north!" Shakira's voice rang out, and he executed some sexy moves, laughing with his crew. Xochiquetzal looked around at the white people—a few Mexican families in groups—they looked like they had a hair ball caught in mid-throat, while some of the Mexicans giggled (those who understood English). As each handsome (in his own way) crew member was introduced, they shook their hips, shimmyed, pretended to strip. Finally, the white folks laughed and clapped to the music.

"If any of you ladies need a Mexican boyfriend just let us know, that's why we're here, to serve you, I mean las mujeres, the women." He smiled right at her, making her look away. Ayy Diosa, do I have Hoochie Mama tattooed on my fregado forehead? Then she laughed out loud, catching his gaze again, and he blew her un beso.

Javier speed dialed linda Lupita, the youngest of his chicas, nineteen; that had always turned him on, fifteen years younger and the sultry body of a mermaid without the fins. An hermosa, wet sea creature between her legs, so young, so fresh, revealed at low tide, la mar.

"Soy yo...It's me," he said, when she answered, surprising him as her answering machine almost always picked up.

He asked how she was and did she want to meet for dinner, his day off. If I call Xochitzalita tonight, I would've already fucked Lupita, ayyy que cabron estoy...what a bastard I am. Her voice was soft, yielding, making him hard, erect. I'm a man, he reminded himself, not a chingado monk.

Javier had no photo of Xochiquetzal to look at, to remind him of her full presence. She's beginning to trust me like Clara did, and women like that, when they no longer trust you, leave. They simply leave.

They'd meet at the seafood place at 7 p.m., an early dinner, an early fuck or two. He couldn't remember her scent, only the feel of her two, huge, natural, firm nineteen year old breasts; her large, brown nipples filling his hungry mouth. He was fully erect, so he'd make himself come with his own oiled hand, making himself think of Lupita.

"Do you want me to wear my purple or red thong, Dr. Gomez?" she teased with that edge of submission. Worship.

"Red, absolutely the red." Javier began to stroke himself, and though he tried to visualize la hermosa Lupita, La Orchid kept intruding with her sad, laughing, direct gaze. No submission. No worship. Her endless gaze of curiosity staring into his eyes; and when his hot sea sperm left him helpless, there was no peace.

After snorkeling, swimming, floating in the transparent, body temperature, so blue water, la mar, surrounding the exquisite island, she spread her towel in the shade, on the white sugar sand. Xochiquetzal thought of her ex-husband of twenty-two years, and dug her hands into the silky sand, thinking how each grain was a second, an hour, a day, a century; and how the twenty-two years was really one, tiny grain of sand slipping through her fingers. She stared up at the young, green palm fronds sprouting from the mother tree, and she thought, That's the secret of eternal youth, eternal re-birth from the source, from the tree that never ever dies. She remembered the wet slices of mango placed all over her willing, trembling, orgasmic body. Her fifty-eight year old body, this life, barely a wink in eternity's endless gaze.

She thought of Javier, the call that he didn't make last night—I've known him for less than a week, but still this lovely grain of silky, white sand...in eternity's gaze, the same, slow, endless wink. "I'm a mango clinging to the tree that never ever dies," she whispered to the young, singing, translucent-green palm fronds, "how long will I cling, ripening?" The sweet island wind caressed her hair, her face, her exposed flesh. She closed her eyes and dreamt a short, vivid dream.

Xochiquetzal...*My mother, Florinda, is dressed in her favorite color, purple, a deep purple sarong that wraps around her body sensually. And I remember the time I saw her this way in life—as I dream, I'm aware she's no longer in this body—the times she was right at home in her very sensual body. I realize this is her gift to me, sensuality. She smiles, her lovely red lips moist, expanding. This is her gift. To me. Her ripening.*

In a flash, barely a second, that splintered grain of silky sand, she saw Javier's eyes staring into hers as though he wanted to tell her something. Gone.

Xochiquetzal's eyes flew open, her heart pounding. Slowly, she calmed herself—It's been eighteen years since she left her body, her still graceful, sensual body, and I miss her, I will always miss her, this woman, this soul, my mother, this time. "Her gift to me, this ripening," she murmured. And Javier, what does he want to tell me? she wondered. Those eyes, tonight he'll call (not knowing it was his day off), or he won't call. Tonight. Ever again. Older woman, younger man, a joke, on me.

She climbed the steps to the outdoor tables and ordered a margarita, waiting for her lunch of chicken mole, with its rich chocolate sauce, to arrive. The view of the calm, breeze-lipped, opal ocean from her small table at the edge of the cliff was simply perfect—and she wondered if she could live on this perfect island every day...Probably not, but what a visit for two or three months, then out into the world again. Her margarita on the rocks, rimmed with salt, arrived, and as she slowly sipped, gazing out to the sheer beauty, she couldn't imagine being any happier, this moment. Now.

Ripening.

She thought of her mother, how she never lived with a man day to day (more of an island visit, Xochiquetzal smiled)—"I've seen how that works," Florinda would laugh. She didn't marry her father, his brief visit to her island, or anyone. "I don't need to, I can support myself, and you will too," her mother's words echoed in the soft air. She was an executive secretary with many boyfriends; a free soul, a woman of sensuality who lived as she pleased. Who danced and suffered. Her gift to me. Her wound to me. Yes, her ripening, my beautiful, sensual mother.

Lupita drew her usual stares as she swayed into the restaurant, and a few Ayyyy mamacitas breathed like prayer. Her chile-red halter top plunged to reveal her perfect, full moon, breasts, and her low rise jeans were painted on; a peek of her red thong rode on her full nineteen year old hips. Red, moist lips smiling expectantly, long dark hair (with streaks of fashionable punk red) falling past her inviting shoulders. She smiled directly at Javier, already feeling his hands on her body, his mouth on her swollen nipples, sucking slowly.

What else could a man, any healthy man, want? he asked himself as she bent over—giving him a full, up close view of the twins—to kiss him, licking his lips with her tongue. Usually, he'd prolong this moment for the drooling spectators, his own pleasure, by holding the kiss, meeting her tongue with his tongue, thrusting it in and out, fucking her mouth. In public. A preview. And he knew every man in the room knew what he was doing to this nineteen year old chica, and it made him hard.

He surprised himself and didn't even meet her tongue, cursing himself pendejo. Her breath, her scent (underneath the thick layer of perfume), was sour to him, and he realized she smelled of other men. I don't have to kiss her, he thought, I'll just fuck her, tell her I have an on-coming cold, a virus, whatever.

"You don't want to kiss me?" she whined sensually.

"I'm getting a fredgao cold, we don't need to kiss, hermosa."

"Tu eres el doctor…You're the doctor," her red lips smiled, parted, open, willing, pliant, submissive. A worshipper.

Javier took out his cell, checked for calls. "I'm being paged," he lied. "I left instructions to call if my patient worsened. I have to go but I'll call later, sorry." He left a 200 peso bill for her meal and strode out the door. By the time he got to the corner of the street, she was approached by two young men.

It was after midnight and he still hadn't called, so Xochiquetzal turned off the lamp and opened the drapes to the fiercely burning stars. These were the beings that had always brought her comfort, at the edge of dreams. Their fierce light, desire. As she closed her eyes, the phone rang making her want to leap out of her skin. "Javier?"

"No, es el tigre muy triste…it's the very sad tiger, Xochitzalita."

"Why are *you* sad? Why didn't you call me last night?"

"Because I can't smell your ripened orchid, because I can't taste your sweet mango, because I'm an ordinary man who misses you, and because I'm a cabron trying to be reborn."

"Qué bien, mi tigre, que bien," she laughed softly. "Why didn't you call last night?"

"I'm going to come next weekend, I can't stand it. I mediate life and death, as you know, and no other thought brings me peace but the thought of seeing you, all of you, a free exam." A smile crept into his voice.

"Do you know who you are?"

"I'm waiting."

"In the Pueblos, in New Mexico, there are sacred clowns, heyokas, who take part in the dances, the rituals. They make everything sacred—with their humor, dancing in the opposite direction, their lightning bolts pointing skyward on their striped chests, smashing the ripest watermelons on the ground so everyone can get a slice. They make everything sacred, profane, sexy and real, always joking, that's you, Javier."

"I'm not joking, Xochitzalita, I'm coming to your door in San Miguel next Friday afternoon so take your vitamins," he said in his doctor to patient tone.

"And you take yours," she answered in the same tone.

"This time it's watermelons, mi amor..."

"It's what?"

"I'm going to cover you in red, ripe watermelon slices, every sabrosita inch, como un heyoka, sabes..."

"Okay, I'll have one here," she giggled, feeling the cool slices on her body, making her want him, making her want him. Now.

"No, I'll bring the watermelon, that's my job..."

"Because you mediate life and death..."

"Exactly," he laughed softly into her ear. "I'm going to tear you limb from limb como El Tigre." Javier quoted Neruda... "Bebo tu sangre, rompo tus miembros uno a uno...I drink your blood, I break your limbs one by one."

A fire rose through her body, starting from her burning, slick vulva, up through her dancing kundalini snakes, erasing her words.

"Xochitzalita, did you hear me?"

"Yes, bring the watermelon," she managed to say, and then the image of the large Pueblo heyoka, body painted in stripes, hair painted the color of fertile pollen, yellow—came to her full force. He was breaking, smashing, the largest, ripest watermelon directly onto the earth in front of her. He was smiling that wonderfully deranged smile as he approached, the ripened pieces in his hands. Then he offered her a fleshy-red, dripping slice, laughing loudly like a grito. Fertile. Potent.

Ripened.

The Energy Child wanted to see the color of fertile pollen, yellow, the fleshy-red, ripened slice of watermelon, and his/her left eye opened, widening, wonder.

Is this   the deepest   sacred play?

Wonder.

Xochiquetzal...*A child wants to play with me, she wants to play Hide and Seek, she wants to hide and she wants me to find her. She laughs so joyously, bubbles of light float from her open mouth. "Okay, hide, I'll find you," I say without words, my light bubbles float to her perfect child ears. I turn my back and listen to her laughter disappear as she runs to her hiding place. "Ready or not, here I come!" my light bubbles shout. I laugh at the silence and sheer beauty of this world, this place where the child lives.*

I'm lifted up by a gentle wind so I forget to be terrified, and as I'm lifted over the ancient tree tops I see that the sun, moon, stars, streaking comets, share the sky at the same time. Wonder. I see someone crouching in a thicket of wild, white orchids below me, so I ask the gentle wind, with just a thought, to lower me. To the thicket of wild, white orchids, and as I'm gently lowered, I smell them.

Rain.   Female rain.   Fertile.

And I thank the gentle, male wind for his violet wings. Potent.

Laughter. The child is laughing.

She springs to her feet, covered entirely by white orchids, and I see she's Clara, mi Mamacita, caressed by the gentle, male wind, his wide violet wings, that brought me to her. To the beauty of this world, where the child lives. Where wonder is always born. He opens his wide, violet wings; one touches a white orchid; one touches a white star. If only I could have those wings, the wings of the wind, I tell myself, remind myself to remember when I wake up from this beauty. Wonder.

Ripened. Fertile. Potent. Violet. Wings. Male rain.   Wonder.

Clara, the child, opens her mouth to sing... "Nina, cuando yo muera no llores...no mi llores, no, no, no mi llores, no...en cambio, si tu mi cantas, yo siempre vivo y nunca muero...Child, when I die don't weep...no don't weep, no don't weep...when I transform, if you sing to me, I'll always live and never, ever, die." Her voice is so pure, the voice of the unborn, the always born, the child, and her laughing/wise eyes tell me she remembers who I am, and that I must always remember who she is. "En cambio, si tu mi cantas, yo siempre vivo y nunca muero..."

A flash of lightning, she becomes a pure, white dove...she flies into wonder.

Ripened.

Her gift to me.

Ripening.

Javier thought of his father (also a physician), mother (a retired teacher), his four sisters, his brother, he the youngest, still not married, no grandchildren to add to the twelve and counting they already had. They wanted more, they wanted his. He was the only one to go off traveling into the wide world: Japan, Indonesia, India, Europe, Spain where he met Clara his lost love. The one he would've had children with, Clara La Rubia, The Blonde. The beautiful girl in the back of the truck, staring into her future, in Vallarta, their lost child. Suddenly, he had the irrational urge to find the little girl, to raise her as his own, a found piece of Clara.

"You're going to be forty with no children, no wife, Javier, it's not good to be tan libre, so free," his father reminded him whenever he saw him. Once a month or less, if Javier could help it.

"I'm not going to marry just anyone to have a batch of babies to prove I'm a man, soy un hombre libre, que me chingan," Javier said out loud to his father's shadow; the man who longed to be free, but never dared to be free, except in the arms of other women. The endless younger women, las chicas. His father. He remembered his father's younger face filled with absolute irritation when one of his children spilled the inevitable glass of milk; and that he had no memory of ever being held by his father. He remembered being held by his mother, then handed to the dark-skinned woman who raised him, Amalia (he'd called her Mama Ama, secretly). He remembered the scent of her strong body, sweat and roasting chilies; her strong, Indian arms.

"She looks like my mother's mother, I think that's why I chose her, but don't ever tell your father. He's only seen photos of my guera, light-skinned, mother," Javier's mother once confided to his young boy's delight, shock, curiosity. I'm an Indian, a mesitzo, just like any Mexican. "Soy mestizo," he let the words live.

Javier couldn't sleep—no watermelon, no Xochitzalita, no orchid scent, no deep orgasmic cries, no entry into molten flesh, no fingers memorizing his face, his trembling body, no arms refusing to let him go, no legs to cradle him tightly, no birth no birth no birth. He oiled his right hand, began to stroke himself erect to bursting. He refused to fantasize Xochitzalita, saving her face for reality, but her face, her body, appeared, her scent engulfed him, as his hot, thick semen puddled the sheets. And he imagined, as he fell into dreams, that his sperm would father fresh orchids by morning.

Potent. Fertile.

Javier...*I'm in Indonesia standing at the lip of a smoldering volcano, night, only the light of stars, no moon, hot sparks strike my face as I gaze into the volcano's core, its womb where all life begins, this is why I travel, wonder, Xochitzalita is next to me, laughing, she gives me one white orchid, and gazes into the volcano's womb with me, where all life begins, "You mediate life and death," she laughs, I throw the white orchid into the fiery center, and lava begins to flow as we laugh, cry.*

Xochiquetzal was the first diner, not quite dawn, her last day, la mar. One more swim, a shower, I'm packed, to the airport, she told herself, waiting for her first cup of coffee to arrive. Then her perfect omelette from the always smiling omelette lady, Juana.

"Estas feliz, señora...Are you happy?" Juana asked, surprising her. "So many people who come here are trying to be happy but I can see that they're not." She sprinkled the omelette with her favorite things (ham, cheese, mushrooms, tomatoes, roasted hot chilies, onions), and heated her fresh, cobalt blue tortillas on another grill.

"Yes, I am, soy feliz, sometimes sad but mostly, truly happy. Are you happy, Juana?"

"I have my work, señora, I'm very happy, but like you sometimes sad, two of my youngest sons are in your country, the U-S-A, and I worry about them. So many young people have died there, never returning home to their own country. They send me money every month, they're such good sons, but I keep saying, 'Come home to your own country, it's time, hijitos,' but they don't listen to their mama. But I have my work here, my own little casita, and you can see that I eat well," she laughed.

"Voy a mi casa in San Miguel ahora...I'm going to my house in San Miguel today, and I'll be very sad not to have your sabrosita omelettes every morning ayy," she laughed. "But I'm sorry to hear your youngest sons won't come home, you must miss them. I have a son on the other side who I miss..." The big difference is that I can cross over to see him, move back if I choose to, or he can just fly down to visit me. Her sons risk being caught, deported, even killed at the border.

"I'll miss making them for you, señora, maybe they'll listen if I get sick, who knows."

"Mi nombre es Xochiquetzal, please call me that." Usually she tipped Juana twenty pesos every morning, but today she handed her two-hundred pesos.

"Ayyy que bonita, Xochiquetzal, your name is beautiful, but this is too much..."

"Please take it, it's not enough y gracias otra vez, Juana."

"Gracias, señora...Xochiquetzal, y que te vaya bien."

"Y tu tambien, Juana." They laughed as the first beam of sunlight lit up the dining room, fully open to la mar. Juana spoke only to the Mexicans, and to this señora pocha, la Xochiquetzal, nombre de India. Only she and some of the Mexicans tipped her, looked into her eyes.

Still wet from her final, silky swim, slightly less than body temperature, rising sun grazing her body, every wave—she stopped to check email. She didn't want to leave la mar; she felt like a mermaid losing her glittery, sensual mermaid tail. She would be dry again; she would forget the scent of salt at dawn. She would forget the sound of Africa meeting Mexico; she would forget Juanito's laughter in the waves. Tears gathered in her eyes, making the screen unbearably bright.

An email from Justin: "I'll call you Sunday, let me know which one's best, this one or the next one, love ya, R U TAN? hate ya xoxo"

And Javier's Spanglish email address announced a message:

Nos hemos recorrido labio a labio,
hemos cambiado mil veces
entre nosotros la muerte ya la vida,
todo lo que traiamos
como muertas medallas
lo echamos al fondo del mar,
todo lo que aprendimos
no nos sirvio de nada:
comenzamos de nuevo,
terminamos de nuevo
muerte y vida.
Y aqui sobrevivimos,
puros, con la pureza que nosotros creamos...

We have felt each other lip to lip,
we have changed a thousand times
between us death and life,
all that we were bringing

like dead medals
we threw to the bottom of the sea,
all that we learned
was of no use to us:
we begin again,
we end again
death and life.
And here we survive,
pure, with the purity that we created...

We will survive on watermelon, will bring two ripe ones. See you Friday around noon, take your vitamins, Xochitzalita, mi Orchid. El Tigre who eats little orchids jajaja
She wrote back:

Tigre, This poem is so stunningly beautiful I almost can't breathe, and so I will find Neruda's Captain's Verses, I owned a copy years ago, and now you bring his words to life for me, with new meaning.. "We have changed a thousand times between us death and life," your first words to me, about past lives, which life is this? Yes we'll live on watermelons, maybe I'm not too old and bitter after all... La Orchid who knows kung fu jajaja xoxo

Traveling within Mexico meant you had to watch out for gate changes as only the international flights were announced; so Xochiquetzal situated herself in front of an airlines desk and a twirling fan over her head. She wiped sweat from her face and neck with a tissue, and like in Bali she knew her thin-filmed make-up was gone. She reached for her lip gloss, that made her lips sparkly and smooth, and applied it. I don't wear that much make-up, but I can't live without lip gloss, she thought, remembering her mother's always red lips, how her red lip mark would stay on Xochiquetzal's face long after she went to work. And the challenge was to wear it all day, to quickly turn her head when Mamacita tried to clean her face—"Ay niña, you look like a clown."

I wonder where Javier's parents live, and Jesus F. Christ I hope they're older than me, him and his two ripe watermelons—she couldn't help smiling and caught herself. Next I'll be fucking drooling, talking to myself, 911 or in Mexico 066. "Ayyy," she sighed, feeling the cool slices of watermelon on every open, breathing cell of her now sweating buckets pocha body. I'll have to ask Javier about his parents, how fregado old they are, it never occurred to me to ask, two red, ripe watermelons...

A handsome young guy sat down across from her with a deep-pink t-shirt that proclaimed: BEST ORIGINAL FOREPLAY. A playful smile greeted her openly and his eyes just stared without shame. Xochiquetzal glanced at his eyes, his face: maybe twenty-two, a student back from a memorable vacation. Look who's talking, me and my chingado memorable vacation—I should be wearing a bright-purple t-shirt with BEST ORIGINAL FOREPLAY WITH MANGOES. She met his eyes and laughed. "Great t-shirt."

He leaped up and joined her in one movement—"I'm Raul, a student from Guanajuato, how was your time in Vallarta?'

"I thought you were a student, what are you studying? I'm Xochiquetzal and my time in Vallarta was wonderful," she smiled.

"Ah, the Mayan Goddess of love, am I right?" He switched to English. "I'm studying engineering but I also snuck in a poetry class, and the Goddess of love would appreciate my t-shirt, so no wonder. And you look like you would appreciate it." His smile was pure, sensual mischief.

Mexican men really live in their bodies, she noted once again, remembering how they avoided her when she first arrived (the kung fu master stride through the cobble streets of San Miguel). "Well, that's embarrassing but I guess gracias," she laughed. "Who's your favorite poet?"

"Ayyy Lorca, como no."

"How about Neruda, I love Neruda," she smiled thinking of El Tigre. She'd always enjoyed being around, talking to students, the young ones with some of their ideals, wonder, still intact.

"Neruda is the king, but Lorca, and his plays like "Yerma," he's a God. Here's one I know by heart, he knew he was going to die young, don't you think so?"

Raul's face became serious, gathering his soul for Lorca's poem. Young Mexican men weren't young like the young men in her country, some still teenagers into their thirties. Here they had go decide what profession (if they were lucky), what work would feed, clothe and house them (and their future families) for the rest of their lives by age seventeen at the latest.

Of course, that's why Javier is such a young resident, he had to push through, give birth to himself in his early teens, no time to be a teenager in this country (and his eyes came to her, looking into her fearlessly). "Yes, I think all of his poetry foreshadowed that knowledge, and Spain is an ancient culture as is Mexico, so death and life are always holding hands in his poetry. Unlike my country where death has a face lift," Xochiquetzal laughed.

"You sound like a professor," Raul smiled.

"I was, now recite me that poem."

He closed his eyes for a moment, seeing the structure of the poem the way he saw the structure of buildings. Then he opened them, staring each life/death word into her eyes.

DESPEDIDA

Si muero,
dejad el balcon abierto.

El niño come naranjas.
(Desde mi balcon lo veo.)

El segador siega el trigo.
(Desde mi balcon lo siento.)

Si muero,
dejad el balcon abierto!"

FAREWELL

If I die,
leave the balcony open.

The little boy is eating oranges.
(From my balcony I can see him.)

The reaper is harvesting the wheat.
(From my balcony I can hear him.)

If I die,
leave the balcony open!

"Dejad el balcon abierto, exactly, the open door, gracias, Raul, that was so beautiful..."

The ticket agent waved at them, and Raul grabbed her carry on. His seat was in the front and hers was toward the back.

"I'll send you one of my inferior poems," he laughed, "if you give me your email address."

"I'd love that, and maybe I'll send you one of mine." Raul waited until she handed him her email address, quickly kissed her on the cheek and got to his seat.

I find my sons everywhere, she thought of her sweet, young driver in Bali, Putu. (And her younger lover in Bali, Wayan, his early forties, not a son.) And then, Thailand, Japan, India, Spain, Greece, Italy; her vacations, sabbaticals, many with her son, Justin. Traveling with Justin was often challenging, but more than anything he was a joyous companion, teller of jokes, and fellow seeker of wonder. Often she liked his photos more than her own; that unblemished eye. Innocence. Wonder. Maybe Justin, my students, spoiled me for people my own age, usually so boring, talking about their endless health problems, pros/cons of being cremated, not realizing they're already dead in the most tragic way. The spirit. She thought of two of her oldest women friends (their twenty, thirty plus year friendships), and she smiled. These women aren't dead in any way, each one alive and sizzling in her own stubborn, outrageous, unique, glittering spirit. "Lara, Tara," she whispered.

Then Xochiquetzal thought of Javier, her body flaring with its sudden, stubborn desire. No, he is not my son. "Best original foreplay with ripe watermelons," she murmured to the smooth, metal wing that would take her home. Home. San Miguel de Allende. And he's coming this weekend, she reminded herself, I have to shop for fresh vegetables, fruit, cheese, freshly baked bread, chicken, maybe some champagne, chardonay, cabernet, brie, los vitamins.

Xochiquetzal sat in the very back of the shuttle where she usually had the entire back seat to herself for the hour and a half ride to San Miguel. For silence if she chose not to talk; to sleep if she sprawled out. She took out his last email; she'd printed it out for the trip home. She read these Neruda lines over and over...

Nos hemos recorrido labio a labio,
hemos cambiado mil veces
entre nosotros la muerta y la vida...

We have felt each other lip to lip,
we have changed a thousand times
between us death and life...

Between us life, death and birth, yes, she smiled to herself, and as
the gringo-mobile introductions began, she stretched out in the back
seat and closed her eyes (Javier's Zapata eyes gazed at her clearly in
that soft darkness). "Ayy mi tigre," she murmured, clenching herself,
the memory of his mouth on hers...labio a labio, si.

"She's gone to sleep on us, "a woman's voice held an edge of
derision, seeing that she'd just disappeared from view.

"One less brain to pick," a man laughed.

Got that right, Xochiquetzal thought dreamily, the air
conditioning sweeping her face clean of sweat, the driver slowing
down for the dreaded topes, cement speed bumps of varying sizes.
She'd taken part in a few of those shuttle exchanges at first, but
the gringo-mind-set irritated and frustrated the fregado out of her
exactly as it did in the USA: Is it safe, Can you drink the water,
You don't live in a gated community oh my, Do you actually drive
down here on these roads, Do you live by yourself oh my, Is it safe
(with all those Mexicans)... Why are you here, she wanted to ask,
but she knew—cheap maids, cooks, gardeners, drivers, labor to
build their fancy houses, the safe, gated communities—the good
and helpful Mexicans (who needed their jobs), unlike herself, the
uppity, arrogant, pocha, *Chicana*, who was better educated than most
of them with her Ph.D. As her mother used to say, "Fuck 'em if
they can't dance," laughing and dancing. She'd gotten her bachelors
degree at night, and bribed and bullied Xochiquetzal into university
directly after high school.

I forgot to tell Javier I'm a doctor too, fuck I forgot I was a doctor
with that best original foreplay with mangoes. "Ayyy doctorcito," she
breathed.

"Senora, estamos a su casa...We're at your house," the smiling
driver shook her shoulders gently. The others laughed, making her

wonder if she had drool on her face, had snored loudly, maybe even farted. I hope it stunk, she thought, grabbing her stuff, to their overly-hearty group chorus of. "Have a wonderful time!"

Then she felt like a grinch—"You too," she waved without smiling. She thought of the 4 a.m. pre-dawn drive to the airport months ago, a gringa mom speaking Spanish to her young children in the tone mothers who love their children use. And her children answering in Spanish... "Vamos a regressar a San Miguel...We'll return to San Miguel," she told them. The children chanted, "Pollito loco," as they passed the chicken restaurant at the edge of town. Their sweet voices reminded her of Justin at that age, that kind of mother love she'd given him, and it made her smile. Then and still now, that love. "Pollito loco, pollito loco..." their sweet, high voices kept singing goodbye to Mexico.

She tipped the driver, closing the double sided Mexican door behind him. "Lighten up, pochita loca," she told herself like a good friend, holding hands with herself, Los Dos Fridas, Los Dos Xochiquetzals. She scanned the walls for scorpions, nothing, yet. The scorpion hunter.

"Javier," she said out loud to the empty casa, invoking his presence, his spirit, his loud laughter and louder gritos. The Energy Child listened with both ears, tiny seashells, listening; gazing out at Xochiquetzal's casa with his/her wide, wondering left eye. But s/he couldn't sing, "Pollito loco"—her/his mouth was closed, not alive. Yet.

Climbing the stairs to her bedroom, she spotted a very large scorpion on the wall, almost brushing it with her shoulder. She shuddered with the always fresh fear and disgust, took off her sandal, raised it, aimed it (waiting for the usual response of other critters, nada), killed it. We don't exist for them, like The Borg, the strange thought came to her, making her shudder again. And if you don't clean them up right away, the next morning there's another one eating its fellow scorpion. "I've become the fucking scorpion hunter, and I think that was Scorpion #32 or so." Who knows, she continued this train of thought, but definitely over thirty, no one killed scorpions before I lived here. She thought of her eighty year old neighbor, laughing at her because she dreaded killing scorpions, "If you don't kill yours, ours will come to live with you, such a nice safe nest," in Spanish.

It was hard to get back into her daily routine of cooking for herself, telling herself she had to go shopping for food (killing two more scorpions); after all of this was taken care of at the resort. Xochiquetzal thought of Juana, the omelette lady, as she cooked her own pretty delicious omelette. She thought of the early morning waves cooling her ankles, knees, thighs, as she walked to the market in Bucerias. She thought of mangoes drizzled with limes, sprinkled with red chile powder, and she thought of mangoes between Javier's teeth, his loco laughter, Dr. Zapata at play. "Will it be the same here in San Miguel, to see him here?" she said out loud.

Well, this time it's watermelons and only three more days till he arrives at my door...will we feel the same here in my house in San Miguel... "Only three more days," she breathed out as the Energy Child dreamt the setting sun in Bali. Where babies were born gods, goddesses, their feet not touching the earth for 105 days. The Energy Child's feet remembered Bali, this Earth, as viewed from a distant star. The Energy Child opened his/her left eye, looking for Javier, his eyes, the dream, his eyes.

Okay, she told herself, today I go shopping for food, the goodies, and tomorrow water, the hot springs, soak and swim. Xochiquetzal grabbed her car keys, her purple plastic envelope with all her driving info—Mexican car insurance, copies of her USA passport, her FM-3 Mexican visa, her USA driver's license.

"As a woman, the whole world is my country, but I'd better have this proof when I'm driving here in Mexico or I could be in deep doo doo," she said to her reflection as she spread lip gloss over her dry lips. "Three more days and he comes here a mi casa, a mis labios...to my house, to my lips...will age matter here?

After Xochiquetzal stopped at her mail service for over two weeks of mail, she stopped at an outdoor café in the Jardin, the main plaza, where the cathedral spires kissed the clear, windy sky. Coffee, wind, desire, kisses; her nipples hardened with the sensuality of memory, this moment. His eyes, she thought, Javier only has to look at me, I'm a fucking goner. She smiled as the invisible wind licked her, el tigre with his soft, raspy tongue. The morning coolness, her favorite time (and then midnight to dawn), scattered people on the benches; a mix of Mexicans, and gringos trying to contact each other. A taste of the states, home, to belong to their own country. I've never belonged to the gringo world in my country, why should I start here? Of course I have white friends, but they're all radical thinkers, artists—and radical as in the meaning of the word... "To the root of the fregado reality," she murmured as the wind's tongue tasted her.

A very good looking gringo approached her. "Do you speak English?"

"Yes, I do actually." Her hackles went up

"May I join you, you look lonely," he smiled invitingly.

Somewhere in his late forties, she guessed, I look lonely, please. "I don't mean to be rude, but I'm enjoying just sitting here with my thoughts..."

His face registered surprise, anger, as he turned on his heel and strode away, tripping once on the cobbles. "Bitch."

"Home sweet home," Xochiquetzal said out loud to a group of well fed pigeons, waiting for a hand-out. "My country man, fuckhead." Her sensuality fled and was replaced by her anti-gringo USA armor. I was lucky to work, teach at a university with the young of all races, it kept my belief in humanity intact. Breathe, she told herself. And then the face of the young woman she'd seen crossing over to El Paso, as she was trying to cross over into the heart of Mexico, came to her, breathe.

A blaring ranchera sliced the air, coming closer, closer. A truck with speakers rolled by the plaza, the middle of town, pulling a large cage. With two staring tigers. Then they stopped in the middle of traffic, staring at people with disdain, or was it hunger... Tigers. El Tigre. She began to laugh, paying the waiter, tossing the rest of her sweet roll to the fat pigeons, and ran down the street. She could smell them, the tigers, musky and wild in the spite of the cage (their stubborn tiger spirits). Traffic began to move slowly. Xochiquetzal stood waving to each truck that passed, blaring the same ranchera, each driver smiling widely, waving back at her (the grown up kid)—one buffalo, two giraffes, two lions, two lamas and monkeys!!!

She wanted to follow them, the music, but her car was parked at the edge of tropical Juarez Parque, a half mile away. "Ayy Javier, mi tigre," she laughed into the invisible, sensual, Mexican wind. Life unedited. And the hungry eyes of the tigers terrified her with wonder. Life unedited. Right through the center of town. La vida.

Xochiquetzal crossed into the rainbow. And the young woman in Juarez crossed, holding her sliver of hope, the rainbow, in her stubborn hands.

At the top of the hill where the supermarket was, where she stocked up on large items for the week—small markets for vegetables, fruit—traffic came to a halt in the growing heat. "What now?" The cars began to move slowly past a man encouraging his cows, with a long stick, to stay off the road. Cars honked, not in irritation, but in friendly greeting. Cows were milk. Mexicans understood necessity. He was guarding the milk. Life unedited. Into the rainbow.

As Xochiquetzal turned into the parking lot, she saw it—rows and rows of cages, kids, families, teens standing and staring. The circus was being built in the large open space for the weekend by a small army of tireless Mexican workers as they laughed, joked and sang in the heat. Into the rainbow.

She walked over to join the small crowd in front of the tigers and she automatically reached for her camera bag...I want to take photos again. "Fertile, potent, la vida unedited," she murmured to the caged tigers. They paced as though preparing to hunt, and then they paused to stare out (fiercely, fiercely), hungrily. Male and female tigers, their wild, musky scent filled Xochiquetzal with a strange desire ("Bebo tu sangre...I drink your blood.") Tears filled her eyes; their undying longing. To be free. To hunt. Hunger.

She thought of the chained eagle in the Ubud Palace in Bali, in the beautiful, orchid-filled courtyard she'd wandered into. The eagle-eyed woman selling amber jewelry, watching her approach the chained eagle. "Madam, do not go near, very dangerous."

"Why is it chained, why isn't it allowed to fly free, it's so beautiful, is it a hawk?" Xochiquetzal didn't move forward or back away, gazing into the large bird's eyes. It was the largest bird she'd ever seen up close, and it's eyes were red with fierceness.

"No, it's an eagle, and you are the second tourist to ask me that this year, the Balinese do not ask, and most tourists don't dare ask," she laughed dryly. "Do you like amber, madam?"

Xochiquetzal turned to meet her sharp eagle-eyes, and asked again, "Why can't the eagle be free?"

Eagle Woman met her gaze like a target, a direct hit of sharp, accurate, deadly talons. "What is freedom, madam?"

"What is freedom, mis tigres?" Xochiquetzal whispered and walked quickly away. Eagle Woman, she'd found out over tea brought by a young girl, was a trance healer, and the chained eagle was her ally in healing. "The eagle aids me in dreaming," Eagle Woman had smiled ferociously into her eyes, daring her to look away. It took all her effort, but she hadn't turned away from those hungry eyes. She looked down to the amber ring she'd bought that day, how the sun filled it like honey. The color of the eagle's eyes, at the very center, surrounded by red. She'd also bought a beautifully made amber bracelet, earrings for herself and friends...she remembered Eagle Woman's laughter. Joyous. Caged. Free. Not free.

The sound of the Mexican workers laughing, singing with the blaring rancheras that sang of lust, love, joy, sorrow, the endless longing for freedom, filled her ears as she walked into the cool entry of the shopping area. "What is freedom, madam?" Xochiquetzal heard Eagle Woman clearly, and then her joyous, dry laugh. Life unedited.

Javier wondered if the young girl would live—raped, beaten, neighbors calling the police, her screams, her cries didn't stop that night. He'd never seen this kind of abuse on such a small, young body. So much suffering for someone not even ten yet. And she looked younger, malnourished obviously—no decent diet, no care, no play. He wondered if she could read or write, if there was any hope if she did live. She was dark-skinned, she wasn't especially pretty, she was poor, female, utterly abused.

He'd followed her up to Critical Care, searching for his favorite nurse; the older one with grown children of her own. "Can you take care of this little bird and call me if she gets worse, Maria?" Javier smiled into the kindness of her eyes, and he suddenly realized that Xochitzalita was older than his favorite nurse—But la verdad, the truth is that Maria looks older, so tired usually, always kind. True kindness, does that come with age, he wondered. Well, I haven't had anymore chica attacks, "Ayyy que cabron estoy," he sighed.

Javier gave the girl a small dose of codeine for pain, so she slept, her small body twitching from time to time. He adjusted all of her drips one more time, and then he smoothed her wild, dark hair from her face, stroking her battered cheek. "Viva, little bird, viva."

He glanced at his watch, it was time to call Xochitzalita. "Call me if she worsens, Maria, call me immediately."

"Si doctor," Maria smiled at his authority, his youth, his kindness. She picked up a soft, wet cloth and began to clean the girl's blood-smeared face—maybe a special sponge bath tomorrow or the next day, she noted, seeing the horror of her small body. If she survives tonight.

Xochiquetzal had fallen asleep with a book in her arms, the lamp still on. She reached for the phone on the fourth ring. "Tigre?"

Javier growled angrily, "Si Xochitzalita, es yo, it's me."

His opening growl was usually playful, not tonight.

"Are you okay?"

"A small girl was brought into the ER raped and beaten, she might die tonight, I'd kill that man if I could." He paused to breathe, trying to remember his doctor-patient rule of detachment. This is how you're able to continue to function, he told himself firmly. "Detachment," he said like a mantra, "without it, I can't do my job."

"Yes, detachment," she picked up the thread, "But how awful, I'll send a prayer to the universe for her tonight."

"Gracias, mi alma, I always forget you're not Catholic, but a Buddhist. To tell the truth, I think that's what I've become, a Buddhist, detachment, como no," he laughed softly.

"Actually, I'm a Buddhist, Earth-Cosmos worshipper," she echoed his laugh and suddenly, desperately, wanted to see his Zapata eyes like thirst, to feel his hands, his hands. His mouth. "Guess what I saw today?"

"I'm waiting," Javier breathed easier now.

"Un tigre, dos tigres."

"Did you take any photos for proof of this outlandish vision?" He smiled as though she were in front of him, tiny pin-points of desire (memory of their lust) at the center of his dark Nahuatl/Spanish eyes.

"I forgot to tell you, I'm a Ph.D. una doctora de fotos," she laughed, "but I took photos only with my eyes."

"Doctora de fotos, que bien, mi pochita," he smiled, "que bien."

"That's what I did at the university, Dr. Zapata, and so I did reach for my camera bag today so it must be time to begin again..."

"Why did you stop, querida?"

Silence.

"I'm waiting."

"My heart was broken. I thought I was getting old, losing my vision, not my eyes, *my vision,* do you understand, Javier?"

"Si tigressa mia, si." His eyes filled with tears of tenderness, the honesty of her words. So naked. "You speak my own truth, mujer tan hermosa, we needed to be born, los dos tigres juntos...the two tigers together."

"Fertile, potent, I miss your mouth, tus labios, your hands, tu locito Zapata sombrero on your head, tu grito ayyy." Xochidquetzal paused. "But I still think I'm too old for you, I'm still fifty-eight years old after all our births…"

"Callate, dame tu boca…Shut up, give me your mouth."

Tears pooled in her eyes; each one contained a world but she didn't know it. "I'm an old and bitter tiger, afraid to love you, afraid to be in a cage, afraid to be free without you now that I know you, yeah that's fifty-eight year old chingada me, Javier the fearless…"

"Callate, if I were there I'd kiss you, I'd fill your mouth with my tongue, with my words, I can taste you, callate mi amor, callate."

Each tear slowly traveled the length of her fifty-eight year old face; one world entered the corner of her lips. Instinctively, she licked it. As Goddess/God does when they're thirsty, when they're lonely in their perfection, when freedom becomes a cage, when love becomes longing, courage, a tiny salty world.

"I can taste you, Dr. Zapata," she murmured, thinking of the sky in Eagle Woman's eyes. Is that where he flies, her eagle, in that sky. "I was wondering…"

"Digame, tell me, mi amor cabroncita."

"Do you have our watermelons yet, I'm hungry."

"I will be at your door on Friday with my watermelons y mi Zapata sombrero tambien…"

"Not the Zapata sombrero, what will my neighbors think?" She smiled, seeing Javier so flamboyant, yet totally at ease, in the huge, black, gold-spangled sombrero.

"That Zapata has been reborn, and is visiting you with watermelons, como no."

"I can taste you, mi tigre."

The Energy Child wanted to taste the world, but s/he had no mouth. Yet.

Xochiquetzal turned off the lamp, looking out to the bright cluster of stars through the high, arched windows. During lightning strikes, and pre-dawn fireworks, she had a front row seat from her pillow. Once during a lightning storm, she woke up in time to see a flash of light enter, fill the room with its brightness. The brightness of dreams. Below the high, arched windows thick, cotton drapes kept out the night, stranger's eyes. But not the stars; she only had to look up. Stars.

Next time there's fireworks, I'll take my camera and tripod to the roof, she told herself, and maybe I'll keep my camera open for a few hours up there, see what appears. Galaxies. "La doctora de los fotos," she murmured to the fierce (reminding us we're in space), comforting stars (always home) framed by the high, arched windows.

Xochiquetzal reached for her dream pouch, filled with so many treasures, gifts: snake skin she found on a trail in Taos, wolf fur from an amiga who raised wolves, eagle down from a wing she found backpacking with an amiga in the Sierras, tiny shells from la mar, small stones with spirals (maps of the universe), Justin's baby teeth, crushed amethyst crystals he gave her in a pouch as a teenager, the woman/man/baby silver milagros...miracles, her ex-husband, Carlos, had given her when she was pregnant with their son, Justin; she kept them because they contained the miracle of Justin's birth, not for their marriage, not for him.

She placed the dream pouch to her dream eye (the invisible eye between our waking ones, as Mamacita had taught her, wearing her nightly red head-band to dream more clearly), and murmured her usual nightly prayer to the universe, the Earth, the stars, the world in a single, salty tear. "Power and wisdom come to me, bring me dreams to guide me, my path, and guide the ones I love." She paused to imagine a small girl, raped, beaten, Javier's hands comforting her. "And may the child Javier's caring for live, may her body and spirit heal, may it be so now, always now."

A black wind, edged in rainbows, covered the stars with thick, dark clouds, and sudden flashes of lightning surprised the sky. Tiny tears of rain from la mar laughed across Xochiquetzal's high, arched windows; each one contained a universe. The Energy Child wanted to taste the universe, so very thirsty, not yet.

Then the sky opened its rusty cage, letting the tigers of desire roam free, tearing perfection limb from limb, drinking perfection's sweet blood, until there was no loneliness left in the world. Only the bones of the most naked love were left, to gnaw on; the sweet marrow of imperfection, perfection, freedom, loneliness, hunger, desire.

She closed her eyes, feeling abandoned. Pregnant. Knowing it was impossible, yet she felt it. Fertile. Potent. Pregnant. The awful burden of freedom. The awful burden of love. Pregnant. Abandoned. Imperfect. Perfect. And though she wept, she also smiled, clutching her hunger, her desire. Dreams.

Xochiquetzal...*I'm sitting by the fireplace, a small winter fire, just blocks from the Pacific, la mar. The sound of Justin playing with his cat, laughing his baby delight as the orange-striped tiger cat softly swats his face, claws hidden in lush fur. He desires that fur and so he pushes his face into her furry stomach. He desires to be an orange-striped tiger cat, and so he crawls after her, making me laugh. He tries to eat her dry tiger food, and I rush to place it out of reach, take dry pieces out of his wet mouth. He begins to cry, then decides to laugh instead. That desire. That baby desire that has no shame, limits, sense of failure or success. He stands, falls, gets back on small hands and chubby knees, following his current teacher, the furry orange-striped tiger.*

Then, as though a million years of evolution had passed, Justin floats by me, upright, on his small, naked, human feet. Something's pulling him upright from the very top of his head. Desire.

I don't breathe, I stay silent. I witness my son's achievement. Pure desire.

His baby gift to me. That's what I want. Shameless. Baby. Pure. Desire.

This is. This is. This is. Deepest play.

———◆———

There was another car when Xochiquetzal arrived at La Gruta hot springs. For some reason it looked familiar, but she couldn't imagine why. She glanced at her watch, 8:05 a.m., a slight chill in the luscious morning air. She looked out at the rose bushes exploding with pink, red, orange, yellow fleshy-petaled blossoms. "I'll stop on the way out," she murmured to the beauty.

"Buenos dias," she smiled at the sweet-faced, older man who took her eighty pesos.

"Buenos dias, que bonita es la dia," he smiled, his wrinkles a beautiful pattern surrounding that smile. She'd seen his frown, deep in his thoughts, then back to an iridescent hummingbird's wing, slant of sun, cast of shadow, a lime-green bird singing its news. Praise, complaint, he couldn't tell, but at eighty-four he knew it was song.

Xochiquetzal paused to allow her eyes to adjust to all the greenery here. Fertility. Grass in every direction, trees, palms, so many flowers— potted in rows, sprouting from the earth, flowers. These mountains were dry with acres of cactus, as well as acres of fertile farmland at 7,000 feet. La Gruta (the farmland) was watered, kept this fertile, lush, with the never-ending flow of thermal water. Potent.

She ran to the main pool (with the dark tunnel leading to la gruta, the grotto), her thick towel warding off the chill. Chill, I love it, she thought shivering, now the warm water. As she eased herself in blissfully, she saw a couple from the corner of her eye, and decided to give them privacy while it lasted. Xochiquetzal slowly
breast-stroked through the warm, morning blue, silk water toward the sound of the waterfall, the dark tunnel.

"Xochitzalita," a man called.

She was standing at the tunnel's entrance and the sound of the waterfall was roaring, soothing. She looked toward the voice: Pablo. Ohmyfuckinggoddess it's fregado Pablo, she realized with a jolt. She waved and continued through the darkness toward the waterfall where (what she called) *the tangible light* lived. She didn't float and take her time as usual through the tunnel, expecting to hear her name again; but she turned once to survey the blue world of light at the entrance. Empty, good.

The roar of the waterfall was loud now and then she saw it: the tangible light. The first time she entered the dark grotto, with the small holes on its roof, she thought there was a glowing, white pipe from the roof to the steaming water. When she put her hand out to touch it (the glowing, white pipe), her hand passed through it: light. The tangible light. That first time, a group of Indian women eased themselves into the hot gruta water (hotter than outside), each woman smiling her way. They made a circle—from teens to grandmothers—and began to chant. Xochiquetzal thought of those women, their sweet, full voices filling the grotto, her heart, her womb. They reminded her of the women in Bali, the temple, who sang so deeply, from their wombs. She'd never heard women sing like that, before Bali, and now she was hearing it again in Mexico.

She stood under the waterfall, surrendering to its stream of power. The tangible light. She chanted softly with no words, just a steady stream, song, from her womb. She sang to Justin who came from her womb, to Javier who knew its taste, to her mother's womb, and her mother's womb, she sang.

The Energy Child wanted to sing, but no mouth, not yet.

When Xochiquetzal emerged from the waterfall, Pablo was standing in front of her with an irritated look on his handsome face. The first thing she'd noticed when they'd met in the outside pool, was that he looked like Antonio Banderas. In fact, her first thought was, What's Banderas doing in La Gruta? as she tried not to stare.

"Why didn't you stop to say hello, are you trying to *ignore me*?"

She laughed at his usual honesty. "I didn't see you at first, Pablo, I just saw a couple and thought I'd give you some privacy before the crowd arrives."

"You could come and say hello, she's someone I'm seeing. I've thought of calling you…"

"She looks in her twenties, very beautiful, so how are you?" she tried to change the subject. Pablo was turning fifty, still handsome, and in command of his sensual, Mexican charm, that confidence, in the body. And he's a Ph.D. in Eastern Philosophy, un doctor tambien, she smiled…Ayyy Diosa, I'm a magnet for the wild doctor type, my first date in San Miguel, almost relationship. What happened, she asked herself…I just wasn't ready.

"I'm going to Thailand, Bali, and probably India, in a month or so, for my buying trips, you know my antique import shop." Pablo's English had that lovely accent and it only made her miss Javier, los ojos del tigre.

"Are you taking tu hermosa amiga? As you know, I love Bali, I was just thinking of Bali, anyway sounds like fun, and how are your daughters?" He's with a woman his daughter's ages, and he's not guilt ridden, but it's *normal* for a man to do it.

Pablo laughed. "Are you trying to point out I'm with someone my daughters' age, but yes they're both fine, at university in Guanajuato. Are you seeing someone, Xochitzalita, you know I miss our talks. I can't find someone like you to talk to, que chingado," he gazed at her smiling his half-smile.

Xochiquetzal looked at the tangible light and decided to tell the truth—Men can do it, why can't women, she told herself, and added, que fregado. "I seem to be seeing someone close to my son's age, just like you," she giggled, dunking herself in the hot, lovely water, then surfaced slowly, opening her eyes. "Shouldn't you get back to your friend, she must be wondering..."

"Ayy cabrona, younger than me, is it serious?"

"He's pretty wonderful, to tell the truth, but I don't know, he's too young for me. Men can do it, in the long run, Pablo, but not women, so we'll see que pasa..."

"Is he from San Miguel, what does he do, a waiter, you know sometimes the young guys go after the dinero, the money, so watch yourself, Xochitzalita, you're in Mexico, the land of the poor young guys," he laughed.

"All I can tell you is that he's a physician, a wonderful person, and I like him."

"Then why worry, you have that timeless thing como La Cleopatra," more laughter. "Come and meet her, you'll like her, Sonya."

"I'd rather not, but you'd better get back there, cabron, are you still insane?" Xochiquetzal laughed remembering their first date, the others.

"Okay, okay, no me chingas, I'll always be muy loco and I'll call you." Pablo caught her eyes, held them, moving closer as though to kiss her, and then playfully kissed her on the cheek, laughing, and disappeared into the tunnel.

"You almost got slapped!" she laughed.

Pablo's grito echoed into la gruta.

Back into the waterfall, she thought of their first date...she'd just ordered a drink at Mama Mia's in the bar area, close to the entrance. A margarita on the rocks. It was a hot night in May (the hottest month of the year, her second month in San Miguel). She was wearing a thin, white, Mexican blouse with vibrant red, purple flowers at the neckline and an equally thin, cool, white, tiered, ankle length skirt, no slip, cool. Sandals. And a light, lacy red shawl just to cover her shoulders. The most immense margarita she'd ever seen arrived, sweating in ice, and on the third delicious, lots of tequila sip, Pablo blew in the entrance.

He had a red scarf tied around his head, dashingly, the way the young men do it at the yearly Sanmiguelada bull run in the central plaza. His white Mexican shirt was open to his navel, tight jeans, nice sandals, muy sexy a el Banderas. "Xochitzalita, hurry, I'm double parked in front, come on, I'll get a chingado ticket!"

"I just ordered this wonderful margarita..."

"Here, I'll help you." Pablo picked up the huge glass with one hand and emptied it in a few long gulps. "Ayy que delicioso, and you look wonderful, very ethnic," he laughed. His Jeep was right by the curb, and he opened her door. "Enter mi reina, my queen, I looked you up on the internet, que accomplishments, una profesora, photo shows, a journalist, it's all on tu web site."

"I'm thinking of taking it down, and so did you get your Ph.D. in Piled Higher And Deeper?" she laughed. "And you drank my entire margarita, Pablo!"

"There's more where I'm taking you, no worries, fear not, mi reina."

"Ay Diosa, you're such a bullshitter, where are we going?"

This only made him laugh louder and drive faster. "You'll see when we get there, it's a surprise, Xochitzalita!" When traffic halted on the cobble streets, Pablo started a conversation with an older man in a leather cowboy hat—"Chinga tu madre, a donde vas, amigo...Where are you going, my friend, with your brand new truck?"

Chinga tu madre means 'Fuck your mother,' Xochiquetzal realized, shrinking in her seat, expecting bullets to fly past her. This guy is insane.

The man in the cowboy hat guffawed loudly and returned the greeting, talking loudly until traffic began to move. "I'm going home to my old lady, where else?"

"Qué te vaya bien...May it go well!" Pablo yelled.

"Y tu tambien, amigo!" The brand-new, white truck sped off.

"I thought saying chinga tu madre was fightin' words, like someone might kill you..."

"Lighten up, gringita reina, you're in Mexico, and that guy is a filthy rich chingadero rancher," Pablo laughed, and continued to insult a few more fellow drivers as Xochiquetzal stayed low in her seat, her face turned away.

"You are insane, Pablo."

"Gracias, mi reina." He smiled as though she'd given him a compliment, and clicked on belly dance music, loudly, starting to dance in his seat. "I learned to belly dance on my travels, do you know how? If not, I can teach you," he laughed, continuing to dance as he drove over and around every pot hole.

He came to a stop in front of an outlandish building—it resembled a surreal Disneyland Mexican dream with a gigantic, gothic frog, and other creatures crawling up and down, what looked like, a luxurious warehouse. A carved wooden chair, made for a giant, waited by the immense, ornately carved, Mexican doors, that were wide open; and a full suit of armor, lance in gloved hand, stood guard at the top of the four cement steps.

"This is my place, how do you like it?" Pablo laughed as he parked the Jeep under a large, metallic sign, JEFE…BOSS.

"My Goddess…"

"Do you mean Kali or Shakti?"

Xochiquetzal laughed, "All of them, I love it, that frog…"

"Guanajuato, the Mexican state you now live in, means 'the place of the frogs,' pochita reina."

"You can call me pochita but spare me gringita, por favor, I got shit in the USA for being a spic, a wetback, then I come here to be called gringita…"

"Calmate, Xochitzalita, calmate, *que genio,* but I know what you mean, I belted someone in Los Angeles for calling me a wetback on a visit there," Pablo laughed.

"What does that mean, que genio?"

"I'll tell you later, but right now I have a surprise por La Cleopatra, you really resemble her, you know…"

"Piled higher, piled deeper, estas loco!"

Pablo became serious, toned his energy down four notches. "I see you're an accomplished photographer and a journalist, I'd like us to travel together, I feel I can talk to you, Xochitzalita."

"I'm more of a photographer than a journalist, though I did some here and there." His sincerity, his offer, took her by surprise.

"And I see you're also piled higher and deeper, okay now for the good part!" Before she could say another word, he was opening her door. "You look like a Mexicana reina in The Place Of The Frogs, women like you usually choose to be in front of the camera, como no."

"Please stop," she gazed at the creatures crawling on the exterior; they were weird and enchanting. "I want to be the creator, not the created, I guess, plus my features don't translate well, I'm not pretty in a photo…"

Pablo took her right hand and pulled her past the full suit of armor, huge planters
with gigantic, dangerous looking cactus standing guard, the giant's chair, and so much more. The sudden explosion of a mariachi band filled the air, her ears, and rattled her bones with its fullness.

"What the hell is that?"

"It's for you, Xochitzalita, in your reina, queenly honor."

"You're kidding, you've got to be kidding."

He pulled her through the wide open doors. A full mariachi band with trumpets, violins, guitars, and a very handsome, older man with full grey hair, a dark mustache, threw out his chest and belted Cielito Lindo. Tears filled her eyes, one of Mamacita's favorite songs to dance to. She'd danced it many times with Mamacita in the kitchen, the radio blaring her favorite song. And Xochiquetzal could hear her singing, "Canta no llores...Sing don't weep," as they danced.

"Canta no llores," Pablo placed the words directly into her ear over the music. Each musician looked handsome in their beautiful, black, edged in a deep red with silver spangles, mariachi outfit. Each man tilted their head in greeting; each one meeting her eyes. In the body, each man, from their teens to their seventies.

There was an ornate, hand-carved chair at the top of some steps, the mariachis taking up all the space below in the showroom. All the beautiful statues from Bali, Thailand, India, large pieces of furniture from Mexico, Latin America, had been pushed back to the walls so the band would fit. And they did, perfectly, as they launched into another song, followed by a few gritos. They were warming up, smiling at her with pleasure, amusement, joy.

"This is your queen's chair, Xochitzalita, please sit down, por favor," Pablo laughed with delight. The mariachis paused for a beat to smile in unison as she sat down, feeling ostentatious, slightly absurd. A young woman appeared to her right with a platter of food and what looked like a margarita. She placed the platter, the icy drink (not as huge as Mama Mia's) on a lotus-carved wooden table next to her. Xochiquetzal sipped, a perfect on-the-rocks-rimmed-in-salt margarita. And then, an older man brought a pitcher of margaritas, more glasses, and an unopened bottle of tequila, which he deftly opened.

"Is your margarita strong enough, Xochitzalita, I'm Pablo's manager, Renee, at your queenly service," he smiled widely. He leaned forward as though to tell her a secret. "I've never seen him do this, que genio, soy impressed."

"Hey, I'm in shock but it's amazing, and my drink is perfecto, gracias, and what does genio mean, Renee?"

He looked at her with amusement and said, "Genio means, mostly, genius, the spirit of a genius, and that he is, el Jefe Pablo, you'll see."

Pablo placed a small, hand-carved wooden chair next to her's, and the young woman poured him a margarita, to which he added a generous shot of the aged, amber tequila. "Ayy que perfecto," he threw his head back and laughed. "Are you happy, Xochitzalita?"

"I should be, I don't lack a thing," she laughed with him.

The beautiful song had come to a halt, and the handsome, older singer stepped forward to ask if she had any requests, his dark eyes gently resting on her hazel ones.

"Sabes esta cancion...Do you know this song, Cu cu ru cu cu paloma," she sang softly, slightly embarrassed by her attempt.

A wonderful smile lit up his dark face and tiny lightning bolts from his eyes flew to meet hers. He turned to face the band, singing the first line in a voice filled with tears and joy. Equally. The mariachis pounced on it as though they were starved, holding nothing back. As Xochiquetzal watched, tears streaming down her face, she saw each man's soul revealed to each note, each word. They held nothing back, que genio. In that moment, there were tears and joy, life and death, body and soul. In that moment, she could hear Mamacita singing without shame as she did with the radio playing very loudly, as the kitchen became Mexico. She opened her mouth to join the lone singer going for the high note, "Cu cu ru cu cu..," and she heard Mamacita's voice blending with his, fully expecting to see her emerge from the shadows. "Paloooma..."

"Finish your margarita and stop crying, por favor, I did this to make you happy." Pablo looked at her closely, smiling his half-smile.

"I am happy, I just heard mi abuelita, my grandmother, singing, she loved this song..."

Pablo took her left hand, and commanded the mariachis to play something to dance to. He pulled her to her feet. "Come on, we're dancing!"

It was a kind of ranchera fandango that made the dead want to dance—the guitarists took the thumping beat, the trumpets wailed pure passion, and the violins tempted the spirit. Pablo grabbed Xochiquetzal by the waist and danced her through the mariachis expertly; she'd never been led like this before. A hard, coiled part of her—somewhere in her womb—resented it, yet she couldn't deny it, longed for it. To be grabbed, to be led, expertly, to be loved. Simply to be loved.

Xochiquetzal reminded herself, He doesn't love me, he just wants to fuck me (her hard, coiled part argued). Pablo continued to hold onto her, holding her at arm's length for a moment, laughing into her eyes as though he knew exactly what she was thinking. And he didn't care.

Pablo slid her red, lacy shawl from her shoulders (wrapping it around his neck), as the mariachis launched into another foot stomping fandango tune. Two of the violin players lowered their violins and joined the singer. They sang about love, loss, jealousy, desire, in the full-throated voices the poet, Lorca, described as *duende* (when the human spirit journeys to the edge of death, joyously).

And then Pablo stopped dancing, and placed the red shawl into her hands. "Here's your cape, Xochitzalita, I'm el toro, the bull, get ready," he smiled with sheer mischief.

"What?' was all she could muster, standing with her red, lacy shawl dangling limply from her hands. She glanced at the mariachis, and each man was smiling at her. They're in on it, Xochiquetzal thought with sudden paranoia; like the first joint she ever smoked, that loss of control. Pleasure, fear, pleasure, fear, pleasure...and at the end ravenous hunger. She pulled the shawl out como un matador, and waited, smiling so deeply no one could see it (her dark, empty womb).

Pablo positioned himself at the far end of the space between them, as the music, singers, went wild. He made two horns with his upraised fingers, pawed the floor with his feet, never smiling, staring at her, intently. Then he rushed forward—ear splitting gritos from the band—barely missing her body, as she swept the red shawl over his crouched-over, horns-on-the-head body. The entire band shouted, "OLE!," which made her laugh, sending shivers up her spine. The lotus on fire tattoo, she flashed, unseen by man. This made her laugh harder, and it felt so good.

The hard, coiled part of herself slightly softened, expanded, as Pablo passed again, making a deep, roaring sound as he slightly nudged her over with one of his horns. She shrieked with surprise as the band shouted, "OLE!"

In his bull-gathering corner, Pablo scraped the floor more passionately with his feet, over and over, aiming his upright fingers toward her, making deep, roaring sounds from his throat. As he came flying past her (and she saw, aiming for her body), Xochiquetzal pierced him with stiffened fingers. He yelled with enthusiasm, and fell, wounded ,at her feet, taking the red shawl with him. It lay over his body, looking strangely like fresh, spilled blood.

"BRAVA!" the band shouted, "BRAVA!"

"You can get up now, Pablo El Toro," she laughed with delight.

"Dame un besito...Give me a kiss." He remained, wounded, on the floor, gazing up at her. "Give me a kiss, Xochitzalita, or I won't get up."

"Not here," she laughed.

"BESO!" Pablo yelled as though he were truly dying, which made her laugh harder.

"Beso beso beso beso..." the mariachis echoed, smiling directly at her, no longer playing their music.

"Ayy Diosa, what a big baby, or should I say baby bull."

"I don't care what you call me, un beso, Xochitzalita, un beso, ayyyy..."

"Beso beso beso beso beso..." the band echoed, laughing.

She knelt down and lightly kissed Pablo on his waiting, pouting lips. As she began to pull away, he held her by the back of the neck kissing her deeply, exactly as she liked it. In public. In Mexico. The Place Of The Frogs. To "BRAVO!"

Then he made her dance with every mariachi, teens to seventies, each one handsome in their own unique way. Each one in their body...

Xochiquetzal heard voices coming through the tunnel, bringing her back to the present. And the memory of the mariachis yelling, "Beso beso beso," her first public kiss in Mexico, made her weep, as her recent memory in Vallarta with Javier, "Regalo regalo regalo." And all the gritos of sorrow, joy—*duende.* She still had the sheer, red shawl that had been her cape; and she also had the body shawl he'd placed in her hands at her door, after their final, lingering kiss that night. It literally wrapped the body; it could be worn alone (if you were daring). It was made of the most sensual, ancient, green silk; as though Marco Polo had brought it from China; with lines of hand-stitched gold beading, red-beaded flowers with purple gems at the center. Pablo claimed it had been made for a Turkish queen, which he'd bought on his travels in Turkey, and now it was draped over her bedroom door. The room he never entered, to see the morning sun cause it to catch golden fire as he returned from dreams, a night of lovemaking.

Why did I open the door to Javier in Vallarta, I barely knew him, why? she asked herself, gazing at the tangible light (the voices much closer). It whispered, *El toro prepared you, his gift.* "Pablo," she whispered, remembering the young, lone mariachi, at the end of the evening, who stepped forward to recite a heartbreaking poem—about love, that wounding you give as el matador, you receive as el toro, el amor. And sometimes el toro wounds, kills, but most often he's the one who dies, *el duende.* The edge of death, that journey to sorrow/joy. His voice had been so full of longing, and at the end of the poem he suddenly laughed, to the sound of gritos.

After a nap, Xochiquetzal checked her email: Justin, Javier, Tara, Raul (the student in the airport, Vallarta), and some others.

Hola La Orchid Xochitzalita,
I'm beyond missing you, I'm dying of thirst, don't laugh at me, I know you are, you and your "In this moment, right now, I love you" mierda. I want to hear the fearless version this weekend or I won't share my delicious ripe watermelon, I can be malo y loco tambien jajajaja...
THE GIRL LIVES!!!! Battered but still breathing, so my detachment has returned for the time being, her father is in jail where the chingadero monstruo, el monster, belongs—or out of the body, dead. Will be working 16 hour shifts, pray for me to your Buddha, so I won't call at midnight, but instead will *see you, touch you, smell you, taste you* this Friday around 5 p.m. as I'll take a nap before I drive to San Miguel. I'll bring the watermelons, take your vitamins, mi amor—see how fearless I am, Tu Tigre.

Hola Mom—I'm still in graduate school, starting thesis paper (in case you had doubts LOL), doing the teen counseling thing while smoking an apple or two, as I taught you in San Miguel. And I met someone actually intelligent, interesting, also not bad to look at, and she also surfs, is a psyche grad student like tu hijo with my journalism minor. Okay, I'm coming for Xmas vacation at least 10 days or so, if you can buy your poverty stricken hijo a tic, cool. I'm also writing some stories, essays for the local mag, what I really want to do is travel with my journalism while psyching people out LOL, and so I'll call you soon, set up day/time,

all one long sentence, love you, don't take any wooden pesos.
Justin xoxo

Hey Expat,
I miss you and will probably be coming for spring vacation,
take in the self flagellation, maybe join in, who knows, pick
up a young Jesus type. Any Man Reports? You're being very
silent, amiga, and bugging the hell outta me. I've gotta list
of emails asking for your current email, but will keep my
lips sealed, or my fingers frozen, until you give me the word.
Even your web site doesn't have it so I'm getting an edge of
irritation from a couple of work shop planners—don't you
need la moola? Also, some int'l email, hey my email's on
your damned web site: Gone on emergency vision quest,
REVISION, email my amiga, Tara, gracias. Girl, yer gettin'
corny but I still love ya. Zip me an email and spill los frijoles,
life at the U ain't the same since we don't hang out no more.
Tara (I need a revision, and I'm coming—any black folks
there haha, a hunky Mexican will do.)

Professora Xochiquetzal,
I wrote this poem por mi novia, girl firend, and I've
translated it into English. If you come to Guanajuato for
Cervantino Fiesta let me know, and If I drop in on SMA
will let you know. I enjoyed meeting you. Also, my girl
friend tore my BEST ORIGINAL FOREPLAY t-shirt
into little pieces, she's jealous, will have to buy another one
next time in Vallarta. She didn't want to come to Vallarta,
or she couldn't, who knows, I doubt that we'll get married.
Okay, send me a poem.
Abrazos, Raul

THE DOVE, THE LEOPARD

I forgive you for destroying
my favorite t-shirt, it shows

how much you love me, Sylvia.
My BEST ORIGINAL FOREPLAY just for

you, no one else, and you think there was
someone else in Vallarta. I'm young.

I have to test my skills, amor, but
there's only you, Sylvia, forgive me

as the spirits roam this town, the ancient
tunnels dark in the noon sun.

Forgive me at 5 in the afternoon, as Lorca
sang "At 5 in the afternoon..." and

"Now the dove and the leopard wrestle
at 5 in the afternoon..." And if you

leave me, Sylvia mi amor, I will wear my BEST ORIGINAL
FOREPLAY t-shirt in Guanajuato.
(ayyyy soy cabron, Raul)

That night as Xochiquetzal tried to write a poem about the
hummingbird she saw at La Gruta, she thought of Javier in the seventh
hour of his sixteen hour shift. I'm fifty-eight, retired from teaching full
time, on a fregado emergency vision quest, she told herself—and Javier
is a young doctor trying to keep his detachment on sixteen hour shifts
in Emergency. What am I thinking, get real, pendeja, revision, what
planet are you on? Her brain wouldn't let her stop. And how will I
introduce Justin to Javier? Will I introduce Justin to Javier? The dove
wrestles with the leopard, only I'm no fucking dove. I'm the embittered,
decrepit leopard—this made her laugh out loud, surprising herself like
a sudden grito. And she wrote another stanza for the poem, with the
great Persian poet, Rumi, as her guide:

I am filled with you.
Skin, blood, bone, brain and soul.
There's no room for lack of trust, or trust.
Nothing in this existence but that existence."

His words at the top of the poem—a few hard won stanzas, with
her new one:

I chant to all that exists, existence. This. A tiny
iridescent hummingbird pauses to sip the tiniest yellow
blossoms, the sexual penis-shaped purplish fruit
dangling from the fertile banana tree,

a crown of tiny bananas begin to sprout,
and underneath the sexual penis-shaped purplish
fruit, the tiniest so sweet yellow blossoms,
the iridescent hummingbird sipping this ripeness,

filling its swift body with this, existence,
this potent fertile blossomed ripening essence,
existence. This. Ripening. This.
Filling (fertile potent) essence.

I want to touch your feet, to kiss
them, to remember your
first steps, your footprints
glowing in the world.

I want to caress your calves, your knees,
your thighs, to lick the salt gathered there,
the years I didn't know you were alive, yet
I dreamt you, heard your voice.

Xochiquetzal finally found the dream (in her dream journal).
Nearly four years ago: "His face, in the dream, commanding my
attention...his eyes staring directly into mine...and he tells me, 'You
will love me like no other, yes you will.' As he speaks light flows out
of his mouth reaching me like a wind." And his eyes, his eyes, from
so many lives, Javier's eyes, young/old/new/ancient/terror/wonder/
endless/curiosity, those beautiful, x-ray eyes.

She could barely keep her own eyes open, thinking of Javier in
Emergency, with nine more hours to go until he could sleep—Will I
give him the poem to read, she asked herself...maybe. "There's no room
for lack of trust, or trust." Maybe. Then, she heard the voice from the
dream, You will love me like no other, yes you will.

Xochiquetzal...*I'm so close to something yellow, I'm becoming blind,*

blind with yellow, and I want it. This blinding, yellow world. Flowers, tiny yellow flowers. A scent of pure, sweet desire. I extend my tongue. Sip. My wings are tireless. My heart a tiny golden sun. Sip sip sip sip pure sweet yellow desire. I'm blind with yellow.

On the walk to the plaza, Xochiquetzal paused to give the older, blind man—always with his grandson—fifty pesos. "Gracias, muy amable...how kind, gracias," he smiled; his grandson echoing, "Gracias, señora," with a child's joy. Further on, she bought a bag of pan dulce for the old women wrapped in their rainbow rebozos; they sat in shady doorways, wrinkled hands extended. As she gave them a pan dulce, twenty pesos, each woman blessed her; and then it was her turn, "Gracias."

She bought two jars of clear, amber honey (which made her think of Eagle Woman in Bali: What is freedom, madam?), from the man who'd brought a bag full in the early morning, from the countryside, to sell on the streets of San Miguel. For tomorrow, for Javier, Xochiquetzal smiled, sweet honey. A man selling strawberries stopped her, and she chose twenty immense, so red jewels—for tomorrow, for Javier. A young woman, with a baby strapped to her breast, offered her freshly made cobalt blue corn tortillas. She bought two dozen (for tomorrow, for Javier), and tipped her ten pesos. The young woman's smile paid her back, every peso. She thought of the young woman she'd seen crossing into El Paso, and Xochiquetzal hoped she was making in one day what she might make in a week in her beloved Mexico.

She paused in the shade of a doorway, and, with one hard tug, opened a jar, scooped a taste of the amber with the tip of her finger... "What is freedom, madam?" she murmured. "The taste of yellow," she answered herself, "the taste of flowers, the tiniest flowers." (The Energy Child tried to taste the amber honey, the yellow, no mouth, not yet.) And to choose your own life, she silently added, for the young woman in El Paso (now in Los Angeles, a maid at the Sheraton, and she did make more in a day than she did in a week in her beloved México lindo, México querido).

"México lindo, México querido," Mamacita would say with such longing. Her eyes staring far away, filled with memories, and tears, never falling. These were the moments she'd silently told Xochiquetzal to take her spirit home someday, to San Miguel de Allende, Mexico. The roof top, April, violet twilight...the pure, white dove.

She walked into the coolness of her favorite church, entirely run by nuns, always filled with flowers, La Virgen in the most beautiful, blue outfit, and her son, Jesus, also dressed in a nice outfit, with a hint of a smile on his face (no wounds, no blood). And the dark-skinned Virgen de Guadalupe had her very own altar to the side, candles lit.

Xochiquetzal approached El Nino Doctorcito, a cute male doll with sweet brown eyes, brown hair, dressed entirely in white with his toy stethoscope draped around his niño neck. His golden halo rayed out around his baby head and his sweet, red heart was enclosed in golden rays. His right hand held a small, black medical bag with a silver, angel milagro...miracle, attached to it (and the silver angel was feminine, sensual, with her outstretched wings). A small wall of silver milagros were pinned behind him: arms, legs, hands, eyes, girls, boys, men, women, hearts...and small photos of people who wanted to be healed, who were healed.

At his baby feet, covered in white shoes, were his toys: a pile of cars, trucks, bouncy balls of every color, a tiny brown bear, and a silver laser gun. The laser gun was wedged tight to the small throne on which he sat. She hadn't seen it before, a gun, it perplexed her. Then, of course, a healer must also have the power to kill (Shakti, Kali, Vishnu, Quetzalcoatl...). Maybe that's the detachment Javier needs to learn, she sighed loudly, superimposing his face over El Nino Doctorcito's. This healing stuff is hard, the killing/death/transformation of the old embittered jaguar (it came to her), for that sip of those tiny yellow flowers. Nectar. Ripeness.

Xochiquetzal's eyes rested on the vividly orange, plastic roses tucked between his toys, and then she carefully placed her cinnamon scented candle between two lit ones. She lit her candle, bending over to smell its cinnamon. "Show me the way of transformation, healing, Nino Doctorcito."

As she placed some pesos in his collection box, an older man with a missing eye approached her, telling the story of how he lost his eye at work. And did she have some extra pesos for El Nino, for him. She understood every word in Spanish; it was the speaking that still wasn't fluent (not since Mamacita, being forced to learn/speak English at six). Our Spanglish, Javier and I, tomorrow, yes tomorrow.

She listened to his story to the end and reached for some pesos, saying, "Qué lastima...how tragic."

Xochiquetzal and the old man placed their pesos into El Nino Doctorcito's collection box and as he paused to say his prayer, she placed forty pesos by his small, tired, brown, worker's hand. "Qué Dios te bendiga....May God bless you, señora."

"Y tu tambien, gracias," she smiled adios and walked the few steps to La Virgen de Guadalupe, always the focus of Mamacita's altars (strewn with silver milagros, old prayers, fresh prayers...really poems, they were so beautifully written...lit candles, some red roses, always red roses, and flowers Xochiquetzal would pick on their walks). "En cambio tu nunca mueras, Mamacita...In transformation you never die," she sang softly, placing some pesos in the collection box at La Virgen's naked feet, lit by a blaze of candles.

She remembered her mother, Florinda, complaining about the lit candles, reminding Mamacita to blow them out before leaving the apartment. "This superstitious stuff, que los altars, will burn our place down." In the early morning Xochiquetzal saw her mother kneeling, candles lit, eyes closed. "En cambio tu nunca mueras, Mama," she murmured.

The sound of the tiny birds that found their way into the church echoed in the beautiful dome overhead; their song was perfect for this place. Sacred only the way bird song can be and it was pitched high like a call to pay attention, be awake. *Let the ecstasy go.* Xochiquetzal sat down on a bench under the high dome to listen, and glimpse their dark wings. At each four corners of the dome was a magnificent painting of a man writing; one was writing with a monster-being at his feet. She imagined Sor Juana writing, a languid jaguar at her feminine feet. Yes, she smiled sadly, creativity must be from an untamed, wild, extravagant source; something never tamed, like love. She put her head back on the bench, gazing up at the monster-being with its wild lion head and human hands. "Qué genio," she murmured.

The central fountain at the Bellas Artes was filled with flowers today and butterflies kept landing to sip—moving their yellow, orange, white, black wings—making the bunches of yellow, white lilies, the deep orange and red roses, come to life. The tall, sturdy stand of luxuriant-green bamboo filtered the cooling breezes and the pregnant, ripe oranges waited to be picked. The overly ripe avocados that fell to the ground were pecked open by birds and the brazen pigeons lined up to wait for their share of her breakfast. Entranced with simple joy, Xochiquetzal sat at her favorite table with this view, as well as La Virgen perched at the top of the dome of her favorite church (where her candle for El Nino Doctorcito burned, a prayer for Javier's sixteen hour shift, his drive to San Miguel tomorrow, with watermelons, Javier, tomorrow). She gazed at La Virgen's metal halo that reflected the sun and moon equally; her serene face, that inward Buddha smile.

"Tonglen," she whispered, breathing in the fear, breathing out some joy, "may all those crossing the USA border today make it alive, in peace, tonglen."

"Talking to yourself again, I see," Roberto smiled, setting her coffee down in front of her. "How was Vallarta, haven't seen you in awhile." Roberto was the head waiter and an art student, a painter. He spoke very good English and had an American sense of humor (like her old students), since he made the journey, once a year, to see his mother who lived in Los Angeles.

"I was doing tonglen, the Buddhist practice I told you about, I was sending peace to everyone crossing the border today." Xochiquetzal sipped the delicious coffee. "Qué rica, esta café, yum."

"I remember tonglen, I'll send some too, yes. I'll keep it coming, I know how you like your morning fix," he smiled.

"Do you ever just want to stay in L.A...."

Roberto looked directly into her eyes (Mexican men in their bodies, she noted), "I'd miss this too much, Xochitzalita." He swept his eyes to include everything, then back to her. "And Vallarta, how was it, did you meet anyone?" he smiled.

"Yes, I see what you mean, this daily beauty." She paused, feeling his eyes on her. "I love Vallarta, actually I was in Bucerias about ten miles north, big stretch of beach, pina coladas at 10am ayy," Xochiquetzal laughed. I want to keep Javier to myself, my very own delicious secret (tomorrow he comes with watermelons, tomorrow).

"I have to go next year, but I stay at this cheapie hotel in Vallarta's centro, lots of fun, too much tequila y muchas chicas," Roberto grinned. "Do you want to go salsa dancing Saturday, we can share a pizza as usual around 8 p.m...." He was even younger than Justin at twenty-eight (and yes, very handsome), but he was truly like her old students, and now he was a friend she went salsa dancing with on Saturday nights from time to time.

"How about next Saturday at 8 p.m., I'll be there...Put on your red dress, baby, cause we're goin' out tonight..." she sang the old blues song that always made him laugh. "Are you still seeing that cutie I saw you with last time, tell the truth."

Being with Xochitquetzal was a little like crossing the border, so it made him feel that extra edge of freedom he felt in L.A. He stayed with his mother and worked as a waiter, visiting the big museums, small galleries, during his three month stay. He traveled the city with his sketch pad, pencils, water colors, and went to the beach on his days off to draw, paint. At night he went to some Latin night clubs, watching out for gang bangers, that kind of violence San Miguel hadn't prepared him for.

"Okay, next Saturday, and this time wear that red dress, Xochitzalita. No, someone else, my Mom says I'm too pinche picky, she wants grandchildren, and I want to paint and travel some more," he laughed. "You want your spinach omelette, right?"

As she watched Roberto walk away, the sound of the fountain constant like la mar, she sighed—Of course, I'm more comfortable with younger people, my students, their wacky view of la vida, their humor, and maybe some of their youth wore off on me, I'm used to it. Talking about the good old days or whatever, bores la ca ca out of me, that's the truth and I can't pretend otherwise. And tomorrow, tomorrow mi tigre, Javier. Would he mind my going dancing with Roberto, ridiculous, we've just met, we're not 'going steady,' she smiled to herself, get real, and Tara with her Man Report, I'm avoiding it, Justin meeting Javier, if it lasts that long, yes get real ayy...

Xochiquetzal felt eyes on her, Roberto. "More coffee?" he mouthed from the doorway. His gaze was unflinching, then catching himself, playful as always.

"Por favor," she mouthed back, nodding yes, laughing, feeling Javier's presence fill the courtyard, the fountain filled with flowers, butterfly wings. His words from Vallarta came to her, "In Mexico there's mama, and then there's *mamacita*." She saw his taunting, sunlit smile—she remembered when Justin was a teen, they'd go out once a week for dinner just to talk, catch up, laugh, and she knew his friends thought it was 'weird.'

"Dude, I wouldn't go out on a date with the old lady." "It's not a date, asshole, she's my mom and she's cool." "Yeah, she's cool but she's still your mom, dude." "Get a life, loser," Justin laughed. She'd overheard once, watching him and his friends file out the door in their wet suits. Justin came back for the sodas, snacks, kissed her on the cheek, laughing, "In case you heard that, Dave's an idiot, Mom." Most of his friends would be tossed out by their parents for doing drugs, drinking; and they'd share Justin's room for weeks, months. They'd learn to sit at the dinner table, talking about real things in their lives, and add their jokes to the usual daily skit.

Here in Mexico teens held hands with their mother, their father; sat next to their grandparents on the plaza benches, talking, laughing, kissing them on the cheek before joining the other teens, as Justin had done with her. And Xochiquetzal realized...I brought him up the way Mamacita brought me up, the way she was brought up, in Mexico. Justin doesn't hate women as Mexican men don't hate women—the clarity of this thought staggered her as she gazed at La Virgen's Buddha smile; she couldn't really see it, she was too far away, but she knew it was there. That smile, gazing down from the very tip of the dome of her favorite church. Where El Nino Doctorcito played with his toys, balancing life and death.

Xochiquetzal had to watch her footing on the cobbles, the various pot holes, sudden steps, on the way to the market where mainly the Mexicans shopped. Once in a while a furtive gringo/a would venture in for their beautiful stalls of flowers and maybe a small bag of vegetables (they didn't trust the food). As she passed the ancient church in this smaller plaza, with one central fountain—only Mexicans on these benches, vendors selling ice cream, snacks, bunches of balloons and toys on their backs—it hit her like a news bulletin...I now live in the seventeenth century, it's terrible (the obvious poverty), beautiful (the ancient dream), and I love it.

"Qué rica," she murmured.

The market was always an assault on all of her senses: sight...rows and rows of red tomatoes, yellow squash, green squash, orange papaya, red/green chilies, onions, mangos, bananas, dangerous-looking fruits and vegetables she'd never seen, tasted—*smell*...the blend of sizzling chicken, beef, garlic, onions, chilies, dark chocolate mole, pyramids of ripened fruit (to be eaten *now*), the endless fresh clouds of sweet-blossomed flowers—*touch*...prickly, tender, fuzzy, slick—taste...hot, spicy, salty, sweet, juicy, sour. Every vendor offering her a taste of mango, papaya, watermelon (oh watermelon, she sighed, tomorrow watermelon); every vendor selling the best, the seduction of every human sense. "Guera...light one, como estas, taste..." they smiled, offering her a slice of something perfect, fresh, on the broadside of a glittering knife. Most of all, today, she needed clouds, flowers. Like the hummingbird, sipping the tiny, yellow flowers of the purplish fruit on the banana tree at La Gruta, Xochiquetzal wanted to go blind with yellow, desire. Today she bought mostly yellow lilies, with a bunch of white roses, an armful. Plus, the usual vegetables, fruits, she packed into her plastic shopping bag; but she didn't buy a watermelon, not even a small one; this was for the mediator of life and death.

(The Energy Child's nose opened to scents, all the scents, in the market, and especially to the small garden she carried bundled in her arm. Scent. Smell. Fragrance. It all made him hungry, though s/he couldn't name it 'hunger,' but that's what it was. Hunger. Every scent fed him through his sea anemone nose, no mouth yet, hunger.)

"Qué rica, qué rica," she murmured. These markets existed before the Conquest, so I've just entered a 1,000 year old dream, probably older, even richer, mas rica, she thought as she headed for the exit, already missing the thick scent of ripeness. Every so ripe fruit, vegetable, offering, waiting for human teeth, human hunger—I'll have to bring Javier, although I'm sure he's seen his share of markets, I want to eat chicken with dark chocolate mole smothering it, an icy Victoria, I want him to place a slice of ripeness in my mouth, here, in this 1,000 year old dream, I don't know why, I just do. "Mas rica," she whispered, as a shifting wind left her breathless.

People kept smiling as she passed with her unruly spray of flowers; she'd added, at the last moment, red and yellow roses, purple iris, and four birds of paradise. One more stop at the drug store, then a taxi home. Shifting her shopping bag, the blaze of color cradled in her arms, she entered the drug store. Why am I buying condoms, I've never even bought them, married for so long, me and my diaphragm, why buy them now, didn't he say he was safe, shouldn't I believe him, will he be offended if I bring them out, why am I buying condoms? she asked herself. Because I've never done it, even in Bali, my last lover, five years ago, had his own, because I've never done it. How do you say condoms in Spanish, maybe I can just point, fuck I hope so, suddenly feeling her ears turn teen-red, hidden by her hair. Oh the fucking virgin rides again, Xochiquetzal laughed at herself, well in the Goddess definition 'virgin' means one unto herself, okay I can live with that. Self-sufficient, self-reliant, self-loving, and, not to forget, self-conscious, she thought as she skimmed the shelves behind the counter for condoms. Nada. "Fregado," she murmured, shifting the fragrant garden.

A young woman walked out from behind the shelves. "Senora?" She was maybe eighteen, Indian looking, and very lovely.

"Tienes Trojans por los hombres?" The young woman gave it some thought, digging deep for the request 'por los hombres.' Nada. Okay, go for it, Xochiquetzal told herself firmly; a patriarchal virgin you're not, a Diosa virgen you are. "Quiero los Trojans, sabes *Trojans* por los hombres, por *sexo*."

The young woman burst into giggles. "Ay si, señora, tengo los Trojans. Cuanto quieres...How many do you want?"

"No se...I don't know," she replied, feeling like a pendeja-dolt, like how about twenty at least, I want sexo at least twenty times. She bought a box of them, which seemed like more than enough, and as she did she knew she wouldn't even use them; but she had to buy them anyway. The virgin, one unto herself, that virgin.

"Qué te vaya bien...May it go well," the young woman offered as she turned to leave.

"Ojala," (Goddess willing) she smiled. They both laughed goodbye. Por sexo, how humiliating and about time, Xochiquetzal couldn't help giggling as she flagged down a taxi.

She took a chilled glass of chardonay to the roof at twilight and, gazing out at the final golden light, she thought of her favorita mesa in Taos, her dawn and twilight walks to the edge. The red-tailed hawk that rested on the wind between her hunting; her graceful, lethal dives that always made Xochiquetzal stop, to record the moment. Memory. Beauty. Hunger. As she tracked the golden light, focusing on the horizon, turning windows in San Miguel to shimmering gold, she thought of Miguel and Hector; the guys who had all of her worldly goods. It made her smile imagining them sleeping in her comfortable bed, complete with sheets, blankets; watching TV on her wonderful black, leather couch; eating on her dining room table, sitting on her dining room chairs. She remembered her promise to send them a dream, so she sent them a dream of ripeness. Whatever that meant to each man. Ripeness. She sent them that dream in the golden fingers of the day and she hoped it would reach them, each golden finger, in dreams. Memory. Beauty. Hunger. Ripeness. For a moment, she saw the red-tailed hawk swoop close to the red mesa earth, ripeness.

"Hey Miguel, Hector The Protector, here comes some ripeness, there's enough for everyone, and tomorrow watermelons," she sighed with longing. To see the naked mesa, no humans in sight, the pure wind slicing sound of the red-tailed hawk's wings in the absolute silence. The milk truck drove up, honking its horn loudly; the man selling corn (slathered in mayonaise, sprinkled with coconut) sang with the confidence of an opera star, "Elllloooottteeee"; some teens came by playing a drum, another one playing a trumpet, as one sang a ballad, and they stopped in front of her house to play. They knew she'd emerge with some pesos, so they played loudly. Two small, grey doves landed at the edge of the roof, huddled together, and gently nuzzled each other's necks, wings. They didn't move as she stood, as she walked to the metal door back into the house, the stairway down.

"Okay, okay, I'm coming," Xochiquetzal laughed, gathering thirty pesos from the kitchen counter. She opened the door and sat down on the top step as they played another ballad, as her neighbors bought the juicy corn, as an ice cream truck came playing its familiar ice cream song, they played.

It was the largest scorpion she'd ever seen; it seemed engorged, pregnant. "Pregnant," she breathed, shuddering with strange pity, fear, disgust. Right by the roof window that looked out over the now lit domes of the churches, Bellas Artes, restaurants in el centro, the bare hills that greeted her each morning in sunlight or in rain; the scorpion didn't move. If Justin were here, would I call him to do it, to kill this very large, pregnant scorpion, or if Javier were here? "Yes," she answered herself as she took off her flip-flop, aimed it—Hard, kill it immediately, it's huge, Xochiquetzal commanded herself—she hit the cement wall so forcefully it sent jolts of pain to her right shoulder. It never moved, it didn't know she existed in its

Borg-scorpion universe, or it simply didn't care, was too stupid, too fearless, too ancient to move.

"Fucking A, I really hate those things, I don't want to get stung, have one fucking climb into bed with me" ... her skin crawled... "so now I'm a fucking hunter." She looked over every wall in her bedroom, bathroom, went downstairs and checked every wall, and the floor, stairs (she'd found them there too); then back up to the roof window, back down to her bedroom. No scorpions. To be seen. They're in the walls, in between the wooden beams, communicating via telepathy, planning their future revolution, Xochiquetzal mused, gazing up at the wooden beams over her bed. The slim, dark spaces they could crawl, slide through, and drop on her dreaming head.

"I give up, scorpianos," (her private name for them) she laughed wearily, opening the bedside table drawer...los Trojans por sexo...and tried to laugh again, but only a dry, winded sound emerged. It's a good thing I don't have a man around or Goddess knows I'd become a wimp and not the fregado scorpion hunter I was destined to become, fuck, and tomorrow Javier, watermelons, tomorrow. She gave one final check to her beautifully carved headboard; when there were no scorpions to be seen, killed, she swept her exhausted eyes over the walls, wooden beams, one more time, turned off the lamp, darkness, stars in the high, arched windows, sleep.

Xochiquetzal...*Two muscular lions are tied to my wrists, left and right, by glowing, silver cords which look flimsy but they're not. They're stronger than metal. Tied to my bony, feminine wrists. They're dragging me somewhere, they're leading me somewhere with their ferocious male lion-hearted energy. They won't stop, they could drag me to death if I let them, they can't stop, they only know where they're going, where they're taking me.*

I must set one free, which one, I can't endure this, it's too much, too much male lion-hearted energy. I quickly glance down and see the silver cords are tied into bows, not hard to undo. As I begin to untie the lion on my right wrist, I hear a voice, "This one will turn on you, not this one." I untie the left lion and he bolts ahead, disappearing. "He will wait for your arrival."

Then, the darkest night, no moon, no stars, and I realize this lion on my right wrist needs no light to guide him. Home. Wherever that may be.

The awful pace slows a bit. I'm filled with new energy. A kind of feminine. Joy.

Only the old man died, a heart attack, no wallet, no name, no pesos, poor old man, but at least he was the only one, he was the only one who left the body, died—Javier comforted himself as he shut out the sun to sleep. Before his drive to San Miguel. "A la casa de la Xochitzalita, la orchid," he murmured.

Javier...*Her eyes, I see her eyes, I know her, yes I know her, she turns from me and runs, she runs away, but I will find her, I always find her, her eyes.*

Xochiquetzal checked her email as she knew...

Javier stopped to buy a chilled bottle of...

PART II

Lovers don't finally meet somewhere.
They're in each other all along.

—Rumi

...she wouldn't check it while Javier was visiting; she knew. She'd be blinded by the yellow. Desire. Till he drives away.

...champagne, and then he saw fresh strawberries, a small round, dark-chocolate-truffle cake; and he knew she'd love this combination. He knew it as though they'd been together for twenty years, twenty lifetimes, twenty centuries. And on the street corner, two dozen, fresh, budding, red roses.

Javier's Spanglish Yahoo address made her smile, and when she opened it:

Soy el tigre.
Te acecho entre las hojas
anchas como lingotes
de mineral mojado.
GGGRRROOOWWRROOLLL Y MEOWSITA, Un
Tigre Mexicano, ABRE LA PUERTA...OPEN THE
DOOR, mi orchid, la feminista
I am the tiger.
I lie in wait for you among leaves
broad as ingots
of wet mineral.

She strained to hear a knock on her front door, nada, nothing, not yet. An invitation to show her photos, the selection entirely up to her, and to teach a workshop, in spring, for a week in Los Angeles, "The Angels," she echoed in English. Xochiquetzal finally relented, put her current email up on her web site. Poor Tara, she smiled, dealing with my 'disappearance,' or as she so concisely put it, my corn ball vision quest, ay Tara, the one who truly, secretly, understands, and wants to do it herself.

One from her oldest friend, Lara: Xochitzalita, either I'm going there or you're coning here, can't wait to hear all the dirt, mujer—tu amiga siempre y la mas joven... your friend forever and the younger one. (Lara was six years older and told no one her age, not even the credit card person verifying a stolen card, she refused, hilarious.)

If I do this L.A. visit, they could meet me, the first time to cross the border back, flying this time, I'd be paid, feted (gawked at, who cares, I should be used to it by now, I'm fifty-eight years old, she reminded herself firmly...but that's why I chose to be on the other side of the camera), stay in a nice hotel with *no scorpions,* now that's tempting. And I think I'm almost ready to do it again, have a show, teach, just for a week, I have to take new photos, get my nalgas and my camera out there...

So that's her casita, two identical addresses on the same street, that's my country for you, but her's has two trees in front, a lion's head for a door-knocker. I hope she told her maid not to come for the next few days, Javier grinned as he slipped on his white doctor jacket, his stethoscope around his neck, and finally the mask.

The loud knock of steel meeting the lion's head (the left wrist lion that waited for her arrival) made her jump. If it was Javier, he was early at 4:17 p.m., she glanced at the clock upstairs in her bedroom (fresh silky, purple sheets, silky pillows, and her Frida doll, with connecting eyebrows, lounged on the sensual pillows). For an instant, as Xochiquetzal checked her bed one more time, the six yellow roses opening their golden hearts on the night table by the windows—Frida winked at her.

She laughed, "And so it starts," racing down the stairs, but also bracing herself for someone selling fresh vegetables, tortillas, tamales, flowers. She usually didn't answer every knock or she'd be answering the door at least ten times a day. But today, today she answered every knock. He hasn't called at all, but he did send themeowsita email.

Xochiquetzal was tempted to peek through the window, to see who it was, her usual trick, but she couldn't stand it, she opened the door, it was after 4 p.m....she almost screamed. Neighbors were openly staring; Mexicans found no shame in staring. She joined them, staring.

A man that appeared to be Javier's height, build, was wearing an extremely garish, very scary, yellow with black stripes, a burst of stiff, tiger-like whiskers, pointy yellow ears with blood-red centers, blood-red tongue lolling out of the mouth, wild eyed, tiger mask. A yellow tiger mask. Doctor jacket, stethoscope around neck, machete in right hand, huge shopping bag in left hand; she slid her eyes down. Jeans, Javier's beautiful, leather sandals. El Tigre. (The Energy Child's right eye blossomed open, the most delicate, yellow squash blossom, open, and s/he remembered los tigres of this world. S/he wanted to growl, to laugh, but the mouth was still uncreated, still unborn, silent.)

"Who in the hell do you think you are?" Xochiquetzal burst out laughing. Her neighbors continued to stare, a few of the kids giggled and pointed.

"El Quetzalcoatl, mi amor," Javier answered in a serious tone, then growled.

"Get your ass in here, you're drawing a fucking crowd, and give me that machete, are you trying to kill me, Javier?" In one swift movement of embarrassment and joy, equally, she took the machete from his grasp, grabbed him by the stethoscope, and pulled him in the slim opening of her Mexican door.

"Hey, I'm carrying ripe watermelons, chocolate truffle cake, champagne, roses..." And, of course, some guy gave a grito, and Javier gave a louder one right back.

"I know, I know, you mediate fregado life and death, and where's tu Zapata sombrero..." The Spanglish began, their connecting bridge.

Javier placed the bolsa, bulging with all the goodies, down quickly. "I knew I forgot something, chingado, I meant to wear it, it's in the trunk of my fancy car," he growled, turning toward the door.

"Are you going out there with that mask on?" she moaned with exaggerated despair, laughing.

"Soy El Tigre, como no, Xochitzalita..."

She grabbed him by the dangling stethoscope, pulling him to her—"No more gritos, these are my fucking neighbors, Tigre."

"I've missed your fucking this and fucking that..." He took off the mask, revealing his dark, laughing, x-ray eyes. "I brought this for you, from una Tigrada, a fiesta de tigres." Javier handed her the mask, taking in all the art, bright Mexican colors, a small purple piñata hanging in the center of the room. "For your hippie house. Is your maid off for the weekend, Xochitzalita..."

"I don't have a maid, I can clean and cook, and what do you mean by 'my hippie house'?" She flashed him that fuck you look he was coming to love, but of course she didn't know this. No woman had ever looked at him that way, not quite that way. It made him smile on his lips, and his serpent stirred.

"No maid, no cook, piñatas in la sala...front room...la Virgen de Guadalupe of course, and what's that?" he pointed to a beautiful, red mask with inlaid abalone.

"A Balinese mask, I brought it back, and I can hang a piñata over my toilet if I want to Dr. Cabron..."

"Callate...shut up...estas una hippie, professora de los fotos, professora de mi corazón." And he kissed her, inhaling her words of protest, laughter, like the mediator of life and death that he was. Like the hungry tiger that he was. Like the impatient young man that he was. He could already taste her on his tongue.

I forgot how young he is, his unwrinkled eyes, face, not an ounce of extra fat on his body, not a fregado sag, and no ocean, la mar, Vallarta, for distraction, just decrepit me—the words flooded Xochiquetzal, she couldn't shut them out, even with his sweet kiss making her want to sip sip sip the yellow. She pulled back. "What do you see, Javier, tell the truth, la verdad, there's no ocean, no Vallarta, just me and you and a million fucking scorpions in my house in San Miguel, what do you see?" She looked away, her eyes filling with tears, and she cursed her vieja, old lady tears...Fuck, if my eyes aren't wrinkled enough this will really help, fuck...

"Ayy Xochitzalita, not that again, you're older than me, I'm younger than you, look at me, look at me *now*," the authority in his voice rose to meet her. The impatient young man would have to hold his ground; el tigre amarillo...the yellow tiger... would have to wait, patiently, hidden by the wide, green leaves.

She gazed back. Those eyes. The dream. *You will love me like no other.*

"Hippie mamacita, professora de los fotos y mi corazón, I see an orchid in the middle of the rain forest, *I see you,* Xochitzalita, I see you, and why do you say you have a million scorpions in this house, I have a scorpion story I'll tell you if you're good, mi India mama told it to me when I was a boy, I hated them too."

The Energy Child's seashell ears opened for his voice, his words, the story. Every wave on la mar was a story, and the shore wiped them clean.

"You don't hate them anymore?" *You will love me like no other.* "And what do you mean, your India mama?"

"You'll have to wait for the story, mi orchid." Javier placed the stethoscope around her neck, into her ears (the Energy Child listened), to his beating heart. "Do you hear it, mi corazón, mi corazón de tigre?" *You will love me like no other.*

"Your heart is so steady, you know I've read that they play a heartbeat in nurseries for motherless children, and I can see, hear, why, it's so soothing, your heart."

Then he placed the stethoscope over her own heart; it was steady but a bit faster paced. "It sounds like I'm heading for a fregado stroke," Xochiquetzal laughed, "that's comforting." Her eyes flashed into his, just joy.

Javier remembered the dream, her eyes, how she ran away, how she always runs away. "Take me to your fucking bedroom, Xochitzalita, take me to your fucking bedroom now."

"Did you say *fucking*?" she laughed, but he ate her words and her laughter.

"I'd make love to you right here on the floor, but these fucking Mexican tiles will cripple us."

"I've really missed you, Zapata, I've really missed tus ojos..." She led him up the stairs to her bedroom, holding his fingertips.

"What is *that* flying over your fucking bed?" He clutched her with his right arm, refusing to let her go. She feels so solid, so alive, like a mountain, a mountain that cradles an orchid.

"My guardian angel from Bali, if you're a good boy she won't take revenge..."

"Ayy mi orchid, callate." They fell into the softness of gathered silk, the deep purple comforter. He pulled her blouse over her head; she tossed his doctor jacket to the floor, and pulled his t-shirt over his head. Her leggings, his jeans, panties, briefs, naked to the purple, silky sheets.

"You're my water in this fucking desert, sixteen hour shifts, tell me."

"What?" she murmured.

"Dime, tell me, tu sabes, de la vida."

"There is no death, mi tigre, only life, this life, now." She wanted to reach for los Trojans por sexo, she really did, but as he entered her it felt like implosions of blinding light. Blinding yellow.

Is this the deepest sacred play joy sorrow joy

"I want you this way, Xochitzalita, you don't know how many times I imagined this, you, this way, doing my all night shifts..."

"The mediator of life and death."

"That's me, yes, this way, this is what they mean by older woman, younger man, otra vez, otra vez...again, again, mi orchid," he moaned, growling softly, burying his face in the back of her willing neck, her willing birth canal, her willing womb, and her womb x-rayed his existence, this life time, calling him padre de la luz...father of the light (and the Energy Child glowed like an x-ray of the sun at noon, eclipsed).

Javier and Xochiquetzal crossed into the rainbow, the burning rainbow, the blinding rainbow, the human rainbow brought to Earth, otra vez, again, together, they crossed.

This   is   this is   this is   this is   the deepest   sacred play

My guardian angel won't seek revenge," she smiled, wrapping herself tightly against his warmth, the contact making her convulse with pleasure. "Tell me the scorpion story."

"You women and your multiple orgasms, I'd be jealous but I've witnessed the birth process too many times and you deserve each one, mi amor Xochitzalita. The scorpion story..."

"I've become the fucking scorpion hunter," she breathed him in, his young man's scent of ripening into sea foam, new salt. "I need a story, Javier mi tigre." She nibbled his shoulder, tasting his new salt.

He gazed at her, smoothing her unleashed hair that covered her like a shawl, and touched the spiral seashell, Vallarta earrings. "One more besito and I'll tell you the story, the scorpion story."

She met his mouth, and he engulfed her with yellow, more yellow. Blinding. Light.

"No, no, tell me the story, Javier, now, and then we're going to eat, I'm starving, for champagne, chocolate truffle cake..."

"Cabroncita, look at me," he exhibited his erect serpent without a trace of shame.

"Tell the scorpion story or I'll toss you out the fregado door, erection and all!" she growled, biting into his neck.

"Ayyy calmate, calmate...calm down...I'll tell you," he laughed softly. "Mi mama India who nursed me with a bottle, took care of me until I was twelve..."

"What do you mean, your Indian mother?"

"You don't even have a maid, pochita, but in upper class families it's common to be fed and cared for every day, by an Indian woman, and she became mi mama..."

"Like the slaves in my country, they nursed and cared for the master's children..."

"Don't start, pochita Yaqui, I'm in paradise, do you want to hear this story or not, digame."

"Tell the story, digame." Xochiquetzal pulled back to watch his face for shadow and light, lies and truth. The story.

"Amalia, mi otra mama, was treated like family, and she lived with us until she died, left the body, cancer. My mother was a little jealous of her, I was the youngest and supposedly she nursed me for a month, then gave me to Amalia, mi otra mama. Amalia didn't nurse me, she had no little one, so I was fed from a nursing bottle. I was about five and terrified of being stung by a scorpion, one of my older sisters was stung and she was rushed to the hospital, she was allergic it turned out, and my father, also a physician, was traveling. I would only sleep with every light on, barely sleeping, watching por los alacrans, los fregado scorpions."

"I know, and they're so hideous and ancient looking, like how can they still be alive in present time. I've nicknamed them The Borg, since they don't even acknowledge human presence, just sitting there, not moving, splat..."

Javier laughed, "I like that, El Borg, estas un Trekie, mi amor." He rearranged his arms to hold her tighter, her orchid scent rising to meet him; not sweet but the tangy scent of something wild. (The Energy Child's seashell ears blossomed open with pleasure, listening to his words, each wave.)

"Amalia came to my room after everyone was asleep and took my head into her lap, stroking my face softly, as she always did when she comforted me. Her voice changed, became soft and secretive, as it did when she told me her stories, she began (Javier's voice became soft, feminine, memory)... Hijito mio, there was an Indian, a very poor, blind man who begged every day for his food on the same corner, on the same street, in the warmth of the sun or the chilling rain, he begged, his little cup waiting for someone's kindness. One day, toward sunset, the priest stopped to give this Indian some pesos, and then decided to take him back to the church to eat, stay the night on a hard pallet on the floor of the church.

"As the priest gave him an extra blanket, he asked, 'Are you afraid of los alacrans, scorpions, they might enter your blankets.' The Indian replied, 'What are these scorpions, Padrecito?' 'Have you ever been stung on your body like something on fire?' the priest asked. 'Yes, many times, Padrecito.' 'Those were scorpions, and you're not afraid?' 'I've never seen them, I've only been stung, Padrecito,' the Indian replied.

"The priest left the church with his candle, leaving the blind Indian in his usual darkness, and then he returned from his quarters. 'I have un alacran, a scorpion, in this wooden cage, never open it or it'll sting you, feed it insects from time to time. Now, listen carefully, if this scorpion *ever glows with a light like gold,* set it free.' 'I'm blind, Padrecito, how will I know if it glows with a light like gold?' And the priest answered him with as much kindness as he had, 'When you're able to see the invisible.'"

Javier paused, still hearing Amalia's voice stirring the air beneath his own.

"That's it, when you're able to see what's invisible, that's it, Javier, so beautiful, glows with a light like gold. Does the Indian ever see it, did she tell you?'

"No, but I believe he did, and that he set that scorpion free, to sting you, Xochitzalita!" He pinched her waist and she screamed so loudly her neighbors smiled, the grandfather giving a young man's grito.

The tray of tamales, fresh green salsa, avocado, tomato, cheeses, ham, the red-jeweled strawberries, the amber honey, slices of dark bread, a large piece of chocolate truffle cake, was spread out between them as they piled their plates. Xochiquetzal dropped a slice of the ripe, red jewel into their champagne glasses, smiling as they fizzed.

"Were you ever stung?" she asked, sipping the dry bubbles.

"Dios mio, no, but I keep watching for the golden scorpion, wait, wait, we must toast, Xochitzalita."

"Yes, you're right, I'm such a barbarian when it comes to champagne, and this is so good, mi tigre."

"Do you want me to wear el tigre mask?"

"I'd rather see tus hermosos ojos, that mask is kinda intense," she smiled with pleasure, his eyes. "And what's a Tigrada?"

"I'll take you, I'll teach you about my country, and so to our travels, amor."

"I'll drink to that, but you can't travel, you're the mediator of life and death." She loved watching how the tiny lights at the very center of his pupils became brighter or dimmer with his emotional spectrum. Nothing about him is dead, dormant, he's the young, fearless tiger eating tamales with green salsa on my bed, and I'm still the bitter fifty-eight year old, battle-scarred jaguar, no matter how you cut it, she told herself.

"Xochitzalita, you're getting triste, sad, stop it, I, El Tigre, forbid it or I'll put the mask on...okay, another toast. If we ever see the golden scorpion, we must promise to set it free." Javier looked at her intently, her turn; the tiny lights blazed. When sorrow and joy merged in her face, it made him want to make love to her. To pierce her depths—Her secrets, her orchid, he thought with a languid shiver.

"Okay, okay, I promise if I ever see a golden scorpion, I promise to set it free, to not kill it..." They sipped at the same time, both aware of the gift. This moment.

"You kill your own scorpions, en serio, you're not kidding..."

"I don't even have a maid, much less a scorpion killer," Xochiquetzal laughed. "I'm it, I'm the fucking scorpion hunter, Javier."

"My mother would *never* kill a scorpion, I mean not ever. There was always one of the maids, the gardener, of course Amalia, then my father. When I'm here, I'll be your scorpion hunter, but we must promise..."

"I know, I know, never ever, the great golden messiah alacran..."

"Ayy cabroncita, mas champagne, por favor, and tomorrow you'll come with me to the girl's orphanage, I promised my good doctor amigo, Carlos, I'd check the girls. Sunday night you'll meet him at the dinner we're going to, my friends here in San Miguel."

She poured the champagne to the brims of their glasses. "I can't wait to see you in action, Dr. Zapata, maybe I can be your helper and do you mind if I take photos?"

Javier laughed at her enthusiasm. "Sure, you can be my helper, but first I'll ask las madres, the nuns, about taking photos, although I'm sure it's okay but we should ask permission."

Xochiquetzal poured him the last drops. "I can't believe I'm being so generous," she laughed softly, "usually I take the last drops."

He reached for her, almost spilling her champagne. "Yes, I want more, I'll always want more..."

"Hey, hold on, speaking of more," she reached for the night table drawer, opened it, and held a row of los Trojans por los hombres (por sexo), "I forgot these puppies."

"Qué puppies," Javier laughed, leaping up to grab his leather duffle. He unzipped a storage area and plucked a piece of white paper out, handing it to her. "It's my bill of heath, signed by mi loco amigo…"

"What in the hell is this?" she fell into giggles, holding the paper to her heart.

"What does it look like, mi orchid?" He joined her, taking her into his boy arms with the strength of a man.

"Ohmygoddess, it's a penis dripping something like a rabid puppy," she howled with laughter.

"Qué rabid puppy, mujer, es un erection fuerte con muchisimas sano, health, and look below, my friend's name, el doctor, es muy loco, you'd like him but not as much as me, Xochitzalita."

"Do you know what I went through to buy these por sexo por los hombres Trojans, it was like *totally humiliating* (a valley girl accent), I need my champagne." She sat up to open another bottle, but he took it from her.

"That's my job when I'm here, I'll be your butler *and* the scorpion killer."

"You have no shame…"

"Es la verdad…that's the truth," he smiled, and the white paper drifted to the bedroom tiles, followed by the row of Trojans.

"Tell your friend I love his drawing, a latent Picasso," she laughed but barely (she was tired from laughing, not crying, laughing). "Those sperm drips, someday you'll have children, mi tigre."

"Maybe."

"You will, Javier, yes you will."

"Maybe the child we create together is invisible, Xochitzalita." (The Energy Child breathed his words in through his/her newly created nose, and her/his twin lungs filled with yellow, yellow joy.)

"You've lost your muy locito mind…"

"To see the invisible, remember, like the blind man with the golden scorpion in a cage, and, you know, I haven't thought of Amalia's story in years."

"Where did that come from, our *invisible child*?" Xochiquetzal's eyes filled with tears, laughter, tears. The spectrum. The invisible.

Is this?   Sacred play?

"So this is your fancy car, a black Jetta, for some reason I was expecting a red hotrod," she laughed.

"My father bought this for me, so can't complain, como no, my next one will be a red hotrod, yeah," Javier grinned like a kid. El Doctorcito.

"Let's walk to the plaza for breakfast, then we can take a taxi to the orphanage, I like to walk."

"Of course you do, estas una hippie, mi amor. I'll put my doc gear in a backpack como el otro hippie," he laughed at her fuck you look.

As they approached the plaza, loud men's voices filled the air with a kind of song. Four young men with skull masks, dressed entirely in black, three on the smooth plaza stones dead, while one sang: "Ven conmigo. La noche al monte sube. El hambre baja al rio...Come with me. Night climbs up to the mountain. Hunger goes down to the river." Then the living, skull poet lay dead as one of the three sprang to life: "Ven conmigo. Quienes son los que sufren? No se, pero son mios... Come with me. Who are those who suffer? I do not know, but they are my people."

Each skull poet taking turns coming to life: "Ven conmigo. No se, pero me llaman y me dicen: 'Sufrimos.'...Come with me. I do not know, but they call to me and they say to me: 'We suffer.'" "Ven conmigo. Y me dicen: 'Tu pueblo, tu pueblo desdichado, entre el monte y el rio, con hambre y con dolores, no quiere luchar solo, te esta esperando, amigo'...Come with me. And they say to me: 'Your people, your luckless people, between the mountain and the river, with hunger and grief, they do not want to struggle alone, they are waiting for you, friend.'"

"It sounds like Neruda, 'they are my people' (tears filled her eyes), I think I'm dying of bliss at 10am in the morning before coffee." Xochiquetzal turned toward Javier but he was speaking to one of the skull poets lying on the beautifully patterned stones of the plaza. The skull poet smiled, "Si, es el maestro Neruda," and closed his eyes, waiting for his turn which was next.

He leaped to his feet, commanding his death, *duende*, to join him, and he sang at the top of his voice: "Oh tu, la que yo amo, pequena, grano rojo de trigo, sera dura la lucha, la vida sera dura, pero vendras conmigo...Oh you, the one I love, little one, red grain of wheat, the struggle will be hard, life will be hard, but you will come with me."

Javier returned to where Xochiquetzal stood, taking her hand; she was crying again. "Yes, it's Neruda, and I think to his lover, que pasa, mi amor?"

"I'm just so fucking happy standing in this place, listening to Neruda in Spanish being sung by poets in skull masks. Lorca called this spirit *duende*, and it is, and you're holding my hand, Dr. Zapata."

"Dame un besito, now."

She leaned into him, kissing him with all the innocence she could muster, all the desire she could muster, now, as the skull poets began a new poem, Neruda. And she forgot he was twenty-four years younger, in that timeless moment, she glimpsed. The invisible.

"Soy el tigre. Te acecho entre las hojas anchas como lingotes de mineral mojado. El rio blanco crece bajo la niebla. Llegas. Desnuda te sunmerges. Espero...I am the tiger. I lie in wait for you among leaves broad as ingots of wet mineral. The white river grows beneath the fog. You come. Naked you submerge. I wait..."

They burst into laughter and said simultaneously, "It's our poem, El Tigre!"

"I don't believe it," Xochiquetzal kept smiling.

"I do, you're in my country, where people still read each other's thoughts, wishes, dreams, where the invisible is as real as Neruda's poetry."

"Okay, you win, you win, and you're right, you'd love Bali, the same thing happens there, mi tigre. Let's go eat, I'm pretty hungry como el tigre, and in need of caffeine." She placed two-hundred pesos into their black, ceramic bowl.

"That's too much, pochita."

"It's not enough, I glimpsed the invisible."

Javier picked up her two-hundred pesos and added two-hundred of his own, handing it to one of the skull poets. They exchanged words, laughter, and the skull poet nodded her way.

"Before it blows away in the wind," he said, taking her hand and kissing it. "You win, mi pochita Yaqui." They went to sit at the outdoor café, facing the plaza, the skull poets, as they continued to sing. At the top of their voices. With so much joy, sorrow, joy. With so much *duende, vida, duende.* They sang to their death, so alive.

"We'll eat breakfast at Mama Mias next time, it's a desayuno feast so you have to take your time, plus tonight we're going for dinner, dancing..."

"Only if I can do the salsa hip hop, como no, y no disco por favor," Javier laughed, gazing out the taxi's window at the old man leading his burro laden with cut wood, explosions of flowers, roses. He told the driver to pull over, and he leaped out to buy red roses. "These are for you, Xochitzalita," he handed her a small bunch. "And these are for las madres." He placed the large bunch next to him, smiling with joy, that she was coming with him, to see him work. I've never allowed anyone, he realized.

"Have you gone before, to the orphanage?" She sniffed the rich, red rose scent, "Qué rica."

I drop in to check on the kids when I'm here, next time the boys. They'll be very healthy now that I'll be visiting la tigressa. We're here, okay, I'll ask las madres about taking photos, but I'm sure it's fine, in fact they'll probably want copies."

"Of course, I'd love that." She opened her camera bag briefly, patting it like an impatient child—It's been months since I've taken you out to play, and now it's time. "Revision," Xochiquetzal whispered. "Con el doctorcito."

Javier handed the huge bunch of red roses to the welcoming nun and Xochiquetzal took a couple shots of her radiant smile, accepting; his radiant smile, giving. "Bienvenidos," she kept repeating, and of course it was fine to take photos of the girls, they'd love it. "They've been waiting for you all week, Dr. Gomez," she laughed like sunlight.

The girls—from toddlers to teens—sat in the open courtyard filled with flowering plants, trees, a small fountain, birds bathing in the fountain, butterflies grazing their, freshly shampooed, flowery scented hair, from time to time. "Revision," she breathed, and began taking photos; and when Javier took the first toddler into his lap, smiling and joking, tears filled her eyes. And they fell, natural as rain. She moved in for a close-up as he put his stethoscope to her heart, first warming it with his hands. Javier's face, the girl's face, his eyes, her eyes; the sheer gentleness in his eyes, in his touch. *You will love me like no other.*

Stethoscope to her back, "Breathe, breathe deeply, niña," he sang to her (as that day when he followed Xochiquetzal to her room, that voice). Her tongue, ears, eyes, reflexes, simple questions of her health.

Each girl photographed; one with a yellow butterfly perched for a few seconds on her head, flying away when she laughed.

I got it, she told herself, it's going to be so beautiful, revision. And Javier's face, his eyes, his hands, so gentle, El Nino Doctorcito. May he never ever change, she wished, silently—may he be this way, exactly this way, at my age, may he. And Xochiquetzal suddenly realized, like lightning on the mesa—If I were his age, younger, I'd have his babies, yes I would, and I would worship him. For his simple kindness. His hands, his eyes. *You will love me like no other.*

As he began examining the teens, they flirted shyly but shamelessly; and when he placed the stethoscope onto their hearts, they shrieked with laughter. Until the nuns made them behave, becoming stern, standing right next to the young woman, la chica. But they continued to flirt with their laughing eyes, and Javier transformed into a gentle but stern doctorcito.

He glanced at her for a moment, sending her *that look* that made her want him, now. That made her soft, wet, that made her want to worship him. Now. El Doctorcito. You gotta be kidding, old battered jaguar, cut the crap and take these wonderful photos, those sweet, not so sweet, flirting eyes. His eyes, stern, but behind them I can hear him laughing, just waiting to cut the watermelon open, el heyoka, we forgot to cut the watermelon open.

"Es su hermana...Is she your sister?" the teen asked as he stared into her left ear.

"Es professora de los fotos," Javier replied evenly, then stared into her right ear. Well, at least she didn't say *mother*, Xochiquetzal smiled to herself. And then, the teen shot her the quickest, dirtiest look, giving Javier the sweetest smile. Yes, you could be his future wife in a few years, an eighteen year difference, perfect, she smiled back at the teen.

After a delicious lunch, prepared by the girls, where Xochiquetzal took her place as witness to Dr. Gomez' presence, enjoying it all, even the flirting, they took a taxi back to her hippie house. Watching the teens, she'd silently wished each young woman a good man, but first an education—Please, an education first. On the way back, Javier held her close, kissing her so deeply, the driver started to stare, smile.

"Later, tigre, we have an audience, I mean it, stop. Do you think some of the girls will go on to university?"

"Some will, there's scholarships available from the Mexican and gringo rich in San Miguel, and many of them are very intelligent, so I hope so. And not get married at seventeen, have babies, make tortillas for the rest of their lives, I truly hope so, Xochitzalita."

"You have a fan club, doctorcito."

"Were you jealous, mi amor?" Instead of kissing her, he stroked her cheek. No man had ever stroked her cheek, that tenderness of touch, the way Amalia had stroked his.

"No, I trust you, tigre, especially in the doctorcito role," she laughed. "We're still getting to know each other."

"Es la verdad…It's the truth, but I was jealous watching you caress your camera, professora, as though you'd forgotten me."

"I was taking *your photos*, idiot."

"Es la verdad…It's the truth," he kissed her again.

"But I imagine those sixteen, seventeen year olds must be eye candy for you, I saw the nun button up the cleavage on that especially well endowed, cute chica. Tell the truth, you do look, Dr. Gomez alias El Zapata, especially as the worship is pouring over you like honey."

"Ayy when you get going you sound like my old professor…"

"I was for twenty-four years, but don't change the subject, *I'm waiting*." Xochiquetzal mimicked his doctor tone when he said this, "I'm waiting."

Javier laughed, "You're too tough for me, pochita feminista, yes I look but I never, ever touch those girls, my patients." His mind flitted to his youngest chica, her lush nineteen year old breasts—But she was never my patient, and I'm going to delete all of their numbers, he promised himself, knowing how easy it was to add new ones. But the promise made something switch in his heart, made him hold Xochiquetzal tighter.

"You are such a bullshitter, Javier, I saw how you soak up the young warm honey…"

He ate her words, her breath, and each time she tried to continue, he ate them again, until all they could do was laugh between each deep kiss. And they realized the taxi had stopped. In front of her hippie, scorpion-ridden casita.

As Xochiquetzal turned the key in the lock, Javier buried his face in her neck, and the driver gave a low grito in memory of his wife's first kisses forty-four years ago.

They made love so gently it surprised them both—they were so tired from the early walk, the light-filled memory of Neruda's poetry sung by the skull poets, the full day at the orphanage, his exchange with over twenty girls, her endless photos (revision), this getting to know the other as they, simply, are. Allowing the other to be as they are. This required a measure of freedom, and it was exhausting. They didn't know this; they couldn't articulate it; but they each felt it. Exhausted.

In each other's arms, legs wrapped together, her head on his flawless chest (with the black crescent moon mark over his left nipple); the words to her poem in progress came to her...

> I want to explore your chest, the map of
> your longing, your vast desire to be free—and
> your back, flaring up to your secret wings that
> dreamt you to the moment we spoke.

She looked at him, so deep in his dreams, and wondered if he was dreaming Spain, his old love, Clara. Let him, she smoothed his moon mark, let him dream freely, he's on loan, a gift. As she breathed in his new salt, foam wave sperm scent, she joined him. In dreams.

The   deepest   sacred   play   yes

Javier...*They appear, each one, one by one by one, each beautiful one, each girl, each woman, I've made love to since I was fourteen, my first experience, my first lover, I still see her, feel her, taste her, her fourteen year old lips, her fourteen year old budding breasts, I lick them, yes I lick them, and I will never ever forget their taste, the taste of rose petals on my tongue, her acceptance of my sex, first time, explosion into light, the feminine, girl, woman, how I love her, the scent of orchids, how I love her, the scent of an orchid in the fertile rainforest, I will find her, I will always find her, orchid.*

Xochiquetzal...*My mother, Florinda, fills the vision of my eyes, what I'm seeing, so beautiful, so strong, I long to be like her, my mother. Yet she betrays me in an unspeakable way, I can't bear to remember in this dream. "Xochitzalita, let it go, let it go, it was me, it was always me, afraid to love, to be loved, you thought it was strength, but you are the one strong enough, free enough, to love the other, and I love you, I always will, tu alma, tu alma, your soul, hija."*

"Javier, it's almost 8 p.m., time to get up and go to Mama Mias, come on wake up." Xochiquetzal saw him gazing at her secretly between slitted eyes. "Wake up, cabroncito..."

"Now for the watermelon," he laughed, placing her beneath him.

"Tomorrow, tomorrow morning you can be El Heyoka con los watermelons, but right now I'm starving, and I want a gigantic margarita sweating ice, tomorrow..."

"Or tonight after Mama Mias, do you promise, I'm waiting."

"Okay, I fucking promise, I promise tonight after Mama Mias." She licked his neck very softly. "Let's make love that way again, mi tigre."

"I'm waiting," Javier smiled.

"So gently, so gently that we become the other, we just slip into the other's skin without fear, you know?"

"You say what I feel, Xochitzalita, and haven't learned how to say yet, into the other's skin without fear."

"The truth is, I'm learning right along with you, but maybe my years of being la professora gives me the words," she laughed softly, rolling him over to gaze into his eyes. "You're the first man in my life to look directly into my eyes, and not look away, you're the first, Javier."

"I told you on the beach in Bucerias, I'm your gift, mi orchid." *You will love me like no other.*

"You either dress como una India hippie or Frida Kahlo, mi amor," Javier smiled with a trace of humor, irony, then caught himself as Xochiquetzal shot him a glare. "And you always look beautiful, you know this, mi feminista," he laughed, "but couldn't you once in a while wear something mas gringa, un-ethnic like modern times?"

"This is how I've always dressed, even before you were born, Javier, you know in ancient times, so get used to it, this is me." Her tone was serious, unsmiling—How fucking dare he? she fumed, gathering the long, to her ankles, black tiered skirt (thin cotton, no slip), for the few steps into the restaurant. The cool, sheer black peasant top with red, yellow, purple flowers was loose and comfortable. Silver milagro hand earrings, a red/purple Huichol beaded necklace with a milagro eye, gold/red Huichol butterfly bracelet, and her Santa Fe Market, Hopi bear claw, silver cuff bracelet (that protected her wrist, her spirit, her journey in the world). And of course, her rings on each hand; each one found on her travels. They spoke of transformations to her, each one.

Javier, dressed up in a crisp, white shirt, creased khaki pants, expensive brown leather loafers, looked more like the upper-class Mexican doctor at home in his own country, and it also made him look older. "Ayy Xochitzalita, don't be angry with me, we just made love so sweetly." He put his arm around her waist, laughing softly.

"You look like a very handsome Muppie in that outfit, if you must know. I've seen your loafers on L. L. Bean, Yuppie Central." She'd meant to laugh but the *Bean* brought back memories of being called, *beaner, spic, wetback,* as a girl; and she realized Javier had no such memories. And she was glad, suddenly and irrationally; she was glad he had the freedom to be a Muppie at home in his own country, whole. With no memory, of these childhood names.

"Qué es this Muppie, como Yuppie, cabroncita?" Javier smiled as she hugged him to her, possessively, he noted, as though she were claiming him.

"A Muppie is a cross between a gringo Yuppie and an upper class Mexican, hence a Muppie," she laughed wickedly. "And you also look a bit older, maybe thirty-eight, Dr. Gomez. So, *if* I look forty-eight, I'm only ten years older than you, I like that."

"Okay, I don't mind being a Muppie if you like being ten years older, and maybe I look ayy forty, so only eight years older, mi orchid tan locita," he laughed with her.

They waited as the hostess found their table, first giving Javier the once-over, the look. Xochiquetzal was getting used to it—As long as he doesn't flirt back when he's with me, fuck it, or I'm referred to as his 'mother,' that would do it, she mused, watching him take in her approval. And he does look older as a Muppie, she smiled.

"Xochitzalita!" she heard, turning to see where it came from, but she already knew. Pablo. With twenty-something Sonya, who was dressed exactly as Javier wanted her to dress (in modern, sexy times). Smiling with real joy, he waved them over.

"Do you know him?"

"He's someone I met when I first arrived, he made me feel welcome, come on, you'll like him, he's a little like you..."

Javier frowned.

"Kind of flamboyant y loco, y un Muppie tambien," she smiled.

"Yippie."

Xochiquetzal laughed, she'd never heard him say this before. It sounded so American. "Yippie?"

"Fucking yippie," and he pulled her to him, kissing her in the crowded entry. And of course, some guy did a loud ass grito—Is that Pablo, ohmygoddess, she realized with a shiver of foreboding. Maybe they're too much alike.

"You know, I'm kind of getting used to your public displays of affection and I think I'm even starting to like it."

"That I'm a flamboyant Muppie?"

"And a delicious kisser, doctorcito."

"So, introduce us, Xochitzalita, before you begin making out in the chingado restaurant." Pablo laughed, standing, his hand extended. Sonya just smiled, beautifully (wearing a discreetly low-cut top, a mid-thigh jean skirt, and gold, glittery earrings that peeked through her dark hair with deep red streaks).

"Pablo, this is Javier, and I'm Xochiquetzal," she extended her hand to Sonya. For a moment, Sonya didn't know what was required of her; then she laughed and shook it.

"Las pochas from the USA shake hands, they can't help it," Pablo laughed with her.

Javier put his arm around her, protectively; after Pablo's jefe-dominating handshake he got the message. An old boyfriend, lover. And he's closer to Xochitzalita's age, he realized, so why didn't it work out? he wondered as he glanced at his hermosa chica, much younger than him.

"I hear you're a physician, Javier, I'm very impressed," Pablo smiled like an indulgent father, pissing Javier off, but he hid it. That detachment.

"I bumped into Pablo at La Gruta, and I told him a little about you," Xochiquetzal jumped in. She'd never seen this edge of anger from Javier, and she knew he was keeping it in his detachment, doctorcito file.

"And what do you do, Pablo, since I haven't been filled in." The waiter came for drink orders, and Javier ordered two margaritas and an extra shot of tequila for himself.

"I'll take a margarita with an extra shot as well," Pablo added, glancing at Sonya's margarita which was still half full. "I see you like tequila," he smiled at Javier.

"I love tequila."

"Bring us a whole bottle, why fuck around, and a plate of limes,"

Pablo told the young, smiling waiter.

"Should I still bring the extra shots, señor?" A contest, he thought, that'll be fun to watch.

"No, bring the bottle with the margaritas, right Javier?"

"Absolutely, why fuck around, and *what* do you do?"

Xochiquetzal gazed at his perfect, young man's face, the twin fires dancing in the center of his eyes; and then she caught Sonya's look of admiration, as Pablo also did. "Oh fuck," she breathed, not a drink-you-under-the-table-fucking-contest.

"I'm an art, antique dealer, with a Ph.D. in something I can't remember," Pablo laughed, taking pleasure in Javier's edge of anger, "and I travel around the world looking for beautiful things to bring back. In fact, I'm going to Bali soon con la Sonya, I asked Xochitzalita to join us, but she declined." Pablo gauged Javier's level of anger from the set of his perfect jaw line; on a scale of one to ten, perhaps a four.

"He's a Ph.D. in Eastern Philosophy, am I right, Pablo?" Xochiquetzal wanted to say *asshole*, but that might ignite the whole situation. So she placed it in her professor detachment file.

A shadow crossed Sonya's lovely face—He invited *her* to join us? Now everyone had their own file.

"Does that qualify you to pull out splinters?" Javier had to know.

Pablo howled with laughter. "Maybe splinters of the soul, chinga tu madre!"

"What did you say?" Javier raised his voice.

"That's the way the idiot talks to everyone, believe me. I thought this rich rancher was going to shoot him in traffic, and then these mutual insults just started flying back and forth, who knows." She could see it, el doctorcito wanted to cause serious harm.

The waiter carefully placed the margaritas down, gigantic ones, and the large bottle of tequila, the plate of sliced limes, and two shot glasses. He could feel it, the contest had begun.

"Pablo tells me he hired a mariachi band for you at his warehouse, a fiesta, como no," Sonya shot him daggers, then she was immediately sorry. In their relationship, he was El Jefe, The Boss—he was in charge.

Pablo let the daggers go; she'd taken them back and placed them into her own heart. "I made Xochitzalita dance with every mariachi in the band, after I got her drunk. Javier, your tequila's gone." He poured their shot glasses full.

"And did she dance with *you*, chinga tu madre y tu padre tambien."

"Stop it, both of you, stop," Xochiquetzal said as evenly as possible. Her detachment file was starting to bulge.

Pablo roared with laughter. "Y tu abuelita, cabron!"

"Y tu puto perro," Javier cracked a smile. "Joven!" he yelled at the waiter, "Dos margaritas aqui…Two margaritas here!"

"Joven, young man, he's maybe four years younger than you, isn't that insulting?" Xochiquetzal asked quietly, but Pablo heard.

"I told you las pochas worry about every chingada cosa, y tu puto gato de tu madre!"

Javier poured the shot glasses to the brim, lifted his, waiting for Pablo to lift his, and they drank together, slamming the glasses down.

The two gigantic margaritas arrived for Javier and Pablo, as the salsa band blasted their opening number. "I'll take another one," Xochiquetzal told the waiter, then asked Sonya if she wanted another one.

"Why not join los pendejos," she smiled shyly, hiding her anger.

"Do you mind if I dance with your date, you're welcome to dance with mine. You don't mind, Sonya," Pablo glanced at her, smiling, that charm.

"It's up to Xochitzalita, I'm not her puto *padre*." The word landed right on target, what he was to Sonya. El Jefe, boss, father.

Pablo didn't laugh, but stood up, extending his hand to her. "Come on, one salsa, and you don't have to dance with every guy in the chingado band this time."

She glanced at Javier. He was staring at a place in the distance, intently. Pablo quickly walked to the back of her chair, pulling it out. If I don't just get up and dance, fuck it, she thought. "Javier, join us with Sonya, come on…"

"I don't feel like dancing, go ahead, Xochitzalita." He looked at her; his detachment file was on fire.

As they began to dance to the bring-the-dead-to-life-salsa, Xochiquetzal leaned into him. "The minute we go back to the table, I'm leaving, you're being a total fucking asshole."

Pablo doubled over with laughter, then quickly returned to dancing. "That's what I miss in my life, being called a total fucking asshole."

"Just give me a call, I'll tell you, fuckhead."

"Stop it, I'm falling in love again," he laughed, giving her a turn, trying to bring her closer.

"If you don't cut it out, I'm leaving you on the dance floor to dance with your own true love, your own pendejo self, Pablo." Then, she saw Javier and Sonya dancing the salsa traditionally, beautifully; and it was evident. What a beautiful couple. Each one young, unblemished. Perfect. A perfect couple. She could have his children, the words came to her. Tears stung her eyes. The truth. (The Energy Child wept her/his first sea salt tears, and longed to taste them, no mouth, tongue, created.)

"Maybe *they're* falling in love," Pablo laughed at their situation. "Then we can go to Bali by ourselves, mom and dad on vacation."

"You may be Sonya's fucking father, but I am *not* Javier's fucking mother. I have a grown son and *I know the difference*." She could almost see her words glittering in the air like tiny stars; this, too, was the truth...I know the difference.

The band began a slow, undulating salsa and she was suddenly in Javier's arms, belly to belly, his face in her hair. "I missed you, pochita, where have you been?"

Sonya was trying to placate Pablo's bruised ego with her perfect beauty, sliding into his arms, whispering something intimate. He was furious and Xochiquetzal had never seen this side of him. Fury. She's perfect, Pablo, she loves you, pendejo, you just want your so-called prize because I never made love to you, she beamed him telepathically.

"I was right here in your arms, mi tigre, but I couldn't help noticing what a beautiful couple you made, you y la Sonya..."

"Callate, mi amor, mi orchid, callate," he moaned, kissing her like they were entirely alone, the tequila short circuiting his usual social restraints (the ones he had).

Gritos, "Vaya a la casa...casa casa casa casa..."

Xochiquetzal pulled away, laughing with pleasure, embarrassment. "Ayy Diosa, deja vu de Vallarta, stop, Javier, I mean it, stop!"

"Here, before you just fuck her on the dance floor, more tequila," Pablo wedged himself between them. Javier took the shot, drained it, and threw the shot glass to the floor, sending little diamonds everywhere.

"How is it your business when and where we fuck each other, Pablo, go fuck your chica, isn't she enough?" Javier's voice was low, in control, watching Pablo's body language, his eyes. El Tigre.

"I'm leaving, Javier, are you coming?" At the entry, Xochiquetzal turned to see if he was following. There were two large waiters trying to separate them.

She finished her second Suenos Rosa...Rose Dreams (strawberry juice, a shot and a half of rum, topped with cream, a slice of lime, delicious), and countered the health risk of drinking rum at 1:44 a.m. with the health fact of vitamin C in the strawberry juice. "I'm such a bullshitter," she said to her flying, bare-breasted guardian angel from Bali, whose staring, black eyes (with red dot in the center of her forehead, dream-eye) were poised directly over her.

"I can never lie to those eyes, that dream-eye, red dot," Xochiquetzal sighed. She picked up a novel she was reading, forbidding herself to call Mama Mias, the local jail—Are they in fregado jail, and with Napoleonic Law in Mexico, both pendejos are guilty. As she put her reading glasses on, edging closer to the lamp's light, going on 1:50am, she missed his muppie mouth, hands, his twin legs wrapped around her, his crescent moon chest, his... Someone began to sing on the street below, "Besame, besame mucho..." A beautiful, male voice, and then violins joined the voice, guitars, trumpets.

"You've got to be kidding, it's almost 2 a.m.," she smiled in spite of herself, opening the metal door as quietly as possible in order to cross the small patio, with potted plants, flowers. The entire band was singing, "Besame mucho," at the top of their lovely lungs as she peeked between the spiky metal bars.

Javier stood in front of them, wearing his Zapata sombrero, singing at the top of his very off-key voice, and his formerly crisp, white shirt was smudged with dirt, but his khaki pants still held their creases. Then, his voice rose alone, "I know you're there, mi orchid Xochitzalita, abre la puerta or I'm climbing the fortress of your walls, I'll always find you, Xochitzalita!"

Ohmygoddess, if the neighbors ever thought I was a pocha loca, now they know, she thought, racing down the stairs before he began climbing the tree to the spiky metal bars. "And he's also bien borracho drunk, what an idiot ayyy, and I had to kill my own scorpion, and it was not golden."

She threw open the door and there he was almost to the metal fence that surrounded her bedroom patio, with spikes. And her neighbors, staring and smiling; who could blame them, what a scene.

"Amor, you opened the door, you don't want me to die, mi orchid..." The band launched into another beautiful song, and she told the neighbors, "I'm so sorry, it's late, I'm so sorry."

"I paid them for ten songs." Javier was trying to decide whether to climb down or just leap. The tequila yelled, LEAP!

"Tell them to stop, Javier, it's after 2 a.m...."

"You're in my country, México, with an authentic Muppie, Xochitzalita, look at these people, they're enjoying the mariachis at 2 a.m., and watching me climb this tree for love, for you," he laughed like the boy/man he was. And then, he leapt to applause and gritos, and to his surprise landed on his feet (loafers) upright, still wearing Zapata's sombrero.

"Besame besame besame besame..." the mariachis chanted, smiling, as they played. And the neighbors joined in after 2 a.m., many giggling, "Besame besame besame..."

"I am so fucking embarrassed, Javier."

"You'll be more embarrassed if you don't just fucking kiss me, then they'll shut up," he smiled that smile as he took her in his arms and claimed his kiss.

"Now I'm really La Pocha Loca, now they really know who I am..."

"Who?"

"My neighbors."

"They always did, mi amor," Javier laughed, holding onto her, so that she wouldn't run away, and so he wouldn't crash to the cobbles.

They finally sat on her stairs, watching the mariachis play with such joy at almost 3 a.m., listening to their rich, diverse, gorgeous, male voices sing more than the ten songs he paid for. And she thought of the Pueblo's flute, drums, song, bringing up the sun, dawn.

"They're bringing the dawn, tigre, they're bringing the sun to us."

"So we can see the invisible." Javier's eyes were half-closed, blissfully exhausted. "And in this moment, this very moment, I'm so happy that I love you, and I want to..."

"What?"

"I want to eat the sun, and then I want to make love to you with watermelons, as you solemnly promised."

Finally, the mariachis—each one so handsome in his spangled outfit, from teens to seventies—paused to yell, "Buenos dias!" laughter, and a song of goodbye. She ran into the house for her purse, found five-hundred pesos right away, and rushed out to tip them, as each neighbor also tipped them what they had

"Buenos dias," everyone echoed, as they closed their doors, and the mariachis climbed into the large van. As they drove off, one of them said goodbye with his trumpet singing sweetly out the window.

"I want to eat the sun, and then I want to make love to you with watermelons, Xochitzalita," Javier repeated. (The Energy Child felt something rise from the throat, from where her/his heart should be, where his/her genitals should be—laughter.)

Xochiquetzal finally got Javier under the covers, where he found one position; on his back, arms spread wide as though he were flying. Toward the sun, laughing. She stretched out next to him, his young man's length, inhaling the blend of tequila and new salt.

"You are my gift, on loan, Javier Quetzalcoatl, I see you flying to the Morning Star, the rising sun, I see you..." She closed her eyes and joined him on that journey, flying, laughing. Dawn.

The usual pre-dawn fireworks announced some daily fiesta, the return of the sun. But first, the Morning Star, Quetzalcoatl.

They didn't stir, their bodies, as they flew, gathering dreams like fading stars. Quetzalcoatl was the final star, the ancient warrior star, bright enough to face the rising sun. To take a bite of its potent, fertile power (that transformed the scorpion into gold). And the Energy Child remembered that gold as they flew to the sun, now, hungry for light, laughing. Weeping. Blinded by dawn's yellow. Gold.

Is this?   The deepest?   Human play?

⊷⊷⊷◆⊶⊶⊶

"Amor, you're drooling," Xochiquetzal heard Javier's soft laughter in her ear. Then she almost smiled: coffee. She opened her eyes to slits, protesting the almost noon Mexican sun with her right hand shielding her. She felt strangely sunburned—My dream, she remembered, and tried to smile. "Is there really coffee?"

"Not only coffee, look, scrambled eggs con chorizo, warm tortillas, and lots of watermelon," Javier smiled with joy. "I don't even have a hangover, I must've eaten the sun."

"You did, I dreamt it. I didn't think you could cook, Dr. Gomez, and I don't believe you don't have a hangover, that bottle of tequila, you and the other idiot."

"When you eat the sun, no hangover, mi amor, but I can't speak for Pablo," he laughed. "I'm capable of just the basics, nothing fancy, scrambled eggs, tacos, burritos, or starve. Here, let's eat, Xochitzalita, let me serve you."

"I'll be right back, I guess I can't be mad at you now that you're feeding me." She ran to the bathroom to pee, wipe her eyes, face, a swish of toothpaste, a stroke of lip gloss, quick lines of green on eyelids— "Honey, you're fifty-eight, no matter what he thinks, and him without a wrinkle," she murmured to the mirror. Well, when he's doing the Dr. Zapata frown, those tiny lines on his forehead, el doctoricito, and last night should cost him a few wrinkles, him and the other pendejo, Pablo, big deep ones, I hope.

"Hurry up, it's getting cold!"

She ran back, "You served me, gracias tigre, I really can't be mad at you," she smiled at him and sipped her first taste of coffee. "It's perfect, strong, American style. So what happened last night after I left, los dos pendejos, was Sonya okay, poor girl, I felt bad leaving her."

"Do you really want to hear this, I could tell you later."

"No, tell me now, also I loved the mariachis y el loco con el Zapata sombrero singing way off key." Xochiquetzal leaned over to kiss him, and he met her mouth, forcefully, gently.

"Let's do this, let's not talk, I knew you'd love them, your spirit can't resist," Javier smiled.

"And now my neighbors know my true name, La Pocha Loca, oh I don't care, tell me what happened, watermelons later. You know, Pablo's not a bad guy, he just takes his ego a bit over the edge sometimes. I think you're both alike in some ways, los dos flamboyant, pendejos, muppies, and he'd be jealous of your Zapata sombrero."

Javier rolled his eyes, muttering, "Yippee, como no, so here's what happened, someone went out and got the colonial policia on his caballito...horsie, very romantic," he smiled (ironically), "since Pablo was losing his tortillas, and I was losing mine, la verdad. So el policia pulls his gun from his colonial outfit, points it at us, joder, we freeze, and then Pablo knows this guy, so he introduces us like we're old friends. El policia, Jorge, has one shot of tequila, looks at us both, and says, 'Finish the bottle and get el chingado a la casa,' and goes out to his waiting caballito. We listened to him race down the cobbles, that sound of horse hooves, I love that sound."

"It sounds like a Fellini film," Xochiquetzal laughed.

"No, a San Miguel film, and so Pablo and I finished the bottle with two more margaritas, y la pobrecita Sonya just watched, never said a word. I think we became friends, chinga tu puto perro y tu gato tambien, and he told me, when Sonya went to el bano, that you were never lovers. Is that true, Xochitzalita? He said, 'Mi dejo en la calle, nunca en la cama de la reina...She left me in the street, never in the queen's bed.' Es la verdad, truth?"

She was tempted not to answer him, to torture him a little for last night's drama at Mama Mias (and all the chicas on his speed dial). She filled a corn tortilla with scrambled eggs con chorizo, spicy green salsa, and slipped it into her mouth. Then, a sip of the just-right coffee, glancing at the watermelon slices...ruby-red, juicy, expectant. Sabrosita.

"I'm waiting, cabroncita."

Xochiquetzal looked directly into Javier's eyes (those twin fires, resting), tauntingly, for a few seconds. "Now I know how out there loco you can get, doctorcito, when the Buddhist detachment flies away, that fire." She paused. "See that beautiful, silk shawl with gold beading on my bedroom door, see how it catches the light?"

It was his turn to be silent, to stare back into her eyes (where he was beginning to see her, his, truth). The dream.

"Pablo gave it to me, I treasure it, but he never saw it draped over my bedroom door, chinga tu puta pajarito. No, he never saw it catch the early morning sun's light."

"Ay mi pochita feminista Yaqui, I'm going to dress you in watermelon slices como una hippie..."

"And then it's your turn today, mi muy malo muppie, I'm going to cover you in watermelon like a heyoka, like the heyoka that you truly are, a muppie heyoka," she smiled as the bright sunlight brought the gold beading to life. Pablo gave me the gold in his own way, but he couldn't see the invisible, with me anyway.

"Qué rica," Javier smiled with pleasure, wondering at her force como un hombre, mi feminista. And it came to him, an *equal*. When Pablo drunkenly asked what it was like to make love to her, he (as drunk) almost punched him. Then, he laughed, "Como una jaguar, amigo."

They were sticky with watermelon, her silky sheets a mess, a wonderful mess of persistent joys, tender violence, brutal orgasms becoming honey, blinding, yellow; kisses threatening to devour the other, kisses threatening to feed the other, embraces that possessed the other, embraces that set the other free; and in that moment, without words, they knew if loneliness were ever to stalk them, find them again, they only had to remember the scent, the taste, the feel, of red, ripe watermelon. In that moment, they were imperfect, not self-sufficient, one-in-their-own-souls; they needed the other in order to live, to take the next breath, breathing into each other's mouths, in order to see light, in order to see shadow, gazing into the other's eyes, the mystery within the other, knowing, not knowing, the other, it was enough, it was a gift, this imperfection.

Xochiquetzal's kundalini serpent filled her, vibrating with insistent ecstasy, wave upon wave, and she wanted him in her mouth. She chose a large, center slice of ripe red, pinched out the center, devouring it, feeding Javier's dripping mouth. She placed it, the circle of ripe watermelon, over his resting serpent, so vulnerable after love, soft soft soft, it fit entirely in her mouth. He moaned, arms spread out, flying, licking him erect, flying, "No no," he moaned, flying, "Yes yes," she hissed, "yes," flying, sucking him gently, mercilessly, tenderly, forcefully, flying, she made him beg, "Yes yes yes," flying, "Yes yes yes," flying, "Yes," he flew into the Evening Star, Venus, Goddess of no shame, flying, Goddess of no shame in love, yes, her, flying, and when his sea salt foam honey erupted, flying flying, she quickly brought some to his mouth, flying, like sudden serpent venom, flying, he tried to refuse, twisting his head no no no, flying, she made him yes yes yes, flying, she made him taste his serpent's wisdom (what kills, what heals), flying flying, she made him taste his sea salt foam honey, flying, potent, fertile, flying, fertile, potent, flying into Venus, her lover, Quetzalcoatal, flying, in the evening sky, flying, filled with the blinding yellow of the ancient sun, flying, into gold, flying, they dreamt, flying flying flying into gold...

Javier...*I'm facing a warrior, an ancient warrior, with a headdress* *of blazing gold feathers, who I simply know comes from the sun. He could kill me, we both know this, but instead he welcomes me to walk into him, and, trembling, I do. I begin to burn with golden joy as I stand in the center of the sun, and he doesn't kill me.*

Xochiquetzal...*Sunset gold, Taos mesa, my favorite, daily mesa, sudden female rain, I'm naked, I open my mouth to taste this female rain, and then it becomes male rain, the taste of fertility, potent, and I begin to sing a song of gold I will always remember, a song that will always give me courage, the courage to love.*

(The Energy Child longed to taste the female rain, the male rain, longed to laugh out loud, longed to sing, and in that longing her/his mouth was created, and then whispered his/her first spoken word. "Play.")

———◆———

Javier glanced at the glowing red numbers, 6:20 p.m., time to get ready for the dinner, his friends in San Miguel, some old lovers in the group, and he thought of Pablo last night. Why did he make me so crazy, I'm not usually so jealous, usually I make las chicas jealous, what's going on, bringing mariachis to her door, climbing the fregado tree, risking my surgeon's hands, my speciality for the next year. He watched her dream, on her stomach, clutching her pillow, suddenly stretching. Then, he knew: *She's my equal and with her I'm not lonely.* The taste of his serpent's wisdom still lingered in his mouth; the taste of raw seaweed, he imagined.

"She made me taste it," he murmured, wanting her again. "Older woman, younger man," Javier whispered into Xochiquetzal's ear until she opened her eyes.

"You've got to be kidding, no way, I'm a puddle of orgasmic jello," she smiled at him. "Plus, it's going on 7 p.m., get your nalgas up and dressed, malo muppie,," now trying to sound stern, but instead pleasure prevailed.

"Older woman makes younger man taste his own semen, which

makes him dream of the warrior in the sun..."

"I love that, did you really dream that?"

"Yes, and did you dream, Xochitzalita?"

She curled into his body, her head on his smooth shoulder, her feet touching his, as he stroked the length of her glowing spine. "I dreamt my favorite mesa in Taos and that I was naked in the female rain, tasting it, then the male rain, tasting it."

"What is female rain, male rain, I didn't study that in biology." He breathed in the scent of her orchid womb and if he had ever been lonely he couldn't remember that time, in this moment.

"Female rain is encompassing, drenching, fertile, and male rain is sudden, joyful, violent, potent. And it's really like that in northern New Mexico, Taos, one or the other, and of course the snow in winter when they marry each other."

"Fertile, potent, the snow, I'd love to see that marriage, it's been a long time, snow. And, you know, I haven't told anyone my dreams since I was a boy with mi India mama, Amalia. My mother said she didn't believe in all that Indian stuff when I tried to tell her a dream once, so I told only Amalia."

"Mi abuela, Clara, and I used to share our dreams in the morning, that's how she taught me dreaming, and how to fly. Then I taught my son, Justin, to dream and fly. And I talked about it with my students from time to time, that kind of vision. I love that I have someone to tell my daily dreams to, mi tigre, but no more tequila for you."

"I flew last night, mi amor, in my dream, to the warrior in the sun, who invited me to walk into him."

"I know you did, I saw you, flying to the sun, but not the warrior, that's wonderful."

"How?" Javier laughed.

"In my dream, flying with you, let's do this from now on, tell each other our dreams, but I didn't see the warrior in the sun, that was just for you, Javiercito."

"Call me that, Amalia called me that, no one else has ever called me Javiercito." Tears filled his eyes for a moment. "But only in private, you and I, mi amor, I don't want to be known as el Doctor Javiercito," he smiled into her eyes. With this woman I'm not lonely, with this woman I fly to the warrior in the sun.

"The warrior wore a headdress of golden feathers, blazing like the sun, and I walked into him. I was afraid but I did it, walked into him, and I burned with, what can only be described as, golden joy." Javier paused. "Xochitzalita, I've never been with an equal, a woman who's my equal. I think Clara, from Spain, would've been, in time."

"If you can walk into the warrior of the sun, you can be with an equal, but I know what you mean, Javiercito, something's shifted in me, yes, that being with an equal. And in my dream last night, I sang a golden song that was joyous, no words, just joyous, and yes, that gold. Now for the puta messiah scorpion," she laughed. Xochiquetzal thought of the dream she had of him, his eyes, years ago, his words, *You will love me like no other.* But she couldn't tell him this, this dream, how could she love him like no other when she knew he was her gift, on loan. My gift, can I afford to receive you, fully, to memorize you fully, like no other, Javiercito?

"Why are you crying, mi amor?" He looked directly into her eyes, an equal.

"How can I love you, love you to your bones, when you're twenty-four years younger than me?"

"Because when you x-ray our bodies, that's what we are, bones, flesh on bones, spirit in the body on loan, and because, most importantly, you know I'm your gift, Xochitzalita."

"And how are you so wise at thirty-four, anyway, doctorcito?"

"Because I met you, you draw it out of me like my semen, and then you make me taste it como una cabrona, I want you one more time, then we'll get dressed, tell me..."

"What, we should get dressed now, we're going to be late..."

"That you love me, no this minute mierda, tell me."

"I do."

"Tell me."

"Love you."

"Tell me, Xochitzalita, now."

"I love you, Javiercito," she murmured into his ear (and the Energy Child said, "Love.")

"If you hadn't called we were going to eat without you, and did you find parking close by?" The good looking, older man grabbed Javier for a hug, glancing at Xochiquetzal with a welcoming smile. About twelve people were behind him in the living room, men and women (all who seemed to be under forty), sitting, standing, talking. Becoming silent as they took her in, Javier's new lover, the unknown entity; and wasn't she older than him, by at least ten years?

"Xochitzalita talked me into taking a taxi, she's an eco-feminista," Javier laughed. "Diego, this is mi amor, Xochitzalita, and this is Diego, el cabron jefe de surgery here in San Miguel. I know, I know, she dresses como la Frida, pero es muy hermosa, como no."

She started to make a muppie comment, but let it pass since he was wearing well worn jeans (not the creased khakis), a Mana band t-shirt, his aged, black leather jacket, and the expensive muppie loafers. Look around, she told herself, you're surrounded by muppies, pendeja.

"She's right about the taxis in this town, too many chingado cars wasting fuel circling around." Diego turned to fully face her, taking her hand, kissing it, then meeting her eyes. "Frida would be happy, bienvenida, are you two hungry, I assume, as new love makes us all," he laughed, some of the others joining in.

What a charming guy, the surgery jefe chief, but as I thought, the women are trying to figure out my age. A few of his old lovers, mid-late twenties, I knew I shouldn't have come, tried to fake a migraine at the last minute, but of course he saw through me, those fucking x-ray eyes. "If anyone's not sweet to you, we leave, I promise, mi amor," and so, here I am, all fregado fifty-eight years of me. And in my Frida Kahlo, pocha outfit, "Yipee," she murmured.

As his friends hugged and kissed Javier—the ex-lovers prolonging the kiss a bit longer—laughing, joking, his friends; she felt, most definitely, like the old, embittered jaguar watching the beautiful young do their greeting ritual. The ex-lovers were obvious as they sent Xochiquetzal their best, icy smiles.

"I've been trying to talk Javier into doing his surgery here in San Miguel, so maybe with your help he'll do it." Diego's smile was dazzling, that god-doctor confidence of course, in his fifties. My fucking age and I'm probably even older, she sighed.

"If Xochitzalita orders me to, I will," Javier announced. The women stared at each other in disbelief; this was the guy who was seeing chicas barely twenty, and we were too old for him, que cabron.

"I don't know you well enough to advise you, much less order you, to do something that crucial in your career, Javier, give me a break."

Javier was momentarily hurt, but she was right—I'm being an ass, cut it out, she's nervous as it is. He put his arm around her waist and laughed, "Time for my medication, mi amor."

"Let's eat, more cabernet for the muy rico pollo con mole!" Diego saved the moment. As they settled into the luxurious chairs, at the beautifully arranged table (small rose, with baby's breath, bouquets ran down the center), an older woman brought out bowls of food, while a younger woman, her daughter, poured wine for everyone. This was Diego's casa (really an immense mansion), and the older woman, the cook, had been with him since before his wife died; before her daughter was born.

"A los pajaritos de amor, or should I say, to the love birds," Diego laughed loudly, raising his glass. He spoke English with less of an accent than Javier, Xochiquetzal noted, and hoped that her face wasn't beet-red. Shouldn't fifty be the cut-off age for fregado blushing, she whined internally, taking sips of the knock-out cabernet that stuck to her tongue with richness.

Javier took her hand and kissed it, holding her eyes. "Pay no attention to this guy, he's just over-sexed."

"And you should talk," the words popped out before she could censor them, and there was a ripple of laughter, easing the tension.

"Where did you two meet? I'm Ana by the way." Where did Javier meet this vieja pocha, she's at least ten years older than him, we're not good enough? She kept smiling, waiting for an answer— attractive, sensual, an old lover of course.

"Vallarta, como no, and very romantic, so I've followed her home to San Miguel," Javier laughed, lifting his glass. "To amor, wherever el chingado it finds you." He gave Ana a stern look of *back off* and finished his wine. She couldn't take Clara's place, no one could, and now they're all dying of curiosity, why her. I shouldn't have brought Xochitzalita, not yet.

"What brings you to San Miguel, tell me your name again, it's Indian right? I'm Juan, an old amigo of este cabron who won't leave you alone." Dark-skinned, Indian features, a very sweet smile; not the god-doctor dazzler.

"It's Mayan, Xochiquetzal, Shweequetzal," she pronounced it. "I'm a wandering photographer taking photos..."

"Es doctora de los fotos, Juan, una professora and a wise woman, mi Xochitzalita, un besito, mi amor." She allowed one quick kiss, whispering, "More later, Javercito, if you're good."

"I'm always good, aren't I, younger man, tu sabes…"

"Hey you two, no love bird talk at the dinner table or I might puke. Xochiquetzal, I'm Feliz, Javier's very old from childhood, pain en las nalgas, amiga, and I'm not an old lover," she laughed wickedly, enjoying turning the energetic tables on the three exes present. They look like a pack of vultures, so what if she's older, big fregado deal.

"Hi Feliz, glad to meet you, and you have to tell me childhood stories sometime." She liked her immediately, beautiful but not vain, and obviously full of life. Feliz, Joy.

"I have something better than stories, mujer, I have photos, proof…"

"Do you still have that pile of black mail?" Javier smiled at her. "Watch out for this one, mi amor, she's a secret sadist, a dentista, but I still love her, and, okay, she's also a very good painter, una artista." He fed Xochiquetzal a piece of his mole-chocolate-rich-drenched chicken, and quickly licked the sauce from her lips. "Do you still have the ones of you and I in diapers, potty training, Dios mio…"

"You bet I do. I'll get your phone number from Javier and we can meet for dinner or something, maybe dancing, do you like to dance?"

"I love to dance, and bring the goods," Xochiquetzal laughed, "can't wait to see el Dr. Gomez in diapers."

"Do you have children?" Ana jumped in (like a vulture).

"I have one grown son, Justin."

"How *old is he*?" Ana smiled as though she were really interested (vulture wants soft, yummy, open eyes).

"Going on fifty actually."

Feliz's laughter rose over everyone else's. Good for her, out-vulture the vultures. "You'll have to fix me up, I simply adore older men."

"Hey, I'm an older man," Diego offered.

"So, how old does that make *you*, and why do you have an Indian name, if you don't mind my being so nosey?" Ana tried for playful laughter, but it was harsh.

"That's enough, Ana, you're being a bitch," Javier said softly, that command.

"I'm eighty-four and I'm a Yaqui Indian…"

"Okay, time to break out the chilled champagne, and, mamacita, you make eighty-four look good, Xochitzalita." Diego stood up to turn some salsa on. "I see what you're up to, cabron, older woman, younger man," he roared with laughter, and offered his hand to her.

She glanced at Javier and he laughed, "Go ahead, just watch out for his Roman roaming hands, no I'll watch out for them, this guy is so fregado sneaky! And I say Roman because I saw those pinche cabrones in action in that city, Rome, kept after the beautiful women, day and night, so I'm watching you, Diego."

Silvia, an ex-lover, pulled Javier to his feet, and Xochiquetzal heard, "Older woman, younger man, is this true?" she smiled seductively.

Very attractive with big breasts, she noted, so this is what he usually likes. Ana has big ones too, Xochiquetzal sighed (with full knowledge of her small, niña ones).

"Nothing like it, Silvia, and what they say is absolutely true, even better than I imagined." Javier looked directly into Xochiquetzal's eyes, held them, smiled.

"Are you really a Yaqui, notice I'm not asking if you're really eighty-four," Diego laughed, taking her hands in his as they danced.

"My great-grandmother was a full-blood Yaqui from Sonora, and I'm not confirming eighty-four," Xochiquetzal laughed with him.

"I'm guessing you turned your age around, forty-eight, it must be your Yaqui blood, Xochitzalita, you look younger. And so, will you help me recruit Javier for his surgery in San Miguel?" He twirled her, catching her hands again, smiling with that god-doctor confidence.

"You are a total charm bucket, Diego..."

"A what bucket?" He bathed her in that smile.

"A *charm bucket,* Diego," she laughed.

"I've been called worse, in fact I thought you'd been speaking to these people, as in a bucket of, well you know what." The smile continued full force, dazzling.

"This is entirely Javier's decision, charm bucket Diego, an important one. Not my place, older woman, younger man," Xochiquetzal laughed. In his fifties, good looking, my age, the thought pounced on her—and if he only knew I'm probably even older than he is, me and my Yaqui blood, oh yeah.

"Do you mind if we share?" Juan cut in with his sweet yet devastating smile.

Dark-skinned, handsome, Indian features. The other god-doctors were dancing with their girlfriends, wives, as the cook's daughter offered glittering, crystal flutes of champagne to everyone. "Gracias," Juan took two flutes. She smiled, eyes down.

"Now, this guy actually steals women on horseback as his ancestors did." Javier danced over with a frowning Silvia. "So you better kiss me goodbye, Xochitzalita."

"Stop it, Javier, later," she said, deflecting Silvia's if-looks-could-kill glare.

"I'll kiss her for you," Juan laughed, kissing her on the cheek. "Do you want to see my splendid horse, and I really do have one. I live in el campo, just outside San Miguel. You and Javier have to visit, and we can all go riding, but I promise not to steal you, Xochitzalita, unless you want me to."

I am really getting the new-comer, get-the-guest treatment, Xochiquetzal realized, but this guy is so handsome, and of course right inside his Mexican skin, mama fregado mia. She caught Javier's gaze, those eyes, so serious as though in pain, and behind them the heyoka with his ripe watermelon. Mi tigre, this beautiful young man.

Someone switched the salsa to Shakira: Feliz. "Okay, I'm cutting in now, so cut the crap!" Feliz bumped Juan out of the way with her lovely hip, grabbing Xochiquetzal firmly by the waist, laughing. They began to belly dance, hands in the air. A fellow mujer loca with crazy joy—Feliz...Joy.

"I love Shakira, I took belly dance lessons a while ago..."

"I can tell, mujer, so I'll follow you, of course I brought Shakira, Mana, Los Cadillacs, or we'd be dancing that worn-out salsa all night. I mean, I love salsa but not the whole chingado night."

They did the bump with their hips touching, pausing to howl with laughter. Diego brought them each a margarita and tried to join them, but Feliz yelled, "No hombres allowed, the belly dance is for women in labor, and you doctors are always hogging everything!"

"I need my teeth cleaned, cabrona!" Diego laughed. "And since I gave you a free dinner, margaritas, and dessert is next, it should be on the house."

"You're on, next Friday, 10 a.m. sharp, no Mexican time mierda." Feliz had a laugh that was entirely unrestrained, wild. She continued to belly dance, arms raised, margarita balanced in one hand, bumping Xochiquetzal's hips with loca joy.

La pocha vieja...old gringa, and la loca Feliz, they deserve each other, Ana seethed. They look like putas, women in labor, que belly dancing, putas.

Javier watched them dance, sipping their margaritas. Dios mio, she's found a play mate, the wild one. Marla, the third ex, had cut in on Silvia, so he pulled her over to the belly dancers and bellowed off key, "Born to be wild!...Hey, I want to belly dance, I'm still doing the fucking salsa!"

"No men, no men!" Xochiquetzal and Feliz yelled at the same time, to their total delight.

"I should tie you two up, las malas mujeres."

Las putas, Ana added, drinking another perfect margarita.

"Why don't you tie me up, doctor?" Marla whined seductively, with a growl of anger. "Remember the time you tied me to the bed..."

Javier walked away to the bathroom, glanced at his watch, going on 1 a.m., time to go, enough.

"Have you met the evil twin yet, I"m guessing you haven't." Feliz's hips were sensual, fluid, a natural belly dancer. It was hard for Xochiquetzal to imagine her drilling someone's teeth at the moment, in a dentist jacket.

"Who's the evil twin?"

"Javier has an identical twin named Xavier, with an X, you know X, A, V, I, E, R. He was born a couple of minutes ahead, so he's older."

She was stunned, *an identical twin*? "Why do you call him the evil twin?"

"He's not really evil, but a true pain in las nalgas. I'll let Javier tell you, they haven't gotten along, I think, since birth. And so, are you a little jealous of all these exes gathered in one spot like a pack of hyenas, or should I say vultures," Feliz laughed that laugh.

"You have a great laugh, and, okay, I'm a little jealous, but we're hardly going steady, like who knows..."

"I'm taking her back, Feliz, for one more dance, then time to go." Javier tried to be stern but shared diaper memories prevailed, and he took Feliz in his arms as well.

"Oh you men, so possessive, that's why I'll never marry, just fool around." Feliz winked at Xochiquetzal. "I'll call you, maybe we'll go out this weekend, I know a great place, you'll love it." When she tried to walk away, Xochiquetzal and Javier wouldn't let her go; so they danced the last dance as a threesome. Laughing like joyous hyenas.

"I can tell Diego really likes you, and of course La Feliz, but I worry about you two going out dancing," Javier smiled. "Gracias, mi amor, for putting up with all the bullshit, shit of the bull, or the cows ayy, tonight. Are you sure you want to walk home, mi hermosa hippie Yaqui?" He held her around the waist, firmly.

"Well, you put up with Pablo and now you're even grande amigos. And I like Feliz, that wild laugh, can't wait to see her paintings." Xochiquetzal paused to gauge Javier's face: peaceful. When he holds me this way, it doesn't feel like ownership, she realized, just a wave coming to shore after a long journey. He's breaking down my long held feminist fear of public displays of affection, that masculine sense of ownership, this is my woman and I want everyone to know it. She smiled, well maybe a little bit, but more so just a wave, coming to shore, after a long ass journey. Am I too old for this, am I? His face, peaceful, his hand on her waist so warm.

"I don't know about grande amigos, but probably friends if we don't kill each other," Javier smiled up at the sky, stars, dreams. I dream with this woman, I dream the golden-feathered, fierce, warrior in the sun.

She took a deep breath. "I hear you have a twin brother, Xavier with an X. Why didn't you tell me, seems like an important detail..."

"I was going to tell you later, of course before you met him, but do you mind if we talk about this tomorrow? There's so much betrayal between us, Xavier with an X, and I..."

The sound of horse hooves bearing down on the cobbles became deafening, threatening. Two colonial police, in their full colonial blue outfits, descended full throttle, like swift thunder, down the center of the street, cars pulling over to get out of the way.

"Wow, what a sight, and what a sound, what the hell's going on?"

"At 2 a.m. anything can be going on, but in San Miguel probably a street fight, or maybe even a robbery, who knows." Javier pulled her even closer. "We're taking a taxi, Xochitzalita." And he hailed one, slowly approaching.

"Our sudden journey into the sixteenth century makes me not argue with you," she laughed softly. "The sound of horses on cobbles, full out, makes me feel like I'm being chased, hunted, do you know what I mean?"

As they sat in the comfort of the taxi, Javier breathed, "I know exactly what you mean, as though we'd entered another life time together. As though someone was going to take you from me, again."

Xochiquetzal gently kissed him, inhaling his sea foam, new salt scent. "Exactly, that's what I felt, like an old dream, an old life, exactly."

"I can't believe I'm not sleepy, I think the horses woke me up. The windhorses, do you know what this is, the windhorse?" she murmured, stretching her body against his, luxuriating in flesh and blood, this life. Now.

"Wind horse," he repeated softly, "dime, tell me, mi amor, wise woman, mujer que sabe." Javier smiled as her orchid scent floated up to him, reminding him he wasn't sleepy either.

"Please don't call me a 'wise woman' in public, it's embarrassing, so please..."

Javier laughed deep in his throat, licking her neck as though deciding if he should devour her. "Dime de los caballos del viento," he growled.

"Do you know my last name?"

"Do you mean your family name, is this a test?" he growled, this time, in displeasure.

"Yes, my family name, and this is a test, I told you in Bucerias when we just met, when you started talking about past lives. Why did you do that, talk about past lives, mi tigre tan malo," she growled back.

"Professora Aguila, and you do have the spirit of la aguila, the eagle, a family of eagles de México, mi pochita Yaqui. I recognized your eyes from a dream, one I've had more than once, and so my mouth started saying things that even surprised me, Javier with a J. I used to dream small dreams, once in a while, and when I dreamt your eyes, a voice said, 'Recordar, remember.'" He paused to kiss her so deeply, they remembered their first kiss in Bucerias. In the shower. When her kimono fell to the tiles. And the red, fleshy rose petals.

"You gave birth to me, Xochitzalita, es la verdad...it's the truth, did I pass the test? Now, tell me about the wind horse."

"We gave birth to each other because we allowed *drala energy,* windhorse, to join us. Okay, in Tibetan Buddhism teachings, drala energy belongs to no one, it's not for you or against you, but the abundance of the universe flowing through us if we let it, and boy did we let it." Xochiquetzal smiled at the memory. She placed her hand over his heart, feeling it pulse his beautiful blood through countless arteries, right next to her, now. "Do you want to hear a paragraph or two about el windhorse, or later."

"Qué bien, wind horse, drala energy, I'm waiting, mi amor."

"Also, wind horse is one word, windhorse, from the Tibetan word *lungta*..."

"I'm still waiting, mi amor, windhorse," he said it quickly, one word.

"Do you realize it's almost dawn, okay, okay, let me read it. I keep the book right here, and my reading glasses," she laughed, and began to read: "'It is possible to contact energy that is beyond aggression—energy that is neither for you or against you. That is the energy of drala...Windhorse is a translation of the Tibetan *lungta*. *Lung* means 'wind' and *ta* means 'horse.' Invoking secret drala is the experience of raising windhorse, raising a wind of delight and power and riding on, or conquering, that energy. Such wind can come with great force,' like the horses on the cobbles tonight, that sound, that energy..."

"Lungta, drala energy, que bien, corazón."

"'...like a typhoon that can blow down trees and buildings and create huge waves in the water. The personal experience of this wind comes as a feeling of being completely and powerfully in the present... Then, having raised windhorse, you can accommodate whatever arises in your state of mind. So the fruition of invoking secret drala is that, having raised windhorse, you experience a state of mind that is free from subconscious gossip, free from hesitation and disbelief...It is gullible, in the positive sense, and it is completely fresh. Secret drala is experiencing that very moment of your state of mind, which is the essence of nowness.' I just read my underlined sentences on these pages, and as you can see my book is an underlined mess. I learned to do this as a professor for my classes, to feel free to ruin my books," Xochiquetzal smiled.

There was a long silence as the stars shifted, as the waning crescent moon set, as the Morning Star, Quetzalcoatl, prepared to climb the sky. Dawn.

"Secret drala, windhorse, is experiencing that very moment of your state of mind, which is the essence of nowness, yes, I love that, I've always known that somehow. When I'm in the Emergency, that nowness, that windhorse, yes, and now my surgery specialty, that secret drala. I'm going to need it, that gullible, fresh mind to learn everything I have to learn. I've never had the words for it, gracias mi amor, mi guru de los caballitos del viento."

"Hey, you're my guru as well, believe me..."

"Of what, tu sabrosita orchid?" Javier smiled with secret drala, enjoying his skin remembering her skin, his soul remembering her soul, now.

"Of joy, that gullible, fearless mind de mi tigre. Without your fearlessness, Javier, we wouldn't be here in my bed in San Miguel at almost 4 a.m. in the morning, waiting for the dawn, again," she laughed, wept softly. I'm sharing my most treasured thoughts with this man, twenty-four years younger than me, my equal.

"Now, tell me about your twin, Xavier with an X. We're waiting for the dawn, mi tigre, you can tell me, amor."

"I can't tell it all, now, Xochitzalita, but maybe a preview. He was born a few minutes before me, he was always jealous of me, he thinks I'm our father's favorite, and our mother's, and I had Amalia all to myself for years. His India mamas kept leaving, pobrecito, it's true, Amalia said he had bad luck from birth, that's what she said with so much sadness, tears, I remember. She even tried to include him, to tell him stories, to hug him to her, but he refused her, saying she smelled bad, running away from us, and now I know, his pride. And so, I was considered the lucky one, the best loved, the youngest, in the family, and he always found a way to betray me, to hurt me. The final straw was when he called Clara, my old love..."

"In Spain?"

"Yes, he called to tell her I had an endless supply of chicas in Mexico, that she was one of many, and she married the wealthy Spaniard who was after her since she was fifteen, when I came home for a month. That's when he called her and he's done these things since we were boys, jealousy, envy, competition, betrayal, but when he called Clara that was my limit, enough."

"Were you seeing someone while you were home, like your groupies at dinner?"

Javier pulled back and looked into her eyes—She spares me nothing. "La verdad es, the truth is, I wanted to, I almost did once, but I didn't. I think he heard the conversation on the extension, and later I cancelled the date. He betrayed me, even if I did why do that, betrayal?" Tears slid down his face, falling on their bodies, wet wisdom.

"I'm so sorry, I'm so sorry, mi tigre. Quetzalcoatl had a twin brother who betrayed him, that's what I remember." Xochiquetzal licked his tears and remembered the betrayal that was still unspeakable, better left to silence. So many years ago, her eyes were now dry. They held each other silently, the wet wisdom shared.

"Has someone betrayed you this way, mi amor, I feel so much sorrow, I feel it, your sorrow, dime...tell me, Xochitzalita, dime." The Energy Child echoed, "Dime."

Harsh sobs broke open from her heart and though the sound was awful, it was time, time for wetness, words.

"Dime, mi amor, tell me." Javier cradled her as though she were a child, as though she were his child.

Finally, the words, whispered words, "When I went to Europe, after graduating with my bachelors, I wanted to go alone, by myself, without my boyfriend, so I did. I also looked for my father in Paris, I never found him, I never knew him." Xochiquetzal's voice was low, calm now, as waves of salt covered them both.

"I loved my journey, I loved traveling alone, and I knew I wouldn't find Marcel Godot, but I had to try, you know, waiting for el Godot," she smiled, tears streaming, creating small, fresh rainbows.

"A French man, Paris."

"Yes, my mother, Florinda, met a handsome, young, traveling artist, a photographer and painter, she said, about to return to Paris, his home, anyway that's what she told me, and I was born. And so, when I returned home, to my mother's house, my boyfriend confessed he'd had an affair with my beautiful mother, Florinda." She paused to catch her breath between tears, but her voice remained calm as Javier stroked her hair. "I was never as beautiful, or as sensual, as my mother, I always knew that, so many men wanted her, not me, her. But for her to seduce Alex was unforgivable to me, so I left and I never lived with her again."

Fireworks exploded in the distance, and then closer, raining down over their heads like prisms of fiery rainbows. Dawn.

"Ayy Xochitzalita, mi amor, mujer tan hermosa, yes you, you are beautiful, professora Aguila, and you became el doctor de los fotos, your father, el Godot."

"And I never forgave Alex, although I also betrayed him in Paris. I didn't find my father, but I did find a lover. When I told him about my lover, I was being honest and all that, hoping he'd forgive me. That's when he told me. How could he, my own mother, and how could she, *her daughter*?"

"She was jealous, mi amor, Xochitzalita," Javier murmured.

His simple reply, words, stunned her; that's the one thing she never thought of. That her mother—beautiful, confident, so free,

Florinda—would ever be jealous of the second rate Florinda. The academic, camera toting, daughter, who just wanted to be loved. By her. The Goddess. And so, she become her own Goddess, Xochiquetzal, Goddess of love, beauty. Yet she was afraid to love, be loved, and she doubted her own beauty—Some Goddess, she'd taunted herself with her new name at twenty-four. Was a Goddess perfect, she'd always wondered in her self doubt, but she kept the beautiful name. Became her own Goddess. In order to survive her imperfection.

"I've always thought of myself as, first, intelligent, then resourceful, pretty strong, good traveler, and of course a pretty good mother, lover of the young, my countless students, and then maybe, on a good day, in good light, pretty, not conventionally so, but attractive in my own way." *To be a Goddess is to love your imperfection*, her orchid womb whispered, but she didn't hear. ("Orchid, womb," the Energy Child sang.)

"Ayy mi amor, you've been sleeping, hiding, in your beautiful orchid petals, in your lost rainforest with your wild, dangerous jaguars that love you. But I've found you again and I love you more than those jaguars, and I'm telling you, estas hermosa, you are beautiful, Xochiquetzal, and muy sexy tambien." Javier continued to cradle her, softly, sensually, so softly, and he realized that this tenderness was new for him. Tenderness, we're teaching each other tenderness it seems. "Esta mujer," he breathed.

"I'll take the compliment, 'Love sees the invisible,' Simone Weil, gracias mi tigre, gracias, and like the messiah scorpion, to see the invisible," she smiled, stroking his chest to his belly button, his soft, matted, young man's hair. "But I'm fifty-eight, don't forget that, I'm twenty-four fucking years older than you, mi tigre."

"You'd better stop that, no don't stop that, don't stop, I want you, all fifty-eight years of you..."

"Wait, I want to finish my story for now, I did forgive Florinda, finally, but I never stayed all night in her house, only when she was dying of cancer did I stay all night. And the night I held her as she left her body, and she was beautiful to the end, Javier, she was my age, fifty-eight, I was forty, she was only fifty-eight, my beautiful mother, Florinda, and I loved her, I loved her." And it came to her that Quetzalcoatl and his twin, one of them had to die, in the story, in the myth. It's a *myth*, she exhaled.

Javier kissed her mouth softly, softly, licked her neck softly, her nipples softly, softly, as she surrendered to his mouth that kept saying,

I love you, softly, to her wild orchid, softly. They moaned as all lovers moaned, they sang as all lovers sang. Someone close by, a few houses away, let loose his supply of daily fireworks, raining fiery rainbows over their heads. Tenderly.

As the Mexican sun rose to meet fearless Quetzalcoatl, the Morning Star, the warrior star flung from the Warrior in the Sun, an immense, red-tailed hawk spiraled on morning gusts of wind, high into silence, on the Taos mesa; whales journeyed south to warm, birthing waters; dolphins leaped into new air along the continent's coast line, no boundaries; humans crossed borders everywhere, this moment; no boundaries to be seen, only air, ocean, wave upon wave, drala energy for all, belonging to no one, existing for every one, to breathe in, like the fiery rainbows over their dreaming heads. Dawn.

Was this   the deepest   tender play...

Javier, Xochiquetzal...*They meet in their dream. They won't remember. This dream. They will remember. The feeling. Drala. Windhorse. Joy. Sorrow. Joy. Each other's. Eyes. Each other's. Souls. This dream. One thousand years old. They will. Recordar. Remember. This soft. Tenderness.*

They crossed   together into   the rainbow...

"I want to take you to the market to eat today, I know, I know, you've probably been to a million markets, a muppie at home in his own country..."

"Cabroncita, I'm proud to be a muppie at home in his own country, let's go, we haven't even had coffee, amor." Javier paused to gaze at some photos in the hallway cabinent, behind glass. "I didn't see this, is this your mother?"

Xochiquetzal brought some out, each one carefully framed. "This is Florinda, my mother."

"Yes, she's beautiful, like you. You still don't believe me, but es la verdad...it's the truth."

"Okay, okay," she laughed with unexpected pleasure, "you see the invisible. And here's my son, Justin, so handsome."

"I see the invisible in the visible, mi amor—and so, how tall is this guy, he must have las chicas lined up on his speed dial," Javier laughed.

"Like you, I assume, but Justin seems to be a one woman at a time guy, anyway as far as I, his mother, knows," she smiled, locking eyes with him, and for once he looked away. "He's six foot two, and why did you look away?"

He sighed, gathering himself, and met her eyes. "Because I just erased all my

ex-chicas from my speed dial, because of you, Xochitzalita."

"But you still know their numbers by heart, right?" she laughed.

"You spare me nothing, mi amor," he smiled. "I can't help it, I have what you call a photographic memory, so they'll slowly fade away, cabroncita." Javier pulled her into his arms, smelling her hair. "Your son is taller than me, I'm barely six feet, but you probably know that..."

"And all your ex-lovers have big boobs, me and my niña, girl ones."

"They fit in my mouth, mi pochita."

"And we fit, just right, mi muppie."

"Do you walk everywhere, hippie girl?" Javier kept trying to stop for coffee, but she wouldn't let him. "It's almost two and no coffee, how can you stand it?"

"I know if we stop we'll never get to the market, come on, we're almost there, in fact we are, right here, muppie in his own country, just follow hippie girl," she laughed. Xochiquetzal wore black jeans, as a concession to her usual Frida skirts, with a beautiful hand-woven top from Guatemala, her dangly, opal earrings from Taos Pueblo, and black moccasin boots, with her jeans tucked in. Javier just threw on his well-worn, black, leather jacket over a purple soccer t-shirt (jeans, the muppie loafers).

As they entered the radiant displays of vegetables, fruits, flowers, he began to smile with joy. "You're right, I've seen it a million times, but it's so damned beautiful every time, my country's abundance, so beautiful, and I smell it, cafecitos."

A vendor thrust out a slice of papaya toward Javier and he ate it, laughing, "Qué rica!" He grabbed Xochiquetzal's hand and led her through the stalls. "Here, this place is perfect, sit, mi amor."

"Si señor, are you giving me ER orders?"

"I am, sit down." He kissed her briefly and ordered them both cafecitos, muy fuerte...strong coffee, chicken tamales con mole, scrambled eggs con chorizo, a bowl of beans simmering con chiles and onions, slices of papaya, mango, pineapple, and a stack of freshly made, cobalt blue, corn tortillas. They drank two cafecitos fuerte before their platters, yes platters, of food arrived.

"Ohmygodddess, I think I'm having a coffee orgasm," she smiled, rolling her eyes in sheer pleasure.

"Me too, los multiples," he laughed. "These marvelous markets have been around for thousands of years, before the Spanish arrived, our great-great-great-great-abuelitos, los Indios, were here making tortillas, tacitos, mole, chocolate, corn, beans, Dios mio, I'm hungry."

"And our great-great-great-great-abuelitas, las Indias, were here selling their wares, cooking that delicious list in these markets." The platters arrived, steaming, cooked to que rica perfection. "Now for the comida, food, orgasms."

"Multiples, te amo…I love you, Xochitzalita." Javier ordered more cafecitos fuerte, some freshly made mango juice for both of them. He put the first bite of the orgasmic mole, rich chocolate, chicken tamale, with chorizo scrambled eggs, into his mouth, and moaned loudly, no shame.

I love you, took her by surprise in public, in this one thousand year old market, this one thousand year old dream. As she took her first bite of the mole-chocolate, spicy chicken tamale wrapped in a warm tortilla, chorizo-chile scrambled eggs, she saw him. A Spanish officer, very handsome, cruel features, but young, so handsome. And she was serving him his food, in this one thousand year old dream. As she served him, she looked down with respect, fear, longing, desire, worship.

"Aren't you hungry, mi amor, I'm ordering more tamales, do you want more, how about more mango juice? I'm so happy, gracias for not letting me stop." He kissed her briefly and they exchanged hints of the deep chocolate mole.

"Okay, one more tamale for me and a mango juice, this is muy sabrosito. I just saw you, Javier."

"I hope so, I'm right here," he laughed, ordering the tamales, mango juice, more fresh, cobalt blue, corn tortillas and tongue-challenging, home-made, red salsa.

"I don't know how to say this, so I'll just say it—you were a Spanish officer and I was an Indian woman serving you in this market, and I think I loved you."

"Of course you did, mi pochita, you always love me and I always find you, and you love me like no other."

"What did you say, the last part." She stared at him, his eyes.

He stared back, her eyes. "I always find you, and you love me like no other."

In this one thousand year old dream, Xochiquetzal remembered her dream of four years ago. His eyes staring fiercely into hers, *You will love me like no other.*

"You said those words to me in a dream I had about four years ago, I could show it to you in my dream journal, in case you think I'm nuts, plus I'm seeing Spaniards."

"I believe you, Xochitzalita, because it's true, I always find you."

Their food arrived and a second wave of hunger hit them, the fresh scent of chocolate mole tamales, blue corn tortillas, cafecitos fuerte, mango juice.

"We're never going to sleep tonight with all this strong, orgasmic coffee." She watched him eat with full concentration, the way he did everything; her womb, vagina, clenched with last night's memory. "In my dream, you said, 'You will love me like no other.'"

"And I will love *you* like no other, Xochitzalita."

"Even though I'm going on sixty years of age, and you're going on thirty-five."

"Callate, tomorrow I leave for my ER duties, callate mi amor. I forgot to tell you that I killed a scorpion for you this morning, as part of my hunting duties, in the entry."

"Was it the messiah, golden one?" She couldn't help smiling, and she realized he made her smile, lighten up, like Justin did. She couldn't resist. Lightness. Their light. The undiminished light of the young.

"Ay Xochitzalita, que blasphemy, do you want one more tamale?"

"I can't resist, okay, what time do you take off tomorrow?"

"Noon at the latest, for the 5 p.m. shift, no me chingas...don't mess with me, I don't want to go, I like it here with you."

"We'll stop at Mama Mias for gigantic margaritas, and there's guitar today, I'm pretty sure." She paused. "I'm going to miss you, la verdad, there I said it." Xochiquetzal looked up quickly to see if the young, handsome Spanish officer would appear, but young, handsome Javier remained next to her.

"I'm going to have to remedy this, there's a way I think, some time off. Would you like that, mi amor, I could take you traveling around my country..."

"Is that wise or even possible?"

"It's wise and possible, let me figure it out." Javier leaned over and kissed her, licking her lips softly. "Qué rica, mamacita, I bet we had at least ten little mestizos in that life," he laughed.

"In this one thousand year old dream," she murmured. ("Dream," the Energy Child echoed.)

Their gigantic margaritas arrived and Javier's extra shot of tequila. Xochiquetzal waited for Pablo's voice and scanned the tables, a bit on edge. Nada, no Pablo, Sonya, Javier's ex-lovers. No dramas, she sighed with relief.

"Are you serious about taking time off, traveling, I mean can you really do that at this point since you'll be specializing?"

"That's why it's time, a break before February when it all starts and I think I'm going to do it here in San Miguel with Diego. Diego is the best all around surgeon I know, so I'm not coming here just for you, Xochitzalita." He kissed her before she could speak.

"I have an inheritance from my father's rich, older brother, a very good man who died in a car accident. I loved him." Javier paused, gathering himself. "I get more than enough monthly, then at forty I get it all. I guess he figured I'd be settled down by then, married, children, an established physician, no more traveling," he smiled.

"We should travel for the next few months, of course bring your camera, how does that sound, mi amor?"

"I can't live with you, Javier, do you understand that?" Xochiquetzal took his hand in hers. "You can't do your specialty here because you think we'll live together, I can't, I'm sorry." Tears struggled to fill her eyes, but she refused them.

For the first time Javier was stunned, taken by complete surprise. By this woman. Who held his hand. Brought his sperm to his mouth. Potent, fertile. Whose scent he loved. La orchid. And trusted. "Why?" was all he could say.

"I've never really lived with anyone, except for my son, Justin, as a grown woman. His father and I lived in different places. He taught and lived in San Francisco, and I in Santa Cruz, about seventy miles apart. Of course, we visited a lot, but we never lived together, daily. It's not my style..."

"Look at me, Xochitzalita." Javier held her eyes. "I'm not asking you to marry me, or to live with me while I do my specialty here. Diego offered me one of his casitas to live in, and while we travel I can leave the bulk of my things in a room at his mansion. So, I'm not asking you to live with me, but only to love me, *do you understand that*, mi amor?"

"I feel like such an old, embittered jaguar bitch, which I am of course," she whispered, tasting her first tear. "I'm sorry I'm not braver, mi tigre, and that I've hurt you, I'm sorry." She'd seen the flash of betrayal in his eyes and then saw him transform it into understanding. Fearless. Understanding.

"Callate mi amor, mi jaguar, let's take our time, let's travel my country together. I want to take you to all the beautiful, secret beaches, and I'm driving you everywhere..."

"Not the burro truck!" she laughed, her face smeared with tears. In public.

"No, we'll take the Jetta so we can lock everything up, plus it gets great gas mileage. I'll bring a tent, sleeping bags, camp stove, vino, tequila—an upper class muppie physician at home in his own country, mi amor. Let's take our time, let's travel, no vows, no leases," Javier laughed, kissing her suddenly, so deeply, tears and laughter merged. In public, she reminded herself, and she was also aware of people enjoying the spectacle (love).

"Okay, okay, but I'm paying for half the gas, food, hotels on the way." She kissed his ear, barely whispering, "You will love me like no other, mi tigre, mi amor." (The Energy Child sang, "You will love.")

The undiminished.   Light of.   The young.   The gift.

A young woman holding a baby was sitting on the front steps, in the shadows, as they paid the taxi driver. Xochiquetzal insisted on tipping him twenty pesos. "Gracias," the driver smiled.

"You're such a pochita, tipping everyone left and right, but not on our travels, promise me, Xochitzalita."

"No vows, promises or leases, and I'll tip people if I want to like the pocha-Yaqui-hippie that I am, take it or leave it, Dr. Gomez."

Javier laughed, grabbing her around the waist. "I'll take it, I'll take it, que jaguar eres, mujer!"

"Are you calling me a jaguar bitch?" She pinched his bare belly, under his t-shirt.

And then, they saw the young woman clearly as she stood up,

holding her baby tightly in her arms.

"Eres doctor...Are you a doctor, I'm sorry to bother you, I'm so sorry, doctor."

"Si señora, how can I help you?"

Xochiquetzal opened the door, turned on the entry light. "Why doesn't she come in, Javier, bring her in."

The young woman walked in shyly, Javier leading her to the couch. Clearly embarrassed, but with a natural grace, she sat down. "Gracias, gracias." She opened the baby's blanket, exposing the sweet face. "She can no longer open her eyes, do you see, doctor?"

The baby's eyes were crusted over, edged in swollen redness, but she was silent and didn't cry.

"Would you get my doc backpack, amor?"

Xochiquetzal ran for it, returning in less than a minute.

"Tomorrow morning you must take your daughter to a very good doctor, a friend of mine. I'll call him tonight and tell him you'll come to his office tomorrow morning at 10am."

"Gracias, doctor, gracias." Tears welled in her eyes, such beautiful eyes, and one slid down her dark, lovely cheek.

"I'm glad you came, what's your name?"

"Maria, doctor." She looked down at her baby.

"Maria, how did you know a doctor was here in this house, and I'm Dr. Gomez." Javier very tenderly swabbed the baby's eyes, using the swab once, dipping the new one into a cleansing solution, over and over, until the outer layer of crust was removed. Then, very gently, smeared a salve over the lids.

"I saw you arrive the other night with your doctor things and your machete," Maria smiled shyly, hiding it with her free hand.

"I was quite a sight, wasn't I?" he smiled back. "Your daughter has an eye infection and tomorrow when you go to Dr. Ramirez, he'll continue to treat her. You will go tomorrow at 10am to the hospital, his office, do you understand, Maria?"

"Si doctor, gracias, gracias."

Javier wrote down Juan's name, the time to arrive, and took out his wallet, handing her 400 pesos, and an extra 20 pesos. "Use this 20 pesos for the taxi, to get you there on time, and the 400 pesos for whatever you may need. Take this salve and gently smear it on her eyes at midnight, and every three hours." He wrote this down as well. "Not too much, just to cover the lids, and be at the doctor's office at 10am.

And no water on the eyes, only this salve, use the clean swabs, Maria. Is all this clear?" He smiled at her with a kindness that made her smile back in spite of her shyness, and made Xochiquetzal forget to breathe.

"I'll call Dr. Ramirez tonight about seeing you, don't worry, cuidate, take care, Maria, you and the little one." Maria tried to return the 400 pesos but he wouldn't allow it—"Gracias," she whispered, pulling the blanket over her daughter's face, "Gracias."

"Did Juan mind seeing her at such short notice, and will he charge her?" Xochiquetzal looked up from her book, taking her reading glasses off. "Hey, you brought some chardonay, right on time, come and join me on your side of the bed," she smiled. I can't believe I just said that, *your side of the bed.* His hands, so gentle, his eyes, so gentle, el doctorcito, I am road kill.

"Juan and I, and some other interns, went down to Chiapas one summer to do some free work, so we're actually secret hippies." That beautiful sun smile. "And we met the great Subcomandante Marcos, women drooling over him, so we were impressed," Javier laughed. He'd taken off his clothing as he spoke, and now he stood confidently naked, sipping chardonay.

"You know, I'm starting to see that, Dr. Zapata, you are a muppie-hippie-hip-hop-salsa-dancer, come here."

"My side of the bed, I like that," he smiled a little victory smile and slid in next to her, careful not to spill the wine. "I'm usually more cautious, to not let people know I'm a physician where I live, or you start gathering a little clinic and you humanly can't be a doc all day and come home to your own private clinic. Of course, the white jacket and stethoscope tipped them off..."

"Also, el tigre mask and the machete, callate Dr. Gomez, just callate," and she kissed him so deeply, so fiercely (their last night), they completely, and utterly, forgot whose side of the bed they were on.

Javier brought a fresh bottle of cabernet, brie, gouda cheese, ham, cold chicken, dark bread, all the fruit he could find, up to Xochiquetzal's bed on a tray. "I can't sleep so we may as well eat, mi amor, I hate to leave tomorrow. Let's stay up till dawn again, make love again as the warrior in the sun appears."

"You look around twelve years old right now, do you know that? I'm not kidding, your eyes, that smile, no older than twelve. Okay, we can try cause I can't sleep either, let's bring up the fucking warrior in the sun with watermelon and flutes like heyokas," she laughed with uncensored joy. *Uncensored joy.*

"I've never heard you laugh that way, and you sound, you look like a twelve year old niña. Laugh like that again, mi amor, I want to hear it."

"Well, I can't laugh like that on command, que me chingas." But she did, she laughed like that again.

He opened the bottle and poured them each a glass. "Do you have flutes for both of us, sounds like fun. There's another chunk of watermelon in the frig, but I may want to cover you with it," Javier smiled, twelve years old. *Uncensored joy.*

"I brought some small, wooden flutes from Taos and a small drum too, I'll get them later. You'd love Taos, that endless sky, hawks hunting on the mesa, and in the summer months a pair of golden eagles would come to nest. The female eagle was older, larger, and the male eagle was dazzlingly handsome, protective..."

"Older eagle, younger eagle," he laughed. "I'll show you that sky, the hawks, and the eagles, here in Mexico, on our travels, but maybe we could also travel over the border, what do you think? I've never been to Taos..."

"Maybe we should, that might be fun, but is it hard for you to get a visa into the US?" she blurted out without thinking, feeling suddenly silly, naive.

"Amor, I've traveled all over the world. I'm an upper class Mexican doctor at home on his own planet, don't worry, although I like that you worry, about me." Perched on his elbow, he gazed at her unwaveringly. This unpredictable woman, doctora de los fotos, madre de Justin, wife who never lived with her husband, la jaguar, la orchid, whose scent is not sweet, wild. La niña en la mujer, mi amor...The girl in the woman, my love.

"Why didn't you live with your ex-husband, mala jaguar, mi Xochitzalita?"

"You know, my mother never lived with anyone either, so I never experienced a daily man in our house. And she always made it clear that she wanted it that way, to be free, her own person. Anyway, Carlos and I tried it in the beginning for about a year." She paused to gauge his eyes, his expression: alert, listening (as though to a patient). But he was *listening*, as he always did, with his full attention. Most men don't listen this way, she reminded herself—but Carlos did most always, he tried to listen.

"Carlos started showing signs of possessiveness, little jealousies, if a male student left a message on the machine he wanted to know why he was calling *our home,* was I going to meet him privately etc and etc. And so, it began to not feel like *my home.* I told him we had to either live apart or separate, I just couldn't stand it. Not being free, my own person. And it worked for a long time, living separately, passionate visits, travel together, and of course travel by myself. That he tolerated because he stopped seeing me as his possession, his wife. But the key word is that he 'tolerated' my traveling by myself, my own life separate from his, yet our passion remained intact."

"What happened, why aren't you still married? That's rare for a long time marriage, passion, mi amor." Javier's voice was soft, non-intrusive. He understood exactly what she meant. That need to be free, your own self—I was only ready to give that up for Clara. Get married, have children, sign on the dotted chingado line, and then she betrayed me, Xavier betrayed me, calling her, telling her a little truth but mostly lies. "I understand the desire to be free," he murmured, mostly to himself.

"Carlos had an affair with one of his students, much younger, and when he wanted to return, to continue our marriage, I realized he'd set me free into the world, my life. But it was more painful, the breaking of that bond, than I could've imagined, that betrayal. There was a few gorgeous, brilliant, tempting students, but I just looked, saving my passion, my lust, for him. All that insane possessiveness, *projection*, he wanted to do it of course." Her voice was sad, far away, memory.

Javier stayed silent, taking Xochiquetzal into his arms, stroking her entire spine, up into her mass of hair, massaging her scalp, her brain, her memories, tenderly, his doctorcito fingertips.

"And so, what does your twin, Xavier with an X, look like, I ask at the risk of sounding very stupid, una pendeja." She smiled under his fingertips, then turned to face him, wrapping her legs around him, drawing him closer, feeling his delicious, dangerous, tigre heat.

He smiled into her eyes. "You ask an intelligent question, mi amor, as at our age physical differences do take hold. Okay, if someone ever comes to your door that looks exactly like me, and I mean exactly like me, yet he's a bit over-weight, chubby face, parts his hair strictly on the side, speaks much more slowly as though constantly speaking to an inferior, an underling, that's my evil twin, Xavier with an X," Javier laughed. "And he has a round, reddish mark over his right nipple, in case he comes in the nude, from birth, a birthmark from our mother's womb." Javier remembered touching his twin's round, red birthmark as a boy, thinking it more beautiful than his own, and it saddened him. The vast distance between them, now. "They're both beautiful," Amalia would smile, "each one is unique, as you each are, Javiercito."

"Like your dark, crescent moon on your left nipple, which I love by the way. Do you have a photo?"

"Are you kidding, that's very bad juju."

"Bad juju, okay, I understand, el malo juju," she giggled.

"He's married to a very sweet woman and she's pregnant again with their sixth child, and his list of chicas puts my list," he paused, "my *old* list, to shame. And, Xochitzalita, this is between you and I. No one else, promise me. I think she knows but why further break her heart with gossip, so when you see my friends here..."

"I see what you're saying, of course, her sixth child, ohmygoddess," she sighed at the thought. "Okay, so if a chubby you with a nauseating voice comes to my door, in the nude with a round, red birthmark on his right nipple, I'll promptly slam it."

"Exactly, now I need your orchid, I need it bad, and it's only 3:20."

"First I want to watch you fly, fly to the dawn, I want to taste you on my tongue as you fly to the warrior in the sun, on my side of the bed..."

"Whose side of the bed, cabrona, and who's in charge here anyway..."

"No one," Xochiquetzal laughed, feeling his lovely, erect serpent between her breasts. Feeling her kundalini serpent dance, stretched between her lotus on fire and her brain on fire.

No one's in charge, the thought struck Javier as so utterly joyous—Yes, I remember, Clara was jealous, very jealous, but I thought that meant she loved me so much, so much that she married someone else, left me, betrayed me. Then, the sheer joy of Xochiquetzal's mouth, her tongue licking him, engulfing him, her hands reaching, her moans deep in her throat; the sheer joy struck him blind with fire, his body on fire, and his kundalini serpent sprouted wings, opened them, and flew to the sun. To the God on fire. The Warrior in the Sun waited for him. And he flew like an ordinary man. He flew. And returned. Morning Star. Dawn, Quetzalcoatl.

They flew.   Man, woman.   Into the.   Fire, sun.

Javier...*Clara so beautiful, Clara in my arms, what love we gave each other is never, ever, lost, Clara...and now, la aguila, the eagle, waits for me, the sun.*

Xochiquetzal...*So many years, Carlos, goodbye, so many orgasms, fights, joy, our love, Carlos, goodbye, goodbye...the young eagle flies into my heart, on fire.*

"I can't believe we overslept and I have to leave in less than an hour, joder."

"I believe it, I'm exhausted, we're going to have to pace ourselves on a daily basis when we travel, ayy Diosa, y el Dios tambien."

"Older eagle, younger eagle, Xochitzalita, I warned you, are you going to miss me?" Javier held her eyes.

"Yes, I'm definitely road kill now, certifiable," she met his gaze. The first man in my life able to do this, to meet my gaze.

"Qué es this road kill, amor?"

"It means no one's in charge, Javiercito, and I mean *no one*," Xochiquetzal laughed, trying to keep from crying. Why does this make me sad and so fucking happy at the same time, she asked herself, memorizing the sweet curve of his left ear, then his right ear. *Surrender.* But I will not live with him, *surrender*, I'm going on sixty, *surrender*, he's going on thirty-five, *surrender*, he'll get married, *surrender*, to a beautiful Mexican woman, *surrender*, have beautiful Mexican children, *surrender*, and I do love this man, *surrender*, his perfect ears, *surrender*, eyes (each one), *surrender*, those lips, *surrender*, his tender healing hands, *surrender*, his sweet, brown serpent, *surrender oh surrender,* the dark crescent moon on his left nipple, *surrender yes surrender. Surrender.*

He took her into his arms. "Why are you so sad, mi amor, I'm coming back in a week, and then we'll journey together."

"Because I'm fifty-eight and you're thirty-four, and our time together is limited, we must always be honest. Do you agree to be honest, and in that honesty not betray the other?"

"Not our ages again, mi orchid, mi jaguar, mi amor..."

"Our time together is limited, Javier, you're going to marry someone wonderful, eventually, have children. Older woman, younger man, yes, but no betrayals."

"Yes, no betrayals, only truth between us, and in that spirit, Xochitzalita, you're not getting rid of me that easily. I wrote my name on my side of the bed," he laughed his wicked twelve year old laugh.

"You didn't."

"I did, and my entire chingaso name, JAVIER OSCAR GOMEZ VILLATORO, EL DOCTOR in capital letters."

"You are entirely wacko, Dr. Gomez."

"And don't you forget it or I'll bring my mariachi posse with me again and serenade you, and all your nosey neighbors, till dawn," he smiled. Like the sun. The undiminished light. Of the young. "In fact, just talking about it makes me want to do it again, to wear my sombrero and sing con los mariachis..."

"Javiercito, you really can't sing," Xochiquetzal laughed as he began to sing, "Besame, besame mucho..." way off key. So, she kissed him deeply, with the memory of their flight to the sun, on fire. Just to shut him up, she kissed him (with the memory of their flight to the sun, on fire). And they surrendered. To the sun, on fire.

The Energy Child's sun-heart caught fire, fully opening to the human realm. Joy, sorrow, joy, sorrow and joy, whispering, "*Surrender.*"

Javier pulled over to read the poem she gave him, making him promise not to read it until he got home. He was a little out of town, in the country, with green fields, yellow flowers, tall cactus, ancient trees. A speeding truck passed him, making his Jetta sway in its wake. He pulled the poem out from the manilla envelope she'd handed to him: "This is for you, don't read it till you get home, and don't think just because you wrote your entire name on my mattress, cabron, that it's yours now." She'd closed the door as he entered his car—It's not her style to stand and wave, and it's not her style to live with someone every day, he reminded himself. Then, he read the poem once, twice, and the third time out loud. First, he read the wonderful quote by the Persian poet, Rumi, who lived in the 12th century, as Xochiquetzal told him: "I am filled with you. / Skin, blood, bone, brain and soul. / There's no room for lack of trust, or trust. / Nothing in this existence but that existence."

ESSENCE

Hot springs, La Gruta (small sacred
grotto where water gushes, where the
tangible light plays, lives), early morning
I swim, float, swim in ecstasy—in la gruta

I stand under the pounding waterfall as
its hard heat massages my wings, my folded
wings that dream the world, the cosmos, my
life, la vida...I stand in the tangible light as

she blesses me, I chant to the molecules of
gushing water, streaming tangible light, my folded
iridescent wings, my unfolding ripening blossoming
heart body heart body, I chant to all

that exists, existence. This. A tiny iridescent
hummingbird pauses to sip the tiniest yellow
blossoms, the sexual penis-shaped purplish
fruit dangling from the fertile banana tree,

a crown of tiny bananas begin to sprout,
and underneath the sexual penis-shaped purplish
fruit, the tiniest so sweet yellow blossoms,
the iridescent hummingbird sipping this ripeness,

filling its swift body with this, existence,
this potent fertile blossomed ripening essence,
existence. This. Ripening. This.
Filling (fertile potent) essence.

    * * *

I want to touch your feet, to kiss
them, to remember your
first steps, your footprints
glowing in the world.

I want to caress your calves, your knees, your
thighs, to lick the salt gathered there, the

years I didn't know you were alive, yet
I dreamt you, heard your voice.

I want to explore your chest, the map of
your longing, your vast desire to be free—and
your back, flaring up to your secret wings that
dreamt you to the moment we spoke.

I want to follow your fearless neck and
pause for centuries to gaze into your open
face, your ancient (always new) eyes that
mirror my own ancient (always new) eyes like

the sun
the moon
the stars
the soul.

I want to touch your mouth with my mouth,
I want to touch your tongue with my tongue,
I want to remember the lava that flows
in me in you in me in you potent fertile-

I want to sip that fertile potent essence-
I want to know your ripened purplish fruit, your
delicate yellow blossoms... my iridescent wings
unfold, dreaming you closer, more clearly, I sip.

I want to make love, yes, to your secret wings that
dreamt you to the moment we spoke. I want to
fill myself with you—I want you to
fill yourself with me.

That potent
that fertile
that essence.
That. Existence.

San Miguel de Allende, México

To Javiercito, mi tigre
(I am officially road kill,
and I can still taste you.)

And then, he read the final stanza out loud, making his voice her voice:

"That potent
that fertile
that essence.
That. Existence."

And, "I am officially road kill, and I can still taste you." He wept with joy, with the joy of surrender—"I am officially road kill," he laughed and speed dialed the final chica on his cell.

"Hola."

Javier read her the last two stanzas, paused. She was silent.

"I still taste you, mi orchid, and you've definitely made love to my secret wings."

"I told you to wait till you got home, where are you?" Xochiquetzal wept with joy, but kept her voice even.

"No one's in charge, mi amor, and, as you say, we're both road kill. If I were there, I'd take you to my bed," Javier laughed softly.

"Where are you, Javiercito?"

"On the side of the road, reading your poem, and don't erase my name."

"Erase your name?"

"On the mattress, on my side of the bed."

She laughed with happy exasperation. "Just get your nalgas back here to the bed, your side of the bed, with your entire fregado name on it, que loco."

"I'll be back to you by Dia de Los Muertos, next week. Will you have an altar?"

"I always build an altar for the dead, the transformed, even in the USA, but here I'm not a weirdo with her altar for the dead, marigolds all over the street..."

"I'll bring my transformed, los fotos, to add to *our altar,* and fresh marigolds, mas champagne, watermelons, Xochitzalita."

Our altar, he said, 'our altar,' no one's ever joined me in this. Remembering my beloved dead, the transformed. "I still taste you, mi tigre, and no one's in charge."

"I left my Zapata sombrero on our bed and you have my permission to wear it."

"Javiercito, you are on dangerous territory, do you realize no one's ever called my bed, *our bed?*"

"Not even your husband?"

"He knew better than to scare me away…"

"Am I scaring you away, amor?"

"Let's just say no one's ever written their name in black, indelible ink on my mattress como un bien loco, but since no one's in charge, who knows."

"Si, estoy bien loco," Javier grinned.

"I forgot to tell you gracias por los mariachis, gracias for risking your life in the tree, gracias even for your awful singing while wearing Zapata's sombrero, and your name is safe on my mattress, for now." Xochiquetzal cradled the phone tenderly, as though it were his face. She laughed softly, tears falling fast.

He had no desire to speed dial his old chicas and their numbers were starting to fade from his photographic memory. My father and all of his chicas during his marriage to my mother, and of course she knew, just the way Xavier's pregnant wife knows, pregnant with his sixth child, que chingon. And Xochitzalita's beautiful mother who refused to live with men, seduced her lover, betrayed her. She's never lived with a man, not even her husband, who also betrayed her.

Well, my full name is on *our mattress, our bed,* and since no one's in charge, "No one's in charge," Javier said out loud just to hear it—maybe it's true, our bed. When she thanked me, just thanked me, no one's ever thanked me like that, no one's ever brought my sperm to my mouth, made me taste it, no one's ever brought me to the warrior in the sun, como esta mujer sabrosita, like this delicious woman. My equal.

"That potent, that fertile, that essence," he quoted the poem's ending; the taste she'd brought to his mouth. "No betrayals, mi amor, Xochitzalita, in this life time, no betrayals." His words surprised him, as though someone else had spoken. Maybe the warrior in the sun, Javier smiled as he sped toward his twelve hour shift in the ER.

"Maybe the Warrior in the Sun is in charge," he spoke to the streaming sunlight. He wanted to call her one more time, tell her this, but he couldn't slow down. "Gracias, mi orchid, Xochiquetzal, gracias."

Xochiquetzal sat on the roof top at sunset with a glass of chilled chardonay, already missing him way too much. "Way too much," she murmured. The green hills in the distance—lightning still brought rain to these mountains and transparent purple flowers bloomed everywhere. Like Taos, she thought, the lightning, the rain, seasonal green, sunflowers swaying in the wind, turning, turning toward the sun. The Warrior in the Sun, she remembered Javier's dream. But these mountains have more people than hawks and eagles, and mariachis, fireworks at dawn, a beautiful man who writes his full name on my mattress, our mattress, who's in charge?

"No one's in charge." The violet twilight was edged in gold; houses, windows, church spires, La Virgen at the very tip-top of the dome of her favorite church, where El Nino Doctorcito lived, all edged in gold; people walking home to dinner, people going out to dinner, the mariachis strolling in the main plaza, the mime telling his story with no words, the blind man with cup extended, children's soft cheeks, the old women, wrapped in rebozos, begging, the small boy in worn out clothing, shoes, selling Chiclets, the blackbird's wings, all edged in gold. The final arrows. From the Warrior. In the sun. And then, she saw them. Two grey doves, side by side, settling into each other, and speaking a language that sounded so soft. Like love.

"The best of love, it sounds like the best of love, these two grey doves, nothing fancy, no hawks, no eagles spiraling in the wind." She spoke to the far hills, waiting for those large, predatory, hungry, beautiful birds; and then her gaze returned to the two grey doves. Speaking.

"Just sitting side by side, I've never known this," Xochiquetzal realized. "Is this the best?" She listened to their grey dove language, so soft. Like love. "But a love I can't keep, yet it's love on loan, isn't all love on loan?" She wept. "I've never known this, this soft language."

She closed her book and, before turning off the light, gazed at his full name: JAVIER OSCAR GOMEZ VILLATORO, EL

DOCTOR. She got up, went to her desk, and came back with the black, indelible ink—BIEN LOCO XOXO She glanced at the clock; he had five more hours to go, and she hoped he wasn't too exhausted. "The undiminished light of the young," she whispered, doing a brief check for scorpions before turning off the lamp. She wondered if the grey doves were still sitting, side by side, on the roof, under the burning stars.

Xochiquetzal...*I'm flying. We touch wings for a moment. The night is dark. I can't see who it is. Whose wing is touching mine. We're flying.*

She went to the feast breakfast at Mama Mias, taking her camera for a walk. Revision. She couldn't bear to be alone this morning, his presence gone. His heat, his laughter. So the people on the street kept her company—the sweet children, joking teens, gorgeous young men, older men, all with that spark of light, the eyes. And the women, young and old, sensual, in their bodies. Revision. Her pesos for the blind, the ancient women, the four year old child begging for his mother holding the baby. Revision. Her favorite waiters, at Mama Mias, posed for her, joking, laughing. Revision. She'd never taken their photos, though she knew most of them by name. Next Roberto at Bellas Artes, revision, and she'd never taken his; so handsome (and in his body, that spark of light, the eyes). She knew he'd laugh as she aimed her camera at him, and she couldn't wait to hear him laugh. Revision. Xochiquetzal felt alive, in her body, that spark of light, her eyes, as she held her camera. "We gave birth to each other, mi tigre, and I can see again," she murmured to the teasing, warm wind. Revision.

Walking through the plaza, el Jardin, a composition of color caught her eyes, as well as a solid feeling in the pit of her stomach that simply said, Stop. She looked at the arresting composition of color: a smiling Mayan man in full costume. A straw hat with dangling rainbow ribbons perched on his commanding head, presence, and his wide, playful smile. A rainbow of birds danced on his white, handwoven shirt and his white pants also were beautiful with flowers. He kept smiling at her, finally waving to her, to come over.

Xochiquetzal pointed to herself, "Me?" smiling back at him.

He continued to wave her over, smiling, somewhere in his sixties to eighties (his age changed with the light, and a light he emitted); still handsome, physically commanding (now he was fifty). He patted the place on the wrought iron bench next to him, "Join me, amiga, on this beautiful day, my name is Don Francisco, from Oaxaca, visiting one of my daughters in San Miguel, my young, energetic grandchildren, so I'm resting here, amiga." All this in one breath, smiling; sunlight leaped out from his dark eyes and held her. Stop. Now sit.

Don Francisco patted the empty space on the bench again and she sat down, breaking his gaze (full of sunlight) to gather herself. Don Francisco as in Don Juan, she suddenly realized, and waved the thought away. It's a common form of respectful address here in Mexico, as well as Spain I'm sure. And besides, I refuse to get caught up in preconceived ideas, look at this guy's smile. "I love your outfit, it's so beautiful. Maybe I'll take your photo later, if you don't mind…"

"Later, yes, where were you walking to so quickly, I thought I was going to have to chase you and I'm an old man," he laughed loudly as though he'd told a hilarious joke. He waited for her to meet his eyes, smiling.

"You don't look, or feel, like an old man to me, Don Francisco," Xochiquetzal returned his smile and met his eyes. Again, that solid feeling in the pit of her stomach that almost nauseated her, yet also made her feel ravenous as though she hadn't eaten. The luxurious buffet at Mama Mias: chile rellenos, chicken mole stew, tacitos, melting pots of beans, spicy green rice, spicy red rice, spinach braised in onions and garlic, cheese tamales, freshly made cobalt blue corn tortillas, platters of mango, papaya, watermelon, pineapple with slices of lime, and her favorite, hot cinnamon coffee that needed no sugar, from a large pottery pot, always simmering. She'd tasted everything, everything, and his unwavering gaze made her suddenly hungry. For more.

Don Francisco laughed as though she'd told him a hilarious joke, as though he knew she was suddenly, so hungry. "I'm an old Mayan Day Keeper from Oaxaca trying to keep up with my four grandchildren, so it's good to sit down and talk to you, have you heard of the Mayan Calendar, and what is your name, tell me." The sunlight just poured from his irises, into hers. Iris in Spanish means rainbow and it felt like she was being flooded with rainbows, an endless supply of rainbows.

(The Energy Child laughed as the rainbows covered him/her like thick, warm honey. With wide open eyes to see the beauty, and wide open mouth to taste it.)

"Okay, my name is Xochiquetzal. I named myself after the Mayan

Goddess of love and beauty, don't ask me why," she laughed at herself.

"I know who Xochiquetzal is and I know why you took her name, Xochiquetzal, but go on, answer my question, please." Don Francisco softened his command as his smile was replaced with sheer listening, while the flood of rainbows continued. It felt like they were alone in the busy plaza, although every bench was filled with people talking, looking at other people, children running and playing, and vendors passing with their mountains of bright balloons and toys perched on their shoulders.

"Isn't a Day Keeper someone who keeps tracks of the days and years of the Mayan Calendar?" And how does he know *why* I named myself Xochiquetzal? She felt irritated, soothed, nauseated, hungry, all at once, and she shifted her gaze from his eyes, irises, endless rainbows.

"Mas o menos...More or less, you're right."

"I've read that when the Calendar ends on December 21, 2012, it ushers in an ancient prophecy of a new, human unfolding, the Mayan Sixth World. Am I right, Don Francisco, because I certainly can't presume that what I've read is correct, the truth..." She met his eyes again, but whether she did or not, the endless rainbows held her.

"Again, more or less, you've got the basics of the truth, that the great Mayan Calendar is ending the Fifth World, the ancient prophecies, birthing the time of the Sixth World, our human evolution unfolding as it should despite all evidence to the contrary. When the great Sun will align with the womb of the Milky Way, every 26,000 years this occurs, so a good reminder to us penedjo humans." His smile became so gentle (like the language of the two grey doves, soft).

Xochiquetzal just wanted him to smile like that at her, forever; to just sit next to him, forever, alone, in this silence created by rainbows. But then, she had to speak, she had to ask, " I didn't know that, every 26,000 years, that's amazing. I'll have to think about that. It sounds like a possible pregnancy—the sun, the womb. And so, you think humanity is on the right path in spite of the mess we're currently creating, the wars, the genocide, poverty, hunger, global warming..."

"We're on the right path, at this time, this is how we humans give birth to each other, through blood and pain, through blood and pleasure, but we must give birth to each other, one way or the other, until we learn who we truly are, all of us on this wondrous planet, entering the Sixth World. The great Sun making la Mama pregnant, making us remember who we truly are, the children of creation."

"Who we truly are," she echoed.

"The children of love, beauty," Don Francisco's smile blazed into her, making her catch her breath—"sorrow, hatred, joy, grief, ugliness, pain and pleasure, that's us humans, what we create, how we choose to give birth to each other, endlessly, and, of course, ecstasy, Xochiquetzal, you're holding so much of it in your body these days, como no," he laughed, jolting her with his light. "You're falling, falling, falling in love and you're terrified to fall…"

"Well, you certainly know (she wanted to say 'fucking' but refrained) everything, how embarrassing," she laughed with him, "like being naked, exposed."

"Let me give you a reading of your birth from the Mayan Calendar, the day you were born, utterly exposed and naked, would you like that, Xochiquetzal?" Don Francisco's smile was gentle again, soft, cradling her in a strange, suspended, so sweet safety. No one looked their way, no one stared at them—at the Mayan man, in full, beautiful costume, with the dark-haired pocha wrapped in a red shawl. At their timeless intimacy, cradled by rainbows. And yet, not his rainbows, her rainbows. An endless supply (drala energy). Of rainbows.

"I'd love that, I think," she smiled into his eyes. Eagle eyes, up close, she realized. "How much more naked and exposed can I get, don't answer that."

"Write your full name down, your birth date, Xochiquetzal, and we'll be silent for a while, no talking, silence, listen to the birds, the trees, the wind." Don Francisco brought a bundle, made from handwoven cloth, to his lap; circles of red and black birds flew into the tightly woven cloth. A wide, sturdy shoulder strap for carrying lay across his legs. He removed various items wrapped separately in cloth: a bark calendar scroll painted with Mayan symbols and animals, and a perfect pink-lipped conch shell were revealed. The other items remained wrapped, but waiting to be used. As he took the paper from her hand, he held her hand for a long moment, gazing into her eyes, iris to iris (rainbow to rainbow). Tears began to fall from her rainbows, but she didn't care since they were entirely alone in the plaza. In the world.

Don Francisco smiled when he read her full name, Xochiquetzal Colette Aguila—Aguila, Eagle, her birth date. He raised the conch shell to his lips and blew, making her almost leap out of her skin; or making her leap out of her skin (naked, exposed). Awake. He put his fingers to his lips, silence, and began to search his beautifully painted calendar. He was also a painter, an artist, a healer.

For the first time since sitting down with Don Francisco, she looked around the plaza and everything seemed glazed in a glistening gelatin—the trees so green they sighed with joy; the water spilling in the fountain wet with pure light; the red, purple, yellow flowers so stunningly beautiful they hurt her eyes. Thick, white, puffy clouds settled over everyone's head in the plaza, and it seemed to her that each person, including herself, was born to be alive, in this plaza, at that very moment. To hear Don Francisco put the conch shell to his lips. To wake them up. A few of the children looked their way and smiled, continuing to play.

When Xochiquetzal looked back to Don Francisco, he was intent on a small leather pouch, drawing something on each side, writing something on each side. As she was about to ask what it was, he put his fingers to his lips, silence. And so, she closed her eyes and listened to the children playing, their laughter, their cries, birds flying from tree to tree, singing of the coming rain, the people's voices, the vendors shouting loudly, lovers voices whispering promises, mothers voices praising, scolding, grandfathers voices echoing long lost dreams, grandmothers voices answering them, fathers voices on the other side of the human-made border, Mexico/USA, longing for their children, their wives, these white puffy clouds pressing down on their heads, this plaza they dream of nightly, fathers voices who stayed home, present in the plaza, singing *México lindo y querido* to their children, their wives; all these voices became the most exquisite harmony she'd ever heard.

"Come back, Xochiquetzal, come back to me." Don Francisco's voice made the harmony perfect, but she didn't weep or laugh. She's ready, she's entered her own silence, the silence of the world, she's ready, to listen, he told himself, watching her open her eyes, finding his eyes.

"This is for you, open your hand." He placed the leather pouch in her open hand. "What do you see on both sides, look carefully, keep listening to the wind, the clouds gathering dreams, lightning, rain, over our heads, keep listening to the sound of the shell from the great ocean, keep listening." Don Francisco's voice, smile, was so wise, gentle, kind, wise, she fell to the very bottom of something. Love. For his voice, his smile, his irises; for herself, her endless stupidities, fears, wisdom, courage; and then, she knew, for Javier's youthful, ancient fearlessness; the optimism, the wisdom, the joy, he kept laying at her feet like ripened roses.

"This side of the pouch has a sexy snake with fangs, almost smiling, a female snake, that's what I see. And, of course, my name, Xochiquetzal, at the bottom. You're an artist, Don Francisco..."

"More or less, yes," he smiled, "go on, turn it over."

"Okay, this side you've drawn a powerful, almost masculine looking, eagle. These stylized feathers are wonderful, Don Francisco, and you are an artist. The paintings on the calendar, are they yours as well?"

He nodded his head yes, and waited for her to continue.

"Over these wonderful feathers you've written, LA GRAN SENORA AGUILA DE COATL, and below the eagle, what's this?"

"Your Mayan name." Don Francisco said it out loud and it sounded like the wind. He began chanting it softly and it began to sound like wings lifting in the wind. She could hear the wings, in his chanting voice, her Mayan name, lifting.

And then, she heard the Balinese healer's voice, "What is freedom, madam?" Xochiquetzal closed her eyes and saw so clearly, as though her camera had suddenly zoomed in, the healer's ally, her chained eagle.

"You hear the eagle wings in the wind and the sound of your endless flight makes you joyous and sorrowful at once, this is true, I see it," he said her Mayan name. "Your nature is perfectly split— Aguila, eagle...Coatl, serpent— into the sensuousness and wisdom of the Earth, the serpent, and your lover loves that," Don Francisco laughed softly, shooting rainbows into her eyes. "And La Gran Senora Aguila embodies the absolute freedom and wisdom of the Sky. She cannot tolerate her freedom to be taken, she will either kill for it or die for it, there's no compromise where her freedom is concerned. So, Xochiquetzal, you are in a pickle, but a marvelous pickle, you were born to love with your entire being slithering up against your loved one, and you were also born to take to the sky, wings spread wide, fearlessly toward the sun..." She opened her eyes to gaze at his face and she saw it: fearlessness.

Javier's dream, the Warrior in the Sun, appeared to her, his golden sun feather headdress blinding her with beauty. She closed her eyes to listen, simply listen, to Don Francisco's soothing voice.

"This is not a common birth reading for either a woman or a man, but when I saw you speeding across the plaza, I saw your wings trailing you, and I saw the bloody trail they leave in your wake, freedom, love, freedom, love, and you've met a teacher, someone who's demanding an answer from you for the first time in your life, and that's your pickle, your marvelous pickle, will you be able to have both, heal your split nature, the serpent, the eagle, that's who you are, La Gran Senora Aguila De Coatl, and a name given to you from birth, la Aguila, so you can't really complain, Xochiquetzal, no you can't and you shouldn't, no one's chained you and I can see no one ever will, but will you allow yourself to love with your entire being slithering against the earth, that wisdom, will you finally acknowledge your own serpent beauty, not your mother's beauty, your own beauty, your wounded eagle wings, will you?" Don Francisco chanted her Mayan name softly as the white, puffy clouds became dark with lightning, rain, dreams at 4 a.m.

"You've entered a time of revision, to see and know all things for the first time, so you've also become like a newly born human being, and this teacher, your lover, a younger man, this is the energy he leaves within you, that ecstasy," Don Francisco smiled with delight, "a man you've journeyed with in other lifetimes, your teacher, and you are his, always this is your exchange, he's with you in this time of revision, and in the future you will not only create images, you will also begin to write, you're a secret philosopher, a poet, an eagle with wounded wings, a wound from your mother who loves you, and I can see that your lover, your teacher, loves your wings, will you allow him to love your wings, will you?" He chanted her Mayan name as thunder sang in the distance, the first strike of lightning. ("Wings," the Energy Child sang, "Wings.")

Don Francisco was silent, so Xochiquetzal opened her eyes and met his direct, unwavering gaze. Of rainbows. He held the pink-lipped conch shell to his mouth, blowing even louder, more clearly, this time than the first. But she didn't jump out of her skin this time; instead, she jumped back into her skin. Into her slithery, sensual, snaky skin, and she felt the weight of her wings. Lift. Slightly, ever so slightly. Lift.

Thunder singing closer, deeper, white zig-zag lightning, first delicate drop of rain. "When you come to Oaxaca to see me, Xochiquetzal, first send me a dream, and if I tell you to come in the dream, here's my son's email address, he knows the way of this magic," Don Francisco laughed, and then he kissed her fully on the lips, blowing his breath into her body. His warm, electric breath filled her body.

She was momentarily stunned, to be kissed right on the mouth, his lips on her lips, his breath in her body; and then she laughed. "I will come to see you, yes, when is a good time to visit…"

"First dream me, then you'll know, and you'll stay with me and my family, no fancy hotels for you, I may be poor by your standards but I am wealthy beyond measure," he laughed with a child's joy. "First send me a dream, and here are the stones for your pouch, open your hands, yes, the amethyst for spirit, the amber for the body, crystal for the mind, coral red for the heart, green jade for wealth, black onyx for protection." Don Francisco chanted her Mayan name as lightning struck over their heads and thick drops of rain began to fall. The plaza was almost empty, people running for shelter, but he continued to chant her name.

Quickly, Xochiquetzal reached for her wallet, finding 500 pesos. "Please take this, Don Francisco, don't argue with me, please take it." She saw he wanted to refuse, and then he smiled, putting the pesos to his heart.

"This is the way you must allow your young man to love your wings, let him give you his gift, el regalo," Don Francisco laughed as the sky opened with full, wet joy. He quickly kissed her lips, murmuring, "Qué sabrosita," and laughed again. He shouldered his white pouch, beautiful with red and black birds flying. "First send me a dream and if I tell you to come, email my son Fernando, the other wizard."

"Okay, I will, Don Francisco, I'll try to dream you but if you don't answer me I'll email your son the wizard," she laughed, grabbing his hand on impulse. She remembered the young Hopi man in Taos, how he suddenly grabbed her hand. The nakwach, holding his hand on top, firmly.

Don Francisco laughed with delight. "You know the nakwach, the hand clasp of humanity, the gift of another young man, and when it's time you'll dream and I'll answer you. Bring your young man, your teacher, when he's recovered, bring him with you." He began to walk away. "Get out of the rain, Xochiquetzal," he laughed.

"What do you mean, when he's recovered, he's fine, Don Francisco."

"Just bring him when it's time."

"He's a physician, Javier…"

"I know, bring him." He turned and waved, sunlight pouring from his wide smile. "And don't forget the nakwach when you enter the Sixth World, Senora Aguila."

"Gracias, Don Francisco, gracias por todo, and I'll dream you!"

And then he yelled like a grito, "Estas madura, bien madura!"

She thought he was saying 'madera,' wood—I'm like wood? "What's *madura*, not madera, right?"

"MA DU RA!" Don Francisco laughed in the pouring rain, drenching them both. "It means ripe, perfect, that's you at fifty-eight, Xochiquetzal, madura, ripe, send me a dream when it's time!"

She stood, watching him run, as agile as any boy, until he simply disappeared. I forgot to take his photo, that beautiful smile, his rainbows eyes, she realized with sudden sadness. "Next time," she breathed his electric breath, "when I see him in Oaxaca with mi tigre." Another deep, electric breath. "When he's recovered," she murmured, shivering with sudden chill.

("Ripe, ripe, ripe, madura," the Energy Child sang, "wings."

Yes   oh   yes   play

Instead of going to see Roberto at Bellas Artes, Xochiquetzal took a taxi home. Too much rain, too much magic, too much Don Francisco, what a presence; it made her hungry for more. In the pit of her stomach. And what does he mean, when Javier *recovers*, when it's time bring him. Fear held her and then Don Francisco's warm breath filled her body, his word 'madura.'

"Madura, ripeness, my wounded wings at fifty-eight, snake and eagle, student and teacher," she whispered, staring out her bedroom window as the rain began to slow and the wind to blow harder. "Do you love my wings, Javier, dare I lift them, completely lift my wings?"

On the roof top across the way, a boy of around seven was perched in the rain, the blowing wind, and, with great concentration, exuberance, he tossed a toy soldier with a plastic parachute into the hard wind. Expectantly. Innocently. His play was innocent as he thought he was alone on the roof, in the wind, with no one watching. His tiny soldier flew over the side of the roof, parachute billowing all the way down. He raised his arms to the sky, laughing, the innocence of flight.

Xochiquetzal wrote a few stanzas of a poem, remembering Don Francisco's words, "a secret philosopher, poet," making her smile. The poem began with sperm, wings, the innocence of flight. To the Warrior in the Sun. She couldn't take it further than four stanzas, so she put it away, tomorrow.

She checked her email and found Javier's Spanglish email address, opened it:

> Amor, I don't have to say it, I miss you and MY mattress jajaja. But I did it, I'm off until my specialty begins in San Miguel, *three months for our travel.* I'll be there on Sunday around noon with more mangoes, watermelon, champagne, and marigolds—are you ready to spread your wings in my country, Xochitzalita Aguila? I'm looking at the map and planning our trip through the butterfly sanctuary, some towns I think you'll enjoy, and then on to my secret, hippie beach, you'll love it, mi hippie. Don't erase my name and I give you permission to wear my Zapata sombrero, but not too much, amor. Let's email until I arrive so I don't wake you up at midnight, and the energy will gather so when we see each other, tu sabes, los tigres de sangre, champagne y watermelons tambien. Te amo, mi jaguar. Unas palabras del maestro, Neruda... Some words from the master. I remember you this way, mi orchid...
>
> From NOCHE EN LA ISLA...NIGHT ON THE ISLAND (Bucerias)
> Toda la noche he dormido contigo
> junta al mar, en la isla.
> Salvaje y dulce eras entre el placer y el sueno,
> entre el fuego y el agua.
>
> Tal vez muy tarde
> nuestros suenos se unieron
> en lo alto o en el fondo,
> arriba como ramas que un mismo viento mueve,
> abajo como rojas raices que se tocan.
>
> All night I have slept with you
> next to the sea, on the island.

Wild and sweet you were between pleasure and sleep,
between fire and water.

Perhaps very late
our dreams joined
at the top or at the bottom,
up above like branches moved by a common wind,
down below like red roots that touch.

Xochiquetzal read out loud, "'Perhaps very late our dreams joined,' wind the eagle, roots the snake, yes, how does he know?" She read the stanzas again, and then Javier's words, "Are you ready to spread your wings in my country?" She heard the echo of Don Francisco's beautiful, soothing voice: "Will you allow him to love your wings, will you?" She still felt his warm, electric breath, the flood of rainbows, in her body. It was early but she was exhausted, filled to the brim, exhausted. So she answered Javier's email briefly. She decided to tell him about Don Francisco, the flood of rainbows, perhaps a trip to Oaxaca (when he recovered), when he was with her. Why 'recovered'? She shivered in the warmth of her bedroom, making herself focus on the response:

Mi Tigre, I'm ready, yes I'm ready to spread my wings with you. Gather the energy, I'm waiting for your arrival, more champagne, ripe watermelons. I still taste you. Perhaps very late our dreams joined, in the common wind, in the red roots that touch, yes, I can hear the skull poets singing these words in the plaza. I'm ready, La Orchid

"Madura alas, me at fifty-eight, ripe wings. Are our dreams, our wings, joining in the common wind, in the red roots, Javiercito?" she asked the newly washed earth.

She woke at 3:54 a.m., sleeping straight through from the afternoon, no dreams, pure sleep, rest, as the rain continued to fall, nourishing the earth all night. She got up to pee, back in the warm bed, scanning the white walls briefly for scorpions. She glanced at the glowing numbers, almost 4 a.m., "Almost dawn," she murmured, putting her face into Javier's pillow, his sea-salt scent. Her body clenched, her womb clenched, her madura, ripe wings opened wide in the darkness.

Xochiquetzal...*I love this earth, the rain soaked leaves, feathery ferns, caverns of orchids cover me as I slide slide slide where I please, I love the taste of the earth, fertile to my flicking tongue, I leave my rainbow skin behind, I slip away, I slide away, new skin, new skin, new rainbow skin, rainbow skin, I love this earth, my lover, ecstasy as I slide in the rain, dawn, sun rising, soft gold fills the sky, soft gold fills the earth as I slide slide slide where I please, warmth sun warmth sun wings, fly from the sun, the Warrior in the Sun shoots me, an arrow, my wings, to the earth, hunger so much hunger, I scan the fertile earth, I see a rainbow sliding so beautifully upon this earth, I want this rainbow I want this rainbow, I swoop, my wings, sun warmth sun wings, new rainbow skin, new rainbow wings, we become one, this hunger, we become one, rainbow skin, rainbow wings, this hunger, this golden hunger of the dawn, and a voice, "I left my body at fifty-eight, you've entered your body at fifty-eight, this is your new body, your new wings, fly my daughter hija, always fly in beauty, in love." Alas madura, ripened rainbow wings.*

"Justin, is this you, it sounds like you," Xochiquetzal laughed with joy. "I was going to call you tomorrow morning."

"Hey Mom, what's up, who's this guy Javier? A very sexy name, by the way," Justin laughed, "right out of a telenovela..."

"Hold on, hold on, do I detect a hint of jealousy, my son? First of all, I think you'll like him, he's a wonderful man, a doctor..."

"And he's how old, Mom?"

"He's thirty-four," she almost whispered.

"Holy shit, Mom, he's only four years older than me, tu hijo."

Silence.

"Does he make you happy, Xochitzalita?" In intimate times between them, Justin would switch to her name, friends.

"It's more than happy, it's joy, he makes me joy, or should I say joyous, joy."

"Sounds like the right guy, hey joy."

"I know it's not forever, whatever that is, he's going to get married, have kids, I know this, Justin, but right now the joy. You'll meet him when you come for Christmas and I know you'll like each other, there's a similar wackiness, of the spirit, with you two. And a similar strength. You're both very strong, centered, fearless hombres, what can I say?" Suddenly she saw Justin's face so clearly, his smile. "You've always brought me joy, Justin." Tears filled her throat.

"Okay, I'm glad to hear you say that, that you see the reality of your ages, but hey Mom, joy sounds fucking good to me. Does he drink tequila, just wondering being a doctor and all."

"Ohmygoddess, he's the tequila king, he hired a mariachi band to serenade me and the neighborhood at 3 a.m., with the help of tequila, a long story..."

"My son, Justin, just called and he's thirty not fifty, but don't tell anyone," Xochiquetzal laughed.

Feliz slowed down for the cement tope, speed bump. "These damned things will take out your muffler, not to speak of the entire underside of your car, if you speed. Wait a minute, your son is thirty, mujer, so he's four years younger than Javier, I love that." She smiled dazzlingly and her red, silky, clingy dress was beyond sexy.

"Justin and I just talked about it and he finally said if I'm happy that's what counts, you know, la joy."

"Qué me chingas, men do it all the time, in fact they flaunt it, so give me a chingado break," she laughed with glee. "What does your son look like, just curious."

Xochiquetzal pulled his photo out of her wallet, in his wetsuit, holding his surfboard as waves kiss his feet.

"I hope I don't offend you, but Justin is a hottie and a half," Feliz whistled. "I'd love to meet him."

"No offense taken, he's had his share of girlfriends at thirty, and he's coming at Christmas," Xochiquetzal smiled. "And, at the moment, he's single again it seems. Anyway, please keep this stuff to yourself, you know the hyena pack energy, I just don't need it."

"I thought you handled it all right on the pesos, but yeah I get it, our secret. And I'll be there at Christmas, maybe we can all go out to dinner, dancing. Okay, we're here, now for parking."

"Justin is the most beautiful man, outside as you can see, but also on the inside."

"Of course, mujer, you raised him, a true feminista's hijo," Feliz laughed, parking the car. "You know, Javier, and his twin with an X, are polar opposites, and from the same mother of course. But Xavier with an X always idolized his playboy father, he's a well-known plastic surgeon in Guadalajara, in case you didn't know. And your Javier was always protective, loved his mother to death, and also his India Mama..."

"He told me about her, Amalia, she sounds wonderful, so two loving feminine beings, madres."

"In fact, Xavier with an X was supposed to follow in his father's footsteps, plastic surgeon, but he's a high priced dentist and your Javier is the surgeon, es la chingada vida," Feliz laughed. "And I must tell you, I've never seen Javier with a J like this with a woman, in love. The truth is, I thought he was becoming like his father, el playboy. Especially after Clara, who he did love, he told you right? He was seeing them younger and younger after Clara, so I thought he was turning into a, well, a jerk."

"He told me about Clara, his lost love in Spain, but I also guessed he had a teen chica speed dial list, I'm not stupid. And so, do you think his parents would mind Javier being with an older woman, and you don't have to answer if it makes you uncomfortable as in too much information."

"There's never enough information as far as I"m concerned, Xochitzalita," Feliz smiled like a twelve year old. "My guess is that they'd be freaked out if you got married, okay I"m just saying the truth here, are you okay?"

"I'm okay, just say it, please."

"I think they want him married with a child by forty, but you know Javier has always done what he's wanted. He's the only one to take off into the world and travel, and he's the only one without a child, not married, the one to claim his freedom. My guess is that his mother wants his happiness no matter what, and his father who knows, but he has absolutely no room to talk, all those women. But in Mexico that's how it is in many marriages, freedom for the man, which is why I'm not married."

"So, you'll never get married, have children?" She doesn't know my real age and that's best, Xochiquetzal sighed, my secret, and Javier's.

"Never say never, but I'm not getting married to some self-centered Mexican who needs his daily dose of worship. It must be mutual worship or I'll die a spinster, but a very sexually satisfied spinster," Feliz laughed. "Here, put this on, I always wear one in this place in case I see any patients."

"Ay Diosa, it's a mask, are you kidding?" The mask was glittery gold with a rainbow of long, graceful feathers erupting from it. And Feliz's mask was a gorgeous, shimmering black with an explosion of perfect peacock feathers.

"Put it on, you'll fit right in, there's so many locos running around this place you'll look weird without a mask," Feliz cracked herself up. "Come on, let's go to el bano so you can see what you're doing, but I'm wearing mine, no more doctora, time for la loca."

They entered a beautifully converted warehouse, a full bar on each side of the immense space, and white cabanas, with comfortable sofas, lined the walls for privacy. And down the center a long, slender fish pond, with exotic fish swimming its length. Comfortable, over-stuffed chairs, with large, silky pillows, small tables for drinks, faced the fish pond, for those wishing to display themselves. And long, sturdy-looking, silky ropes hung from thick beams; each rope a different, vivid color.

"What are these ropes, Feliz?"

"It will all be revealed, and now do you see why you need a mask?" Feliz never stopped smiling, exuding a kid's desire to play. They stood in front of a full length mirror, staring at themselves, each other. The bathroom was beautiful, every detail obviously chosen with care, to the stage-like lighting that had equal amounts of shadow and light. A place to hide; a place to be revealed. The flowing sound of a cubist style fountain at the entry, soothing.

"Well, you look like a sexy loca mujer in your slinky, red dress, and I look like a teen runaway in my twirly skirt with black leggings, and an old teen," Xochiquetzal laughed at herself. "Do you have more of that gold glitter, it looks great on you, maybe that'll help."

"I think you look *dangerous* in that outfit, yeah definitely a Frida Kahlo teen runaway with that flowery top, and not so old," Feliz laughed, handing her the gold glitter. "Okay, put on your mask and let's get our groove on, mujer, I hear the music. If I didn't dance I'd shoot myself, la doctora this, la doctora that."

Gold glitter on all exposed flesh—neck, chest, arms, traces on cheeks, eyelids. Xochiquetzal clipped the mask on, wiggled her head as the long, rainbow feathers swayed. "The Warrior in the Sun," she murmured. I bet Don Francisco would love this mask, but what would he think of this place, she wondered. I bet he'd dance, into the Sixth

World.

"Perfect, you look perfect, a dangerous loca Frida teen on the run from la policia ready to get her groove on, come on Xochitzalita!"

"I think you're right, I'm a madura teenager and a dangerous loca as well, mama fucking mia," she laughed. "Justin would kill for a photo. And you look fantastic, down to your gold hoop earrings, glitzy high heels, me in my black boots ayy. Do you know what madura is, Feliz?"

"And so would Javier, hold it," Feliz took her cell out and clicked. "Ripened to perfection, madura, that's us, mujer. Oh this music, come on let's dance, women dance together here, and also with men if they're brave enough to ask. Here, put your jacket on your chair, and mine, our table, come on!" Feliz was already dancing to a kind of techno-disco-rock, enjoying the hell out of herself, when a gorgeous guy joined her.

Xochiquetzal gave her the thumbs up signal as the waiter, another gorgeous guy, approached. Is that all there is here, knock-out men, she thought, looking around. Pretty much, she answered herself, but no one as knock-out as mi tigre. She ordered two margaritas on the rocks, keeping time to the non-stop music—one segment merged into the other—with her black, ankle booted feet. The gold glitter on her arms, down to her hands, made her smile. "Qué dangerous," she smiled.

Beautifully costumed acrobats appeared in front of each long, silky rope, smiling, waving, turning, to the crowd. Exquisite. Each acrobat, two women and two men, were stunning in their unique, skin-tight, leotard costume; their faces etched in glitter, catching the spotlights as they climbed. The lights switched to deep red, purple, blue, and shimmering gold, silver, as they climbed to the top of their vivid, rainbow ropes. Wrapping the ropes around their bodies, the ropes looked like sensuous serpents; then suddenly, they dropped, extending their arms in flight, twirling to the music, their bodies on fire. They slowly, sensually, climbed again, wrapping the rainbow serpents around their bodies, twisting, dancing, flying, making love to their infinite space, exquisitely.

"Xochitzalita, is that you?"

She was transfixed by the acrobats, the lights, the music, but the voice sounded so familiar—she shifted her eyes. "Who else, Roberto, you know I was going to see you the other day but I got waylaid, in a good way, then it started pouring rain. You look great, very handsome, where's your date?"

"I came alone, so come on let's dance. Are you going to wear that mask all night?" he laughed. "Actually, I like it, and here you add to the festive atmosphere." He smiled into her eyes.

"I like this music but I wish they had a live band like Mama Mias, I can only dance for so long to techno, but this is nice, kind of techno Brazilian." Now it was Feliz's turn to give her the thumbs up sign, and she mouthed 'amigo' in reply. Feliz fanned herself with her hand, the code for hottie, and Xochiquetzal laughed.

"I came with a friend, Feliz, the beautiful, sexy woman over there with the peacock mask. So, where's that gorgeous woman you were seeing?"

"I'm on to the next one I guess, and are you still seeing el medico?"

"I still am, yes, and we're going to do some travel here in Mexico, taking my camera along..." Suddenly, out of the immense, surround speakers, James Brown, "I FEEL GOOD..."

"Ayy Diosa, real music at last! And hey, this is our dance night, Roberto, let's dance to some James."

Feliz dragged her very handsome dance partner over to dance with them, and as they exchanged names Roberto burst out, "Doctora Santana?" "It's our secret, Roberto, and you're due for a cleaning," she laughed, seriously getting her James Brown funky groove on.

Roberto laughed, bringing Xochiquetzal in for a spin, enjoying the rhythm of her hips in her twirly, black skirt. "I like your leggings, very stylish," he said into her ear.

"I don't look too much like an old teenager?" she laughed as James Brown tore up her body, her soul—Please play more, she begged the DJ telepathically, please.

Roberto smiled, shaking his head no, and they all danced together, changing partners, as the DJ played an entire soundtrack of James. Xochiquetzal and Feliz did the hip bump thing and Roberto and Alex did a kind of dosey-do move. Then Roberto and Feliz, Xochiquetzal and Alex.

Three mariachis strode in together, single file, onto the dance floor, just standing there, each one painted the colors of the Mexican flag: green, red, white. Clothing, faces, hands, all exposed flesh, their instruments, even their shoes, each mariachi vibrated with green, red, white. Standing side by side, not moving, not speaking.

The epitome of machismo, Xochiquetzal thought, stoic, unfeeling, not in their bodies, as when men make war. Unlike the sensual Mexican men I've been seeing, experiencing; machismo, the sliver of ice in the heart of all men, and women, be honest, when we're not present, in our lovely, sensual bodies. And I don't have a fucking camera, damn and fregado.

"Pretty weird and interesting, I'll paint this later," Roberto was also taking it all in.

"I was thinking que machismo and wishing like hell for my camera, damn!"

"You're right, machismo it is, great colors."

The music changed to a technoish Brazilian samba—flowing, smooth, hypnotic. The red mariachi grabbed Xochiquetzal, the green one Feliz, and the white one another woman, dancing briefly, sensually. The sliver of ice melted, they moved their hips, laughter in their eyes. And then, they lined up and strode out of the club without a word.

Roberto went to the bar, and Feliz and Alex sat down, leaving Xochiquetzal swaying gently to the Brazilian sound. She closed her eyes, swaying, moving, aware of the long, graceful feathers moving with her. Don Francisco's voice sang to her of rainbows, serpents, eagles, her Mayan name, her rainbow skin, her rainbow wings. She opened her eyes, still hearing his beautiful voice, the music entering her body, her body entering the music, and she lifted her wings and danced to the warrior woman in the sun, to the warrior woman in the moon, to the warrior woman in the stars, to the warrior woman in the earth, the great universe. She lifted her hands into the changing light of dark purple to shimmering violet, fluttering them like birds, unaware of being watched, only aware of the music, the light turning red, then blue, silver, gold. Shimmering gold.

She remembered the taste of sperm, bringing it to her lover's mouth, and then she danced to the warrior in the sun, moon, stars, earth, the great universe. She lifted...

Everything was packed into the Jetta and Javier stopped for the goodies, watermelons, champagne, and her favorite, the chocolate truffle cake. He did it, he was off for three months to travel with Xochiquetzal, before the full force of his surgery specialty. I'll do them all, he thought, try them all, then decide on my personal specialty. Plus, I've done so many different emergency surgeries in the ER, and now I wonder if I'll miss that. He thought of his going away party last night at their usual club—Those idiots, I love those guys, I don't want to leave, not really, but it's time, it's really time, and I want to travel with

Xochitzalita, mi orchid.

The drinks kept coming, trying to get him drunk as usual, teasing him mercilessly, him teasing back mercilessly. "Who is this woman who's bewitched you, hombre, tell us who this bruja puta is."

"Watch your diseased mouth, she's a Goddess in disguise."

"They're all goddesses in disguise, when the pussy's still a novelty." They howled with laughter.

"I remember when my wife was a goddess, and now she's worn it out with four kids, no novelty there I tell you."

"So we're left to our goddess chicas, Dr. Gomez, and you know all about that, no me chingas, cabron!"

"You guys aren't in love anymore, so you're bitter, old farts!"

"Love, what's this love shit, you are bewitched, pobrecito Javier, you'll see."

He'd never danced alone, but he couldn't help it as he joined the dancers, alone.

"Ayy Dios, es Zorba!" his friends started yelling, busting a gut.

Yeah Zorba, Javier thought, raising his hands to the music, what do I care what these hijos de la puta think, plus too much tequila. He laughed like a loco, arms raised, hands poised like birds in flight. Poised. For. Flight. And he danced to the drums, the rising flute, alone—"Zorba," he murmured, arms raised, hands poised.

"Hermoso, why are you dancing alone?" She was incredibly beautiful, with the usual, large, lush breasts trying to escape the skimpy halter, maybe seventeen, with the eyes of a child prostitute, irresistible as usual.

"Hija, I want to dance alone."

"Hija? Chinga tu madre!" She stormed off, as all his doctor-god friends began to howl like coyotes, laughing.

He thought of his dream of the Warrior in the Sun, his golden feathers, he wished he had some golden feathers as he raised his hands and continued to dance, alone, as he remembered the taste of sperm she'd brought to his mouth, making him taste it, making him remember the Warrior in the Sun, making him raise his wings. To the golden sun, the rising golden sun, rising that moment in Asia, at the edge of dreams, bringing gold, shimmering gold, to the world. Javier lifted his wings. He danced...

Part III

Birds make great sky-circles
of their freedom.
How do they learn it?

They fall, and falling,
they're given wings.

—Rumi

...her wounded healed wounded healed wings, falling.

...arms raised, alone, for joy, and he remembered wings, falling.

"No stethoscope, no machete, this time," Xochitzalita laughed.

"I'm incognito, let me in and fucking kiss me." They kissed, nearly crumbling to the hard, tile floor. "I told you the energy would build without phone calls, I'm dying of starvation por tu orchid, mi amor."

"All your stuff's in the car, you'd better bring it into the second bedroom or it'll be gone by morning..."

"You don't mind if I leave it in your *space*?" He gave it an American emphasis, laughing.

"I give up, bring it all in, I'm fucking road kill, but it's only temporary while we travel..."

"You're falling for me, amor, yes you are, you're falling for me *bad*," he sang, smiling directly into her soul, making her womb melt. "I've fallen for you, Xochitzalita, accept this gift, this time, just let me love you, let's just fall, tu sabes, into our bed..."

Javier pulled her up the stairs, removed the bedspread, as she always did, picked her up, kissing her as though she were food, water. "Give birth to me," he sang.   *This is...*   She kissed him as though he were her last breath. "Give birth to me," she moaned.   *Deepest play*

"Birth," the Energy Child remembered, whispered.

"No one's in charge and I'm road kill," Xochiquetzal sighed, heading for the stairs.

"Feliz sent me your photo with the mask de el Club Z. I don't trust you with her, a bad influence. She talked me into finger painting con la caca at three, the future artist, visionary!" Javier yelled, laughing.

"She wants to meet Justin and I really like her, a fellow loca!" she yelled back from the kitchen, grabbing everything delicious she could find.

"Dios mio, Feliz y tu hijo Justin. Mi Mama called, they want to meet you. Apparently, some blabber-mouth at Diego's called her..."

"One of the vulture-exes I'm sure, but I'm not ready to meet your parents, no way, we're not getting married..."

I know, amor, I know," Javier winced, her words. "I told them probably after Christmas as your son was visiting."

"Wait, I'm coming!" Watching her footing on the cement stairs and balancing the over-loaded tray, Xochiquetzal entered the bedroom, sunset. "Would you light the candles?"

"I brought photos of my transformed, Xochitzalita, so tomorrow we can build our altar and buy marigolds."

"That's perfect, just right." Javier placed two candles on both night stands and a large purple one in the center of the tray.

"You didn't tell them Justin's thirty, right? I mean, what if we hate each other after our journeys, by Christmas…"

Tears sprang to Javier's eyes, but he held them tightly behind the dam of his ER training. He grabbed her shoulders, staring each word directly into her eyes. "Xochitzalita, I will never ever hate you in this life time, if anything we're teaching each other how to love."

Tears slid down her face and she wondered where his courage came from, to be this vulnerable. Translucent. She couldn't stand his gaze and tried to focus on the purple candle's flame.

"Look at me, mi amor, look at me." He held her weeping face between his open palms. "If we're going to break the cycle of betrayal—remember the Spaniard at el mercado—this is the life time to do it, and you know, Xochitzalita, you know I always find you, mi amor."

"I love you, Javercito, es la verdad…it's the truth, and I'm road kill." Unable to bear his fierce, tender, open gaze of love, unable to break away, she pulled him to her, devouring him so he couldn't speak. So she couldn't speak. They devoured each other's words as though centuries of starvation leaped forth from that truth. Javier's courageous words, truth. Translucent. (The Energy Child laughed, wept, "Translucent.")

Is this fierce   Is this tender

Xochiquetzal put a sliced, jeweled strawberry into his mouth as they sipped the last of the cabernet, ate the last of the cheese, ham slices, dark bread. "Did you tell them Justin's age?"

"It's none of their business and they didn't ask, why should they? Amor, the bottom line is they're truly gracious people, especially my mother, you'll see. But if Xavier is there, only leave my side to pee," Javier laughed.

"Will he murder me with a poisoned dart or what?" She collapsed into his arms, giggling. "Okay, I honestly dread meeting your family, but after Justin leaves, and after our travels, I think I'll be ready."

"Dame tu boca…Give me your mouth, Xochitzalita."

"First we have to unload your stuff, unless it's already been done, no no I mean it, Dr. Gomez, then we'll bring up more food, wine, I promise, back to our bed." She smiled teasingly, then leapt to her feet, dressing quickly.

"To *our bed,* okay I'll follow you anywhere, even to the fregado Jetta. Tomorrow we make our altar, te amo, mi orchid." Slipping his feet into sandals, he ran down the stairs, grabbed her from behind, buried his face in her neck, exposing his teeth for a second (that primal instinct to bite, kill, what feeds you), and licked her flesh.

"Ayy sabrosita...delicious one," Javier smiled.

"Do you love my wings?"

"Qué?"

"Do you love my wings?"

"Always, mi amor, do you love mine?"

"Always," she laughed, "always, come on, let's unload the fucking Jetta, then more comida, vino."

"Do you promise, cabroncita?"

"Always, Dr. Zapata." Xochiquetzal thought of Don Francisco. Later, I'll tell Javier later about his beautiful voice, the conch shell returning me to my body. But not about his hot breath filling my lungs, my body, she thought, smiling to herself.

"Don't come in yet, it's a surprise!"

"I can hear you, you're running a bath, don't leave me, cabrona, let me in!"

"Count to twenty y callate."

"Uno, dos, tres..."

The over-sized tub was surrounded by candles, four red roses in a vase, lavender bath salts in the almost too hot water to bear, with rose petals floating...champagne with two flutes, sliced mangoes, strawberries, crackers, brie. "Perfect," she murmured. "If we weren't burning all these calories we'd be morbidly obese."

"Veinte, cabrona, open el fregado door, sabrosita Xochitzalita, veinte-uno..."

She let the door swing open, laughing. "Come in, mi tigre, but do tigers take baths?"

Javier laughed, pulling her close. "This tigre does and he loves to eat rose petals, your rose petals..."

"Callate and get in, ayy Diosa, maybe I'll die of exhaustion, as in Woman Murdered By Too Much Sexo Y Amor by Christmas so I won't have to meet your family. Xavier and his poisoned darts, and I don't even know about the rest..."

"I brought photos, stories, for our journey, so by the time you meet them you'll know all the secrets, mi amor." Javier put his right foot in slowly and jerked it back. "Do you actually get into this cauldron, amor, mis huevos will be hard boiled, not to speak of el gran chorizo, por favor." He ran some cold into the steaming tub, bending over gracefully. The inherent grace of health, youth. The undiminished light of the young.

My Goddess, he's so beautiful, not a sag, not a wrinkle, on that yummy body. She kissed his smooth, brown shoulder, where his wings were folded, and entered the cauldron, submerging herself. "Not too much cold, tigre, here, that's good, join me."

Javier moaned loudly as he entered the water inch by inch. "Ayy mis probecito, sabrocito huevos...My poor, sweet testicles." He poured a full glass of water, sharing it with her, then the two flutes of champagne. He took a slice of mango in his mouth, bringing it to hers. "This is the way tigers and jaguars feed each other, amor, la boca."

"Qué bien, yum," Xochiquetzal growled, spreading her legs to accept his sweet body between them. Spread wide, like giving birth, she thought, his head resting on her niña breasts, her feet circling around his boy legs.

"I did something weird the other night, and in front of mis amigos in the ER." He put a rose petal in his mouth and ate it; then he put one in her mouth. "Eat it, vitamin C, mi amor."

"What, what weird thing did you do, Zapata?"

I've never done this with a woman, between her legs, in a tub floating with roses, like sharing a womb, together—he sighed loudly, deeply, from his huevos.

"First of all, Xochitzalita, it's Zorba, and I danced alone, by myself in a club como un 'weirdo,' como tu dices...like you say, so my friends yelled, 'Ayy Dios, es Zorba!'"

"I love it!" she laughed, putting a piece of brie in her mouth, nudging him till he turned around to eat it. "You know, I danced by myself at the Z Club as well, raising my hands like little birds..."

"Like wings," he echoed, "like wings."

"Maybe we were dancing alone at the same time, around midnight..."

"Exactly, mi amor, we were, like wings." He thought of the gorgeous chica, calling her 'hija' as she stormed away. "We're falling, Xochitzalita, do you know what I mean?"

"As in road kill..."

"You and that road kill, callate, we're falling..."

"I mean no one's in charge, Zorba, and I've never seen such beautiful wings, I actually see them spreading like light around your shoulders, edged in violet..."

"Better than seeing Spaniards," Javier smiled. "Mas brie and a cracker too, amor. I can't believe I'm off for three months to travel con la Orchid."

"Okay, goddamn, you're getting spoiled, I'm creating a doctorcito monster," Xochiquetzal laughed.

"Then I'll bring you mangoes, strawberries, more rose petals, to your spoiled, sabrosita mouth, and when all the rose petals are gone, I want yours..."

"I've never been spoiled, not like this, Javier," her voice caught, weeping. "Me, the old, embittered jaguar being fed mangoes."

"And a mango surgery is also scheduled and you know how expert I am, mi monstrua sabrocita." He turned to face her, licking her tears before they disappeared into the water. "You know, I'm starting to like your tears, they don't scare me anymore. It only means you're feeling your passion, tu alma...your soul. I don't even care if you say, 'Older woman, younger man,' and weep even harder. I'll just keep licking like this, like this, like this..."

The fierce, close stars rained their light down on them through the sky light, over their thirty-four and fifty-eight year old bodies; and when they finally rested, her inside his spread open legs, they saw the deep, red gash of a comet leave its mark. Forever.

"I see your wings spread out in light, Xochitzalita, ringed in violet. I really do see them." He thought of his dying patients, the violet light that encircled them, comforted them. But he'd never seen their wings. "I think your talk of seeing my wings has triggered my seeing yours, who knows."

"Do you love them?"

"Like my own. Wings," Javier smiled so peacefully. We don't have to die, leave the body, to fly, these wings, esta mujer, we're falling.

"Javiercito, you're more beautiful than I am. You're the brand-new star shining over our heads, look do you see it..."

"Amor, you're going to make me lick you again."

"And I'm the ancient comet leaving red trails, my final journey across the sky..."

Javier started to laugh, holding onto her in case she became offended. "I told you, I'm not listening to this young star, old comet mierda, and you are beautiful, Xochitzalita, I see men look at you..."

"I see women drool on you..." He laughed harder as she tried to move forward.

"Where are you going, cabroncita?" he gasped, still laughing.

"More hot water. So you think this is funny?"

"It's not a competition, *do you see that?*"

"Will you let him love your wings?" Xochiquetzal heard Don Francisco's deep, playful voice, felt the surprise of his kiss on her mouth, the roar of the conch shell.

"Someone kissed me in the plaza the other day..."

"Was it that puto perro Pablo, que me chingas!" Real anger rose in his voice. She turned to gaze at his twin fires, those perfect eyes.

"No, no," she laughed. "An old Mayan Day Keeper, a wonderful man, he wants to meet you, for us to visit him in Oaxaca..." *When he's recovered*, she remembered and let it go. Maybe if I give it no further energy, maybe it was just a warning to be careful on our travels, no speeding on those crazy roads, maybe.

Javier relaxed as she turned off the hot water, steam rising toward the stars. "This guy kissed you, que cabron," he laughed softly, bringing her back to the circle of his body.

"His name is Don Francisco and he gave me a Mayan Calendar reading, my Mayan name. I'll show you the pouch he made me later. He asked me if I would let you love my wings, he knew you were a physician, that you're younger than me, that you're my teacher and I'm yours..."

"I like this guy, so when did he kiss you, this viejito perro?"

"It was a quick, sudden kiss, look, like this." Xochiquetzal kissed Javier briefly, blowing as much of her breath into him. "Did you feel that?"

"Let me do it to you." Slowly he came to meet her mouth, holding her eyes, not letting her go, his mouth devouring hers, his tongue seeking hers, twin serpents, blowing a long, deep breath into her body. Fire. She felt beautiful, full of his fire, loved, adored.

"Will you let me love your wings, Xochitzalita?"

Fear, love, fear, love, fear, love—tears ran down her face as she began to sob, but he didn't let go or try to stop her tears.

"Will you, mi amor?"

"Yes," she managed to say between sobs. Gathered thirty year old tears, sorrow.

They built the altar on the tiled divider between the kitchen, living room space. His dead, transformed; her dead, transformed. Their photos, little messages on strips of paper, candles, seashells, a Huichol beaded bowl with a light-filled deer edged in sky blue, and a beaded rainbow stretching across the deer's belly. Xochiquetzal placed two silver milagros inside of the bowl. At the top eyes for vision; at the bottom a heart for understanding. And two tiny packets of Chiclets she'd bought from the children at the plaza, for generosity of the spirit. Water in front of her grandmother, Clara, and Javier's India madre, Amalia—their photos. A shot glass of tequila in front of his uncle Hugo's laughing face—clearly a sensual man.

"You can *see* the strength in Amalia's eyes, una India como mi Mamacita...an Indian like my grandmother. They have an ancient strength you don't see in my country anymore, sadly."

"They could be sisters, yes, those eyes. You have those eyes, Xochitzalita, but with a dose of cabroncita, you like to play." Javier held her to him from behind, nibbling her neck softly. "Tu Mamacita was beautiful as a young woman, those liquid eyes."

"I almost forgot, the woman who came with her sick baby came by." Xochiquetzal disappeared into the downstairs bedroom and returned, holding two handmade shirts—one white, one black. "One for you, one for Juan, and look at these abalone buttons, the beautiful stitching."

Javier laughed with pleasure. "I'll wear one, the black one, what do you think?" He took off his t-shirt to put it on.

"Perfect, black suits you like your black leather jacket, but you also look good in your white muppie shirts, Javiercito." She placed the bunch of densely, fragrantly, blossomed, orange marigolds behind the altar and the heavy blossoms leaned down to their dead, their transformed.

"Our altar is perfect, mi amor, I've never built my own altar, leaving it to my mother. Now I build it with you, our altar for our dead, beautiful."

Tears filled her eyes. "I've never built an altar with anyone, mi tigre, never."

"Do you agree that our altar is perfect?" He held her from behind, cupping her small breasts.

He's not afraid of my tears, my passion, mi alma, she told herself as she lit the candles. "Yes, our altar is perfect."

After their feast at el mercado, the one-thousand year old dream (she kept looking away to see if the Spaniard would appear; not this time)—they bought two bunches of marigolds, perfumed lilies, red roses, two vases, more candles, a hand-full of silver milagros. All in the market. Days could be spent here and still there would be mysteries. The extended mercado that ran down steps, the street below, sheltered from the weather by a sturdy tin roof. Aisles and aisles of handmade beauty, sellers extending their wares. To hold, to feel, to admire.

"I'm taking you somewhere special to me, Javiercito."

"Can we take a taxi with all this stuff, hippie girl?"

"It's only a couple of blocks away, and we can take one home, okay?"

"Home, I like that," his little victory smile again. "Lead the way, hippie girl."

"I'd smack you if my arms weren't full," she laughed. "And I saw your sly, little smile."

"So, the secret is to distract you, mi amor." Javier blocked her way and kissed her deeply, to scattered gritos.

"A donde vas con el jardin...Where are you going with the garden?" a man asked, smiling.

"A la casa de mi amor...To my beloved's home," Javier smiled back.

"Here's El Nino Doctorcito, I think he brought you to me. Just before Vallarta, I lit a candle here to him. Isn't he sweet, his tiny doctor bag with his sexy milagro angel?"

Tears filled Javier's eyes. "Amalia took me to her Nino Doctorcito, to her church, the church of the poor. She'd tell me, 'This is you, Javiercito, el doctoricito, this is you, and you will heal people, mark my words.' Then she'd buy us the richest, most rica, ice cream from the vendor outside. Hers small, mine huge, que rica, and now you bring me to your Nino Doctorcito, mi amor." One tear escaped his eye, caressing his cheek all the way down.

Xochiquetzal caught the tear with her fingertip and ate it. "Ay tigre," she murmured, "I love your tears. Amalia was your second mother, your India mama, and she obviously knew who you were." She lit a candle for El Nino Doctorcito, and for Amalia.

"You're right, he brought me to you and he wouldn't let you ignore me, tu regalo...your gift. I'd lick you but we're in a church," he smiled. "Do you want water for the vases? I'll ask the nuns." Javier rang a bell at the convent door and an angel appeared, smiling shyly, gazing down, taking the vases from his hands. She returned with water in them, that smile. "Gracias, Madre," his voice was soothing, sweet.

"Gracias tigre, women love you, even the nuns, that voice of yours."

"My bedside manner, mi amor," he smiled. The sun.

"It worked on me," she laughed softly. "This church is run by nuns, my favorite church in San Miguel." The red roses went into the clear, gold vase and she placed them in front of the dark-skinned Virgen de Guadalupe. The Indian mother of God. The fragrant lilies for El Nino Doctorcito, and more marigolds for the house.

"And here's the other reason this is my favorite church." Xochiquetzal led him to the front of the church to sit. "Look up."

Javier rested his head on the thick, polished, wooden back rest, placing everything beside him. "I love church domes, the chandeliers, the play of light, the singing birds that find their way in, and all these flowers."

"Do you see the four paintings in each direction—north, west, south, east."

Javier sat upright to focus on each one. " Each painting a writer is writing, yes, I can see why this is your favorite church, poeta."

"And the one with the monster at his feet."

"The monster has human hands, of course. El monstruo es el genio...The monster is the genius," he smiled. The sun. The undiminished. Light of the young. "My monster does surgery," he laughed.

"Of course," she laughed with him, taking his left hand in hers. They sat in peace, in the spilling gold sunlight, as bird wings circled the top of the dome, singing. "Will you let me love your wings, doctorcito?"

"I will let you love any part of me you choose to love." He looked at her and she believed him. Then he looked up to the monster with human hands, el genio. Yes, those are my hands, mi genio manos, a gift from the monster I've come to know—life, death, life, death. All my failures. A wave of pain caught him; then the memory of those that lived, joy. Javier brought Xochiquetzal's hand to his lips and kissed it. "Qué genio," he smiled, "mi amor."

On the Ancha, the wide main street just a few long blocks from her house, they followed the crowd of families walking to the Guadalupe Cemetery. The large, somber, yet gently smiling, crowd left the Ancha, turning right down a side street which opened up to a crowded bazaar. Stalls of yellow, gold, orange marigolds, vases, buckets to carry water, plastic crosses, ribbons, little lambs, children's toys, plastic flowers, to decorate the beloved's grave. Javier bought a small bunch of marigolds for each of them since they had no graves to decorate. They carried their dead's photos in plastic bags, holding them to their hearts instinctively.

"I suddenly feel like an orphan, my photos, no grave," Xochiquetzal almost whispered.

"You can't be, Xochitzalita, you're mine." Javier put his arm around her. "I know what you need—a taco and a café fuerte." The food stalls smelled delicious as the women chopped fresh vegetables and stirred the spicy meat, scenting the air.

"Okay, but just two, the blessing is in twenty minutes. The café fuerte sounds good, tigre." She leaned into him as he ordered, nestling onto his chest. How does this thirty-four-year-old man make me feel safe, at home, not an orphan, in his arms, how? She breathed in his scent—the sharp-foam scent of la mar mixed with the watermelon musk she'd dabbed on him, laughing. "The heyoka scent of watermelon for you, Dr. Zapata."

"Una cerveza con limon, madre, por favor." His doctorcito voice, a sweet request, held up by all of his voices. His many faces, roles—the healer, the ER surgeon, the one in command. That voice. The older woman smiled with delight, just to serve him.

Where have I heard that voice? Xochiquetzal wondered, gazing at his perfect young man's beauty. The Warrior in the Sun shot to Earth, visiting her, picking up the Victoria to squeeze in the lime, focused on his task, not allowing one drop to escape his icy beer.

And Don Francisco's face came to her, making her laugh out loud. For a few seconds, she watched Don Francisco's face become thirty, forty, then eighty, ninety, then thirty again as his inner light matched the outer light. This moment. Perfectly.

"Why are you laughing, cabroncita?"

"That face of yours, how everything you do, including making love, is like how you're not letting one drop of that lime be wasted."

"That's called passion, mi amor, el pasion." He grazed her mouth with his tongue, slowly, holding her eyes. "And we've just begun el pasion, mi orchid."

"Will I survive this?" she laughed.

"Not only survive, thrive, look at you, Xochitzalita, you're in full bloom. Older woman, younger man."

"Callate...Shut up, you're making me want you, right by the cemetery, que blasphemy."

"Qué genio, I'd make love to you in the middle of the cemetery, and I know the dead would rejoice, the good stuff of being human, alive, chinga los marigolds..."

Maybe later I'll tell him he sounds like Don Francisco, maybe, or when they meet, I'll listen to each one. Full bloom, yes, that's how I feel.

Javier felt eyes on him and as he looked, she mouthed *Tan hermoso*, smiling, bending over to expose her full breasts. He glanced quickly at Xochiquetzal. She saw nothing and he gave la chica a quick half-smile of appreciation, for beauty.

"I've never in my life seen this, entire families sitting on the graves of their loved ones, and children—look, Javier—resting on a fallen tomb stone, no fear of death." She took out her small digital camera and took some quick shots, not wanting to make them feel self-conscious, observed.

"No fear of living, yes I see. After my mother's more formal Dia de Los Muertos, I went with Amalia to her mother's grave. She brought candles, food, so much food, warm blankets, and we'd spend the night. Musicians wandering all night, playing to each family for some pesos, the sound of prayer, laughter, singing. And after the dead ate the essence of the food, we ate every bite, and more, she always brought more to share with those who had little. And she'd speak to her mother of Oaxaca, their home, their family there. She'd always planned to go home, then the cancer."

"She was from Oaxaca?"

"Amalia was todo Maya de Oaxaca. She came here with her mother to find work for a season and then her mother died suddenly, so she stayed on with my family."

"Agua por las flores...Water for the flowers?" a boy of five asked, beautiful eyes huge in his open, brown face.

"We don't need the water, niño," Javier answered with a tender smile.

Xochiquetzal handed him twenty pesos. "Gracias señora!" His smile paid her in full. His five-year-old body balanced itself with the full bucket of water as he tottered away to the next grave, family gathering.

"Ay pochita, people pay him maybe three or four pesos for some water..."

"Javier, he's only maybe five, it breaks my heart. I can't imagine Justin at five with a full bucket of water, trying to sell it. Did you ever do it, sell water at a cemetery?"

A sharp anger flickered in his eyes, dark obsidian, then understanding. "I've told you, mi pochita, mi amor, I'm an upper class doctor, once boy, son of a doctor, at home in his own country. You were right to give him twenty pesos, absolutely right. I never had to sell water in a cemetery, ever." Javier took her hand in his as some musicians approached. They'd placed their photos on some stones, their bunches of marigolds in front of them.

"I know, I know, I'll tell them," Javier laughed. "Mi amor quiere el canto, 'La Paloma,' por favor amigos."

"How does every singer hit that high note?" She smiled with pleasure (He remembered Mamacita's favorite song, he remembered), her hand enclosed within his. The white dove, la paloma, on the roof, Mamacita, she remembered, weeping, as they sang, "Cu cu ru cu cuuuu paaaalllooommmmaaaa..." Enclosed within his doctorcito hands; her hand a trusting, trembling bird. *Am I too old for this?* Her scarred, embittered, so fierce, jaguar hissed, *Beware you don't fly too high, beware...* Then she turned her tail to Xochiquetzal and melted into her lush jungle.

A family joined the singer and the children hit the high notes with him, smiling with the joy of children. Surrounded by all of the families and their dead. Transformed.

"Bring your photos, join us," one of the grandmothers waved them over.

Javier smiled back at her, the entire family waiting for their response. "Come on, Xochitzalita, let's join this family." They brought their photos of their dead, transformed. The bunches of marigolds. The grandmother that waved them over, picked up Javier's photo of Amalia.

"Tu Mama era India...Your mother was Indian."

"She was my second mother, mi India Mama."

"Qué bien, hijo, que bien." Then she picked up each photo, gazing at each face, asking who this loved one was. Javier's uncle, Xochiquetzal's mother, grandmother.

Javier asked the guitarist to play México Lindo y Querido, and the singer launched passionately into the first words—"México lindo y querido, si muero lejos de ti que digan que estoy dormida...Beautiful and beloved Mexico, if I die far from you tell them I'm sleeping..."

The grandmother began to quietly weep, tears filling her deep wrinkles. She brought a photo out of her dark red rebozo, the smiling face of a young man. "This was my husband when he went to el norte so many years ago. He continues to sleep, to dream, in el norte."

Xochiquetzal took his photo in her hands, tears filling her eyes. "Do you have children, señora?"

"These are his two sons, his daughter, his grandchildren, his great-grandchildren." Her eyes lit up with love; no room for loss. He lived in them.

"Your family is so beautiful," Xochiquetzal smiled, still weeping, thinking of Mamacita's young mother, baby brother, swept away in the current of the river. As they crossed. The border. They never crossed. Only Mamacita, Clara.

The singer sang the final stanza, alone in the silence, as people paused to listen, heads bowed. The ones who traveled north. That never returned. Home. Who were still sleeping, dreaming. "México lindo y querido, si muero lejos de ti que digan que estoy dormida y que me traigan aqui, que digan que estoy dormmida y que me traigan aqui, México lindo y querido...Beautiful and beloved México, if I die far from you tell them I'm sleeping, and bring me here, tell them I'm sleeping and bring me home, beautiful and beloved Mexico."

The pure white dove, the memory, the singer's voice, his words, comforted Xochiquetzal, and she murmured, "México lindo y querido."

Paper plates were passed around, then freshly made tamales, beans, rice, tomatoes, avocado slices, still warm corn tortillas. Javier bought large bottles of soda, four six packs of still cold Victorias, and a chocolate cake a woman was selling. It became a feast, a celebration of the living and the dead.

The musicians continued to play and sing songs she'd never heard—of love, loss, death, reunion. If not on Earth, then in heaven. And they sang La Paloma again, even more sweetly. People gave them bottles of water, Victorias, a plate of bulging with food, and they continued to sing.

After they hugged and kissed everyone goodbye, and as Xochiquetzal kissed the grandmother's feathery cheek, the old woman asked, "Estas del norte, hija?" "Si Mama." "Qué bien que vienes al tierra de su gente, que bien...It's good that you come to the earth of your people."

She took photos of the entire family, the musicians stopping to rest and eat. What beautiful smiles, what beautiful people. "Regalar los fotos," they joked, and she wrote down where to mail them. "I don't want to go, Javier, but I guess it's time. I feel at home here, México lindo y querido."

"I know, pochita, I know. I feel at home here as well." He paused to kiss her, and then he shouted, "Qué te vaya bien...May life go well!" "Qué te vaya bien," followed them as they walked away. Then the full-throated, joyous gritos of the musicians, and of course Javier answered with his.

At the entrance they stopped to admire the most beautiful, heartbreaking, beautiful grave. Childhood toys, from every stage of childhood, covered the mound of the grave. And so many flowers. The entire area was transformed. Into life. A celebration of life. A photo of a young man in his twenties, toy cars surrounding his laughing face.

"Is this your son?" Javier asked the man sitting with the grave, lowering his voice in respect.

"Si, es mi hijo," he smiled with joy, as though he were alive. And he was. Alive. Transformed. Into life.

There were people stopping to take photos of the beauty, so Xochiquetzal brought hers out for two quick ones, not wanting to intrude.

"Would you take my photo with my son?" the man asked, smiling.

"Of course," she returned his beautiful smile. "If you give me your name and address, I'll send you a copy. She took six shots to make sure one turned out perfectly, and he smiled in each one. Perfectly.

As she put her camera away, the father, Tomas, handed her something. An orange splashed butterfly wing. "La mariposa siempre vive...The butterfly always lives,'" he smiled each word into her eyes. And Javier thought, If my father loved me this way, if.

All the way home they scattered marigold petals—a trail for the dead, the transformed—right up to the steps, the door, through the door, to their altar. They placed their photos in their proper places and Xochiquetzal lit every candle.

"Tomorrow we take off for the monarchs, so we should get to bed early, pack the car while it's still dark, my precaution for theft, so no one sees me leaving..."

"Callate, mi amor, I agree it's time for bed." Javier led the way, scattering marigolds up the stairs, guiding her feet to the bed. Their bed. His full name on the mattress. He thought briefly of la chica, exposing her full breasts to him. I've had plenty of those fucks, sweet and empty, empty and sweet.

He pulled the silky bedspread off, tossing it onto a chair; tore the blossoms of a red rose from its stem and scattered them across the silky sheets. He pulled her to him as they fell across the rose petals, covering her mouth with his. "Tu boca, tu boca, your mouth, es mio, is mine," he breathed into her. This woman takes me to the Warrior in the Sun, to the fullness of the sun, to the danger of the sun, esta mujer, mi orchid.

"I saw how the men watched you, wondering how it was me who was with you, Xochitzalita."

"I stopped counting las chicas after the first five minutes, give me a break, Dr. Gomez."

"Callate, mi amor sabrosita, I'm going to lick you, fuck you, until the grandfather next door does a grito when you can't help it, when you scream."

"You may not scream," she laughed, "but you will sing, you will fly, as I take what's mine."

"What's yours?" His breath caught as her tongue traced his crescent moon nipple, the other nipple, licking, sucking, so gently, then down, down the center of his chest, his slender boy-man belly, down.

"The gold, your sperm."

"This way, mi amor." He guided her on top of him, her mouth to his gold, his mouth to her gold, so gently, firmly, forcefully, madly they sang, yes, the golden sun of their making, yes, the healing sun of their making, yes, the dangerous sun of their making, yes, she brought his gold to his mouth, yes, he brought her gold to her mouth, yes, and then they danced, two butterflies circling the great Sun, four months to live, four centuries to live (Who can judge the joy of a life time?).

As fragile.   As a butterfly.   Wing.   Yes.

"Gold," the Energy Child sang with them, "yes."

Javier, Xochiquetzal... *They gaze at the map of Mexico, planning their trip to the monarchs, the coast, the pyramids. They gaze at the map of the USA, up to Taos where Earth and Sky marry. Snow. They gaze at the map of the world, pointing to Bali, Thailand, India, Tibet, Bhutan, Japan, all of Europe, back to Mexico, Oaxaca, all of Latin America. They gaze at the map of the Universe, wondering at the flight of the monarch, the joy of its flight. They laugh, its life span, they weep, and laugh again, as the Universe blazes with awe-full, golden wonder.*
"It's not about maps, it's about blood, I'm getting lost, I'm getting found, in your blood, Xochitzalita."
"This is how we keep finding each other, each life time, our blood."

They were on the highway before dawn, deciding to stop for breakfast on the way. "We'll be there in about three hours and I know a small town on the way with a morning market, desayuno y café fuerte. I murdered a scorpion for you this morning, amor, a big one, Dios mio."

"Where?" Xochiquetzal asked sleepily, yet her excitement to be leaving, traveling, with el doctorcito squeezed her heart, sharply. Joy.

"The downstairs hallway, joder," Javier laughed softly, aware of the pulsing sun beginning to rise between the dark mountains. When have I been this happy? The first light met his eyes. As a boy, around eight, when each day glistened with wonder. In summer, yes, in summer. Play. Sun to moon to sun. The sound of Amalia's voice at bedtime, her stories, always her stories. If only I could remember. All of them. Her stories.

The sun devoured every shadow, every secret the night had whispered to the earth; and the earth opened her legs to the sun's warmth. Life.

"I killed one too, upstairs by the roof, also big, el fucking Borg, it never fails to creep me out..."

"Was it gold?"

"Was yours?"

The Warrior in the Sun shot his golden arrows into the heart of the day, as Javier sped toward the monarch sanctuary. Two golden arrows reached their targets. Their beating, pulsing hearts.

When he's recovered, Don Francisco's voice echoed. "Slow down, amor, slow down, I'm not ready for transformation, yet."

The stalls in the market were being set up in the morning sunlight as they ordered chicken and pork tamales—and Javier a bowl of spicy goat stew—beans in fresh sliced tomatoes, cilantro, and of course café fuerte sprinkled with cinnamon.

"How can you eat goat meat in the morning? I mean, it looks great but in the morning." She took a shot of the steaming bowl in his hands, his pleasure in eating.

"Smell it, Xochitzalita."

"Smells sabrosito, delicious."

"Taste it." Javier placed a small piece in the spicy broth, into the large soup spoon. He brought it to her mouth. "Taste it, mi amor," laughing at her pocha-gringa ways.

"Ohmygoddess, it's fantastic."

"I'll order you one."

"Not in the morning, but for lunch or dinner with a beer, tortillas, okay. I'm still in the pocha-transition-phase," she laughed.

The motherly cook brought them two steaming drinks, smiling at Javier like a favorite son. She quickly gave Xochiquetzal a sly wink, woman to woman.

"What's this?" She sniffed the thick looking liquid.

"Taste it, pochita."

She sipped it carefully, trying not to burn her tongue. "It's a thick, yummy chocolate, damn, it's good." Xochiquetzal leaned over and kissed Javier.

"It's a pre-Conquest drink made from chocolate and corn meal, called *atole,* really a meal in itself. You can eat it with a spoon, ayy I love this stuff. Amalia used to secretly make it for me, or we'd buy it in the market, but hers was the best atole."

"Why secretly?" A flicker of the Spaniard, serving him this drink.

"My mother said only los Indios drank it, and the poor ones at that, to sustain themselves. It's very healthy of course, and the chocolate zaps you with energy."

She took a deeper sip as it cooled. "I love it, it's so comforting, delicious." She took a shot of the woman bringing the steaming serving pot of atole to warm their cups. Her smile was dazzling.

"Exactly, mi amor, comforting." He'd never had atole as good as Amalia's, and wherever he traveled in Mexico he'd never found one to equal hers. A darker, richer chocolate; a thicker, sweeter corn mush that actually required a spoon to eat. Amalia would add more chocolate so he could drink it, and it always made him dizzy with joy.

"I've been looking for Amalia's atole since my childhood and I've never found it. This is good, muy sabrosito, but not her Mayan atole, that dark, rich, thick chocolate, cinnamon, ground chiles, con maize, ayy." He heard Amalia's laughter, vividly, saw her face for a moment as she blessed his life with her eyes.

"This looks like the Sierras in northern California." Xochiquetzal's digital camera was out, clicking. "Or the Sierras in northern California look like this. Or they look like each other, since it's all las Sierra Madres, right?" she laughed. "The pine smells, these trees, the lake, how beautiful, I could live here."

Javier smiled, nodding 'yes.' "Maybe for a month or two, Xochitzalita, but I think you need a town like San Miguel for doses of excitement. But, yes, it is beautiful, and I'd live here for a month or two with you, to make sure you get your minimum dose," Javier smiled at her knowingly. "You know, el prescripcion."

"I've got yours too, you know, Javiercito."

"Es la verdad...It's the truth, amor," he smiled. "The people here are poor, but they're rich, do you know what I mean? Of course, you know what I mean."

"You're starting to know Hippie Girl, mi amor, older and wiser too," she laughed.

As they climbed further into the mountains, the air became thick with pine scent as though they were bees in a jar of honey; or butterflies dripping from trees in winged clusters. Dripping and dreaming after their long journey—life time after life time—to this sky of golden sun. White sun to golden sun, they winged their journey south—dying, birthing, dying, birthing their wet wings—then north. Migration.

Only sky. No borders.

"I can't believe it yet, that I'm free to travel with you for three months, three years, three centuries," Javier laughed, swallowing sweet honey. "We're riding the Windhorse, mi amor."

Xochiquetzal looked at him, his sheer morning beauty, and she forgot to breathe. She aimed her camera at his young man's beauty (this moment), clicking each shot, and inhaled deeply. Honey.

"Do you want to go to Taos, those mountains, Sangre de Cristo, snow, the marriage of Earth, Sky..."

"I want to have a snowball fight with you, then soak in a tub with you, walk in the snow, drink cognac with you, mi amor."

"By a chingaso blazing fire, yes, and I know just the place, you'll see."

"Como no, the marriage of Earth and Sky with you, Xochitzalita mi pochita."

"I love watching you drive, at home in your own country, doctorcito, and I know exactly where we'll go. First Taos, then the hot springs, maybe a Pueblo dance if we can find one. I miss them, the dances, the men singing in winter, the early morning, snow on the peaks, the drummers in ribbon shirts..."

Suddenly, a boy of fourteen grabbed onto Javier's open window and began to sing at the top of his lungs. A song of honey, a song of pine, a song of butterflies. A sun song. From the Warrior in the Sun. Three smaller boys chased after him, begging for a ride.

"No, no, you're all dirty," Javier scolded them, trying to be stern.

"Let them in, doctorcito, I want to hear the rest of the song."

"Ay pochita," he laughed. "Okay, to the sanctuary, do you live there?"

"Si señor, with our families who take care of las mariposas," one of the younger boys answered shyly.

The older boy continued to sing without a trace of shyness, smiling ear to ear, eyes shining, the most haunting song. Of love, longing, a long journey. Migration. Wings.

Xochiquetzal's eyes filled with tears. He's singing our lives. He's dreaming our lives as he sings.

Javier glanced at her, laughing with the boys, and, seeing her tears, reached for her hand.

"Listen, he's dreaming our lives, Javier."

He brought her hand to his lips. "I know," he murmured, kissing it, a butterfly's wing.

They entered a wide, dirt road with a parking lot ahead. "Aqui señor, right here is good," the boys chanted as though still humming with the older boy, giggling among themselves. They'd ridden in a car today, what luck.

"Wait, wait." Xochiquetzal stopped them as they were about to spring out the door. "For the song," she smiled at the singer, giving him fifty pesos. Eyes liquid with light, he smiled 'gracias.' She gave the other boys twenty pesos each.

"We didn't sing, señora," the smaller boys said in unison.

She lined them up for a photo—switching to her old, professional camera— as they laughed, surrounding the singer. "How do you say, You were his back-up?"

Javier translated and the boys howled with laughter, yelling "GRACIAS," disappearing into the trees.

"They live in such a beautiful place, there's literally light coming out of their eyes, their faces. You don't see that in my country, well maybe in the Pueblos or people on the land far away from cities, or the very young who haven't had it snatched away." She thought of Justin and she saw the light at the very center of his eyes, at thirty.

He pulled her close, just holding her, smelling her hair. "I saw the same light in the children's faces in the mountains of Oaxaca, Chiapas, in the adults as well, and in the eyes of El Subcomandante Marcos, el jefe. The Warrior in the Sun loves them, mi amor."

"And his lover, the Warrior Woman in the Sun."

"Ay cabroncita, come on, you're in for a treat, for a spectacle, but try to put your beloved camera down once in a while to just *see*."

———◆———

A teenager led each of their horses and Javier rode in front, he and his teen talking, laughing. On his last visit years ago, he'd come with a chica who was terrified of horses, so she'd ridden on his lap. In a short skirt. He remembered putting his hand up her thigh as they rode, jostling in the saddle, the teen looking away, smiling. He looked back at Xochiquetzal and waved, blowing her a kiss, proud of her strength, her feminista courage. To ride by herself. Yet wishing his hand was on her thigh, her pollen soft thigh. In that moment.

"You're right, I'm going to sit right here on these rocks, this spot, it's perfect, and not take any photos. For at least twenty minutes," she laughed into the sweet wind. Clusters, thousands of butterflies, dripping, dreaming, from thousands of branches, trees. The view through the trees, to the valley, held the vision of infinity. An infinity of monarchs. Dreaming. Were they dreaming of snow? she wondered. And if they didn't dream the snow, would snow continue to fall?

Then a warm wind woke them up and they rose in clouds of stained glass orange painted wings, filtering the golden sun, flying toward them, grazing their faces, their bodies, as they sat absolutely still. Silent. Shoulder to shoulder. That moment.

"Now the rocks are our Windhorse, Xochitzalita. I think las mariposas love us, look." One perfect monarch landed on his right hand, as he slowly brought it toward her. "And one is at the top of your head, don't move, mi amor, don't move." They sat still in the silence, afraid to disturb the wonder.

"I'm going to make mariposa love to you tonight, mi orchid, I'm going to taste you with all my feelers, I'm going to lick every speck of pollen from your secret orchid places como una monarca."

"Listen, do you hear their wings, listen."

They were silent, still. In. Wonder.

"I hear the wind, amor, and you have two more monarcas on your head."

"You have one on your shoulder, you look like Saint Francis of Assisi," Xochiquetzal started to giggle.

"Come here mi chica mariposa...my little butterfly." Javier thrust out his tongue suggestively and then leaned into her, circling his tongue over her lips slowly.

"Where," her breath caught as her womb clenched for him, "are we staying tonight?"

"By a lake, you'll love it, oh look." Javier bent down and touched the fallen butterfly very carefully, with his fingertips, in case it was still alive. "For you, Xochitzalita, it dreams its next life." As we must, he thought, as the boy sang. Will she dream with me, this life, or will she leave me. Again. Will I leave her, again.

She held the intact monarch in her open palm, its vivid colors undiminished. She thought of the boy's song, dreaming their lives. This moment.

"I'm getting lost, I'm getting found, in your blood, mi amor. This is how we keep finding each other, each life time, our blood. Where did that come from, it just bubbled out of my mouth," she smiled with surprise. She held the monarch, cupped in her hands, trying not to bruise its still perfect wings.

The butterfly.   Always lives.   This dream.

"Look at these casitas, they're obviously poor but each one is surrounded by flowers, trees, views of the lake, the surrounding mountains. I could live here, Javiercito, I could." As they slowed for a curve, they saw two women washing their family's clothing on flat rocks in a small creek.

"Could you wash your stuff in a creek?"

"No, but I still could live here with a washing machine," Xochiquetzal smiled. "Look, there's some fancyish houses out by the lake."

"Yes, the upper classes always get right by the lake, and, yes, I'm talking about myself, el muppie, and you la pochita," Javier smiled with a sigh. "We could live here for a month or so, let's do it, let's dream it, I'll look into it. We'll rent a muppie mansion, mi amor," he laughed. "Let's dream it together."

"Wake up and look, Xochitzalita, we're here." Javier parked in front of the hotel. "I called ahead and our room's ready. Are you hungry, amor?"

She opened her eyes to a wind rippled lake glittering with the Warrior in the Sun's final arrows. It was wide, immense, ominous. Magical. Full of dreams, poetry, stories. This lake. "What's the name of this place again?"

"Patzcuaro, isn't it beautiful?" he asked as though he'd created this billion year old gift just for her.

"It's more than beautiful, it's wondrous, gracias for bringing me here, corazón."

"You've never called me 'corazón,' I like it, mi amor."

"I imagine if I stayed here for a while, this lake would give me dreams, poetry."

"We can stay for a couple of days before the hippie beach, write some poetry, dream, como no, mi corazón. Let's unpack the basics and go eat, tengo hambre...I'm hungry por pollo con mole, una Victoria y un chingaso margarita ayy."

"Mole, let's get going, and why do you keep calling it hippie beach?" Xochiquetzal faced the lake, stretching her entire body, breathing in its musky magic. Fertile. Potent. That scent.

"You'll see, mi amor, it's a surprise but you'll love it because you're a pochita hippie girl."

She picked up a small rock and threw it at him, laughing. "You like keeping a secret from me, don't you, a mild form of torture."

Javier ducked, laughing. "The mild form of torture tonight will be when I withhold your orgasm with my feeler"—he flicked his tongue—"until you can't stand it, truly can't stand it, and burst from your safe, cozy cocoon, mi corazón."

"Ohmygoddess, you are so full of shit!" She picked up another small rock and threw it at him, but this one connected to his heart, a tiny plink, then joined the earth again.

Corazon. The Energy Child remembered, listening to the heart.

"The scent of pine is following us everywhere, all these pine trees, the flowers, all this green," Xochiquetzal breathed it in. "Have you been here before, well I'm sure you have." She sipped the chilled chardonay as they waited for dinner, pollo con mole.

"A couple of life times ago, yes, but now I'm here with you in this life time."

The sky and the lake merged into one endless mirror as the birds flew from tree to tree, settling in for the night. Large, white egrets slipped gracefully, white kites against the darkening sky. And blackbirds trilled, invisibly, in the tree tops. An ancient song of conquest after conquest, as the wind became still.

"There's such a brooding quality to this place in contrast to its beauty. I can smell the mole, is it good here, and did you always come with a chica?" The candle between them caught a flicker of impatience in Javier's dark eyes, fastened on her.

She felt the subtle threat of a public scene, a leap from his chair to pull her to her feet; that deep kiss that rendered her speechless, helpless. What a pocha I am—she tried not to smile, and a fifty-eight-year-old pocha, ayy Diosa.

"Xochitzalita, you've even met some of my old lovers and I don't even know who your last lover was."

"You don't want to know."

"I do, tell me." He held her eyes. "Tell me." The center of his dark eyes held the light of the candle, burning. Let's balance this fregado power and get it over with, he thought, waiting.

"Do you really want to know?"

"I'm waiting." The Zapata look, gaze.

"In Bali, five years ago."

"I'm your first lover in five years?"

"Yes, I think I'd given up on a deep level. If I couldn't really love someone, why fuck, no matter how lovely it was to, you know, fuck." Xochiquetzal looked directly into Javier's eyes, the light. Calm. Waiting. Dr. Zapata in the ER. Detachment. She looked away for a moment to the dark, still lake, then back to his waiting eyes.

"I was staying in Sanur, right on the coast, at this sweet hotel by the sand. It had its own little restaurant facing the sea, beautiful."

"And your lover?"

"He owned the hotel, passed down for generations. He invited me one night to join him for wine on the beach. He'd brought blankets, pillows, food, wine." She could see him—slender, graceful, gentle, beautiful as young Balinese men are, and Wayan was handsome even by Balinese standards. Beauty.

"Was he Balinese?"

"Yes."

"Young and handsome, mi amor?"

She looked away to the lake, the icy stars beginning to reflect their poetry on its dark, calm surface. "Yes."

"Was he a good lover, mi amor?"

She looked into his twin fires. "Yes."

"As good as me?" Sadness flooded his eyes.

Xochiquetzal stood up, bringing Javier to his feet, kissing him so deeply, finding his tongue with her own, breathing her breath into him. "No, mi corazón, no."

The cook gave a long, low grito which they couldn't hear, as he watched them. He added one more ladle of rich, dark mole to their tender, sabrosito pollo, sighing, "Qué bien, el amor, que bien."

"I can't believe our room faces the lake, this lovely balcony, and where did you get that wine?"

"An upper class doctor at home in his own country," they said simultaneously, laughing.

"Ay mi muppie, what wine did you get and where are the wine glasses." Xochiquetzal watched him unwind the glasses from rainbow, handwoven cloth.

"Vino tinto, el cabernet, a dark-earth taste like the earth we're visiting." A gentle knock on the door. Javier went to answer it, and a shy teen brought in a tray with platters of fruit, cheese, tacitos.

"Tip him, Javier."

"Ay pochita," he flashed her a smile and tipped el joven, the teen, forty pesos.

"Gracias, señor, gracias." His sudden smile was dazzling in contrast with his sweet, chocolate-skinned face. Innocence. Still that innocence.

"That mole was the best, maybe even better than the San Miguel market, so fucking rich I can still taste it all over my mouth. How are we supposed to eat this, mi muppie?"

"After we make love and I apply the full torture of my mariposa feelers upon you everywhere, that mole's going to be a distant memory, amor." He smiled his young man's smile; the smile she'd seen when she opened the door to him the first time.

"You are so arrogant, I swear!"

"Don't mistake confidence for arrogance, corazón, and why am I a better lover than your last lover, the handsome Balinese?"

Xochiquetzal paused to take him in, exactly as he looked, at that moment, the dark lake behind him reflecting the almost full moon rising. The icy stars giving way to the ripening, golden moon. Rising.

"You know your anatomy, Dr. Gomez, and I've known you for a thousand years, a million moons, a million orgasms, a million tears."

"You're starting to write that poetry, poeta, yes, write about tonight, mi corazón, write about tonight, the next thousand years, amor."

Javier refused to give her an orgasm as he felt her peak each time; he paused, waited for her to stop climbing, over and over. He edged her to the peak, both of them sweating liquids they didn't know their bodies contained; and exactly at the moment she was about to ascend, explode, he stopped, waited, her wildness driving him crazy, their breaths searing their lungs, he waited. El Tigre, he waited.

"Javier," Xochiquetzal gulped air, "I can't stand it, I really can't stand it, my entire body's an orgasm, I have to, I have to, now, Javier, right now..."

"Tell me you love me, Xochitzalita, tell me."

"I do, love you, cabron Javiercito, I do."

"Louder, I can't hear you, louder." He began to taste her again, slowly.

"I fucking love you!"

"Louder." Slowly.

"I love you, right now, this moment, forever, I fucking love you!" she screamed as she merged into white light. The risen, floating moon. Holding the lake, their bodies, their souls, lifetime after lifetime, conquest after conquest, orgasm after orgasm. Love. Torture. Pleasure. Pain. Laughter. Tears. The moon swallowed them into her white light belly, her white light womb; and they'd be born between her silvery legs when Quetzalcoatl faced the blinding, rising radiance. Of the Warrior. In the Sun. Born together. This life. Time. Twins. Spirit. Twins. Together.

They woke up famished, 4 a.m. Javier laughed deep in his throat, his body a lake of pleasure, knowing hers was a lake of pleasure. He brought the covered tray of food, the bottle of wine, to the bed where she waited for his return. I love that she waits for my return, he smiled in the dark velvet his body sliced through.

"You're so beautiful, I must tell you, you're so beautiful in the night, this air."

"That's because you love me, amor, you make me beautiful, now I'm writing la poesia." Tears came to his eyes, they fell. "No one's ever told me that, not like that, mi amor." Not even la Clara, she never told me. He poured the wine in each glass and exposed the delicious food.

Xochiquetzal leaned over and licked his tears. "Yum, they taste lovely, tigre." She reached for a piece of mango, a tacito.

"No, we have to feed each other, we can't feed ourselves, amor, I'll feed you." Javier placed the slice of mango into her open mouth, the tacito bite by bite. A sip of the dark-earth wine. Then she fed him a slice of mango, juicy pineapple, a tacito bite by bite. A sip, two sips of the dark-earth wine.

They finished the sabrosito feast, the entire bottle of wine, laughing, as the pregnant, white light moon set. Into. The golden. Radiance. Into. The rising. Sun. Radiance. Born together. This life. Time.

Spirit.   Twins.   Sacred.   Play.

"How much to take us to the island, amigo?" Javier asked the dark-skinned man sitting in his wooden boat, enjoying the breeze. He smiled as though expecting their arrival, taking them in at a glance. The warm caress of the sun on his face made him happy—New love, he thought.

Javier grabbed Xochiquetzal as she entered the boat, nearly tipping it.

"Puedes nadar... Can you swim?" the boat man asked, laughing.

"I can swim, but I don't know about the entire length of this lake," Xochiquetzal answered with a trace of worry. "Can you swim, Javier?"

He laughed, tilting his face to the sun. "He's just giving you a bad time, joking, in fact here's a life vest, a little beat up, mi amor."

"Ha and ha, very funny, I'll sit on it." She kept her hand in the water as they slid silently toward the island. "We've done this before, you know, here."

"I know, Xochitzalita, I feel it too, a peaceful life together."

Tears stung her eyes in the blinding radiance. "I think this lifetime is a gift, to remind us love is possible, peace is possible, and that's why we returned, this time." She paused. "Together."

The boat man, Geraldo, felt their memory and smiled. "Los reyes, the kings from ancient times, called this place The Gateway To Heaven." Men in small wooden boats began casting their nets, billowing butterflies.

"The Gateway To Heaven," Xochiquetzal echoed, smiling, weeping.

"When she's very happy, with too much joy, she weeps, amigo," Javier laughed and Geraldo joined him.

"Do you want to stay one more night or take off tomorrow morning for the coast, corazón, I leave it up to you." Javier drove to the next village, where they were known for their masks. The last simple, poor, yet lovely, village offered handwoven textiles and Xochiquetzal was in ecstasy touching the cloth, buying a sunburst table cloth and napkins rimmed with tiny yellow suns. Sunflower stitched blouses, silky rainbow skirts (to Javier's "Ayy Frida."); and four handwoven shirts for him, which made him look at home in this place. Indio y guapo...Indian and handsome. Which provoked her to give him a soft wolf whistle, making the women smile. She took photos of the beautiful, sensual Indian woman, young and old; a teenager, smiling shyly, with her sleeping baby wrapped into her red rebozo.

"Why don't we leave tomorrow, I'm dying to get to this hippie beach," she laughed. "But why don't we come back for a week or two, maybe in January. We could stay in some of the villages, what do you think?"

"It's better to stay in the hotels, amor, believe me, but a week or two sounds good."

"Why not the villages?"

"You might have to squat over a hole in the ground," Javier laughed.

"I did that in Bali, in the only Buddhist temple on the island. A magnificent temple, but with an awful hole in the ground for a toilet, I squatted and aimed. There's a sign at the temple's entrance—'Freedom is like the sea, the taste of salt. We yearn for that taste of freedom.'" She closed her eyes to better see the golden letters carved into wood, in a language she couldn't read, then in English.

"The taste of salt," Javier smiled, "and soon the coast, la mar, the hippie beach, corazón. Do you want to drive the Jetta? Try it, it's very smooth, my father chose a good car."

"Maybe later, as I'm thoroughly enjoying watching you drive, this light, you in that sexy, handwoven, rainbow shirt." She took out her digital camera for a few shots. She'd used an entire roll of film, with her Pentax, in the textile village. The beautiful young mother, her baby, their life. In the Gateway To Heaven.

Javier smiled with unadulterated joy. "Do you desire me in this shirt, mi orchid?"

"I think I do." Xochiquetzal moved closer, putting her hand under the rainbow shirt, massaging his hardening nipples with her fingertips, the soft hairs of his chest; then down to his waist, the thicker hairs on his belly. She grabbed them and pulled softly, teasingly.

"I'm going to pull over, Xochitzalita, I'm not kidding, if you don't stop, but I don't want you to stop," Javier laughed with deep pleasure.

Last night. A new level. Of torture (the monarch feelers). Trust (this lake). Feeding each other (this lifetime).

"You think this is torture? I thought I was going to die last night, my last breath, cabron." She took his serpent in her hand, as it lengthened, erect, and licked the rim of his ear slowly.

"I'm going to pull over."

"There's no where to pull over, mi tigre, keep driving, pay attention to the road, it's unpredictable and so am I," she laughed directly into his ear.

"Are you getting revenge, mi amor?" He gasped as his view blurred with orgasmic beauty.

"I'm the female monarch and I want your pollen, your sweet, sticky pollen."

Javier swerved off the road, barely missing an ancient tree, losing his breath, the radiance exploding behind his eyes.

"It's mine, you know," Xochiquetzal whispered, laughing.

"What?" he breathed jaggedly.

"This." She brought his pollen to his mouth, kissing him, mingling their tongues, their feelers. Then she saw a sight she'd never seen; so many hummingbirds.

"Look, Javier, look in the flowers, hummingbirds, sipping nectar, so many."

Xochiquetzal spread the four masks on the bed—black jaguar with red markings, orange monarch with wings, yellow-black striped tiger, and a topless mermaid, her tail dangling from the side. Javier placed the jaguar mask over his face, growling, and waited for her to choose one. She placed the butterfly mask over her face, sighing. He felt playful; she felt sad.

"We could've hit that tree today, tigre, no more auto sex scenes." A smile tugged at her mouth under the monarch mask, and she remembered Don Francisco's words: "Bring him to Oaxaca when he's recovered." But she couldn't bear to say it, fearing she'd join in to create that reality. She refused.

"Next time we'll pull over immediately for an auto sex scene," he growled, grabbing her by the waist, feeling her sadness. "You have the boy's phone number, the place we can reach his mother, right?"

"In my wallet, tigre. Do you think his harelip can be fixed?" Watching Javier examine the four year old boy's mouth, his teeth;

holding him on his lap, tenderly. The boy's trust in those hands. Xochiquetzal forgot to breathe, once again. I'm beyond road kill, who is this guy? One minute he's a sex maniac, the next he's Dr. Zapata. Eros and death, she sighed, death and Eros. A whole human being, at thirty-four. Yes, I'm truly beyond road kill.

"He's the right age for surgery and his mouth looks healthy. I wish I could do it, but not yet. My father could but he only deals with the wealthy. I'll talk to Diego about it, we'll fix him up, what a beautiful boy. Hijo de la chingada, my father, my greedy, self-centered father, those skilled hands."

"You're a beautiful boy," she paused, smiling, "man, doctorcito. Maybe you should just mention this boy to your father, see what happens, you never know."

"I tried years ago, more than once, so that's enough for me. Diego will find someone excellent, don't worry, mi amor."

"Maybe someday he'll change, people change, tigre, at least once in a while," she smiled, the memory of his tenderness with the boy. "You know, I'm starving but I'm also in great need of a shower."

"I'll join you, Xochitzalita." Javier stripped off his clothing in seconds, taking her by the hand.

"Hey, I'm still dressed, start the fucking shower," she laughed, picking up his beautiful rainbow shirt and placing it over the back of a chair.

"Come on, the shower's warm, just right, mi amor."

"Wear the black rainbow shirt tonight, for me."

"I'm waiting."

"I bet you are."

"I'm waiting, mi orchid."

"You're such a whiner," Xochiquetzal laughed at the exaggerated look of need on his face. "Does this face always work with las chicas?"

"No, this one does," and he shot her his most sultry, hottest look; then the dazzling, doctor-god, sun-smile.

She stepped into the warm shower, his arms. "That is truly scary, you have control over that look, that smile, like the time I opened the fucking door to you in Bucerias, ohmygoddess, and now I'm beyond road kill, fucking A." She shivered, a part of her meaning every word— He knows what works. I used to be a feminist, she sighed. I love the feel of his arms around me, who fucking cares anyway.

"Amor, you have control of various looks, gazes, that drive me muy loco, that knowing smile of yours," Javier laughed. "We're both beyond esta cosa, road kill, and as you pointed out previously, no one's in charge. So I'm scared too, just a little, but I'm happier than I'm scared, es la verdad, mi amor, Xochitzalita." I love the feel of her against me, her skin, my skin, our skin, that's all I know, that she sets me free, and con esta mujer, with her, I'm not lonely.

"I love traveling with you, I love being with you, I love feeding you, I love you feeding me, I love my sperm in your mouth, I love your mango in my mouth, I love your wings, mi orchid." Javier kissed her shoulder blades, slowly entering her from behind as she clung to the wet tiles. The warm shower rain blessing them like the first time in Bucerias. Then he thrust suddenly to the center of her open orchid womb, making her cry out. With pleasure, a slight, subtle edge of pain. Pleasure and pain, joy and sorrow, feast and famine, love and torture, Eros and death, youth and ripening. Whole human beings (at thirty-four, fifty-eight), teaching each other. How to love.

Xochiquetzal sobbed as her orchid womb orgasm rippled throughout her body, buckling her knees, as he held her up, close to him, his skin, her skin, their skin. He pulled the shower curtain open to reveal the large mirror over the sink, smiling at their images.

"Look at yourself, Xochitzalita, look at yourself, how beautiful you are, tan madura, in love, and me, I'm ripening, I'm ripening in this love, look at us, mi amor."

At first she couldn't take it in, that this was herself, this adored, being loved, madura woman, being held by this beauty, this beautiful, tender man. Finally, she looked into the mirror—We are both beautiful, ripening into Eros, death, at thirty-four, fifty-eight, ripening into death, Eros.

"I love your wings, Javier, I love your serpent, and I think we've both crossed the boundaries of road kill into some unknown territory, I have no words for it..."

"We keep setting each other free, mi amor, we keep giving birth to each other, falling into this love."

"Is that it, and no one's in charge, fuck," she laughed, weeping, turning around to face him, to watch his face (not the mirror's image) for truth.

"I killed a scorpion this morning in the closet, so shake out your clothing, amor."

"Was it a big one?"

"Yes."

"Was it the golden one?" She smiled, watching his face, his eyes, absorb the last arrows of the Warrior. In the Sun.

"The Gateway To Heaven, yes, let's return for a week. The Aztecs never conquered these people, just like you, Xochitzalita, my undefeated Yaqui pochita." He smiled his arrows into her watchful eyes.

Javier reserved a table facing the twilight lake, the white egrets still floating between the ancient, deep-rooted trees, the first stars appearing. "Venus in the west," Xochitzalita says. I love to watch her taking in every detail. How wonderful to not be on call, kind of weird but wonderful, my cell turned off. He sat at the bar waiting for her, checked his messages: his mother, some friends, two persistent chicas, and one from Xavier. He sipped his icy Victoria, saving the tequila shot con limon for the end of the beer, when she would arrive through that entry, so beautiful. Her dark hair just washed, full and long the way I like it, beautiful. For me, he smiled, still hearing her sobs, her orgasm. For me. And I for her, my pollen, as she calls it.

"What makes you smile, hermoso?"

Javier looked up half expecting to see Xochiquetzal, but it was the wrong voice. Dark-haired, large dark eyes, maybe twenty, sweet breasts, not too large, revealed, white lacy tank top, tight jeans.

"My lover, and she's due right now." His voice was slightly stern, detached, as he looked away toward the lake, then the entry where Xochiquetzal should be.

"I saw you with that vieja, that old woman, you should be with someone my age, hermoso, and I saw you looking at my breasts, don't lie." She touched his face, grazing his cheek, just as Xochiquetzal walked into the room. At that very moment, Javier took hold of her hand, the young woman laughing.

He threw down her hand, rushing over to Xochiquetzal who looked ready to leave. He grabbed her by the waist, taking her into his arms, murmuring into her mouth, "I love your hair down, wear it this way more often, mi amor."

"Was I interrupting something?" she murmured into his ear. "I could leave you to your newly found chica, no problem."

Tears of anger came to Javier's eyes. "How can you say that after what we just said to each other, in the shower, how we keep setting each other free, falling..."

She heard the tears in his voice. "I am setting you free, Javier, no betrayals, our promise..."

"Callate mi amor, I want us to be free together, I want us to feed each other our dinners, callate." He led her to the table; the dark, still lake filling their eyes. "The Gateway To Heaven for us to witness, I'm starving." He still held her waist, his hand spread open, touching her breast under the thin blouse.

"I'm only going to say this once, Xochitzalita mi orchid. I've had so many sweet chicas like that, an endless supply since my teens. Beyond the newness and novelty of their lovely bodies, I know exactly what they're going to say and do after the first time, the first fuck, and I really know after the second, the third, the rest. They didn't give birth to me, they didn't set me free. I didn't give birth to them, I didn't set them free. We were not ever road kill," Javier smiled a sorrow into her eyes, truth.

"I was always, and I mean always, in charge. Except for Clara in Spain, like you mi amor, we are falling and I want to fall with you. No one's in charge, do you understand, Xochitzalita, not me, not you."

"Did Clara give birth to you?"

"Then she set me entirely free. I wanted to be free with her, as we are, mi amor."

"Were you trying to take that woman's hand from your face, was that it?"

"What do you think?" He covered her right breast entirely, making her womb clench.

"Let's eat, I'm truly starving." Xochiquetzal pulled away to sit down, but he refused to let her go.

"Do you believe me, mi amor, I need to hear it now."

She faced him, looking directly into his sad, unflinching eyes, where joy played in the twin fires. "You are relentless, Dr. Zapata, okay *I believe you.* I believe you," she repeated more gently. "And both of us must remember this—no betrayals, this lifetime, no more Spaniards, por favor, do you promise me?"

"Again? I already promised, que me chingas, amor."

"I need to hear it, now."

He pulled her to him—both of them realizing they were becoming a spectacle in the restaurant, but they didn't care—and slowly grazed her lips with his tongue. "Te juro, mi orchid, I promise."

Someone gave a low-pitched grito, laughter, then, "Vaya al

cuarto...Go to your room!"

"Primero tenemos a comer por fuerza...First we have to eat for strength." Loud laughter. Javier and Xochiquetzal joined the laughter, sitting down, as the waiter appeared, menus in hand. Smiling. Enjoying this new, shameless love.

"How long has it been since you've been to Oaxaca?" Javier brought his chair to sit next to her, facing the lake. Stars bloomed in the calm, dark mirror, scattering billion year old light years of poetry. I want to write poetry like that, like the stars, Xochiquetzal wished silently.

"As I told you, el hippie Juan and I went there, then on to Chiapas, around four years ago, why, and what are you ordering, mi amor?"

"I told you, Don Francisco, the Mayan healer, wants us to visit him, his family, maybe in the summer."

"For the Guelaguetza, I've never seen it, it's in July." He looked for the waiter and caught his eye. That look of command that she resented—*Señor Muppie at home in his own country,* he heard her voice, the echo, her teasing laugh. But this is who I am, he sighed, and why she opened the door in Bucerias.

"Why don't you order for me, I know it'll be maravilloso. Isn't the Guelaguetza the ritual of gift giving, as I remember."

"Si señor," the waiter stood ready.

"You know I'm your gift, Xochitzalita," Javier murmured. Then turned to the waiter and began to order.

"I don't get service like this by myself, it's somehow more formal. It's like they're under your command, General Zapata."

"They are, mi amor, and I'm at your command, a muppie at home in his own country, tu regalo...your gift. And yes, it's a ritual of gift giving, let's go."

"Don Francisco won't be under your command, he's his own person, that's all I can say. But I think you'll like each other once the power struggle's over," she laughed. "Seriously, lighten up, tigre, you're not on call, you're not in the ER, you're with me on this magic carpet."

"I used to pretend to fly, on my parent's handwoven rug from India, when I was a boy. It was a beautiful rug, so smooth, a kaleidoscope of color. I used to close my eyes and fly, often falling asleep, dreaming, and Amalia would carry me to bed. When I woke up in bed, I thought I'd flown there in my dreams."

"I love that, the magic carpet—I remember after a Sinbad The

Pirate movie, literally sitting on a small rug, nothing as fancy as your parent's, waiting to fly for hours, and then I got hungry, thirsty, had to pee," Xochiquetzal laughed at the memory. "But some deep, stubborn part of me vowed I would fly awake as I did in dreams. And the first thing I did when I graduated with my bachelors was to fly to Paris, I told you. And I was never afraid to fly, I just loved it."

"Leaving your boyfriend behind, by yourself." Javier paused, realizing he was about to mention her mother, Florinda, the betrayal.

"With my mother, yes, but I'm never ever sorry that I flew to Paris, traveled by myself."

He put his arm entirely around her, his hand under her hair, feeling the vulnerability of her neck. He wanted to lick it, but refrained. "That's what I did, Xochitzalita, I also took off on my own magic carpet and flew around the world."

The waiter opened the bottle of Mexican chardonay, pouring a taste into Javier's glass, and he motioned to Xochiquetzal's glass as well. They both tasted the golden liquid—fruity and so rich it clung to their palettes. He placed the bottle in a bucket of ice on a metal stand and turned to leave.

"Gracias," Xochiquetzal called after him. The waiter paused, nodded. Una pocha con el señor, he confirmed it silently. Only a pocha would thank me like that with a man. Younger man, older women, he remembered those days in his twenties, his youth. The older gringas bringing him gifts, traveling with them as a guide. But with them it's different, he has his own money, it's apparent. "Sinverguenza... shameless," he muttered, "que bien."

"Will you share your magic carpet with me, Senora Aguila?"

"If you're good, Javiercito."

"I'm always good, you know that by now, my anatomy. Give me your mouth, Xochitzalita, now, or I'll have a fucking fit."

She laughed, leaning over, giving him her mouth, la boca, and his slow, wet tongue made her instantly wet, want him. "I'm sorry I taught you to say *fucking*," she breathed, "now you use it against me." They played, kissed and teased each other—pausing to stare at the Gateway To Heaven—then back to play.

The waiter cleared his throat, their dinners on a carved, wooden tray. An immense platter of fajitas, a covered, clay bowl of spicy beans, a large fresh salad, and a basket of hot, homemade, blue corn tortillas wrapped in a rainbow cloth. An assortment of salsas—green, red, whole jalapeno, and one so hot, full of flavor, it sang seductively in its small clay bowl.

"Gracias amigo, que sabroso," Javier smiled, visibly taking the waiter by surprise.

"Do you want anything else, señor?" His smile was reserved, taking in la pocha's laughing eyes.

"Another bottle of chardonay, amigo, in maybe fifteen minutes."

This pleases her, his kindness, que bien—"Buen provecho...Good appetite!" He smiled without reserve, like he did in his twenties.

"All those roses, what a scent." Xochiquetzal stood on their room's balcony facing the gardens, the star-mirrored lake. "All those hummingbirds today, I've never seen such a diversity of them. Blue, green, red jewels zipping everywhere, pausing to sip." She thought of the lone hummingbird at la Gruta, the hot springs; how it sipped the tiny yellow flowers beneath the phallic shaped purplish fruit of the ripening banana. So thirsty. For yellow.

"There's usually even more, but they're entering their hummingbird comas. They actually find a perennial, leafy tree and push their beaks into a crack as far as possible, staying there in their comas for the winter."

"That's amazing, how do you know that?"

"A tour guide, I pay attention, mi amor, and if you're lucky enough to see them they appear to be dead, that coma. In the spring, when the tree is reborn, so is the hummingbird, sipping new life from the tree."

"Did you see one?"

"I did only because the guide knew where to look, they blend perfectly with the tree, and they do look dead. When we return in January, we'll go with a guide and witness a hummingbird coma," Javier laughed softly, holding her from behind, breathing in the roses.

"Have you seen a human coma?"

The image of a tiny hummingbird, with its beak stuck deeply into a crack of a leafy tree, was replaced by a human face breathing air imperceptibly, seemingly dead. He saw the sixteen year old boy brought in from a motorcycle accident, how he lingered in a coma for almost three months. So young, still breathing, then gone. He remembered his face, every youthful feature. The fractured, cracked open skull, damaged brain. His young, peaceful face dreaming his life, the coma.

"Alejandro, I remember a sixteen year old named Alejandro. There have been others, but I still see his face, hear his family wailing, then quiet, absolutely quiet for months. Until he died. Left the body. Transformed. I really saw it, the transformation, with Alejandro. Maybe his age, his struggle to live, his finally letting go." Tears fell, surprising him.

"I'm sorry, corazón, you've seen a lot, that's why I love you. Are you crying?"

"I never did, cry."

"Let's bring the sofa here, some wine."

"Sip, sip, sip, I'm the little hummingbird, mi amor, and only your juices keep me alive." Javier licked her neck, down to her breasts— She allows me to cry, esta mujer, not lonely, not lonely, con esta mujer fuerte.

"Don't say that!" Her anger was sudden, irrational. "I mean, not the hummingbird in the crack, *of the tree*, oh I give the fuck up."

They laughed and dragged the sofa to the wide open verandah doors. And as they both sipped the essence of the other, the scent of roses drowned them; and finally the ancient poet stars took them dreaming.

Javier...*I can't stand it, I can't stand it, she's dying, there's nothing I can do, nothing I can do, nothing. My father won't pay for her treatment, she refuses in advance, my mother battles my father, Amalia refuses saying "No, it is time, it is time." I sleep next to her, bring her water, warm broth, a tacito to smell, she smiles, brushes the hair from my eyes, so tenderly. I remember I remember I remember. "Javiercito mi corazón, you will meet a woman who will guide you to the Warrior in the Sun, follow her, doctorcito."*

His eyes flew open, her face turned away from him. "I remember," he whispered, closing his eyes, gathering her naked body tightly against his own.

Xochiquetzal...*The sound of ranchera music, singing, guides me into the kitchen, gritos, feminine gritos, laughter. My grandmother, Clara, lifting her skirt over her knees, dancing. My mother, Florinda, clapping, a louder grito, laughing. They see me, extend their hands to me, the child of eight, I take their hands, dancing, laughing. I remember. These women loved life. I remember. They danced with me. I remember I remember I remember.*

"Recuerdo, recuerdo, remember el corazón de las estrellas poetas," the Energy Child whispered, longing for her/his ancient wings.

They stood on a ridge, the last view of Patzcuaro. The vast green, brown-red earth, so many flowers (with the still-awake hummingbirds), the light-rippled lake. The mirror of the sun in daylight; the burning arrows of the sun. The mirror of moon and stars at night; the soothing, ancient light.

"We entered The Gateway To Heaven, mi amor. What a dream I had last night. I remembered Amalia's transformation, all of it, why I became a physician. She always called me doctorcito, saying, 'It's your path, doctorcito.'"

"I believe it, El Nino Doctorcito, his tiny doc bag with the sexy angel, that's you. She was your spirit mom, like my Mamacita Clara was to me."

Javier nodded, gazing at the singing lake. "Amalia," he whispered, "Mi mama India."

"I dreamt my grandmother, my mother, dancing in the kitchen to rancheras, gritos, maybe I was eight years old, and I danced with them. I once read that the best thing a mother can give a child is her love of life." Xochiquetzal paused to listen to the wind, gaze at Javier's face. He was listening.

"They gave me their love of life, la vida. In spite of Florinda's betrayal with my boyfriend, she loved life, she loved sex, she loved beauty, his beauty, it's enough."

"You sound so peaceful, mi amor, here in The Gateway To Heaven," Javier smiled as he pulled her closer, his arm around her waist. "I dreamt what a bastard my father was to Amalia, how he refused to pay for her treatment, the cancer, how my mother fought him, his fucking money. Amalia's wise words, 'It is time.' I'm not so peaceful in The Gateway To Heaven, Xochitzalita, but I'm glad I'm here with you. Tu eres mi reglao...You're my gift."

"Look up, look, a red-tailed hawk!" They stood silently as her wide wings gripped the sky, as she caught an updraft of wind and spiraled upward. Then a young male hawk joined her. Opposite her. Confident in his power. His wings. Spiraling. Upward. The sun filtering their spread wings. Dancing on the wind. The Gateway. To Heaven.

"I remember her last words to me, from the dream, I'd forgotten.

'You will meet a woman who will guide you to the Warrior in the Sun, follow her.'"

"She actually said that?" All the hairs rose on Xochiquetzal's body, chilling her in the sun's warmth. She turned toward Javier, his eyes. "I find it hard to believe he wouldn't pay for her cancer treatment, and your Mom without a say in it, how awful. Did Amalia actually say that, what she said in the dream."

"I'd forgotten but, yes, those were some of her last words to me." He met her eyes, nothing to hide. The wound. The healing. Memory.

When they looked up to the sky, the hawks were gone. Through The Gateway To Heaven, into the sun. They left the silence, the memory of their dance. Flight.

"Do you want to hear a poem I wrote, still in rough draft, but you might like it. The hawk's spiral dance reminded me of it, or I could show it to you later when it's more polished..."

"Amor, read it to me now, right now, in The Gateway To Heaven." Javier smiled with joy, trying to see where the hawk lovers had gone.

Xochiquetzal reached into her large travel purse and brought out her notebook; then followed the line of vision he was seeking, the hawks. "They're hunting is my guess, but they revealed themselves to us, a gift. Okay, you asked for it, my still rough poem. Are you sure you want to hear it?" She glanced out to the sky, hoping to see wings.

"I'm waiting, mi amor, and maybe your poem will entice them back." He smiled to the open sky, holding the waist of his lover.

She waited for a few moments, to hear the silence between them. "No title yet...

> A million moons.
> A million suns.
> A million orgasms.
> A million tears,
> this lake,
> that's how I've loved
> you, life time after
> life time, a thousand
> years ago we met by
> this lake,
> a life of children,
> grandchildren, survival,

love and joy, I
remember you by
 this lake,
do you remember me,
your lover, sister, mother,
your wife of forty
peaceful years, a thousand years ago,
 this lake.

In the far distance, on the edge of the horizon, the hawks hunted life. Their hunger, the joy of flight, drove them on. To hunt. Spiral. In the wind. Into the. Blinding sun.

"I remember, Xochitzalita, one thousand years ago, this lake," Javier murmured, closing his eyes for a moment. The blinding Warrior in the Sun. And he also remembered that although the Aztecs never conquered these people, the Michoaques, the Fisherman, the Spaniards did. There was once, five hundred years ago, thousands of lakes which they drained, torturing and killing their king, King Tangaxoan. But he couldn't bear to tell Xochiquetzal after her poem. In The Gateway To Heaven.

Javier slowed the Jetta on the narrow road winding down the mountain, through the thinning forest, scattered lakes. Men on horseback waved; then a young woman on horseback smiled and waved. An old man leading a burro with sacks of fresh vegetables, his seven-year-old grandson riding the burro, both of them waved. Their smiles of sheer joy, as though their swollen sacks of vegetables were sacks of gold.

"Where I come from, kids only smile like that when their parents break down and buy them the newest video game. Their eyes, the lights in their eyes, not a metaphor, mi tigre." Xochiquetzal grazed his cheek with her fingertips, thinking—How beautiful he is in this dappled light, in the sun, how beautiful this man is. *You will love me like no other,* the dream came to her. His eyes, his voice, these words, in the dream; and his dream of Amalia—*She will guide you to the Warrior in the Sun.* Tears stung her eyes.

Javier glanced at her, smiling. "I love my people, Xochitzalita, es la verdad...it's the truth. Traveling the world taught me that, how I missed them, those eyes, that light. Amalia had those eyes, the soul light of my people. I think that light comes from centuries of suffering, we're all, most of us, mestizo. But mi Amalia was pura Maya and I think that's why she remembered so many of the ancient stories, mi mama Maya." He thought of the Spanish in The Gateway to Heaven, and the Spanish in his own blood.

"She taught you to love your people, to want to heal, that's what I think. And you know, your father might want to help with the plastic surgery, the boy we met, you might ask. He might change, or be inspired to change, if you include him. I mean, maybe, you never know."

"He's never done a free surgery, ever, it's his greed-first policy, mi amor. He thought me and my friends were insane to go to Chiapas and donate our time. He called us a bunch of pendejo hippies, and he threatened to not give me my monthly allowance if I went. And as I said, he refused to pay for Amalia's cancer treatment. Tears filled his throat, but he swallowed them. "She needed radiation therapy, her breast removed. He refused, to pay." Javier remembered how his father never spoke directly to Amalia, but always through his mother. He refused to speak directly to an Indian, or to save her life. He was the great, Spanish plastic surgeon, destroying all evidence of his Indian grandmother; but she lived in his haunted, hungry eyes.

"I think that's the wound that made you a healer, doctorcito, the wounded healer. The hole in your heart that either kills you or heals you."

"I'm not lonely with you, mi amor, digame, tell me."

"What?"

"De la vida, digame...About life, tell me." His eyes contained that light. Sorrow and joy. At the center.

"Oh that," Xochiquetzal smiled. "There is no death, only transformation, always transformation."

"I love you, Xochitzalita, like my people." Javier swerved wide to avoid an entire family walking home, laughing among themselves, smiling widely to the strangers in the car. The mother carried a baby strapped to her back with a deep blue rebozo, and the father held the hand of the youngest.

"I feel like stopping to give everyone a check-up, but they all look healthy. It's weird to not be a physician in my daily life, to be on vacation, traveling again. But I'm getting used to it because I'm with you, mi amor, and the Windhorse," he laughed, speeding up a bit.

"I love you, doctorcito, but I don't know if it's wise to love me like your people. To love me like that..."

"Should I limit how much I feel for you, *to protect you*. I don't care about protecting myself, Xochitzalita, so I'm going to love you as much as I want. Will you let me?" Her face was turned away from him, refusing to look at him. She gazed at the beauty she had to keep letting go of. To survive.

"Will you let me?" Javier repeated.

Xochiquetzal heard Don Francisco's voice, "Will you let him love your wings, will you?" Her desire to be free, her desire to be loved. Her fear of love, her fear of freedom. She heard the conch shell, his hot breath filling her lungs. "Yes, mi tigre, but I don't know what it'll mean."

"Look at me, amor, your tears don't scare me anymore, in fact they make me happy. It means you feel this moment, our love, deeply."

"Is that what it means?" A tear slid into her mouth and she realized it was delicious. Her first delicious tear. The tigers of desire and loneliness. Were free. In The Gateway To Heaven. Now.

"But I don't think I can live with you, and even if we did our time is limited, tigre. I am twenty-four years older than you and we can't change that, you'll want children." The tigers of desire and loneliness refused to leave The Gateway To Heaven; refused to return to their sad, rusty cages. They simply. Refused.

"As I grow older, Xochitzalita, you grow younger, didn't you know that? And we can live like Frida y Diego with a bridge between us."

"You'd do that?" Fresh, delicious tears erupted.

"It would be so erotic, mi amor, I think I'm going to have to pull over so I can cross that bridge right now."

"No way!" she laughed, weeping. "Save it for hippie beach, tonight, you know, I think you're over-sexed."

"Older woman, younger man, the bridge of Eros, tonight, the future, our house, we'll paint it gold, glittering gold with silver wings."

"Don Francisco is going to love you, the healer from Oaxaca. Silver wings, the golden bridge of Eros, estas bien loco."

"That's why you can't resist me, mi amor, if I were boring and sane you'd run away. For you, that's the cardinal sin, boredom. Don Francisco saw that, the old lecher from Oaxaca," Javier laughed, gulping the last of the mountain air, as they descended into fertile fields of earth, small towns, larger towns. Where the light in people's eyes were slightly dimmed, the poverty, but not diminished.

After lunch Javier drove straight through to the coast, the first scent of the sea telling them, *faster, welcome home*, where they'd met, by la mar. "You drove well on the toll road, mi amor, I wasn't even afraid."

"I drove all the way down to San Miguel from Taos, Dr. Muy Macho Cabron, with literally the essence of my life crammed into my Toyota." Xochiquetzal gave him the fuck you look for good measure as she looked out the windows to lush jungle. Centuries of fertility softened her irritation. That scent of lust.

"You're so quick to call me bad names, mi feminista," he laughed, "but you're right, I was trying to be a muy macho muppie, always clobber me, por favor."

"Does your mother drive, and okay I forgive your muppie ass."

"Ay cabrona, come here." He drew her to him as the tangled scent of fertility made him want her orchid, now. "No, she always had a driver, my father absolutely forbade her to drive como una gringa, the old dictator. But all my sisters drive of course, and they all stand up to him como las gringas, how do you say, la karma." Javier smiled as he thought of each sister, their strong, beautiful faces.

"My mother was, is, strong, Xochitzalita, don't misunderstand me, she just never unfurled her wings. But she loves life, as you say, her gift to us."

"You love your mother, Javiercito."

"As I loved Amalia, my sisters, women. They taught me to love women and now I love you like the male hawk loves the female hawk in The Gateway To Heaven."

"You should write poetry, I mean it."

"Maybe I will on the beach and you can critique it, professora."

Los Fabulosos Cadillacs came blasting through the speakers just as a slice of the ocean came into view. A small, sparkling diamond that widened as they approached. Xochiquetzal danced in her seat, raising her arms to the music, putting her window down all the way.

Javier raised his left arm to the music as he steered them toward the immense diamond. La mar. Almost sunset. "Now for the dirt road with potholes the size of cows, hold on as I'm going to have to swerve, amor!" Javier laughed with joy. He'd turned his cell off after calling his mother, left a message for Xavier, as in mind-your-own-business. "We'll visit, Mama, after Christmas, Xochitzalita's son will be in San Miguel, I know you'll like her, yes I'm happy, I love you, take care of yourself, Mama."

"Hey, that one almost threw me out the fucking window, slow down! Los Fabulosos are too inspiring," Xochiquetzal laughed.

Javier slowed down. "When I used to drive this road with my friends we were todos locos, but we were also driving real junkers not a good Jetta, courtesy of my father," he sighed. "And no orchids on board."

"You found las chicas here, so I assume there's a good supply on hippie beach."

"There's people from all over the world, you'll see, people tell each other and they all come to hippie beach, mi amor."

"Oh how beautiful, those cliffs, that stretch of beach, these palm frond villages, and the sound, the sound of the waves."

Small, brown boys and girls, women over cook fires, men sitting in groups, laughing teens; some waved, some looked away.

Javier thought of las chicas he'd met here, the people from all over the world—Sweden, England, France, Spain, Thailand. Las chicas from Thailand, he remembered, smiling to himself, tan hermosa. They all made me want to travel, to see, smell, taste, feel the world, and I did. A muppie at home on his own planet—he laughed out loud.

"What?"

"This is why I started traveling, Xochitzalita, this place, I just remembered, and now you're here with me, un muppie y una hippie."

"The beach looks deserted, is there usually more people?"

"It's a long beach and usually the families with kids take that side." Javier pointed to the left where a distant camp fire blazed. "In the middle are the hippies that wear clothes, and over there," he pointed to the right, past a cliff, "are the hippies that wear nada. Where do you want to place our tent, amor?'

"Where the clothes are worn," Xochiquetzal laughed. "I don't mind folks without clothing, in fact I love to photograph them, but I prefer an option. Where did you stay with your friends?"

Javier beamed her that smile of utter innocence, utter confidence. "You have to ask?"

"Pendeja me, no clothes for you."

"I was studying my anatomy, mi amor."

"This is why you worry me," she couldn't help laughing. "You are so full of shit, mi amor tan cabron."

"Hey, the fire's over here, join us after you settle in!" a tall, blonde guy with a Swedish accent yelled, smiling a lovely smile of welcome.

"We could sleep in the car tonight with the back seats flat..."

"Oh no, let's sleep in our tent out in the sand."

An old Indian woman came to welcome them and take a rental fee for the slightly raised platform, with thatched roof, for the tent. "Quieres cervezas frio y tacitos...Do you want cold beers and tacos?" she asked.

"Si mama, gracias, y tienes algo a fumar...and do you have something to smoke?"

"One hundred pesos for la bolsita and we grow it here, very strong, very sweet." She took Javier's pesos and brought the small, plastic bag out from her apron. "My name is Celia and I will cook your meals, cold beer, bottles of water, whatever you may need."

"I'm Javier and this is Xochitzalita, gracias madre."

"When you're ready, join us to eat." Celia's smile transformed her into a young girl. No pretense. Just life. La mar. Those visitors from far away, yet this young man, Javier, could be my son, the eyes. And the woman feels strangely familiar, she noted—not like a foreigner. As long as they pay they're welcome, but I like these two.

Javier carried the tent, a small lantern, and Xochiquetzal carried their sleeping bags and pillows to the thatched roof platform. The sea was undulating gently and Venus had her prongs set firmly in the west; the brightest diamond in the amethyst-purple sunset. Facing the white shadow of the waxing, full moon. Three more days to full. Venus waited. So patiently. In love. With light. And dark. Equally.

"What a beautiful smile Celia has, that strong face. I have to take photos of her cooking tomorrow morning. I'm a photographer again, doctorcito."

"Una doctora de los fotos," he laughed. "The people here are Nahuatl and they are beautiful, inside and outside beauty, you'll see. Only the teens get tempted by our things, so in the day we lock everything in the car if you want to keep it. I always pay a teen to watch my car and they guard it with their life. Ayy Xochitzalita, my people are poor."

"Do you consider the Nahuatl to be your people as well?" Xochiquetzal watched him pitch the dome tent under the thatched roof quickly, tying it down to the sides of the platform. She squeezed the still warm sand with her toes. La mar, we're back to la madre mar.

Javier jumped down, grabbing her by the waist, making her drop the sleeping bags and pillows. "We're all Mexicans, so yes they're my people. My mother showed me an old photo of her grandmother, she kept it hidden in her treasure chest. I used to love to sit and have her show me her hidden treasures." He smiled with the memory.

"Did Xavier with an X sit with you and your Mom those times?"

"He'd get bored and leave like it was girl stuff, that's Xavier. My great-grandmother was pura India, Maya my mother said. And my grandmother was Nahuatl, mestiza, but she looked very light-skinned. Pues, we're all mestizos, es la verdad. But my great-grandmother was pura Maya and she was dark-skinned, beautiful, una India."

"Maya," Xochiquetzal echoed, "like Don Francisco."

"And like Amalia, she was from Oaxaca and she missed it endlessly."

How did Don Francisco know he was a doctor? the thought exploded suddenly, irrationally, making her mouth dry. And why did he say to bring him when he's recovered? "Why didn't she go home, mi amor?" She wanted to tell him about Don Francisco, these details, but it felt like he'd given her secrets to keep. Until they saw each other again. In Oaxaca. The future. The dream.

"I was her boy, she stayed."

"Don't be sad, doctorcito, I know she's proud of you, who you've become."

Javier threw the sleeping bags and pillows into the tent. "Let's walk on the tide before we join the others, but first give me your sabrosita boca."

The well-tended fire revealed everyone's faces as they spoke their names, smiling their relaxed, stoned smiles of welcome. Two couples from Sweden, one from Italy, from France, two from the USA, three young, single Mexican men, and a lovely, lone Japanese woman. Floriana, the woman from Italy, in a bra top that barely covered her nipples, kept her smile fixed on Javier. When they passed over the Japanese woman, she said to Javier, "Her name is Ai, from Tokyo, she's traveling by herself for a year, and she's taken a vow of silence. She'll give you a card later, I'm sure, explaining." Her husband, Tony, put his arm around her in an attempt to claim her, but she pulled away.

Someone passed Javier a sweet-smelling joint as Celia gave them a plate of tacitos de pollo, beans, rice, sliced fruit, two Victorias, bottles of water (for less than $5usd).

"We just smoked some on our walk, very mellow stuff, gracias." He passed it to Xochiquetzal and she took a short hit since it was pretty strong for her.

"You're Mexican?" Floriana asked, glueing her eyes on him.

"And you're Italian, what part of Italy?"

"Rome of course, the sex capital of Italia," she laughed, licking her lips. She leaned forward, revealing her nipples.

Oh marvy, Xochiquetzal thought, I can see exactly where this scenario is going, Fucking A and B too.

"How nice for you and your boyfriend," Javier smiled at him.

"Husband," Tony smirked with pain. He tried to put his arm around her again and she pulled away again.

"Where do you come from and how do you say your name?" Floriana stared into Xochiquetzal's eyes.

"Shweekwetsssal," she said it slowly, drawn out. "From Santa Cruz, California."

"We're from Los Angeles, so neighbors," Pete said.

Celia gave Javier another Victoria and two more tacitos. "Gracias madre," Javier smiled. The Mexicans call me 'madre' and to the others I'm a servant, a cook. "De nada, hijo." And she served them both more sliced fruit, another tacito for his woman.

"We're supposed to be getting some magic mushrooms either tomorrow or the next day, in case you're interested." Pete held his girlfriend close and she didn't pull away. "Have you been here before?"

"I used to come in my youth," Javier laughed. "One of my favorite places, and for Xochitzalita it's the first time."

"I bet you came here in your so-called youth, Javier, how old are you anyway?" Floriana's gaze was fixed on him.

"Time for the tent, Floriana." Tony stood up to leave. "Come on."

"I want to hear his answer first," she whined.

"Not so young anymore," Javier laughed, bringing Xochiquetzal into his arms. "We forgot to feed each other, amor."

"You *feed* each other?" Floriana asked.

"Come on, bed time." Tony waited.

"Sounds like hot, new love to me. Why don't you feed me anymore?" she asked Tony, while staring a hole into Javier.

The young, Mexican men had wandered off to sit by the waves, disappointed at the lack of single chicas; but probably by the weekend. Patience. The Japanese woman was beautiful, but more like a monk they joked.

Tony bent down to pull Floriana up by the arm pits, setting her large breasts entirely free to the wind's warm tongue.

"See what you've done!" she laughed loudly, enjoying herself.

"Right on schedule," the French woman rolled her eyes.

"Come on, Floriana, now," Tony raised his voice. He grabbed her hand and pulled her to her feet.

"See you all in the morning for the pancakes, we'll feed each other," she said directly into Javier's eyes.

Javier met Tony's eyes. "Buenas noches, you two, good dreams."

"Yeah, that's all I have to look forward to, dreams," Floriana whined as Tony pulled her along.

"What's wrong with you, shut up," he whispered sharply. Then he switched into an angry tirade of Italian.

Ai caught Xochiquetzal's eyes with a gaze of profound sadness. Then her eyes lit up with hilarity, as though she could barely keep herself from laughing out loud.

"Why are you laughing, mi amor?"

"I think Ai just made me," she laughed softly, their secret.

Ai waved to her and Javier, standing up in one, smooth movement, and walked slowly toward the tide.

"Let's face la mar, our faces to the opening, here," Xochiquetzal turned their zipped together sleeping bags around. They felt like two kids on their magic carpet, watching the Mexican guys take a final swim, doing gritos to the swelling, golden moon.

"She gave me tonglen, you know."

"Who?"

"Ai, the Japanese woman, first the face of sorrow, pain, breathing it in, then the face of laughter, joy, breathing it out. The Buddhist practice of tonglen—breathing in the pain, breathing out some healing. And that woman, Floriana, is a royal fucking pain in las nalgas, and I'm wondering if there's enough tonglen for her ass, or should I say her bazooka boobs ayy. And her name, Floriana—my mother, Florinda, oh the karmic dance, fuck," she sighed.

"Will you ignore her, mi amor, but I felt sorry for her husband, pobrecito. If she's on that side of the beach, we'll be on this side of the beach, but I liked the Japanese woman, Ai, her vow of silence, her tonglen to you. I need your orchid and I'm hungry again, Dios mio,"

Javier laughed.

"It's the grass, you're stoned but I like it, it makes you kind of mellow. We have snacks in the car…"

"You're my snack, mi amor, feed me." He pulled on her nipples softly with his lips, circling them with his wet tongue, making her entire body shiver expectantly.

"We have to be quiet, there are no walls and our neighbors are all around us, I mean it, Javier, quiet," she said as he started to laugh a bit too loudly with joy.

"Soon the cave, mi amor con las chi-chis de niña…with young girl breasts."

"What cave?" Xochiquetzal smiled with tired joy and fresh lust as he turned her over onto her belly, slid into her and into her, her wide open womb, orchid, as she watched the womb of the sea sparkle. With her usual abandon.

Javier…I'm being served a feast, everything I love spread before me—Mexican food, Thai food, Italian food, French food, Indian, Japanese, Greek food, Amalia's rich chocolate mole con pollo, and I eat it all, her mole the best thing, I knew it would be, the best thing. I begin to weep with happiness as the rich mole fills my mouth. Amalia appears, smiling, a bit sternly as is her way—"As fragile as a butterfly's wing," she says, opening her hands, a monarch flies free.

Xochiquetzal…*The Gateway To Heaven welcomes me back, the thick scent of roses, hummingbirds stop in mid-air as I approach, this dream, I know I'm dreaming, and I begin to laugh. Monarchs cover the roses, fluttering their wings slowly open, close, open, close, and then I see a slender twig, leaf, hummingbird, its delicate beak deep in the tree trunk, dreaming its life, its death, rebirth, dreaming. I watch the monarch's delicate, orange splattered wings filtering warm sun, open, close, open, close, and I know I'm dreaming this dream. That I wish to be in this dream watching the monarch's delicate wings open, close, open, close, open.*
"What is freedom, madam?"

Eagle Woman's voice, the healer from Bali, wakes me up. I breathe in Javier's sea foam scent. I watch the ocean come to her knees, praying for more, singing for more, laughing for more. I watch her beauty dissolve, only to return to Japan, China, Africa. I watch la mar gather herself for the long journey. I watch the golden moon begin to set on the horizon. I feel the sun's longing to rise. Here. I feel Javier's strong, sweet hands claim me as he dreams. I know I'm dreaming.

Is this   yes   Is this   yes   Is this   yes   Is this   yes

———◆———

"Buenos dias Mama, dos cafecitos por favor, and we'll return to eat soon." Javier smiled at Celia, who calmly cooked with a naked two-old at her feet. "Is that your grandson?" The boy's eyes were sea-green, translucent, as they met Javier's.

"Un guerito...light-skinned, yes he's my grandson. I have six grandsons and four granddaughters, and this one has a rash I can't get rid of."

Javier picked him up and the boy laughed, poking at his eyes with his chubby fingers. "He's very healthy, so I see he eats well, and it's not measles. It's just a heat rash, his light skin, but it's making him uncomfortable."

"How do you know all this, hijo?"

"Soy doctor but don't tell anyone, I'm on vacation, mama. I'll give you some ointment for it and at night bathe him in cool water with two tablespoons of corn starch, or flour if you have none. I also have some extra sun screen, this little guerito needs his sun screen." Javier laughed as the boy leaned back in his arms playfully.

"I knew you were special, doctorcito, you have the hands of a healer, and I'll tell no one so you can rest, gracias doctorcito, gracias."

"Doctorcito, you're a physician?" Floriana came up behind him, pushing her breasts into him, as though trying to see the boy better. She was already in her combat string bikini/thong gear, with no sarong as the other women wore to walk around.

Javier moved out of the way, handing the boy back to Celia. "I'll bring the medication after we have our cafecitos, madre."

"I asked you a question, are you a physician?"

"Good morning," he responded curtly and walked quickly to the platform with their cafecitos.

Celia ran after him with pan dulces, putting them in his vest pocket. "That one's a snake, watch out, doctorcito," she laughed, but her eyes were serious.

"Es la verdad...That's the truth," he laughed with her. "Gracias madre."

Floriana's voice reached him—"Well, that was rude!"

He wanted to shoot back, "Well, you're a brazen bitch," but he kept his silence. The warmth of her breasts was nice, he caught himself thinking involuntarily—stop it, cabron, now.

"Amor, cafecito, wake up," Javier whispered into Xochiquetzal's ear, laughing.

"Ohmygoddess, coffee, the smell of coffee," she opened her eyes slowly to the light, to the sea, to this beautiful man with her coffee in his hand.

"I dreamt I had a feast last night and Amalia's mole was the best, but the food from all my travels, mi amor, places we'll go together," he smiled. "Celia has our breakfast waiting for us."

"You told her you're a doctor I bet, what happened?" She took her first sip, moaning with pleasure. Strong and blended with cinnamon, her favorite.

"You're beginning to know me, amor, her grandson has a rash and at first I was worried it might be measles, but it's only a heat rash."

"You brought a duffle bag of meds and stuff, right? And now you're going to have your own clinic by la mar, Dr. Zapata."

"I asked her not to tell anyone else as I'm here on vacation con la Xochitzalita, but tu amiga Floriana heard..."

"And I imagine she'll be in dire need of a doctor, Fucking A to Z."

"Let's go eat, I am famished, and later the cave, Xochitzalita."

"What are soldiers with M-16s doing on the beach, holy shit!"

"They patrol for drug dealers trying to land on this coastline, but they don't bother us. In fact, they get their bolsitas of Maria Juana and eat the pancakes Celia mixes with it. They'll patrol during the day, it's their job, but it's best not to make eye contact or smile, just know they're doing their jobs."

"Okay, I get it, but it's pretty surreal to see a fully uniformed soldier shouldering a weapon of war, strolling the beach."

"If they didn't the drug cartels would take over these natural ports and beaches, complete with heroin, cocaine and dead bodies."

"Weird, the wild Mexican west."

"It's my country, mi amor, and in your country the drug cartels do the same thing, maybe worse with your inner city drug addiction, branching out to the nice suburbs, the meth use, the young."

"You sound like Justin when he talks about the drug addiction mess. Yes, it's all true. I'll see these young soldiers as sentries, taking care of business."

"They patrol maybe every three hours or so, not constantly. Let's go eat, we'll feed each other, but first I have to stop at the Jetta to get the ointment for Celia's grandson. You'll love his sea-green eyes, un guerito." My son with la Clara, the thought came to him.

They ran to the car and Javier found his medical duffle bag, and also his sun hat. A white, floppy hat that shaded his eyes.

"Ay Diosa, the muppie hat!" Xochiquetzal giggled. "Please not the muppie hat."

"Should I get my Zapata sombrero?" Javier gathered her in his arms. "Estas mala. Anyway, you're wearing your Taos feminista sombrero."

"El muppie y la hippie feminista, what a fucking pair." She screamed as he picked her up, twirling her. "Okay, put me down and let's walk back to la mar first, then to breakfast. I swear I can smell it, yum the chorizo." As they strolled slowly on the tide toward breakfast, letting the warm waves wash over their ankles, the young soldier made his way back across the beach and turned toward the scent of Celia's breakfast.

She piled his plate with food, slipping the small plastic bolsita to him smoothly. "Let me know if you want more to eat, hijo, I'll take your cafecito to you." Celia beamed a smile to Javier and Xochiquetzal as they aproached, and Floriana pretended not to see them.

Good, Javier thought, keep it that way, we don't need your loca drama in this beautiful place. Floriana sat with her legs wide open, exposing her labia to the sun.

"Don't look now, but Floriana's pussy is getting a tan," Xochiquetzal giggled.

"I'd rather look at your pussy getting a tan, amor." He licked the inside of her lips, laughing. "And give you my expert mango surgery," he breathed into her, making her womb clench.

"Mango surgery," the Energy Child sang, "butterfly wing."

I wonder when this stops, my womb loving the sound of his voice, his breath in my lungs, his tongue in my mouth—I can't remember when all this stops. Or when he leaves, we part, how will I live without it, I wonder. She watched Javier pick up the boy, spreading the ointment over his face and chest, and she lifted the camera to her eye. Tears blurred her vision—What a wonderful father he's going to be, she thought, zooming in for a close-up.

"Look at these eyes, Xochitzalita." The boy laughed sweetly, the tickling of Javier's fingers spreading the ointment.

"I know, he's so beautiful, I just zoomed in, you're both so beautiful."

Javier put the boy down, giving him a piece of banana. He put his arm around her waist. "Why are you sad, mi amor, I see your tears."

"Because time will take you from me, as it should, but right now, this minute, I'm so happy we're together, Javiercito, so it's okay."

"Callate, mi amor, callate."

Xochiquetzal took shots of Celia cooking, serving their breakfast on two large plates, her beautiful smile in the morning light. The smile of a young girl, loved by the sun.

"Close your legs, Floriana, that young soldier can't tear his eyes away!" Tony said in Italian, but the meaning was clear to everyone as he tossed her sarong into her lap.

"Let's sit over here, keep our distance," Javier said, rolling his eyes in mock terror. "Okay, we're feeding each other, mi amor."

"I'm so fucking starving," she laughed.

"I'll feed you fast, you feed me fast, Celia says there's more in the pan. Madre, tienes una Victoria?" Celia smiled, nodding yes.

"I'll take one too, sounds good with the chorizo."

Javier leaped up to get them, saving Celia a trip. "Gracias mama." As he passed Floriana and Tony, he heard her voice—"There goes the doctor," thick with sarcasm.

"Here's limes for the chorizo, our morning Victorias, I think I'm in fucking heaven, mi amor."

"You'd better not get used to saying 'fucking,' I'm a bad influence on el doctorcito. What if you say to a patient, 'I think you have a fucking fracture.'"

Javier leaned over, stopping her words with his mouth. "Callate and let me feed you." He put a fork-full of scrambled eggs con chorizo, sprinkled with lime juice, into her mouth.

"Put it into a tortilla and take off your muppie hat, mi amor."

"Take off your Taos hat, mi feminista." He scooped the fluffy, yellow eggs, drenched in juicy, red chorizo with onions, into a piece of warm tortilla, straight to her laughing mouth.

"Okay, okay, you're right, we'll each keep on our weird ass hats, and now it's your turn, Javiercito." Xochiquetzal placed the warm tacito into his mouth as he grabbed her hand to lick her fingers. And then he surprised her with a perfectly ripe slice of mango, from his mouth to her mouth. All this in the morning sun, shot through with arrows. The golden arrows. Of the Warrior. In the Sun. "Chorizo, mangos, arrows, Warrior Sun," the Energy Child laughed, tasting it all, tasting.

"Look at those two," Floriana said to the just arrived French woman. "It's pornographic, this feeding each other, showing off what they do in bed."

Isolde glanced over, smiling. "We're going to feed each other, Claude, it's been a while."

"I'm your slave," he answered, smiling into her eyes, "and you're mine."

Floriana strode over to Celia, demanding a beer—"Make sure it's cold."

Celia took her pesos, saying nothing, keeping her eyes down. The unhappy ones, she thought, sighing. She raised the warm pan with simmering eggs con chorizo, cubed potatoes, sweet corn, nopales, to el doctorcito, la novia.

"Por favor mama, and another Victoria," Javier beamed his joy to her. This day, this day, this day, the golden arrows that kept falling.

Xochiquetzal laughed, "This is so delicious, Celia, gracias," as she served Javier most of it. Exactly the right portion for each one.

Floriana headed for the nude beach, hoping Tony wouldn't follow her. Maybe a single guy had arrived or one of those cute Mexican guys, she thought, taking off her skimpy top, feeling the sun tease her erect nipples.

Ai, the Japanese woman, arrived for breakfast. Her waist length hair was secured with stylized chopsticks, and she wore a black/fuchsia sarong around her waist. Her large straw hat dangled from her shoulder. She smiled at everyone, taking her time with each person, bowing slightly.

Javier and Xochiquetzal returned her smile, bowing slightly, motioning her to join them. After Celia served her a small portion of everything, she took Ai's face in her hands—"Bonita," she murmured. Ai laughed very softly and sat down to join the newlyweds, as she thought of them.

"Do you want some coffee, I'll get it for you," Javier offered.

Ai shook her head no, lifting her glass of fresh mango juice, and then she laughed. A child's tinkly laugh. With the stunning beauty of a woman.

Xochiquetzal wondered if she was safe traveling alone in Mexico. "Are you taking buses?"

Ai shook her head, yes, as she took her first bite, eyes closed, ecstatically.

Javier and Xochiquetzal dove under the waves, then floated faces to the Warrior. In the Sun. They watched the families with kids on one end of the beach, fathers carrying the little ones on their shoulders into la mar laughing.

"Look, there's Floriana *a la natural* with the Mexican guys and one's groping her," Javier laughed, remembering his own groping days on this beach. Who could blame them, a beautiful woman offering herself to them.

"And there goes Tony, holy shit!" Xochiquetzal ducked under a small wave, then surfaced wiping the salt from her eyes. The Mexican guys scattered as he approached, grabbing Floriana by the arm, dragging her toward her tiny pile of clothing.

"We shouldn't watch, Javier." Suddenly she felt sorry for Floriana, for what she was seeking to fill up in herself. That emptiness. That sadness.

"Dame tu boca, mi amor, and I'm taking you to my secret cave."

"Let's make love there, not in our public platform." She shivered in the warm ocean as his tongue claimed her mouth. "Ay tigre," she moaned.

Xochiquetzal floated on a wave, leaving Javier to la mar, his private joy with her. As the waves let her go, claiming her legs again to walk, she spotted Ai kneeling on the sand with her broad-brimmed straw hat on her lovely head. Walking closer, she realized Ai was making a sand castle. She looked like a happy child at play, that focus.

She wrapped her sarong around her body, placing the Taos hat on to protect her face, shoulders.

"May I join you? My son, Justin, and I used to make sand castles together when he was little."

Ai smiled with joy, yes. A friend, she thought, a friend who doesn't think I'm weird because of my vow of silence. This year of travel around the world before I reach the age my mother died of cancer, my grandmother died of cancer, thirty-two. The legacy of Hiroshima, Nagasaki, and I will have no children, no more children in my family. But now this friend, this friend, Xochitzalita, her lover calls her Xochitzalita. She has a son, Justin, a son, how wonderful, a child.

"Did Celia give you these cans?" She packed a large one with wet sand.

Yes.

"Where should I put this, Ai?"

She gestured in a sweep, anywhere, smiling.

Xochiquetzal added her round, wet sand to the beautiful forms embedded with tiny shells, already created. "Are you from Tokyo?" She filled the large can again, picking out tiny, broken seashells for the outer decoration.

Yes.

"Do you feel safe traveling alone here in Mexico, it can be tricky."

Ai wiped her hands on her sarong and brought out a pen and notebook. *I'm a heyoka, the Native American clown who rides backwards, trust, that's me. A heyoka. I'm on a year long vow of silence and journey around the world. I'll write you more later, I promise, but let's finish the sand castle, okay?*

"Okay," Xochiquetzal laughed, "later, tell me more. I lived in New Mexico by the Pueblos and I've seen the heyokas in action at their sacred dances, so yes, the heyoka, I understand."

Ai took Xochiquetzal's hand in hers for a moment, tears gathering in her eyes, and then she laughed, putting away pen and notebook. She removed the chopsticks from her hair, creating a shawl of beauty and silence all around her as it fell to her waist. She hadn't cut her hair since a child to remember the feel of her mother's hands, stroking it.

"Do you mind if I take some photos? I'm a photographer and you are so beautiful, this moment, right now."

Yes, Ai smiled shyly.

When Xochiquetzal returned with her camera, Javier was kneeling next to Ai scooping the wet sand into the large can. Silently. They played, created, in perfect silence. He knows that's what she wants, mi doctorcito, he reads her mind, her heart, and doesn't insist on words. That's why I love him, mi doctorcito, he reads your heart.

She shot a full roll of film with her professional camera, caressing each image. The light and shadow dappled on Ai's face from her straw hat; her shawl of hair reaching her waist, grazing the sand as she played. And Javier, with the absolute focus of a boy of eight, creating sand castles, his muppie hat, his twin fire eyes coming to meet hers from time to time. "How beautiful they are," Xochiquetzal murmured. What a lovely couple they would be, she smiled to herself. And, be honest, what a lovely couple Javier and Ai are in this moment, creating sand castles and silence together.

And then Javier read her heart—"Amor, let me take some photos of you y la Ai, dos sabrosita mujeres," he laughed.

As she handed her precious camera to him—"It's all set to go, here's the focus."

"You know I'm your gift, Xochitzalita, you know." Javier grazed her lips with his tongue as he took the camera from her hands. "Okay beautiful mujeres, pretend I'm not here, no look up, both of you and smile, give me a smile, you two hermosas!" He laughed as the Warrior. In the Sun. Pierced his heart, lungs, abdomen, genitals, knees, finally his feet. With his golden arrows.

He carefully placed her camera into its padded bag, back into the large camera case, zipping it up. "Your baby's sleeping, mi amor." And he ran into la mar shouting like a boy set free from school, all expectations; he dove under wave after wave, surfacing to laugh. At the Warrior. In the Sun. "She sets me free, Xochitzalita sets me free, and Amalia knew I'd find her, who's the gift, we are, the gift." Javier floated on his back, suddenly craving an icy cerveza. "I'm so fucking happy this moment, this moment, right now!" he shouted to the dazzling arrows of light. Holding him up.

Xochiquetzal watched him swim into shore, each wave bringing him closer, closer. And when he stood, so brown, wet, beautiful, lost in his own joy—she saw him. The Spaniard. Shoulder length hair, hard and handsome, his piercing eyes. Looking for her. His cruel, beautiful eyes. She saw his ship anchored in the distance. She saw the row boat that brought him to shore; the dark-skinned men who served him. The dark-skinned men who feared him. She saw. The Spaniard. Standing in the waves.

Ai reached over, touching Xochiquetzal's hand, concerned, bringing her back. To the present. To Javier. Who reads the heart. El doctorcito. Dripping with his joy. "I was just thinking, Ai, probably too much," she smiled at her new friend. This heyoka from Tokyo, maker of sand castles. "Do you want a beer or some juice? I'm guessing Javier wants one."

Beer sounds good, gracias, Ai wrote.

"Javier, I'm going for some cervezas, are you hungry?"

"You know I am, mi amor!" He sent his joy, his lust, into her body. Straight into her body. Like the Warrior. In the Sun.

When Xochiquetzal returned with the cold Victorias, a large plate of tacitos de pollo, a clay bowl of fresh guacamole with tortilla chips, salsa, limes—Ai was walking slowly around the sand castle with a rake in her hand, as Javier stared out to la mar. So peaceful, both of them, so peaceful. And no Spaniard in sight.

Only the gentle, sweeping sound of Ai's rake creating spirals of movement, spirals of memory, spirals of sorrow, spirals of joy, spirals of time. Spirals of peace. Beauty. Peace.

Finally, Ai joined them, taking a sip of the still cold beer, and Javier handed her a bottle of water. She coiled her hair back up with the chopsticks and reached for her pen and notebook. *Under the sand castle I placed a crystal, a crystal of peace. Even as war rages around our planet, this little crystal of peace. My grandmother was 12 when Hiroshima was bombed on August 6, 1945 at 8:15 a.m. as she and her sister were about to leave for school. Her father was closer to the center of the bomb so he burned up immediately. When they ran outside they saw people with their skin melting, dying. My grandmother died at 32, my mother at almost 32, cancer everywhere, and I'll probably die at 32 so I only have about 4 years to take the crystals around the world and to live. I'd love to live until 12/21/12 when we enter the Sixth Mayan World. They foretold a spiritual unfolding, but I will have no children. So this is my vow of silence as I travel around the world, starting in Mexico, the Mayas, then to New Mexico, the Pueblos, their Fifth World. And to where the atomic bomb was created, I'll plant my crystal there. Then to Europe, that continent, later, more crystals. The heyoka from Tokyo, me, Ai.*

Xochiquetzal read Ai's words out loud, tears flooding her. She looked at Javier; a single diamond slid slowly down his cheek. They flanked her, each one taking a hand. They sat in the silent peace Ai's crystal, the flowing spiral design, created. The perfect sand castle. Waiting for the tide.

After a while, Javier spoke in a voice that barely broke the silence—"I'm a physician, I don't know everything, but, Ai, you might live forty more years. You're the third generation of that horror, you carry peace."

Xochiquetzal opened her mouth to speak, but Javier had spoken for her, so she squeezed Ai's hand. A young soldier patrolled at his leisure; his M-16 slung on his shoulder. He glanced at them, smiling briefly, then back to the horizon that began to bleed. Sunset.

Over by the fire, Floriana gazed at the threesome. "Looks like a menage a tois to me, at last something juicy in this place."

"You wish you were Ai, but they just look like friends, stop talking, Floriana," Tony replied in irritation.

"If you don't like me talking, take the car to Mexico City, I'll meet you there later…"

"And leave you here alone, you'd like that, you bitch."

Floriana smiled. "Whatever makes you happy." Bastard, she breathed out.

"A young Hopi guy in Taos showed me this, the nakwach." Xochiquetzal took Ai's hand in hers, grasping her wrist, twisting her hand to be on top. Then she did the same to Javier's hand. "He said when we enter the Pueblo Fifth World, this is how we'll know each other, the nakwach."

"Gracias Xochitzalita," Ai whispered.

They kept Ai between them as they ate Celia's sabrosita mole enchiladas, taking turns feeding each other, nearly choking with laughter, as Floriana's face registered disgust. Envy. Xochiquetzal almost felt sorry for her, but she also knew if they included her she would only feed Javier. I'm not that generous, she sighed with joy—in fact, I'm normally a jealous, bitter, old jaguar, ayy la verdad, the truth.

"Estas locos," Celia laughed, serving them another round. For Javier and Xochiquetzal cold cervezas; for Ai her juice.

The blaring sound of salsa-rock came thumping toward them, carried by a tall, dark Mexican guy. He carried the large boom box in one hand, a black leather backpack over his shoulder, and a six-pack of Victorias in the other. He wore a purple shirt, unbuttoned, exposing his broad chest, tucked into his well-fitting jeans. And his huge, silver belt buckle was engraved with an enormous scorpion. As his face came into view, reflected by the fire, he was attractive as very masculine men can be. No prettiness in his features, but a history of his defeats. His victories. A dark, Indian face that absorbed the light of the fire.

"I'm Pompeii," he bellowed. "I've brought dance music, the promised mushrooms and they're free, I feel generous tonight!" He laughed directly into everyone's eyes, placing the boom box onto their make-shift table. Strands of gold chains draped around his neck, as well as a large, gold cross that emphasized his broad, muscular chest. Gold chain bracelets, an expensive watch studded with diamonds, all glittered by firelight. And in his right ear, a large diamond earring set in gold.

"Ohmygoddess, here's the guy the soldiers are looking for," Xochiquetzal giggled. "I'd love to take his photo, but then he'd probably have to kill me."

Pompeii reached over to Floriana, "May I have this dance?"

"You'll have to ask my husband." She indicated Tony, taken by surprise.

"I'll return her to you unharmed, amigo," Pompeii smiled widely. The smile of a man used to getting exactly what he desired.

Tony scowled, waving his hand in agreement, a kind of 'take her' gesture.

Floriana wore a red-flowered sarong around her waist, her bikini top barely containing her lush breasts, and her dark hair was pinned up with butterfly clips. She began to grind her swollen hips to the music; suddenly she was a confident, sensual woman. All female, lovely, dancing to the fiery, sexual salsa beat.

Pompeii brought her close for a moment, inhaling her female scent, feeling her breasts against his skin, her thighs moving rhythmically between his legs. "What's your name, bonita?"

"Floriana, from Italy, and where did you get that name, Pompeii, the volcano," she smiled at him with undisguised sensuality.

"I named myself after the volcano, when I was in Italy, traveling in that country. Where are you from in Italy, Floriana?" He smiled at her like the hunter smiles at his prey; just before he pulls the trigger, sinks his fangs, his claws, into soft flesh.

"Rome, of course, the city of sensuality." She returned his smile, translating the hunt into play. She wanted to play. So desperately. She looked for Tony; he was gone.

The other couples got up to dance, talking, laughing, as Celia added more wood to the fire. Tiny chispas, sparks, leaped to the stars. The almost full moon. Swollen, pregnant, fertile with gold desire, promise, as she revealed herself nakedly. Golden. Fertile. With desire.

Pregnant.

"Let's dance together, come on!" Xochiquetzal got to her feet, pulling Javier and Ai with her. She held hands with both of them, dancing in the soft sand, but Ai gently pulled away, laughing.

She began to dance to the fertile, golden moon, her arms upraised with sensual joy. Ai remembered her mother's gentle face, still beautiful in death. She remembered her father's grieving face, and she remembered the photo of her grandmother's face, the raw pain in her eyes. She danced to remember, arms raised; she danced to forget, as her fingers reached for the shimmering gold orb, dead planet, where the dead of Hiroshima, Nagasaki, waited to be born. Where I'll plant my crystal, the Sixth Mayan World, she breathed, she danced, arms raised.

When the song ended, Pompeii reached for Ai. "Join us, hermosa, you shouldn't be dancing by yourself."

"She'd rather dance by herself and she's not talking to anyone either," Floriana laughed.

"Why not, hermosa, you can talk to me, you can dance with us." He wouldn't let go of her hand as she tried to back away. Fierceness, not fear, came to her eyes.

Xochiquetzal recognized the kung fu stance Ai began to assume and, before Javier could step forward, she leaped between them. "I'd let go of her if I were you, Pompeii, now." She took Ai's hand from his and Ai continued to stand, feet apart, ready.

Pompeii laughed, the center of his dark eyes cold, ruthless. "And what's your name, madura bonita?" He brought Floriana in, close to him, and she luxuriated in his sense of power. The hunter. Prey.

She wanted to say, Yo mama, but decided not to trigger more aggression. "Xochiquetzal, a Mayan name."

"A beautiful name, a beautiful woman."

Javier wrapped his arm around her waist, claiming her. He took her into his arms, dancing to the slow, sexy salsa. Ai remained standing, but away from the group.

"And who are you, amigo?" Pompeii tried to gain control of the situation, his power, questioned. By this skinny kid, younger than her, que me chingas.

"He's a doctor, Javier." Floriana tried to pull him into her arms to dance.

"You're a doctor, amigo, maybe you can look at an old wound that won't heal," Pompeii laughed loudly. He spoke English almost with no accent. Then he said in Spanish, "I have many wounds that won't heal, doctorcito, I could use your help."

"He's here on vacation, not as a physician," Xochiquetzal answered.

"Are you his nurse?" Pompeii exploded with laughter. A laughter without warmth.

Javier stopped dancing, facing him. "Okay, that's enough, what are you doing here, amigo?" Everyone stopped dancing, absolute silence, and Ai continued her stance. The slow salsa switched to a fiery one, and the almost full moon flooded them with light.

Pompeii threw his head back, laughing. "Ay doctorcito, I'm here to share my music and los free mushrooms." He let go of Floriana and picked up his backpack. "Here, this is for you y la bonita." He handed Xochiquetzal a plastic bag of mushrooms. She tried to return it, "We can't take this," but Pompeii gathered Floriana in his arms and began to dance full throttle. He brought Floriana in close to him, her full breasts against his naked chest.

The other dancers disappeared, expecting gun fire, Tony reappearing, a fight, and Ai was no shrinking violet.

"You can see my wound later, doctorcito," Pompeii laughed as Javier, Xochiquetzal and Ai walked away, leaving them to dance alone.

"I wonder if Tony's coming back, good fucking grief. Well, we have some mushrooms, tigre, and for you too, Ai."

She shook her head no, kissing each one on the cheek goodnight. Ai walked slowly to the tide, letting the almost full moon light wash her feet, ankles, legs, over and over. Peace. The crystal. Buried. Hidden. The Sixth. Mayan World. Hiroshima. Nagasaki. Waiting. To be. Born.

"Ai was in a kung fu stance back there, in case you didn't know," Xochiquetzal whispered. "I'm almost a brown belt and can do some harm, and something tells me she's a third degree black belt. Her eyes, her stance, were absolutely fearless. She was absolutely ready to main or kill, mamacita."

"I saw she was unafraid, but yes I think you're right, of course you're right. That's why she's not afraid to travel by herself. She's a joder kung fu master," Javier laughed softly. "Well, we have los mushrooms, mi amor, even if they're from a pendejo drug dealer named Pompeii."

As they settled on top of their sleeping bags, face to la mar, they watched Ai swim in the smooth waves.

"If I didn't know that was Ai, I'd swear we're having a mermaid sighting. What a beautiful and amazing woman she is, her story, la heyoka de Tokyo."

"It looks like Pompeii lured Floriana to his lair and it looks like Tony gave up, who can blame the guy." Javier smiled in the moonlight, which made him look younger. A moon man. Of twenty-four. "I bet you y la mermaid, las mujeres, would've kicked his nalgas," he laughed softly, caressing her smooth thighs, making her moan with sudden pleasure. Joy. His hand seeking her wetness, his mouth seeking her mouth.

"Javier," she caught her breath, "I saw the Spaniard today as you were leaving la mar, after your swim."

"Do I turn into this guy? Don't talk, Xochitzalita, don't talk."

She pulled away slightly. "It looks that way and it scares the shit out of me, his eyes are so hard, cruel, terrible, really terrible, and he's looking for me. That's what it feels like, he's looking for me, and he's also handsome, cruel but handsome. And I think I want him, to find me, tigre."

"If it happens again, talk to me right then, let's see what happens, but for now chinga el Spaniard, callate, mi amor, callate."

"We should wait for tomorrow, the cave..." He caressed her wetness, his sea foam scent rose to meet her, his sweet tongue engulfed her, his mouth his mouth his mouth.

All night they woke, tracking the moon, the voice of la mar, the other's face. He twenty-four, she thirty-four. In the moon's light. Moon man. Moon woman.

Javier...*She's pregnant. With my child. Perhaps a son. I must. Find her. I must. La India. Mi amor. La India. I must. Find her.*

Xochiquetzal...*He'll take my child. From me. I know. He will. When he sees me. With his friends. The cruel soldiers. He laughs. At me. He laughs. He'll take. My child. From me. I'm his. India mujer. He laughs.*

Her eyes flew open just in time to see a scar of light welt the onyx sky. Shooting star. Make a wish. "Don't betray me, Javier, this life, and I won't betray you, this life, mi amor, mi amor, with your gentle eyes, with your twin fire eyes, mi amor." She watched la mar stretch herself under moonlight, under starlight, like a woman welcoming her lover. Javier's arm drew her close—"Amor," he murmured.

I'll paint your faces after breakfast, for your cave ritual. Ai handed Xochiquetzal her note and laughed, that hint of her voice.

"Okay and I'll paint yours. You know kung fu, I saw it last night." Ai nodded yes, smiling.

"I'm almost a brown belt and I could tell you're a master, right?" The coffee was just right, so was the day, la mar. She glanced at Javier, no Spaniard, just right.

I've trained since a child, first with my father, the true master. I'm going to make a sand castle today for Rwanda, Palestine, Tibet, the people of China, the world. For the Sixth Mayan World. Does your Mayan name have a meaning?

"We'll join you for awhile, it's too gorgeous to go straight to a cave," Xochiquetzal laughed as the Warrior in the Sun caressed, kissed, her face. "My full name, Xochiquetzal, is actually the Mayan Goddess of love and beauty. I had the audacity to name myself in my twenties after my heart was broken, ayy youth."

*My name means **love**, so we have similar names. The Goddess Quan Yin is tattooed on my back, I'll show you later, the Goddess of compassion. My teacher. How wonderful, our names mean **love**.*

Javier brought their plates over, steaming with omelettes, rice and beans. "Celia says Tony's car is gone and that Floriana went with Pompeii to his hotel, the one up there on the cliff. A nice hotel, I've stayed there a few times."

"Why don't we stay there tomorrow night to shower and stuff? Maybe we'll run into the new couple, ay Diosa," Xochiquetzal laughed.

"I hope she's okay, that she knows what she's doing. This guy, Pompeii, is used to getting what he wants, buying what he wants."

"I imagine at this very moment, Floriana's in fucking heaven with El Jefe, but you're right. She might not know what's really going on, not that I do, but I know better than to go off with a drug lord in Mexico."

"Celia says Pompeii, his group, protect her business, her place, so that's a good thing. And I'm sure he likes the soldiers to look the other way where he's concerned, and to keep other drug dealers off this beach, his beach. Anyway, tomorrow I'm thinking of doing a kid's clinic, just some check-ups to see how things are here."

"Ay doctorcito, you can't stay on vacation, but I was wondering when you'd bring out your doc backpack. Maybe Pompeii will show up for his check-up," Xochiquetzal laughed, kissing him lightly, playfully.

"Both of you can be my assistants, if you want."

Ai smiled into the arrows. From the Warrior. In the Sun. Yes, she nodded.

Ai painted Xochiquetzal's face with small rainbows, butterflies. Javier's face with suns, birds. She painted a tiny, yellow eagle, with wings spread, in the center of their foreheads—the dream eye—for their cave ritual. The sacred mushrooms. Xochiquetzal painted Ai's face with blossoming red, purple flowers, shooting stars; not as beautiful as Ai's face painting, but the meaning was clear.

Ai unwrapped the crystal meant for Rwanda, Palestine, Tibet, the world. *I'm going to take more crystals to Patzcuaro Lake, Teotihuacan Pyramids of the Sun and Moon, Oaxaca, Chiapas. Then I go to New Mexico, the Pueblos, north where the atomic bomb was created. Then Europe, back to Mexico, the Sixth Mayan World.*

"Will you be here for Christmas, in Mexico?"

I plan to go to Europe in March or April when it warms up, so probably yes.

"Spend it with us, Ai, come to San Miguel, and you can meet my son, Justin. You'll like him and he's cute too."

Ai laughed. *Are you trying to fix me up? Maybe I can come to San Miguel at that time, I'd love that, but I'd stay at a hotel.*

"You can stay with us, we'll find room."

Ai smiled no, touching Xochiquetzal's hand lightly. Javier already had a circle of perfect sand mounds and his look of total, boyish concentration was that of a surgeon slicing open a patient for surgery.

"This is what a surgeon looks like building a sand castle, a perfect sand castle, Ai, in case you didn't know. Javier specializes next year in San Miguel," she laughed, and then realized what she just said. He'd be in San Miguel for a couple of years to specialize—With the erotic bridge, she told herself.

"I don't see you two kung fu mujeres building anything thus far, so don't mock my sand castle mounds. I think I'm going to expand my kingdom, then build higher. I wish we had some flags for the towers." The bright birds, small yellow suns, danced on his face. With simple. Joy.

Ai took out a piece of purple cloth, tearing it into strips. She gathered twigs, tying the purple strips to them. She handed them to Javier, laughing.

"Perfect, these are perfect." The surgeon was pleased.

They began to work in silence, each one expanding their kingdom, queendom, until their territories met. Rows of smooth stones created bridges to each territory; the purple flags perched on the towers. Their territories becoming one land, one country, one vast sand castle universe. Then Ai raised the crystal to the Warrior. In the Sun. Her blossomed flowers, shooting stars, laughing. With simple. Joy. She handed it to Xochiquetzal.

She raised it to the Warrior. In the Sun. Her rainbows, butterflies, slightly smeared with tears. She handed the smooth crystal to Javier.

He raised it to the Warrior. In the Sun. Then he placed it to the eagle on his dream eye; pulling Xochiquetzal closer, and placed the crystal to her dreaming eagle. And the tiny birds on his face flew into the tiny suns, singing.

Ai carefully walked to the center of their linked universe, to the very center, kneeling down. She raised the crystal one more time. To the Warrior. In the Sun. His sweet, golden arrows. Blossoming her flowers further. Open. Dazzling her stars further. Open. She opened the earth in the center of their universe with her hands, and dropped the shimmering crystal into the dark, wet womb. "For the dead, for the living, for the ones being born, for the ones waiting to be born on the moon, for the Mayan Sixth World, for the Pueblo Fifth World, may we become new, may we become forgiven, on this miraculous Earth, this miraculous universe, this miraculous life, no matter how long or how short. May we become forgiven, may we forgive, may we become new," she sang in a low whisper.

They carried water and juice in their backpacks as they climbed to Javier's secret cave. They climbed a narrow, dirt-stone trail, hidden by lush greenery, flowers. It overlooked the entire beach, as the young soldier began his leisurely patrol. Later he'd stop at Celia's to be fed her wonderful mole enchiladas, a cool Victoria. Maybe two, he decided.

There were candles perched on stone, waiting to be lit; some burned to puddles of wax. Straw mats on the stone floor, signs of use, but well kept, clean. In a mayonnaise jar, eight red roses on the threshold of their final bloom. Petals dropping. Still beautiful. Their blooming, dying scent was subtle, yet full, in the enclosed space.

"I love this cave, tigre, how did you find it?"

"The woman who used to cook and do Celia's job years ago told me, all the young lovers use it for privacy."

"And beauty." Each word spoken sounded distinct, just born. For a moment she wanted to ask if he'd brought lovers here—Let it go, she told herself.

"Yes, and for beauty, mi amor." Javier picked up a large square of hand loomed rainbow cloth and walked to the cave entrance.

"What are you doing, don't jump!" she laughed. Her laughter echoed into the cave's darkness, beyond their eyes.

"Maybe I'll fly. Like the Warrior in the Sun." Javier turned to smile into her eyes. Those golden arrows. "I'm hanging up the signal that the cave's occupied by lovers seeking privacy."

"Or dreamers seeking visions."

"Bring out the water, I'll light some candles so we don't get lost in our dream, Xochitzalita, mi mujer tan linda."

"The sound of your voice, each word."

"Como un sueno, to share a dream, our voices." He thought of his dream last night, the Spaniard, but decided not to speak of it. Yet.

She remembered her dream last night, not yet.

They sat in the cave's narrow entrance, partially concealed by dangling vines, small violet flowers. They ate their first earthy mushroom, first raising it to the sun. Swallows of cool water.

"Ohmygoddess, there's Pompeii y la Floriana going to Celia's, so she survived her drug lord fiesta," Xochiquetzal giggled, enjoying the strange taste of earth in her mouth. The sacred mushroom made her tongue tingle, so she scratched it with water.

"And you can bet she's got, as they say in your country, a shit eating smile on her face, ay at last properly fucked by a cabron Mexican drug lord." Javier laughed softly, offering his second mushroom to the sun, placing it on his tongue. He let it rest there, allowing it to tingle his tongue.

"You are so fucking bad, tigre, but you may be right, who knows what their real problems were."

"Mexicans love the taste of a woman's secret honey, amor, and you can bet he's still tasting her on his tongue."

She offered her second mushroom to the undying sun, placing it in her mouth.

"Hold it on your tongue, Xochitzalita, these are talking mushrooms, do you feel it?"

"I sure do, okay I'll try it, talking mushrooms, I believe it. And after you, doctorcito, I also believe it about Mexican men loving the secret honey de las mujeres. I wonder if the Spaniard loved the taste…"

"Don't even talk about el cabron, mi amor, you'll conjure his presence in this cave, our dream."

"I agree, you're right, but maybe we both need to see him, Javier."

"As long as I don't fucking disappear and you'll be stuck with a cabron who doesn't love the taste of tu sabrosita orchid, mi amor," he laughed, shooting his arrows into her.

They raised their third sacred mushroom to the undying sun—if not this sun, this world, the next sun, the next world. The Sixth Mayan World.

"Por Dios, Pompeii just waved at me, of course he knows about this cave, but I'm sure he also knows the rule of privacy. Don't wave back, Xochitzalita, or that cabron might just come up here," Javier laughed dryly. "And then I'd have to push him off the edge, que me chingas."

"They're going to the hotel, it looks like."

"Okay, for our fourth mushroom, but wait, I forgot the rattle, it's back there." Javier got to his feet, heading for the darkness. "I came here with an old shaman from the village the first time I took mushrooms. His altar, his things are still here, look, Xochitzalita, look. Help me light the candles, it's hardly changed."

"You came here with a shaman the first time you took mushrooms, how wonderful."

"He was at least ninety when I met him in the village, and I was barely twenty. For some reason he singled me out, to come to the cave with him."

"El doctorcito, he saw you, Javier. Oh how beautiful, all these feathers, the designs of the shells, this conch." Xochiquetzal picked up the conch shell, bringing it awkwardly to her mouth and blew softly. "When Don Francisco blew the conch shell, I leaped out of my skin, so this is pretty pathetic."

Javier shook the old shaman's rattle rhythmically, like a heart beat, the way he had years ago for him. He turned toward the darkness at the back of the cave, shaking the rattle, and a glow of light appeared. "Blow louder, more breath, mi amor." His voice sounded strange, not his own, the old man's voice. A thick darkness began to spiral in his dream eye where the tiny yellow eagle flew, as he shook the rattle, tiny stones, tiny bones, calling an ancient human, inhuman, dream. To heal, to harm, that power.

The sudden blast of the conch shell made him jump and laugh out loud. "One more time, mi amor, that was perfect." Now his voice blended with the old man's trembling voice—What a gift he gave me, the old shaman, Don Jose, and now I remember that I fasted for three days. Well, we didn't eat that much, we've been eating lightly. The way he guided me through the darkness, his lightning eyes laughing. Always laughing at me, the young man stumbling in the dark.

Xochiquetzal put the conch shell to her mouth, seeing Don Francisco's face, his smile, his eyes, that light, and blew with all the breath in her lungs. Violently. With longing. For love. For freedom. The clear voice of the shell roused her yellow eagle, edged in red—she remembered Ai's note. *Your eagle must be dipped in blood, the power of your blood, amiga.* And the black spiral began to pulse in her dream eye where the tiny, yellow eagle flew dripping blood from her wings, her body, her hungry talons. Her violent longing. To love, be free.

"Amor, he's here, the old shaman Don Jose is here, I'm going to sing you a song he sang to me fourteen years ago, if I can remember it...Pajarito en sus suenos, volando, siempre volando, por la luz...Little bird in your dreams, flying, always flying, to the light..." Javier's voice sang with the rattle and he paused to light copal, filling the cave with the thick, dark scent of the ancestors. To heal, to harm, that power.

"I need to be by myself for awhile."

"I'm with you in spirit, Xochitzalita, I'm here. Take a candle with you, there's an opening to the sky at the back. Follow the glittering stones, mi amor."

Xochiquetzal followed the glittering stones by candle light, the darkness of the cave swallowed her as she walked deeper into its silence, darkness, silence, darkness. Fear swallowed her. Longing swallowed her. Love swallowed her. Freedom swallowed her. "What is freedom, madam?" Eagle Woman laughed harshly.

A shaft of light shimmered in the absolute darkness. Her candle flickered. I have no matches, I forgot to bring matches, maybe I should go back, I forgot to bring fire, my own fire, I should go back...but the shimmering light wouldn't let her. Go back. "I'm in the womb," she whispered. "I'm being born, I'm dying, always dying, always being born, in this undying light." She began to smile as her tears fell uncensored. She had no choice but to weep in this undying light.

Carefully, she placed the burning candle on a sheltered stone ledge, and slowly walked in the darkness to the shimmering, undying light. It fell so peacefully on the stone floor, growing wider as she approached, so slowly. She sat down inside the patch of sky, the undying light. Every person she'd ever loved came to her; every spark of love she'd gathered came to her. In light. Clara, Florinda, Carlos, Justin Justin Justin... the memory of her womb, full of his sweet weight, came to her. Each beloved friend came to her, each one, in light. She looked up to the patch of swirling sky, changing by the second, and a violet butterfly floated by in the warm wind.

"This is freedom, Eagle Woman, to love and to be loved." She wept and laughed. The joy. The sorrow. Of being fully human.

Javier sat by the opening to the cave, facing the unending, dancing mirror of light. Each wave sang, *Heal*, then *Harm*, then *Heal harm heal harm heal harm heal harm heal*, endlessly. Every person he'd ever healed came to him. In light. Every person he'd ever lost, who had left as he struggled for their life, came to him. In light. Amalia came to him as a beautiful, young woman. In light. Smiling, laughing. In the undying light. "I am your flawed, human healer, Amalia mi mama India."

He wept and laughed. This joy. This sorrow. Of being fully human.

Two yellow butterflies spiraled, wing to wing. Their fragile wings. Enduring relentless sun, gusting winds. Their fragile wings. Enduring. "Mariposas en sus suenos... Butterflies in your dreams..." Javier sang softly as they disappeared from sight. Entirely in his own human voice. Weeping, he also laughed. And his hands longed to touch her, his eyes longed to see her, his mouth longed to taste her. He followed the glittering stones by candle light. Fearlessly. He carried one ripened rose. For her.

The shaft of shimmering light, she sat in it gazing up at the sky, her face shining with strange joy. She didn't hear his silent footfalls coming closer. Then he stopped, standing still.

"You will love me like no other, Xochiquetzal, mi amor."

She turned her face to him. "And you will love me like no other, Javiercito." She saw the light stream from her mouth, reaching him (as in her dream years ago).

He walked the few steps toward her, sitting next to her. "I missed you, amor." Light streamed from his mouth, reaching her. They kissed very lightly, soft lip to soft lip, wing to wing, and the undying light poured over them from the patch of shifting sky. The dome of sky that contained them life after life after life.

Fragile as a butterfly's wing.

Enduring as a butterfly's wing.

Their long migration to this moment.

Life after life after life after life.

His tongue met her tongue. This is what tongues were for. His hands clenched her hair. This is what his hands were for. Her mouth opened wide to him. This is what mouths were for. Her hands reached under his shirt, his warmth, his firm, fleshy warmth. This is what her hands were for. He undid her blouse, found her niña breasts, her erect nipples, each one, in his warm, wet, sucking mouth. This is what breasts were for. She licked his dark, crescent moon nipple, his head thrown back, moaning. This is what dark, crescent moons were for. His fingers grazed her body like a blind man, finding the hot wetness of her orchid. This is what fingers were for. He entered her blindly, weeping with dumb joy, and they danced with creation, they danced. This is what creation was for. This dance.

Nothing separated them. In this moment. Each moment. Was complete. They lacked nothing. In this naked vulnerability. They lacked. Nothing. In this. Moment. Naked. Vulnerable. This is. What freedom. Is for.

"Creation," the Energy Child sang. "Freedom," the Energy Child laughed. And her/his genitals, both sexes, vagina/penis, orchid/serpent, found creation's blossom, dance. S/he lacked nothing. In this. Moment.

This is   what freedom   is for

They slept briefly, a sleep of no dreams. This moment was a dream. He led her to the hole in stone in the back of the cave, and they took turns peeing. Laughing.

"This must be true love, we're peeing together." Xochiquetzal squatted, keeping her balance with both hands on the stone floor.

Javier guided her back to the patch of sky with his lit candle. "I brought a gift for you, Xochitzalita, and a poem as well. Sit with me here in the light, facing me, mi amor, yes."

"I feel like I'm dreaming awake."

"You are, we are." He handed her the ripened, wilting rose. "I forgot to give this to you."

She tore the ripened petals from the stem, tossing their red flesh between them. The waves below took her voice. Silence.

Javier held white light in his hands, looked directly into her eyes—his fire to her fire (this is what eyes were for)—and began to read/sing from the white light pages in a new voice. A voice trying to contain the enormity, th e essence: love. In Spanish first, then in English.

IN YOU THE EARTH

Little
rose,
roselet,
at times,
tiny and naked,
it seems
as though you would fit
in one of my hands,
as though I'll clasp you like this
and carry you to my mouth,
but
suddenly
my feet touch your feet and my mouth your lips:
you have grown,
your shoulders rise like two hills,
your breasts wander over my breast,
my arm scarcely manages to encircle the thin
new-moon line of your waist:
in love you have loosened yourself like sea water:
I can scarcely measure the sky's most spacious eyes
and I lean down to your mouth to kiss the earth.
El maestro, Pablo Neruda, mi amor, como no.

He paused, letting the silence engulf them after the tidal wave of Neruda's words, song, words. Then he got to his knees, leaned over, and kissed her. Softly. Butterfly. Wings. He wept. She wept. This is what tears were for. Still on his knees, Javier reached into his vest pocket, and brought out an old, black, velvet pouch. Shook it out into his open hand. Golden. He offered them to her, weeping. She took them, weeping. Golden. Earrings.

"These were Amalia's, mi amor, and now they're yours."

Xochiquetzal examined their beauty. Lacy, large, slightly heavy. Pure gold. She looked up to meet his eyes, to speak. The Spaniard. But his eyes weren't cruel. They were wounded, ashamed, unforgiven. Suffering.

"I forgive you always," she whispered. The Spaniard wept, faded, leaving Javier.

"What did you say, I couldn't hear you, amor."

She could barely speak above a whisper, as though her voice was a knife shredding the sacred silence. Only poetry should live in this sacred silence, she thought, but Javier was waiting. To hear her voice.

She held onto his eyes and whispered, "You became the Spaniard for a moment." She paused, listening to the silence between them. The red flesh of a rose between them. "His eyes weren't cruel, but suffering. I told him I forgive him. Always." Xochiquetzal leaned over the silence, the red rose petals, kissing him. Javier. Butterfly. Wings. Fragile. Enduring. Life after life after life after life.

"It's time, mi amor," Javier whispered.

"Yes, it's time, finally, it's time." She stroked his beloved face with her fingers (this is what fingers were for). "And these exquisite earrings were Amalia's, so beautiful. Are you sure you should give these to me, Javiercito, aren't they gold..."

"They are pure gold, what the Spaniards came for, the gold, and now these are yours, Xochitzalita mi amor. Pure gold, always yours."

"Put them on me." She reached for the seashell earrings he'd given her in Bucerias, to remove them.

"No, let me do it." Javier removed the seashell earrings, replacing them with pure gold. Amalia's special earrings, not for daily wear. Her daily earrings had been pure gold hoops, given to her by her mother as a girl. The special earrings, given to her by her grandmother, from her mother and her mother. "She gave them to me, saying, 'Don't let them bury me in these, give these to the woman you love someday. Tell her they're from me, Javiercito, but only give them when you know who this woman is.' Now I know." He paused. "What she meant. These earrings were meant for you, Xochiquetzal, mi amor."

Javier stood up, pulling her to her feet. "Tan hermosa, so beautiful."

Long, deep, butterfly wings, besos, kisses. "Let's go back to the altar, light the candles, it's sunset." He took her by the hand, laughing softly with butterfly joy (fragile, enduring), and led the way. The small candle he held in front of him became a star in the black sky of the cave, and the star led them to the cave's entrance.

The horizon held colors they'd never seen before. The ocean held music they'd never heard before. And new stars, constellations, had taken their place in the twilight sky. The world, the cosmos, had rearranged itself while they dreamt awake under the patch of sky. The undying light.

Javier lit all the candles on Don Jose's altar, then returned to sit next to Xochiquetzal. "I finally realize, fully realize, that I was supposed to lose my great love, Clara, in order to find you again, and to treasure you, our time, this life. It was my lesson, mi amor." His voice merged with the waves, as though the sea had spoken. She met his gaze briefly, then back to the new world.

"And I realize I had to give everything away—my marriage of all those years, being a mother, a professor, all my things in Taos, to pack my car with the essence de mi vida. And even my vision, my gathered vision, for that time, had to be given away. In order to ride the Windhorse, and drive my car to San Miguel," she smiled, leaning into him, feeling his warmth, as his arms encircled her. "I had to let everything go, mi amor, so I could find you, or you could find me, again, this time." It felt like she spoke—her words, her voice—yet she was listening. To the sea.

"The world is new, mi mujer tan hermosa, with pure gold in her ears. The world feels new."

"Maybe this is the Sixth World. Maybe we helped to create it." Xochiquetzal thought of Ai. "As Ai creates her sand castles, her sacred worlds with crystals." This was what worlds were for. To be created. Recreated. Entered.

A final, golden arrow suddenly flew across the horizon. Pure gold for a moment, through dark purples. New beauty. They laughed with delight. Like children. They lacked nothing. In this moment. This is. What freedom. Is for.

As they waited for the full moon to rise, to light the path down the steep trail, they ate the still delicious tamales, two ripe mangoes, Celia had packed for them. "Eat slowly and not too much, or you might get sick after our mushroom feast." Javier licked the rich salsa that dripped from his fingers.

"Yes, doctorcito, and that goes for you too. Isn't that your third?" Xochiquetzal placed a piece of her sweet chicken tamale into his mouth.

"I forgot to feed you, mi amor, I'm such a cabron, here." He fed her a piece of his, and then began peeling one of the large, ripe mangos.

"I was just thinking about how I went to my grandmother's funeral with a red shawl, everything else black, but people stared at me as though they were shocked, hypocrites. Most of them from her church, who thought they were better than her because she claimed being Yaqui. The others wanted to forget they were Mestizos, Indian."

Javier remained silent, watching the full moon rise, golden. Immense. Being born through the horizon's spread legs, it rose into the sky's midwife hands. Wet. Golden. Full. Moon. Dripping blood. Dripping sperm. Newly born. "New beauty," he murmured. And the memory of Amalia's funeral came to him; the long, sad walk to the cemetery, following her wooden coffin. Her tired body entirely cradled by fresh flowers within, and a white, silk pillow under her head. His mother had added the pillow, making sure only the most beautiful, fresh flowers surrounded Amalia. He remembered the red roses that circled her peaceful face, the white, silk pillow in contrast to her dark, Indian skin. The musicians that led the way, singing her favorite songs. His mother had hired them, and she'd walked with Javier, trying to hold his hand, but he'd pulled away. Seeing her tears fall, he'd put his arm around her as they walked to the beautiful song of lament and praise being sung. He remembered that his father had been away on a business trip, as he always called them; spending money that could've been used to save her. Javier remembered all of this, and how he decided not to punish his mother who wept for his second mother. The woman who had loved him perhaps as much as herself: Amalia.

"I think I wore that red shawl as a symbol of blood, of life, as though to wear all black was a final goodbye."

Javier put a piece of dripping mango into her mouth, then into his. They'd never tasted mango like this, the ripened, sweet fullness in their mouths.

"I just remembered Amalia's funeral, how my mother and I followed her coffin in the streets, how we covered her body with flowers, the musicians singing her favorite songs, and I wore red as well. Secretly." He smiled with the memory he'd forgotten until this moment. "Black socks with red stripes in my black shoes, under my black pants, yes, I think for the same reason, mi amor, no final goodbye, yes. I actually remember choosing them, and I had no memory until this moment, gracias," Javier smiled with sadness, joy.

"You know, in the stories of Quetzalcoatl, black actually symbolizes life and red symbolizes death, as in blood sacrifice, that's what I read. Maybe we were trying to unite red/black, death/life. How wise we were, Javiercito." He fed her another explosion of ripe mango flesh, and she fed him, until both mangos were devoured, piece by piece.

They slid down the trail, laughing, moonlight guiding their way. They paused to hold onto each other—butterfly wing kisses, tongues—laughing at the moon's beauty. They'd never seen a moon like this; the clarity of this moon guiding them. When they reached the bottom of the trail, Javier stripped off his clothes. "Come on, Xochitzalita, let's swim, come on!"

As they floated in the dark, warm waves, they began to miss the sacred sanctuary of Don Jose's cave. "We'll return in a year or so, mi amor, to the cave." Javier took her hand and kissed it.

"Promise, I love this place, so peaceful, even with armed soldiers," Xochiquetzal smiled.

"Te juro, mi amor, I promise."

"There's light coming out of your mouth, like in my dream, and I think I'm going to love you like no other." She wept her delicious tears into the delicious, salty sea.

"Te juro, mi amor, te fucking juro," he laughed. "We're both road kill, both of us, and I love your tears. It means you love me like no other, as I love you." Javier gave a soul shattering grito to the full moon's light caressing each never-ending wave. Someone in the distance returned it with that perfect balance of sorrow, joy (Pompeii).

Your grito reminds me of one of my favorite poets, Rumi's words—'Dance in your blood. Dance when you're perfectly free.'" They touched fingertips, not clinging to the other.

"That's what we did today, isn't it? We danced in our own blood, and in this moment we're perfectly free. To love each other, to be road kill," Javier laughed with joy as la mar held them in her warm, salty, light-filled blood.

What is freedom, madam? Xochiquetzal heard Eagle Woman's laughter. Delight. Joy and sorrow. Equally. And she screamed a grito that gave the white light moon all her sorrow, all her joys. Equally.

Venus' subtle light pierced the waves, creating a trail that reached them. Pierced them. Transformed them. As they danced. In their own. In la mar's. Blood.

From the shore, someone returned her grito, so full of raw longing. To live. A woman's grito. Ai. She watched them swim, feeling their joy wash over her. Reminding her. Her Longing. Desire. To love. Ai, her name, Love. "Ai," she sent her name out over the waves, to the other side of the world (dawn), and back. She cupped Venus in her open hands, weeping. Then left her friends to love each other in privacy, smiling, their joy.

━━◆━━

"Doctor, los niños are waiting for you," Celia repeated until he finally answered.

"Ayy Celia, fix un café muy fuerte for me. I'll be there in ten minutes." Javier could barely open his eyes, and his watch told him 10:17 a.m.

"Como no, doctor, and there's a few adults with los niños as well."

"Okay, es bien, fix el café fuerte y gracias."

"I'm coming to help you, remember, and Ai is too. If I can open my eyes that is." Xochiquetzal tried to laugh but only a dry croak emerged.

"Tres café fuertes, Celia!"

"Si doctorcito!" she laughed.

"You look beautiful, mi amor."

"You are such a fucking liar," she croaked, laughed, choked. "Don't stop."

Ai was waiting for them, dressed in white pants and top, smiling in the sun. Her hair was held tightly in a bun with the carved chopsticks, and she conveyed an air of professionalism. She'd given everyone numbers so they wouldn't lose their places in the intimate jostle of their waiting. A mother had to chase a child, a child had to pee, children wanted to play. Under the Warrior's golden arrows.

Javier wore his extravagant, black with glittering gold trim, Zapata sombrero from Vallarta, and everyone began to laugh. "El doctor mariachi!" a small boy yelled, and his mother covered her mouth, smiling in spite of herself. "Dios mio," she murmured, "que guapo, el doctor...how handsome, the doctor."

They hugged Ai quickly, and she handed Javier a note—*I'm a nurse, Javier, maybe if I live past thirty I'll go to medical school. Put me to work, doctor.*

"Ai is a nurse, Xochitzalita, que bien!" Celia handed him his café fuerte first and the first swallow jolted him to full life. "Perfecto Celia, perfecto, gracias."

"No wonder everything is so orderly, this is your work." Xochiquetzal put her arm around Ai's waist, as Celia gave them their café fuertes. Ai refused hers and Javier claimed it.

The sound of rousing ranchera music drifted toward them as Pompeii approached, boom box in hand, Floriana beside him. Smiling. "Doctorcito, some music to keep you going!" he laughed loudly. Some of the kids started to dance, kicking up puffs of dust with their bare feet.

"Lower it, Pompeii, por favor!" Javier ordered him, in his clinic.

"I love your sombrero, doctorcito," Floriana purred, holding onto Pompeii like her first meal in ten years. Dressed, as usual, in her skimpy bra top, but a sarong wrapped around her waist. Her skin glowed with last night's pleasures.

"I told you I want a check-up," Pompeii growled, lowering the music. "And I see your camera, bonita, no fotos, por favor."

"You'll have to wait your turn and you're at the end of the line," Javier said without looking at him.

"I'll be by the water, drinking my first cerveza, doctorcito," he laughed.

Floriana laughed with him as they walked away, her hips swaying with fresh orgasms. "I want a check-up too, doctorcito."

"Good for her," Xochiquetzal smiled, "a satisfied customer." She was tempted to capture those hips, Pompeii's large hand claiming them, but she lowered her camera. Then she watched Javier and Ai begin to work together as though they'd been doing it for years. Ai opened his doc bag and began handing him exactly what he needed, without a word exchanged. As Javier held a baby, listening to her heart, tears filled Xochiquetzal's eyes. He held the baby as though she were his own (she began to take photos, being careful to not be intrusive). He touched every child as though that child were his own. (Click) And the adults like family members. Tenderness. (Click click)

Since Javier and Ai were such a smooth team, Xochiquetzal handed out cups of water from the large container Celia had provided for the wait. November was the beginning of cooler weather on the Mexican coast, but the Warrior in the Sun continued to shoot his golden arrows. So accurately.

The final child waited under the shade of quickly erected palm fronds, covered with a light cloth. The father carried him to Javier, holding him in his lap with a shawl covering the boy's legs. Javier greeted the father and gently removed the shawl. The boy had lost a leg from the mid-thigh down, and it was infected.

"How did this happen?" Javier asked with gentleness. He saw the father's fear and sorrow. And he veiled his own outrage at the loss of the boy's leg, so young. How did this happen?

"My son was given a small chain saw to help with construction, by a visiting gringo. A good man but he didn't teach my son to use it properly." The boy stared blankly, without emotion, as the fever of infection rivaled the sun.

"When did this happen?" And the gringo didn't bother to take him for medical care, not his personal responsibility. Javier could just hear those words, 'not my personal responsibility.' The mantra of the wealthy, the well-to-do, gringo or not. The shock of being an intern hadn't left him, that sense of outrage.

"Over two weeks ago. The healer took care of him with herbs, that's what we do here, doctor."

"I understand, señor, and that's why your son doesn't have gangrene, yet. I'll give him antibiotics, and I want you to take him to Morelia, to a doctor there. Your son needs a specialist." Javier saw his father's question in his eyes, How? And before he could offer his own car, and time, to take them...

"I'll take them!" Pompeii's voice boomed. "And I'll pay for the doctor as well. If I'd known about the boy, I would've taken him earlier, but I just arrived three days ago."

Javier met Pompeii's eyes. "Gracias, you're a good man, when you want to be."

Pompeii laughed loudly. "You too, doctorcito, you too." Floriana never left the shadow his large body created for her. Safety. Pleasure. He was large in every way, and his tongue desired her.

"He's going to need a brand new leg in a few months," Javier smiled at the boy, trying to give him hope. "It'll be a special leg made just for you and you'll be able to walk on it. Qué es tu nombre, hijo… What's your name, son?"

"Carlitos, doctor." A tiny smile played on his lips, in his eyes. A special, new leg just for him. "I'm going to be twelve next month."

"You're very brave, Carlitos, como un hombre…like a man of twelve." Javier gave him his first capsule of antibiotics with water. Then gave his father a week's supply, telling him how to dispense them.

"I'll call some physicians in Morelia, see exactly who to take Carlitos to, Pompeii. Can you take him within two days, that leg needs to be looked at now."

"Of course, doctorcito, just make the appointment and he'll be there." Pompeii's left hand fondled Floriana's left breast as though he owned it. She shivered under his fingertips, moaning softly.

"You two better go to your room right now," Javier laughed, "I understand entirely." He smiled at Xochiquetzal, remembering their fan club in Vallarta—"Vaya el cuarto…Go to your room!" Gritos. "I'll meet you there in an hour or so and give you that check up, or whatever it is you need."

"I like the way you think, doctorcito," Pompeii laughed, leading Floriana back to the hotel.

"He's a good man," Celia said. "He brings food, clothing, books for the children when he arrives, and he also pays for a teacher so they can read the books he brings. That's how Pompeii pays for his sins, doctorcito. Better than confession, como no." She smiled with her common sense wisdom. "And he protects us, not the soldiers, those boys." She nodded to the young soldier, arriving for a cold Victoria.

"I agree, mama, better than confession," Javier smiled with understanding. "I'll take a Victoria tambien. Would you pass along the word that no child under fourteen should be given a chain saw to use under any circumstances, or it's going to happen again to some other young boy. No one under fourteen should do work like that, just look at Carlitos."

"I'll tell them and remind them, doctorcito. You're right, of course, but as you know when someone offers them some pesos for work…"

"I know, Celia, just pass it on, and I'll say something about it as well."

"I'll take a cerveza too, Celia. Ai, do you want one?" She nodded no, smiling, but Celia knew what she wanted, mango juice. Xochiquetzal put her arm around Javier's shoulder, reading his face. Sorrow. "I love that Pompeii pays for a teacher for the kids, so much better than confession. And that he's taking Carlitos, so there's goodness there."

"But a man like that must have total control, ultimately. A double-edged sword, mi amor, and his sword is sharp."

"I see it in his eyes, those dark, twin fires, ruthless. And I see the same dark, twin fires in your eyes, Dr. Zapata, especially in your sombrero tan sexy. It's a good thing you called a clinic today, that poor kid, and you're right, no one under fourteen. Find an older boy for those, let's face it, much needed pesos." She grazed his lips with her tongue, tasting him. "If you weren't a healer, a physician, you might need to do that, total control."

A shiver of recognition went through him; first anger, then laughter. "You should see me in the ER, I'm a tyrant, es la verdad... that's the truth, mi amor. Wait until I'm a full fledged surgeon, Dios mio, but it's our secret."

Ai laughed and began to write—*I'm a surgical nurse and you surgeons think you're Zeus, but I love you guys anyway. The work you do, how could I not.*

"Two women that know me too, well, I give the fuck up!"

"Are you going to Mexico City with us tomorrow, Ai? We're taking off early, around 8 a.m. or so. A surgical nurse, of course you are and Kung Fu Woman as well," Xochiquetzal laughed. "We have this guy's number for sure, but yeah, we still love him and his Zapata sombrero."

Yes, Ai nodded. *You're going to be a wonderful surgeon, Javier. That's what I really wanted to be. Maybe if I live past 30.*

"You will, watch and see, you will," Javier smiled at her.

"And you better do it, no excuses!" Xochiquetzal gave her a quick hug. She feels like my daughter, the daughter I always wanted. "Come on, I'm starving, and then on to Pompeii and Floriana. Are you ready for Pompeii, doctorcito?"

Javier groaned, "Mano a mano, que cabron, but it seems a good heart is in there. Leave your camera in the car, mi amor, he's not that good. You know, his wanted posters."

The room smelled like sex and gardenias as Javier and Xochiquetzal entered. Ai went swimming; they'd join her later. Their last day by la mar. There was a large bucket of Victorias in ice, and bottles of chardonay among them, on the tiled patio facing the beach. The horizon.

"What a beautiful room and the view, perfect," Xochiquetzal noted.

"This is where I really live, so it's my personal suite year round. There's two bedrooms, a small kitchen, room service, I'm happy," Pompeii laughed, squeezing Floriana to him.

"There's Victorias, chardonay, and food will brought up in an hour." Floriana couldn't stop smiling.

"And tequila, the good stuff," Pompeii winked at Javier.

"I'll take a Victoria now and tequila later, como no. Y la Xochitzalita wants the chardonay." Javier stroked her cheek with his fingertips. Then he brought out a folded piece of paper—"I made an appointment for Friday at 10am, here's the information, and again gracias. Okay, where's this wound, cabron?" He met Pompeii's twin fire eyes, so much like his own.

Pompeii laughed, "Qué me chingas, doctorcito," unbuttoning his freshly ironed shirt. A bandaged section on his lower abdomen was revealed, and he stood, legs spread, belligerently.

"I keep asking him if it hurts," Floriana winced.

"Not enough to stop me from making love to you, hermosa!" He pulled her close, laughing.

"Okay, okay, cut it out or I'll see you later, cabron," Javier laughed with him. He carefully took the bandage off; a knife wound with inappropriate stitches.

"The wound is pretty clean, but the doctor should've used dissolving thread. This stuff never dissolves, causing the wound to welt, itch, and often infect. And it looks like a terrified intern did them, where did you go?" Javier shook his head, trying not to laugh. In his role as doctor.

"He was a hack, doctorcito, can you fix it?"

"How did you get this wound, just curious."

"How else, in a fight. I don't fight often, but I always win. I'm a pacifist by nature, but will fight to the death if aroused," Pompeii laughed, enjoying himself immensely. "Can you fix it, Dr. Javier?"

"Gomez. I can but you'd be more comfortable in a doctor's office."

"You do it, Dr. Gomez, I like you, chinga tu madre!"

Oh no, not that again. Xochiquetzal remembered the Javier-Pedro show at Mama Mias and held her breath.

"Chinga tu padre y tu perrito tambien, cabron, okay it'll be a pleasure to cause you discomfort, even some pain," Javier laughed, giving up the role. "I'll put the skin to sleep, around the wound..."

"No, no pain killers, doctorcito, just do your job!" Pompeii put his arm around Javier, squeezing him with affection. "Floriana, two tequilas and keep mine coming. Andale, doctorcito Gomez, give me my dose of pain!"

Javier joined Pompeii's booming laughter, swallowed the rich, smooth tequila, poured from a crystal decanter. "I'll have another after I finish torturing you, Pompeiicito."

"You two look like twins, not physically of course, but in a chinga tu madre kind of way." Xochiquetzal shook her head, laughing.

"You're right, they do," Floriana giggled. "I'm having a tequila, it's really smooth. Do you want one?"

"Okay, let's take it to the patio, I don't want to witness this muy macho moment."

———————

"How did we get here, Xochitzalita?" Javier grinned with drunken delight.

"Pompeii's flunkies literally carried you back, you should be proud."

"How did I get undressed, mi amor?"

"How do you think?" Xochiquetzal laughed.

"Did you abuse me this time?" He kept smiling.

"Of course, do you remember giving Floriana a fucking breast exam? For a lump supposedly. It definitely made her day."

"Were you jealous, dame tu boca...give me your mouth, mi amor, now."

"Go to sleep," she laughed. "I decided, then and there, that I had to get over your examining women, even if they were enjoying it, and she was definitely enjoying it. You're a physician, that's what you do."

"But tell me, were you jealous, mi orchid, tell me." Javier closed his eyes. The marvelous taste of that rare tequila soothed him. The stubborn song of the sea soothed him. Xochiquetzal's hands undressing him, soothed him. The sudden vision of their years together, soothed him. "Ayy pochita cabroncita Xochitzalita," he murmured happily.

"Do you remember giving Pompeii your cell number in case of emergency?"

"I think so, yes, but he has to come to me, I'm no drug doc ayy, the cabron got me drunk."

"And he says they're coming to San Miguel for Christmas, him and Floriana, she's staying in Mexico."

"Of course, he probably runs Immigration."

"And we all did the nakwach, ay Diosa, I don't know why but I like them. I just warned her to stay aware…"

"I want to torture you with my hands, my tongue, mi amor, I want you to beg me for an orgasm, el prescripcion." Javier reached for her, pulled her to him and licked her neck. "Qué sabrosita…How delicious," and passed out.

Xochiquetzal stayed awake listening to people singing, a couple fighting in the distance, a couple making love close by, the sweet, stubborn song of la mar. And she realized she was dazzled. With joy. With love. Javier's love of life. She licked his neck, his open mouth, his quivering eyelids. "Sabrosito."

"Javier, wake up, wake up, Javier, it's after 8 a.m.!"
"No me chingas, por favor, no," he moaned.
"Ai is waiting for us, Tequila King, get the fuck up!"
"Xochitzalita, mi amor, have some mercy."

———◆———

Ai was waiting with coffee, laughing at the sight of them, as Xochiquetzal led Javier toward her, los cafes fuertes. "Do you know how to drive?" she asked Ai. She shook her head yes, laughing, as in of course.

"If you drive the first lap, I'll drive the second, then el doctorcito borrachito...the drunken doctor... can take us to his friend's apartment in the D.F." Ai gave her a perplexed look. "Mexicans call Mexico City the D.F., as in Districto Federal." Ai smiled with understanding and mimicked herself driving, turning the wheel with effort.

"I need menudo, Celia, con limon, ay Dios my head is bursting." Javier reached into his vest's zippered, inner pocket for his stash of vitamins and aspirin, as Celia laughed. He pulled out a wad of pesos wrapped in a rubber band. "What the hell is this?" He held the pesos up like an offense.

Xochiquetzal took it and counted it. "3,000 pesos total, from Pompeii I'm guessing, for torturing him."

Celia served Javier a bowl of freshly made menudo with lime slices, and some hot tortillas in a covered basket. Javier bent his face over the hot menudo and breathed in his favorite fragrance after drinking too much. "Ay Celia, que bien, gracias."

"I'll take some tamales, Celia, gracias, I'm not suffering como tu hijo," Xochiquetzal laughed.

Javier took the 3,000 pesos from her hand, adding 3,000 more pesos from his wallet, and gave them to Celia. "This is por los niños, mama, for whatever they need. And here's my cell number in case of a drastic emergency. Even if I can't come, I can contact people to help you." Xochiquetzal added 2,000 more pesos, and Ai 1,000.

Celia couldn't talk as gratitude took her words, so she simply took him in her arms, and wept. Then she held the women in her arms, weeping until they laughed.

Everything was finally packed into the black Jetta, but people kept stopping them to shake their hands, changing their minds to hug them tightly. The small children clung to Javier's legs, and the older ones stood in a playful circle surrounding him. "Where's your sombrero, doctorcito, put it on for us," they joked.

"We're coming back, I promise, and next time longer." Javier couldn't stop his tears.

"El doctorcito loves us," a man laughed with joy. As Ai drove slowly away on the rutted, dirt road, swerving to miss potholes that would break an axle in half—they heard the first grito. Then the second, third, fourth; a chorus of gritos. Filled to the brim with joy, sorrow. Javier leaned out the window and gave the loudest grito of his life; so balanced between joy and sorrow, it wasn't quite human.

The chorus of gritos stopped, silence. They watched the car move away in the thick, red dust, and they waved back to el doctorcito who loved them. Then Xochiquetzal and Ai gave their very human gritos, one after the other, and the grito chorus began again. Laughter, waving, weeping, laughter, until there was only clouds of red dust filtering the Warrior in the Sun's golden arrows.

It was almost 3 p.m. when they arrived at Teotihuacan; after breakfast in the Zocalo and stopping to watch the immense group of Indian dancers. Ai had burst into tears at their beauty; their feather headdresses, exposed brown skin as they danced, their feverish smiles. Copal burned at the edges of their huge circle—north, south, west, east, and the very center. Where the drummers glistened with sweat in the Warrior's heartbeat, as his golden arrows pierced them. Their hearts.

"Vicente, is that you?" Javier laughed, recognizing one of his doctor friends from the hospital.

"Hey mestizo, why aren't you out here dancing in your tribal costume?" Vicente smiled, continuing to dance, sweat mixing with sprays of rainbow feathers.

"I don't know what tribe I am, cabron!" Javier howled with laughter, rejoicing in his friend's dancing. He was wearing his muppie hat, but also a black t-shirt, Xochiquetzal had bought him, with the Mayan Calendar in glowing gold.

"Estas Toltec, pendejo, look at your face, your eyes, no me chingas, Dr. Gomez!" And, with a laugh, Javier leaped into the mob of Indian dancers, next to Vicente. For a moment he wished he had a headdress, yes, like the Warrior in the Sun. Ai and Xochiquetzal watched as Javier's face became transfixed with joy. He stopped caring if he looked out of place in his jeans, as the golden arrows pierced him, Vicente, all the sweating dancers. The drummers caused their hearts to beat as one heart, as they danced to the pulsing heartbeat of the Sun.

"Dance with us, come on, mi pochita Yaqui, and you too la Japonesa Ai, come on, dance with us!" Javier shouted, followed by an ear shattering grito of sheer joy. Returned by a tidal wave of gritos. Joy.

"Come on, Ai, let's fucking dance," Xochiquetzal laughed, pulling her into the sweating, pulsating, ecstatic mandala of Indian dancers. Welcoming the Sixth World into their circle, Mexico, this continent, this planet, Earth. Dancing.

On the ride to Teotihuacan, the pyramids, they were tired, happy, silent, calming down from the Warrior's heartbeat. Now they stood at the bottom of the steep, stone steps that climbed the Pyramid of The Sun, and they all silently wondered if they had the energy to reach the top.

"Hey, I'm older than you guys so no complaints, to the top. Let's get a view of the Sixth World." Xochiquetzal looked at Ai. "And we're all going to make it." They began to climb, laughing. "You know, Vicente is right, Javier, you're a Toltec mixed with the Spaniard. You're a mestizo like me."

They climbed the steep, stone steps of the ancient home of the Sun, stopping to rest, drink water, and gaze at the Pyramid of The Moon in the distance. The November chill began to claim the air as the Warrior's arrows barely reached them; and it also gave them a boost of energy. To move.

"Okay, I admit it, I'm probably a Toltec, the people who built this place," Javier smiled, catching his breath. "And when those two Eagle Men dancers, all in black, those long black feathers growing out of their heads..."

"With eagle skulls on their staffs, amazing." Xochiquetzal interrupted him.

"When they got on both sides of you, mi amor, I thought I was going to have to become a Toltec warrior and fight for you," Javier laughed, pulling her to him.

Ai handed Xochiquetzal a note—*They gave you jolts of energy. I could see it shooting into you. I've seen surgeons do this with patients, and I bet you do it, Javier. They gave you a gift, mujer.*

She read it out loud, tears filling her throat. "Gracias, Ai, I felt it too, it actually made me dizzy yet filled with a weird strength."

"If anyone's going to shoot energy into you, it' me, Xochitzalita," Javier smiled at Ai, then fixed his eyes back on the horizon. The great Sun was mellowing as the Warrior put away his golden bow, arrows. One by one. "I know what you mean about surgeons, that energy. I think I've done that a few times, or I hope so, yes a gift."

"Let's get going to the top, no stopping, or we won't be able to see the Palace of Quetzalcoatl," Xochiquetzal coaxed.

"Or climb the Pyramid of The Moon, I think they kick you out at sunset, fregado," Javier sighed. "To not climb The Moon would be a sacrilege, so we have to."

Ai was already climbing, enjoying her body's strength. The flow of life that filled her. She wanted to tell her friends all this, but she'd promised to be silent. "For one whole year," she muttered. Silence, she told herself, silence, look at this extravagant, stunning, ancient beauty. Silence.

"Go Ai!" Xochiquetzal gave her a quick grito.

"I'm glad the Eagle Men gave you their jolts of energy, mi amor, but I'm still fucking jealous, so you'll have to make love to me with that extra energy."

"Estas malo, mi tigre," she laughed, licking his lips teasingly. "Come on, Ai's beating our asses."

"That woman's going to live to be one hundred and one, mark my words. She's sprinting, Dios mio!" Javier paused to give a quick grito to the horizon, then began leaping the steep stone steps trying to catch Ai.

As Ai reached the top of the Pyramid of the Sun, she wanted to send out a grito but her lungs were on fire. So she collapsed spread eagle, laughing, even though it hurt to laugh. Soon Javier joined her, then Xochiquetzal. All three on their backs watching immense, white clouds gather, float by, gather, as their lungs gathered breath.

"Do you see the gold outline of the clouds, barely perceptible..."

"I see it, yes, mi amor, stupendous." Javier got to his feet, pulling Xochiquetzal to hers. Then together they pulled Ai to her feet. They heard it at the same time. Silence. *Fifty-two centuries of silence* gathered in this place, outlined in gold. Light.

"Sacred," Ai had to say, sounding more like breath.

"This is why we got here so late, otherwise the crowds, yes sacred." Xochiquetzal took Ai's hand in hers.

Tears filled Javier's eyes—the horizon, the beauty, the memory of time. He took Xochiquetzal's hand in his, brought it to his lips, kissing it. "We all must make a wish in this sacred place, this time. We're here together at the same time, together, and there's a reason for that. Our separate paths brought us all here, Xochitzalita, Ai."

"You first, mi tigre." She saw the full, ripened sun reflected in the salt of his eyes. Tears. Falling. Slowly. Sun. Setting. Slowly. Beauty. Memory. Time. Salty. Tears.

Javier couldn't take his gaze from the Warrior's horizon—he

began. "I wish to be the kind of man Amaila saw in me, a true healer, el doctorcito, the one she loved. I wish to be the kind of man my mother sees in me—a man of strength who simply loves. I wish to be the kind of man my father's not." He paused as tears overwhelmed him, feeling Xochiquetzal's hand squeeze his. "A man who honors women, especially the woman he loves, that kind of true man. And I wish the same for my brother, Xavier."

He looked away from the Warrior's horizon to meet Xochiquetzal's eyes that wept. "I wish to love Xochitzalita for as long as she lets me, for as long as she allows me to love her wings."

Ai was openly weeping, sobbing, as the horizon welcomed her. Xochiquetzal's hand held her's tightly, and she was grateful, these friends. "I wish to let go of my anger, my sorrow, my grief." Her voice was soft, beautiful like song, raw with her truth. "I wish to transform grief into joy, death into life, life into birth." She held up a small, clear crystal to the ripened Warrior's Sun, and one golden arrow reached it, so slowly.

"I wish," Ai sobbed without shame, "to have children and to see my grandchildren born into the Sixth World, I wish." Javier and Xochiquetzal took Ai into their open arms, holding her close. "You will, you will," they echoed.

Finally, they separated, still holding hands, and the Warrior waited for Xochiquetzal at the edge of the horizon. She gently removed her hands from theirs and stepped forward, alone. "I have to do this by myself, I'm sorry," she said, facing the patient deep gold, bleeding-red Warrior.

"Te amo, mi orchid."

"I love you too." Ai took Javier's hand in hers, shyly; and he smiled at her like a brother.

"I wish to remember this moment, the man I love, who I've always loved, and this beautiful woman who feels like my daughter and my friend, this sacred place, this sacred moment. And Amalia, gracias for your gift to me, these golden earrings from your mother, from this man we both love. I wish that my beloved son, Justin, find a woman to love him as I love Javier, his undying soul. I wish to acknowledge the wisdom of my grandmother, Clara, her love for me—the desire and passion for life, my mother, Florinda, her love for me. To my French father, all the grandfathers, his sweet sperm that gave me life within my mother, his desire and passion for life, gracias. I wish to remember, to know this longing, this joy, fifty-two centuries from now, this moment, as we enter the Sixth World." She paused to breathe the chill, violet air.

"I wish to love and to be loved." Xochiquetzal raised her arms, weeping, "Father Sky"—and lowered them, "Mother Earth. Eagle and Snake, I wish to be your daughter. I love this life, gracias," she wept with sorrow's joy. She returned to Javier and Ai, holding their hands in the nakwach. They were silent as the Warrior descended into gold, purple, violet, blood red. Venus glittered in the west, as the waning full moon climbed the sky, still invisible to their eyes.

Ai took a small, white, tinged with purple, crystal from her shirt pocket and held it up. "I may as well speak, it's getting too dark for notes," she smiled, her face shone with fresh tears. "I have to find a spot for this crystal, a powerful spot, so help me find it." A clear, magnetic force pulled them, simultaneously, to the center of the Pyramid of The Sun, where it held up the sky. For fifty-two centuries.

Javier was on his knees. "Look," he pointed to a thin crack in stone.

"Perfect." Ai kneeled next to him.

"Will it fit?" Xochiquetzal wondered. Their voices barely pierced the silence. The ancient silence swallowed words.

Ai passed the crystal to Javier, Javier to Xochiquetzal, and back to Ai. Each one raised it to the slim wing on the horizon, the Warrior left glowing with gold and blood. "To the Sixth World," she sang, and they echoed her.

Then Ai placed the small, white, tinged with purple, crystal into the thin crack in the ancient stone, whispering, "To the Toltecs, their living spirits, take our small gift to the Sun." She felt the stone swallow the crystal; the clear sensation of it being taken from her fingers.

A quick, slim shadow ran, or flew, from the east to the west. Playful. Greeting. Toltec. Power.

"Did you see that?" Xochiquetzal breathed.

"Yes, the Energy Child sang, laughed, "yes."

The short, stocky caretaker waited for them as they climbed back down the Pyramid of The Sun. His skin and clothing were dark, so he blended with the gathering twilight. Usually he blew a piercing whistle to make stragglers descend, but every time he'd raised it to his lips, he'd lowered it. He'd liked Javier, his manner. Kindness. His wife would heat his meal, warm the tortillas, and his children would wait for the sound of his old, much patched, car. The distant sound of that struggling, loyal motor.

Gustavo smiled as they approached him; he could see the great Pyramid of The Sun had spoken to them. "I'm closing, amigo," he said in Spanish to Javier. "In fact, I should've closed an hour ago."

"Oh no, Quetzalcoatl's Palace, the Pyramid of The Moon," Xochiquetzal murmured, "but it is late, poor guy. And I didn't take one photo up there, not one."

"Yo soy Javier, and what's your name, amigo?"

"Gustavo, señor."

"Qué señor, call me Javier." He took his wallet out of his inner vest pocket, pulling out two five hundred peso bills, one thousand pesos. "Can we stay for one more hour, but only if it doesn't inconvenience you too much, Gustavo, if you can." Smiling, he held up the two bills.

"Get going," Gustavo laughed, "one hour."

"Gustavo, would you take our photo?" Xochiquetzal set the camera to flash, gauging the available light. "If you'd take two, gracias." And then Javier took a photo of Gustavo standing in the middle between Xochiquetzal and Ai, his arms around them, laughing. I'll stop and buy bottles of soda for the kids and cake for dessert, que bien, he smiled as they walked toward the Pyramid of The Moon. And maybe even flowers, roses, for my wife, Marta, it'll be good to see her smile, mi corazón.

By the time they climbed to the top of the Pyramid of The Moon, the still pregnant, golden, melon moon began to rise. "Of course we had to be here at this moment," Ai laughed softly. "We're right on time, look at that moon." And, for the first time, the full moon doesn't make me sad. That the dead are waiting to be born, as they should be.

Xochiquetzal began taking photos of the melon moon, of Ai and Javier, of Javier suddenly leaping in ecstasy, of Ai laughing like a child. Then Javier took a photo of Xochiquetzal dancing in the golden light. An ancient dance she couldn't remember, but her body did.

As the moon became translucent with light, they danced together, as though they knew exactly what to do, dance. Only the pregnant with light, waning melon moon watched. And the quick, slim shadow that flew from the west to the sleeping south, took note of their joy, before it disappeared into dreams.

They paused at the Jaguar Temple, but didn't go inside. Their hour was almost up, and they wanted to enter Quetzalcoatl's Temple. As they stared at the outer jaguar mural, they began to smile.

"I see it's muscles moving," Ai whispered.

"It wants to escape the mural," Javier added.

Xochiquetzal looked up to the sky. "And take a bite out of Venus. That's what my jaguar looks like, the one I always dream."

"I believe you, mi amor, these are Quetzalcoatl's jaguars. Now it's time to visit el jefe, Quetzalcotal."

"I've dreamt butterflies since a girl and these stylized butterflies remind me of the ones I've dreamt, who knows. But come on, our time's almost up." Ai started to walk. I was born on August 6th, the day of death. Of course I had to dream butterflies. She paused to place a small crystal, in a crack, at the entrance.

Quetzalcoatl's Palace was alive in moonlight. The stylized murals of Feathered Serpent, Quetzalcoatl, and the Rain God, Tlaloc, stood guard to the fearful, and welcomed the trusting. Moonlight shifted and followed them as they entered the two thousand year old temple; and it was as though their lives, their memories, vanished. Cleansed. Healed. This timelessness. The place of remembering, and the place of forgetting.

Ai felt their longing, their desire to merge with it. "I'm going to keep Gustavo company, maybe he has some tequila, so take your time," she whispered.

"You don't have to go, stay," Xochiquetzal whispered back. "Talking seems like a sin, doesn't it?"

"Don't talk, mi amor." Javier held her hand.

"I'll see you back with Gustavo." Ai turned toward the entry, unafraid of the dark, to be alone. And she saw a butterfly mural, with humans swimming and playing—These are the ones I've dreamt, *these butterflies.* Tomorrow I go to Oaxaca, Monte Alban, alone, Chiapas, the Isthmus, Vera Cruz, who knows where else, all my little crystals, all alone. Maybe I will go to their house in San Miguel in December, before I leave for the Pueblos, New Mexico—face it, I'm lonely. They've shown me, I'm lonely. For friends. For, be honest, love. She imagined them in an embrace, in the moonlight, under Quetzalcoatl's gaze. It didn't make her envious, but it did remind her of her own. Desires.

Transformation. Butterflies. Dreaming. Desire.

"Dreaming butterfly," Ai traced the ancient, faded wings, and placed a tiny crystal in the soft earth under her feet.

"Here, under Quetzalcoatl y el Tlaloc, I want you here, Xochitzalita, here," Javier moaned, entering her standing up. No gritos. Silence. Their ecstatic breath. The scent of life. The Gods remembered. Human pleasure, ecstasy. Desire. Quetzalcoatl's wings spread and slithered, and Tlaloc gave his moisture, his lightning, to their human dance.

As ripples of womb orgasms shot through her, the Eagle Men's eyes came to meet her. All in black, black with rainbow tinged feathers, staff of eagle skull, each one. As the radiance exploded behind Javier's eyes in the darkness; as his body memorized her body...the sound of one flute, one drum, soothed them for two thousand years.

"I marry you here, mi jaguar, look at the jaguars right there, dancing," Javier growled.

"Gustavo, it's me, la mujer con Javier, Ai."

"Si, la Japonesa," he smiled. "Where are the other two?"

"Tu sabes, el amor," she smiled back at him. I'm talking, she realized, I'm saying words out loud, not only in my mind. And the vow, que me chingas, she laughed.

Gustavo gave a soft grito, el amor, and laughed with her. Yes, tonight roses for mi corazón.

"Tienes tequila, Gustavo?"

"Y limon tambien...And limes too."

People continued to talk and laugh, drinking free juices, sodas, beers, wine, tequila and rum drinks. The woman behind them peacefully breast fed her baby, barely covering her breast, and the sound of the baby's urgent sucking reached them.

"It makes me want you, Xochitzalita, and I'm jealous de el bebe," Javier slowly traced her lips with his tongue. Making her womb clench deliciously. Making her wish she had that nourishing, warm, sensual milk.

"What a beautiful sound, that sweet sucking. I remember breast feeding Justin, but in public I had to cover my breast or people would become fucking offended. But I never hid, ever, I breast fed in the open, wherever I was when he got hungry. In a USA plane, she might be asked to go to the toilet..."

"Callate, you're making me jealous of Justin," he blew his breath into her. "I suppose that's why my visits to your country have been short, only twice about a month each time. If a mother can't breast feed her baby in so-called public, some spark plugs are missing from your national motor," Javier laughed.

The gorgeous Mexicana flight attendant appeared with a tequila in her hand, smiling. "From the gentleman," she pointed to a beaming, good-looking guy his own age.

"I see you're drinking tequila, amigo!" He lifted his glass in a toast as the USA/Mexico border drew near.

"Gracias, you read my mind!" Javier lifted his glass, laughing.

The older woman across from them offered them homemade chocolate cookies, urging them to take more than one. She made them Oaxaca style with cinnamon, chile, the darkest chocolate. "Gracias madre," Javier smiled, taking a bite of the rich chocolate, and chasing it with tequila. He gave a soft grito of pleasure and took another bite.

"This cookie is orgasmic, mama mia." Xochiquetzal watched the older woman offer Javier's tequila amigo some of the amazing cookies, and as he bit into one he did a grito. "I still can't believe we're on a plane going north, over the border, the USA, Taos, with you, mi tigre. And Ai in Oaxaca..."

"And she found that guy, Don Francisco..."

"The Mayan healer, you'll meet him when we go. Yeah, the email to The Wizard, as he calls his son, worked," she laughed. "He told Ai he's been dreaming us, and that he knew she was coming."

"And why does Don Francisco sound like he knows me, frankly it's a little weird, but then la vida is weird," Javier joined her laughter. "I fucking give up, mi amor."

"I really worry about you and that 'fucking' thing, doctorcito, and I guess we'll find out when we visit. Don Francisco is mysterious with no effort on his part, so there's no bullshit, I'm sure you'll like him. He seems to already like you, the mystery at work. And don't start saying 'bullshit,' I'm corrupting you, the nice Mexican muppie ayy."

"This is not corruption, mi amor, this is called trading our bad habits, and now you also have some of mine. Do you think I've lived in a bubble? I'm a slick muppie with a low tolerance for bullshit," he laughed and caught the attendant's eye, signaling for another shot of tequila. And then he sent one to his new amigo, and they lifted their shots in a salute and drank. The plane began to descend into Los

Angeles, as the pilot's voice welcomed them over the border in his sexy accent.

"I'm sure you know the USA planes aren't like Mexicana Airlines with free drinks and food. Be prepared to have tiny bags of peanuts tossed at you..."

"Give me your mouth, mi amor, callate." Javier took her breath, her words, in the sky that belonged to no one.

Xochiquetzal pushed him away, laughing. "And we go to different lines in Immigration, obviously. You to the Visitor, me to the citizen of my own fucking country."

"Callate, mi amor pochita."

"I'm serious, listen Javier, so I'll meet you at the start of baggage claim so you don't stand in the Immigration area. I've seen Mexicans questioned there, or you don't get lost."

"Amor, calling mi amor, I've traveled the world, remember? An upper class Mexican doctor at home on his own fucking planet, mi amor. Neither one of us will get lost, now kiss me, Xochitzalita mas locita."

She wanted to say, to warn him—They haven't seen many Mexicans like you, intact, whole, proud, kind. With no desire to come north, to leave your beloved country, *México lindo y querido.* No echoes in your mind, heart, spirit, soul, of *wetback, greaser, spic.* You are intact and they will sense it, Javiercito, mi amor, beware. But she didn't say it out loud; her eyes said it to his eyes.

"If you don't get lost, I won't get lost, Dr. Zapata," she murmured, kissing him. "México lindo y querido."

"You miss the pyramids, Quetzalcoatl's jaguars, Don Jose's cave, la mar, Celia, Dia de Los Muertos, mariachis singing till dawn, and of course the Golden Scorpion," he breathed into her mouth.

"I haven't found it yet, the mythic Golden Scorpion," she breathed back.

"You will, mi amor, you will." Javier held her close, keeping their mutual arm rest up, and the flight attendant only smiled as she passed by.

The plane touched down smoothly, over the border, and the old merchant, wanderer, shaman, Kokopelli, laughed. The idea of borders marring his ancient trade routes, he laughed. Kokopelli pulled out his beloved flute and began to play so beautifully, so sweetly, the birds wept.

Xochiquetzal's line was moving fast, but Javier's much slower—Torture the fucking visitor, especially from Mexico, she thought. It was her turn, so she handed her passport to the good looking black man.

"Business or pleasure?" His voice was neutral but his eyes sparkled.

"Definitely pleasure."

"I hear you," he laughed quietly.

"You're now free to move around the country." He handed her passport back. "Ms. Aguila, means 'eagle,' right?"

"Yep, means eagle, and the same goes for you, Officer Johnson. You're free to move around the country, enjoy la vida."

"Get outta here," he grinned, waving her off.

She tried to find Javier but couldn't see him in the line. Fear struck. Are they fucking questioning him? the thought flashed through her. Are they trying to make him feel like a fucking wetback, greaser, spic? Then she saw a woman with her five children—an infant in her arms, to a teen boy—sitting together on a long bench. Fear shadowed her face, and the teen looked like he wanted to run as he nervously checked the exit. There were two boxes at her feet tied with rope, some precious things, Xochiquetzal imagined. The woman felt her eyes on her and looked up—fear, despair—and looked away. She breathed in the woman's fear, despair, and breathed out, "Let them cross over the border, now."

She disobeyed her own instructions and waited in the Immigration area. One of the guards started to eye her, as in what are you doing lady. Just as he began to walk over, she heard it. A grito, but a civilized grito; not a blood-curdling one of sorrow/joy. Xochiquetzal walked quickly toward baggage and waited at the entrance. Waited for his beloved face, body, presence, to fill her eyes. And he did, smiling like the Mexican sun.

"Was that you, cabron, that grito?"

"It was the Custom's guy, his family is from Guadalajara, as mine is, so we started talking..."

"Don't talk, fucking kiss me, I was worried..."

"Callate." And he did kiss her, to a couple of low-pitched gritos. "I like Immigration, mi amor, let's do it again," Javier laughed, holding her close to him.

As they waited for the baggage to appear, Javier began talking to some young Mexican men. She watched him with joy, desire, joy—

He's so damned beautiful, me the old, beat-up jaguar. She sighed, then remembered the ancient, alive jaguar at the pyramids. Lighten up, take a bite of Venus. Her eyes fell upon a sign, warning travelers of huge fines for a list of items, including fruit.

The banana in my purse, my snack, my Mexican banana. And she remembered the Mexican woman with her five Mexican children, wondering where they were. Big deal, she told herself, I have a banana. Xochiquetzal pulled it out quickly, peeled it and began to bite and chew her Mexican banana.

"You are not allowed to eat anything in Custom's! Put the banana down!" the voice of Jehovah boomed over the loud speakers. She wanted to laugh, but she realized Jehovah might fine her a million USD for her Mexican banana. So she stuffed it in her mouth, as an over-weight, red-faced, white guy ran toward her.

"I told you to stop eating in this area!" he yelled, but failed to sound like Jehovah. The veins in his neck stood out and his eyes popped.

"The banana in question is now in neutral territory, my stomach, sir." Xochiquetzal met his eyes, feeling Javier's arm encircle her waist. Scattered Mexican giggles, just as the first luggage started to appear. Her tongue wanted to say 'fuck you,' but she sent the message, tonglen, to her brain.

"I could take you into custody for having that item in this area!" His face was

stroke-like, pulsing-red, rage. "But I will leave it as a warning!" He spun on his heel and clomped away. People struggled to not burst into gut-splitting laughter, their hands over their smiling Mexican mouths.

"I can't take this woman anywhere," Javier said in Spanish. Laughter. "And you're worried about me, Xochitzalita, you almost got thrown in jail. Was that pinche, Mexican banana good, cabroncita?" He hugged her to him as their luggage came into view.

"The best banana de mi vida, mi tigre, the very best platano de México lindo y querido," she laughed with the tinny echo of anger. Tonglen, she told herself, breathe in the fear of that family probably still sitting there or being questioned, and breathe out some hope. That they cross. Now. She'd tell Javier later, when they were safely on the road. Free of Immigration. The illusion of man-made borders.

Kokopelli continued to play his beloved flute for the weeping birds. Their ancient sky routes. Undisturbed. Wings. Instinct. Ancient.

Song.

The Energy Child sang, "México lindo y querido, si muero lejos de ti, que digan que estoy dormida, y que me traigan aqui....Beautiful and beloved Mexico, if I die far from you, tell them I'm sleeping, and bring me home again."

Kokopelli paused to listen, weeping. Then laughed as he played his beloved flute. To the freedom. Of the wind.

On the New Mexico border, that stretch of killing desert, a coyote abandoned a padlocked truck, filled to the brim with people. Their money in his pocket. Families with children, teenagers, young men and women. From all over Mexico, a few from Guatemala. They sat on patches of filthy carpet as the small ones slept or cried fitfully from the stale air, hunger. No food. And the water was almost gone. They waited for the engine to start. The coyote was able to relieve himself in the desert. They had two buckets with lids, almost full. The sound of a helicopter in the distance, as they waited for the coyote to return, start the motor, drive them to a better life. El otro lado...the other side.

The harsh desert wind made the truck sway slightly, and a woman began to sing, "México lindo y querido..."

Wings.   Instinct.   Ancient.   Song.

"How does it feel to drive in the USA, Dr. Zapata?" The red cliffs, horizons of mesas, afternoon vault of sky, welcomed her back. To her old home. To Pueblo country. It belonged to them, the Pueblo people. After all these centuries. It belonged them. This vault of sky, earth.

"Crazy Mexican drivers everywhere, feels like el otro lado," Javier laughed. "I feel like I'm riding tu amigo el caballo del viento...your friend the Windhorse, and the land is beautiful, mi amor."

"When I first moved here from Califas, I had to get used to the no speed limit and the muy loco drivers. To tell the truth, it freaked me out at first, coming from law abiding California." Xochiquetzal stroked his neck, his cheek, with her fingertips.

"And then you moved to México where the real locos live, que genio, mi amor," he laughed, lowering the window to give a shrill grito. The car next to them, with an older, white couple, sped away. Fear/disgust registered briefly on their faces—gone.

"Ride the Windhorse, do another grito, louder!" she laughed. And he did, even louder; that chilling balance of sorrow, joy.

This time the car next to them was filled with young Pueblo guys, and they honked their horn, gave a group yell back, and sped away laughing.

"I do love New Mexico where the Pueblo people and the Mexicans roam, you know like, Oh home on the range where the Pueblos and Mexicans range, grange, aren't strange, rooooaaaammmm wherever the fuck they want to." She fell back, laughing at the awful sound of her voice trying to sing.

"Estas locita, Xochitzalita, but I like it, the sound of your laughter, but what an awful song, mi amor, please don't sing it again," Javier laughed with her, shaking his head. "The sign says Santa Fe's coming up soon."

"We're driving straight to Taos, remember? We're staying at a great place, you'll love it, tigre. And Taos might have snow on the ground, as it keeps the snow when Santa Fe's melts. We'll stop in Santa Fe on the way back, but I want you to see Taos first, then the hot springs." Up ahead on the side of the highway, by the off-ramp, a lone, slim figure caught her eye, and grabbed her heart.

"Stop Javier, this guy up ahead, stop!"

"Why?" He glanced at her.

"He's pulling my heart and we should give him a ride."

"Should I be jealous, mi amor, this pulling tu corazón?" Javier began to slow down, pulling over.

"I think you know by now, as in the way Ai pulls my heart, mi tigre."

"I know, I know," he laughed softly. "Estas una bruja Yaqui... You're a Yaqui witch, but I love you anyway."

"You should talk, you and your Toltec self, I saw you dancing in the moonlight on the Pyramid of The Moon. And I even have photos, mi amor." Xochiquetzal rolled the window down. "Do you need a ride? We're going to Taos."

"Yup, that's where I'm goin', where I live. My jalopy's being fixed by some friends a mine, or at least that's what they keep tellin' me," he laughed dryly, revealing white teeth in a dark, appealing, warrior's face. A fierce face that battled for gentleness, with a direct gaze tempered by humor.

"Get in, amigo, we're at your service," Javier smiled. "I'm Javier de México and this is Xochitzalita from Taos."

"Actually California, but I lived in Taos for four years before moving to Mexico where I met this guy," she laughed.

"I'm Hank, like a hank a hair, beef jerky, stray songs, a hank a burnin' love that's me, Hank. Say your names again, por favor," he laughed that dry laugh.

"He's Javier and I'm Xochitzalita, try Shweetsalita."

"Cool name, Shweetsalita, does it mean anything? Sounds Indian to me."

"Brace yourself, it's from the Mayan Goddess of love and beauty, Xochiquetzal, Shweekwetsal. My friends call me Xochitzalita, but both are hard at first."

"I thought so, about the meanin,'" Hank half-smiled. "And does Javier mean anything, and where do you come from in old Mexico?"

"No, just a name given to me from my mother, amigo, we're from San Miguel de Allende in Guanajuato..."

"It's about the center, the heart of Mexico, in the mountains, about the same elevation as Santa Fe, seven thousand feet, only no snow. Are you a poet, Hank, the way you use words." She was turned around in her seat, smiling, and taking in his presence of contrasts. A man who's responsible for his shadow, and his light, she thought.

"Xochitzalita's a poet so she can spot them a mile away, that's why we stopped," Javier laughed. I like this guy, he realized, a solid human being. And around my age, a freshness of spirit. He beams salud, health, que bien.

Hank grinned. "Yup, I write some songs now and then and sing 'em too, but my favorite thing is this." He looked to the sky. "Clouds startin' to gather, some snow soon, count on it." He pulled a small, eagle bone flute out of his backpack. It was wrapped in a soft, deer-skin travel pouch and, when it emerged; a delicate eagle feather dangled toward the mouth piece, held with rainbow yarn. He gave a quick smile, warming it in his hands, and put it to his lips and played. He played the songs of the red cliffs bleeding with the Warrior in the Sun's arrows, the mesas praying for lighting, female rain, male rain, Thunder Being Sky, the marriage of Earth/Sky snow, the sacred Blue Lake...he saw wind rippling its surface...the Hopi Fire Clan, Eagle Clan, Bear Clan, Snake Clan, Parrot Clan, Spider Clan, Water Clan, Badger Clan, Pumpkin Clan, Bow Clan, Coyote Clan, blue-white-yellow-red corn, corn pollen offerings, harvest hunger, feast, drummers and singers entering the plaza, deer-men, buffalo-men, eagle-men, bear-men, sacred women and children, all dancing, heyokas smashing ripe, red-fleshed watermelons on Mother's fertile body, he played…(on his great-great-grandfather's eagle bone flute)…

Tears slid down Xochiquetzal's face—the beauty, the beauty of his song. Javier took her hand in his, squeezing it gently. And tears stung his eyes, surprising him. The beauty.

They reached Taos in the dream of the eagle-feathered, rainbow flute, and Hank took it from his lips.

"I could hear you play forever," she breathed, "gracias."

"I know you could, I could feel it from the both a you, so hey I kept on playin'. Could you drop me at the Pueblo, that's where I live." Hank slid the ancient eagle bone flute back into its deer hide pouch, tenderly, his child.

"Of course, so you live in Taos Pueblo, it's a beautiful place. We're staying close by in a casita, you should join us for dinner. You know, payment for the wonderful and free concert," she smiled.

"Nah, I can tell it's been a long day for ya, but hey tomorrow come by for coffee in the mornin'." They reached the entrance to the Pueblo, as the ancient adobe dwellings gathered darkness. "Meet me here, say 'bout 10am, give ya time to screw yer heads on straight," Hank laughed. "And hey, me too."

"Okay, amigo Kokopelli, see you here at 10am, but tomorrow you can join us for dinner." Javier met his gaze.

"You know 'bout Kokopelli, Javier de México?" Hank grinned.

"That guy's been playing his flute since time began, from South America to Alaska, como no."

"I didn't know you knew about Kokopelli, fucking A, that's surprising," Xochiquetzal laughed, both men joining her.

"She says 'fucking A' a lot, Hank, and now so do I, que fucking joder."

Hank did the half-smile as he slid out of the car. "I fuckin' love it." He walked to the entrance of the Pueblo and faced them. "Okay, tomorrow 10am, strong, hot coffee waitin' for ya and don't keep me waitin' in the snow. Sleep well, good dreams, and snow tonight, bet on it, hay-ya!" He waved once and was gone into the darkness of the Pueblo, where no electricity was allowed, as it's been for centuries.

"It really does look, feel, and smell, that dry snow smell, like it's going to snow tonight. I forgot to tell you about a woman with her five kids—from a baby she was holding, to a teenager—all sitting on a bench in Immigration. She looked so worried, Javier, I just hope they made it across, and they *flew* over the fucking border..."

"I saw them as well, but someone was talking to her, speaking Spanish to her, and she looked hopeful. I'm not just saying this, mi amor, it's true. But with five kids, I felt the moment as well, and the ones crossing with some pendejo coyote, ayy. Let's send them that tonglen energy, all of them, as they cross."

They sat silently for a full minute, breathing in, breathing out. Both imagining the woman, her five children, in Los Angeles with a welcoming relative. And the thousands crossing, always crossing, Kokopelli's ancient trade routes—they saw them arriving healthy and alive, ready to work. Ready to dance, *México lindo y querido...*

"Hey, that dry snow smell is getting sharper and the temperature is definitely dropping, do you smell it..." A sudden burst of tiny snowflakes exploded, like the pre-dawn fireworks in San Miguel, making them both laugh. "Suddenly I'm so excited, not tired anymore." She found a rock station and began to dance in her seat.

"Lovemaking energy, mi amor, save it for me," Javier smiled. "And I really like this Hank a burnin' love guy, a special feeling, spirit."

"He pulled my heart, como no, and now he's pulling yours. You know, I'm thinking why don't we stop for food and wine for our casita tonight, and there's a fireplace..."

"Amor, you read my fucking mind y mi corazón tambien."

The lights were on revealing the earth-toned adobe casita with its deep turquoise wooden door. Two large bouquets of bright, red chiles hung on both sides of the door. And over the door, an antlered, bleached skull, a la Georgia O'Keefe. It reminded her of the O'Keefe Museum in Santa Fe, and she made a mental note to take him, that beauty.

"I've seen photos of these adobe casitas, and Taos, the town. This is beautiful, Xochitzalita."

"Wait until tomorrow, the mesas, maybe even a blanket of snow like Hank said. Feel the temperature dropping? It might really snow." She danced in place for warmth. "Look at those stars, quick, before the clouds cover them!"

"Amor, open the fucking beautiful, turquoise door! Mis cajones are freezing and you don't want that to happen," Javier laughed. He had the luggage, she had the food. She slid the key into the lock, turning it once, and the door swung open. One rose-colored, stained glass lamp threw its circle of rose-light. Leather couch and chairs, hand-loomed rugs on the walls, floors, thick blankets strewn for warmth, and a thick, lush rug by the fireplace was covered with large, welcoming pillows.

"I stayed here for a month when I first arrived. Isn't it beautiful?"

"More than beautiful, perfecto, mi amor, perfecto, but still pretty cold, mis cajones."

"I'll start a fire for your sweet cajones, and you open the wine, our feast, Javiercito."

"And then the real feast, later, by the fire, perfecto, y mis cojones cantan 'gracias.' And gracias for bringing me here, mi amor, we are the lucky ones, the fortunate ones, in this life time." He grabbed her hand, pulling her to him. Kissing her with gratitude. With joy. The lucky ones. Who cross all borders. At will. Hank's flute was still full in his ears, as Kokopelli continued to play, to sing, to the wild birds. And all wild humans. Those who continued to migrate, south to north, north to south. West to east, east to west. At will.

Wings.   Instinct.   Ancient.   Song.

Xochiquetzal woke at almost 4 a.m., the fire down to red coals, still throwing out flickering waves of heat. The red coals became Taos Pueblo at sunset, one thousand years ago, as she dreamily stared. Javier's face was hidden by the thick, winter blanket, but she could see his thick, dark eyelashes, his eyelids. Flutter. With dreams. She uncovered his slightly open, tempting mouth, and softly, so softly, kissed it. He moaned and shifted.

The sea-foam scent of his semen comforted her, and her thighs were sticky con ternura, tenderness. His body's warmth enveloped her. "One, two, three," she whispered, and was on her knees adding two pieces of pine at the bottom, over the pulsing coals, and a large piece of oak on top.

As it burst into the warmth of flames, she wrapped herself around Javier's sea-foam body, and joined him in dreams, one thousand years ago, fire and ice. Snow.

"It's snowing, Xochitzalita, wake up, its snowing," Javier whispered into her right ear. "Wake up, mi amor, it's snowing."

She opened her eyes to slits. "What?"

"It's 9:05, Hank has el café fuerte and it's snowing, mi amor."

She wrapped the blanket around herself and limped to the window. Delicate, white butterfly wings flew to the earth without a pause. Fragile, enduring butterfly snow. "Pour us a sip of that cognac, tigre."

"Perfecto," he laughed, "a sip of cognac, the marriage of earth and sky, and us, perfecto."

Xochiquetzal reached for the pyramid photos she'd placed on the table, but they'd forgotten to look at them. Eating the feast, the earth-rich cabernet, the tenderness of love, had distracted them. "I can't get over this photo Gustavo took of us—you, me, Ai. The shadowy figures behind each of us, like dark ancestors..."

Javier took it from her hands. "All our lives gathered in that moment, that sacred place. There is no death, Xochitzalita," he smiled. "Look at that whiteness falling and it's so silent. I'm remembering the silence of snow, it's been a long time, mi amor." He sipped the smooth cognac, as the memory of skiing in Italy with Clara came to him. And he wished her well in that moment of silence; her, her husband, her child with him. His sorrow, anger, sorrow simply lifted, as the delicate, white butterflies fell to earth.

"The marriage of earth and sky, yes, it's always weirdly silent when it snows. I love this silence, like we're the only people alive on the planet," she smiled at the thought, and then remembered. "Hey, we'd better get dressed and over to Hank a burnin' love or he might not give us café fuerte." The cognac numbed her lips, filling her mouth with its essence.

"I love you, Javiercito, like the earth loves the sky." She pulled him into the blanket with her, weeping with the strange fullness of joy.

"Don't do that or we'll never get to that café fuerte, mi amor."

"Those photos of the three of us—I think, I feel, Ai is going to mean a lot to us both. Okay, I'm going to run and get dressed now, right now." Xochiquetzal screamed as Javier tried to hold onto her, leaving him alone in the blanket. "Get dressed, tigre, and no more cognac, but we'll take it with us."

The sight of the pure-white butterflies falling, flying, to earth, mesmerized him. He thought again of Italy, beautiful Clara laughing within the falling pure-white butterflies, the sudden feel of her in his arms; and, for the first time, sorrow/anger was replaced with gratitude. "I love you like the sky loves the earth, Xochitzalita," Javier murmured.

Hank was sitting on a wooden chair by the entrance, wearing a down jacket, a wool cap, worn jeans with thermals, and sturdy boots with wool socks. His face was to the sun, with the air of someone lying on a beach sun tanning. He waited until their car stopped to stand and stretch. The silence. The snow. My ancient home, always waiting, home, he thought as he half-smiled a welcome. The peace of the Pueblo in snow. The ancient peace, always waiting, home.

"Have you been waiting long? We were bad and slept in a little," Xochiquetzal walked up and hugged him. "I forgot how beautiful these mountains are in the snow."

"Nah, me'n the sun were having a few words. Ain't the snow a giant jewel, and there's more comin', bet on it."

"I talk to the Warrior in the Sun too, now that I know Xochitzalita," Javier laughed.

"You two look good together, yeah, a spirit connection, hay-ya. Okay, you two hungry lovers, follow me." Hank led them to his family's ancient, adobe casita, where a small fire greeted them. He added a piece of oak gently, making the child fire dance.

"This is my ancestral home, it belongs to my people. No electricity, no runnin' water as in plumbing, just peace. Whenever I leave, I return here first for a few days. Then I join the modern world with the house me and my friends built, hay-ya, TV, ster-eo, el web and hot showers," he chuckled.

"This is beautiful, Hank, I love it, so peaceful, the absence of electricity." Xochiquetzal took in the warmth of animal skins, a large conch shell on a side table, mural-like paintings on the walls, and one table covered with beads, gems, silver.

"Yup, electricity makes us humans jumpy, get rid of it'n we start ta chill out'n talkin' to the sun, Taiowa, the Creator. Even in my modern abode, I don't watch much TV, but I do listen ta music, yeah."

"It smells sweet like earth or wild flowers," Javier smiled, enjoying the unique beauty of Hank's home.

"That's the dry sage hangin' over there, smells good, don't it? Okay, my Mom cooked us a real-deal meal and brought it all over wrapped like mummies in tin foil. She'll meet ya later, she's Hopi and shy of strangers. My Dad, us Taos, more out goin' like lightnin', hay-ya!" Hank smiled and reached for a charred, metal coffee pot, banked in the glowing, child fire. "This'll wake ya up, been simmerin' in its grounds for awhile."

"Your Mom's Hopi? How did that happen, a nice mix Hopi and Taos. Hey, I'm a mix too, as in la Mexicana and French. My father from Paris, but I never knew him, a long sad story, so will spare you the details for now." Xochiquetzal smiled as she watched Hank pour the dark, potent liquid.

"I'm always one for a story, so anytime ya feel like tellin' it, Xochitzalita," he returned her smile. "Anyways, my Dad was a wanderer in his youth, a flute player who wormed his way in everywhere he went," Hank laughed, enjoying his family story. "He sold, bought, traded, and spotted my Mom in Hopi Land and lured her here. But my Mom and me spend time with the Hopi too, so we're back 'n forth, me and my Mom. The Hopi are her first people, so she's there at least half a the time, and I join up with her and my Clan there. The Fire, Blue Flute Clan, that is, from my Mom. Which is probably another reason why my Dad got her attention, playin' that sweet flute to her, hay-ya!"

"This is the best coffee, Hank, muy fuerte, strong." Javier did a restrained grito and Hank echoed it. "We even brought some cognac, want some?"

"Pour it on the side like a shot, my man, andale. I ain't heard a grito in a long ass time, since I was in Mexico, Baja, then to Acapulco, down that way. I took off after my Dad died, time to think..."

"I'm sorry, Hank, about your Dad." Xochiquetzal extended her clay cup for more café fuerte. "Por favor, it's really good stuff."

"He loved me, I loved him, he loved my Mom, he loved everyone and that's the truth. He taught me to play the flute, so he lives in my flute." The half-smile. "Time to unwrap the mummies, let's eat, and more a'that cognac, amigo." Hank threw his head back and did a proper grito, that perfect balance of sorrow/joy.

His love for his father is so honest, to hear him talk about his father, Javier sighed with slow sadness. I may never have that with my own father, and that's also honest, my truth. His disregard for my mother and Amalia, really all women. Yet he makes women beautiful to look at, como un Dios, that power. People die under my hands, some live, I'm no God, the thought came to him. And yet I love him, el cabron. Javier answered Hank's grito; that blend of sorrow/joy.

"What will your neighbors think of all these wild Mexican gritos, Hank?" Xochiquetzal laughed, giving a subdued one of her own.

"We should be hearin' some a their's 'bout now."

Xochiquetzal met his gentle gaze, which she also saw hid his fire. "I love that he lives in your flute, and I believe it. Your music is so beautiful. Oh, look at those tacitos...." She picked one up.

"Stuffed with spicy chicken, the beans with pork bits, scrambled eggs with stray veges, and my favorite, dried corn plumped back to life con la leche and spices. You can keep this corn for over two centuries and it'll spring right back to life with moisture. Well, the Mexicans knew that, the migration trail our people were on. Those borders are bullshit, and you look Indian, what tribe are you?" Hank asked Javier, then bit into half of his tacito, and a spoonful of corn, savoring it with his usual joy.

"Pues, the gathering evidence," Javier laughed, "is that I'm a chinga tu madre Toltec."

"Chinga tu madre, don't that mean fuck yer mama?"

"Don't waste your breath, Hank, it seems in Mexico 'chinga tu madre' is an endearment, a way of saying, 'I love ya like a brother, dude!' Ohmygoddess, this corn is total bliss!"

Hank quietly cracked up, that half-smile. "Well okay, so yer a chinga tu madre Toltec, hay-ya dude!"

"And I'm a chinga tu gato Yaqui, my people from Sonora, México," Xochiquetzal laughed, then put another spoonful of sweet, spicy corn into her mouth.

"A fuck the kitty Yaqui, hay-ya!"

"A mestiza, a mixed-blood of Yaqui, Spanish, hence the Mexicana, and French from my unknown, drive-by padrecito from France, hay-ya. And you must tell your Mom this meal is the real-deal, way too yummy. I could live on just this corn, give me more."

"You can tell her later, she'll love hearin' it, she's proud a her cookin'. Like I said, she's from the Fire Clan, which is why my flute has the eagle feathers on it, just a piece of Taiowa, Creator Sun. And my Dad's animal spirit was the eagle, so his feathers too." Hank's face darkened for a moment, then he half-smiled. "Us Hopi are matrilineal, from the Mama, so don't go sayin' that chinga tu madre stuff 'round her. She knows enough Spanish to figure that one out 'n she'll sure as shit brain ya," Hank laughed.

Xochiquetzal carefully held a large, exquisite, wooden flute with intricate, carved designs. A piece of long, thin fur was wrapped around its center.

"That's my Dad's ceremonial flute, ain't it a beauty? He carved it as a teen and wrapped it with his first rabbit fur, his first kill, his first meal for the family. He was an expert flute maker, carver." Hank walked slowly to the other side of the room, pausing to kneel and place another small piece of oak into the laughing, child fire. He returned cradling a wooden carving like an infant, alive. He handed it, with obvious care, to Javier, saying, "So what d'ya think, Toltec?"

Javier took the carving with both of his hands, feeling its weight. "Puessss..." he extended the word, "it looks suspiciously like Kokopelli with a chinga los cojones male member." He laughed and executed a grito of admiration. "This guy is hung."

"I'll say," Xochiquetzal giggled. "Can only men hold him?"

"Nah, ya'll get yer turn, Yaqui girl," Hank smiled playfully. "To us Hopi, he's Kokopilau with his hump of seeds, la vida, probably dried corn too, wanderin' and playin' his sun-warmin' flute, lurin' the fertile women as he goes. Sounds like my Dad in his bad ass youth..."

"But not this well endowed, or I hope not, for your mom's sake," Xochiquetzal laughed. "Sorry, but as a woman it had to be said."

"Everything's sacred, nothin's sacred, that's our brand a humor, yeah all us Indians, so speak yer mind, Yaqui spirit woman, hay-ya!"

"He's beautiful and very sexy tambien," Xochiquetzal smiled at Javier. He blazed the look into her eyes, and she blazed it back. He softly stroked the long, erect penis; then the hump full of fertility.

"Medically, he'd be in big trouble with one this size, but mythically I'm jealous," Javier smiled.

"Javier's a doctor, so naturally he has to consider both sides. I want to hold Kokopilau, come on, share."

"I felt that healin' energy from ya, a doc, and I bet a good one, yeah."

"He might take you from me, Xochitzalita." Javier stood up to hand her Kokopilau.

"Here, give me my Dad's flute 'n I'll play ya a cloud gatherin', snow gatherin' song. Not as good as him, nah, but okay." Hank gently took his father's sacred flute from Xochiquetzal's hands and began caressing it, heating it, with his hands.

As Javier gave her the sexy Kokopilau, he grazed her inner lips with his tongue, sending little jolts of lightning to her womb. "Don't fall in love, mi amor, cabroncita."

Hank put the flute to his lips, sounding a note; short, long, short, long. He did this with each round opening his father had carved as a teen, until each one came to life. Breath. "In Hopi, *huiksi* is the Breath of Life." He gazed at the dancing child fire as he began, then followed the path of sunlight to the window. The Warrior in the Sun—or as the Hopi called the Creator, Taiowa—aimed his slender, pale-gold arrows, one by one, to meet Hank's song. Breath. His father's sacred flute, as the clouds gathered. Snow.

Kokopilau played his flute, an echo to Hank's weeping, singing, laughing flute. He smiled as he remembered his endless journeys from fire/south to ice/north, the ancient trade routes. He watched Xochiquetzal cradle his image—The beauty of women, their sweet moisture and ecstasy, their dark wombs full of life, their cries of joy, he thought with longing. And he added his ancient, always new, desire to the gathering clouds, snow. Breath.

Wings.   Instinct.   Ancient.   Song.

The final note was high and sharp; an eagle's cry as he played in the wind. Hank held his father's flute in silence for a few moments, gazing at the child fire's embers. The child had grown old and was now resting before it became pure smoke, memory. Before it entered the womb and was coaxed to life again. Chispa...spark. Breath. Life.

Hank felt his father's boyhood spirit, his first kill, the tender rabbit, in his hands. His father's undying song. Breath.

"Do you mind if I take a photo, this moment is so beautiful," Xochiquetzal whispered in the silence.

"Sure, that's okay, but not my father's flute." Hank reached for his eagle bone flute, placing his father's flute down safely. "You can't take photos outside, of the Pueblo, but inside it's okay, Yaqui girl." The half-smile.

"She's una doctora de los fotos, photography, so she can't help herself, amigo." Javier understood exactly why she reached for her camera, this moment. Hank had delivered them to sacred time, this place. Beauty. Breath.

Hank held his eagle bone flute in his hands, caressing it, greeting it (his great-great grandfather). "So, yer a Yaqui woman spirit of vision, hay-ya! Hurry up, take my photo, and then I'll take yours, you and lover boy, el Toltec doctor."

"You look wonderful, Hank," Xochiquetzal said as she worked. "Do you mind if I take a few of tu casita, inside, as well?"

"Knock yerself out, woman spirit of vision, and there's a Hopi name for you, tuawta, meanin' 'vision, one who sees the magic,' hay-ya!"

"Say it again and you'll have to write it down for me, I love that name."

"Tuawta. Okay, my turn, and I want you two to hold Kokopilau between you. That he may grant you years of erections, you know great sex." Hank laughed very softly. "And that your journeys be full of seeds, dried corn, scattered life on this planet of ours. And that we become good friends, north to south, south to north, the old trade routes."

"Are you sure Kokopilau won't lure her away from me with his obvious magic? I can't compete with this medical marvel," Javier smiled into the camera.

"Hey, where's your Taos, easy-goin' accent, Hank a burnin' love?" Xochiquetzal laughed, keeping her fingertips on Kokopilau's enormous penis. Full of semen, potency. His rounded hump full of seeds, fertility. A true Creator—male and female—as Quetzalcoatl was, is, she realized.

"You caught me, Tuawta, this is my chinga tu perrito teacher's voice. I use it when I teach, can't have my kids talkin' like no easy-goin', flute playin', wanderin' Taos hick," Hank laughed at himself. "Or should I say, easy-going, flute playing, wandering, Taos-Hopi hick teacher."

"What do you teach, and don't cheat, stay in your teacher's voice, I want to hear Hank a *burning* love teacher." Xochiquetzal smiled into the camera as Javier kissed the back of her neck, then licked it for good measure.

"I teach high school history, from an Indian point of view, as few lies as possible. And some art, as in jewelry making, some painting, and I sneak in flute playin'," Hank grinned. "But I haven't taught since my father passed on, spirit at large, so I've been out wandering, playing my flute, making my jewelry, selling it, and sometimes playin' in a band. Floatin', healin', makin' love ta beautiful women here 'n there. Like my man, Kokopilau, a Taos-Hopi hick can't complain, hay-ya!"

"Put El Koko down, mi amor, I want un besito without someone's penis between us."

"Ay Diosa, you're jealous of Koko..."

"No, but I'm getting some extra energy from him, like the black Quetzalcoatls gave to you, mi amor."

Hank captured the kiss. "Hey, I can leave you two here for a while and come back," he laughed.

"This guy's way over-sexed." Xochiquetzal pushed him away playfully.

"We just met, Hank, and I had to talk her into it, no dignity for Dr. Gomez, hay-ya!"

She ran to the door and flung it open to fresh snow. No footprints. The ancient Pueblo looked brand-new covered with Taiowa's gold and silver, blinding, glittering arrows. "Oh, look at this beauty!" Tears came to her eyes. These mountains, Sangre de Cristo, covered in snow, I've missed this beauty.

"Go ahead, Tuawta, take a few shots but make it quick, hay-ya the beauty! Here's a Hopi name for this beauty, like a snowy white owl's wing...masawistiwa, means 'wing spreading over earth.'" Hank put his eagle flute to his mouth and played a song to the snowy white owl's wing spreading over the earth, masawistiwa.

Wings.   Instinct.   Ancient.   Song.

"Here's the dishes, Mom, it was the best as usual, hay-ya!"

"Hay-ya yourself and you ate it all, good." She smiled shyly at Javier and Xochiquetzal, but her eyes revealed her spirit. Sky-root strength, and earth-brown joy.

"Mom, this is Javier, a doctor from Mexico, and his love interest, Xochitzalita, a photographer, woman of vision. I just named her Tuawta..."

"One who sees magic, good name for her, and what about the doc?"

"You can name him," Hank laughed.

"Okay you two, you can call me Joy, closest to my Hopi name, and I don't want you calling me Hank's Mom." She laughed and began to cough. Paused, caught her breath. "You two have a spirit connection, it jumps right out."

"That's what I told them, didn't I?"

"He did, right away, kind of surprised me, but I think you know your son is unpredictable," Xochiquetzal shot a smile at Hank. "And thank you for that yummy breakfast, Joy, ayy those tacitos tan sabrositos. And the corn, I could truly live on that stuff."

"Gracias madre, everything hit the spot, and that corn is magical. In fact, Hank and I arm wrestled for the last of it." Javier took Xochiquetzal into his arms, placing her in front of him, smelling her scent.

"I'll give you some double-bagged so you can smuggle some over the old trade route, the damn border," Joy glowered for a moment, then sighed.

"And they're always makin' out," Hank teased. "I let them hold Kokopilau, the one I carved."

"And by the way, you don't have to tell me about this guy, Hototo, he's been this way from birth. We had him later, in our forties, so he had to entertain us old folks." Joy gave her son a smile of pure love and play. And she coughed again, a bit longer.

"What does Hototo mean?" Xochiquetzal asked. "Sorry to be nosey but he told us his name is Hank a burnin' love," she laughed.

"Oh yes, he's that too but his real name's Hototo, means Spirit Warrior Who Sings. In his case, with the flute, like his Dad." Sorrow filled her eyes briefly, a cloud that swept her sky-root strength; but the sorrow in her heart was permanent. Their great love, undying. Sorrow/joy. She remembered his touch, his scent. Undying. Another coughing bout, pause, breath.

"Madre, do you mind if I listen to your lungs? Do you cough that way often and does it hurt to cough, to breathe?"

"She won't go to the clinic, I've even tried to kidnap her there, but she's pretty stubborn and sneaky too, just won't go," Hank groaned.

"Go ahead, listen, I like your eyes, doc. The docs at the clinic have eyes like starving wolves, greedy..." Joy began to cough.

"Don't talk, madre, just nod. Does it hurt to cough?"

Joy nodded, yes.

"Where?"

She pointed to her chest.

"And to breathe?"

Yes, the chest again.

"Would you take off your sweater, madre? Good, that's good." Javier placed his right ear directly to her back, bending her forward slightly. "Breathe in and out, slowly, yes, good, breathe."

He listened for awhile and in the silence her breath filled the room. It's rhythm, the slight struggle, her desire for air.

"Okay, breathe in as deeply as you can four times, madre."

She began to cough.

Javier sat up and faced her, taking her hand in his. "Your lungs are congested, madre, you need to go in for a chest x-ray and get a firm diagnosis. My guess is that you need antibiotics to clear something up in your lungs, but first you need a chest x-ray and a lung capacity test. Also, have them test you for allergies as allergies can trigger coughing. You don't smoke, I hope."

"That's one bad habit I don't have," Joy smiled.

"Good, that's good, now do you promise to go to the clinic for this check-up?" Javier continued to hold her hand.

"I wish you were my doc, damn!"

"Me too," he smiled into her eyes, "but a Mexican doctor can't practice in this country."

"You aren't in the USA now, hijo, you're on Taos Land." Joy returned his smile.

"Hay-ya, that's the truth." Hank did a little dance step. "I wrote down everything you said, doc, *for the clinic visit.*" He stared these words into his mother's stubborn eyes, then had to laugh.

"In Mexico he travels with his doc bag, giving check-ups as he goes. But trying to cross the border with it, Joy, he'd be in jail. I almost got tossed in jail for eating a Mexican banana in baggage." They all laughed at the absurdity, the notion. A dangerous Mexican banana.

"It's true, she told the Customs guy the Mexican banana was safely in her stomach, neutral territory, la cabroncita."

"Hay-ya!" Hank added an exuberant grito and a few more dance steps.

"How safe is it down there with all the talk on TV about drug lords and kidnappings," Joy asked.

"I live in San Miguel de Allende where families are out walking at night, buying ice creams, tacos, food from the street vendors. The central plaza is full of families and teenagers lookin' for love, as Hank would say," Xochiquetzal smiled. "Kids play in the street after dark, women walk in groups or alone at midnight, and there's always something going on at the plaza. Students reciting wonderful poetry, puppet shows for the kids, live bands and dancing, mariachis, fire eaters, drummers, Indian dancers from all over Mexico like the Pueblo dancers here. I feel so much safer in San Miguel than in this country, our cities. Of course, I'm not speaking of Taos Land," she laughed.

"I think you can tell I love San Miguel, and once you leave the border towns there are these kinds of havens, the smaller towns. But, in truth, I'm wary of Mexico City which is about three hours away from San Miguel, where there are kidnappings and robberies. It's the largest city in the world with lots of poor folks, hay-ya. Excuse my lecture, Joy..."

"She was a professor, still is," Javier quietly laughed, "but I still love her, la professora de los fotos."

"No, no, I was there walking in the plaza, sounds lovely," Joy smiled with pleasure.

"I'll send you some photos of San Miguel to Hank via la web, or do you have an email address and I can send them directly to you."

"No, just send them to Hototo, I'd love that."

"Okay, madre, back to business. Do you promise to go to the clinic?" Javier met Joy's eyes.

"Okay, okay, I promise." Joy paused, eyeing Javier with her direct eagle gaze that she used when she needed to see something just as it was. Head slightly tilted, eyes on target. Nothing personal. The truth. "I promise to go to the clinic. Huiksi, means Breath of Life."

"This is the mesa I used to walk every sunrise and sunset, these cliffs, my old friends. Do you see the face there, framed by the snow? I used to come and pray, chant out loud, and I never felt lonely here." Tears filled Xochiquetzal's eyes; then they fell naturally as female rain.

"I see the face, Xochitzalita," Javier whispered, "que hermosa, how beautiful."

"I see the Spirit, hay-ya," Hototo breathed. "We're all welcome here. This sacred land, it's all Taos Land, and, yes, we're never lonely here." He reached over to touch her tears, smiling. "Your tears are welcome here, but you know that, Tuawta."

"Hey, that's my job," Javier joked, but it did take him by surprise. To see another man touch her face. Road kill, he smiled.

"I know, I used to come here and cry quite a bit," Xochiquetzal smiled, still weeping. "This place just opens my heart, the truth. If I ever moved back, it would be here. But something tells me I'm staying in Mexico..."

"Hay-ya," Javier murmured, putting his arms around her.

There was such a luminosity in Hototo's face as he gazed at the Spirit's face, and she remembered Don Francisco's light in the plaza. "You know, in fact I'm sure you know, about the Mayan Calendar ending on December 21, 2012, the upcoming Pueblo Fifth World..."

"And the Mayan Sixth World, oh yeah, I teach it as part of our true ancestor stories, the ancient trade route stories of all the people on this continent. The no lies or bullshit version of so-called American History," Hototo half-smiled. "We're already doing ritual, kiva time, both here and in Hopi Land. We've already begun the journey of transformation into the Fifth World here, so now for the rest of our planet. And I know the southern part of our continent is doing their part of the transformation, the tribes."

"Hay-ya, yes, y gracias for sharing that with us, Hank a burnin' love," Xochiquetzal laughed softly. His sheer presence makes me happy, like Justin, mi hijo, she thought. And Javier, mi amorado, I've truly memorized him, every cell. Look at those eyes gazing at me, oh fucking road kill.

"You'll both have to come when it gets closer to 12/21/12, when the Solstice Sun, Taiowa, makes love to the center, the womb, of the Milky Way. Happens every 26,000 years, what a pregnancy, hay-ya, the unfolding of human Spirit." The Spirit in the cliff began to sing high, so sweet, like the wind. "Sorry, my turn to be el professor. I can get permission for you to be present at some of the ceremonies, but not all, you understand. You'll be the few non-Hopi people, if you come, and you can't use your camera."

"We'll come, Hototo, gracias, amigo!" Javier clasped his shoulder. "Why don't you join us for Christmas or longer?" He glanced at Xochiquetzal for support.

Join us, the words resounded in her ears—But he's right, join us. "Of course, I understand about the camera. It would be an honor to just be present, if it's okay. And absolutely, yes, come join us, it'll be a blast. My son, Justin, is also coming and he's thirty. How old are you, if you don't mind my asking that is."

"Thirty one goin' on thirteen, can't lie ta' ya, and I'll be there probably by bus. See the land, then fly back like an eagle." Hototo gave an eagle cry that circled the cliffs and returned to them. "I think ya saw the eagle in my Mom's eyes, her fire clan, where the eagle keeps its nest, and my Dad was an eagle, is an eagle. This tiny eagle feather's pretty old, belonged to my Dad, but it still flies." He took the eagle bone flute from its deer-skin travel pouch, and began caressing it, warming it with his hands. The small, delicate eagle feather—hinged at the lip—dangled in the wind, and the larger ones waited within the dark-womb pouch to cradle it.

"I also play with the Flute Clan at rituals, and you'll probably see, hear, when you come to Hopi Land, hay-ya, a piece of my spirit with you two on this perfect day. And when we all play together, my Flute Clan, you'll realize how sad it is to hear only me." The secret, half smile. "Next time we meet in Mexico..."

"Aren't you going to meet us for breakfast tomorrow in town, hang out, damn, Hank a burnin' love. And, yes, I saw the eagle in your Mom's eyes, that beautiful, scary strength. Reminds me of my grandmother, her eagle eyes." She paused to remember those eyes— Mamacita, Joy. "But you know, I didn't notice that little eagle feather before, so sweet, and it does fly. Oh look, those steaks of red on the horizon," Xochiquetzal pointed to the changing sky.

"The Warrior in the Sun, the Mexican Sun of my people, buenas noches, Sol Mexicana!" Javier gave a perfect grito—joy and sorrow, married. Sky and Earth, married. Flesh and blood, married. Past, present, future—married. The Spirit, the cliff, married. Life and death, my surgeries, always married, he thought. The imperfect doctorcito, me.

Hototo threw his head back and did his own perfect grito, laughing softly. "I can't tomorrow, too much goin' on, catchin' up, but I'm comin' at Christmas, stayin' till you evict my ass. And I'm comin' to eat with ya tonight, my favorite place in town, you'll love it. And here's a couple of gifts, made by Hank a burnin' gems." He reached into the flute pouch for two small, black, velvet pouches. Dangle, fire opal earrings for Tuawta, and a large turquoise ring for Huiksi, with a raised eagle, wings spread.

"Opals are my birth stone, these are beyond beautiful, Hototo!"

"And an eagle in the turquoise, this is too rare, we should pay you for your work, amigo."

"And insult me, chinga tu abuelita, no fuckin' way." He blazed his words into their eyes, then gently smiled. "Yeah, look at that deepening red, there it is, palatala, red light of sunset." Hototo put his eagle flute to his laughing lips and played—to the sacred, red light of sunset, palatala, to Taiowa always shining somewhere on the spinning Earth, to the Pueblo Fifth World, to the Mayan Sixth World, he played. He played so sweetly, Kokopilau sat down on a large, red rock to simply listen, remembering every world there ever was. And ever will be.

(The Energy Child joined Kokopilau in the ancient memories, but it was the human memories that were lost, forever. The memory of this flute would be lost, in time, and s/he wept for that loss, in time. S/he waited for the firing, the bonding of his/her human brain. Maybe this time, maybe.)

Hototo lowered his flute and listened to the pure silence, broken only by night birds. Soon the owl would hunt. He slid the eagle flute into its deer-skin travel pouch, the waiting mother feathers, and as usual he heard his great-great-grandfather's flute sigh.

"Bring your eagle flute to San Miguel, please. That was so exquisite, gracias. You can play on my roof..."

"On *our roof,* Xochitzalita."

"This guy's trying to live with me," she smiled, rolling her eyes.

"I think he is." Hototo half-smiled at both of them, and then he grabbed their hands in a nakwach. Xochiquetzal grabbed Javier's hand, completing the circle.

"HAY-YA!" they all shouted, with all the longing and desire they could muster. To Venus, holding her glittering place in the darkening, slashed by purple, sky. Then they collapsed into laughter, and tears, holding on to each other.

"Okay, calm down," Hototo wiped his eyes. "Tomorrow at dawn, and you have to get up at pre-dawn for this, look for the first, sweet flash of red, talawva. And look for Talawsohu, the Morning Star."

"Quetzalcoatl," Xochiquetzal had to say.

"Yeah, I think they're related," Hototo smiled with happiness. "We'll do the whole dawn ritual on your mutual roof in San Miguel, and I'll bring the eagle bone flute for sure. And I'll hide it in case the border folks think it's some kind a terrorist secret weapon, like Tuawta's Mexican banana. I love ya, dudes, chinga tu perro y tu gato tambien!" He laughed briefly, then whispered, "Hay-ya." He took a small pouch from his shirt pocket. "Here, take this for the sunrise tomorrow morning, and don't forget you have to be up and ready at *pre-dawn*, love birds, so no sleepin' in. It's sacred corn pollen, so bless each other exactly when you see the first, sweet flash of red, talawva. Sprinkle it over each other's crown chakra, the open door, kopavi, and you will be born with the sacred Creator Sun, Taiowa, together."

Hototo placed the small pouch into Xochiquetzal's hand, squeezing it. "Hay-ya," she and Javier whispered at the same time, taking hold of their friend's hands for one more nakwach.

"We pray that Saquasohuh, the Blue Star Kachina, never, ever, dances in the plaza, we pray, Taiowa." Hototo's voice was suddenly sad, and it was rarely sad.

"Why should the Blue Star Kachina never dance in the plaza?

And I can't pronounce the Hopi name, sorry, it sounds so beautiful like poetry," Xochiquetzal asked, as the glowing, crescent moon took its place next to now blazing Venus.

"It would mean destruction of this place, this continent, as the Hopi Prophecies warn of a terrible, atomic war, World War Three. In the Prophecies it's a warning to us all on this continent, the world at large, this beautiful, blue-green, spinning planet we all live on. As we enter the Fifth, Sixth Worlds, hay-ya." Hototo almost chanted the information in a low, sad voice. "And so, we pray that the beautiful, far away, Saquasohuh, Blue Star Kachina, never, ever, dances in the plaza, we pray."

Javier felt a strange energy travel his spine as he held the nakwach with Xochiquetzal and Hototo. "We pray," he echoed.

"Yes, we pray as we transform into the Fifth, Sixth Words, we pray." Xochiquetzal thought of Ai, the bombing of Hiroshima, Nagasaki; her journey around the world planting her clear, white crystals of peace. "No Blue Star Kachina, ever again," she breathed out softly. For Ai.

Wings.   Instinct.   Ancient.   Song.

"Are we sleeping here again, mi amor?"

"I think so cause I can't leave this fucking fire, but you can go to the comfy feather bed with fluffy quilts."

Javier pulled her to himself possessively, deliciously, burying his face in her neck, as they both faced the blooming fire. "No way, cabroncita, you're stuck with me cause I can't leave the fucking fire either."

"I love it when you say 'fucking' in your Toltec accent."

"I love it when we fuck in any language." He licked her neck delicately; a tiger tasting for freshness, tenderness.

"Everyone knew Hank in that restaurant. He's like the chingado mayor and he loves it."

"The guy is definitely a ham when he gets in the spotlight," Javier laughed.

"Like you, Dr. Zapata, you just didn't have your sombrero." Xochiquetzal smiled at the memory of his gorgeousness in Zapata's sombrero. I've memorized this man, she realized suddenly, like lightning on the mesa. He's alive in me no matter what happens—he lives in me.

"And how he played the guitar with that hermosa chica, a nice duet, como no."

"You can bet she's at his modern home at this very moment. I think I love that guy, Hototo, alias Hank a burnin' love, and I hope Joy is okay."

"More than me, cabroncita? We'll know after her full check-up, and Hototo is keeping me informed via email." The question was habit, he knew the truth. Con esta mujer, no soy solo...With this woman, I'm not lonely.

"I'll have to think about that and get back to you..."

"Xochitzalita, mi amor, no te haces mala, and why do you taste so good?" He pulled her hips closer, holding them firmly, gently. He entered her warmth that bloomed hotter than any fire. They made love simply, directly, in the realm of very young lovers. Tenderly.

Javier... *Look, the Blue Star Kachina is so beautiful, look. A glowing, Blue Star dancing in the distance. Look. Everyone I love is here, look. We're all in danger, look, look. Xochitzalita takes my hand, the nakwach, and we look away from the beautiful Blue Star. We look into each other's eyes, and I say, "Tell me, mi amor, tell me."*

"There is no death."

And we refuse to look at the dazzling, beautiful Blue Star Kachina, dancing. Far away but visible. We refuse. To look.

"Wake up, it's pre-dawn, wake up, Javier, or we'll miss it."

"What?" he groaned, reaching for her. "Come back to bed, it's still dark."

"Remember *talawva*, the red light of dawn, get up now, Javier."

"Qué me chingas, okay, okay."

Xochiquetzal laughed as he stumbled to his feet, naked. He's so beautiful, completely beautiful, first thing in the morning. Not like the decrepit, old jaguar, me, ayy Diosa and fuck.

"Do I smell café fuerte, mi amor?"

"Put your clothes on and I'll pour you some. We're going out on the patio when we see talawva, so unless you want to freeze tus huevitos get dressed."

"Qué me chingas, but I still love you, ayy café fuerte, por favor," he begged.

The Warrior in the Sun began to glow on the horizon. Just a

feeble glow against the frozen snow. Then his first golden arrow reached them.

"Come on, outside, I have the corn pollen, and put down your coffee."

"Not el café, Xochitzalita."

"We'll have more later, Javier, put it down, come on." She dragged him out to the freezing patio. "The only thing missing is Hototo's eagle flute. I bet the entire dawn ritual is amazing, can't wait. Okay, watch for the first red light of dawn."

"If I don't freeze to death..."

"There is no death."

"You said that in a dream last night, as we refused to look at the Blue Star Kachina dancing, and what a beautiful star. I see it, Xochitzalita, look, *talawva*, look."

"There it is, the red light of dawn. Take off your wool cap so I can sprinkle your open door, kopavi."

"I don't want to open my door, I am fucking freezing, mi amor."

"Take it off, okay I will," she smiled, kissing him briefly. She poured the silky corn pollen into her hand and said, "I have memorized you, I love you, you live in me, Javiercito, no matter what happens, you live in me." She sprinkled the sacred corn pollen over the crown of his head, dissolving—the open door, kopavi.

He took the small pouch and carefully poured some corn pollen into his hand. "It's so delicate," he murmured. His warm breath, little clouds, in the frozen air amused him. Only for this woman do I stand here, freezing, without café fuerte in my hands. The red light of dawn began to pulse into the Warrior in the Sun, rising.

"Your eyes connect me to the earth, to my life, Xochitzalita, and with you I'm not lonely. I need you, I want you, like breath, y te amo siempre jamas...I love you always and forever." He slowly released the molecules of sacred corn pollen over the crown of her head, dissolving. The open door, kopavi.

"Kopavi," the Energy Child sang with longing, "Kopavi, the open door."

"Tonight Ojo Caliente and you're going to love that water, tigre. I just wish we could say goodbye to Hototo, better yet take him with us."

"We'll take him to La Gruta when he comes to San Miguel..."

"Are you nervous to meet mi hijo, Justin, tell the truth."

"With you I always tell the truth, que fregado, I do. Just a little maybe, but I bet we go out drinking like hermanos y amigos," Javier laughed, seeing Xochiquetal's slight frown of disapproval.

"Just don't bring back any live mariachi bands or try to climb that fucking tree again, and don't get my son in jail under Napoleonic law..."

"I'm just kidding you, Xochitzalita mi amor, estoy jugando...I'm playing." He pulled her to him on the Taos sidewalk and kissed her. Silence. No gritos. A few stares.

She pulled away, keeping hold of his warm hand in the cold morning air. "We aren't in Mexico, we might get fined."

"For kissing, que barbaro...how barbaric."

"Just kidding, but notice not a grito, and where's your gloves anyway?"

"You're keeping me warm and I think they're back in the car. Right now I need café fuerte con huevos rancheros, mi amor."

"Hey, don't I know you?" someone yelled. "Hey!" A tall Indian guy was standing by a large, black moving van with MIGRATIONS painted in bright yellow across it width.

Xochiquetzal squinted her eyes—a gesture that made her memory clearer—and the word *Hector* came to her. The Canadian Indian, Hector, his Guatemalan friend, Manuel, the Goodwill truck.

He walked toward her, grinning ear to ear. "You're that lady going to Mexico for her vision quest, am I right?"

"Hi Hector, yeah it's me, Xochiquetzal, and what are you doing with MIGRATIONS?" she laughed. "Oh Hector, this is Javier visiting from Mexico."

"Welcome brother, I'm a visitor too," Hector laughed, offering his hand. Javier shook it, smiled, and gave a quick glance to Xochiquetzal as in, Who is this guy?

"Hector came with his friend, Manuel, from the Goodwill, and liberated me from all my worldly possessions, hay-ya!" she laughed. "What's with MIGRATIONS and where's your Guatemalan amigo?"

"Don't worry, I ain't smuggling illegal aliens over the border. It's a moving van, my own little business. You know, migrations, like the old trade routes, that unbroken treaty, man," he cracked himself up. "And the illegal dude, Manuel, now works as a chef here in Taos, and the dude is good."

"So Manuel and his family are doing okay, the furniture helped?"

"Oh yeah, and he's even learning some English. He's a pretty smart guy and a great cook, excuse me, chef. He gets pissed off if you call him a cook," Hector laughed.

"And you have your own moving business, very cool, I love that name, the old trade routes, yeah." She smiled at Javier and he returned it...their current migration together. "Tell Manuel el chef, I said hola, that's hi, and that I'm still on that vision quest. And it looks like I'm sharing it with this guy, Javier."

"Hey, thanks for those dreams you sent, Xochiquetzal, they helped, hay-ya," Hector laughed, grabbing her for a bear-hug, then Javier.

"Do you want to join us for breakfast?" Javier asked, enjoying this large, laughing, generous man.

"Nah, already ate but gracias como no, amigo. I have a moving schedule today, folks movin' far away. You ever moving back, just let me know, I'll come get ya, both a ya, Xochiquetzal. Good ta meet ya, Javier, keep migratin'!" He walked toward the van, then turned. "Send me more dreams!"

"Any requests?" Xochiquetzal laughed.

"Somethin' with eagles, yeah eagles!" Hector climbed into MIGRATIONS, turned on the rumbling motor, laughed, waved, and drove away singing loudly to the radio.

"I never thought I'd say this, mi amor, but I love your Frida blouse today. All the bright, flores Mexicana here in the snow, under your leather jacket."

She smiled with pleasure. "México lindo y querido. I think you're missing your country, and a pochita like me can remind you. I'm going to remind you someday that you loved my Frida outfit in Taos," she laughed. "And you continue to look like uno hermoso muppie, always at home on his planet, tigre."

Javier kissed her again in the middle of the sidewalk, no gritos. Some stares. Then they continued the short walk to the restaurant.

"This place has good huevos rancheros, good homemade salsa, and hot tortillas in a basket..."

"Will you really send Hector eagle dreams, and of course I want huevos rancheros y mas café fuerte tambien." Javier gave a quick, joyful grito; y como un milagro...and like a miracle, someone answered him.

"Maybe it's Hector," Xochiquetzal laughed as Javier opened the heavy wooden door to the restaurant.

"Or maybe the eagles. Ay café fuerte, por favor, y tortillas caliente."

"We're almost to Ojo Caliente. You'll turn left at the sign, so slow down right here. We're entering the village and we're almost at the sign for the hot springs, can't wait." Xochiquetzal did a loud, quick grito.

"Sangre de Cristo, the red blood is everywhere the snow isn't sparkling. The mesas, the ravines, the rocks covered in el sangre. I can see why you lived here, Xochitzalita."

"Okay, you're going to turn left now. Down this road, over the bridge, yeah, and park right ahead. I bet it's going to snow tonight, Hototo's right, I can smell it, Huiksi."

"I can't remember your name, mi amor, tell me." Javier parked the car, letting the motor idle for warmth.

"Tuawta, One Who sees Magic, I guess that's me," she smiled. "I like it even better than Profesora Aguila, although I can't imagine my students calling me One Who Sees Magic. And your name, Breath of Life, it's you Dr. Zapata. Joy *saw* you, that's for sure, and I hope she's okay. What a sweet woman and strong too, talk about an eagle."

"Hank also gave me her phone number, so I'm calling her to make sure she goes to the clinic with him. He thought if I goose her, as he put it, it'll help him get her there," Javier smiled, leaning into her mouth. "Give me your mouth, Tuawta." And she did. She gave him her mouth. In the silence of the snow. That marriage. Earth. Sky.

They opened the cabin door to a large, comfortable room, warmth. "Isn't this nice, tigre, a little kitchen for our treats. I've stayed in these cabins for a week, hey even a small stove. I'll put the wine in the frig, so are you hungry?"

"Los huevos rancheros were good, maybe some wine, cheese, bread, mi amor. And you?"

"Okay, sounds good, open a bottle. The woman at the desk liked you, tigre." Xochiquetzal began slicing the cheese, opening a package of ham.

"I'm charming, what can I say?" Javier smiled into her eyes, as he pulled the cork from the bottle of cabernet. "But my bedside manner is only for you, Xochitzalita."

"Ohmygoddess, you are so fucking corny," she laughed. "But women do like you, from young to old"—like me, she thought—"and you know that, Dr. Cabron."

"No te haces mala...Don't be bad, mi amor. Men like you too and I wouldn't have it any other way, cabrona."

"Like your now friend, Pablo, right, chinga tu puppy."

"Callate." Javier kissed her, the breath of life into her. Into him. "Let's eat, pochita, and get to the water." He poured the wine.

"There's different pools, *you'll* see. You're going to be a noodle tonight, no sexo for you," she teased.

"It'll energize me, mi amor, you'll see. We've only been together for two months, I can't help myself. Older woman, younger man, and I want you."

"We'll see, these waters are pretty intense, Dr. Zapata."

Javier changed into his trunks as he gulped the last of the wine. He started to put on his warm clothing over them.

"Wait, I have a surprise." Xochiquetzal found the gold glitter in her purse and walked over to him. "Just a little bit, not too much, so I can find you in the dark, mi amor."

He laughed as she rolled the gold glitter across his cheeks, forehead (the dream eye), chest, a bit on his arms and legs. "Will they throw me out of the pools, Xochitzalita?"

"I'm wearing some too, hay-ya, it's just glitter to find each other in the fucking dark," she laughed. "You know, right now in those trunks, you look exactly like the day I met you."

"Two months ago, older woman, younger man—only now I'm glittering. Do you mind if I go ahead, mi amor?"

"No, in fact it's a good idea to see it for yourself the first time. I did, so go on. I'll be there in ten minutes or so."

Xochiquetzal found Javier in the upper pool facing the dramatic, red cliffs. Her favorite pool. He was talking to two young women in Spanish and, catching sight of her, waved her over.

"Amor, these women are from Barcelona, come and meet them."

Barcelona, where Clara is from, she thought, walking slowly toward them. And they're gorgeous, of course.

"Ana, Sara, this is Xochitzalita, mi amor." Javier beamed his love to her and the old, bitter jaguar gave up and slunk away.

"Mucho gusto," they both said, smiling, but she saw it. A trace of envy.

As Xochiquetzal lowered herself into the delicious, hot, mineral water, she reminded herself how open Javier was to Hank's friendship. Inviting him for Christmas. Pompeii, Hector, and even finally making friends with the dreaded, outrageous Pablo (his twin in outrageousness). Breathe and relax, she told herself. And this tempered their envy; the competition of younger women with older women for the gene pool. And a handsome gene pool, she smiled back at them, entering his open arms. "Mucho gusto."

They began talking about Barcelona, the beautiful places in Spain. The beautiful places in Mexico, where they wanted to travel next.

Xochiquetzal surprised herself by saying, "Javier, I'm going to swim before our massages. There's the clock," she pointed to it, "so in twenty minutes be at the desk where you got your towels." She kissed him briefly, licking his inner lips, glancing at the women. Envy.

"I'll join you in a few minutes, swimming sounds good, mi amor."

"Or I'll see you at the desk in twenty minutes." As she walked away, bundled in her thick towel, she resisted the urge to look back. If he prefers younger women, anyone else for that matter, I'd rather know it now. A sleek, muscled jaguar led the way and Xochiquetzal growled under her breath. This is called trust, she told herself. Without trust, no love. Or a false love, which I no longer want. "Trust," she murmured. And confidence in my own damned self, finally at fifty-eight. She smiled. Her secret smile.

As she swam laps in the warm pool, clouds gathered shielding the Warrior in the Sun. Silence. Only the sound of gliding through mineral-silk water. A couple in the hot pool behind her spoke quietly, laughing intimately. How beautiful, how peaceful, this place is. I've missed it, just coming by myself to soak and swim for a few days. The red cliffs, the sacred silence. And the friends I've also brought with me, now mi tigre, Javier. I can see him smiling, talking, laughing with Ana and Sara, let him.

Trust, trust, trust, her hands parted the water as she swam. "Beauty above me, beauty below me, beauty behind me, beauty in front of me, beauty all around me." Words, weeping, swimming, trust. "Beauty inside me, trust." Each whispered phrase was one complete breast stroke, pushing her forward. Into beauty. Trust.

Javier looked at the large clock bolted to the wall—five more minutes. He felt strange in the sudden freedom Xochiquetzal had left him in con las dos hermosas, de Barcelona, chicas. From Barcelona, la Clara. In the past, I'd choose one, focus on her, straight to bed. I like them both, but they're overly impressed that I'm a physician, and didn't I always use that to my advantage, ay que cabron, he smiled. His secret smile.

"It's time for my massage, but perhaps Xochitzalita and I will meet you for dinner if we're not in bed by then."

"Ah yes, we understand," Ana laughed. "The gold glitter couple."

Javier almost corrected her by saying, I mean sleeping, but he realized they wouldn't be sleeping if he could help it. And he felt strangely lonely. Without his equal. La feminista, mi amor, he thought as he climbed out of the hot pool.

"If you get hungry, we'll be at dinner around seven, a bottle or two de vino, and the food is good here," Sara smiled seductively. But his eyes continued to convey only friendship.

"I'll ask Xochitzalita, but if not tonight, tomorrow…"

"We leave tomorrow at noon." Ana pouted playfully, thinking, Nothing works with this guy, and she's obviously older. Attractive but definitely older.

"Have fun, chicas, if not dinner, see you in the morning, I'm freezing." Javier ran for the door, his towel wrapped tightly against the gathering clouds.

"Amor, I missed you and I'm not kidding." He opened his towel to include her and she let out a small scream.

"You're wet and freezing and I'm glad you missed me," Xochiquetzal laughed, kissing him quickly. The older woman at the towel desk looked away, smiling. "Exchange that frozen towel for a dry, warm one or you'll catch a cold, Dr. Zapata." The woman handed Javier a dry, warm towel without him asking for it.

Javier handed her the wet one, "Gracias, señora." And sighed with the pleasure of the dry, warmed on the heater towel. "We've been invited to join Ana and Sara for dinner, if we feel like it, mi amor. They leave tomorrow at noon…"

A good looking, blonde, younger man came out and called Xochiquetzal's name, trying hard to pronounce it. And then, an older, dark-haired woman came out and called Javier's name, saying it perfectly.

"Do you want to switch therapists, same sex, it's up to you," the woman at the desk offered.

Xochiquetzal glanced at Javier, seeing he was about to say yes. "No, I actually like opposite sex therapists. See you at the pool after, tigre, enjoy."

"Ay cabroncita, mi amor," he murmured into her ear.

And she walked toward Eric with a smile. "I've been here before, I used to live in Taos."

"Do you like your massage soft, medium or hard?" Eric waited for her to walk ahead, smiling with his usual charm.

The women looked at Javier, waiting for him to greet his therapist. "Senora, I'm from Mexico and I'm enjoying this beautiful place. Lead the way, I'm yours."

"Bienvenido a New Mexico, Javier, and I'm Miranda. How long has it been since your last massage?" She led him down the hall as he peeked into open doors for a glimpse of Xochiquetzal.

"About ten years ago in Tokyo, so I'm overdue." Javier followed her into a small room with soft flute music playing. He imagined Xochiquetzal stretched out nude, under the gringo's hands, and for two seconds he wanted to find her and haul her out. Grow up, he told himself, grow up, breathe, breathe, breathe, breathe.

"Trust," he murmured. "Trust."

"How was your massage, tigre?"

Javier opened his eyes to half-slits, taking in her relaxed face. The thick clouds hid twilight and the slicing air dipped into the low thirties. Tiny flurries of snow drifted into the hot pool, melting. Merging. "I've had the pool to myself for the past forty-five minutes. I thought our massages were for an hour, but yours was almost two hours. Mine was a marvelous one hour massage, que paso...what happened?"

"Eric extended it and I sure didn't say 'stop.' I tipped him extra, so worth every cent. I love this place, tigre, I'm in fucking heaven..."

"Was it more than a fucking massage?" Javier hated himself for saying it, but he had to know—Forty-five extra minutes doing what, he fumed.

"I left you with Ana and Sara from Barcelona. I chose to trust you. I thought of you with Hank, crazy Pompeii, even making friends with Pablo. So I told myself to stop being an old, bitter jaguar. You know, me at fifty-eight, you at thirty-four. Time to trust you and, most importantly, myself." Xochiquetzal wanted to weep but it felt like such an old response; she was tired of weeping. As an apology for who she was; those kind of tears, the bitter ones. She stayed on the opposite side of the pool from Javier, facing the sacred, red cliffs.

I can be alone, she told herself, yet it's true, you will always live in me. No tears. Instead, delicate white snowflakes wept to earth, stone. Silence. Each one in their own mind. Their own heart. Their own body. Weeping, laughing, merging, delicate starflakes, falling. Flying. Into silence.

(Kopavi. The Energy Child's brain ignited, caught fire. The delicate, white starflakes. The journey of the human mind, human memory. The ancient journey, the human journey. The Bering Strait, the glacier wall. The opening. Crossing. Into this continent. Kopavi, the open door. The mind on fire. "Trust," s/he sang to the flying ice. "Kopavi.")

"This is why I can't live with anyone again, but I've memorized you, Javier, I love you, I can't lie, I love you."

"It's time for me to grow up, Xochitzalita," Javier whispered.

"I didn't hear you."

He met her eyes. "I said it's time for me to grow up, to stop wanting everything my own fucking way, ultimately my own ER doc way. I'm sorry, Xochitzalita, I'm sorry I didn't trust you, mi amor." Tears filled his eyes; a new response, sadness.

The snow was thicker, falling faster, covering them like pollen. She swam toward him. He opened his arms. She entered the warmth of his arms. He held the warmth. Of their trust. Sheltered in icy pollen. Trust.

A low cry, spread of white wing, gliding from snowy cliffs. Swooping, silent Snow Owl. Masawistiwa, wing spreading over earth. Wing spreading over their heads, over their lives. Trust. Masawistiwa.

"Huiksi, give me your breath." She covered his mouth with hers, breathing.

"I still can't remember your Hopi name, mi amor."

"Tuawta."

"You see the magic," he wept, breathing into her. Breathing. Into her.

"I'm sorry we're late, but hey we're here." Xochiquetzal smiled at Ana and Sara.

"No problem, we have wine and we just started eating. In fact, in Barcelona dinner starts at 10 p.m., but they stop serving at 10 p.m. here. Isn't that right, about Barcelona, Javier?" Ana poured a tongue-rich cabernet into their waiting glasses.

Javier glanced at Xochiquetzal, squeezing her hand. "Ay, es la verdad...It's the truth. And when we travel to Barcelona, mi amor, we'll eat at the proper hour. Until midnight, then go dancing till dawn, right Xochitzalita?" He spoke Spanish as Ana and Sara had a hard time grasping everything in English. In conversation. They spoke English well for the basics, their travel needs. They spoke French and Italian better than English; so Spanish it was.

"I've been to Barcelona once, with my son, Justin, when he was a teen. So, yes, it's time to go back and dance till dawn." She smiled at the memory of traveling with Justin; their endless jokes, play, punctuated with a few fights. Standing up to her, becoming himself at sixteen. She spoke Spanish slowly, carefully, trying not to bungle her first language.

"Javier is from Mexico, but he forgot to tell us where you're from." Sara's eyes lingered on Javier's, smiling. "And a teenage son, how wonderful." I knew she was older, la vieja.

"I'm from California and Spanish was my first language, but I was punished for speaking it in school. They don't teach foreign languages to the young here, which they should. Kids learn languages so quickly, so truly a tragic waste. My son, Justin, learned Spanish from the beginning, private teachers, so his Spanish is pretty good."

Javier brought her hand to his mouth, kissing it. "But I'm teaching her to speak it fluently again, mi amor," he said directly into eyes. "Her understanding is perfect," he looked back at Ana and Sara.

"Qué barbaro...How barbaric, they actually punished you for speaking Spanish. In Spain you learn French, Italian and English in the primary grades. Yes, the little ones don't have any barriers to any human language. Your Spanish will improve with Javier's help, I'm sure, " Ana laughed, letting go of her envy. She has kind, strong eyes, I like her, she thought. I hope I have her pizzazz in my forties, and a handsome, younger lover.

"How old is your son now?" Sara had to know. Ana kicked her under the table, shooting her a shut up glance.

"Xochitzalita is a photographer, una doctora de fotografia, and a wonderful poeta as well. Her son and I are the same age, exactly." Javier stared the information into Sara's eyes. Sara's mouth dropped open, and Ana burst into gut-splitting laughter.

"Do you mind tonin' it down a notch or two, *people are eatin' here*," a red-faced man with a Texas drawl announced. Then he turned back to his wife, the other couple, who backed him up with their dirtiest looks of disgust.

"Sir, we are having a conversation with a little laughter. Surely that can't be a disturbance to your meal, or anyone else's," Javier responded evenly, calmly. Edged with respectful warning. Dr. Zapata reined in.

"Wetbacks think they can come here and change the damn language of this country," the other man said with that Texas drawl, loudly. Smiling. Enjoying himself, showing off what a patriot he was. In comparison to a *wetback*. Javier's beautiful accent, warming the English language.

"They wade the Reeo Grandee and think they own the place," his dyed-blonde wife laughed.

Xochiquetzal walked over before Javier could stop her. "What did you say, exactly what did you say? This man you're referring to is a Mexican physician, a doctor, *visiting* from Mexico, and he has *no desire* to live here."

"Well, that explains it, a real *doctor* from Mexico," the first man laughed.

Javier stood next to her, holding onto her, but she jerked away.

"You fucking ignorant cow fuckers can kiss my California ass!" Xochiquetzal picked up the pitcher of water and drenched them. Two large waiters ran over, both Mexican.

"Call the police!" one of the women yelled.

"This is an outrage!" the other woman joined her, wiping water from her overly-done eyes.

"You goddamn spic bitch!" The second man stood up and suddenly began to choke on the extra rare steak he'd been chewing. He doubled over as his air was withheld, choking.

Javier glanced at the steak knife in case this didn't work; to quickly cut a hole into his windpipe. He grabbed him from behind and with three, quick, firm jolts, the steak flew, landing in the center of the table.

The Mexican waiters looked at each other, one muttering, "Qué joder, el gringo cabron de Texas."

"Gracias, doctor, gracias," the other one said, putting his large hand on Javier's shoulder.

"What's this graceeass shit, call the damn cops!" the first man yelled.

"You're very lucky, señor, that we don't ask you to leave at this moment," the waiter replied in heavily accented English. He leaned into him for emphasis. "You should be thanking el doctor for his services, señor."

"I could've done that!" his wife screamed shrilly.

"Please leave the dining area," the other waiter ordered, "or I will call the sheriff to remove you."

"We'll be checking out this minute and get the hell to Santa Fe!" the first man boomed, as they quickly filed out. The second man still struggled for breath, allowing his wife to lead him.

"They speak Spanish in Santa Fe too, amigo!" a diner called out. Laughter.

"And we'll be contacting the manager!" the first man's wife hissed, bringing up the rear.

"That would be la Senora González," one of the waiters called after her.

"Qué barbaro la gente...What barbaric people," Ana said in disbelief. "Mas vino, por favor!" she raised her glass to the smiling waiters.

"Amor, I'm impressed, la jaguar in action," Javier laughed.

Xochiquetzal burst into tears. "They called you a *wetback*, you, a wetback, those fucking scumbags! You've never been called a wetback or a spic in your entire life, I'm so sorry, I'm so sorry..."

"Hey, there's a first time for everything, mi amor tan amazon, mi mujer." He kissed her tears, laughing softly. "I think you love me, Xochitzalita."

"De la casa...On the house." The waiter began to open the best cabernet they had to offer. He poured each glass full as tears stung his eyes, wetback.

Sara yelled like a grito, lifting her glass, "Qué viva!" Then everyone—the other diners, mostly white—joined in, "Qué viva!"

The two Mexican waiters gave a spine-tingling grito, sorrow/joy; and Javier answered them. While Kokopilau danced back and forth over the border, laughing.

Xochiquetzal woke up moaning—Javier was inside her, deep inside her, holding her from behind. "Little jaguar, mi amor, little jaguar, mi amor," he sang, holding her so close their skins merged.

Their souls danced, merged.

"Ay tigre," she wept as her womb rippled with orgasms. Why did my womb wait so long for this, these orgasms, at fifty-eight, why...

(The Energy Child's genitals pulsed with wonder, and s/he waited for a miracle—"Orgasm.")

"Let's get up for the pollen ritual, red light at dawn, *talawva*, I'm probably saying it wrong. We passed out last night, that's for sure, too much fucking excitement. Except for when you woke me up, tigre, que dulce," she licked his lips. "But I must admit, I thoroughly enjoyed emptying that pitcher of water on them," Xochiquetzal smiled.

"You're my little jaguar, mi amor, but do we have to get up?" Javier growled deep in his throat and closed his eyes.

"We can go back to sleep, have a late breakfast, soak in the pools. We don't have a schedule and we should get up in a few minutes to see it, talawva." She paused, trying to find the right words. "I have memories of being called wetback, spic, greaser, dirty Indian, me and my beautiful, dignified grandmother. When she picked me up at school, the kids of course saw she was an Indian, and of course I had to fight them." Tears filled her eyes as she saw her grandmother's face, the small stones she picked up to throw at them, yelling, "Ninos malo...Bad children!" And they'd run away laughing; later she'd fight the leaders, mostly boys, making them cry.

"Did you really fight them, little jaguar, don't answer, of course you did," he laughed.

"And they were mostly boys, the ones I fought, beat up. I made them cry, punching them right in the face." She smiled in the darkness as she nuzzled his sweet, brown shoulder and stroked his breathing chest. "Okay, I love that no one ever called you such names growing up, Javier. You're so..." Pause. "...intact."

"Amor, I'm still intact. I know who I am—I'm a Mexican at home on his own planet." Javier kissed her wet eyes. "And so are you, little jaguar, at home on your own planet, intact. When you called them cow fuckers, que cabroncita, mi amor. I think you punched them right in the face, little jaguar."

"I don't know where cow fuckers came from, but hey it worked," she laughed. "I love your confidence, your doctorcito confidence, from that first day in Bucerias. I was a little scared of it, I have to admit, that doc/God confidence. I guess I've always equated that kind of confidence with male, God-like arrogance. So I avoided guys like you, the truth."

"I almost had to break down your door, Xochitzalita, and I would have…"

"Come on, the red light of dawn is coming, I'll get the pollen." She dragged the naked, unblemished Javier to his feet, facing him. "Do you see me as intact, tigre?" She became a small girl facing him—the girl who had been called wetback, spic, greaser, dirty Indian.

"You are my equal, little jaguar, and with you I'm not lonely. Amalia's last words to me, at sixteen, were to find you. The woman who would guide me to the Warrior in the Sun, and you have, mi amor. Now let's go meet, how do you say it?"

"Talawva, the red light of dawn…"

"Two intact human beings in the red light of dawn, talawva," Javier smiled, kissing her lightly, sweetly.

"Okay, I'm going to stop crying so we can greet the dawn properly. Hototo said there's more lights to the dawn and that he'll show them to us in San Miguel. But talawva, the red light of dawn, announces the fully formed human being. I guess that's us, tigre. Two intact, wetback humans, yes, that's us." Xochiquetzal's tears slid down her face unselfconsciously, as she held the small pouch of sacred corn pollen in her hand, lifting it slightly in the warming air of the wall heater.

"I love it when you cry, mi amor, it means you love me, and now you also know who you are, the little jaguar. Look, the sky is changing!" They quickly bundled up against the ice, stepping out onto the wooden porch, as the first, thin red light of dawn was born. The fragile sliver of a waxing, virgin, almost half-crescent, moon trembled before the Warrior in the Sun; but she held her place, trembling. Translucent.

Xochiquetzal poured the delicate pollen into the center of her palm, cupping it gently. "Why don't you start this time, tigre."

It took him by surprise to be first, but he began. "To all the intact humans on our planet, like Hototo who gave us this great gift, hay-ya. And to you, little jaguar, hay-ya otra vez." He opened his palm over her open door, *kopavi*, as the first, pale-gold arrow reached them.

"For the first time in my life, I feel truly intact, whole, at home in my skin, in this world, with you, Javiercito," she wept. "Yes, to Hototo, to Ai, to mi hijo Justin, Don Francisco, Amalia, my mother Florinda, Clara mi Mamacita, Clara your old love, your mother…these people

I love and know, all those I don't know but that you love." Then she remembered. "What about your twin, Xavier, tigre?" Xochiquetzal opened her palm over his open door, kopavi, as two golden arrows reached them.

Tears stung Javier's eyes, but he refused to let them live. "I love Xavier, I always have, I always will. Amalia told me stories about the Sacred Twins to understand him better, and myself better. We're both necessary, twins, that balance. I can't explain, Xochitzalita, her stories told the truth of our lives as twins much more deeply."

Javier looked at his empty palm and tiny specks of pollen still lingered. He lifted his palm to the Warrior in the Sun—"To my older brother, my twin, born seconds before me from our mother's womb, Xavier." The pain of loving. His tears were born. The joy of loving.

"To your twin, Xavier, hay-ya," she echoed, entering the warmth of his arms.

"Kopavi kopavi kopavi," the Energy Child sang to the warrior in the Sun. Her/his mind on fire, the taste of pollen from brain to tongue. S/he sang, "Kopavi."

Wings.   Instinct.   Ancient.   Song.

"I'm glad we checked our email in Santa Fe and I'm even more glad we didn't run into the cow fuckers. My so-called president, Alfred E. Neuman, also from the Big Star State, shock and fucking awe. Of course, not all humans from Texas are cow fuckers, ohmygoddess, send me tonglen." Xochiquetzal made an exaggerated effort to breathe in the negative of the world, and it actually worked. The out-breath was much lighter. "Gracias, Buddha," she murmured.

People in the long, impatient line, waited to be x-rayed... taking off all metal, their shoes, leaving the just bought bottled water behind, and be scanned while standing spread-legged if the metal detector screamed. TERRORIST. Others turned to stare. Some with undisguised disgust; some smiling in agreement; some with human sympathy.

"Quien es this Alfred guy?" Javier acknowledged the stares, his brown skin in the mostly white line, where they stood waiting. He smiled his calm physician's smile. The one he wore for terrified patients, and he thought—The whole Los Angeles Airport feels terrified, yes, like terrified patients waiting to hear the worst. Terror.

Terrorist. Terrified.

"In the olden days of the sixties, before you were born, Javiercito, Mad Magazine featured a little retarded guy with floppy ears and a goofy grin—actually, they still do, I'll find him for you online." Xochiquetzal kept her voice low in case a lynch mob mentality was brewing, and she suddenly, and fully, realized the *terrorist threat* had made every stranger suspect; the 'other' carrying a computer chip bomb in the heel of their innocent shoe.

"Ay como no, el presidente Bush," he mimicked her low voice. No more cow fucker show downs, por favor, he told himself. "Them wetbacks just wade the Reeo Grandee, que barbaro!" The mix of his bad Texas drawl, with his languid, Mexican accent was in direct contrast, opposition, fighting for his tongue. Javier laughed with delight.

"Ayy Diosa, you are so locito and don't ever try that again," Xochiquetzal laughed with him. "Anyway, it was good to hear from Hank a burnin' love, that he's really planning to join us, and Ai is coming too. Hey, maybe the burnin' love for those two, wouldn't that be amazing? Ai with her peace crystals and Hototo the Taos-Hopi, the people of peace."

"Amor, you're a match-maker," Javier smiled, amused. "And he'll bring his eagle bone flute for our roof top, the full dawn ceremony." He looked into her eyes without a trace of guile and smiled. So innocently. As only the young can do.

"I heard that *our*, muppie boy, and that charming smile doesn't work on me, by the way..."

"Maybe this will, little jaguar." Javier pulled her to him, kissing her, licking her inner lips (her womb on fire).

A Mexican, way behind them, going home to Aguascaliente— México lindo y querido—gave a low, sensual grito, like a wolf whistle. Most of the people laughed, finally meeting the other's eyes.

"I'm going to hang out in this bar and have a margarita for the road, maybe two," Xochiquetzal indicated the bar stools.

"Mexicana will have free drinks, mi amor, so no more pinche peanuts. Come and help me choose some regalos de Navidad," Javier smiled the smile.

"It's not going to work, tigre, see you back here. Take your time, enjoy this crazy place. It's a lot like the Mexico City Airport, only with the terrorist alert mania," she laughed. "But then I'm talking to a muppie at home on his own planet and you've been in plenty of airports, so I'll shut up now."

Javier's face clouded for a second. "Okay, mi feminista, save a margarita on the rocks, double shots, for me." He walked slowly away toward the shops and disappeared into the crowd.

As Xochiquetzal pulled her carry-on luggage, stuffed to the brim, behind her, it got stuck in a table leg. I have to buy a more compact, back-packer, roller style, she told herself—this is absurd and I bet we do lots more travel, mi tigre...

"Here, let me give you a hand," a low-pitched, soothing voice interrupted her thoughts. Clear, hazel eyes smiled into her own (hazel eyes).

"I was just thinking that I have to replace this over-stuffed, designer dinosaur, although this shade of purple helps me keep track of it," she laughed. "Thank you so much, how nice of you." Xochiquetzal distinctly felt eyes on her, so she looked around. People were staring— the women with envy, the men with obvious admiration.

"No problem," he smiled, "although I'm surprised it's under the weight limit." Then he went back to his Blackberry—texting and calling. He spoke Spanish, Italian, french, German, and some other languages she couldn't identify.

She took him in sideways—he was built and bulked like a slender wrestler, yet had an air of—the only word was—grace. He had a knit cap pulled down, hiding his hazel eyes that she'd caught for a moment.

"I'll be in Stockholm tonight, so count on it, tell everyone I'm coming. Then I go to Italy for a week, yeah..." He switched back into Swedish, Xochiquetzal realized, Stockholm, of course, I didn't recognize the Swedish language. Who is this guy, Einstein's nephew, all those languages.

He put the Blackberry down as his slice of pizza arrived, which he dabbed with a napkin, taking off the excess grease. He poured bottled water into a glass with ice and sipped. "Raul, una cerveza, por favor." He smiled so winningly, she forgot to order a margarita. As though reading her mind, he asked, "Do you want a drink, I didn't catch your name, I'm Ari." He extended his large, brown, firm hand.

It was warm, muscular, yet friendly. "I'd love a margarita, on the rocks, and I'm Xochiquetzal. I forgot to order, sorry to admit this, but I was listening to you speak every language known to humankind." She smiled back, knowing her smile wasn't even half as winning—Look at him, maybe twenty-five, the beautiful young, but at least I'm still fucking smiling.

"Isn't Xochiquetzal from the Mayan Goddess of love and beauty, if I remember right." Ari paused to order her margarita, "A special one," he added with a wink. "I asked Raul for a good double shot in code, in case you're wondering." That smile, flash of absolutely perfect teeth against the cocoa skin.

Javier has some smile competition, she thought, almost laughing. "Listening to you speak all those languages, I was wondering if you were Einstein's nephew, and now you also know the origin of my name. So is it Ari Einstein or what?" she finally laughed.

A deep, charming red landed on his high cheek bones for a few seconds, and then turned into simple pleasure. "Gracias, Xochiquetzal, but I'm trained to speak all those languages," Ari lowered his voice, loud enough for her to hear. "I hope I wasn't blasting my voice all over the place, not cool." He looked very young, his teens, vulnerable, just for a moment.

"No, no, it's me, Ari, I have supersonic ears and plus I'm very nosy by nature. But damn, how many languages do you speak, and what do you do, the training. Sounds very intriguing..."

"You are nosy," he laughed softly, his large hand touching hers briefly, that grace. "Gracias, Raul, put it on my bill."

"You don't have to do that, Ari."

"I want to, let me," he smiled. "Taste it and tell me if it's a good one." The bartender also waited, a smile in his eyes. It was a big margarita, sweating its coolness as she picked it up and sipped.

Xochiquetzal closed her eyes with pleasure. "Ayy tan sabrosito, gracias, both of you, it's so good!" She sipped again.

"Es doble, señora...It's a double with the best tequila, my family recipe, the special. El señor Bernstein, Ari, orders it sometimes, que bien!" Raul went to take a new order, smiling with a job well done. Pride.

"Senor Bernstein, well almost Einstein," she laughed, "but you don't look Jewish to me, as in, you know, white. My Goddess, I'm a pain in las nalgas, sorry, but do you know what I'm trying to say?"

Ari's smile was so gentle it made her want to weep; not a rational response but true. His hazel eyes held her hazel eyes (the second man in her life to do so, she noted). "My father was Cuban so I grew up in my favorite place on the planet, Miami. And my mother is Jewish, so my full name is Ari Bernstein Ruiz. She came to Miami from Israel as a young woman to study at university and met my Dad in one of her classes. The professor of Latin American Studies, and a very handsome, charming dude, so how could this little Israeli resist?" Ari laughed deep in his throat. "She'd finished her military training, served her country, and came to Miami, I think to just live for awhile, travel. I used to love to hear about Israel, her stories. Now I'm talking too much, and you know what it is, Xochiquetzal? Most people don't *listen*. You listen, you'd make a good spy," the smile.

"I was a photography professor for twenty or so years, so it's one of my skills, that listening. Plus that nosy thing, I love to listen to folk's stories. And so, what do you do with all of this language training, I'm dying to know."

Ari glanced around briefly, as though taking that moment to decide whether to tell her. "I work for Israel, special assignments world wide, so the languages come in handy." He pitched his voice just for her (supersonic) ears.

"Wow, how did that happen?"

"Do you have a hidden mic on you? I'm sure you have your camera, profesora," Ari smiled. "I think it was my mother's stories about Israel, growing up there, her love for Israel, the constant threats, suicide bombers. In a place like this in Israel, the bartender would have his weapon within reach, that's how it is, the constant threat to drive Israel into the sea." His eyes glistened, high tide, breathed in deeply, smiled.

"My mother's mother was ten when she and her mother were liberated at Auschwitz. Everyone in the family exterminated, murdered, but them, so they were two of the lucky ones in so many countless ways. They went to the promised land, Israel. The things my grandmother experienced, witnessed, as a child, never, ever again. And so, I work for Israel, my country, dual citizenship. My fiancee is Israeli, here's her photo." Ari reached for his Blackberry and brought up a photo of a beaming, gorgeous, sensual, strong-looking young woman.

"She is absolutely beautiful, Ari. Is she meeting you in Stockholm? Sorry, it's my ears," Xochiquetzal laughed.

"No, I still have girlfriends, hey I'm only twenty-six, but we're planning to get married next year. I want a child by the time I'm thirty, maybe two." Ari fastened his wide pools of hazel directly onto her own (not so wide, not so fresh). "I want to know I'm leaving children behind in case something happens to me. This kind of work can be hazardous to your health," he smiled very gently. "Do you want another margarita? I think I'll have one with you, be a little wild since I'm babbling non-stop. I usually stick to water, or try to, but Raul makes the best."

As Ari caught Raul's attention, Xochiquetzal searched for her travel protection; a carved, stone, translucent Quan Yin. She found the black, velvet pouch which also held Kokopelli, who was carved onto a circular black stone. Quan Yin fit in the palm of her hand. "Here, take this, she'll protect you."

"Quan Yin, the Goddess of Compassion, right? But what about you, Xochiquetzal?" She looked tiny, so fragile, in his large, muscled hand.

"I have Kokopelli, who's also good at his job," she laughed, showing him the carved, black stone.

"Gracias, Xochiquetzal, I'll carry this everywhere." Ari leaned over, kissing her very softly on the cheek. As a son would.

"What do you think of the Palestinians, their situation, I have to ask..."

"Yeah, it's pretty bad, that's for sure, and an understatement. I met a Palestinian physician with two young children. We became involved, to make a long story short, and I helped her immigrate to London. We stay in touch, still friends."

"Do you take part in that, Ari?" It felt like they were speaking under a dome where no one could hear them; where only the truth was asked, answered.

Raul brought their perfect margaritas and set them down with a slow smile. Ari handed him his credit card. "I have to get to my gate fairly soon, Raul, gracias." He took the first sip, Xochiquetzal's question making him remember, everything. Like a film fast-forwarding. Truth and secrets.

"I don't know how he makes these, but these are the best I've had anywhere, even in Mexico."

"I live in San Miguel de Allende now," she sipped. "México lindo y querido, but yes absolutely, these are the very best I've had."

"What they do in Palestine is soldier's work and Israel must retaliate after an attack. It's an on-going war, that's the reality. But I can tell you, Xochiquetzal, that I've never, not ever, killed a woman or a child. Although I know what I do might result in their deaths." Ari met her gaze. That clarity, fearlessness, grace. And then la mar filled his hazel eyes, just for a second.

"Israel will not be driven into the sea, *I won't allow it*." His voice was pitched low with passion, his own deep truth.

"Amor, did you save me a margarita?" Javier sensed the intimacy of their exchange, so he paused to chant, *Grow up,* inwardly. Silently.

Ari stood up, dwarfing Javier with his sheer bulk, those highly trained shoulders, his height at six foot three. "I have to catch my plane to Stockholm, Xochiquetzal, and I'll treasure this." He held the opal-lit Quan Yin up for a moment, putting her in his travel wallet.

"Wait—Ari this is Javier, and I wish you two had more time together. You have more in common than you both might think. Javier's a Mexican physician," she told Ari. "And Ari works for Israel world wide," she told Javier in a low voice. "He'd have to fill you in of course, but you're both agents for transformation, in my opinion."

Javier and Ari extended their hands simultaneously, smiling with some kind of instant recognition. Both equal in their passion, their work.

"Raul, one more margarita por mi amigo, Javier el doctor de México lindo y querido. These are special, ask Xochiquetzal," Ari smiled into Javier's eyes.

"Here, take my email in case you come to Mexico, bring your fiancee or whomever you want," she laughed.

"Come at Christmas, join us. We're going to have beautiful Hopi dawn ceremonies on our roof," Javier smiled the invitation into Ari's eyes.

"Hopi dawn ceremonies, you have my attention, Javier. Is this a real invitation, cause I just might come," Ari laughed. "That's the Mayan Calendar on your ring, Xochiquetzal, isn't that right?"

"This guy's Einstein's nephew, I warn you, he knows every human language and this too, my ring," she smiled at Javier. His beauty, his confidence, extended to Ari, making her see him more clearly... Mi tigre. "Yes, it is and do you know about December 21, 2012?"

"I have to go or I'll miss my plane, Xochiquetzal." Ari kissed her on the cheek, grabbed Javier in a quick hug, put down ten dollars for Javier's margarita, and turned to leave. Paused. "The Sixth Mayan World," he smiled.

"It's a real invitation, so email me and come!" she yelled after him as he trotted gracefully. Sheer power. People stopped to stare.

"I will! And I'll bring Judith my fiancee, you'll love her!" Then he was gone.

Javier sipped his margarita. "Mama fucking mia, this is perfect. Who was that masked man, he looks like a Samauri. I felt like a little kid next to him, yet he's obviously younger."

"You're right, that's it exactly, Ari's a Samurai. I bet he could kill someone like Spock on Star Trek, just a touch of those well trained hands. But he's also so gentle, a beautiful guy..."

"You aren't falling in love, mi amor..."

"He's twenty-six with girlfriends waiting for him in Stockholm and probably all over the planet, a fiancee in Israel. Plus, I'm not a twenty-six-year-old -molester, and I'm cutting it pretty close with you, doctorcito ayy." Xochiquetzal took a sip of the perfect margarita.

"I'm just kind of kidding, being the jealous type, but yeah I could see the mama-hijo cosa, but more, a real connection. I understand, mi amor, I make those with my patients. I just start to love them."

Xochiquetzal leaned over, touching Javier's lovely lips lightly with her own. "We've both been going through the kind of jealous thing, especially me, let's face it." A knot of tears in her throat made her pause. "But I want you to know that your true openness to the world, Javiercito, sets me free. To be able to love you while being myself, no apologies, what a gift, tigre." She heard Eagle Woman's words, "What is freedom, madam?" To love and be loved, open to the world, and to love my own wings...she sent the words to Bali.

"My ex, Carlos, would've freaked out on the spot with Ari..."

"Callate." Javier leaned into her, engulfing her mouth with his own, finding her tongue. "That's what you do for me, Xochitzalita, you set me free. But not too free, mi amor," he smiled into her eyes. "I don't want you to give me away, I want you to keep me. In *our bed,* our escorpion casita."

"Don't remind me," she laughed, tears in her eyes. "I haven't thought of scorpions in over a week, damn. Your full fucking name written on our mattress in black ink, yeah I said it. *Our mattress.*"

"Let's go to a bathroom stall, mi amor, or in the plane..."

"You are insane, doctorcito, and we'll get arrested. They'll take away my visiting privileges to México lindo y querido," she laughed. "So what's in that huge upscale shopping bag?"

"I'm going to get you drunk and kidnap you to the bathroom in the sky," Javier said in a serious tone. Then the smile that rivaled Ari's lit up his face (Warrior in the Sun). "I bought everyone in my family a techno gadget, and something for you, mi amor."

"You have a beautiful smile, Huiksi, I have to tell you. Way too chingado charming," she sighed. "What did you get me, show me..."

"No te haces mala, niña...Don't be bad, little girl," Javier laughed, moving the shopping bag out of her reach. "All I can say is that it's for, how do you say your Hopi name?"

"Tuawta."

"Tuawta, she who sees magic, for you, Xochitzalita."

"I have to wait till Christmas, damn, and it looks like it'll be quite a gathering if everyone shows up. I wonder how I didn't meet Hototo, The Hank, while I was living in Taos. I wish I had..."

"It just wasn't time, Tuawta, it just wasn't time." Javier grazed her lips with his tongue, holding her eyes with his. "I want you to keep me, mi amor," he breathed the words into her.

"It must be time," Xochiquetzal breathed back into him. She reached into her purse for the gold glitter, smiling wickedly like a kid.

"Not here, mi amor, por favor."

"Didn't you want to kidnap me to a bathroom stall, Dr. Zapata? You don't have your gold glittery sombrero so callate, hold still."

"Ay Xochitzalita, tan mala," Javier smiled, holding still as she spread gold glitter over his forehead (pin-pointing his dream eye). His cheekbones, a dab on his laughing lips.

"Okay, your turn, mi amor, callate and hold still." He spread a line on her forehead, the dream eye, her eyelids, her cheeks, blending it gently with his fingertips. Finally, her mouth, kissing her, sharing the gold.

Raul did a low-pitched grito, but it was filled with so much longing. México lindo y querido. "Do you want another one?" he asked. "Where do you live in Mexico, doctor?"

"In San Miguel de Allende right now, with Xochitzalita, but I'm from Guadalajara, amigo."

"Me too," Raul beamed, tears filling his eyes. "My family is still there and I go back at least once a year for a month. I send money home para mi familia tambien, ayy Guadalajara!" Raul did another low-pitched grito, so full of longing.

Javier threw back his head and gave a full-throated grito— México lindo y querido! People laughed and clapped, no chorus of *wetback* here. A couple of people thought it, but no one gave it a voice.

"I'll take another one but with only one shot or you'll have to get me a wheel chair," Xochiquetzal laughed. "This guy did gritos all over Vallarta, very embarrassing, can't take el doctor anywhere."

"I'll take one too, Raul, pero con todo poder...full power, por favor."

"Wait Raul, come here." She held the glitter.

"Oh no, señora, no puedo...I can't."

"Just on your cheekbones, be brave!" she teased. "Come here!"

"Just a little, señora, ayy," Raul laughed, facing her.

Xochiquetzal dabbed the gold on his high cheekbones and between his eyes. "One for your dream-eye, Raul, so you can dream your home more vividly."

"I understand, señora, canta no llores...sing don't cry," he...

Wings.   Instinct.   Ancient.   Song.

PART IV

Make peace with the universe. Take joy in it.
It will turn to gold. Resurrection
will be now. Every moment,
a new beauty.

—Rumi

…smiled with joy as the light caught the gold.

"We haven't looked for talawva, the red light of dawn, since we've been back, sleeping in, being flojeros ayy lazy." Xochiquetzal smiled in the darkness of pre-dawn, as fireworks exploded, blessing the town. Over and over, immense, shimmering blossoms of gold, red, purple, rainbows, gold flowers of light, exploded. Then silently shimmering, filtering into dreams; into their upturned eyes of wonder.

"Fireworks and talawva, can't ask for more, mi amor, and Justin arrives in a few hours, tu hijo." Javier took her hand in the pre-dawn chill and kissed it. He sipped the hot café fuerte, waiting for the next explosion of light. The first streak of red light, talawva. Dawn.

"Do you remember what Hototo said about the three phases of Creation, the first colors of dawn?" Javier asked, almost whispering. "The purple light of mystery, the yellow light of breath, let's try to see the purple and yellow…"

"And the red light of human form, as the rising Warrior in the Sun, Taiowa, seals the dream-eye and the kopavi, the open door, the soft spot at the crown of the head. I used to love to place my fingertips on Justin's kopavi when he was so new. To feel his heart beat on my fingers, to smell his baby smell, that innocence. I remember the series of dreams from that time, the gift from his kopavi, his soft spot. They're in my dream journal, thirty year old dreams, still so new." Xochiquetzal could see Justin's tiny, newborn face, and a sudden sadness pierced her—I'll have no more babies in this life, but Javier will, he'll have his babies in time, he will. One final blossom of light exploded, shimmering gold.

"Do you think he'll like me, Xochitzalita, I know it's important to you that he like me or at least tolerate me." Xavier came to mind as they waited for the purple streak of sky, how they could barely tolerate the other. And then he saw it—"Look, the purple light, the mystery!"

"Hay-ya, the mystery! He's going to love you, I know he is, don't ask me why, it's a mystery," she smiled, stroking Javier's worried face. "The yellow pulsing light, oh look, I wish Hototo were here with his dawn flute."

"The breath of life, the yellow. Well, Justin may not love me, mi amor, but I think we'll like each other, y una hay-ya tambien." His voice was low and sad.

"Huiksi, give me your breath, he's going to love you because I love you, callate." Mouth to mouth, they exchanged breath, warm kisses. "You know, you are one of the most lovable and loving people I know, el doctorcito..."

"Amor, talawva, the red light of dawn expanding, look. I guess it's Xavier, always back to Xavier, that he doesn't seem to love me. Yet I know," tears strangled his words, "at the bottom, I love him. Always have, always will, my necessary twin in el mundo, the world. Amalia used to pronounce Xavier's name 'Shavier,' the way your name is pronounced with the 'X'—but my parents forbade it, too Indian." Javier paused to face talawva, raising both hands to the sky. "Shavier and I, the Toltec twins," he laughed softly. "And both of us necessary, as Amalia's sacred twin stories told us, both of us loved."

"That's why you're el doctorcito and that's why Justin's will love you, hay-ya," Xochiquetzal murmured.

They silently watched the Warrior in the Sun, Taiowa (Hopi Creator, Sun God), reveal the kopavi, open door, as it rose. Slowly rose. Humming its Sun Song. In the silence. In that moment. Silence. Song. The sun bloomed. A golden rose.

"May the Blue Star Kachina never ever dance in the plaza." Xochiquetzal took Javier's warm, brown hand in hers. "For all us humans, every color, may the Blue Star Kachina, Saquasohuh, continue to dance far away from us, from Earth. As we enter the Hopi Fifth World, the Mayan Sixth World..."

"Dance beautifully, invisibly, far away, Saquasohuh," Javier joined in quietly. "Dance the Fifth, Sixth Worlds into being, beautifully, Blue Star. Not enough physicians, not enough medicine, not enough preparation for nuclear war. Dance beautifully far away, Saquasohuh, ojala." Tears streaked his face in the chill dawn.

"Mi amor, you're a poet, I love that word 'ojala,' God/Goddess willing, ojala." He enclosed her in his arms. Warmth. Simple. Human. Embrace. She licked. His tears. Salty. Delicious. Sweet. The tigers of loneliness and desire laughed, and leaped to the far

sun-song horizon.

"Hay-ya," they murmured simultaneously. As the first golden arrow. Pierced them. Gold.

("Saquasohuh," the Energy Child danced, sang, "Blue Star.")

Darkness shimmering.   *The gold.*

Playful knocking on the thick, oak Mexican door with bare knuckles. Then the metal lion knocker, louder. Xochiquetzal rushed to open it, flinging it wide. "Justin!" She laughed with so much joy it made her dizzy.

"Gracias amigo, see you on the return trip!" He waved to the van driver, then began shoving his suitcase inside the slim opening of the door. "Hey Mom, es tu hijito," Justin laughed at the sight of his mother's welcoming eyes.

"Wait, I can open the other one, it's getting stuck. Okay, you did it! For my monstrous one I have to open both doors, hey you are here, Justin!" She grabbed him in a bear hug, dancing in place.

He'd been slightly dreading this meeting with his mother's lover—A guy around my age, fucking A. But he picked his mother up, as he always did, dancing with her. Laughing at their ridiculous joy of seeing each other, again.

Javier stood, smiling, taking in the fullness of their joy; and as he quickly searched his feelings, he felt no jealousy. Nada. This is her son. Her beloved son. Justin.

"You must be the one and only Javier," Justin smiled, offering his hand. "I hear you're an ER doc, that's incredible as we're almost the same age. No offense intended, just the truth..."

Javier laughed, taking Justin's hand in his, meeting his eyes. His mother's direct gaze, that strength, mi Xochitzalita, how can I not love him. "I took off traveling for a year, but the main focus, before and after, was medical school..."

"Where did you travel, that's so cool to take off for a year. In fact, I'd love to do that before I graduate, just for three months even." This dude's no wimp, those eyes, kinda like Mom, and he looks a little older than thirty-four but not much.

"You're just in time for a fresh pot of café fuerte, an omelette with blue tortillas, and help yourself to the bowl of mangoes and melon sprinkled with lime. So, do you want a chorizo omelette as usual?" Xochiquetzal kissed Justin on the cheek and hugged him again, then turned toward the coffee. She walked into Javier's arms waiting in ambush, and he kissed her softly on the mouth, letting her go.

"I'll take everything, yeah it all sounds muy sabrosito, but first el café fuerte, por favor. The driver, Jorge, stopped for some pretty good coffee and pan dulce around 7 a.m." Justin felt their energy, the attraction between them, and to his surprise he wasn't jealous or up tight. They fit together, the thought came to him. They belong together somehow, their eyes, and I've never seen her so happy. Never, Justin realized. I love my dad, but she never looked like this. This is what it looks like, to see my mother happy.

Javier spread out the world map on the coffee table in the front room as Xochiquetzal poured two cups of café muy fuerte. "Do you want some kahlua in it, mi amor?"

Justin and Javier answered at the same time, "Si, gracias, Xochitzalita." "Si, como no, Mom." They looked at each other and laughed.

"We'll do the dishes, mi amor, right Justin?"

"You know the way to my mother's heart, dude, and I always do the dishes when she cooks." Justin smiled at Javier in code, *You are sly, dude.*

"I saw that smile, Justin," she laughed, pouring a shot of kahlua into both cups.

"I traveled east first, stopping in Hawaii, all the beautiful islands, and I even witnessed some flowing, black lava closing the highway on its journey to the sea. I've never seen anything like it, new land steaming into the sea."

"Mom and I went when I was around fourteen, but no cool lava, and it was pretty gorgeous for sure."

Xochiquetzal served their cafes con kahlua, smiling at their mutual intensity as they gazed at the map of the world. "Everywhere Justin and I traveled he gathered his fan club, but I'm sure you did that too, Dr. Zapata. Are you giving my son ideas?" She put her hand through Justin's thick, dark, spiky-gelled hair, pausing at his kopavi, his beloved open door. "I like your hair all spiky like this, it suits you."

"You're screwing it up, Mom," Justin laughed, enjoying her touch. "And is your name really Zapata, Javier, like Javier Zapata?"

"Nah, it's my code name for el doctor when he gets a little wild y locito. I'm sure you'll get to know him as well, el Dr. Zapata," she laughed. "Okay, now for chorizo omelettes, muy sabrosito, por los dos locos."

"I like your spiky hair, dude," Javier teased Justin.

"And you have a doc hair cut, am I right? You oughtta try this one, up to date, Zapata dude."

"I like it actually, but my patients might run out the door, dude, just kidding." They smiled at each other, slyly, a secret between them.

"Then I went to Japan, traveled all over Japan but I loved Tokyo. Then down to Hong Kong, what a city, I loved the energy, overwhelming." Javier's finger traced it, then journeyed to Thailand. "Bangkok, the beaches, all the Buddhas. Have you been to Thailand, mi amor?"

"Only to Bangkok, a five day stop-over on my way to Bali, but I hear the beaches are wonderful. Justin was around sixteen on this trip to Bali, then on to New Zealand. And later I went to Bali by myself, as I've told you, mi amor, and Justin returned to New Zealand by himself and had way more fun, right Justin?" Xochiquetzal laughed.

"And I bet you had more fun in Bali by yourself, right Mom?"

For a moment she wanted to get angry, as in how dare he; but she caught herself. He's right, I did have more fun by myself; and she ever-so-slightly blushed with the memory of her sweet Balinese lover. The cooling night wind. By the Bali Sea.

"Okay you two, behave!" Javier laughed, but he knew she was thinking of her lover, and if they were alone he'd pick her up. And take her. To their autographed mattress. And what about me? he reminded himself. Everywhere I went, women, my lovers. Grow up, he breathed, grow up.

"I'll take you to the Thai beaches, Japan, Hong Kong, and you can take me to New Zealand and Bali, after my surgery speciality, mi amor."

"It's a deal, I'd love that. So I guess we're traveling..."

"Of course we're traveling." Javier winked at Justin as though they'd been

co-conspirators forever. "And then to India where I traveled for over a month, a truly boggling country. Then parts of Africa, a truly boggling continent, and I stayed in Morocco for a couple of weeks, the food, oh the food, such a sensual place." He remembered his lovely, sensual Moroccan (Indian, African) lovers and smiled. I think I'm growing up, yes, finally.

"Where haven't you been, damn, I'm getting very jealous. Okay, I'm taking off three months to fucking travel, I feel deeply deprived. We went to India for a couple of weeks, yeah, boggling, that's for sure, and I loved the food in India. But seeing all those hungry people on the streets took some of the joy out of it, all those hungry kids. We kept giving money until we ran out of cash, remember Mom? And we kept getting mobbed, so we left for the countryside, one of the beaches."

"I remember, Justin, way too well. India was hard to take in the immense city of Bombay," she sighed, tasting the spicy chorizo, now ready for the eggs, onions, tomatoes, slices of Oaxaca cheese.

"And I remember Bangkok, the way beautiful women, real knock-outs, but at sixteen still too young to be on my own, damn!" Justin smiled at the memory of such longing.

"I must agree, dude," Javier returned the smile. "Then I went up into Europe and traveled, I mean every country in Europe, down to Greece, staying on the islands for a couple of weeks. But my favorite place was Spain—Barcelona, Madrid, Seville—so I ended up living there for a while before I came back home to Mexico."

With Clara, Xochiquetzal thought, your beloved Clara, who gave you to me—gracias, Clara, for this beautiful man, mi tigre, Javiercito.

"I went to Europe by myself in my early twenties and I loved Spain, especially Barcelona, what a party town that place is, sorry Mom," Justin grinned, remembering.

"Tell me about it," Javier laughed.

"What are you sorry about, Justin, damn, enjoy la vida every fucking second. And yes, take off for three months, I'll even make a donation."

"I can see that *fucking* runs in the family, and Xochitzalita even has me saying it. I hope it doesn't pop out in fucking surgery, mi amor." Javier and Justin met eyes for a moment, slyly smiling. Yes. They liked each other.

"Show me your trip, Justin, you know the dream stage, which I love to do. And let's plan our first big journey together, mi amor, I think I'm catching your son's wander lust."

"Okay, first Japan, then India, South Africa, maybe Morocco, yeah..." Justin traced his fingertips across the map, dreaming. "Then up to Europe, taking trains everywhere, carrying a backpack, staying in hostels, drinking cheap but good vino, eating the local, daily bread, the cheeses, and of course checking out las mujeres..."

"Come and get these perfect, fucking chorizo omelettes, you guys!" Xochiquetzal paused to look at them bent over the map of the world and burst into sudden tears. They're so beautiful, so very beautiful, and I love them both like the Sun. Taiowa, the Hopi Sun God, so beautiful these two men.

"Mom, are you okay?" Justin watched Javier take her into his arms, laughing quietly. I've seen her cry maybe twice in my whole life, he thought with some alarm. And here she is just about bawling, damn.

"I've come to understand that this means she loves us, Justin, when she cries. So it doesn't scare me anymore. In fact, it makes me happy, she just loves us and can't help herself, tu mama." Javier kissed her tears and smiled into her eyes. Like the sun. The Warrior. In the Sun.

Xochiquetzal blew her nose. "He's right Justin, I seem to cry more these days, like my heart's breaking open, fuck, what can I say, I love you both."

"It's a little weird since I've seen you cry maybe twice in my whole life, but I kinda like it," Justin smiled. Her heart breaking open, that's it, she loves this guy. I wish my heart would break open, he thought with that stab of familiar pain. Loneliness. The soul. The longing. For his. Unknown. Beloved. He placed his finger on Tokyo—Yeah, first Tokyo, Japan, visit Hiroshima, Nagasaki, and make paper cranes of peace, Buddhist temples, hot springs in the countryside, night life in Tokyo, yeah.

Then he joined his mother, her lover, the feast. As she poured them fresh coffee, placing the bottle of kahlua and a shot glass on the table, Justin said, "I love seeing you happy, Mom, and I think Dr. Zapata's growing on me, damn!" Suddenly embarrassed, in an effort to change the subject, Justin added, putting a fork full of chorizo omelette in his mouth, moaning with pleasure—"How many scorpion corpses have you collected thus far?"

"I heard you about Dr. Zapata, Justin, but I think the body count's going on forty." Xochiquetzal paused to look into Javier's smiling eyes. "Javier told me a story about a golden scorpion..."

"A *sacred*, golden scorpion," Javier interrupted in a serious tone, trying not to smile.

"Roger, as I was saying, if you see the *sacred*, golden scorpion don't kill it, let it live."

"Why?" was all Justin could say.

"My second mama, la Maya, told me as a boy, to never ever kill the golden scorpion and it will grant you your heart's desire." Javier smiled like a kid revealing a secret.

"You never told me that part, about the heart's desire," Xochiquetzal whined, throwing a piece of cobalt blue tortilla at him. He caught it, putting it in his mouth.

"You never asked me *why*, Xochitzalita mi amor," Javier laughed deep in his throat, enjoying her real irritation.

"Qué cabron estas, Dr. Zapata, chinga tu gatito tambien! And I won't throw any more tortillas at you as you seem to enjoy it too much," she laughed.

"Come on, mi amor, tengo hambre…I'm hungry." Javier opened his mouth. "Or kiss me, even better un besito, mi amor, no mas uno, only one." Javier leaned into her, grazing her inner lips with his tongue.

"Hey you two, get a room!" Justin laughed, enjoying the sight of his mother's play. Joy.

"You should've been in Vallarta when this loco was wearing his black with gold spangled sombrero and people doing gritos all over the place when he'd, well…"

"When I couldn't keep my hands off tu mama tan hermosa, Justin, es la verdad, and we'd just met, hey I kissed her on the streets of Vallarta and I'm proud of it, como no."

Justin gave a subdued grito, pouring some kahlua in the café fuerte. "I wish I had someone I couldn't keep my hands off," he muttered.

"I heard that, Justin, and you will." Xochiquetzal reached over and traced the sweet curve of his cheek.

"Okay, all sacred, golden scorpions are spared, but they better come through with the heart's desire contract, damn it!" Justin smiled and took a sip of the coffee, kahlua mix, sabrosito.

The phone rang and Javier reached for it. "Hola, Quien, who? Ai, where are you, mujer? So, you're in town, how long have you been here, cabrona?" he laughed.

"Ohmygoddess, it's Ai, she's here! Justin, this woman is amazing, I know you'll like her. She's from Tokyo and she's traveling the world burying little crystals for Hiroshima, Nagasaki."

"That's amazing, Mom, what's her name?"

"Ai, it means Love in Japanese."

Javier handed her the phone. "Ai yi yiiii, it's Ai," she laughed. "Where the hell are you and why aren't you here? Hey, my son's here, yes, Justin."

"Slow down, Xochitzalita, I'm staying at a nice but cheap hotel that includes desayuno, breakfast…"

"You have to stay here, mujer!"

"No, no, I'd rather stay in this place but visit you most of the time, okay? I've been here for two days getting a feel for the place and

I really like it. I see why you live here…"

"Hey, it just dawned on me, you're talking, so you broke the vow of silence."

"You and Javier made me break it, damn you!" Ai laughed. "Oaxaca and Chiapas was awesome, and I got together with Don Francisco for a few days. He told me to tell you that he's waiting for you and Javier, and that he received your dream of me coming. He found me before I could even send my email to his wizard son, but I'll tell you more when I see you, my travels. Don Francisco is a truly amazing man, him and his family. What a gift it was to be with them, but I'll tell you more later, Xochitzalita."

"Why don't you come over right now, I'm dying to hug you and you can meet mi hijo, Justin."

"I'm going for a massage as it seems I threw my back out of whack carrying too much stuff while traveling. But how about dinner tonight, and then you'll be stuck with me indefinitely," Ai giggled wickedly.

"Okay, take care of your sweet back, enjoy the massage, get very spoiled, and I'll see you tonight at 7 p.m., a place called Mama Mia…"

"I've been there for pizza, the live music at night, I love it, my favorite place so far."

"Of course you found Mama Mia, so see you at 7, can't wait and you'll get to meet el Justin, que bien, see you then, mi chica."

❖

"I can't believe I let you put gold glitter on me." Justin rubbed at his face briefly. "Do you always let her have her way?" he asked Javier, laughing.

"Yes," he joined Justin's laughter. "I'm wearing it too, dude."

"Oh come on, you guys, it's not a fucking tattoo, you can wash it off, but don't you dare! My theory is that the gold glitter entices the golden scorpion to show up…"

"Well, in that case, I'll take some more, just kidding." Justin led the way into Mama Mia's looking for a Japanese woman named Ai.

Suddenly, an uncensored grito and a woman rushed past him, meeting his eyes briefly. Her face was ecstatic, beautiful, laughing. Ai grabbed Xochiquetzal by the waist and they danced for a few seconds. "I missed you. I swear by Quan Yin and my tattoo, I missed you both way too much!" Then she grabbed Javier in a dancing hug, laughing. "Are you being good to this amazing woman, Dr. Zapata?"

"If I weren't she'd toss me out and you know that, cabroncita," Javier laughed, picking her up and twirling her for joy.

Xochiquetzal watched Justin's face light up with a sense of recognition, as though remembering something he'd forgotten. His strong, gentle, hermoso cara, face.

Ai turned to face him, meeting his eyes calmly. "You must be the famous and beloved Justin, son of Xochitzalita," she laughed, grabbing him in a joyous hug. But no dancing. They stood still as their hearts mirrored the other's welcome, and their blood danced.

There's no seduction on Ai's part, Xochiquetzal watched their meeting—It's not necessary with her beauty, her spirit, that recognition, she realized, tears clouding her eyes. Then she saw Justin simply take Ai's hand in his. It was involuntary. It was inevitable, so natural. And she let him. Hold her hand, as she held his. Their hands. Remembered. The other.

"Do you two already know each other or what?" Javier laughed.

"Remember when you started talking about past lives on the beach," Xochiquetzal interrupted, wanting to protect their meeting. This moment.

"And I kept having to tell you I was your birthday regalo, your gift, almost breaking down your chingado door, yes I remember, mi amor."

"You know, Javier, she's never really lived with anyone, so I'm pretty impressed by your persuasive powers." They continued to hold hands as the handsome waiter led them to a table close to the stage. Where the salsa band would soon play, after the wonderful flamenco guitar player.

"I'll show you my personal autograph on our mattress sometime, dude," Javier laughed as Xochiquetzal punched his shoulder.

Javier ordered bottles of cabernet and chardonay, and a shot of tequila for himself. Paused. "Do you want one, Justin, a shot?"

"Does a chicken got lips?"

Javier laughed. "¿Qué? Say that again."

"Does a chicken got lips?"

Javier translated for the waiter, making him smile, and told him to make it two shots.

"Does a wild man shit in the woods?" Xochiquetzal added, laughing.

"Does a bear have hair?" Justin continued.

"And what's the sound of one hand clapping?" Ai giggled.

"You're all way too existential and Zen-like for me," Javier smiled at everyone. And he realized he loved everyone at the table. That they belonged together, this moment.

"You know, you and Justin look like twins in your black leather jackets," Ai smiled at them both, meeting Justin's eyes fully. "Handsome twins."

Ohmygoddess, Xochiquetzal thought, this is it, I can feel it, this is it. *They recognize each other*, yes, the way we did.

The tequila shots arrived with a small plate of sliced limes.

"We'd better take off our jackets, dude, I already have a twin."

"Seriously?" Justin asked.

"His name is Xavier with an X, seriously."

"Okay, just to say it, no tequila contest tonight, Dr. Zapata, por favor," Xochiquetzal said, meaning it.

"Come on, Mom, we have to have the ceremonial tequila shot contest como los hombres."

"Last time this nut case loco did one he ended up in a brawl here, then he hired a mariachi band to talk me into letting him back into the house, and he also tried to climb the tree to my bedroom patio…"

"How romantic," Ai laughed. "I wish I could've been there for that show."

"Picture Javier in his glittering gold, black Zapata sombrero— you know the one he wore at the beach—very drunk and singing, I mean, way off key…"

"You loved it, big fat liar!" Ai laughed.

"I hear you're traveling the world with peace crystals, and I gotta tell you that sounds pretty amazing." Justin wanted to take her hand again; he could barely resist. Next I'll be hiring a mariachi band and climbing trees, he told himself.

"Yes, it's all true," Ai smiled into his waiting eyes. "I buried crystals in the earth at Monte Alban, in Chiapas, and I placed one on Don Francisco's altar, Xochitzalita." She turned to meet her eyes. "I stayed with him and his family for six days in Chiapas. In fact, I was held kind of captive," she laughed. "He stays with his wizard son in

Oaxaca, but the family home is in Chiapas, you'll see."

"Was it all wonderful, I'm sure, that sneaky Don Francisco." Xochiquetzal met Ai's gaze and she realized something was changed in her. Something subtle. Something healed.

"He did rituals, cleansings, I'll tell you later, and his family, what loving people. He told me to tell you and Javier he's waiting for you, and he received your dream of me coming. Of course, he made it all into a huge, cosmic joke, that this little Japonesa was traveling the world with her little peace crystals. I loved him immediately, yes sneaky."

"This guy, Don Francisco, sounds spooky and why is he waiting for me, chinga tu perro. Justin, should I order us a bottle of tequila, I see you're done."

"Chinga tu poodle, si, the contest is on, and I want to see that autograph, dude!"

"Don't start with that chinga tu gato, perro, now poodle stuff, you guys. Javier, remember last time, you and Pablo…"

Javier leaned over, whispering, "Callate, mi amor, callate," grazing her lips with his tongue.

"Who's this Pablo, Mom?" Justin arched his eyebrows in mock surprise.

"Okay you two, keep it clean," Ai giggled. She returned to Justin's waiting, hermoso eyes. How can I turn away from those eyes? the thought zapped her. "As I was saying, Justin, next I'm going to New Mexico where the atomic bomb was developed, to bury a humongous crystal there for sure. Probably stay in Taos for a couple of weeks, as your Mom and Javier tell me how beautiful it is. Then off to probably Europe first, then India, Tibet…"

"Why are you doing this, Ai, and do you find crystals as you go?" I want to go with her, Justin realized—I want to go with her.

"I brought some with me from Japan, but now I find them as I go. Otherwise I'd look like Kokopelli with a hump of crystals on my back and, as your Mom knows, I'm already a chinga tu pajarito heyoka." Ai tried to smile.

"A heyoka with Quan Yin on her back," Xochiquetzal added, feeling Ai's sudden sadness. "And a black belt in kung fu, hey I'll take a shot of that tequila, por favor." Javier signaled the waiter, then ordered a shot glass for her and Ai just in case.

Ai gathered herself, looking down at her folded hands. "My grandmother was caught in the bombing of Hiroshima, and I don't want that to happen again," she almost whispered.

"May the Blue Star Kachina never ever dance in the plaza," Javier murmured.

("Saquasohuh," the Energy Child sang, "Blue Star Kachina.")

Javier poured a shot for himself, Xochiquetzal, Justin, and for la Ai, to the brim.

Justin's hands flew—two swift birds—to cover hers. The handsome waiter returned for their orders, his presence making them remember hunger, the scent of food from the kitchen.

"How does pizza and salads sound, todos, everyone?" Javier took charge.

"Javier and I met a Taos guy on our trip there last month and he's probably going to be joining us this week. Actually, his mom is Hopi, so he's a Taos-Hopi mix. We call him Hank a burnin' love and you'll soon know why." Xochiquetzal smiled at Ai and her son. The undiminished beauty of the young.

"Listen to that guitar, flamenco, my favorite, and next salsa. Do you know what's missing, Ai, mi chica bonita?"

"Dime...tell me, Xochitzalita." Ai returned the smile, suddenly pierced by joy. And sorrow. Equally.

"You need gold glitter and I'm the one to do it," she laughed.

"Bring it on, mujer!"

"Can I do it, Ai, do you mind?" Justin blurted out, a bit embarrassed, but he didn't care.

"Okay, I don't mind," Ai smiled into his eyes. "And you need a freshening up yourself, you're losing your glitter."

"First we must toast el escorpion de oro, and the true reason why we wear el pinche gold glitter," Javier laughed, raising his shot glass.

("El escorpion," the Energy Child laughed, "de oro.")

"El escorpion de oro, if you ever spot one, will grant you your heart's desire, so don't kill it," Justin said directly into Ai's sad/laughing eyes.

("Heart's desire," the Energy Child wept, laughed.)

"We've murdered around ten regular escorpions since we've been back, ayy Diosa, but we await el escorpion de oro!" Xochiquetzal raised her shot glass. Then Ai, Justin, Javier—they all ceremoniously took a lick of salt, a slice of lime in the mouth, drinking their shot in one gulp.

Javier let loose a grito, then Justin matched it. Ai and Xochiquetzal did one together, giggling. Scattered gritos, laughter, echoed in response. "One more shot, todos?" Javier raised the bottle and poured shots for all. "The rest is for me and el Justin and this contest, right dude?"

The flamenco player left the stage to a round of loud applause, whistles, more gritos. Mama Mia was warming up for its journey toward dawn. And the salsa band arrived, laughing with anticipation and an abundance of overflowing energy. For salsa. They talked and laughed among themselves as they set up their instruments, tuning them. The suave lead singer began joking with the crowd.

"I see you bonitas, are you ready to dance?" He smiled, focusing on a table of young, single women.

"Start playing and singing!" a beautiful, bold one answered him, as they all laughed.

Justin held Ai's face with his left hand (loving the electricity of her skin), and very slowly traced gold glitter across the ocean of her cheeks, her forehead. "Close your eyes for your eyelids," he murmured, wanting to kiss her. Those soft, full lips. Now.

"You're next, dude," Ai smiled, closing her eyes. Wishing he'd kiss her. Now. I don't know what Don Francisco did to me, those cleansings, but I feel so alive, so alive. "Sana, sana, sana, sol, alma, sol, alma...heal, heal, heal, sun, soul, sun, soul," his beautiful, deep voice came to her.

"Isn't this a million percent better than that night in Ojo Caliente, los chingaderos de las vacas, the cow fuckers?" Xochiquetzal laughed softly. "Look at those two, Javier," she whispered into his ear, licking it quickly.

"I think they've found each other, Xochitzalita, just like we did. I can see Justin wants to pounce on her como un tigre, like this." Javier kisser her, meeting her tongue with his, breathing into her. Huiksi, Breath of Life.

Justin placed a careful dash of glitter on her soft, soft lips, barely able to stop himself. From kissing her. "You look beautiful, Ai, you really do," he breathed. "Do you salsa?"

"Does a chicken got lips?" she laughed. "Okay, your turn, close your eyes."

"Why, first my cheeks..."

"You're burning a hole in me, Justin, and I might fucking explode, as Xochitzalita would say." She met his gaze, those eyes. "Okay, close them, now."

"And then will you dance with me, bonita, I feel the same." His voice was ragged with longing. He couldn't hide it, and he closed his eyes.

Ai slowly traced her fingertips across the continent of his forehead, his eyelids, his cheeks. This face, I remember this face. Then the gold glitter across his forehead, his cheeks, his eyelids (as tears gathered, fell—one, two—the caged tigers free). And very softly, so gently—a butterfly wing—she kissed him. "A little glitter for your lips," she murmured, "from mine."

Justin opened his wet, amazed eyes. He wanted to hold her, to feel her next to him. Her warmth. "Let's dance, bonita, come on." He took Ai's hand, pulling her to her feet. To the dance floor. A salsa, but they danced so slowly, sensually, innocently.

Javier jumped to his feet, extending his hand to Xochiquetzal— "Dance with me, bonita."

"Only if you promise not to do the salsa hip-hop," she laughed.

"Ay cabroncita, baile con Dr. Zapata but without my sombrero. I knew I should've worn it, fregado."

Xochiquetzal let him pull her to the dance floor, and for a moment she met Ai's gaze as Justin held her to himself. And she knew. Ai was going to have her grandchildren, with her son, Justin. They would love each other for many years—Don Francisco's gift, *sana heal sana heal sol sun alma soul.*

Javier pulled Xochiquetzal into his arms. "You're too far away, corazón, ven aca, come here." He breathed into her ear, "You know, the gold glitter may entice el escorpion de oro, but my glittering Zapata sombrero is the true key to your heart's desire, mi amor."

"Callate and kiss me." Scattered gritos. But they may have been for Justin and Ai as they merged within the music. Butterfly wings. Kisses. The undiminished. Beauty. Of the young. They danced. Their unfolding. Life together.

Javier and Justin each wore a borrowed mariachi sombrero—gold on maroon—and they both sang at the top of their lungs. Off key. "Caaaantaa nooo llloorresss…"

Xochiquetzal and Ai held onto each other, howling with laughter. "Should we be embarrassed?" Ai caught her breath.

"You said it would be romantic, as I recall," Xochiquetzal wept with laughter.

"Baile, baile, baile," the mariachis chanted, teased, Javier and Justin. "Con las mujeres, hombres...Dance, dance, dance, with the women!" As they were dancing with each other, or rather stumbling around with each other.

"They can barely stand up, much less dance, Xochitzalita. I feel something for your son, I can't explain it."

"You don't have to, mi bonita, I just went through it myself, as you know. Ayy Diosa, here they come. Come on, Javier, we're catching a taxi, no more dancing for you, mi amor," she laughed.

"I'm going to walk Ai back to her place, Mom, it's pretty late and she needs protection..."

"You need protection, dude!" Javier laughed, trying to turn to the music, almost falling. "And so do I, but hey, estas mujeres know el kung fu and Ai es un black belt!"

"Guide him over the cobbles, Ai, and see you both tomorrow, I love you both!" Xochiquetzal called after them, listening to their laughter.

"I love you too, Mom, maybe even el Dr. Javier dude, later!"

"I love you, Xochitzalita, Javier, hasta la manana, maybe breakfast, good dreams you two!" Ai yelled, laughing, and they were gone. Justin stumbled on the cobbles and Ai held him up, guiding him to the hotel. To her room, her warm, waiting bed, her small pouch of gathered crystals from Oaxaca. They sang inside the dark-womb pouch of the journey ahead, in the language of crystals.

"Let's do a killer grito, Ai, come on, just one." Justin pulled her into his arms, sniffing her hair, her scent. This is my home, my home.

They turned their faces toward the ancient stars, laughing, and did one more joy/sorrow, love/loss, full-fledged, woman and man grito.

A group of teens, sipping their beers, a couple of blocks away, paused to answer them. Then they started to howl to the open sky, sensing (like the wild young) the very beginnings of love.

Justin willed himself to stay awake as he waited for Ai to emerge from the bathroom. The softness and warmth of the bed lulled him, but he refused to close his eyes. If I even close them for a second, I'm a goner, come on Ai...

She emerged wrapped in her red kimono with purple-gold lotus flowers on the back. She thought he'd fallen asleep, so she removed the kimono, tossing it on a chair. Her hair was loose, covering her breasts, to her waist; and covering her back. The Goddess. Quan Yin.

"You are so beautiful, Ai, please come here, please..."

"I thought you were sleeping, passed out, sneaky boy," she smiled in the darkness.

"I'd rather die than go to sleep, please come here, bonita."

Ai slid in next to Justin. He'd taken off his t-shirt, shorts. They reached for each other simultaneously, as jolts of joy arced all around them.

"I guess they're not coming for breakfast," Xochiquetzal smiled at Javier.

"Remember those first days, who can blame them," he returned her smile. "In fact, let's go back to my autographed mattress, mi amor."

"Okay, I got an email from Hototo," she ignored his suggestion, but her womb still flared. "He's flying in tonight. We told him to come any time and he's coming. Also, an old student, now amiga, Muriel, will be in San Miguel in two days. She's in Mexico City right now, so I sent her the phone number..."

"It's my cell that's ringing, and I know you're ignoring me, mi amor." Javier gave her a mock-hurt look and answered his cell.

"Qué me chingas, Pompeii, where are you, cabron, y la Floriana."

Xochiquetzal answered the house phone. "Justin, is that you, I was wondering where you two are," she laughed.

"The truth is, we just woke up and I'm bringing Ai some café fuerte, Mom." Justin's voice was languid, happy.

"Hey, that's fine, take your time, in fact if you want to come for breakfast tomorrow morning, that's fine. Javier and I totally understand, like does a bear have hair. And that Taos guy I told you about—Hank a burnin' love—he's coming in tonight, so why don't you come tomorrow at around 6 a.m."

"You're kidding, right Mom?"

"No, I'm not kidding, he's bringing his eagle bone flute and we'll do a dawn ceremony. You'll love it and I promise to have some killer café fuerte. Tell Ai I love her, and as usual I love you too."

"Well, it looks like Pompeii and Floriana are coming to San

Miguel in a couple of days. They're still together and he sounds, what can I say, happy. Also, he says Carlitos was fitted with his new leg, que bien."

The house phone rang again and Xochiquetzal wondered if it was Justin changing his mind; or Ai changing it. She smiled as she answered, "Hola." Then she laughed, "Ayy Diosa, chinga tu madre, Pablo, where the fuck are you, and that beautiful chica, Sonya?" Javier leaned over, doing a grito into the receiver, and Pablo promptly returned it.

"Okay, look, should I just give the phone to Javier so you two can continue your secret love affair?"

"No, no, first you, then put el otro cabron on so I can insult him," Pablo laughed loudly. "Sonya and I have been back from Bali for a couple of weeks, and we just moved into this chinga tu padre palace. I bought it a couple of years ago and I've been getting it ready just for a party like this, you'll see, Xochitzalita. So I'm calling to invite you, el cabron, tu hijo, all your friends, here for Navidad. This place is huge and I'm going to have mariachis, flamenco, and a rock band for modern dancing. And my friends will be here, as well as my beautiful daughters for a few days, with their chingado *boy friends*, so they tell me."

"Their boyfriends are staying with you overnight, wow."

"Are you kidding, nunca, just for the fregado party, and that's enough for el papa," Pablo growled low in his throat.

"You're sure proper with your daughters, cabron," Xochiquetzal teased him, laughing. "Are you sure you can fit everyone, plus these bands?"

"I could land a jet in this place, you'll see, and bring some champagne, nothing else, and come around 8 p.m. or so. We'll stay up till dawn, who knows maybe longer. Okay, now put el joder Javier on, mi Xochitzalita bonita."

"Estas muy loco, Pablo, but you're growing on me, I think. I'm bringing a great guy we met from Taos, he's part Hopi..."

"Bring the whole chingado tribe, Xochitzalita, and some champagne, nothing else. Everything will be taken care of, from the soup to the chutney."

"Okay, you asked for it, cabron—here's el otro loco." She handed the phone to Javier.

"What's this about bands, cabron, and stock up on the tequila so I can kick your ass again, chinga tu perro...."

Xochiquetzal shook her head—There they go and I just hope Justin doesn't join in on the ass kicking contest. Justin. Ai. She smiled as she climbed the stairs to the roof, keeping an eye out for scorpions. "The golden scorpion," she murmured, "my heart's desire." Then she sat in her favorite chair, gazing out at the sweet, human-sized town; its church towers that lit up at night to comfort lovers and insomniacs. The circling mountains, the perfectly painted clouds that held to the endless blue morning sky.

"Maybe this is my heart's desire, what more could I possibly want," she whispered to the perfection of the moment. This ever changing painting.

"I'm surprised you're up after the late shuttle, the tequila," Xochiquetzal smiled at Hank in the pre-dawn darkness.

"I don't think I made any sense last night, I was so tired, no sleep for almost twenty hours. I can't sleep on planes and that delay in hella L.A., but I ain't complainin', the ride was pretty cheap. Especially when I figured that the bus ride would take up most of my time here, hay-ya! I'll do the drive next time, on my own wheels, but the eagle does like to fly," Hank laughed. "Then I got a cheap drunk on those four shots, man I was pretty dead last night. Where's the doc, still sleeping?"

"I have la café fuerte, amigo, so you better be nice to me." Javier appeared in the doorway to the roof, still groggy with sleep. He placed the basket tray of cups, pan dulce, down on a low table. A small brass lantern with a lit candle was at the center and he held the thermos of strong, hot coffee in his right hand.

"I smell la café fuerte, dude, hay-ya! I think I'm still kinda alive, so pour that puppy!"

"So, you couldn't talk your Mom into coming, I would've liked to have seen her again, but I'm glad to hear her breathing problem was only allergies," Xochiquetzal said, waiting for her coffee.

"You can bet she'll drive down with me next time, she just ain't no flying'eagle like me, more of a nestin' eagle, my Mom. Yeah, she can't stop talkin' 'bout you y el doctor, what a beautiful couple blah blah blah, and when am I gonna find someone to hang out with," Hank laughed softly. "She wants her grand-babies like now, hay-ya."

The lion knocker rang loudly in the silence. "It's Justin and Ai, he probably forgot, or lost, his key..." Xochiquetzal started to get to her feet, taking one more strong sip of coffee.

"Hey, where's *my key*?" Javier leapt to his feet to answer the door.

"You don't deserve one yet," Hank smiled.

"You can't have any more of my café fuerte, dude," Javier tossed behind him as he ran to the front door. "Come on up, you two, café muy fuerte on the roof and also Hank a burnin' love." He led the way back to the roof, hoping his coffee would stay hot.

Xochiquetzal poured coffee for everyone, listening to their quick footsteps. "Look, the sky is slightly changing, Hank."

"Yeah, pretty soon but first a sip, por favor."

"Hey Mom," Justin smiled sheepishly, joyously. "Coffee, coffee, coffee." He hugged her with a small laugh, then straight for coffee.

"I'm Hank, dude, and I know you're Justin the favorite son."

"The only son, yeah. Glad to meet you, Hank, my Mom tells me you're from Taos. And this is Ai, she's from Tokyo..."

Ai rushed Xochiquetzal, hugging the breath right out of her.

"Hey, no one hugged me," Javier whined with a sharp laugh.

"Oh man, I forgot." Justin grabbed Javier in a bear-wrestler's hug.

"I was only kidding, dude, stop!"

"Okay, my turn, move away, Justin!"

"Ayy la Amazon de la black belt," Javier complained, loving it, as she grabbed him.

Hototo warmed the eagle bone flute in his hands briefly, eyeing the far horizon. Their chairs faced the east where Taiowa would soon claim the dawn. He began to play a high pitched song of longing, as Quetzalcoatl blazed, reborn, in the darkness. The longing for first light. The longing for Creation. He paused as the sky flashed streaks of dark purple. "Qoyangnuptu, the mystery of Creation, purple light of dawn."

The eagle flute sang ragged with breath—high and low notes— then less ragged, smoother, smoother, singing breath. Traces of yellow shimmered on the far horizon, reaching, flying, toward them. "Sikangnuqa, Creation's breath of life, yellow light of dawn." Hototo began to laugh, his head thrown back with joy. The eagle flute began to fly with joy; the joy of simply being. Alive.

Existence.

The red light of dawn struggled for a moment—that birth— then spread itself, fresh red blood, across the birthing sky. "Talawva, human beings, fully formed, now created, O sacred red light of dawn." He continued to play the carved bone eagle flute—carved by his great-great Hopi grandfather, blessed by his beloved Taos father. Father,

Hototo thought, as the eagle flute praised every breathing being on Earth—father, I see you in Taiowa's first light. He paused to breathe, "Kuivato, the three lights of dawn, we greet you, Taiowa."

Then more softly, "Father."

Ai quietly wept as the first, so slender, golden arrows reached her. "Talawva, human beings, fully formed, now created," she whispered, remembering the day when the Sun fell to Earth.

Xochiquetzal saw her tears at the same moment Justin did. And as he took her into his arms, she said, "May the Blue Star Kachina never ever dance in the plaza, ever."

"Hay-ya!" Hototo answered, watching Taiowa rise, pulsing pale gold. They stayed silent until the Warrior in the Sun's arrows reached them without effort.

"What is the Blue Star Kachina?" Ai asked softly.

"In the Hopi prophecies, when Saquasohuh, Blue Star Kachina, dances in the plaza, he'll bring the great Sun energy to Earth." Then Hototo reminded himself, Not good to make things a reality. "And so, we keep prayin' he keeps dancin' way the hell out there in mama space. Or better yet, that he ventures into a black hole journey of two-thousand years at least. Give us humans some time to get it together, hay-ya!"

"For the Sixth World," Ai added.

"And for the Hopi Fifth World, yeah," Hototo grinned at Ai.

"The last time Saquasohuh..." Ai paused to struggle with the word, "...when Blue Star Kachina danced in the plaza my family was in Hiroshima, August 6, 1945, and of course the people of Nagasaki." Tears flowed from her eyes, but she made no effort to hide them. If I can't cry here, where can I cry?

Justin held her hand tightly, squeezing it. He met Hototo's eyes and found a depth of understanding rarely found in daily life, the white world. If people don't talk like this, believe this, these prophecies, Ai's memories, her family's stories, the Blue Star Kachina will return. To dance. He trembled in the chill, dawn air and brought Ai closer to him.

"You need a Hopi name, Ai, and we just greeted Taiowa, perfect. What do you think of *Yamo' osta*?" Hototo beamed her a sun smile, as his stomach starting to clamor for food.

"What does it mean, it sounds so beautiful." She tried to smile, but her tears continued, and she heard Don Francisco's voice, "Sana, sol, sana, sol...heal, sun, heal, sun."

"It's very special, Ai, as you are, I can see it, feel it. Yamo'osta means Mother People."

She could barely speak. Not even to say gracias. She put her palms together and bowed her head slowly.

"And Justin, you've got to be Kwahu, the eagle, the way your eyes hunt the horizon. The way you protect your woman, yeah you're Kwahu, dude," Hototo laughed softly. We're all the same age, except for Xochitzalita, yet we're all ancient. He smiled to himself. Maybe Xochitzalita is the only one who's young here, yeah.

"Thank you, Hank, our names are perfect, gracias. Can you write them down for us so we don't forget like idiots." Justin returned Hototo's sun smile.

Ai and Xochiquetzal were the last ones on the roof, as all the men insisted on fixing breakfast for the 'mother people.' "I'll make scrambled eggs con chorizo," Javier tried taking over.

"Show me the flour and I'll make Pueblo tortillas," Hank joined in.

"Well then, I'll peel mangoes and whatever, and sprinkle lime juice over it," Justin laughed.

"Do you like chorizo, Hank?" Javier asked as he opened the frig door.

"Is the Pope a Catholic?" Hank answered, and they all cracked up on themselves.

"Hey, there's cold Victorias in here!" Justin reached for one. "Do you guys want one? No, don't tell me, Does a chicken got lips?" And he passed out the icy Victorias, turning back to find mangoes and the ripest papaya begging to be eaten.

Ai and Xochiquetzal watched pure white cranes float by; then immense flocks of ducks migrating to their day lake in the east, from their night lake in the west. Their dark designs evolved in flight; no leaders, only flight.

"Don Francisco told me to give you this when we were alone, and we're definitely alone now." Ai reached into her day pack and brought out a tiny box wrapped in a handwoven rainbow fabric, tied with red/black yarn, which she'd cushioned in a sweater. "He said to only open it when the time comes, and that you'll know when that is." She carefully handed the tiny box to her friend. "He also said he'd send you a dream and not to worry, you'll know when it's time, when to open this. And as I told you, he's gotten your dreams, the one about me coming," Ai smiled, tired but so happy.

"I wasn't even aware of sending him any dreams, but if they're for him I'm sure they arrive. I did have a dream of him chanting, "Sana, sana, sana," in the dark, some candles..."

"That's exactly what it was like, his altar, then our walks. I might be sano, healed, Xochitzalita wouldn't that be amazing? Maybe I'll live to be forty or so, maybe I'll go to medical school when I finish this journey..."

"You'll live longer than forty, Ai, I can feel that, and you'll have children too." Tears stopped her words as she cradled the tiny, beautifully wrapped box.

"I think I'm beginning to love your son, Xochitzalita, he's such a gift, this son of yours..."

"He's been waiting for you—what's your Hopi name?" Ai handed her the names written on paper. "He's been waiting for you, Yamo'osta, and you're right on time," she smiled, weeping rainbows. "Like the poet, Rumi, wrote, let's see if I can remember." She closed her eyes to see the words: "Lovers don't finally meet somewhere. They're in each other all along."

"That's it, exactly, that's how I felt when I first saw Justin and although it was kind of weird, I also loved it, you know, deep down." Ai wept her own fresh rainbows.

Xochiquetzal took her hand and kissed it, laughing. "Boy, do I know, the weirdness when love wakes up inside of us, yes, I know."

"Are you curious, what's inside the tiny box? I don't know if I could stand it. In fact, I had to kick my own butt not to open it," Ai laughed like a girl, still weeping. Rainbows.

"The truth is, I am fucking dying of curiosity, but I also know if I open it when it's not time it'll be some pretty bad juju. I mean, if Don Francisco specifically said that, I'm going to hide it from myself," she laughed with frustration.

"Oh Quan Yin, I almost forgot maybe the most important thing he said to tell you. 'When the sacred scorpion appears, you'll know it's time.'"

("Sacred," the Energy Child whispered, "scorpion.")

"Feliz, are you hungry? We just finished breakfast, cooked by los muy macho hombres, and it wasn't too bad." Xochiquetzal grabbed

Feliz for a hug.

"Whattaya mean it wasn't too bad, you had seconds, hay-ya!" Hank yelled.

"I'll take café fuerte if there's some left and some of this pan dulce, yummy. And who's yelling like a wild Indian, Dios mio."

"A wild Indian from Taos, Hank, or as he's now widely known, Hank a burnin' love a la Kokopelli. That womanizer and wandering flute player," Xochiquetzal laughed. "And this is Feliz, everyone, and she's a very wild woman."

"You didn't tell me this cute Indio was going to be here, and you shoulda, especially after you told me el hermoso Justin is now taken ayy," Feliz leaned into her, whispering with a giggle.

Hank stood to greet Feliz, extending his hand. "Feliz, Joy, ya gotta nice name, hay-ya, my mama's name is Joy." He grabbed her hand in a nakwach greeting, putting hers on top. Smiling into her. The fully risen. Sun.

Feliz yelped in surprise, laughing her wild laugh. "Watch the hand, por favor, I'm a painter and a dentist."

"Well, I'm pretty impressed, damn, I'm a lowly high school teacher..."

"He teaches Taos kids their real history, and he makes the most beautiful jewelry, he's being shy. That's a new one," Xochiquetzal laughed. "Show Feliz Hototo's ring, mi amor, the one he gave you." That's right, Joy and Feliz, she realized, smiling.

"Who's Hototo?" Feliz looked slightly confused. "Oh, what a gorgeous ring and you made it, or this guy Hototo made it?"

"It's Hank's Hopi name and I'll let him tell you," Javier joined in. "And yes, he made this ring and gave it to me in Taos."

"If you're Hopi, what are you doing in Taos?" Feliz met Hank's laughing eyes.

"I'm Taos from my father and Hopi from my Mom. He was the real Kokopelli womanizer and wanderer, and how I got here, when he wandered into Hopi Land and enticed my Mom, hay-ya!"

"Okay," Feliz laughed, enjoying his voice, his loud laughter, his presence. Xochiquetzal put café fuerte, pan dulce, a small serving of still warm scrambled eggs with chorizo, Pueblo tortillas, and the bowl of mango/papaya slices in front of her.

"Those are my tortillas, my Mama's sacred recipe, tell me what you think, and about the handshake I just gave you, the nakwach, that's reserved..." Hank paused.

"Reserved for?" Feliz prodded.

"Reserved for the trust worthy, hay-ya," he said softly. Into her eyes.

Feliz blushed, full body—Not since a teen, Dios mio, she realized. "Well, I feel honored, do it again," she giggled, "so I can see exactly how it's done. Hey, maybe a nakwach painting..."

Something lovely stirred in Hank's belly, a tiny yellow bird pecked through its protective shell. He took her hand gently in his this time, feeling the weight of it, turning it over on top of his, not letting her go. "It would be a beautiful painting, Feliz, I can see it, hay-ya."

"And then she could give you a root canal, dude!" Justin couldn't resist, guffawing.

"Callate, estas malo," Ai smacked his face playfully, lingering to trace his cheek.

Javier met Xochiquetzal's eyes, widening them and making his eyebrows go up and down, as in *muy caliente.* He took her in his arms. "It's the fucking love train or love boat, tu sabes, mi amor," he laughed, whispering into her ear.

As Hank walked down the cobbled street, he kept smiling and greeting people as though he were on the rez—Taos Pueblo, Hopi Land. "Everyone looks like an Indian,

hay-ya, couldn't get rid of us, we're takin' back Turtle Island!" He gave a short grito, throwing his long-haired (loose, past his shoulders) head back, laughing. He wore the traveling turquoise earring he'd made at sixteen, those years he'd dreamt of travel. It dangled in his left ear as he walked; Taiowa's golden arrows danced with the spiral of silver, traveling up to its center. Where the deep, blue turquoise waited.

"Callate, locito Taos-Hopi hombre, you might get your Indio nalgas...your Indian ass...arrested," Feliz laughed, holding on to his hand as he almost dragged her down the cobbled street. Look at that beautiful hair, longer than mine—she smiled to herself—so chingado hermoso, but my parents would think I'd lost my mind, una loca.

Justin and Ai led the way to the Arts and Crafts Fair, held in the wide open courtyards of the Instituto Allende. They walked through the immense, two-story, hand-carved, 17th century wooden doors, flung open to the crowd. Every space was filled to the brim with every hand-made object a human could create. Woven rugs, clothing from Oaxaca, Guatemala, all over Mexico, Peru (the entire southern continent), sold by wandering Indios, Mestizos. Handmade jewelry in traditional designs, and unexpected designs, glittered in Taiowa's arrows. Paintings by local artists in so many styles, visions, with one thing in common. Each one held its own unique rainbow, vision of the world.

A mural of Mexico's ancient history—the Mayans dreamt the zero, astronomy, magical pyramids that held the Earth's Solstice lights, great cities, written history, while Europe still crawled on its knees—commanded an entire wall at the back of the courtyard. Each amazing section had to be discovered with the lingering eyes of a lover; and Ai stopped in her tracks in front of it. Justin stood next to her, bringing her hand to his lips. Their bodies ignited with joy's lust as his mouth grazed her hand. Slowly.

"Look, at this amazing mural, look," Ai leaned over, kissing him playfully. "There's plenty of time for that later, muchacho malo. Look at those faces, those bodies, those stories in time..."

"I'm coming with you, Ai, I'm going to travel with you and that's all there is to it. We're going to travel the world together in the next year and I won't take no for an answer, I'm not kidding, bonita..."

"Okay," Ai smiled, gazing with rapture at the mural.

"Okay? Is that it?"

"Yup."

Justin did a soft grito laughing, "Yup."

"Look at the woman," she pointed, "her vagina, the umbilical cord still connected to her child, so beautiful." Tears filled her eyes. "I want a child someday, after the travel, if I'm truly healed, I do. I want a child."

"Okay." Justin took her into his arms, picking her up so easily, spinning her. "And I know you're healed, bonita, look at you," he laughed.

A guitarist sat down in a chair behind them and began to caress chords of fire. Flamenco. He smiled at the shimmering air that held the fire leaving his fingertips; and his fingertips sang of love found, love embraced, love lost, only to be found again. The ancient cycles of earth, fire, ocean, volcanoes erupting, cleansing lava, new earth. He played.

Xochiquetzal saw Justin pick Ai up and spin her, bringing tears to her eyes so suddenly. Javier stood next to Hank and Feliz as Hank spoke to the Huichol man, Salvador, about his beautiful yarn paintings and beaded bowls. His wife, Maria, beaded extravagant bracelets, necklaces, earrings, sitting to the side, listening, smiling. They both wore the beautiful, hand-loomed with birds, butterflies, flowers, Huichol clothing.

"This yarn painting reminds me of the Hopi Blue Flute Altar in spring," Hank breathed, "so beautiful." He picked it up, Taiowa (Creator, Sun God) at the center. His warrior arrows blessing every breathing creature, and the painting held a circle of beautiful deer with glowing horns. One tiny human being, arms spread wide, mouth open in song, praise, at the edge of the Sun's sacred circle.

"You're a Hopi, hermano?" Salvador smiled.

"And Taos Pueblo de mi padre, Hopi de mi madre, the Blue Flute Fire Clan." Hank reached for the eagle bone flute in his inner vest pocket, safe in its leather travel pouch. He warmed it in his gentle, brown hands. His child. The eagle. He closed his eyes and began to play the eagle song to Taiowa, the longing to reach the Creator. To burn. As one. He opened his eyes and found Feliz gazing at him steadily. On fire.

He continued to play his child; the eagle's long journey home. A small crowd gathered and just as the eagle began to circle the Sun, Hototo stopped. Soft applause. You'll reach Taiowa tomorrow morning, little kwahu, eagle...kuivato, when we greet the great rising Sun, Taiowa. And he put his child away, into its soft deer skin, travel pouch. Cradled by eagle feathers—from the wing—the child fell asleep, dreaming. Flight.

"I want you to have this, hermano, my gift to you for your song." Salvador had wrapped the yarn painting in plastic, handing it to him.

"No, no, I was going to buy it, mi hermano, you work too hard to not be paid. Hay-ya I know, because I make jewelry to sell in Taos..."

"If you don't accept my gift, hermano Hopi, I'll be insulted. We're relatives, the Huichol, the Hopi, you know this. Please accept my gift."

"Well, I'm buying a few for my house and my office," Feliz broke in energetically. "I really love these two and also these."

Maria stopped beading, taking the yarn paintings from Feliz's hands to wrap them. "My husband is one of the best, señorita."

"I can see that, claro que si," Feliz smiled, reaching into her purse for pesos. And luckily, she'd just been to the bank. "And I also want some of your beautiful jewelry, like this necklace, ayy que bonita."

"Gracias, hermano Salvador, gracias." Hank touched the sacred yarn painting to his forehead (his dream-eye). "There's a migration story the Hopi tell of our lost Hopi clan to the south, mi Huichol hermano. They didn't complete the migration back to us in the north, but they remain Hopi in spirit." He lowered his voice. "May I call you Cheveyo, Spirit Warrior, in Hopi. My name in Hopi is Hototo, Spirit Warrior Who Sings," he smiled, hoping he hadn't offended him.

Xochiquetzal and Javier watched in silence; both recognizing a historic moment that would never be recorded in any history books. They watched. Listened.

A long moment passed between Hototo and Salvador. The small crowd dispersed to the market. Feliz and Maria spoke in whispers, then paused to listen.

"Say my Hopi name again, hermano, and your name too."

"Cheveyo, Spirit Warrior, and my Hopi name, Hototo, Spirit Warrior Who Sings." He reached for his small notebook and pen tucked in his vest pocket, and wrote out the names, their meanings.

"You live in the north, Hototo?" Cheveyo asked.

"In the very north of a state called Arizona, the final migration of the Hopi, my mother's people and mine. The old trade routes of Kokopilau, our continent." Tears stung his eyes—My Huichol brother to the south. Hototo took his Fire Clan ring, with its Fire-Sun symbol, from his finger and offered it to Cheveyo.

"This has been passed down through time, and I'll make another to pass down, a new time."

Cheveyo shook his head no, with an ancient sadness. Beyond words.

"If you don't accept my gift, mi hermano, I'll be offended. We're ancient relatives, the Huichol, the Hopi." Hototo gently smiled as tears blessed his face. One blessed the ring.

Cheveyo reached for the wet ring and slipped it over two fingers. The third finger fit, perfectly.

"It's from the Fire Clan, Taiowa's gift to the people."

"Quien es...Who is Taiowa?"

"The Creator, Sun God, mi hermano."

"Como el Huichol, Tatewari, Grandfather of Fire who gives us light, and Tao Jreeku, Father Sun." Cheveyo pointed to the pulsing Sun in the center of Hototo's yarn painting.

"Si, si, el Sol...Yes, yes, the Sun, Taiowa and Tao Jreeku," he smiled so widely.

Hototo's smile broke Feliz's heart. Who smiles like that, no defenses, she asked herself. And I forgot my own defenses, me, la doctora, as he held my hand.

Hototo gently grabbed Cheveyo's right hand. "Esto es el nakwach, hermano...This is the nakwach. When the Hopi meet a relative, a long lost brother, sister, they offer the nakwach. Like this, Cheveyo." He quickly turned Cheveyo's hand to rest on top of his; both hands on each other's wrist.

"I see," Cheveyo laughed. "This is a firm clasp, hard to break, el nakwach, que bien."

They released the clasp and hugged, patting each other on the back. Like long, forgotten brothers. Each one laughing with ancient tears: joy.

"To the Fifth World emerging like *lomahongva*," Hototo pointed to the thick, white clouds over their heads. "In Hopi it means 'Beautiful clouds arising.'"

"And to the Sixth World in the south, flying through our hearts, Wealika, Madre Aguila...Mother Eagle. Show me the nakwach again, Hototo."

Xochiquetzal had to do it, she couldn't help it. La profesora de los fotos—"Do you mind if I take some photos, please, you look like brothers," she smiled, waiting.

Cheveyo looked at Hototo for the answer. He was used to tourists taking his photo, but he always held something back, in reserve. In this moment, with his ancient brother, he held nothing back.

Hototo smiled back at her, the sun at zenith—"We're two old Indians who want to escape, Xochitzalita, but we'll trust you to return our spirits intact. And I sure would treasure a photo of me and el Cheveyo together, hay-ya, so give it your best shot, hermana Yaqui!"

"La señora es un Yaqui, que bien!" Cheveyo laughed in surprise. "Send me un foto la web way, por favor."

"Do you mean the internet?" Hototo laughed with him.

"My sons taught me its use for fiestas like this, el web camino."

"Qué bien, we'll email from the north to the south, south to the north, like lightning, the old trade routes, hermano! We'll meet in *tangakwunu*, the rainbow!"

"Okay you two, look at me and smile or cry, whatever you want to do!" Tears clouded her eyes for a moment as she gazed at their ancient/new sun smiles. Exposed, revealed. Brothers. Then she took shots of Cheveyo, Maria, Hototo, Feliz, and Javier took some of Cheveyo, Maria, Hototo, Feliz, Xochiquetzal. An onlooker took two shots of them all, including Justin and Ai. Exposed, revealed, laughing, weeping.

Pablo swung the door open, then slammed it shut, laughing; then opened it again. "So I see you brought this pinche cabron with you, lovely Xochitzalita, que lastima...what a shame."

"Where's the tequila, pendejo?" Javier clasped Pablo in a fierce hug. "I don't know why I like an idiot like you, but I do, que me chingas!"

"Maybe it's this way with hermanos, you can't help it, pinche pendejo," Pablo laughed, picking Javier up for a moment. "And I'm the bigger brother, doctorcito!"

Javier laughed with irritation/pleasure—he and Xavier never played like this.

"Okay, okay, enough bonding! Ayy Diosa, this place is a fucking palace! And you bought it a while ago, sneaky you," Xochiquetzal laughed, gazing around.

"I could keep a mistress here and Sonya would never know it," Pablo grinned wickedly. "Later on you'll have to take the tour, in the day is best, and it's almost complete, but still more to go. And yes, it's ours and we're going to be married here, so another fiesta in a few months. Hey, your friends are here waiting for you, and who's el pinche gladiator looking guy?"

"That's Ari, and you'd better not keep any mistresses here or I'll help Sonya kick your butt," Xochiquetzal glared at him, then grinned. "This is Hank, high school teacher from Taos Pueblo, New Mexico, the old trade routes. And this is Feliz, talented painter and local dentist. Mi hijo, Justin, beloved since the womb," she smiled into Justin's eyes. "And his newly beloved, in this life anyway, Ai from Tokyo, Japan, traveling the world with her peace crystals."

"Welcome, welcome, join la fiesta in progress." Pablo clasped everyone's hand, meeting each one's eyes. And with Justin, he said, "I was hoping you'd take one of my daughters from their pendejo *boy friends*," he growled with mischief. "A good man is hard to find, just look at mi preciosa Sonya, she's stuck with me."

"Welcome Xochitzalita, Javier, todos los amigos y amigas, welcome!" Sonya beamed her shy smile. "Is Pablo talking about hiding his mistress again, que barbaro!" She smacked him lightly on the shoulder, and then followed with a quick kiss.

Javier and Xochiquetzal hugged Sonya and repeated the introductions. "Your son is so handsome, ay!" Sonya laughed as Justin squeezed Ai's hand. But he didn't have to; her confidence was supreme.

"I thought the same thing, Sonya," Ai smiled at her.

"I'm getting slightly embarrassed," Justin smiled shyly, holding Ai closer.

"And he's shy tambien, lucky you!" Sonya giggled.

"The daughters, Justin, not the wife to be." Pablo slapped him on the back teasingly. "Okay, okay, the champagne's flowing, your friends are waiting, my friends are waiting, and my mistress is waiting in her secret rooms, como no!" Sonya and Xochiquetzal smacked Pablo at the same time, making him yelp, "Hey, that hurt, mujeres del diablo!"

"Don't kiss him, Sonya, he deserves a little pain," Xochiquetzal giggled.

"Qué cabroncita," Javier grabbed her around the waist.

"Maybe a room of S and M with little whips and hand cuffs, mi amor," Pablo leaned into Sonya kissing her.

"See, he likes the pain, Sonya," Xochiquetzal rolled her eyes.

They walked into a sweeping room the size of a film set a la Hollywood, and an entire wall opened to an equally sweeping outdoor patio. The Mexican tiles in the room proper were blends of dark purple, brown, red, streaked with gold; and the patio was hues of sky-blue with a radiating, golden sun in the center. A flamenco group played guitars, drums, and sang as the seated women dancers clapped in rhythm—smiling, laughing, joking. Waiting to dance. Waiting for *el duende.* The spirit of the dance; the edge of death. Life. *Duende.*

A series of connected tables, against a vaulted wall, held every delicious food in the world—of course, Mexican, every state (the richest, darkest mole from Oaxaca)...Europe, the Middle East, Asia, Indonesia, India, Africa. Pablo's palette-tongue was tuned to the world after traveling, tasting each country's breast since he was a ravenous teen.

Xochiquetzal tried to find Ari in the growing crowd, but was side-tracked by a yell, "Xochitzalita," and Muriel seized her in a hug, laughing.

"I got in last night from the D.F., so I slept in, but hey we're both here at the same time, como no!"

"Damn mujer, I haven't seen you in over three years, so are you in Mexico on assignment or what?" Xochiquetzal had forgotten Muriel's beauty, the strength of her features. Where Nicaragua and Africa told their stories in her fearless, open, witnessed-the-world face.

"I was in Mexico City, el chingado D.F., for pleasure, if you must know, a muy sexy mujer, dang! Next Chiapas to find and interview the very compelling y also muy sexy, for a man," Muriel giggled, " Subcomandante Marcos. I'd love to get his photo without the joder mask, fat chance, but I can try."

"Muriel, this is Javier, it seems the man in my life, ayy Diosa, and he met Marcos a few years ago, right Javier?"

"I very briefly met him, if you can call it that, as an awe struck intern, but I could tell las mujeres thought he was muy sexy," Javier laughed.

"Girl, you are blushing, que bien! About time, Javier, I ain't never seen this woman blush. And I can see why, Xochitzalita, you old, sexy huntress!"

Javier extended his hand to Muriel, grinning—"And I also wrote my entire name in black ink on *our mattress,* so she's not getting rid of me, amiga..."

Muriel pushed past his hand, hugging him. "I love this man, Xochitzalita, he's a keeper, dang, and a doctor tambien!"

"Where's this dang-thing coming from?" Xochiquetzal laughed.

"I was seeing a gorgeous Texan for awhile, so slap me upside my head when I do it, dang!" Muriel leaned into Xochiquetzal, whispering, "If you throw this one back, give him to me. I could try to be bi for that kind of male beauty," she grinned. "He wrote his full name on your mattress, please girlfriend, *please.*"

"I'll get us all some champagne," Javier smiled, pausing to kiss Xochiquetzal, thrusting his tongue to meet hers, making her womb blush. Clench. Blush.

The younger woman dancer slowly rose to her feet, hands over her head, lush breasts thrust forward, held in her form-fitting, blood-red gown that swept her ankles. Her hands began to clap over her head as the guitarists and lone drummer spelled out the pulsing rhythm. Her feet kicked the wide, black flounce at the hem, her ankles, and the older woman singer, sitting behind her, called *el duende* in her raw, open-throated voice. Her eyes gazed out, piercing the unseen, singing.

"Where did you find this guy, Xochitzalita, dang, I mean damn, tell me all, mujer!"

"It's a very long story, amiga, but in Vallarta where *he* hunted *me* down. So he's the sexy, young hunter, and he's a physician, a healer, so there's a wonderful mind and heart as well..."

"Girlfriend, *please*, and please know this—he looks a few years younger, but love has slashed the years from you, I swear, go on with your bad self!"

"Xochitzalita, is that you?" a lovely, low-pitched, masculine voice asked.

"Ari! I was looking for you and hey you'd be hard to miss! Where were you?" A stunning, young woman stood next to him, holding her own with his presence.

Another dancer, an older woman, took the younger woman's place. Her form fitting dress was dark purple, gathered memories, and she stood absolutely still, slowly clapping her hands over her head, calling *el duende*. To stay. The man singer ruptured the air with ferocious longing, and she began to thrust her hips to an unseen lover. To offer her fully blossomed breasts to his lips. *El duende.* Paused. To dance.

"We've been here for two days but decided to wander around our first time in San Miguel de Allende, and what a beautiful town. Like Spain but with the warmth of Mexico, it feels far away from the USA border." Ari smiled sensually, holding his lover close.

"I'm so glad you wandered around, and did you and your gorgeous girlfriend go to La Gruta, the hot springs, if not..."

"I'm so rude, perdoname, Xochitzalita, this is my fiancee, Judith, from Israel, como no. We're getting married next summer in Israel and my Mom will come to stay for awhile. Of course, you and Javier are welcome to join us, I'll send you a formal invitation via email when it's a few months away.' Ari's sensual smile widened into joy.

"Ari tells me he met you in the Los Angeles Airport, instant recognition," Judith smiled, stepping forward to hug Xochitzalita.

"There's strength in those arms," she laughed. "And this is Muriel, Ari and Judith, an old photo student who's entirely out-stripped the professor. You've been to Israel, right Muriel?"

Muriel exchanged polite hugs with Ari and Judith. A body like that, she thought, an Israeli soldier. That presence, a commando. "Yes, and also to Palestine, covering both sides, my job as a photo-journalist." She watched carefully for Ari's and Judith's responses. Interest but no offense, she noted.

"Muriel's also been to Rwanda, interviewed survivors there—also, Bosnia during that awful genocide..."

Justin and Ai stood behind Xochiquetzal, champagne glasses in their hands. The word *genocide* made Ai flinch internally, but when Justin met her eyes she smiled. This is life on our planet, our world, and now I have this beautiful man to journey with me. To plant peace crystals with me. To leave some love where fear and pain was the reality. Yes, the word 'genocide.' Bitter word.

"Okay everyone—a repeat for some of you—here's my son, Justin, my first true love, and his new love, the beautiful and dangerous, Ai," Xochiquetzal laughed with joy, "from Japan. She's traveling the world planting peace crystals in honor of Hiroshima." Hiroshima melted everyone's heart and Israel, Palestine were momentarily forgotten.

"Ari, cabron, is that you?" Javier laughed, handing out glasses of freshly poured champagne from a tray. "I'm your Mexican waiter today and I'll give you some ER care if you need it as well."

"This is Judith, my wife in six months—Judith, this is Javier, Xochitzalita's love interest y un doctor," Ari slowly smiled. More hugs, quick kisses.

"Do you know this pinche ladron...thief, Javier? This guy says he knows you!" Pablo's voice rang out over the flamenco, followed by booming laughter.

"Pompeii, Floriana! You guys made it, welcome!" Xochiquetzal walked over to greet them. "What do you mean, ladron?" She shot Pablo a warning look.

"No me chingas, mujer, I know this guy, El Pompeii," Pablo laughed. "He used to live in San Miguel in his youthful, gangster days, and I finished his pinche mansion with my impeccable taste."

"Qué *impeccable taste*, cabron, I felt sorry for you and your fledgling import business," Pompeii laughed from his lower belly and seized Pablo in a mock headlock, giving the top of his head knuckles for good measure.

"Ohmygoddess, los dos jefes...the two bosses," Xochiquetzal had to laugh, grabbing Floriana in a hug. "So, you survived being with this guy!"

"It's more than survival," her faced clouded in momentary offense. "Okay, I'm surviving *and* thriving," she laughed. "You know, Mexican men," Floriana whispered.

"Oh yes, I know. Come on, lots of folks to meet!"

"The tequila competition is going to be interesting tonight, cabrones, look at the competition." Pablo indicated Ari who was shaking hands, then a quick nakwach with Hank.

"I could use a guy like him in my business," Pompeii did a low whistle of sheer masculine admiration. "Is he a professional wrestler or que? He just needs the mask, the name, and he's ready to go."

"He's from Israel, or that's where he works from, but from Miami originally. My lips are sealed," Xochiquetzal giggled, bumping her hip into Floriana's as Javier walked toward them.

"Pompeii, Pablo, los cuates...the twins, los pinche pendejos!" Javier laughed, approaching them. "So you two coyotes know each other, of course you do. And to remind you both, I beat you con el tequila."

"You call that a beating, I had to put you in a taxi," Pablo grabbed Javier, putting him between them.

"And my men had to carry you to Xochitzalita's tent, doctorcito!" Pompeii gave a sudden grito of such joy, every man in the room responded, including Justin, Hank, Ari, as well as la bonita macha, Muriel.

(The Energy Child trembled, surrounded by such joy—than added her/his own grito that sounded like tiny, golden bells.)

"Look at my beautiful daughters dancing con los pinche pendejo *boy friends*. They're just waiting to get out of my sight to slip their fregado panties off, and they already look like they're fucking, in public." Pablo poured himself another shot of excellent tequila. And then a shot for Pompeii, Javier, handing the bottle to Ari to pour for all takers. "There's more on that far table, amigo, so just keep pouring, como no. It looks like you might win tonight, Ari, ayy!"

"It's the rock band, Papacito," Javier laughed. "It's that funky music, gets the hips pumping, the blood flowing, dude. Look at Xochitzalita and Muriel, I think I'm getting jealous," he smiled.

"I could have los novios disappear, Pablo, just give me la palabra, the word." Pompeii smiled but his tone held an edge of truth. "But look at your daughters, cabron, who could blame them. You were the same, even worse, as I remember," he laughed so loudly, a ripple of laughter answered him like an echo. He was a man who'd learned to die, and to live full-tilt, in his twenties. So everything he did—laugh, cry, dance, sing—was contagious. And every time he made love was the first time—Why do it otherwise? was his personal religion. Floriana's lushness, sexual scent, her ripe black-olive eyes, wounded red mouth, was what he prayed to. Daily, nightly.

"Where's Floriana?" Xochiquetzal approached, still holding hands with Muriel, dancing. Javier intercepted her, pulling her into his arms, and she allowed them, his arms, to possess her. I never knew a man's arms could be so delicious, so fucking addictive, road kill for sure. The stray chicas who've been asking him to dance, him laughing, that sheer charm. The young, fearless tigre—"Ayyy," she sighed. But she stayed within his arms, and in that moment she knew she couldn't leave them with her usual will.

"Here she comes, Xochitzalita, and good sex becomes her, doesn't it? She glows like a Goddess, thanks to me!" Pompeii exploded into laughter.

"And Sonya's with her, that can't be good," Pablo smiled warily. "All that secret woman's talk, que me chingas. And now you're getting hold of la dulce Sonya, Xochitzalita." He gave up and laughed, watching his daughter's mimic sex on the dance floor.

"What a humongous ego you have, Pompeii, and your only rival is Pablo..." Xochiquetzal shook her head.

"Just because Javier is quiet, more refined, el doctorcito, he's still a Mexican who thinks he's a God!" Pompeii boomed with laughter.

She laughed with him—as did the rest of the room. "I already know about this guy's humongous ego, cabron, I was just commenting on yours!"

"I love you, Xochitzalita, estas mala!" Pompeii dragged her from Javier's arms, picking her up for a twirl. Then carefully placed her back, laughing. He quickly seized Floriana away from Sonya, holding her softness from behind, smelling her deep woman's scent on her neck.

The rock band paused for a break and the crowd was thinning out, going on 1 a.m. Ai, Justin, Feliz, Hank, Ari and Judith wandered over, as one of the waiters opened a bottle of chilled champagne.

"My pinche friends are going to see their families," Pablo laughed. "And my daughters are off to their mother's, who I will call to confirm in no more than twenty minutes."

"Bye Papa, I'll see you in a few days," the older daughter smiled. The younger one let her do the talking, but sent her father a sly smile.

"Do you think I've never seen a young woman smile like that, and you two pendejos, if you *touch* my daughters, either of you idiots,

Pompeii here will make you two disappear, y tu mamas will only have a photo as memory!" Pablo growled, no laughter. "And your bodies will not be found, he's a pinche professional, right Pompeii?"

"Papa, calm down, we're just going to Mama's house now..." the younger daughter finally spoke.

"And I'm calling her to make sure you arrive within twenty fregado minutes, no me chingas!"

The young men glanced at Pompeii nervously, then back at Pablo. "Senor, we'll drive your daughters directly to their destination, their mother's home," the brave one said.

"I know you will, pinche cabrones, or your ass is mine, or Pompeii's, now get el joder out of here!"

Both daughters kissed Pablo quickly on the cheek, giggling.

"Do you think I'm kidding, chicas?"

"No Papa, we know you love us," the older one smiled. They held their laughter down (in their ripening wombs). "Bye Sonya, you're like our big sister, we love you!" the younger one yelled as they fled, laughing. The young men, however, didn't laugh, but glanced nervously over their shoulders. Waiting for the meaty hands of Pablo, Pompeii.

"You terrorized them, Pablo, you should be ashamed!" Feliz laughed.

"Wait until you have grown daughters and you'll do the same thing, a curse upon you!" Pablo finally smiled, glancing at his watch to time his call to his ex-wife. "The young man that gets my daughter pregnant, in other words marries her, must ask my permission first, que joder!"

"I think you're worse than my father," Ai laughed, leaning into Justin. "He didn't want to let me travel alone, but now I have Justin..."

"That's exactly what I mean, once out of sight..."

"Hey, that's my son you're talking about, and look who's talking, the coyote in the chicken coop, get real, Pablo! Okay, okay, I've noticed we're all lacking gold glitter, so it's gold glitter time, and I know you love your daughters but lighten up just a tad. I think you made those poor kids pee their boxers."

"Our heart's desire," Javier added. "The gold glitter I mean, not peeing our boxers," he laughed.

"I loved los mariachis, Pablo, will they return?" Judith asked.

"Not tonight, but they're my favorite band in town. If you're planning to be here for New Year's, it'll be them and the rock band, maybe two." Pablo walked over to the returning band and asked them to play some slow rock, no more funky music tonight. Something to ease them into 2 a.m., the lone Spanish guitarist, and a surprise.

"Put out your hands and I'll put some gold glitter in the palm of your hand. Then put some on your partner, friend, victim, lover," Xochiquetzal laughed softly as she sprinkled the color of dreams into their open hands.

Heart's desire   Deepest play

The handsome, young band members watched as los locos began painting gold glitter on each other's faces. The gorgeous, brown-skinned singer with his electric green/gold eyes—eyes burning youth, often wasting it. Just to burn. He'd gotten Pablo's older daughter's cell number—*No chica's off limits to me, and it's clear she's tired of being la virgen.* Alejandro turned to the band, smiling, "Stairway To Heaven, amigos." He gave an intimate grito into the microphone, and began to sing, thinking of his tongue circling her nipple. *Just to burn.*

Heart's desire   Deepest play

"I have a surprise, follow me," Pablo took Sonya's hand and led the way to an adjoining, secret room. He took a key out of his pant's pocket, facing the immense,

hand-carved wooden door, slid it into the lock, and flung it open to a sprawling,

high-ceilinged space. It wasn't a room; it was a space.

Silk fabrics—purple, red, gold—hung, draped from the high, domed ceiling to the tiles, billowing slightly in the night wind. A huge, ornate, round oak table in the center of the space was surrounded by large, plush cushions; each one handmade, unique with its own beauty. And candles of every size burned everywhere, creating the illusion of stars in the night sky. Creating the tone of another world. A world of dreamers.

"This is my secret room, bienvenido, welcome, sit where you want. It's a marriage of Asia, Indonesia, especially magical Bali, my home away from home," Pablo smiled, enjoying the obvious pleasure being displayed as everyone tried to take in the diversity of sheer beauty. "And Africa, Egypt, India, and of course this beautiful continent, all my travels. The prayer mats, under your pillows, to lounge, rest, plot adventures or revenge, dream, are from Mecca," he laughed quietly in the stunned silence.

"This is the most beautiful room I've ever been in," Ai broke the silence. "The church spires in the distance lit up and, damn, just the magic you've created here, Pablo, gracias, I'm honored to be here."

"What's that in the center, a water pipe or what?" Ari laughed with recognition.

"I see you've used one, amigo," Pablo smiled, "on your travels. A very wise balance for a soldier, discipline tempered with sensuality."

"Where's the pinche dope, cabron, and what are we smoking?" Pompeii broke the silence further with a burst of loud laughter. "No me chingas, I brought a small pouch of los magico mushrooms in case such a moment arose." He laughed again, pulling Floriana to the luxuriant cushions with him.

An older woman began to place platters of food around the table, and a young woman plates, glasses, cutlery, napkins in front of each person. Pitchers of water, bottles of wine; the white wine in icy buckets, scattered around the immense, beautiful table. Everyone found their place, their cushions, sitting around the table.

Xochiquetzal stared in wonder, the exit door to the main room, an entire, sculpted, stone doorway from a Balinese temple, with a bare-breasted Goddess over the entry. Flowers, gods, humans, streaming down the sides in stone. An entire Barong stood to the right of the entry, with its mirrored, golden body, the lion-like tail upraised with confidence, and it wore the immense Barong mask with its playful blend of lion/dragon. Only the Balinese were missing to give it life—their feet showing under the Barong, dancing down the street. A stone statue of the Goddess, Saraswati, to the left, standing on her fierce, cosmic goose; her four hands held the tools of literature, music and beauty. And over her head flared a red, fringed in gold, Balinese umbrella. In the corner next to her, an altar to the Supreme God, Atintya—tiny, golden, dancing in flames—with baskets of fruit, dried corn, beans, rice, stacked to the top as offerings. Fresh flowers surrounded the baskets, and a pottery bowl of water for his thirst, as well as a shot of tequila. Which Pablo would drink at the end of the day and refill it in the morning, while lighting incense. As is done in Bali, the entire island, daily—the offerings, the incense.

And then Xochiquetzal saw, in the farthest corner of the space—

more like a temple courtyard, she realized—a Balinese pavilion with a royal-sized bed for lounging, sleeping, dreaming, making love. There were wooden steps leading up to it and the pavilion was complete with its stunning, ornate, hand-carved, wooden canopy. She could glimpse Balinese masks, winged statues, paintings, but she controlled the urge to leap to her feet and see it all up close. To sprawl on that sensual, glorious, royal-sized bed—Later, she promised herself, I'm sleeping there.

"I'm so fucking impressed, I can't even speak, Pablo, Sonya—what can I say but gracias. It's so beautiful as though you've read my definition of beauty, hey *wonder*," Xochiquetzal wept with joy. "You've created a Balinese courtyard and I swear I'm going to sleep in that bed!"

"Don't worry, this woman weeps when she loves you," Javier laughed, kissing her.

"I wouldn't believe this room is in San Miguel, but now I do. Of course, I'm going to paint it, "Feliz smiled. "Can I return in the sunlight, Pablo?"

"The afternoon is best, call me."

"The Navajo sand painting next to the Tibetan scrolls are perfect together, and the Heyoka Kachina, hay-ya I'm right at home!" Hank chanted a soft Hopi prayer of gratitude, to beauty. "There's a word my Hopi grandmother used to say to encompass beauty, the moment, *kuwanyauma*. It means 'Butterfly showing beautiful wings,' hay-ya what a magnificent butterfly! I'm glad to be here, Pablo, gracias amigo."

"I want to take photos, set up my tripod, work with flash, but I think I finally know enough to leave the magic's wonder alone," Muriel sighed with that certain sadness born from the sharp-edged sword of wisdom. She'd seen the world's wonder, and its awful terror, in equal measure. "Gracias, Pablo, Sonya, gracias."

"Where's the pinche dope for the hookah, pendejo!" Pompeii demanded, sending laughter around the circle.

"Don't mind him," Floriana giggled, "he saves his best behavior for the bed, if you know what I mean." She placed a stuffed date into his mouth, with her mouth, kissing him deeply. Unashamed, in fact, enjoying the momentary spectacle. "And this is the only way to shut him up, but I don't mind," she smiled, catching her breath.

"You're glowing like a Christmas tree, mujer, claro...clearly," Muriel laughed.

"Okay, okay, el cabron is right, but first the peace pipe and it's loaded with the best blend of visionary weed and hash, and later the water pipe. It's the blend that makes you want to tell stories about your childhood, lost loves, found loves, the journey of la vida, the journey of your lover's body. This stuff provokes you to tell all, the stories, tu sabes, smoke and tell," Pablo laughed.

"I've smoked some weed, remember Ari? But I've never tried hash, especially the visionary kind..." Judith stared at the water pipe nervously.

"Just smoke a little, see how you like it, I'm right here, baby," Ari held her close, kissing her gently. He wasn't into public displays, but he wasn't above watching. He enjoyed the passion between Pompeii and Floriana, which reminded him of those parties he'd been to. Where you simply began fondling a woman, taking turns with her partner, another woman joining in, and another. I've made love, well lust, to four women at the same time...okay, I'm not into public displays with my future wife, mother of my children. Pablo's right, sensuality has always been a good balance to my discipline, but I sure don't want to talk about it via the visionary weed, he smiled to himself.

"Okay, I'll try it, but just a taste, sweetie. You can carry me back to the hotel, I trust you..."

"No need, stay the night in one of our guest rooms, breakfast when you awake. And that goes for all of you, although you might misplace my secret mistress."

Sonya punched him, hard.

"Ayy calmate, corazón," Pablo laughed, rubbing his shoulder. "She got this from you, Xochitzalita, the idea of torturing me..."

"She would've come to it all on her own, something about you requires it, cabron."

"Okay, pues, we start with the peace pipe, which means no hitting, mi amor," Pablo laughed, giving Sonya his best Bandera smokey gaze. "The eagle feather for visions—what do you think, Hank?" He held the large eagle feather up, bound with leather and turquoise beads dangling. He lit the pipe, taking one deep hit of the strong, sweet smoke. Then passed it to his left, Sonya.

"Eagle, Kwahu, Justin's Hopi name, hay-ya, kwahu flies closest to the sun, so the eagle's vision is the vastest vision on Earth. If we dare to fly to the Creator in the sun, yeah the eagle feather's powerful stuff, so just be aware of that as you smoke, dudes and dudettes." Hank laughed at his own joke as Sonya had a coughing fit, handing it to him.

"A good thing to remember is to take small hits, ladies. This visionary stuff smells good but pretty strong, hay-ya!" Hank paused to lift the eagle feather with dangling turquoise, briefly, to the cool night wind. He took two deep hits, holding them in his lungs and exhaled slowly. A slight after-taste of dark cinnamon lingered on his tongue, and as his lungs swelled with it, his brain lit up. With cinnamon. And he began to see the tip of an eagle's wing—"*Masawistiwa*," he laughed. "Wing spreading over earth."

"Hay-ya!" Pompeii boomed. "Pass the pinche pipe, amigo!"

"Callate, pendejo, this is a ritual," Pablo shook his head.

"Qué ritual, I want a hit of the hookah..." Floriana kissed him, shutting him up.

Feliz held the clay peace pipe and raised the eagle feather, as Hank had done. "I smoked a few times at university," she giggled.

"Small hits, it's nice, and hold it in your lungs," Hank encouraged her, smiling, wanting to swoop in and kiss her.

"It smells good, sweet." Feliz took one small breath and held it in her lungs for a few seconds. "What's that word you used?"

"Masawistiwa, 'Wing spreading over earth,' a Hopi word."

"Masawistiwa," she echoed, feeling her body glow. With cinnamon. Feliz felt the intensity of his gaze, but she couldn't meet it, yet. She passed the pipe, the eagle feather, to Judith.

Judith caressed the eagle feather, feeling its smooth softness. Flight, the word came to her. She took a small but deep breath into her lungs, holding it for a few seconds. Cinnamon. Shoulder blades. Itching. Then she saw it. In the darkness, lit by small candles. But she couldn't be sure—a child's coat with the Star of David suspended over the candles. I must be seeing things; fear clutched at her for a moment. Relax, you've been to war, relax, and later I'll investigate this so-called vision. Her shoulder blades. Began to burn. Judith passed the pipe to her beloved, Ari.

"Pues, I can see from the line-up at this pinche table that I'm going to be the last one to get a hit of this stuff, joder!" Pompeii growled, then shadow-smiled.

"You have enough altered chromosomes to get blasted on their memories, callate! Keep him occupied, Floriana, Dios mio! Listen, pendejo, I could give you your own private joint, but we're sharing a peace pipe here, a ritual..."

"You can say that, you were first, chinga tu madre!" Pompeii sulked, but continued to breathe in the rich remnants. And his chromosomes remembered his mother's voice—tired, loving—just the voice, no words.

Ari passed the eagle feather across Judith's face, her eyes; then his own eyes. He took two deep breaths, holding each one in his lungs, expanding cinnamon. He saw his grandmother, a girl, at the gates of Auschwitz, and when he blinked his eyes she was gone. He passed the pipe to Muriel, who met his eyes with recognition. When a human being witnesses horrors beyond naming, the eyes become cameras. The spectrum. Of existence.

Muriel caught sight of Pompeii's impatient gaze and started to giggle. "Oh Pompeii, without you we'd die of boredom."

"What's so funny!" he demanded.

"Your wonderful, endless impatience." Muriel took a deep breath of smoke and handed the pipe to Justin. He reminds me of my father, his wonderful, endless impatience, his love of la vida. Him and my mother, both of them, always dancing, in love. Until they were killed, murdered, walking home one afternoon from the market. Both of them teachers, so a threat to the US funded government at that time, Nicaragua. So now I wander the world witnessing in their names, their memories, their passion. Their laughter. Their daughter.

"I think I've been insulted, chinga la pipa de paz!" Pompeii laughed.

"Muriel's right, your raw truth fuels the world of us humans, if we're honest, hay-ya, and I actually want s'more that visionary stuff myself," Hank laughed, then did a brief grito.

"Give me the peace pipe." Pablo got up to get it. "It needs a refill by now, and hay-ya we'll give it a fresh one just for you, Cantinflas!"

"I was wondering why it wasn't drawing too well," Justin smiled, handing the pipe to Pablo. "I was going to ask for a match."

Pablo quickly refilled the bowl and handed it back to Justin, and then Hank gave the eagle feather to him, noting how the feather flew from his hands to Justin's. "It probably needed more fire as well, but now you have both. Here's some matches, enshalla, God willing. Enshalla, ojala, the same, God willing. I'm a Mexican Muslim, in case Xochitzalita didn't tell you, and my entire family is embarrassed by me." Pablo laughed as he settled into his silky cushions.

"No, they're not," Sonya tried to whisper, but it echoed around the circle.

"They love that I make money, corazón, but I should be a normal Mexican, a Catholic. Let it go, I have. I've been this way for years!" he laughed.

As Justin handed the pipe to Ai, he leaned into her—"May we fly together." He'd raised the eagle feather as Hank had done, allowing it to graze the top of his head. Hank met his eyes, smiling, "Kopavi, the open door, yeah, the crown chakra, Kwahu, keep knocking, it'll open."

The top of his head tingled as he watched Ai hold the peace pipe with absolute tenderness. Tears streaked her face, and he saw her in old age. And he still loved her.

The two serving women quietly built a warming fire in the fireplace, and Pablo found the remote for the next surprise. The roof slid partially open to reveal stars, the waning moon.

"Kopavi for all of us, man, cool!" Hank laughed with delight. "You thought of everything, Pablo, hay-ya!"

The sudden silence announced the band was gone, as they hadn't been listening for a while. Now they all stared up to the sharp-edged winter stars. The explosion of the Milky Way, their home galaxy. Everyone lay back on their cushions, prayer mats. Everyone but Ai.

Ai got to her feet, face tilted to the star-washed sky. The ancient sky. The always new sky. The same sky that had held death over Hiroshima, Nagasaki, in August 1945. She raised the peace pipe, the soft eagle feather, to that same sky—"Pointing at your own heart, you find the Buddha. Sana, sol, sana, luna, sana." Her words were quiet but clear, circling the table. Each heart. Each human. Under the same sky. She wept freely as only the very strong are able to do—freely, no shame. Sorrow's simple rain.

Justin wanted to stand up and hold her, but a wiser voice (in his heart) whispered, *Respect this woman's strength*. He remembered the standing warrior, Japanese Goddess, Benten (Quan Yin was her sister, she'd corrected him), tattooed on her full spine. Goddess of love, luck, wisdom, compassion, Ai had told him that first night together. Benten stood on her roaring, singing, terrible, loving, green-gold dragon. This Goddess propelled her around the world and out of her safe life in Tokyo. Her daily life as an excellent Critical Care nurse, but she (truly) wanted to be a physician. If she had the time. Life.

Ai slowly sat down, saying, "Pablo, Sonya, gracias for this beauty, this sky, this time." She handed the pipe to Xochiquetzal and then leaned into her son's warmth.

Xochiquetzal gazed at Ai and Justin, then at Javier who waited to meet her eyes. As he did in the beginning. As he always would. Meet her eyes. She burst into tears. "I'm too happy, if that's possible, too fucking happy."

"Give the pinche pipa to me, Xochitzalita," Pompeii whined, "I'm not happy, joder!"

"You're not?" Floriana asked, feeling betrayed.

"Of course I am, you know I'm just bien loco, te amo." Pompeii enveloped her in an embrace and a kiss everyone could experience.

"Get the hose for these two," Xochiquetzal laughed, still weeping. She swept the top of Javier's head (kopavi, the open door), and raised the eagle feather to the burning stars that always saved her. From her early twenties to this moment. She offered the pipe to Javier and he drew two deep breaths. Some went to his cinnamon lungs and the rest he kissed into her mouth.

Javier swept the top of her head with the eagle feather, kopavi, then higher to the Windhorse that danced between the stars. He could see the trail of glittering stars flying, the tail, the mane. The twin eyes. Xavier, he thought briefly. And offered the pipe to Xochiquetzal's lips—two small breaths. Half for her lungs, half for his. The taste of cinnamon on their lips, together, breathing.

"Pass the pinche pipa, you two *love birds* make me look bad con mi Floriana, who is mi paloma de amor." Pompeii's hands mimicked two birds that flew to her breasts, cupping them, following with a resounding grito.

"Ayy Pompeii, you are such a pain en las nalgas," Xochiquetzal sighed. Then she saw it across the room—a child's coat with a yellow star and what looked like a sitting Buddha. Gold. Shimmering with candles. Buddha. She wanted to walk over to the yellow star, the golden Buddha; but she didn't want to disrupt the circle. Later, she told herself, and she continued to gaze at the Buddha, further illuminated by the young flames in the fireplace. *I'm indestructible,* the young flames laughed. The ragged, yellow star on the worn child's coat echoed, *I'm indestructible.*

Pablo handed the freshly filled and lit peace pipe to Floriana, over Pompeii's protests—"Qué joder, hombre, I'm next!"

"Look where you're sitting, pendejo, Floriana's next..." Pablo began.

"Let me handle this hermoso idioto," Floriana smiled. The small, pure gold cross between her lush breasts glittered in concert with the gold on her face. She swept Pompeii's kopvai—the top of his frustrated head—took two small breaths, met his protesting mouth, and gave it all to him.

"Amor," harsh tears came to his eyes, "you gave it all to me."

"Everything I have is yours, Pompeii."

He heard his mother's voice filled with love. The words. He'd unbuttoned his shirt so the night breeze would soothe him; his body always ran too hot. The blood. Too hot. The large, gold crucifix on his neck, dangling to his thick chest hairs, caught there, and winked in the candlelight. His childhood prayers. For food. Warmth. His beloved mother. That the cruelty of his father. Stop. No more. Beatings. He never. Stopped. Beating her. Mama.

Pompeii took the pipe from Floriana's open hands. Her words in his ears, "Everything I have is yours." He took two deep breaths, passing the eagle feather gently over her smiling face. He took the first one into his cinnamon lungs, and the second one into her delicious mouth. He didn't trust himself to speak, this moment. His mother's cries. Long ago. I killed. My father. He took another deep breath of cinnamon.

"Don't speak," Floriana whispered into his mouth, "I know."

Pompeii's body jerked in surprise as though evading a punch. Floriana's hands flew to his face, "It's me, Pompeii, it's me, Floriana, it's me."

"Ayy this stuff brings back memories you thought weren't there anymore, you know the sad childhood stories." He took one more deep breath of cinnamon and then handed the pipe to Pablo, giving a short grito that held no joy. Only sorrow. Killing sorrow. He took Floriana into his arms and stroked her face with his fingertips, softly, so softly.

"You cry like a boy in your dreams, in the darkest hours, 'Mato mi padre, mato mi padre, no mas golpes a mi mama, yo te cuido mama, no mas golpes.' Spanish is so close to Italian, I understand, mi amor, I understand todo." One renegade tear escaped Pompeii's left eye and it glistened on the gold cross between her breasts.

Pablo held the pipe with one hand and the eagle feather with the other, the turqoise beads swaying. "I've never shared this room with anyone but mi Sonya. In truth, I created it just for me, but your company, your diverse energies, made me unlock the door..."

"Pass the pinche pipe, pendejo, no me chingas!" Pompeii bellowed with threat and joy. "And here's los magico mushrooms, enough for two each I think."

"Including este cabron Pompeii, I look around and see a loco Hopi, Israelis, Catholics, a beautiful Buddhist, me the Muslim, Muriel the world witness de Nicaragua, el Toltec Javier doctorcito, la pochita Yaqui Xochitzalita, el aguila Justin, las Mexicanas Feliz y mi preciosa la Sonya. Yes, I think we're all here as we approach dawn," Pablo paused. "Do you have your dawn flute, Kokopelli?"

Hank smiled, "Como no, right here." He reached for the deerskin travel pouch.

"The guitarist must be gone, it's so quiet," Feliz whispered as the candle's thin flames swayed in the dark wind.

Pablo passed the pipe to Hank. "There's some left, amigo take it and pass it on. And now, I'll also light the pinche hookah." He reached for the bucket of ice, bottled water, mango juice; mixing it all in the ceramic bowl, carefully.

"I'm very moved that we're the first people you've invited into this incredible space, gracias," Ai smiled at Pablo.

"You really can't take it all in, cabron," Xochiquetzal laughed, "it's amazing. This is your real Ph.D, this beauty." She rose to her feet, going directly to the imposing, golden Buddha in the far corner.

"I've been watching him too." Ai stood up to join her. "And those Japanese scrolls, so exquisite. These are pretty old, right Pablo?" Then she saw the photos on the wall, in the darkness, illuminated by two small candles. Mushroom clouds. Atomic blasts. "Hiroshima, Nagasaki," Ai gasped. Memory. Cells. Exploding.

"The Blue Star Kachina dancing," she sobbed quietly as Xochiquetzal held her.

"I can't believe this, Ai, do you want to sit down?"

"No, no, I want to look at the Blue Star Kachina—what's the real Hopi name?"

"Saquasohuh," Hank offered, standing behind them. "Yes, this is Saquasohuh dancing in the plaza," he whispered, holding the eagle bone flute.

"Ari, look at this child's coat with the Star of David, look. Where did you find this coat, Pablo?" Tears streaked Judith's face.

"And the Torah, look, wrapped in purple, the ornate silver shield, or that's what I call it." Ari stroked the purple silk, the silver, and the 'yad.' The handmade silver arm, with its perfect hand, one finger pointing. It dangled on a fine silver chain, waiting to be used; to read each word of the Torah.

Pablo joined them, facing the Star of David on a child's coat. The golden Buddha witnessing the Blue Star Kachina dancing in the plaza of the world. "I bought an old trunk in Poland years ago. It yielded handmade lace curtains, bedspreads, a wedding dress, women's clothing and a fur coat. The family was obviously wealthy—old china, silver. And this child's coat. Once an expensive coat, for a boy…"

"The Yellow Star of David weeping in the plaza," Ai breathed. "Too many Yellow Stars dancing and weeping."

"Why did you create this shrine, Pablo? You say you're a Muslim, I don't understand," Ari asked with an edge of defense. Aggression. Yet his Samurai body displayed only grace, peace.

"Why shouldn't he create this shrine?" Muriel interceded. "I've been to Israel and to Palestine, and both sides are at fault. But it's come to this—Israel is the aggressor. Becoming what it hates, fears…"

"You're not Israeli! You have no right to judge us!" Judith seethed, keeping her real fury contained. "You come to visit, your so-called interviews, take your journalistic photos, and then you catch the next flight out…"

"My family was murdered in the US funded genocide in my country, Nicaragua, and yes I'm African as well. I *interviewed*, spoke to, women who survived the rapes and genocide in Rwanda. Children forced to cut off their parent's hands, women who witnessed their entire family, their children, hacked to death before their eyes. Then held for months of gang rape. I interviewed, spoke to, looked into the eyes, of the survivors in Bosnia…"

"Hay-ya, we've all suffered, all of our people have suffered, man, that's for fuckin' sure! Have you heard of the genocide of Native People on this here Turtle Continent, and I mean the entire continent, north to south, up to seventy million souls, seventy million!" Hank was almost shouting, then caught himself. "It's the human experience and the real question is, can we fuckin' evolve into the Fifth World? That is if Mama Earth doesn't kick us all out, courtesy of our very own human stupidity, global warming…"

"I still don't appreciate being compared to a *Nazi*," Ari's voice was low and modulated. Calm. Where he went. Before full battle. He thought of the men he'd killed for Israel. Those who would take away his grandmother's country; the small girl at the gates of Auschwitz. Once he'd taken off the ski mask of a man who'd shot at him—a boy of fourteen or fifteen.

Judith recognized the tone and put her arm around his imperceptibly tense, slim waist. "No Ari, I owe Muriel an apology. She's lost her own family in Nicaragua, and she's seen, witnessed the worst. She has a right to speak her truth." Judith met Muriel's eyes in silent apology.

"You all need some pinche magico mushrooms before you kill each other in Pablo's puto paradise!" Pompeii put one into his mouth, swallowed, and fell back laughing. With an edge of pain. He refused. To see. His father's. Face.

"I'm sorry," Muriel almost whispered, "I didn't mean to say the Israelis are Nazis. But it's our human condition to become what we fear, hate. I know, I went through the same thing, which is what sent me to the US, California, Xochitzalita's photography class, journalism, and then out into the wide, beautiful, terrible world. The fear I'd be swallowed by hatred, revenge. I *hated* the US for funding the genocide, so it brought me there to study..."

"And my best student." Xochiquetzal took Muriel's hand in hers. "You were a little scary at first, mujer, those killer eyes of yours."

"Yeah, they had to go out into the fregado mundo and witness, and to witness until they became—how else can I say it—cameras of some kind of compassion."

"That's why I'm traveling, Muriel, yes, that's why. I'm planting these little, pinche peace crystals wherever I go. My grandmother died of cancer when she was thirty-two, and the same with my mother, thirty-two. So instead of shriveling into a little ball of fear and hate, here I am. Next California with Justin to pack his stuff, and we're off to New Mexico where the atomic bomb was created." Ai felt Justin's arms encircle her, and she leaned into his warmth.

"You're staying with me, you two, in Taos. Just let me know when you're comin', you know as in mi casa es su casa." Hank took a deep breath. "You're startin' to feel like relatives." He paused to sweep his gaze at everyone.

"Stay at the modern house," Javier quietly laughed. "That's where he keeps the good stuff."

"But the Pueblo casita is so beautiful too, full of spirits. Only Taos people can stay the night, sleep there, right Hototo?" Xochiquetzal suddenly realized she might not see Justin for a long time. Tears filled her eyes.

"Who's this Hototo guy?" Pompeii growled.

"It's Hank's Hopi name, pendejo!" Pablo laughed with tenderness. Pompeii was a boy, a dangerous boy, but a boy. He'd seen that immediately when they'd met years ago. And the part of him that was a protective father, instinctively shielded the wounded, generous boy.

"Too many chingado names, Pablo, if your name is still Pablo El Cabron." He continued to sprawl on the prayer mat, the silken cushions, his head in Floriana's lap. She stroked his face with her fingertips, listening to the conversation.

Pompeii remembered—like tuning into a clear TV channel—his mother's gentle face. Her fingertips on his boy's face, calming him to sleep. The sound of his father's drunken entrance, when she would hold her breath, stop stroking his boy face.

"I understand and appreciate everything that's been said—your family in Nicaragua, Muriel—your family in Japan, Ai—and yes, the millions of Native People murdered on this continent. I understand." Ari paused to compose himself inwardly; his words were making him angrier. Why? he asked himself and continued.

"This once expensive coat with its Star of David, now ragged and dirty, once belonged to a Jewish boy of maybe nine or ten. In some death camp. His family murdered and so was he. This is all there is of him, this ragged, sixty year old coat. With the Star of David. His brief life created Israel. This boy with no name, no face, and millions like him." Ari's perfect Samurai body trembled with anger. Sorrow. And he saw his thirty-three-year-old grandfather walk into the gas chamber, stripped of his clothing. Hungry, thirsty, cold, terrified—his head held high. I will not allow Israel to be driven into the sea, to not exist, these millions of lives, I won't allow it, ever, he promised the ragged, intact Star of David on the boy's coat.

"Hay-ya, his spirit is here, let's name this boy," Hototo's voice pierced Ari's vision—*Let's name this boy.*

Judith stroked the Yellow Star of David—"Sweet boy, hungry boy, frightened boy, son of Israel..."

"Solomon, my grandfather's name. Only my grandmother, my mother, survived from the entire family. Solomon, my great-grandfather's name, Solomon." Ari's voice cracked with sorrow and his shoulders, his chest, his arms, stopped aching. To explode.

"Solomon," Ai echoed.

"Solomon," Justin.

"Solomon," Javier.

"Solomon," Hototo.

"Solomon," Xochiquetzal.

"Solomon," Muriel.

"Solomon," Sonya.

"Solomon," Feliz.

"Solomon," Floriana.

"El niño Solomon," Pompeii.

"Si, Solomon," Pablo.

"Solomon, oh sweet Solomon, our Solomon, Ari," Judith wept.

("Soloooomon," the Energy Child sang, wept, sang.)

Quetzalcoatl, the Morning Star, was zenith, preparing to face the Warrior. In the Sun. Taiowa. The chill, pre-dawn wind gusted, ruffling a black silk curtain. Pablo placed two more logs into the fire and it leapt to full life. He walked over to the black silk curtain and pulled it open, tying it to a tasseled hook, revealing an antique Japanese screen.

"Masawistiwa, Wing spreading over the earth—Hania, Spirit Warrior, Solomon, I see your spirit, your spirit wings, Solomon, son of Israel, Solomon." Hototo warmed his great-great-grandfather's eagle flute with his hands, and the fire hissed, Kuivato, Greet the Sun, Taiowa, Kuivato. He licked his dry lips and put the eagle flute to his mouth, the small feather dancing. Gathered breath. Played. *Talatawi*, song to the rising Sun, Taiowa, the first sacred lights.

Feliz stayed at his side, watching him—listening to him play the beautiful, eerie eagle bone flute. And she realized, though it terrified her—she wanted to hear this long-haired hippie, Taos-Hopi Indian play for the rest of her life. And she couldn't stop smiling, como una idiota. "Ayy," she breathed, and her eyes followed where everyone else's were fastened.

Pablo carefully folded the antique Japanese screen with exquisite white cranes in flight, and leaned it into the far right wall. Exposing a shimmering rainbow material that caught the candle's light. He stepped away and sat down by the fire. The open roof over their heads allowed the chill, pre-dawn breezes to soothe them. Wake them. Tempt them. With curiosity.

Ai glanced up. "Oh look, a shooting star, look!" The eagle flute played, talatawi, song to the Sun, Taiowa.

Javier was on his feet, walking smoothly as though in a dream (the nightmare of their human his/herstory), and pulled open the shimmering rainbow material. He laughed. With joy. Poster-sized photos of the ocean at dawn...the Himalayan peaks icy with snow... orchards in full spring bloom...fields of summer harvest...expanse of desert silence...rainforests thick with life, green so green life...the living ocean at sunset...the perfection of the planet gathered in this tiny space, always born...the wonder...hope.

"And the Bible, the Koran, facing each other, the feuding twins," Xochiquetzal murmured, noting the rainbow silk cradles they were placed within. As though dreaming the other, the twins.

"The Hopi twin story goes like this," Hototo said in a voice that merged with the

pre-dawn winds. "In the beginning when Taiowa created life from *Tokepela*, endless space, he instructed Kokoyangwuti, Spider Woman, to create two beings. And she did, from the same earth and her own saliva. She molded two beings, the twins, and covered them with a cape made of whiteness, the creative wisdom itself. And she sang the Creation Song over them. When she removed the cape of whiteness, they came to life. One twin, Poqanghoya, was sent to the north pole of the world axis, and the other twin, Palongawhoya, was sent to the south pole of the world axis. They were commanded to keep the world rotating properly, in balance. 'These are your duties,' Spider Woman told them, 'you must send out your call for good or warning through the vibratory centers of the earth.'"

"Play the pinche flute, stop talking," Pompeii complained, smiling secretly.

"Callate...shut up," Floriana kissed him, laughing.

"And Kokoyangwuti created from the earth, her saliva, trees, plants, flowers, all the birds and animals, covering them with her cape made of whiteness, and she sang the Creation Song over them. She instructed them to spread to all four corners of the earth, to live. Then it was time for human beings, created from earth, *tuchvala* her saliva, and once again she covered them with the white cape which was the creative wisdom itself. Four male human beings, four female human beings—red, black, yellow, white. And Spider Woman sang the Creation Song over them...my Hopi grandmother sang it to me...

'The dark purple light rises in the north,

A yellow light rises in the east.
Then we of the flowers of the earth come forth
To receive a long life of joy.
We call ourselves the Butterfly Maidens.

Both male and female make their prayers to the east,
Make the respectful sign to the Sun our Creator.
The sounds of bells ring through the air,
Making a joyful sound throughout the land,
Their joyful echo resounding everywhere.
On this path of happiness, we the Butterfly Maidens
Carry out the Creator's wishes by greeting our Father Sun.
We call ourselves the Butterfly Maidens.'"

"Hay-ya," Hototo wept. "It's longer but this is what I remember, hay-ya." He stood to face the dark purple light. The mystery. As he placed the ancient, eagle bone flute to his lips and began to play a note so high, so alone, and sweet, it seemed impossible—everyone stood up and gathered around him. Even the reluctant Pompeii. They faced the dawn together—the dark purple light, the mystery; the clear yellow light of breath; and the pulsing red light of *talawva*, life. The Creator's warmth, love. And finally, Taiowa the Sun rose as Kokopilau's song poured through Hototo's eagle flute. His ancestor's eagle flute. Kokopilau's ancient song sang of Creation, always newly born: wonder.

When the first long, pale arrows of the Sun reached them, he placed the precious flute into its deerskin pouch, cradled by wing feathers. Silence. They could hear The Twins calling north to south, south to north—each one on their axis—and the Earth continued to spin in perfect balance. Hototo took hold of Feliz's hand to his right in the nakwach, and then Justin's hand to his left in the nakwach. "Grab the Pahana's hand next to you this way." He held up their hands to see. "This is the Hopi symbol of brotherhood, sisterhood. We are all related, hay-ya, into the Fifth World..."

"Into the Mayan Sixth World, hay-ya!" Ai added with so much joy it made her dizzy. "Wakhiru-me, oh Wakhiru-me, Goddess of the rising sun, send this to my ancestors. I'm going to live, have children, sana sana sana sol."

Javier leaned into Xochiquetzal, whispering, "Which twin am I? Which axis do I keep in balance, mi orchid? And my twin, Xavier?"

Tears filled his eyes and fell as all their sorrows, all their joys, were transmitted. Their clasped hands. Nakwach.

Xochiquetzal raised Javier's hand to her lips and grazed his sorrow with the softness of butterfly wings.

"And may the pinche joder Blue Star Kachina stay way the fuck out there in space dancing or whatever it needs to do, hay-ya! We have some plans down here, como no, maybe some kids, Floriana." Pompeii tilted his head upward to the warm-winged sky and gave a perfect grito that started from his feet. Rising up his ankles, calves, genitals, spine—pausing for his chest, his heart—and flew from his open mouth. Longing, gratitude. Sorrow, joy. Hate, love. And remorse. But mostly—most of all—gracias.

Without prompting or warning, everyone opened their mouths and gave a grito that made The Twins (each on their axis), smile.

"Where's el café, where's el chingado desayuno, breakfast!" Pompeii bellowed. And instantly, everyone remembered hunger.

A new pair of women servers brought in trays of food—enchiladas de pollo, chile rellenos, stewed chicken in a green chile sauce, tamales, red chorizo folded into rich scrambled eggs, spicy black beans, red rice with sliced hard boiled eggs on top, and piles of still-hot, yellow and deep blue tortillas wrapped in bright cloth. Pitchers of café fuerte, juices of every kind, and chilled, freshly made sangria to extend the celebration.

As they sat to eat under the wide open sky, the Warrior in the Sun flung his golden arrows relentlessly, joyfully, to the far horizon (where Spider Woman laughed)—Xochiquetzal had to ask, the moment so complete. So ripe. "A trance healer in Bali, an eagle woman, asked me, 'What is freedom, madam?' She had a chained eagle, her ally in healing, and it broke my heart, those huge, folded wings. So I asked her why the eagle couldn't fly free, why it was chained. And then her eagle eyes dug into mine, and she asked, 'What is freedom, madam?'"

Xochiquetzal paused to sip the rich, cinnamon spiced, café fuerte, as Javier served her everything he also served himself. "So, after all that, fellow travelers of the universe," she softly laughed, "and Pablo's magical lair, what is freedom for each of you?" Silence. The sounds of forks touching plates and sighs. The sighs of the well-fed and the well-traveled. Through the long journey of night. (The Energy Child dreamt the eagle's wings spreading, lifting, flying, free.)

"What a wonderful question, Xochitzalita," Ai smiled, swallowing a bite of luscious tamale. "I've traveled a long way to say this, and I say it also for my mother, my grandmother, my grandfather, all those who disappeared in Hiroshima, Nagasaki, in 1945." She looked down to her faithful hands. "To live your life out in failure or success, in joy and sorrow, in pain and pleasure. To die while climbing a mountain or giving birth or old age. To manifest your love as fully as possible, this life, this time. To have no one and no thing steal it, that human possibility. To me, that's freedom." Silence. A burst of bird song. The risen sun. The new day. White egrets winging, dazzling the eyes. Silence.

One by one, in hushed voices, "She spoke for me...That's my answer...Gracias, Ai, la pinche verdad...Yamo'osta, you are the Mother People." Ari added, "I read this once, by the French philosopher, Jean-Paul Sarte, 'There are two ways to go to the gas chamber,' (he saw his grandfather, Solomon's youthful face, his final smile)... 'free or not free.'"

"Hay-ya!" Hototo raised his sangria for a toast. In that moment, a small yellow-blessed butterfly flew into the room, circled the table, and landed. In the huge, still wet bouquet of flowers, picked in the dawn garden. It landed in the center of a blossoming, red rose, fluttered, and landed in the pollen-center of a wide open, ripe-pink lily.

"Then we of the flowers of the earth come forth to receive a long life of joy." Hototo whispered the next words to Ai, smiling like the sun.

"We call ourselves the Butterfly Maidens," she laughed as the yellow-blessed butterfly opened and closed its wings. Opened and closed its wings, freely. In the golden light.

"Kuwanyauma," Hototo sang to the small butterfly.

"Butterfly showing beautiful wings, Kuwanyauma," Kokopilau sang (making the Energy Child long for wings). He played the ancient butterfly song (of all winged beings), masawistiwa...wing spreading over earth...to all of the vibratory centers of the Earth. The Twins called north to south, south to north, for good (winter spring summer fall winter spring summer...) and for warning (warming warming Earth *warming*)...

Wings.   Spirit.   Ancient.   Song.

"I can't believe Justin and Ai are gone, damn and fuck, I miss them," Xochiquetzal wept.

"How can you miss them, mi amor, when they keep emailing you their latest photo, updates?" Javier gathered her in his arms, laughing. "And we're going to meet them in Paris in less than two months. Before my surgery begins and hay-ya you still have me, or don't I count?"

"Of course you count, tigre, without you I'd be the old, embittered jaguar, la verdad. And how can I thank you for the $3,000. dollars you chipped in to match mine, for Justin's travel." She quietly laughed, tasting her tears, burying her face in his neck. Smelling him. Licking his neck once, his young man's salt.

"Yes, I'll take my payment in trade for your pleasure. What a good idea, mi amor, there's time. We meet Xavier at the entrance to the Plaza del Toros in an hour."

"No way, maybe you can get there in an hour after making love, but not me. Plus that gives us thirty minutes, not counting foreplay, forget it, tigre." Xochiquetzal pulled away slowly, reluctantly. "But tonight, all night, there'll be time. All the wonderful company did interrupt our so-called luna de miel, honeymoon. And besides, I want to pay you in full," she laughed, enjoying the play of sensuality between them.

"You're right, an hour is ridiculous, so tonight all night, mi amor, you must pay me in full, no credit for you," Javier laughed, then remembered. "And speaking of time, I haven't seen Xavier in over six months."

"That's why I think a bullfight is kind of crazy for your get-together. In fact, you two should go out to dinner somewhere quiet and just talk. You know, North Pole, South Pole. Earth in perfect balance." She smiled into Javier's worried eyes.

"I actually suggested we do that, get together by ourselves first. But he insisted on the bullfight, as in what's New Year's Eve without a bullfight. And he wants to meet you, Xochitzalita, so later a dinner together, just me and my axis twin. But tonight he's made reservations for dinner at his 'secret place,' as he calls it. He says it's very private and he won't tell me the name of this place. Xavier in charge, so like our father," Javier groaned.

"And so like you, Dr. Zapata. I had to reform you to stop scaring innocent waiters, don't forget."

"Cabrona!" Javier grabbed her into his arms, but she escaped, laughing.

"Do you think Xavier's going to be an asshole? Sorry, but from what you've told me...."

"Of course he's going to be an asshole, that's who he is, mi amor. But he's also going to see why I love you."

"I don't know if I'm prepared to see you in duplicate, ohmygoddess, the fucking twins, hay-ya y ayyy Diosa!"

Xochiquetzal saw him immediately—Javier's duplicate, twin. Xavier. He was a bit chubbier in the face but still handsome. He was impeccably dressed in a custom-made, black leather jacket, well-fitting black trousers, black silk shirt, and a blood-red silk tie. A gorgeous, blonde woman, in a form-fitting, red dress with deep cleavage, was draped to his side, clinging. Claiming him.

"Is that his wife? I thought she was pregnant, so if that's pregnant, hoochie mamacita!"

"That's not his wife, Xochitzalita, here we go. The usual ego centered bullshit. I'm sorry, mi amor, I thought he'd have more class than this, joder!"

Xavier laughed as he saw his brother's face register disgust, alarm. "Hermanito, no te haces como una viejita...don't act like an old lady. You look like a Goth with only black, at least I have a red tie! And you're still wearing that old, worn-out leather jacket , buy a new one, let go of the *old*." He clutched Javier in a violent hug and his laughter sliced like a sword. Then he locked eyes with Xochiquetzal as Javier positioned his body between them, instinctively.

When Javier holds my gaze he gives me something; when Xavier holds my gaze he takes something. She put her hand out as a greeting. "Well, we finally meet, I'm Xochiquetzal."

"Your reputation precedes you," Xavier smiled coldly, dismissing her with his eyes like a servant. A Frida Kahlo pocha and older than him by at least eight years, who knows maybe ten, la vieja, complete with her black shawl. "This is my *good friend*," his English was perfect, "Angelica, and she's no angel." The cold, detached laugh. He placed his hand over her large right breast for a moment, squeezing it.

"Stop that, Xavier, Jesus! This guy hasn't been potty trained yet," she tried to smile.

"I'm Javier, the twin." He reached out his hand to her and saw it—fear.

"Okay, come on, I have our tickets, let's see some bloodshed.

Have you seen a bullfight before, Xochiquetzal?"

"Just twice, so I'm still getting used to it all," she answered without looking at him. Two can play this dumb game, she told herself, stay cool, distant and dignified, please.

"Qué pocha but that's okay, so is Angelica..."

"Where are you from, Angelica?" Xochiquetzal asked her, smiling into her eyes.

"From San Diego but I've been in Guadalajara for almost two years..."

"Her *older husband*," Xavier sliced a look at Xochiquetzal, "el viejito died and left her a wad at twenty-two, so how could I resist? She was our father's patient for the most perfect breasts, gracias Papa!"

"Tone it down, Xavier, and I won't bring up your wife," Javier hissed into his ear.

"Angelica knows about my wife, we have no secrets." Xavier flashed Xochiquetzal a perfect smile, winking at her. "Joven!" he shouted at an older man, ordering four

double-shot margaritas from the bar.

"You're a real fucking charmer, Xavier." It was out of her mouth before she could call it back—What a fucking prick (Xochiquetzal said this silently).

A flash of sheer rage glazed Xavier's eyes for a moment; but without warning, he threw his head back, laughing. That awful laugh. Of swords. Slicing flesh. "This is why Javier's with you, yes, of course. As they say in the states, you're a real pistol, Xochiquetzal!"

"She's right, sweetie, you're being a jerk," Angelica said. Very quietly. The look he gave her made her step back. For a moment, she looked like she wanted to weep. Or run.

"You don't mean that, honey." Xavier put his wide hand around her slim neck, guiding her to the entrance of the bull ring. He whispered into her ear, "Shut the fuck up, mi gringita." And then he laughed, intimately, as though he'd just told her how much he wanted to make love to her.

The laugh caught Xochiquetzal by surprise. "Maybe things are picking up, a turn for the better, his human side," she murmured to Javier.

Javier let his brother walk ahead. He could see the tension in Angelica's body; his fingers on her neck. "Don't bet on it, mi amor, and please let me handle this shit. What else can I call it, and this is why

I don't see him. I don't want him to have an excuse to disrespect you because, what can I say, I will kick his fucking ass, mi amor, mi orchid." He held her for a moment, kissing her softly. Butterfly wings.

"Hermanito," Xavier's voice boomed, "you always were a sentimentalist! Come on, the bull and death wait for no one!" The laugh. Of swords. Sharpened swords. Her and that Frida Kahlo shawl and I'm sure she's wearing an authentic Indian blouse under it, pocha puta, Xavier seethed, tightening his fingers on Angelica's slender neck.

Xochiquetzal caught Angelica's eyes briefly—fear. And an endless sadness. From the beginning, like a birthmark. And it made her, irrationally and suddenly, furious; she wanted to slap that bully's smirk right off of Xavier's face. She's a grown woman, she can walk away, Xochiquetzal chanted inwardly.

Javier took her hand and they slowly walked toward them. The sound of the band began to blare, announcing the opening of the ritual. The dance. The matador, the bull, and death. "Let me handle things, Xochitzalita, mi amor, promise me. She's with him by her own choice, and she also knows he has a pregnant wife with five children, que monstruo, como el padre...What a monster, like the father," his voice verged on tears for a moment. "So promise me, Xochitzalita."

She squeezed his hand but promised nothing as the two matadors entered the ring, strutting, assured. The sharpened sword. Waited. For the bull.

The older man brought them their strong, icy margaritas and Xavier instantly ordered another round.

"Not for me," Xochiquetzal said, raising her voice over the crowd's roar.

"I'll drink it if you don't want it, so bring it on, old man!" Xavier ordered, without tipping him.

"Wait!" Xochiquetzal stopped him as he turned to leave. She tipped him fifty pesos, as his eyes lit up with gratitude. His barely audible, "Gracias señora."

"He makes that in a day, if he's lucky, and the gringos come to Mexico and disturb the natural order of things." Xavier wanted to say more—the ignorant, liberated pocha gringas are the worst, but he stopped, feeling Javier's eyes on him. He looked up, meeting them, and laughed.

"How would you like to make fifty pesos a day, if you were so-called lucky?" The words seethed out of Xochiquetzal's mouth, calmly.

"If you don't cut it out, Xavier, I'm leaving right now. I tried, I always try, but you remain an idiot," Javier said. For the first time. Openly.

"Hermanito, come on, I'll be a good boy, the entire evening is waiting." This pocha bitch has made him this way—he struggled for control and found it. "Come on, I promise to be a gentleman." Xavier tried to smile but it was more of a grimace, stretched tight across his face.

Javier didn't respond, but stayed seated. "Let me deal with him, please, mi amor," he murmured into her ear.

"Okay, since you're doing it, but what an ass."

"I told you, he can only be who he is. Now for the bullfight, and today there's only two matadors. One from Mexico and one from Spain, and I hear the Spaniard is fearless."

"Mexico and Spain, that'll add an interesting twist." She thought of the ancient Spaniard and briefly looked around at the crowd. "Who are you betting on?"

"The Mexican, of course," Javier smiled, kissing her.

"Okay, I'll bet on the Spaniard," she laughed.

"Just don't bet on the chingado bull, someone's got to die!" Xavier brought out a silver flask of tequila, pouring a generous shot into his ice. He leaned over Xochiquetzal to pour some into Javier's half-full drink, grazing her body.

"Can you say, 'Excuse me,' I'm not kidding, Xavier." Javier met his brother's angry eyes and held them.

"I'm such a pig, please *excuse me*." Xavier paused. "This one has you trained, hermanito," he switched to Spanish.

"Xochitzalita understands Spanish, hermanito."

Xavier laughed loudly and poured himself another shot as the next round of margaritas arrived. He pulled a one-hundred peso bill from his wallet and tossed it to the old man.

"Gracias Jefe," he said solemnly, without gratitude.

"He knows who's el jefe, the boss!" Xavier didn't hear the lack of gratitude as he was tuned only to power. Over someone else. He kissed Angelica roughly, and laughed.

After the graceful, and very guapo, handsome, caballero on his pure-white stallion—the bull chasing its sleek haunches—the young Mexican matador cautiously strode into the center of the ring. The overweight lancers, on their well-padded work horses, had pierced the bull's powerful neck and shoulders, repeatedly. And as he bled, his large, fierce head lowered toward the ground. The tendons that held up his head had been cut, weakened. But the bull was large and still had a share of his old power; and as he charged the trembling, red cape in the Mexican's hands, the pass lacked bravery. He stepped ever so slightly back, and the crowd roared with disapproval. His maroon traje de luces...suit of lights, sprinkled with beaded mirrors, only diminished him. Reflecting back his fear.

"Sin pasion te haces viejo...Without passion you grow old!" a man in his seventies yelled to the young, trembling, dishonored Mexican matador.

A lone lancer speared the bull in his profusely bleeding shoulder, neck, repeatedly, and the crowd went wild. "TORO TORO TORO..."

Xochiquetzal joined the, "TORO TORO..." Then Javier, laughing. "I've only been to two bullfights, but there was four matadors in each one, and I've never seen a bull tortured like this. It's so unfair, it makes me want to puke."

"El matador is a coward, mi amor, so the bull must suffer." Javier's eyes softened with this truth.

"Chinga el toro, someone has to die here today, and not the one with the sword!" Xavier laughed as the coward easily killed the bleeding, dispirited bull.

The large, beautiful bull fell to his knees, as though begging for death, and the trembling Mexican matador suddenly became brave, thrusting the sharp sword into the bull's spine. Scattered boos, loud jeers. He cut off the bull's ear and threw it into the crowd, the prize; and they threw it right back, booing loudly this time.

"'Sin pasion te haces viejo...Without passion you grow old,' I love that, the truth." Xochiquetzal's eyes filled with tears, but she refused to cry in front of Xavier (she felt him watching her, closely).

A magnificent quarter-horse was led in by long, leather reins, held by a striking man with long grey hair pulled back in a pony tail. He, and some waiting men, chained the dead bull, held by the huge horse, and swiftly dragged the bleeding body out of the ring. The subtle smells of fear, anger, blood, the beautiful bull begging for death, lingered.

"I hate bullfights," Angelica quietly said. "I've only gone to around five of these with Xavier, but this was truly awful."

"Do you think we can all choose our death, my spoiled little gringa? Watch and learn, you're not in politically correct America," Xavier laughed with disdain.

Angelica saw the cruelty and the beauty in his face; and then she glanced at Javier. What happened to Xavier? she wondered. "But we can choose how to live, Xavier."

"Hay-ya!"Xochiquetzal almost shouted.

"It's the Gringa Liberation Front, Dios mio! I need another margarita. *Joven!*" He motioned the older man over.

"You might cool it, hermano, and wait for some food," Javier advised.

"Chinga el toro y el muerte tambien...Fuck the bull and death too!" Xavier ignored the warning and added a large shot to his melting ice.

The band launched into a trumpet-blaring Mexican song, announcing the next matador. A violet twilight had unfurled and flashes of white-winged egrets cast their swift shadows on the swept smooth earth of the bull ring.

The slim figure of the Spaniard strode, with a balance of grace and fearlessness, into the ring. His golden traje de luces...suit of lights defined his stature. His presence. He turned slowly, glittering with confidence, and the crowd roared. The gate opened and an even larger bull thundered out, being met by apprentice matadors to deflect his first powerful energies. They took turns teasing his horns to their fuchsia capes, then leapt behind the thick, wooden barriers.

The lancers surrounded the bull and as one drove his lance deep into the bull's powerful neck tendons, the crowd roared, "TORO TORO TORO!" Xochiquetzal joined in, and Angelica spoke the words, "Toro, toro." Some long-lost part of her spirit returned. A small, glittering piece. "Toro," Angelica whispered.

The lancers were called to the edge of the ring, and told something they didn't want to hear. The Spaniard nodded his head, yes. The fat, disgruntled lancers rode out of the ring to cheers. The Spaniard turned to face the beautiful, still powerful, bull. Silence descended. And for a still moment, they met. The man. The bull.

"Javier," Xochiquetzal gasped.

"I know, mi amor." He took her hand, kissing it. The bull rushed toward the Spaniard, his thunder-hooves beating in his human blood. From his feet to the crown of his head (kopavi). The Spaniard stood like a thousand year old tree, rooted to the center of the Earth, the twilight caressing the leaves of his hair. And everything loved him. Even the beautiful bull.

The dance began. The bull grazed the Spaniard's slim, arched body so intimately. Like a lover. Over and over. "OLE!" the crowd roared as one, "OLE!" With each graceful, dangerous, intimate, lover's pass of his red cape. And Xochiquetzal realized—He's *allowing* the bull to graze his body, to feel the power of those horns passing him.

"They're dancing," she whispered into Javier's ear, weeping. She couldn't help it. She didn't care.

"Now *el duende,* death, dances with them. Now there's three. Do you see it, mi amor?"

Javier held her close.

"Yes, I see it, and they're one being."

"One passion."

("One," the Energy Child echoed, "passion." S/he somersaulted in the empty darkness of Xochiquetzal's womb; the size of the tiniest hummingbird.)

When it was time, the bull died quickly—it could've been el matador, but *el duende* chose the beautiful bull. They were equal in that intimate dance. *Duende.* The Spaniard faced the roar of the crowd, their cheers, with gratitude. His bearing held no boast, no arrogance, only gratitude. He turned, holding his small, matador hat high, and the spirit of the bull lingered. To taste this moment. With the man.

"That was too slick, not enough bloodshed for my taste, too artsy for me!" Xavier complained loudly. They all ignored him, rolling their eyes and sighing.

The crowd continued to cheer as red roses, people's hats, even shoes, and a bota de vino, were thrown into the ring. The Spaniard laughed, picking up the bota and began to drink as the crowd counted... "Uno, dos, tres, quatro...doce, twelve." And they loved him. For revealing. His death. Their death. *El duende.*

"Someone has to die," the Energy Child wept.

The taxi dropped them off on a quiet, dark street high on a hill that overlooked the central plaza, the bullring, the lit church domes.

"Where's this restaurant, Xavier? These are houses," Javier asked, as Xochiquetzal snuggled for warmth. In the plaza, el Jardin, handmade, towering displays of fireworks, castillos, were ready to explode at midnight; and rainbow fireworks were poised to be shot into the air toward the stars. New Year's Eve, Feliz Ano—México lindo y querido.

"I told you, it's a secret place, follow me," Xavier smirked with satisfaction. Being in control. His true passion.

"You've never brought me here, Xavier." Angelica stumbled on the cobbles as he

semi-dragged her toward the stairs.

"We've only been to San Miguel twice, together. I've been here many times, and knowing you, you'll like it." He knocked loudly with the brass knocker, in the shape of a bull's head. A small, wooden slot opened, behind an ironwork grill. A man's face appeared, his eyes, but he said nothing.

"Soy el Dr. Xavier Gomez and I have a reservation for four, open the door," he commanded. A moment's pause and the ornate wooden door opened wide.

The man smiled in welcome, bowing his head slightly, but continued to be silent. He led them through an immense dining area with crystal chandeliers, two huge fireplaces blazing, bouquets of flowers everywhere. Candles lit every table and corner of the room to perfection. Pure luxury. And every table was claimed. One immense, long table was filled with powerful looking Mexican men, and a stunning women next to each man. The men ranged from their twenties to their seventies, but all the women were in their teens to mid-twenties. Waiters were positioned around the table, waiting to serve, and serving at the most subtle signal of command.

"That's the Mafia, smile ladies like you mean it," Xavier said a little too loudly, drunk. He tipped his head in their direction, and an older man raised his glass to him. "I've joined them on occasion and those gangsters know how to have fun. They have a room upstairs for privacy, like a sultan's dream..."

"Lower your voice, pendejo," Javier warned.

Xochiquetzal felt eyes on her, probing her—she found dark-mooned eyes set in a ruggedly handsome, Zapotec face. Long black hair to his shoulders, loose; a contrast to the impeccable, dark suit, rose colored shirt, dark purple tie. He smiled at her, revealing a perfect smile; and his eyes conveyed only a hint of amused flirtation.

"All the women seem to be around the same age, that's kind of strange." Angelica smiled at the group, receiving more than her share of stares.

But the long-haired Zapotec kept his eyes trained on Xochiquetzal, no longer smiling. Still amused. She shuddered with an unexpected loneliness, and leaned into Javier's warmth. A small flamenco group played, sang and danced on an upraised stage in the center of the room.

As Xochiquetzal's eyes adjusted to the dim lights and the countless candles on the tables, walls, even the floor, each stair—she began to see the paintings on the walls. Some blown-up photos. Erotica. A woman on her knees, filling her mouth with a man's erect penis, while another man filled her from behind. Two perfect women together; one licking the other's clitoris. Groups of people in an orgy of ecstasy, lust, and every painting, photo, was of a sexual preference, pose. She wanted to stop and examine the photos, but still felt that wind of loneliness and didn't want to let go of Javier's hand. A sudden, irrational fear of losing him, swept her.

"I think we've entered the Kama Sutra Express," she giggled, removing her thick, black, wool shawl. She paused to kiss Javier, breathing him in.

"We'll take notes for later," he laughed into her open mouth. "With you I'm not lonely, mi amor," he murmured, grazing her inner lips with his tongue. Xochiquetzal released a deep sigh as his words reached her, but she didn't look back at the Zapotec, though she still felt his eyes on her, laughing.

They were led to a spectacular, private room. A small fire threw its heat, and an extremely handsome, young waiter stood next to it. The table was scattered with candles and small bouquets of red roses circled the crescent-shaped table. A lush, dark-purple, crescent-shaped sofa with gold-purple brocade pillows enticed them to lounge, enjoy. Take pleasure.

"Something to drink?" His eyes voice was pitched low, seductively, as he met each woman's eyes.

"Why don't we have champagne, it's New Year's Eve," Javier said, resenting the waiter's eyes lingering so long on Xochiquetzal.

"Yes, make it two bottles, Alejandro, and pitchers of ice water. You know my favorite appetizers, the usual," Xavier smiled curtly. Then he passed around the hand-written menus. "A couple can share a Moroccan banquet, or Japanese, Spanish, French, Italian, and of course Mexican. I suggest the Moroccan and you eat with your fingers, very primitive. You'll love it, Angelica, my primitive little gringita."

"I'm not your primitive little anything, chill out, Xavier, it's starting to get old..."

Xochiquetzal's attention was on the photo of a naked, hooded woman being led with a thick chain attached to the jeweled dog collar at her throat. By a fully dressed, smiling man. In the next photo he was beating her with the chain, welts rising on her full breasts. "Is this the S And M Room or what? I mean, it's a little hard to look at while you're eating, like a little too fucking primitive," she said (her thoughts out loud). The gorgeous waiter returned carrying a large, silver bucket with three bottles of champagne. He smiled at her. As though he knew her.

"This is from one of the gentlemen, a gift for the ladies, he said to tell you. And you're all invited to join their party." He slowly popped the cork off the third bottle, the gift from the handsome Zapotec, leaning into view and tipping his head. That smile. Of amusement.

And the waiter poured the champagne into the women's crystal flutes, leaning into them ever so slightly, feeling their heat.

"Thank the gentleman, and tell him not this time, although it's tempting, Alejandro," Xavier replied. Their eyes met in understanding. "It's my favorite room, Xochiquetzal, but notice the photos over there depict a dominatrix having her way with the men," he laughed. Knives.

"I think it sucks," Angelica breathed.

"And that's why I didn't bring you here last time, but if we were in a different room with the women having their orgasms, and in very unique ways, you'd love that. And you'll also love the food here, trust me." Xavier spoke slowly, as though to a child, then turned away from her.

"What do you think, Javier, the Moroccan?" Xochiquetzal gave Angelica the you-have-my-sympathies look, but told herself, She has to fight the idiot, not me.

Alejandro popped the cork on the second bottle of champagne smoothly, not a drop spilled. Every move he made conveyed a graceful sensuality, seduction.

"What do you think, mi amor, you choose for us," Javier smiled at her.

"Be a man and order, no me chingas, hermanito."

Javier focused on Xochiquetzal as the waiter poured a bit more champagne into her flute, and he saw his arm graze her shoulder slowly. He almost said, "Watch yourself, cabron," but he knew she'd be irritated—as in 'I can take care of myself with a waiter.' Plus, it would amuse Xavier to see his protectiveness. Jealousy.

"Italian, I'd love Italian." Xochiquetzal leaned away from Alejandro imperceptibly, and then leaned into Javier, kissing him. Whispering, "Tigre."

"I'd love the Chinese banquet," Angelica smiled with joy, taking a sip of champagne.

"No, you'll really enjoy the Moroccan and I haven't had it for awhile," Xavier quickly said, taking her joy. "And bring a bottle of tequila, you know the one, two glasses, Alejandro." Things were blurry but that was how he liked reality. Blurry. No commitments. Easy and good sex. A big breasted, tight pussy chica, no kids yet, the tight pussy intact. And younger, always younger, no viejas for me. The sixth kid about to pop from my very tired, sainted wife, more tequila, he smiled, secretly.

"Why are you such a jerk, Xavier? I know you're already drunk, so why not order the Chinese? For Angelica, your date." Javier looked at his twin, seeking for a moment, the boy of four, five, six... His playmate, friend, mirror. But only a stranger, who looked like himself, stared back. Enraged. Beneath the smile. Enraged.

"She's not my date, she's my *puta*, my whore. You only bring your whore here, and later Alejandro will fuck her for your viewing pleasure."

"I know our father was, and still is, a prick, but you've surpassed even him, Xavier." Javier's voice was falsely calm as he thought of their mother, always waiting, always understanding that their father was un hombre, a man. That he couldn't help it, the way he behaved, so she always forgave him.

"Who do you think brought me here? Of course, he wouldn't bring you, the *good son*, the one who never tried to please him. Look at me, with five kids and one about to pop, a highly paid dentist. But I'm not the M.D., the joder *surgeon*, the mama's boy, I'm not the good son, so fuck you, Javier!" He continued to smile; cruelty the only pleasure.

"Let's get out of here, now!" Xochiquetzal stood to leave. "I'm sorry, Angelica, and good luck, you really need it."

"And you, the handsome surgeon, you should be with a very hot, mindless, twenty-year-old chica, not a viejita, an old lady, hermanito. In fact, I really liked that nineteen-year-old and I bet Alejandro would too!" Xavier's laughter danced with sorrow, madness, rage, death.

Angelica threw her champagne into his face, but before she stood to leave, he slapped her, hard.

Javier leaped to his feet, clenching his fists, trembling with years of his own rage. Wanting to. Kill. His twin. His mirror.

"Go on, Mr. Hero, hit me, go on, que puto."

Xochiquetzal grabbed his arm. "Don't do it, Javier, don't do it, he *wants* you to do it, don't."

Javier's body slightly relaxed, his fists slightly softening. "Come on, Angelica, you're coming with us." He pulled her to her feet, holding onto her, putting his body between her and Xavier, as she held her bruising face, weeping. "Go home to your wife, Xavier, your five children—do you hit them as well? Only a real macho hits a woman, coward."

"Go on, Mr. Hero, take la puta, I was getting bored with her anyway! I'll join my friends and order a fresh, younger puta! You don't know what you're missing, hermanito, time for fresh pussy!" Xavier's laughter filled the room, trailing after them as they fled. The flamenco group never skipped a beat, playing and singing louder. The dancer's feet pounding, playing with passion. *El duende.* Xavier gave a grito filled with only rage, and no one answered him. *"Chinga tu puta madre!"* Silence.

The Zapotec stood as they rushed by, as though he were going to speak. But he only smiled as though to wish them chispas…sparks, fire, passion. To be in love is rare, he told himself; and to see it ripen even rarer. He softly laughed and sat down next to his stunning, waiting, eighteen-year-old, perfect, blonde chica.

After settling Angelica into a new hotel so Xavier couldn't find her, they got home after 3 a.m.. They'd shared a dinner, bottles of wine with Angelica, after Javier checked her for injuries. She was badly bruised on the right side of her face, but not injured. They talked and finished four bottles of wine.

"I'm going back to university. I'm going to do something with my life. You both must think I'm just awful, his pregnant wife, five kids. I think I'm awful, he's right, I'm no better than a whore." After she calmed down, had her share of rich red wine, Xochiquetzal led her to bed and tucked her in.

"You're not a whore, Angelica, you're just very young, and yes, go to university, yes."

They'd fallen into bed exhausted, holding onto each other, directly to the dream.

Someone was banging on the front wooden doors, almost 4 a.m. "Abre la puta puerta...Open this whore of a door!" Xavier.

"Stay here, amor, it's the idiot." Javier got to his feet.

"How does he know where we live anyway?" Xochiquetzal asked half-asleep.

Xavier's pounding and yelling was waking up the entire block— "Un loco," people murmured and waited for the hurricane to pass.

"I told him, of course, in case he wanted to drop by, and here's the pendejo now."

"Be careful, Javier, he's kind of insane."

"I know, he's my brother, Xochitzalita." He bent over and kissed her. Then he went quickly down the stairs, as Xavier's pounding and shouting became louder.

"ABRE LA CHINGADA PUERTA..."

And in that moment—the center, the utter silence of the hurricane—Javier felt his twin's killing loneliness. The caged tigers were eating his beating heart, alive.

Javier flung the door open, dragging Xavier inside. "Callate pendejo, you're waking up the entire town, it's after 4 a.m.!"

"I want to wake up this pinche, artsy town, fuck this town and fuck you too, hermanito! You're like a trained poodle for that vieja, or should I say, with due respect, a trained surgeon." Xavier tried to laugh but it caught in his throat, swaying in the middle of the room, barely able to stand. But he stood, feet wide apart, as the hurricane kept battling him. "Where's that puta, Angelica, where is she hiding, is she here, are you hiding her from me! PUTA!" he yelled, stumbling toward the downstairs bedroom.

"She's not here, Xavier, quiet down, calm down, everything will be all right. Look at the bed, fresh sheets, stay here, go to sleep here, hermano, it's time to sleep, hermano mio, time to sleep." Javier tried to take off his made to order leather jacket, but he spun away—violently, drunkenly.

He stood facing Javier, his mirror, the good son—the twin he hated. And loved. Equally. "Our mother gave me to him, our father, so she could keep you. She had to sacrifice one of us and it was me, Javier," he almost whispered. "Someone has to be sacrificed, someone always has to die, hermanito."

The secret, the truth of those quiet words, picked Javier up and flung him to their childhoods, their teen years. Their separation. The devastation. To Xavier. The unloved boy always having to prove his masculinity. To his father. An impossible, insane task. If he didn't, he was punished, ridiculed. And if he did, the same, even worse.

I was protected by my mother, by Amalia. I was loved. I was spared. Tears filled Javier's eyes and he wanted to hold his brother. To embrace his brother. To protect his twin. To keep him safe. "It's time for sleep, hermanito, it's time for sleep," he said, slowly reaching for him.

"Don't touch me, puto joder, Papa always said you'd become a puto joder." Killing. Laughter. Choked him.

"I'm sorry our mother gave you to him, our father, hermanito, I'm sorry." For a moment, Xavier looked at the empty bed with sheer longing as though he might collapse. Surrender.

"Take me home, I need to go home to my wife, my children, take me home, Javier. My car's outside, take me home." A trace of emotion entered his voice—*Take me home.*

Quickly, Javier left a note—Xochitzalita, mi amor, I'm taking Xavier home to his wife, Guadalajara. I'll take the bus back and I'll see you tomorrow probably by 10 p.m. or so. I'll call you in the morning, corazón, and I'll hold you in my arms tomorrow night. Dream beautiful dreams—Tigre

She was asleep as he grabbed his old leather jacket, his muppie shoes, wallet with credit cards, Physician ID, pesos—so he placed the note under a seashell from Bucerias. The last time they swam together in la mar, as they heard Juanito singing in the waves; this small, battered seashell had lodged itself in her hands.

He followed Xavier's weaving, stumbling walk to the brand new, red convertible BMW sports car, and as his brother stumbled on the cobbles, he noticed his blood-red tie was askew. For a moment, he wanted to straighten it or take it off his neck. But he knew if he tried to touch him it would only provoke him. Javier sighed as he opened the door for him and, ever so slightly, he grazed his twin's lost, drunken face with his butterfly hand.

Xochiquetzal woke up in a sitting position, tears beginning to drown her. Shadow dream, not clear, sudden violence, and Xavier's crazy voice—"Someone has to die." She saw the note under the small shell, picked it up and read it. "Guadalajara," she murmured, running down the stairs to the phone. She glanced at the clock, 5:42 a.m.. She speed dialed Javier's cell and it rang. And rang. No answer. She dialed again. It continued to ring.

Maybe the ringer's off with Xavier going bonkers on him, that's it, she told herself. She made a cup of green tea and carried it to the roof. Bundled in her black, wool shawl and fleece-lined Ugg Boots, she waited for Taiowa, the first dark purple streaks of Mystery; the yellow streaks of Breath; the red warmth of Life. "Love," she could hear Hototo, his eagle flute warming in his hands. Soon he'd put the eagle-dawn flute to his lips and sing to Taiowa, Creator, Warrior in the Sun. She heard the first pure notes rising to meet Taiowa, coaxing the Creator to rise for humanity. Spider Woman's saliva still wet on the twin human clay; her white, sacred substance surrounding them. Their life in the balance, this moment. The sacred, white substance—the creative wisdom itself—was always her love.

The phone rang and she flew down the stairs, picked it up. "Javier, where are you?"

"Xochitzalita, it's Diego, I'm here at the hospital..."

"At the hospital, why?" She wanted to scream. *Someone has to die.*

"Javier and his brother were brought in, a bad car accident..."

"Is Javier alive, tell me the truth, Diego," she whispered.

"He's alive, Xochitzalita, and his brother's not doing as well. Should I call you a taxi?"

"No, I'll drive but thank you, Diego, gracias, I'll see you soon."

As Diego's arms enfolded her, he said, "Let me prepare you, Xochitzalita. His forehead is severely bruised, swollen, and his face has multiple cuts. Not very deep, so I closed them up. He has a breathing tube to prevent loss of oxygen to his brain, and the scan shows a subdural hematoma, multiple fractures. There's bleeding between the brain and the skull due to the impact, trauma, to the head, his temple..."

"How are his hands, Diego, his hands?" Xochiquetzal wept quietly—his expert, surgeon's hands. She watched Diego's face for grief, alarm—desperation.

"Only minor cuts, so his hands are intact, Xochitzalita. And the scan revealed no spinal injury, so he's pretty intact. But he's going into surgery for the brain bleed, and when that's taken care of he'll be ready for his residency..."

"Are you bullshitting me, Diego, please don't lie to me. I mean, his brain is bleeding. What does that really mean, please don't lie to me, Diego."

"Okay, the whole truth—I've done this surgery so many times and it depends on what it really looks like once I'm in. There have been deaths due to trauma to the brain, and some people go into comas and wake up not quite the same. And some are fully recovered, that's the brain, Xochitzalita, unpredictable. But he's young, very healthy, and I know he wants to return to you. To life. He has a strong spirit. When he was brought in he kept saying, 'Don't open the door, Xavier, don't open the door,' and 'How is Xavier, where is he?'"

"Xavier was drunk and pretty crazy, Diego, and he must've been trying to jump out of the fucking car. Javier was driving him home to Guadalajara, that fucking idiot. You said he was worse." Tears flooded her but she remained calm. Strangely calm. The center of the hurricane. I should've stayed awake. I shouldn't have allowed Javier to drive him home. I should've knocked Xavier out, made him stay the night, but I went to fucking sleep, I went to sleep. I went to sleep.

"That's what I figured, and Xavier's on life support, beyond surgery, nothing more to do. It seems he went out the door, broke his neck when his tie caught, snapped spinal column, with deep multiple injuries. His poor wife, five kids."

"Six, she's pregnant, full term, as I understand it."

"Qué lastima, what a tragedy, I called Javier's mother and she should be here by noon or sooner. What a night, New Year's Eve, but now it's time for Javier's surgery. And I've done this surgery many times, Xochitzalita, trust me."

"I do, of course, I trust you, Diego. Can I see him, quickly?"

"Three minutes and no kissing," he tried to joke. "I'm going to prepare for the surgery, so they'll come for him in about five minutes or so."

"Gracias, and may Taiowa be with you."

"Taiowa?" he smiled.

"The Hopi Sun Creator, and also every divinity known to humankind be with you."

"Okay, take a deep breath, he *looks* injured, Xochitzalita, and I gave him something to prepare him for surgery, so he's not conscious. In fact, he lost consciousness soon after arrival, but this will keep him under until the surgery for sure."

As she walked to the door, she told herself, No crying, he can hear you, no crying. She almost didn't recognize him under all of the facial cuts; the stitches that held them shut. The deep too-purple bruises and massive swelling on his forehead; the breathing tube down his open mouth. But then she saw his hands. It was him, Javier.

"Javier, mi amor, it's me, Xochitzalita, I'm here. I'll be waiting here for you to wake up, mi amor. Diego is the surgeon, you're in good hands. I love you, Javiercito, come back to me, come back to me. I want to see you in your Zapata sombrero splendor. I want to hear your embarrassing grito, come back to la vida, Javiercito, mi amor, mi tigre. I'll be here waiting for you to wake up." Don't cry, she commanded herself, or you'll start sobbing, he can hear you, don't cry.

His eyelids fluttered as though he wanted to open them, and then he took a deep intake of air. His chest moved, breath, and the breathing tube answered loudly.

"Breathe, yes, breathe, tigre, I'll be here waiting for you to wake up, mi amor." She heard footsteps approaching, the sound of smooth wheels. She very carefully stroked each hand, and as they stopped at the door, she kissed his cut, graceful, perfect hand. "Come back to me, Javiercito, I'll be waiting here for you, come back, breathe."

Xochiquetzal suddenly had a stab of pure fear—What if this is Xavier, not Javier. She pulled back the blanket. There it was. Among the deep bruises. The tiny, black crescent over his left nipple. Rising with his breath. And she remembered, whispered, "Huiksi, Breath of Life."

"Huiksi," the Energy Child wept, "breathe."

Xochiquetzal stood next to the bed where Javier was resting after his surgery. His skull was bandaged, and the swelling had gone down slightly. His face cut and bruised, but she recognized him. She held his fingertips. "Diego says you're going to be fine, so keep resting, that's good, but then come back to me, Javier, come back to me."

Javier... *We're laughing, we're playing. Six years old. Soccer players. The ball rolls out of sight. Xavier turns to chase it.*
"No!" I yell. "No, stay here. Don't go!"
He pauses. Looks at me. His eyes. Laughing.
He chases the ball. Laughing.
Gone.

"Pardon, are you Xochiquetzal?"

She turned to see the kindest face and she knew this was his mother's face.

"Si, soy Xochiquetzal, Senora Gomez. My Spanish isn't perfect but I can understand everything if you speak slowly," she said in Spanish, trying to smile.

Diego came in, his face in shadow without his open smile. Then a stern-faced, older man in an impeccable suit—Javier's father. He shook hands with Diego briefly, ignoring Xochiquetzal's presence.

Diego caught her eyes for a moment in recognition, obviously poised to speak. No smile. Only shadow. "Your son, Xavier, stopped breathing. He didn't regain consciousness and I think he left peacefully. He sustained too many injuries, trauma. I'm so very sorry."

Javier's mother collapsed with grief, sobbing, and Diego caught her in his arms.

"My son is dead!" the father yelled angrily. He glared at Xochiquetzal with sheer hatred and strode out the door.

Javier's mother pulled free of Diego's support and stumbled to her son's side. "Will Javier live, doctor?" she wept.

"I believe he will, Senora. The brain pressure is normal and I stopped the bleeding. Now it's up to him, and knowing him he'll begin his surgery residency in March."

"Gracias, doctor, gracias. Javier's often spoken of you and your kindness to him." She glanced at the door her husband had exited. "His father should be here with him. I've lost a son too, but this one lives."

"Maybe I should go so he's more comfortable staying, Senora." Xochiquetzal bent over to gather her things.

"No, no, you've been here with my son and when he wakes up he'll want to see you, Xochiquetzal. He's told me about you and I know he will want you to stay."

"But your husband, Senora."

""You stay and keep me company, Xochitzalita, Javier calls you Xochitzalita." The warmth of her wounded eyes conveyed the message. Xochiquetzal put her things back in the corner.

"Look at Javier's hands, just a few small cuts. I've been touching them, talking to him..."

"Do you love my son?" Her gaze was unwavering. Like her son's.

"Yes," she almost whispered.

"Then we understand each other," she smiled briefly, tenderly.

Quietly weeping, she took Javier's right hand in both of hers. "We're here, hijito, we're here, two women who love you."

Javier's father returned, taking a few steps inside the room. Refusing to acknowledge Xochiquetzal. "We must return to Guadalajara with Xavier for burial. His wife is waiting for him, his children." He stared at his wife, waiting for her to move, to join him.

"Javier was driving him home last night, I'm sure you know, and Xavier was very drunk. He tried to stop him from leaping out of the car, but he obviously didn't succeed. I'm so sorry, his family." She had to say this much, at least this, in English. I can't find the words in Spanish right now, so maybe he doesn't understand me. And Angelica's made to order breasts, the secret, scumbag restaurant he introduced his son to, the endless pursuit of trying to pleasing his father, poor Xavier.

"This is none of your business, señora. This is family business and you are *not* in our family," he said in perfect English. Like Xavier, he took lessons to lose the demeaning Mexican accent. He met her eyes briefly, then looked away with undisguised disgust. You don't treat putas like family, our family, he seethed.

"You are being rude, stop it, Javier loves this woman, and her name is Xochitzalita, stop it!" She faced her husband squarely, and a hint of shame crossed his harsh, still handsome, face.

"I don't know you, señora, my apologies," he muttered tensely, enraged.

"Come and speak to your son, Fernando, he needs to hear his father's voice."

He quickly crossed the room to stand next to Javier's bed, but he didn't touch him. "Hijo," he began, realizing it was always plural, 'hijos.' "Your brother is dead, now you must live." Tears blurred his vision, but he banished them. In that moment, he banished sorrow. He banished grief, death. But he didn't touch his living son. He strode out of the room without another word.

"I must return with Javier's father, Xochitzalita, for the funeral. Here in Mexico there's a twenty-four hour law for burial, Dios mio, mis hijos," she wept. Quickly, she straightened her back, composing herself—"Here's my number and please call me when he wakes up, if anything changes. I'll be back as soon as I can and maybe he'll be awake when I return. I know you'll take good care of my son, and that you'll persuade him to return to the living."

"I'm going to sleep here, Senora, and I'll call you immediately when he wakes up.”

“Call me Eva, Xochitzalita. Javier tells me you have a grown son as well. Keep talking to him, tell him we love him, and to return to us.”

“I will,” Xochiquetzal paused, “Eva, and I’ll call you when he wakes up.”

“Qué bien, hija,” she wept, hugging her son’s lover. Then she turned toward her son, bending over him, and she stroked a small section of Javier’s uninjured cheek, close to his mouth, and whispered things only for him.

Diego made clear to the staff that Xochiquetzal was staying the night, and they brought her a cot with fresh sheets. And dinner on a tray—Diego had brought it in. “Here’s a glass of my own wine I keep in my office, enjoy. You have to eat, Xochitzalita.”

Pablo, Sonya and Feliz had come by briefly, not wanting to intrude. The room began to fill with roses of every color, fragrant lilies.

“Mom, are you sure you don’t want us to come back? We could catch a plane and be there in four hours.”

“Give me the phone, sweetie,” Ai said. “We can come right now, Xochitzalita, what do you want? I can’t believe his brother tried to jump out of a moving car, if he weren’t dead I’d call him names.”

Justin took back the phone. “Okay Mom, tell me the truth, how bad is Javier?”

“Diego stopped the bleeding in his brain. I know that sounds awful, but the worst is over, Diego says. He says the coma is the way the brain is recovering itself. Some people need therapies, memory loss, and some people wake up fully recovered. Confused of course, probably some time and memory loss, but the wonderful thing is Javier’s hands are fairly uninjured, just small cuts.”

“The surgeon, yeah, that’s good news, Mom. We can come just to *be with you.* You don’t always have to be Wonder Woman, you know,” Justin smiled. He’d never seen his mother cry until this visit. With Javier. “She’s crying because she loves us.” He heard Javier’s laughter.

“I know, I love you, Justin, but let’s be honest. It’ll be crowded in this little room and we’ll start acting like people in a stuck elevator, fuck, you know what I mean...”

“You’re telling me to shut up and get out and travel, but we can always travel *after* Javier wakes up, Mom.”

“Look, if it starts to look bad for any reason, I’ll call you to come.

Otherwise, we'll meet you in Paris in early March or so. Diego said he could start his residency as late as April..."

If he wakes up, Justin thought, and he knew she was thinking it, holding it in the place of the impossible. "Okay, we'll stay in New Mexico, hang out with this loco dude, Hototo, until Javier wakes up. We ain't leavin' till doctor dude wakes up. And Mom, call me if he gets worse, we want to be there, me and Ai. I think we love the guy."

"Kuawta, mujer who see la magic, you know who this is, el loco Hototo. Give this message to Huiksi—tell him I'm his twin now," his voice broke, paused. "I'm his twin, Poqanghoya, to the north axis. And he's Palongawhoya, to the south axis. And remind him to send out his song for good or warning through the vibratory centers of our Mother. Remind him, this is his sacred duty now, to wake up."

"I'll tell him, Hototo, I love you."

Ai took the phone. "We'll stay here until Huiksi wakes up, and we'll come anytime you say, Xochitzalita, we love you."

"I love you, Yamo'osta, Mother People. What a perfect name for you. Have you buried any crystals yet?" She could see Ai's calm, playful face, filled with sorrow, worry. And she was so glad Justin and Ai were together. To hear another woman call him 'sweetie' made her smile; and then she thought of Javier's mother. "We're two women who love you."

"I buried some crystals along the fence at the Alamo site, and Hototo drove us to Bandalier. I buried one in the Sky Kiva—the place you told me about—as he played his beautiful flute. A Pueblo man joined us and sang, what beauty. Like Pablo's secret paradise, but not as ornate," Ai laughed very softly.

"How wonderful, I love the view from that Kiva. Whenever I sat out beyond it, close to the edge, that sky opening view—I could hear spirits singing. And no stragglers either, but full-voiced kind of spirits. Gracias for reminding me it's there, that beauty. Listen, I'll put each of you close to Javier's ear, so you start, Yamo'osta."

"What a good idea, I love you, Xochitzalita."

"I love you more, go ahead."

"Huiksi, mi amigo Javier, dream good dreams, connect all the tissues in your brain, then wake up cause I love you."

"I'll see you in Paris, Javier, and we'll have a tequila drinking contest with champagne chasers. I love ya, dude, wake up! And a special message to your brain cells—connect all the dots, just as he was, we like him that way, wake up!" Justin imagined each word reaching his ear, traveling to his brain.

"Palongawhoya, I can hear your song faintly, but I can hear it. Now sing it louder as Spider Woman's white sacred substance surrounds you, brother. I'm waiting to hear your song at the north axis, wake up, Palongawhoya," Hototo wept silently. A small smile (hope) in his tears, the rainbow.

After Xochiquetzal called Javier's mother, Eva, she finished the last of the rich cabernet in the bottle Diego had brought to share. Mostly in silence. The comfort of a friend in silence. Tomorrow I'll bring books, Neruda's poetry to read out loud. A mi tigre, mi amor, Javier. I'll bring The Captain's Verses, the love poems, he'll love that. And Neruda's The Heights of Macchu Piccu, the great epic poem. "Talk about sending out your song to the vibratory centers of the Earth, Neruda's epic poem does that, you'll see, mi tigre, you'll *hear*."

She licked her right forefinger with her saliva and brushed it on Javier's dream-eye. The inner vision chakra, just below the fresh bandage, between his dreaming eyes. "Dream beautiful, healing dreams, bathe your beautiful brain in healing dreams. And come back to me, to all of us who love you, Javier Gomez Villatoro. Come back to me, doctorcito, I'm waiting for you to wake up, intact and entirely your own self, come back, wake up, mi amor."

"Wake up, Palongawhoya, sing," the Energy Child sang toward the dawn. Taiwoa.

She kissed both of his hands and licked them as well. She sat down on the cot and picked up her watch, almost 4 a.m., turned off the small reading lamp. The hospital sheets felt so smooth and clean; she lifted her head one more time to see Javier, eyes closed, still dreaming. Her head met the pillow and a dream swallowed her, whole.

Xochiquetzal, Javier... *They were standing in the waves at sunset, trying to hear Juanito's voice in the waves. Silence. Only the sound of the tireless desire of the sea to possess the sand, her endless journey.*

"Where have you been, Javier, I've missed you."

"I'm in your heart, mi orchid, hold me there. I have to cross la mar."

"Where's your ship, I don't see it."

"I have to swim, Xochitzalita mi amor, but I can do it. Hold me in tu corazón."

The second week of Javier's coma. Diego was getting worried. With his powers of recuperation he should've woken up by now. Even with memory loss, his brain should be firing him awake. He's breathing entirely on his own now and his lungs, heart, his body, is strong. His spirit is strong. He hid his worry with his warm, tired smile.

"Do you think he'll remember me, Diego? Does that ever happen?" Xochiquetzal asked. They were finishing a bottle of his favorite, rich cabernet before he went home for the night. Three surgeries today, he was so bone-tired—But I'm going home to my king-sized, foam-enhanced bed, he told himself, and a hot, violet-essence bath first thing.

"It can happen, depending on short term, long term, memory loss. But then you can help him to remember, Xochitzalita. Get a good night's sleep and take a break tomorrow. The nurses tell me you've been showering here, barely leaving. Go home, take a long bath, promise me. Remember, if you fall apart you can't help him."

"Okay, I promise, I'll take a break tomorrow and come back in the afternoon." Eva had come for three days, but she returned home. To help with Xavier's wife and children. She was due any day and her grief and stress had put her in the hospital. She had to take over with the children and relieve her oldest daughter, who was with them.

"You tried to save your brother, it's not your fault, it's not your fault, Javier, hijo, come back to us," she'd murmured her goodbyes. "I'll return in a week, wake up, precioso, wake up, m'hijo."

Maybe I'll ask Justin and Ai to come, maybe I need them here, maybe... Javier's bruised, healing face, the swelling almost gone, came to her in the darkness of the hospital room as she lay within the small cot. Only the lamp next to Javier remained lit, as though guiding him back. To his warm, pulsing, living body. Then his face receded, drawing her to a far distance.

Javier, Xochiquetzal..._He was swimming, stroke by stroke. Swimming. Exhausted. No sight of land. Only the waves lapping over him. Threatening to engulf him. To take his breath. His memory. His_ *body. Stroke by stroke. Each stroke. Exhausted.*

She was on a ship. She could see him swimming, exhausted, wanting to stop. Swimming. She climbed to the top of the ship, the very top, and she saw it. Land. Earth. So far away still. The brown, smudged line. And she couldn't help him. She couldn't save him. Pull him into the ship. She began to sob with grief and fury. "Keep swimming!" she shouted as her tears merged with the ocean he battled, endured. "Don't give up, mi amor, keep swimming, I see the land, it's there, I can see it!"

He didn't turn his face, his eyes, to acknowledge her. Her words, her grief, her love. But her salty tears held him up as he stroked. One more time, stroke, one more time, stroke. Beyond exhaustion, beyond endurance, one more time. Stroke, his hands wouldn't stop, refused to stop, even as he asked them to, begged them to, stop, he stroked...

Suddenly, a conch shell in her ear, **wake up***...*

She couldn't open her eyes, but she was fully aware—Don Francisco's face, eyes, his words. "The hummingbird, bring him the hummingbird."

Xochiquetzal's eyes flew open and she reached for her watch, 5:21 a.m. She tried to remember where she put it, the box, hiding it from Javier, from herself. Wait for a dream. It must be in the very back of the closet where the towels are stacked, she told herself, dressing quickly.

"I'll be right back, mi amor, don't stop, don't stop swimming, you're almost there, the land is there." She carefully, softly, barely kissed his healing face. Butterfly wings. And the words from Hototo's song came to her—"We call ourselves the Butterfly Maidens," she murmured. " The purple light of Mystery, the yellow light of Breath, now, Huikski."

It wasn't hidden behind the towels or the sheets or her folded sweaters, shawls, or her stacked purses, her leggings, behind her shoes, her box of stashed vitamins. "I know I put it here, this closet, I know it, I remember opening this closet door, the small box in my hand, oh Francisco, where did I fucking put it, where?" Her hand reached for the large, canvas travel purse where everything fit—passport, wallet, coin purse, make-up bag, emergency items, a black stone with Kokopelli carved onto it, notebooks, pens, books, reading glasses, extra sunglasses, snacks, water bottle, juice bottle, small camera, so heavy it dug into her shoulder.

Xochiquetzal picked it up, light as a feather, unzipped the long, sturdy zipper. Opened the center section wide. There it was, so small, a tiny hummingbird (Francisco said in the dream, "Hummingbird"), in the rainbow wrapped box. Sleeping, she thought, dreaming like Javier. She sat on the bed—with his full name on her mattress, his mattress—and she carefully, so delicately, unwrapped the rainbow cloth box tied with red/black yarn. She opened the lid of the small box—white cloth. She lifted the nothingness out, holding it in her right hand; and she remembered. The hummingbird is the symbol of rebirth, the coma it endures, awakens.

She opened the white cloth—"The white sacred substance from Spider Woman," she breathed. The tiniest, intact, preserved flash of iridescent-green hummingbird, rested on the word—*Despertar...* awaken. She wrapped it in the white substance, placed it back on the word in the small box, and wrapped it in the rainbow cloth, tying it with the red/black yarn. 6:06 a.m., pre-dawn. She looked down at the books she'd scattered while searching for the box, and reached for the book with the Mayan Calendar on the cover. I'd been meaning to re-read this, it's been years. Xochiquetzal opened to a marked page, the underlined words, and read out loud: "After her self-sacrifice, Xochiquetzal is shown in the center of the painting with a large rayed disk on her belly whose center is the hieroglyph of the *chalchihuitl* drawn as a human heart. From it issues a tree whose branches end in flowers, and on top perches Quetzalcoatl in the form of a hummingbird. For six months of the year it is dead, and for six it is alive. The *huitzitzilin*, the hummingbird, then, is a symbol of rebirth."

"Gracias, Frank Waters, gracias for this book, I remember," she murmured, tears falling. And her fingers opened to another marked page with these underlined passages—"There appear now two Quetzalcoatls, one black and one red—Mictlantecuhtli, a black skeleton with eagle claws; and the red Tezcatlipoca, goddess of the moon and of birth. The division of Quetzalcoatl into two beings, *the black destined to live and the red destined to die.*" She thought of the black Quetzalcoatls with their eagle skulls, talons, feathers, in Mexico City, flanking her at the Zocalo dance. And then, Xochiquetzal realized both Javier and his brother were entirely in black that night. Except for Xavier's deep red, silk tie. That caught as he leapt and broke his neck.

Tears kept falling, the salt to keep Javier floating—I'll never tell him this, he doesn't need to know. "If it's true, if it's not true, he doesn't need to know," she said out loud. She rushed to the roof to see the horizon, and as she flung open the roof door the chill

pre-dawn sky embraced her. Warned her, dawn was coming soon. And she suddenly knew she had to take the tiny, dreaming hummingbird to Javier. Now. Before the three sacred lights appeared. The horizon. Taiowa.

She closed and locked the roof door and turned to run down the stairs. The largest, most awful, scorpion she'd ever seen. On the wall. Next to her. She took off her boot, steeling herself to kill it. Smash it. Dead. It looked engorged. Pregnant. Her stomach turned. Pregnant. She steeled herself. To kill it.

"NO!" the Energy Child screamed, "*NO!*" And the dream-eye bloomed between her/his eyes, shooting an ultraviolet light out like a laser. Through Xochiquetzal's eyes, focused on the scorpion, the raised boot in her hands. It began to glow. A translucent, golden light. The ugliness became beautiful. She heard Javier's voice, his laughter—"Let the golden scorpion live, mi amor."

"To love the self, the other," the Golden Scorpion sang so harshly.

"My heart's desire, yes." She slid her boot onto her foot, raced to the bedroom for the small, rainbow covered box, and ran to the car. 6:24 a.m.

Xochiquetzal placed the small box behind Javier's lightly bandaged head. The tiny, fragile, spring-leaf-green hummingbird within dreaming, upon the word, Despertar (awaken, enliven, remind, revive).

"Amor, Javier, listen to me, listen. Don Francisco, the Mayan healer, sent a tiny, so beautiful, green hummingbird to you, and it's time to *despertar*, mi amor. And I saw it, your sacred, golden scorpion, I swear, and I didn't kill it, it lives, amor mio." The horizon revealed a subtle smear of dark purple, the Mystery. A thin line of yellow, The Breath of Life.

"Huiksi, it's time, now, it's time, *despertar*, Huiski." She tried not to cry (as he swam, stroked). His eyelids fluttered, deep in his dream. A hummingbird circled him, tiny and jeweled. The blur of its wings gave him hope—land.

A streak of blood-red flashed on the horizon, the warmth of Love. Only his eyelids moved, fluttered, dreaming. The tiny, jeweled hummingbird paused in mid-air, and he reached for it.

"Huiksi, Javier, mi amor, wake up, wake up, despertar," she quietly wept. And as she'd done first thing in the morning for the past two weeks, she brushed her lips on his dream-eye, between his fluttering eyelids. Soft, soft, butterfly wings. She picked up Neruda's book and, sitting down, close to his right ear, she read, sang, wept:

ABSENCE

I have scarcely left you
when you go in me, crystalline
or trembling,
or uneasy, wounded by me
or overwhelmed with love, as when your eyes
close upon the gift of life
that without cease I give you.
       (Wake up, Javiercito, *despertar*.)

My love,
we have found each other
thirsty and we have
drunk up all the water and the blood,
we found each other
hungry
and we bit each other
as fire bites,
leaving wounds in us.

But wait for me,
keep for me your sweetness.
I will give you too
a rose.
       (Come back, come back, doctorcito, *despertar*.)

His eyelids continued to flutter, and she knew he swam, and swam. La mar. Maybe he'll never wake up again, the thought came to her. Those people who enter the vegetative coma state. Maybe the hummingbird can't reach him, or Don Francisco, certainly not me, not me, not me. Tears just rained. Down her face.

Xochiquetzal reached for a red rose and carefully placed it beneath Javier's nose. To breathe. The scent. She'd noticed that his breath would slightly quicken, the scent. "I will give you too a rose," she whispered, weeping, seeing him swim toward a shore he'd never reach. She crushed the rose to her throat and one sharp thorn pierced her flesh. Blood bloomed. Red rose.

The tiny, jeweled, iridescent-green hummingbird lifted him from the waves and flew...

"Amor," Javier barely murmured. His eyes took her in as the Warrior in the Sun, Taiowa, pierced her with his arrows.

Joy   Joy   Joy   Joy   Joy   Joy   A L E G R I A   Joy

The Energy Child's translucent-violet wings erupted from her/his shoulder blades, and in that joyous moment, he/she emerged from the empty, fertile darkness of Xochiquetzal's womb. Laughing, singing. Gone. One more angel. The Ancient Child. Waiting for love. To bloom. The invisible. Ultraviolet. Translucent. Golden. Light. Ultraviolet wings. Gone. Winging. Laughing. Weeping. Singing...

Into the Sixth World...　　　*　　*　*　　　*　　*　　　　　*
　*

　　　　*　　　　*　　　　　　　*　　　　　　*

　　　　　*　　　　　　*

　　*　　　　　　　*

　　　　*　　　　　　　　*

　　　　　*　　　　　*　　　*

　　　　　　*　　　　*　　*

　　　　　　　　　　*

Part V

There is something above all else that needs to evolve: the gap. Fetch the world back from the brink of disaster; steer the future off a collision course with chaos. Dharma, the upholding force in Nature, will support any thought, feeling, or action that closes the gap because the universe is set up to fuse the observer and the observed.

—Deepak Chopra, *The Book of Secrets*

Solstice Sun, Taiowa, makes love to the center, the womb, of the Milky Way, every 26,000 years, December 21, 2012...when the Mayan Long Count calendar ends, only to begin...

Wings.   Instinct.   Ancient.   Song.

Thirty years later, 2035, the Sixth World...

Javier...*The tiny, jeweled hummingbird pauses in mid-air to stare at me, its wings a blur of fury, and the wings tell me one word,* **Xochiquetzal***.*

"It's me, Ai, Javier—and Xochitzalita wants to see you. As Justin told you last time, she's preparing to leave her body, and now she's in the final stages. I'm acting as her physician at this time..."

"Are you sure she wants to see me, are you absolutely positive?" Tears of anger and sorrow gathered in the corners of his eyes, making them shine brightly.

"I know you haven't seen each other in over eighteen years," she said so gently, "but now that she knows she's leaving her body—she refuses to say the word 'die,' you know her," Ai laughed softly. "She asked me to call you, and so will you come, Javier, and Justin and Hototo are also here. It'll be a kind of reunion, we'll have a dawn ceremony..."

"I haven't seen Hototo in at least four years, since Feliz, but I see you and Justin pretty regularly," he smiled. "Okay, I'll come, I obviously have to come. Should I bring anything, do you need any oxygen, supplies, an extra doctor, you know, me?"

"I forgot to mention this, Javier, but she's refusing anything to keep her alive beyond her own body's function, and that includes oxygen. I've tried to give her oxygen as it would help with her breathing, but she continues to refuse it. Damn, she's one stubborn woman, but maybe that's why we love her...I'm sorry, I didn't mean to include you..."

"I don't know if I still love her, certainly not as I used to, but I agree, she's a pain in las nalgas and to the end, and I'll be there tomorrow around 2 or 3 p.m.. Should I fly, do you think it's an emergency, or should I just drive?"

"I don't think it's an emergency. I think she's waiting for you, to be honest, Javier, so I'll leave it up to you. Take your time, I love you, we all love you." Justin and Hototo did a sudden grito in the background, making Javier laugh.

"Make sure there's some tequila, doctor, and tell those locos that I'll see them tomorrow." He paused. "And tell Xochitzalita that I'm coming. To wait for me."

Javier decided to drive—Only five hours and time to think, he told himself. Besides, flying should only be a need, not a luxury—he checked his batteries one more time. I'll recharge in Morelia on the way back, after Xochitzalita leaves her body. After Xochitzalita leaves her body—I haven't seen her in eighteen years. She refused to see me again, so why am I going now that she calls for me to come—because she's leaving her body, that's why. Our twelve years together in San Miguel, and I signed every new mattress in black ink, he remembered, smiling, as the toll road welcomed him at top speed, sixty miles per hour. But she left me anyway, she was going to be seventy, it was time for me to marry...

The glaciers had melted, flooding coastal regions, small island countries gone, changing the world's map. Many species were extinct, and polar bears were only in the encyclopedias. Whales could still be seen, after hunting them had been finally and firmly banned; but their birth numbers kept dropping. Madre mar's womb was becoming too warm, too sun-filled, drowning her children. Wolves flourished where left alone, not hunted for sport and cruelty, and their voices remained beautiful on full moon nights. Every weather was still extreme and human beings continued to suffer, but their global suffering kept them working, struggling toward global solutions. Slowly, very slowly, a thousand years. The accelerated energy of the Sixth Sun, the next one thousand years. One planet, one people. If Saquasohuh continued to dance, still far away—the beauty, the horror, Blue Star Kachina. Saquasohuh had danced closer a few terrible times, but human beings changed the tune and the Kachina returned far away, dancing. If not, the Earth would reclaim herself, begin again, without the human voice. The sweet, human song. And the Twins, north to south, south to north, calling, singing warning and praise. Human song.

Perhaps, as a butterfly wing can tip events light years away, their gathering in Pablo's paradise thirty years ago tipped the Blue Star Kachina's dance just a little, perhaps.

He thought of things as he drove; things he'd pushed out of his daily consciousness for so long. Javier remembered their journey to Paris to see Justin and Ai, after he'd regained his strength. The joy of it. And mourning Xavier that first year (the sorrow of it). Their love-making even deeper, which surprised them both; their mutual road kill. The joy of it. Their trip to Paris alone a few years later, after he'd completed his surgery residency—a top general surgeon who was also able to repair a child's harelip, and a list of ER surgeries. Their journey to Chiapas, to meet Don Francisco; his shock of laughter upon meeting him. Amalia, his beloved Amalia, in Don Francisco's face. Her brother, sharing dreams all those years; of course, he knew el doctorcito. And every summer, for two weeks, he trained Javier in his ancient medicine—"You physicians don't know everything, doctorcito, so I'll show you a few tricks, and we'll heal your still open spirit door, the top of your hard head," his booming laughter as he grabbed Javier like a son. In his arms, playfully. Tenderly gazing into Javier's eyes, proud, like a father. He missed Don Francisco freshly, an open wound; yet his voice continued to speak to his heart, his dreams.

He remembered their travels to Bali, to meet Justin and Ai toward the end of their journey—later by themselves. The joy of it. He'd helped Xochiquetzal tolerate India's poverty and pain, and showed her its beauty as well. Greece, Italy, and of course Spain. And I stopped looking for la Clara in Barcelona with Xochitzalita, mi amor, he remembered as though for the first time. The joy of it. Their trip to Japan, Tokyo, to meet Ai's father after she and Justin were married. The joy of it. She lived, the first woman in her family since 1945, beyond forty, a surgical oncologist, a healer, a mother. Yamo'osta, the Mother People, her people witnessed the Blue Star Kachina dancing in the plaza, Hiroshima, Nagasaki. Her children—Keiko (after her grandmother) Perla, twenty-four, and Sachio (after his grandfather) Helio, twenty-one, lived. The joy of it. He remembered their births in San Miguel—They stayed with us the final months so their Mamacita would be there, and I was her doctor back-up with the mid-wife. I helped Justin cut their cords, and I felt like their grandfather (tears filled his eyes), I still do...la Keiko Perla, el Sachio Helio, now grown. Both of them threatening to be physicians—the thought made him smile.

They're still my grandchildren—"I held them at birth, Xochitzalita," Javier said out loud. And Justin, now a published novelist and professor, often journalist, taking off to wander—Kwahu, Hototo named him, Javier thought, el aguila in flight. Like his mother, that need to be free. Their children know my children—Xochiquetzal Dulce, la Xochitzalita, fourteen, Xavier Fernando Francisco, twelve, and Eva Amalia, nine. And my strong, sweet wife, Yessina. The joy (and sorrow) of it. A family physician, a healer, the mother to my three beautiful children, Yessina. She found me and healed me with her strong, sweet love. I was so broken, lost, set free, and she claimed me, found. The joy. Of it. Yet didn't Xochitzalita teach me how to love, that deeply…the sorrow. Of it.

Javier looked out at the dry, almost barren, October landscape, but it remained beautiful to him (México lindo y querido). He feasted his eyes on patches of green farmland where only the sturdiest harvests grew, painstakingly cared for by the earth's treasure—water. Drought and flood were the terrible, sacred twins now; yet Poqanghoya at the north pole of the world axis, and Palongawhoya at the south pole of the world axis, continued their sacred duties, their songs throughout the vibratory centers of the Earth. And each world axis remained true. They sent out their calls and songs of good or warning through the vibratory centers of the Mother, the Earth. "One people, one planet," they sang, north to south, south to north. The rising pulse of the Mother, 12 cycles per second, her dance of energy. The next one thousand years, "One people, one planet." The human voice.

I hope they have the roses I ordered, Javier reminded himself—I called la casa fria…the cool house, in Patzcuaro to reserve eighty-eight red roses. The guy thought I was joking at first, but then he became worried he might not have enough good red roses, but he'll try he said. I told him to add any color of rose if he came up short, but I hope they're all red. For Xochitzalita's eighty-eighth birth day last week. The day we met thirty years ago on the beach in Bucerias, older woman, younger man—he smiled at the memory of following her to her room, refusing to be ignored. "What arrogance," he murmured, laughing softly. He remembered eighteen years ago, the same month, October, when she neared her seventieth birth day. On the roof of the large house he'd bought in San Miguel (with a cook, maids, gardener, not a hippie house), she said it was time to set him free. He remembered the small, rainbow bridge between the main house and her two room Zen retreat, as they'd joked. Once in a while, she'd stay there for three or four nights, and then Javier would patiently knock until she opened the door. Then he'd pick her up in his arms and carry her over the rainbow bridge, laughing. The joy. Of it.

He remembered that sunset on the roof of their beautiful home—his full name on the king-sized mattress, black ink—when she'd turned to him, tears falling, and said, without looking away, into his eyes, "It's time, mi amor, I'll be seventy this month and you'll be forty-six, it's time."

"Time for what, your seventieth birthday fiesta? We'll throw one to rival Pablo's pinche parties, mi amor…"

"No, it's time for me to go, set you free to your own life, tigre. To get married to a wonderful woman, who I know is waiting for you," she wept without shame, the truth. "And to the children you were meant to have with this wonderful woman, it's time, mi amor."

He remembered how they fought for those four months, and then made love as they had in Bucerias twelve years ago. But deeper, more exquisite. Torturous. The joy. And sorrow. Of it. She remained firm (while weeping, sobbing, shamelessly)—it was time. For her to go. To set him free. The sorrow. Of it.

The first year returned so vividly, he almost pulled over to the side of the road. I was so angry, so hurt, so alone—worse, much worse, than mourning Xavier that year. I was completely alone, no dreams, not one, of Xochitzalita. She left me. Completely. "It's time," Javier murmured. I hated her that first year, as much as I'd loved her, so I steeled myself to my work, my surgeries, sometimes around the clock for days, then I could finally sleep, no dreams. Not one. And the mindless, beautiful fucks, las chicas on my speed dial once again—no dreams, not one.

And then, Yessina, my wife, my patient lover, my patient healer, began to hold me in her heart. Strong and sweet, mi Yessina, she held me in her heart until I allowed her into mine. Our perfect children, Xochitzalita Dulce (so heartbreakingly beautiful and strong)…Dulce after her mother, and I told Yessina about the woman who taught me how to love, after I stopped hating her, after Yessina took me into her heart. Xavier Fernando Francisco (a fierce and gentle boy) and Eva Amalia (los dos mamas, a girl of fire and ice)…I feel their spirits all around me, every day. They heal me, their father, the physician. And now I dream.

After Xochitzalita was born, I began to dream la Orchid—not as lovers, but as souls. And I began to understand her gift to me, "It's time." My words to her in Bucerias, filled with so much youthful arrogance, "Maybe I'm your gift," when she told me she was old enough to be my mother. Javier smiled at his thirty-four-year-old, young man's boldness, his refusal to be ignored, turned away. Chasing after her, still wet from la mar, knocking on her door persistently. Patiently. "I always find you, Xochitzalita," he whispered. "I'd do it again, for those twelve years, Tuawta," he said louder, hoping the rising wind would carry his words to her, and that she'd wait for him to arrive. Before she left her body.

"She's waiting for you," Ai had said yesterday. "And you know how stubborn she is, don't worry."

"Drive carefully," Justin took the phone. "She'll wait for you, hermano."

Then, "Hay-ya, Tuawta's full of spirit and she ain't goin' nowhere, Huiksi, see you soon, bro." Feliz had left the body four years before, cancer. Their children remained—Joy Feliz, twenty-six, and Franklin Antonio, 23, after his grandfathers...and he now carried his grandfather's hand-carved flute.

And then, everyone came back to him—that night at Pablo's paradise. He and Sonya had a son—Alejandro, twenty-eight. Ari and Judith had three sons—Solomon, twenty-five, for his Jewish grandfather...Ernesto, twenty-three, for his Cuban grandfather...and David Ari, twenty—before he was killed on a mission for his beloved Israel. Muriel was kidnaped covering a war zone and never seen again. Pompeii fled to Rome with Floriana, with enough money to open a successful Mexican-fusion restaurant—two sons and a daughter. The last I heard, over ten years ago, Javier laughed out loud. "The living and the dead, the joy and the sorrow of la vida. Wait for me, Xochitzalita, I'm coming."

"Are you sure you want all those roses, doctor?" the vendor laughed. "The order says *Eighty—eight red roses for Doctor Gomez..* Are you sure?"

"Exactly," Javier smiled, "eighty-eight red roses, and they're all red, gracias amigo."

"They aren't all perfect, doctor, but there are eighty-eight red roses," he smiled as he took the most cash he'd seen in one sale for a long time.

He was in the Gateway To Heaven, Patzcuaro. The lake was diminished, but still deep in the center. Xochiquetzal had moved to

Oaxaca when she left San Miguel de Allende, and lived there for nine years. Then she had to move to the Gateway To Heaven, after she could bear the memory of their times there—bringing the orchid plant he'd gifted her for her seventieth birthday. She'd dug it into a shady, fertile spot, and her gardener tended it like a child. Set free into the dark earth, it had spread its furious roots and bloomed with undying, purple-winged desire.

Javier glanced back at the tightly wrapped in plastic, eighty-eight red roses, and he thought of his father's sudden death. He'd had a sudden, violent stroke, and he left without saying goodbye. *We had our moments, especially after Xavier was born—of course, he disapproved of me naming my daughter Xochiquetzal. But when he held her, his sternness melted, and with Xavier he almost wept. He didn't see Eva Amalia born. My mother did the year before her cancer. She insisted on receiving no treatment—"I'm old enough and I want to die with some hair on my head, hijo." And when she told me, as I shifted her body into a more comfortable postion—"Xochitzalita promised me you'd have your own children, when you were in that coma years ago, mi corazón Javier. She promised, one mother to another, and she kept her word. She's a good woman, m'hijo, and she loved you."*

"I know, Mama, she is. A good woman," he managed to say, to comfort his mother. *Her secret all these years. Only his children's eyes comforted him in that moment. I was betrayed. By them both. And when I bought her book of photos and poetry, there was nothing from our years together. Which is why Justin kept it from me—betrayal.*

⟶•◆•⟵

"Javier, where did you find all those roses, Dios mio!" Ai laughed, opening the door wide. "I'll hug you after we find a container!"

"I ordered them and just picked them up, all eighty-eight red roses for la Xochitzalita's birth day."

"Oh, you sentimental, beautiful man, hold still so I can at least kiss you."

"Hay-ya, the rose garden arrives and my twin from the south axis." Hototo's eyes filled with tears, joy, as he squeezed his shoulder.

"Justin's with Xochitzalita and we've all said our goodbyes, lots of crying and some laughter. Keiko and Sachio were here for a week as well, and they made her smile. We let her go as they do in Bali, remember? Remember how we witnessed the entire family letting go of their beloved grandmother, each person who loved her," Ai smiled, the memory.

"I do remember, and now it's my turn." Javier met her eyes, but he couldn't return her smile. "Why don't we use that huge pot holding the paper flowers in the corner. I want to bring them in to her."

"How long has it been? Since you've seen her, I mean," Hototo quietly asked.

"Eighteen fucking years, as Xochitzalita would say in the old days. You know, when she left San Miguel for Oaxaca."

"Yeah, I remember now, but I thought you might've seen each other..."

"Let's put these beautiful roses in water and here's some scissors to cut them, Huiksi, if you want to." Ai placed the immense, Oaxacan, black-glazed pot on the dining room table, and Javier placed the tightly wrapped red roses on the floor. He slit the plastic wrapping and cut the string that tightly bound them, releasing the abundance of blood-red offerings.

"There's a photo, bro, so beautiful," Hototo smiled, breathing, "hay-ya. These days it's a luxury to see so many roses gathered in one spot, but only in México lindo y querido, as Feliz used to say. Her México lindo y querido, hay-ya to beautiful women, my daughter included, la Joy Feliz, and now the future dentista is also pregnant." He met Javier's eyes with so much kindness, knowing the name of his oldest daughter, Xochiquetzal. This healer. His south axis twin.

"You're going to be a grandpa, we'll celebrate later, que bien!" Javier did a quiet grito, and picked up a long stemmed rose, smelling it.

"Do you want me to cut them, peel the old leaves while you arrange them, bro? You'll be one soon enough, bet on it."

"He's Keiko and Sachio's abuelito, from the beginning," she smiled at Javier, so tenderly. "Her eyes remain the same, Huiksi, look into her eyes, she's right there." Ai began cutting the stems with a knife, slowly, with the precision of a surgeon.

"I always did, Dr. Yamo'osta, thirty years ago in Bucerias, la mar, when she tried to escape, run away from me." But I found her, I always find her. Javier smiled, remembering her face, her eyes, when she opened the door.

"I don't understand, Huiksi." Hototo handed him a perfect red rose.

"What?" Javier paused to smell the lush, red center before he placed it with the others.

"Why you two didn't stay together."

"Me either," Javier whispered.

"But you love your wife, your children, I know you do." Ai looked at him, handing him another, almost perfect, red rose. Its stem was a bit crooked, but the rose remained lush.

Javier nodded his head, yes, as he placed the almost perfect, red rose into water.

The birds had settled into their nightly trees, the Warrior in the Sun's arrows returned to his radiant quiver, and Venus held her place in the newborn night. Her searing light reflected on the lake, in the Gateway To Heaven. Her ancient light. Remembered. Human love.

"Javier, she just woke up from a nap and she's rested." Justin quickly walked over to him, hugging him tightly. "You just missed Keiko and Sachio, they were here for a week, but we'll get together, all of us. They miss seeing your kids."

"They're going to miss visiting Xochitzalita for their summer month, and of course she spoiled the hell out of them," Ai laughed softly. "But she gave them the house, their dual citizenship, so we'll return for longer visits, all of us, Huiksi."

"Come on, she's rested and she knows you're here. Holy shit, where'd you find all those roses, let me help you." Justin laughed as he watched Javier balance the huge, black-glazed pot. The eighty-eight womb-red roses sprayed wide against the deep, black glaze.

"I can handle it, I think," Javier smiled nervously as he walked through the door, balancing the stunning beauty in his hands. He saw a very old woman, watching him closely, smiling. Her face was finely wrinkled and her long, grey hair hung loose in a single braid. Freshly washed, with a bright purple ribbon twining its length. For a moment, he panicked, he didn't recognize her. Javier placed the roses down on the floor next to the bed—Breathe, he commanded himself, breathe.

"So you can smell them, Xochitzalita." He arranged the roses that had shifted, staying on his knees. Then he stood, facing her, this eighty-eight-year-old woman.

"Tigre," she whispered, meeting his eyes.

Her eyes, her eyes, *her soul*—"I see you, Xochitzalita, I see you," he wept quietly.

"I'm going to bed, a long day, see you all in Taiowa's light, hay-ya." Hototo quickly kissed Xochitzalita on the cheek, and whispered, "Tuawta, do you see talasveniuma, the butterfly carrying pollen on her wings? Are you this butterfly, Tuawta, I think you are, hay-ya."

Justin and Ai glanced at each other—"We are too," Justin said, walking over to kiss her goodnight. "I love you, Mom." Then Ai, "I love you, Xochitzalita."

"Nakwach," Xochiquetzal whispered.

"What, Mom?"

Hototo laughed. "The nakwach, Tuawta wants the nakwach." They gathered around the bed—Javier with her right hand, Justin with her left. Nakwach. "Hay-ya, to the journey!"

"Hay-ya," everyone echoed, "to the journey."

"See you in Taiowa's light, Mom, you know I love you." She waved Justin over as Hototo and Ai left the room. He leaned down to hear her more clearly, and she clasped his face in both hands.

"I'll always be with you, m'hijo," she held his eyes, paused for breath. "You've been the sun in my sky, always."

"I love you, Xochitzalita, Mom." He kissed her forehead, butterfly wings, stroked her wrinkled cheek. No tears, their long talks of goodbye. This peace, he thought, her final gift to me. Her love. My love. Our love. This peace.

Justin hugged Javier, "See you in Taiowa's light, Huiksi." He paused at the door. "You were always the Earth surrounding me, Mom, I love you always. Good dreams and see you in Taiowa's light, Xochitzalita." He briefly smiled like the sun, as he did in his youth, and closed the door behind him.

I can smell the roses, beautiful, Xochiquetzal wrote and handed the notebook to Javier.

"Good idea, yes write, speak only when it's comfortable, Xochitzalita." He glanced at the wall behind him, facing her bed—every inch was filled with photos, her photos. "There's eighty-eight red roses in honor of your birth day, but if their scent becomes too strong tell me and I'll move them over by the window."

No, leave them, 88 red roses, perfect, a garden. Light the candles and look closely at the photos, tigre.

After Javier lit the scattered candles, and the ones lining the large wall of photos, the ones on the long, low table facing the wall, from which an altar flowed to the tiles; he stood and stared at each photo. Their twelve years together in San Miguel, their family of Ai, Justin, their children; their friends, Don Francisco, at his home in Chiapas, with his arms around them both, and one with only Javier and him, the pride in Don Francisco's eyes. Their travels all over the planet, their meeting with Justin and Ai in Paris after the coma; Europe, India, then in Bali, California, always Mexico. Keiko and Sachio at birth, in their home in San Miguel—Justin cutting the cord, Javier holding each one, Ai breast feeding each of her precious babies, La Yamo'osta. Keiko and Sachio at every stage of their growth. The visits to Taos, the photos of Hototo and Feliz, their newborn daughter, later their son. Ari and Judith's dizzy with joy wedding in Israel, and later their three beautiful boys. Pablo and Sonya, Pompeii and Floriana, Diego in his scrubs, the last photo of Muriel, her visit before she took off on another adventure—so many good friends. And then, Javier saw it— the photos he'd sent yearly of Xochitzalita, Xavier, Eva Amalia, next to her grandchildren's. And my grandchildren—Keiko and Sachio remained my grandchildren. And at the very center of the wall, the photo of Dr. Zapata in his flamboyant sombrero and La Feminista in her Taos hat, kissing in Vallarta thirty years ago. Taken by the throw-away camera, it glued thirty years together. On this wide, candle lit wall.

Javier stood with his back to her, weeping. She didn't betray me, no, she set me free to the fullness of life, this life she captured on this wall, mi Xochitzalita. "These are so beautiful, Tuawta, so unexpected. You saved everything, every memory, gracias." Then he saw a kind of spiral galaxy of photos, spreading to the right—her nine years in Oaxaca, her friends there, her lover. Emiliano, the Zapotec healer, his dark-skinned face serious, about to laugh, holding her by the waist. He'd heard from Justin and Ai that he was very kind, a sweet man, her only lover in all that time, but they'd never lived together. He never wrote his full name on her mattress, Javier smiled to himself. His eyes like Don Francisco, burning, full of la vida, he saw at once.

"Es la vida, tigre," she smiled, motioning him over. "He was a good man," breath, "a healer" breath, "like you," breath. Emiliano made me want to live again, after you, she remembered. "Earrings," she whispered, pointing to the night table. In the soft lamp light, candle light, her fine wrinkles caught their light. And, for a moment, she was twelve.

"Right now, you look like a girl, I told you you'd grow younger as I grow older. Look at me at sixty-four, greying hair," he smiled, as tears still clung to his face, glistening.

"Callate, you're still handsome," a hint of her full voice reached him. "Earrings," she pointed again. *You still have Hototo's eagle ring, so beautiful*, she wrote.

Javier's heart stopped—the seashell earrings from Bucerias, la mar, and Amalia's pure gold, filagree earrings (he'd placed in her ears in the cave at Maruata), shimmered. Salt stung his eyes as he faced her, but he stopped these tears. He held both earrings up in each hand, reading her message. "I take it off only for surgery and sleep, yes beautiful."

Xochiquetzal pointed to Amalia's gold—"Tu hija," pause, "Xochitzalita." Then to the seashells and her ears, "Tigre."

La mar filled his eyes and these tears couldn't be stopped. He didn't turn away, but continued to meet her twelve year old gaze. He sat on the bed, placing Amalia's earrings back on the night table. He stroked her face. "You want the seashells in your ears, mi amor?"

Yes, she nodded, exuding peace. This is why Ai didn't speak, this peace. But his words, *mi amor,* were more. Than peace. The scent of the eighty-eight red roses lulled her, embraced her. "Mi amor," she breathed.

Javier brought his doc backpack close to the bed, as he'd packed an oxygen supply in case he needed it. Ai told him she was still refusing oxygen and that she had made it clear she didn't want to be kept alive artificially. *I'm so grateful for my old amiga, mi cuerpo, but now I have to let her go, this time, this life, mi bonita, mi Ai.* But he'd brought it anyway, in case she changed her mind—that fear of not being able to breathe at the end. He'd seen it too many times and he wanted to ease her final breath.

"Do you mind if I stay sitting on the bed with you?" The twelve year old smiled, welcoming him. Javier carefully placed each silver-spiral seashell, with their blood-red garnets, into each soft earlobe, remembering the first time he'd placed them in her earlobes. Thirty years ago. The mango surgery. Her multiple orgasms, his constant erections. Swallowing the juicy, so ripe, mango, still warm, her birth canal. Vulva. Orchid.

"I'm smiling, mi amor, remembering the mango surgery, do you remember?" She nodded yes, smiling, that peace. "You gave birth to me, Xochitzalita." She pointed to him, herself, no tears, smiling, that peace. Light.

"And I gave birth to you, yes," Javier wept, stroking her light-filled, wrinkled face. "You're beautiful, mi amor."

"Fucking liar," she whispered, smiling, that peace.

"I brought you some gifts, this one from Yessina and she sealed it, so I don't know what it says." Javier handed her the sealed card, but she handed it back, touching his lips.

He opened the card—of mountains, a lake, trees, the sun rising— and read: "Querida Xochiquetzal, mi amiga, mi hermana, in this life. Although I've never met you, I know you from Javier's stories. The man we both love. I know this, hermana, y gracias for setting him free. To me, our children. I wish I'd met you. I wish I'd known you. But I understand your choice not to see him again." He paused, her wisdom. "As a woman I understand, gracias Xochiquetzal. Con todo amor, Yessina."

For the first time, tears filled her eyes and fell, smeared with light. "I knew you'd find her, mi amor," long breath... "Yessina," she whispered.

"And these are from my children, for you." He almost wanted to tell her that he knew; the promise she'd given to his mother, but he let it go. "This is from Xochitzalita." Javier handed her the wrapped in tissue gift—a Frida Kahlo doll with connecting eyebrows, earrings, a gauzy shawl. "Ayy Frida," she smiled. "From el Xaviercito." She opened the wrapping paper, a small box, to a delicate glass horse—"Windhorse," she whispered. "He chose it on his own, mi amor, el caballo del viento. And from Eva Amalia." She tore the tissue away from a beautiful photo of a single monarch butterfly, wings spread, on a blossomed purple thistle. "It looks like she's going to be the artist, Xochitzalita. I've told them about you, as you can see, and that we were such good friends, but the oldest, your namesake, has guessed..."

"Yessina," Xochiquetzal whispered. She paused to write—*Tell her I knew you'd find her, your wife. Justin will give you my new book of photos, poetry when it's published, our time together, travels, my gift to you, tigre, and to Yessina tambien, she'll understand.*

"I will and she knows, Xochitzalita, and a new book of our time. Someday I'll share it with my children, corazón." Javier paused to stop fresh tears—she remembered our time. She remembered every thing. "One more gift." He reached into his backpack. "May I lay down next to you, mi amor?" She wept, smiled her welcome. He very carefully placed his body next to hers, the length of her eighty-eight year old body. He could feel her fragility even with the hand-loomed, sky-blue with golden stars, blanket between them. He leaned on his elbow and handed her a small box wrapped in a slightly faded rainbow cloth, tied with red and black yarn.

"Hummingbird," she murmured, "open it, Huiksi."

Javier removed the red and black yarn, the faded rainbow cloth, and brought out the tiny body wrapped in white cloth. "Open your hand, Tuawta." He placed the tiny streak of green into her open hand, still intact with the beauty Don Francisco had gifted it with. His magic, so alive.

She brought it to her throat, so tenderly. "Yours," she paused, long breath, "is the only sperm I've tasted, this life," she whispered.

Javier took her into his arms, cradling her. "You brought my sperm to my mouth, you set me free, mi amor, Xochitzalita," he wept. "And you were the only one I ever tortured with multiple orgasms, this life," he smiled. "Yessina would have been offended, but not you, mi amor, not you."

"Glitter, drawer," she whispered, remembering their bedroom garden in Bali. The profusion of flowers—their fertile/potent, mysterious, sweet scents. All night. The exquisite torture. Of their lovemaking. Her orgasms. La orchid. All night. His sperm. On her tongue. To his tongue. Only him. El tigre. All night.

"Glitter?"

Yes, she nodded, "Drawer."

Javier gently placed her head onto the pillow and reached for the drawer, opening it. Gold glitter. "I know what you want, mi amor." He slowly traced gold glitter onto her forehead, the dream-eye, cheeks, eyelids. And she did the same to him, his mouth, his laughing sixty-four-year-old mouth. She saw the lines of living on his face, the undiminished light of his soul. And he lightly kissed her mouth with his gold, weeping, laughing.

"Tell me, mi amor," she whispered as he cradled her again.

"What, mi corazón, dime."

"You know, tell me," she met his eyes. And he remembered, the words.

"There is no death, only transformation, life after life, no death, mi amor." Javier cradled Xochiquetzal, and she cradled the tiny streak of green between them. "I'll find you again, mi amor, and next time we'll meet as children, a whole life time, next time, I'll find you, Xochtizalita."

"I believe you, Javiercito." She closed her eyes, her head on his heart, home.

Javier, Xochiquetzal... *"How did you become a child? she laughs with joy. "How did you become a child, Xochitzalita?" He runs over to play. To kiss her on the cheek. "I told you I'd find you, hide and seek!" he laughs and laughs.*

A tiny, green-jeweled hummingbird circles them, pausing to sip a lily's nectar. Then it circles the girl, its blur of wings the only sound in the pale-gold sunlight.

"No, no, go away!" he yells.

But the exquisite, tiny, green-jeweled hummingbird lands on the crown of her head. The open door, kopavi.

"Tigre," Xochiquetzal shook him gently, "tigre."

He woke up, her head still on his heart. "I'm here, mi amor."

"Toilet," she breathed with effort.

"Do you want me to carry you?" She nodded yes, small smile, child's smile, no shame.

He waited outside the door, listening to the thin, brief stream of urine—Good, he noted, her bladder's functioning, but she only drinks water, juices, no solid food. Stop it, he told himself, she's choosing to leave her eighty-eight year old body, mi Xochitzalita.

He carried her back to bed, light as a handful of feathers, and she struggled to breathe. Then found it again—in and out, breath.

"I have your sombrero," breath, "I took it," she smiled, the twelve year old.

"I thought so, cabroncita."

"I have," long breath, "a lightning bolt in my lotus."

"The tattoo on your lower spine, mi amor?"

Yes, she smiled, nodding her head. "Secrets." She wanted to laugh, but she knew her limits.

"Ayy cabroncita, mi amor." He stroked her soft, wrinkled cheek.

Her eyes, her eyes, her soul, there she is.

I didn't see you all these years, I wasn't strong enough, forgive me, doctorcito.

Javier held the notebook with trembling hands; it felt like a cold wind of truth was setting him free again. Setting her free again, this time. "I read this, the poet William Blake—'I forgive you, you forgive me, eternally.' Next time I'll find you as children, cabroncita, a long life of forgiving each other, mi amor."

She gathered herself, a long breath. "I didn't want to," breath, breath... "set you free, Huikski." Tears ached in her eyes for a moment, and then peace returned.

"Huiksi, Breath of Life," Javier wept quietly, "but you won't let me give you oxygen, cabroncita, it'll ease your lungs, let me, I don't want to set you free, right now, this moment..."

No, she nodded. "Neruda," she pointed to a pile of books. The roses had slightly opened in their warm, womb water; their thick, sexual scent reached her. And she remembered. The first time. He held her. When he. Found her. "You know I'm your gift." His young man's smile of utter confidence, el doctorcito.

"Here, I've found Neruda." Javier lay back down next to her, full length, cradling her fragility in his left arm. "I know, this one, are you listening, Xochiztalita?"

She nodded yes, smiling, aware of each breath, her chest, lungs, tired of breath, effort.

"Should I read it in Spanish, mi amor?"

"Si," she barely whispered. And she remembered, *You will love me like no other,* smiling, her ear directly on his heart, home.

The sound of a flute carried on the pre-dawn air—Hototo's eagle bone flute coaxed the first purple light of Mystery to spread itself on the horizon, over the dark lake. Justin and Ai stood next to him as the flute sang so high and sweet, their arms around each other, waiting for the Mystery.

"Do you hear Hototo's eagle bone flute, mi amor?"

"Purple light," breath... "Mystery."

And he began, joining his voice to the flute—

AUSENCIA

Apenas te ha dejado,
vas en mi, cristalina
o tremblorosa,
o inquieta, herida por mi mismo
o colmada de amor, como cuando tus ojos
se cierran sobre el don de la vida
que sin cesar te entrego.

Amor mio,
nos hemos encontrado
sedientos y nos hemos
bebido toda el agua y la sangre,
nos encontramos
con hambre
y nos mordimos
como el fuego muerde,
dejandonos heridas.

Pero esperame,
guardame tu dulzura.
Yo te dare tambien
una rosa.

ABSENCE

I have scarcely left you
when you go in me, crystalline,
or trembling,
or uneasy, wounded by me
or overwhelmed with love, as when your eyes
close upon the gift of life
that without cease I give you.

My love,
we have found each other
thirsty and we have
drunk up all the water and the blood,

we found each other
hungry
and we bit each other
as fire bites,
leaving wounds in us.

But wait for me,
keep for me your sweetness.
I will give you too
a rose.

Xochiquetzal's heart exploded with the memory. Reading it to him that morning. The golden scorpion. Her heart's desire. And she forgot to breathe.

"Amor, you need oxygen!"

No, she shook her head, holding onto him as he tried to reach for his backpack. She struggled for breath imperceptibly, but he saw it. He put his mouth to hers and blew his breath into her. The sound of wings. A rapture of wings. Eighty-eight red roses erupted into bloom. Releasing their final, fleshy scent, each petal fell. Slowly. Fell. Flew.

"There is no death, only transformation, mi amor." He cradled her body, so gently. "And I'll find you again, Tuawta, I let you go, mi amor." But he continued to cradle her body, fully blossomed. Fully ripened.

Wings   Instinct   Ancient

Song...

The jaguar stirs from dreams. The comfort of the orchid roots. The woman calls her. As she had at the hour of her birth. The jaguar stretches her powerful muscles. The scent of the rising Sun. The first purple light, Qoyangnuptu, the Mystery, streaks the horizon.

She begins to run. Toward the Morning Star, Quetzalcoatl. Burning white with light. Becoming gold. She leaps.

Into gold.

A man stood outside his small, clean casita. Tears fell quickly as he faced the first golden arrows. That first warmth. The newborn. Warrior in the Sun. After the long, dark night. Of labor. Dar la luz... Give the light. His wife. Gave birth.

Is this   Is this

He gave a full-throated grito. His heart on fire. Joy. Gratitude. The newborn child. On the Earth. The Sixth World. As Taiowa blessed all in The Gateway to Heaven. With Mystery, Breath, Life. Golden arrows. Dawn.

Is this   Is this   This is

the deepest sacred play...

Alma Luz Villanueva was raised in San Francisco's Mission District, mainly by her curandera/healer Yaqui grandmother, Jesus Villanueva. Jesus taught her to recite poetry by heart (in Spanish) for church. Though she writes in English, Villanueva says that "the language/meaning is rooted in Spanish, and the Yaqui prayers I heard my grandmother sing every morning to the new Child Sun. Without Mamacita Jesus, no memory, no poetry, no stories."

Villanueva began to publish poetry in the late 1970s, winning first place in poetry with the University of California at Irvine's Chicano Literary Prize. Her books of poetry include *Bloodroot, Mother, May I?, Life Span, Planet* (Latin American Writers poetry prize), *Desire, Vida,* and *Gracias,* which will be published simultaneously with *Song of the Golden Scorpion.*

Villanueva's novel, *The Ultraviolet Sky,* received the American Book Award, and was listed in *500 Great Books by Women.* Her second novel, *Naked Ladies,* won the PEN Oakland fiction award, and was excerpted in *Caliente: The Best Erotic Latin American Writing.* Her third novel, *Luna's California Poppies,* was recently excerpted in the anthology, *Califlora.* Stories from Villanueva's collection, *Weeping Woman: La Llorona and Other Stories,* have been included in several anthologies, most recently in *Coming of Age in the 21st Century.*

Her fiction and poetry have been included in numerous textbooks, from elementary school to university, and has been the subject of Masters/Ph.D. thesis papers in the USA and abroad.

Villanueva taught fiction/poetry at the University of California, Santa Cruz, as well as Cabrillo College in Aptos. She has been a guest writer at the Naropa Institute, the University of California at San Diego, Stanford University, Pacific University, and many other institutions. She now teaches in the MFA in Creative Writing program with Antioch University in Los Angeles.

When she is not traveling to do readings, workshops, seminars, etc., Villanueva lives and writes most of the year in San Miguel de Allende (Mexico).

To find out more, visit her blog at
www.almaluzvillanueva.blogspot.com

Wings Press was founded in 1975 by Joanie Whitebird and Joseph F. Lomax, both deceased, as "an informal association of artists and cultural mythologists dedicated to the preservation of the literature of the nation of Texas." Publisher, editor and designer since 1995, Bryce Milligan is honored to carry on and expand that mission to include the finest in American writing—meaning all of the Americas, without commercial considerations clouding the decision to publish or not to publish.

Wings Press intends to produce multicultural books, chapbooks, ebooks, recordings and broadsides that enlighten the human spirit and enliven the mind. Everyone ever associated with Wings has been or is a writer, and we know well that writing is a transformational art form capable of changing the world, primarily by allowing us to glimpse something of each other's souls. We believe that good writing is innovative, insightful, and interesting. But most of all it is honest.

Likewise, Wings Press is committed to treating the planet itself as a partner. Thus the press uses as much recycled material as possible, from the paper on which the books are printed to the boxes in which they are shipped.

As Robert Dana wrote in *Against the Grain*, "Small press publishing is personal publishing. In essence, it's a matter of personal vision, personal taste and courage, and personal friendships." Welcome to our world.

Colophon

The first edition of *Song of the Golden Scorpion*,
by Alma Luz Villanueva, has been printed
on 55 pound EB "natural" paper contain−
ing a percentage of recycled fiber. Titles have
been set in Pide Nashi and Bremen typefaces,
the text in Adobe Caslon. This book was
designed by Bryce Milligan..

On−line catalogue and ordering:
www.wingspress.com
Wings Press titles are distributed to the trade by the
Independent Publishers Group
www.ipgbook.com
and in Europe by Gazelle
www.gazellebookservices.co.uk

Also available as an ebook.